Wallace Family Affairs
Volume VIII
Just A Friend

Carey Anderson

DEDICATION

To my A.J. Garrett love is a force that can never be stopped.
Thank you for the wonderful example of love and humility.
We don't always know what to do, but we can rebound as long
as love is the motivating factor.

Cover design: Cover Couture

Join me on Facebook –
www.facebook.com/careythewriteranderson

Twitter - @CareyTheWriter

Blog - http://careyanderson.blogspot.com

Website – http://www.careythewriteranderson.com

Editorial – Treasures of Joy Editorial

Photography by – Carey Anderson

ACKNOWLEDGMENTS

I would like to thank my baby-girl who is my life's ultimate expression of a dream realized. Thank you for sacrificing mommy time so that I could have the time to work some things out on paper.

I would like to thank my Soul Sistah #1 who has been my captivated audience since middle school. Without your love, support, encouragement, and FIRE I never would've completed Volume I or II, etc. Thank you for bringing me laughter when I couldn't get outside of my head.

I would like to thank my Sister-In-Law for taking time out of your busy family life to humor me with a read through of my latest thoughts and expressions. (SS1 & SIL THANK YOU for the trip to St. Helena where we spent the day lost in my imagination. I will never forget it, and it was exactly what I needed. THANK YOU!)

I would like to thank my dear cousin for reassuring me that my little hobby was relatable and entertaining. You are definitely a speed-reader, thank you for taking time out of your busy life to be entertained by my imagination.

I would like to thank last but not least Mrs. Laverne Dyes! Mrs. Dyes the day that you read my short story to my class changed my life. Thank you for giving me a positive outlet for all the angst going on in my life. You have forever changed my life, I am so thankful to have ever known you.

Chapter 1

Ethan

All I ever hear people saying is how good the genes are in my family. How beautiful the women and how handsome the men are. Some of my family members in my opinion act like this is all we are. A group of attractive family members. The fact that there are a bunch of us stands to try to prove some people's point. My cousin Tatum was going on and on about how there's no one ugly in our family. That's when the fight started. I asked her why couldn't she brag that we were all good people and hard workers? Matthew and Ryan are in law school; Jennifer's going to be a doctor. They set the bar high as far as achievements for our generation. I don't want the pressure of someone's life in my hands so neither one of those fields hold my attention. Although I paid attention enough to pick up a couple of things in both of those regards.

"You never do it right! Do you have to be so.... So.... White!" I said laughing at my brother.

"I've got soul, just cause your skin is browner than mine means nothing." Dito said laughing, "one of these days you'll dance somewhere outside of the living room!"

"Why are you arguing?" Georgette said rushing out the bedroom to shush us. "Franky is trying to sleep!"

"He should know better than to try to sleep in the middle of the day!" I said loudly.

Then there was a rhythmic pound on the door. "T!" Dito and I said in unison.

Georgette ran to the door, "Timothy please keep the noise down Franky's trying to sleep."

Timothy frowned at her, "why is Franky sleep in the middle of the day?" He said loudly on purpose.

"Ok!" I said giving him a high five.

"Cause she just depleted me of all my juice and she was hoping I'd fall into a deep coma like sleep, and forget I was going out tonight." Franky said standing in the doorway.

"Baby are you hungry? I can fix you something to eat." She said rushing to Franky.

"Nope, you've served your purpose. Put your clothes on and go!" He said coldly.

Everyone covered their mouths to try not to laugh. We used to feel sorry for her, but no matter how rude Franky is to her she keeps coming back for more. It's hard to respect someone like that. Georgette got dressed and walked out looking like a wounded kitten.

My brother Franklin aka Franky is the ladies man. Girls flock to him like nobody's business. He literally has to beat them off with a stick. Tall dark and handsome is what they call him. My cousin Timothy aka T is the next runner up, I don't think he even knows what it's like to be single or rejected by a girl. My brother Fernando aka Dito doesn't fair badly with chicks, but he's too sweet kind and gentle until they get on his nerves. Then there's me, I guess I'm handsome. I'm smart; I've got a great personality. However, I share my father's love of food. My momma calls me husky, but most of the girls around here call me fat. I'm always friends with these chicks who think they're using me to get closer to my brothers and cousins, or for my *talents*. Normally it's the four of us, but our other cousins Matthew aka Matty, Darren who we only call Darren, and a few others step out with us from time to time. Although we spend most of our time here Franky and Dito live together. T and I share an apartment a couple of buildings over. This arrangement works cause T and I are more the same as we have to have neat and order in our home. Franky and Dito are more *relaxed*, but normally some chick from school volunteers to clean their place for them.

As we walked to Franky's car I announced, "I think I should grow my hair out. You know be my true hippie self."

"Is that the plan? Grow your hair, catch a woman?" Franky said.

"I catch girls all the time. This is not about girls. I think I want this for me." I said.

"Momma always wanted a girl, kind of figures it would be you. Dito came close."

"Forget you! Just because I don't beat my chest and roar like the rest of you, Momma says I'm just fine."

"Of course she's going to say that. You remember when she asked you if you liked girls?" Franky was still pushing.

Dito turned red, "that's not funny. You always bring that up. It was just a question; she asked it's over. Why do you harp on it so much?"

"Because she asked the question the rest of us had been thinking but didn't know how to ask."

"T and Blu, you guys think I'm gay?" Dito asked in frustration.

"You are whoever you say you are. It doesn't matter to me." I wanted this to stop.

"It matters to Dad and it matters to me!" Franky said not laughing anymore.

"Let's change the subject. How many girls you think are going to be at this party?" I was trying to keep the peace.

"Doesn't matter you're not going home with any of them." Franky laughed again.

"Franky you're in rare form tonight. Don't treat your brothers like that." T was about to snap.

"It's ok T, Franky needs to have something to feel good about. Mister can't declare a major. Maybe if you devoted as much time to studying as you do to these females you'd decide what you want to do with your life besides being a career student. Dito and I will settle in our careers before he picks a major. Franklin the third turned out to be a big fat dud!" I dared him to say something else.

Franky had no response; he drove angrily to the party. When we stepped into the party T and Franky went to the left, Dito and I went to the right. "Hi Ethan!" The girls on the couch sang to me.

"Ladies."

"Come sit with us!" One drunk girl said.

"I need a drink."

"Barbara will get it for you!" One girl said pushing Barbara to go play fetch for me. "Come sit down." She said patting the now vacant spot on the couch next to her. I sat down; she immediately put her hands in my hair. "I love your hair, it feels like cotton."

Another girl touched it, "kind of like wool?"

"No Darla! Wool is itchy and scratchy. His hair is soft like cotton." The first girl said.

"Since when are you the expert on black people's hair?" Darla snapped.

"Since now!" Then she shot her friend a look. Then she smiled at me. "Ethan," she gave me that smile.

"Nope, if you want it you know what you've got to call me."

She folded her hands in front of her face. "Please Big Daddy, did you bring us any snacks?"

All of the girls smiled at me. "How much money you got for the Baker-man?"

They deflated, the first girl spoke up. "How *about*?" She smiled seductively at me. "You let me do *something* for you, and then you do *something* for me?"

"Not interested, I've had you and it wasn't all that great." I said honestly. "If I was going to barter with you I want to feel like it's worth it. I'd only give you a corner of a cookie, forget about any blow."

The girl looked insulted. "What did you bring?" She asked me.

"I might not have brought anything. Impress me." I sat back.

The girls huddled, then a different girl sat next to me. She flipped her hair as she started touching me. She threw her leg up. "Ethan, I mean Big Daddy. If you share your goodies with me, I'll share mine with you." Then she bit my ear.

I was intrigued. This girl was about ready to go right here in front of everybody. "Where we going?"

The girls clapped excitedly. This girl stood up and led me by the hand. "Blaine can we use your room for a little bit?"

Blaine looked at me, "what's in it for me?"

I looked at the girl who looked frustrated, "I'll share. Can we go or not?"

Blaine held his hand out, "enjoy!"

"Don't hurt her!" Franky called out from across the room.

This girl who didn't feel it was important for me to know her name, went in. She was kissing all over me; I thumped her when she got too close to my mouth. I don't kiss these girls. She got on her knees and went to work. I tried not to laugh when she tried to take me all the way in and gagged. I told her to watch herself. She drank my mess like it was Kool-Aide. Feeling good about herself she stood up. I told her that was just my warm up and now it was time for the show. She looked at me in disbelief as I stood at full attention waiting for service. I put on a condom and told her to come on. I guess she thought because I'm a big guy this would be easy. Clearly, her friend didn't give her the full disclosure on who I am. I may be big, but I know how to handle my business. Her blue eyes stretched wide in shock as she exploded. Snowflake came so hard you would've thought she was having a seizure. When I finally blew my top, she screamed in surrender to her Big Daddy. I rolled over and caught my breath. "How did I do?" She asked still trying to catch her breath and get control over her body that was still shaking.

"I'll give you a C+"

She shot up, "a what?"

"You were average, a good average but average. C+ little girl." I said wiping myself on the bed and then fixing my clothes.

"I demand a redo!" She said pulling on her dress.

I tossed a couple of brownies, rice treats, a joint, and a little snow on the bed. "You gonna end up strung out like your friend. I'm good for now." Then I walked out.

Jenise

My parents were so proud of me. The first person in our family to go to college. The fact that I got a full scholarship to go to one of the most prestigious colleges in the country gave them so many bragging rights. I was never the prettiest or the smartest; my out going personality is what always put me ahead. I was only ever the center of my parent's attention. If it weren't for my personality, most people would pass on by. A lot of people say I'm real animated and entertaining to watch. I like making people laugh, when appropriate of course. My parents always say I made the most interesting friends. I've always taken that as a compliment.

My parents saved all year to give me money to make the trip out here; we were excitedly surprised when we realized that they actually saved enough to come up with me. I'm from Stockton, a farming town, a little hole in the wall city in California that people don't know about unless they're from here. My parents drove me to school instead of the bus like we originally planned. They stayed in a motel nearby for the weekend as they took me to get the few things we could afford for my dorm room. My roommate arrived a day later. She was nice, and we said they stuck the minorities in the room together. Everybody at this school was basically white. Stuck up little spoiled rich kids.

Grace's family is from San Francisco. Her uncle owns a grocery store and her family works in the store. He happens to own the apartment building that they live in as well. In exchange for their help at the store. He also gives them a small allowance. She's here on scholarship like me; it helps to have someone who understands the struggle. We can't pick up the phone and say mommy and daddy *I need*. We work in the cafeteria and we help each other out. These idiots around here ask the dumbest questions. Especially about my hair. Dickey calls me Angela Davis because of my Afro. I wasn't insulted; he didn't know what to say to me. Since he knew about my girl Angela I figured he was at least on the righteous path to enlightenment. Dickey and I actually ended up becoming good friends. Along with the other people in his inner circle. Grace is still my number one. She says we gotta get out and network; meet new people, make connections cause they might take us somewhere one day. Seems like we connect with people all the time.

"Mail call!" Grace said coming in with the mail from my cubby.

"Gimmie! Gimmie!" I said happily.

Grace gave me the latest letter from Jamal. My "*boyfriend*" back in Stockton. Jamal and I are a lot alike in a lot of ways. He's not silly or out going, but the person at the heart of him is a good person. His parents are getting up there in age, and it's expected that he will take over the farm now that they can't handle it. I haven't seen him since I came out here. During vacations I stay here and work, and my summer. Grace and I got an "apartment" and worked our behinds off to afford it and try to save money for the next school year.

One time I applied at this department store, and they had a problem with my hair. I held myself in a polite and disciplined manner while Grace went completely off; I love that girl so much. I never have to wonder if she has my best interest at heart. She shows it constantly.

Jamal and I keep each other up to date on the latest with each other in our letters. I know my parents think we're going to end up together, but I don't know if I see it anymore. I tell myself I'll figure it out when I graduate.

"You got gum?" She asked as we got off the bus.

I reached in my purse and gave her a piece. "How long we gotta stay? Blaine's parties always turn into big orgies and I'm not interested."

"Let's give it an hour, and then we'll come home. I want his friend to partner with me in that class. Let me talk to him for a minute then we can go." Then she turned the knob to enter Blaine's place.

As usual most of the girls in these parties are stuck up. I end up talking to the guys and waiting for Grace. Tonight seemed no different.

"Grace who's your friend?" Blaine said looking at me like I was lunch.

"This is my sister Jenise, I introduce you every time."

"No, no! I would remember this flower." He said kissing my hand.

"You say that every time too." Grace said looking around the room. "Is Braxton here?"

Blaine focused on me, "I like your hair like that. It brings out your eyes."

I looked at Blaine's red and sleepy eyes. "You're high!"

"Is that a crime?"

"As long as you're not in public, no. Being in possession is."

"You want some?" His eyes pleaded with me to say yes.

"No thank you."

"Jenise you need to relax. I can help you with that."

"If it's not dancing, I don't see how."

"Keith!" He called out, "turn on the stereo, this one wants to dance."

Some whiter than white music came on and Blaine started dancing. I looked at Grace and she shrugged. So I two stepped to the music I don't know why I was expecting Motown.

"WHAT IS THIS?" A guy I didn't know said to Blaine.

"Music!" Blaine said dancing all off beat.

"Where's the Motown?"

"What you know about Motown white boy?" I said with a smile.

"Everything!" Then he turned to Blaine. "Turn this off! Turn on the radio! You know what I'll do it!" The guy walked over to the stereo. He turned off the record and turned on the radio. He turned the dial until he got to the station then he adjusted the antenna. When soul music came on he came back to me. Bumping Blaine out the way he danced with me. Grace jumped in when we started doing the hustle. He wasn't a bad dancer at all and we had a lot of fun. So much fun that I didn't pay attention when he brought me *punch*. I was so thirsty I gulped it down without tasting it until my drink was gone. The fire! This punch was beyond spiked. Grace looked at me with big eyes as we both realized what I did. My body is a temple that I have been very adamant about keeping clean. AND NOW! Now it has been defiled! "It's spiked!" I yelled grabbing my throat and dropping to my knees. "Temple violated! No! Lord Jesus please forgive me!"

The guy looked at me with a goofy look, "you're crazy! I like you!"

"Water! I need water! Please save me before I drown in a pool of my own vomit because the demon liquor got me and made a fool...." My lips got numb! "Lord! It's happening! Grace tell my parents I'm sorry! Tell them I tried! But it's true, bad association spoils useful habits!"

Grace put her hand on her hip, "who's the bad association?"

"You are if you don't help me!" I said coughing dramatically.

She looked at the guy, "what's your name?"

"Dito."

"Thank you Dito for poisoning my sister. She will now be forced to become a wino and live out her days as a drunk homeless person doing anything for a drink."

"You're freshmen?"

"No sophomores, but my sister promised God she would keep her temple pure."

"Your sister?" Dito smiled at us.

"Can you please do this later? Help me!" I said stretching out my hand.

Grace stood me up off the floor. We went to the bathroom and she sprinkled water on my face. "Jenise I think you're going to live."

"You want a refill?" Dito asked with a smile.

"No she does not!"

"Yes!" I said smiling at Grace. "I might as well since I had the first one."

"Bye Jenise! You get on my nerves." She laughed as she walked away.

I sat on the edge of the tub chatting with Dito as I sipped my drink. The more I drank the more I wanted to talk. Dito grew up between Walnut Creek and Oakland. He has two brothers and a cousin out here. I asked him how that was possible and he said he was the middle child. He was eleven months older than his younger brother and five months younger than his older brother. He said his parents never treated him like he was different. He said his little sister on the other hand was born different. He said they have the same mom but you would never know it. He said for one reason or another they don't get along. I told him I was an only child and first person in my family to go to college. I told him Grace and I consider each other sisters because of how close we are. "What's it like being friends with a Chinese girl?"

"I wouldn't know, Grace isn't Chinese." He looked at me confused. "Not that it matters but she's Filipino. Completely different culture. Asian is an umbrella just like white or black. Are you Irish, Italian, British?"

"Part German and I don't know what else. My parents didn't focus on it. What about you?"

"My grandfather was from Nigeria. The rest of my folks are American and you know how that goes. The only real connection I have to my roots was through my grandfather."

We talked for a long time, getting drunker and drunker. I remember laughing with Dito and being silly. At one point he had to pee so he closed the door and went. Eventually his girlfriend showed up. I don't know why I expected her to be black. Dito wasn't nice to her like he was to me. He made her get her own drink and he looked irritated when she interjected in our conversation.

When I stood up my legs wobbled. Dito insisted on driving Grace and I to the dorm. His brother gave him keys to his car. It was a really nice car. Dito gave Grace and I his number. He said if we ever needed anything to call him.

Chapter 2

Ethan

T got off the phone and he threw his body backwards on the couch and exhaled loudly. He said his momma always asks him when he's coming home to visit. Then she asks about girls. He said in high school no one was good enough for him. Most of the girls had hidden agendas. I asked him if that was true and he said yes. I told him my momma was like that with Franky too. T said he warned his younger brother Malachi not to bring his girlfriends home. He said no matter how much he liked the girl it didn't matter, his momma was going to find something wrong with them. "Blu, man, I need a pick me up." He smiled at me.

I sucked my teeth. "This batch is for the game." I said cutting my rice treats.

"I'm a lightweight, all I need is a little piece and I'll be good." I tossed him a corner. "Gracias mi Amiga!"

Homecoming game was a pretty big deal. Our football team wasn't any good, but we had enough school spirit to make up for that. I pressed my clothes and made sure everything was the way it was supposed to be. Tim said Dito was bringing friends to the game so he was going to meet us there. Franky picked us up and we were off. As soon as we got out the car here comes the girls. They come for my brothers and cousins looking for relationships. All of them dreaming of the day they will be crowned Mrs. Wallace, but for me they only sacrifice their bodies for the sake of getting high. Then once they had a taste they come back begging for a hit of both. I'm tired of being invisible to these girls but not tired enough to stop doing what I do. The girl with no name was foaming at the mouth looking at me. I knew that look; she wanted to feel me again. She didn't want me, there was a difference. We were almost inside the game and she said she needed to talk to me. I don't even know this girl's name. I told her she was going to have to wait. Her big blue eyes filled up with tears. Franky and T looked at her and laughed. Franky patted my shoulder and said he was proud of me, and then they walked away. "What do you want?"

"I want to do it again!"

"You want the fat man?"

She didn't like the phrasing. "I can't stop thinking about you. Ethan, please!"

"Girl with no name, I gotta buy my ticket to get into the game. I gotta go make this money."

"I'll buy your ticket. Please! I'll do whatever you want!"

"Like that girl? Why?"

"I've never been with a black man. You're amazing! I.... I.... I need to know that wasn't the affects of the alcohol I drank that day."

"Go buy my ticket."

She happily ran towards the gate to comply with my request. A couple of customers came by, we exchanged goods. Another strung out customer began her plea for the

E man. When the no name girl came back, she walked up to me and put her arms around me. She licked my cheek then she looked at the girl. The other girl said she'd come looking for me later. I looked at the first girl and I asked her where we were going. She led me by the hand to her dorm, which was nearby. Everyone was at the game. She locked the door and dropped to her knees. I almost saw stars when I released, I told her that was much better. She screamed loudly as I went in further than any man has gone with her before. I flipped her backwards, side ways, at one point she turned purple she was so red. She was gone, and I knew this girl wouldn't be right after this. As she was still coming down from her high I pulled up my pants and then I walked out the door. I patted myself on the back for being good at what I do. However, the overwhelming emptiness that settled over me was a buzz killer. I've never had a girlfriend, not since I was a kid. Ever since Junior high school, it's been this empty barter back and forth. The girls I liked, never liked me. It's not easy being Franky's little brother. It's like everyone expects me to be like him, and I'm glad that I'm not. Sometimes I wonder what it would be like to be away from him. I'm strongly considering going to graduate school in Berkeley to be my own man, to stand on my own. Franky is a very smart guy, but he lacks direction and conviction. He doesn't know what he wants to do. He should've graduated with Dito last year. Maybe when I'm out of his shadow I can meet someone of my own.

Jenise

"It's Dito!" The knocker said jingling the knob. I opened the door. "Darn! You're dressed!" He joked.

Grace smiled at Dito. "Was that comment in reference to me or Nise?"

He put his hands up, "it was only a joke. I have a girlfriend."

"That you don't even like. What's the deal?" I asked.

"I like you two as friends, nothing more promise. You two are like sisters to me."

"Good cause we feel the same way." Grace said.

"Still doesn't explain why you're with a girl you don't even like." I eyed him.

"She gets on my nerves when she acts like my mother!" He tried to hold back his irritation.

I frowned, "I thought you loved your mother?"

"Mother NO! Momma YES! Guys I don't want to talk about this. I want to have fun tonight. I'm taking you out to eat afterwards."

"Um, I can't afford to go out to eat. I...."

He cut me off. "Read my lips! I'm taking you two out to eat! You better come hungry too."

"As long as we're back by curfew." Grace said.

Dito frowned, "I can't promise it. If it gets too late you two can take my bed, I'll sleep on the couch."

"Dito? You're not a rapist right?" I had to ask.

"If I were I would've got you when you were drunk. It's Friday night; I don't want to punch a clock. Let's go have fun!"

Grace and I packed a few things for our sleepover then we put our bags in Dito's trunk. At the game Dito bought our tickets and then we followed him to the stands. We sat down and then he looked around, he said his brothers would sit with us. He said he'd be back with popcorn and sodas. Dickey came over and chatted with us. As Dito was walking back Grace grabbed my leg and then she mumbled under her breath. She said it was the guy! The guy that she dreams about from around campus. I asked her which one, cause both of them were cute. She said the one with the black jacket then she straightened up cause they were approaching. Dito introduced us, T looked at Grace but I didn't know if she caught his attention.

"I thought I knew all the Sistahs on campus?" Franky said.

I shrugged, "I guess not. I've never seen you before either."

"Where did you meet my brother?"

"Blaine's party."

"The one a couple of months ago? I was there!" He said like he was insulted.

"They were on the other side of the place. I found this pretty little thing dancing with Blaine." Then he smiled at his brother.

"Blaine was dancing? What was that like?" He said laughing at the thought.

Dito made us laugh as he mimicked our dance. The three of us were talking and making each other laugh when Dito asked why Grace and T for that matter were being so quiet. T blushed, "this is my watcher."

Dito and Franky gasped, "What does that mean?"

Grace didn't say anything she looked at T. "Whenever I feel someone is watching. I look up and it's her. She doesn't even look away. Why do you do that?"

Grace blushed, "you are so beautiful. You've never had a woman admire you before?"

"Admire yes, watch no." He blushed.

"Guess that makes me different." Grace said not looking away.

"Very different." He looked away.

"It's your turn to watch me boyfriend. Jenise come with me to the bathroom." She commanded.

I stood up and walked behind her. Even her walk was different. When we were out of eyeshot, Grace started screaming to the top of her lungs. She was excited that he noticed her. I laughed from my stomach at her excited silliness. She immediately told me how beautiful her babies were going to be. When we came back there was another guy with them. Dito introduced him as Blu. Blu looked at us, said hi and looked away. Grace took her seat next to T and stared at him. T started laughing and he made her talk to him, so she'd at least have a reason to look at him. Apparently we were sitting with the ladies men. Almost every girl had to walk by and say hi. People kept coming up to Blu talking lowly and then leaving. A few girls came up to him promising whatever and he said no shutting them down and sending them off crying. After the third one I asked him if he was Georgie Porgie. He didn't even think about what I said before he replied no. He seemed troubled, Franky shook his head at his brother and then he returned his attention to the game. After the game Dito told his brothers we were going out to eat. T rode with us while Dito's brothers followed us in their car. Grace kept smiling really big at me and then trying to look normal when T looked at her. Dito took us to a nice restaurant. It wasn't so fancy that we were under dressed, but nicer than any place I've ever been able to afford.

Dito and his brothers seemed very interested in knowing what life on a farm was like. They asked me question after question. Everyone was interested except Blu. His non-interest in us made me curious about him. He wasn't rude or dramatic but it seems like he's upset about something. When our food came he wasn't even focused on his plate. I could tell when he was satisfied, but he forced himself to finish, and then he ordered a big dessert. The only reason I noticed is because when I was younger I used to do the same thing. My mother would ask me why I felt like I needed to finish everything on my plate. I told her it was because I didn't want to waste food. So she started putting her dishes on the table. She told me to start out with small portions. I could have as much as I wanted, but if I was satisfied why should I force myself to continue? She said the leftovers always tasted better the next day anyways. Once she did that I remember how my little bit of chub melted away. Blu looks sad, and he also looks guarded so I didn't say anything. I can see that Franky likes to be the center of attention. Dito likes and needs to feel included, Blu is holding back, but so is T. T sits over to the side quietly observing everyone, and then he becomes very lively.

"Do you know how to drive a tractor?" Franky asked like he couldn't believe it.
"Yes."

"Let me see. Make a muscle." Franky said holding his arm up showing off his beautifully sculpted arms.

I took my jacket off and then I mimicked Franky. The entire table oohed me. T said my muscle was impressive, and then he asked Grace if she had muscles too. She smiled at him and said of course, but she had long sleeves on her shirt. She'd have to take it off to show him. T smiled at her and got quiet again.

When I mentioned Jamal they all paid attention like the name triggered something. Dito said I needed to invite Jamal out for a weekend of fun. I couldn't tell if T was feeling Grace or not. Or if he was only paying attention to get in her panties. Dito invited us back to their house. Franky leaned over and whispered that the cleaning lady hadn't come yet. Dito asked T if we could come back to their place. T said of course and Blu looked like he could careless.

When we got to T and Blu's place, Blu told us to make ourselves comfortable. He asked us what we would like to drink. "What do you have?" I asked, honestly thinking he was going to say they had grape, lemon, and fruit punch flavors of Kool-aide.

"You look like a wine drinker, we've got Riesling, Chardonnay, Cabernet, Merlot, Zinfandel, Port, Sherry. If you'd like something stronger we got that too. Pick your poison." Blu said matter of factly.

"Whoa! There's a list. I was thinking Kool-Aide honestly."

"You don't drink?" Blu asked like the thought of it annoyed him.

"No, I drank with your brother by accident."

All of them stared at me, and Blu frowned. "You religious?"

"I am religious, but that's not why I don't drink."

Blu rolled his hands, "you waiting for me to ask you why?"

I didn't know why my non-drinking seemed to bother him, but whatever. I sighed, "There's a lot of alcoholics in my family. I'd rather not start the habit."

"What are you in school for?" Franky asked with his face all scrunched up.

"To get an education."

"Come to the kitchen and pick a flavor, I'll make you some Kool-Aide."

I followed him to the kitchen, there was a plate with rice treats, brownies, and cookies individually wrapped on a plate. "Who bakes?" I asked hoping he'd share. "I do, but if you don't even drink you don't want none of those." He pulled out the Kool-Aide packets he had. "I'm glad we still got these, which one would you like?"

"You only have one lemon packet?" I frowned at the foreign concept.

"Yes," he looked at me like he didn't get it.

"I don't know how you make Kool-Aide, but at home we mix lemon with whatever flavor we're making for the ultimate drink."

"You can't talk to me about Kool-Aide mixology cause I'll have to put you to shame."

"Challenge accepted, you got enough sugar and two pitchers?" I looked around the kitchen.

"Guys! She's challenging me to make a pitcher of Kool-Aide." He announced.

"Blu is the King of all things edible!" Franky called out. Blu frowned at the counter, "what? Well he is." Then you heard whispering. "What I mean is Blu makes a mean pitcher of Kool-Aide, she's bitten off more than she can chew." When no one said anything Franky came in the kitchen. "Ethan you know what I mean right?"

I could tell Blu was trying to suck it up by the way he was looking at his brother. "Has anyone ever mistaken you two for twins?" I decided to change the subject.

"No!" Blu said opening the cabinet to get the second pitcher.

"When we were young they did." Franky said.

"I guess," Blu said still irritated. "So you get the lemon and pick whatever flavor you think will help you. Then I'll pick my flavors." He mixed the packets up in his hand without looking. I picked the grape and then I hid the packet behind my back. He didn't even look at the packets he mixed them again and then he randomly picked a flavor, only ONE! He went to the refrigerator, when he didn't find what he was looking for he put a teapot on. I raised an eyebrow at him and he shook his head yes at me. Using a measuring cup he measured two cups of hot water to two cups of sugar. Then he made sure the sugar melted and he brought it to a slight boil. He poured some of the liquid in his pitcher then he put his Kool-Aide packet in mixed it really well. Then he added lots of ice cubes. He got six glasses down and then he gave each person a glass. Everyone tasted mine and they said they really liked it. I smiled at Blu, then he had everyone taste his and as he poured it, he added a maraschino cherry to their glasses. His did taste smoother I guess cause the sugar was melted. In the end it was a draw Franky, Grace, and I voted for mine. Blu, T, and Dito voted for his.

We spent the rest of the night talking and having a good time. Eventually Dito turned on the music and he and I started dancing again. Franky shook his head at his brother and asked him why he was always dancing. Blu sat over to the side watching us and I told him to come dance with us. He said no, and then his face that had a somewhat relaxed look, went back to irritated.

Grace flirted with T all night long. He seemed opened to her flirtations, and he flirted a little back. However, I couldn't tell if he liked her as much as she was making it known that she liked him. I basically hung out with Franky and Dito all night. Blu kept sitting over to the side, not overly concerned with what was happening with us. Dito took us home in the morning. He thanked us for hanging out with them. He told us we would have to do it again soon.

Ethan

"What's wrong with you? You decide to go monk or something? Why you turning down all this catnip. You got females throwing it at you, and you acting like you too good." Franky fussed at me.

"I'm tired!"

"Of catnip?" Franky bucked his eyes like he couldn't believe me.

"Of females who want to have sex with me, but none of them want to be with me. Like you said when do I ever bring a girl home?"

Franky felt bad, "don't take my ignorance out on the females. I was just jiving, you know. Mad cause I can't get it together and both of my brothers got it. I'm still gonna be in college when Gwen graduates." He patted my back, "ok? Feel better? Now go get some!"

"Franky when was the last time you had sex?"

"Today?" He looked at his watch, "this morning, but I'm on my way out. So..."

"How long can you go without?"

"Why on earth would I want to know that?" He frowned at me.

"It's been mechanical, I need love."

Franky stared at me. "You talked to momma while you were high again didn't you?" I laughed. "She'll have you thinking you need to settle down and start a family. That woman wants grandbabies like nobody's business."

"I want to give her some, but she's not going to get any if I keep going like this."

"Dad says to wait for love."

"Dad says a lot of things. I don't want to end up like him. Living miles away from my wife passing time with idiots."

Franky was quiet for a minute. "Maybe I should look for a wife. *Maybe*! A good woman will be just what the doctor ordered for me."

"You aren't ready to be a good man."

"I could be a good man."

"*Could,* doesn't mean you're ready Franky."

"What you think about Dito's friends?"

"I don't." I said honestly.

"I guess the black one is kind of pretty in a very plain way. She mostly stayed under that jacket I couldn't see if she had anything else going for her."

"That's Dito's friends."

"Dito ain't looking at them like that. The other one got it bad for T."

"Does he like her?" I asked.

"He'd be crazy not to, she's gorgeous. I think he trying to run that shy guy jive on her though. He don't say nothing when she come around."

"He don't have to say nothing, she's open." I said.

****

"Next time you see Whispers tell him to call me. Just in case you see him before me." My dad told all of us. Then he looked at his namesake. "I don't know what I'm going to do with you. I should've given Ethan my name." He said with his eyes locked on Franky.

"Technically dad the naming rights would've passed on to Fernando." Franky replied sarcastically.

Dad didn't smile; he stared at Franky for a long time. "Everything is a joke to you? When are you ever going to take anything serious? I'm wasting money sending you here."

"It's not like you're hurting for the money. You can afford it." Franky sunk in his seat.

"Spoiled little rich kid, is that what this is? You think the world owes you something?" Dad said getting angrier.

"I didn't say I thought that." Franky sulked in his seat.

Gwen came back to the table and sat down. "Daddy take it easy on Franky." She said matter of factly while looking at her menu.

"You don't even know what they were talking about." Dito snapped.

"No, but I know them. Those two are always fighting."

"You need to be quiet." Dito said.

"I'm the only one who understands Franky."

"Speak for yourself." I said.

"All of you look down on him. Just like you do to me." She volunteered.

Everyone looked at her. "Why would we look down on you?" I asked.

"Because I'm the only girl, and you'd prefer to have your own boys club."

"That's your assumption."

"No it's a fact you ding dong."

"Look here you ho ho!"

"ENOUGH! Gwen shut up! Ethan don't talk about your sister like that. Franklin you need to get your act together. Your momma has that I told you so look plastered on her face whenever we discuss you. I'm tired of it! If it weren't for her I would've cut you off a long time ago! You're setting the wrong example for your sister."

"The only time she pays attention is when I do something wrong."

"That's not true!" Gwen protested.

"As long as you're the center of attention at all times. Can't dad scold me without you interjecting on my time?" Franky halfway teased.

Dad glared at Franky, then he looked at Fernando. "Are you going to finish here?"

"Yes," he said quietly.

"Yes?" Dad mimicked him. "What's wrong with you? You got your period or something?"

"Dad!" I said sticking up for my brother like I always do.

He looked at me. "Don't Dad me, why don't you go run around the block a couple times then come talk to me."

"I'll do it when you do!" I said matching his tone.

Franky and Dito smiled at me while Gwen looked at me in horror. "You can't hang with me little boy!"

"And you under estimate me." I said not taking my eyes off his. I was tired of the insults and reference to my weight from all of them. If this man goes for it I'm not giving up until my air completely leaves me.

"Alright, then show me. Let's go!" Dad said.

Franky and Dito got excited. "Daddy why does it always have to be a battle of the men? Why can't we just eat dinner and be kind to each other?"

Franky and Dito stared at her, "you're the main mess starter!" Dito said.

"There can only be one Queen Fernando!" Gwen blurted.

"Leave him alone Gwen!" I barked at her.

"Dinner is over! Let's go!" Dad said dropping money on the table.

We followed Dad in Dito's car to the track. Dad gave his jacket to his driver and then he walked over to the track. I took a deep breath; I was going to give this everything I had. Even if he beats me like he normally does, I will be proud of myself for standing my ground with him. Franky told me he was proud of me, and no matter what happened here he was going to remain proud. I thanked him, but I knew if I didn't win this I wouldn't hear the end of it. I had on jeans and sneakers at least. Dad had on dress shoes, slacks, and a shirt. He looked at me coldly and said I better not give up, I thought to myself YEAH RIGHT! Ain't nobody giving up. I asked how far we were racing and Dad said until I gave up. I told my heart to slow down; I needed to save the adrenaline for when Dito said Go! I kept looking at Dad's shoes like he was going to fall, but he showed no concern. When Dito said go, we took off. Dad was watching to see how hard I was going to go while I was watching for the same. I always knew he was fast, but this was on a whole other level. Whoever told the lie that fat people were slow never met my Dad. We were neck and neck and if I sped up so did he. He was toying with me, but I was doing the same. We were halfway around the track and my Dad was floating, the old man's still got it. When we hit the home stretch I decided to finish big instead of trying to keep going lap for lap. I could feel a cramp coming on in my stomach from my undigested food. My legs were tightening, and I kept telling myself to breathe. I gave it everything I had and to my dismay he was still right there on my side. I kept going and going until I felt like I was going to vomit. We passed everyone and I couldn't do it anymore at this speed, I slowed down then I proceeded to vomit on the grass on the side. Dad stopped a little ways ahead of me breathing heavy but controlled. I HATE HIM! "TIE!" Dito yelled.

"You better get your eyes checked son." Then he looked at me. "You ok?"

"I'm fine!" I said as I spit in the grass trying to clear my mouth.

Dad came in and gave me a big bear hug, "I'M PROUD OF YOU SON!" Right as I was about to feel good about myself, "next time you challenge me. You better win!"

Jenise

"You're on the Dean's list." I whispered as I took a seat at Blu's table in the library.

"Of course I am." He said matter of factly.

"How come I haven't seen you around?" I asked.

"Because I'm on the Dean's list. You only see me at social events when I'm making money." He said watching my eyes.

"Do I want to know what that means?"

"No," as I took paper out of my bag I saw him scan me out the corner of my eye. "Jenise, what do you want?"

"I want your brain matter to rub off on me." I smiled, "all the tables were full. You mind that I'm sitting here?"

"I guess not!" He looked down at his book, then back at me. "Franky ask you out yet?"

I swallowed air, "why would he do that?"

"Don't you like him?" He asked like he knew the answer to that question.

"Franky's not my type."

"He seems to be everyone's type."

A girl came out of nowhere, as she stood in front of our table she flipped her chocolate hair that she perfectly ironed. "Hi Ethan, I was wondering…" She stopped talking when she saw the look Blu was giving her. "What?"

"You are so rude! We were talking." He grumbled.

Her eyes darted to me, "I'm sorry. I…."

A man approached our table. He told Blu he needed to leave immediately. Blu exhaled, "Whispers. I need to finish this."

"You know the drill, let's go." The man said with a deep and raspy voice.

Blu looked at me, "let's go."

"Me too? Where are we going?" I said packing my things right back up.

"Come on." Blu said waiting for me.

The girl stood there looking irritated that Blu completely ignored her. When we went outside, Blu gave his car keys to someone and we got in the car with the man who came inside the library. I asked Blu where we were going and he said to another library that would be less crowded. When the guy dropped us off, he gave Blu a number to call when we were ready. This library wasn't as crowded as the one we were at. I asked Blu why we had to come to another library and he said there were too many people at that other one. I told him I felt like the secret service just relocated us. He didn't say anything to that; he went back to his schoolwork. We were working hard and I got a lot further on my work than I thought I would. The assistants to the librarians pulled whatever book I needed which saved me time. When my stomach grumbled one of the assistants told us that the library was closing soon. I looked at the clock and it was five minutes until curfew at my dorm. We were twenty minutes away. I tried to hold in my scream. Blu looked at me and then he looked at the clock. He said he didn't realize it was that late, he apologized for not keeping a better eye on the clock. I used the pay phone to call Grace. I told her I was going to miss curfew. Blu said he'd let me sleep in his bed and he'd take the couch.

"So," I leaned forward. "Is Whispers your birth given name?"

He looked at me in the rear view mirror. "Why do ladies always ask that?" His voice smiled even though his face didn't.

"You seem mysterious and a name like Whispers adds to the mystery."

Whispers looked at Ethan in the mirror. "Is this your girl?"

"No, she's Dito's friend." He said nonchalantly.

"Ethan? We're not friends? Our Kool-Aide battles were our bond I thought."

"If that's what you call a friendship. I thought you and Franky were going to give it a go."

"Franky? Why would I be in to Franky?"

"All girls are in to Franky."

"I guess that's why I'm not all girls. Franky and I can only be friends."

"You too good for my brother?"

I thought about it for a second. "Yes I am!" Ethan looked surprised and then we both laughed, even Whispers chuckled a little. "Every girl is after Franky, I don't want that aggravation in my life. Franky has so many girls he'd never appreciate me."

"That's what you want?"

"Isn't that what everyone wants? To be loved and appreciated?"

Ethan looked at me like he was looking for a put on in my eyes. "Things virgins say."

"Is that supposed to be an insult, compliment, or your assumption of my situation?"

"How could being a virgin be an insult?"

"Cause your comment wasn't meant to make me feel good." I said looking at him.

"All I'm saying is sometimes you connect with people and it has nothing to do with your future."

"That doesn't make sense to me. Who you sleep with today sticks with you tomorrow. Especially if you end up pregnant."

"There's ways to protect yourself from pregnancy."

"It doesn't always work." I said.

"It does most of the time."

"Most of the time isn't always, and if I don't mean anything to the person that's two people heart broken now. If it isn't love I'm not interested."

Whispers laughed, "Most is definitely not always. I've got tons of kids to prove that, and some I don't know about I'm sure."

"Speaking of that my dad's reached out to you?" Ethan said to Whispers.

"Yeah, he called me." He exhaled, "I don't think that's me directly. I need to do some more digging."

"Have you seen him?" Ethan asked.

Whispered exhaled, "I got a good look at him." He exhaled again, "I'm doing my homework."

I looked at Ethan waiting for him to share. "I always wondered what my life would've been like if I didn't know my father. My dad said he's a dead ringer for you."

Whispers gripped the steering wheel. "He's not a dead ringer for me, but he has my coloring and things. He doesn't have to directly be my son for that to happen."

Ethan started to say something else. "Ethan! Go ahead and talk to your pretty little friend."

I blushed, "thank you Whispers."

Whispers looked at me then Blu in the mirror. "You're welcome darling."

When we got to Blu's apartment T looked surprised to see me. Blu explained that the library we were at got too crowded so Whispers moved us and we lost track of time. Blu asked what I wanted to eat as he held the refrigerator and freezer open for me to see my options. He had steaks, chicken, ground beef, pork, lamb, turkey, you name it, and he had it. He also had the individual goodies on that special plate as well. I chopped the potatoes as he made the patties for our hamburgers. Blu finally warmed up to me a little, but I could tell he was guarded like I wanted something from him. When I told him his burger was good he genuinely smiled which was nice for a change. "If you think this is good, you should try my Salisbury steak. My gravy will have you licking your plate."

"So you really know how to throw down in the kitchen?"

"Look at me and tell me you didn't know that?" He said sarcastically.

"What is that supposed to mean?"

"You know I eat well."

"Whatever, I didn't know you knew how to cook."

"My mom owns a shop in Oakland. Sometimes she would work late, and most times she was tired from being on her feet all day. So I would make dinner. I liked to be able to dazzle her taste buds with new tastes and flavors. Whenever she comes over or I go see her, she gets excited when I cook."

"I can see why, this is just a hamburger and it's delicious. Can you pencil me in for your Salisbury steak dinner?" I smiled at him.

Blu's eyes danced around the kitchen. "Yea, I'll ask Dito if that's ok with him."

"Why would you ask Dito? Matter of fact why do you keep doing that?"

"Doing what?"

"Every time you can you bring up your brothers, like I belong to them or something."

"I don't know which one you're interested in."

"Dito has a girlfriend."

"So, most females don't care about a man's dedication unless it's to them."

"I'm not most females. You will never meet another Jenise Wright. I thought we were all friends. I didn't realize I was only Dito's friend."

"My friend? Whatever! Have you ever reached out to me?"

"Um, I sat at your table today. We don't have to be friends Ethan, I thought we were though."

Blu chewed for a minute; "we can have dinner this weekend. BUT! I'm not serving Kool-Aide with my meal. That's an insult to everything. If you can't handle wine the whole thing's off."

"BUT! BUT!" I said with big eyes.

"You'll drink plenty of water before and after. You will be fine."

"I'm not twenty one yet."

"So!"

"But what if I get a taste and then the next thing you know I'm strung out? Doing everything I can for my next drink! All my hard work to get here washed down the drain. A total embarrassment for my parents!"

He blank stared at me, "you came here to be a theater major?"

I laughed, "no. You think I should be an actress?"

"No, I didn't say you were good." Then he smiled.

Blu gave me his pajama top and he took the bottoms. Even his closet was immaculate. His bed was big and fresh, like his linens were washed minutes ago. I snuggled under the covers, I dozed off for a minute and then I had to pee. I cracked the door and Blu was up turning the channel. I thought I opened the door quietly, but he looked at the door anyways. "What?"

"I gotta potty." I said hurrying to the bathroom as Blu watched me walk. When I came out I walked towards the couch. "What are you..."

He cut me off, "go to bed." He didn't look at me.

"Huh?" I was confused.

"You don't have a bra or bottoms on. You can't walk around here like that. Go to bed!"

Instantly I felt embarrassed. "Oh, I didn't think of it. Sorry." I said hurrying to the room. I got in the bed and chuckled to myself. Does my nakedness affect him?

Chapter 3

Ethan

She has to have some kind of agenda. She keeps popping up wherever I am. She keeps talking to me, complimenting me? I don't have time for some jive time fun thing. I tried to sleep but I couldn't. What does she want? When I knew she was sleep I cracked the door and I looked in. The light from outside was shining on her in the middle of my bed. I gasped as it looked like a tornado hit it. She spent the night with Grace before, I saw what they did to T's bed and I naturally assumed it was like that because of the two of them. Now I see she's a wild sleeper. Nice try, but I'm not falling for it. I will not play the fool again thinking a girl likes me and she doesn't. She ain't gotta do all this just to get the dick. I think she's a virgin though, so she got all these ideas of what she thinks sex is. Virgins are the worst! They take a year before they let you feel on them, another year just to put a finger in. They run from you acting scared the whole time…. At least that's what Franky says; I've never had a virgin so I wouldn't know. I'm not worrying about this girl. She wanna be friends, fine. I'll be the best friend she's ever had. She's not getting over on me; I don't care if she walks around here… dang near NAKED! See! Virgin stuff! She didn't realize she was asking for me to come in here. I quietly shut the door. I went back to the couch and I told myself to go to sleep.

My phone rang at eight o'clock exactly like the person was waiting. It was a customer calling and needing an entire pan of brownies for a party tonight. I quoted them a price and I told them that included my gas and the RUSH order. I needed to replenish my stash to fill this order. If I would've had classes today, it would've sucked to have been them. I called my Dad and I told him I needed more *cake mix*. He gave me a number to call. When I called he answered on the first ring. I simply said this was Blu. He told me where to meet him.

When I knocked on the door Jenise stirred in the bed. She looked around the room like she was trying to remember where she was. I told her I needed to ride out to Oakland. I asked if she had classes this morning and she said no. I asked if she wanted me to take her home. When she stood up and stretched, I turned my eyes as my shirt kept going up showing her underwear. I handed her a toothbrush from our guest stash, and then I closed the door. I got in the shower and she came in to brush her teeth. She was still brushing when I stepped out in my towel. "Ethan!" She said staring in the mirror. I looked at her, "you're solid!" She said like she was surprised.

I didn't say anything I kept walking to my room. I put on lotion and my clothes. As I made my bed I could smell Jenise in the sheets that fast. She didn't smell bad, but I wasn't expecting it. I told myself I'd deal with it later.

"Can I go with you for the ride?" She asked with a smile.

"Why?"

"I've never been to Oakland." She batted her eyes at me.

I started the car to let it warm up. "Are you a cop?" I watched her eyes for a hint that she was lying. I didn't want to hurt a girl, but I would if I had to.

She put her hands up to her chest, "me? No! Why would that matter?"

"Just checking. You want me to take you to your dorm?"

She thought about it for a minute. "No?"

"I don't have time for indecision, I have to go!" I growled.

"Calm down, I'll go with you." Then she looked out the window. "Are you mean because you didn't eat breakfast?" I didn't respond, "You know it's the most important meal of the day."

I didn't say anything. I drove to Oakland to the rendezvous spot. Jenise watched with big eyes as I got out the car to talk to my father's runners.

"How's it going Blu?" Troy said shaking my hand.

"You know another day another dollar."

"Who's the girl?" Malcolm said looking in the car.

"Just a friend. You got it?" I said changing the subject.

I opened the trunk to my car; Troy took a brown paper bag out of his trunk and put it in mine. "Blu is that your girl?" Troy asked looking back at Jenise.

"Just a friend."

Troy looked at Malcolm. "I know you're Frank's son and all, but you can't bring friends with you. You shouldn't bring your girl either." Troy said

"I hear you." I said looking at Jenise. "Dad talk to you yet?" I asked them.

"You got your order." Troy said not knowing what I was talking about.

"About your mom."

"Pam's in jail, she'll be there for awhile. I told him that." Malcolm said.

"Ok, I was making sure."

Troy smiled at me, "there's more to it than just that isn't it?"

"Man! I got to get to school. Anything involving Pam is more than I want to talk about." Malcolm said unattached and walking towards the passenger side of the car.

"Alright then Blu! Later!" Troy said walking towards the car.

"Later!" I said.

"Those guys weren't big and scary looking at all." Jenise said sarcastically.

I looked at her but I didn't say anything. I started the car then I heard her stomach grumble. "You're hungry again? Didn't I feed you last night?" Then I smiled.

"I can eat when I get back to my dorm."

"Hold on, let me see what time my momma starts today. Maybe we can eat with her."

"Your mother!" She stretched her eyes big. "Ok! She won't get the wrong impression will she?"

"She's a mom of course she will." Then I drove to my momma's house. I almost turned around when I saw my father's car and driver in the driveway.

I knocked on the door and my momma opened up right away. She gave me an excited hug. My Dad was sitting on the couch looking annoyed that I was interrupting his time. I asked my momma if she could join my friend and I for breakfast. "What friend?" My Dad said walking to the window.

My momma's face got really excited. "She's just a friend momma, please don't assign anything else to her."

"You brought a friend with you on your run this morning?" My Dad said burning me with his eyes.

"What's wrong with that?" My momma asked not knowing what we were talking about.

"You gonna ride with Dad or me?" I asked my momma ignoring my dad.

Dad pulled my momma into him, "she's riding with me."

When I got in the car I told Jenise my parents were leading the way. Jenise watched my parents, but I knew she was looking at my Dad. We went to a cafe and my momma hugged Jenise. My Dad barely said hi, he was dissecting everything about her. I guess when he realized Jenise was harmless he turned on the charm. My Dad had Jenise and my momma blushing. Jenise kept stressing that we were just friends and nothing more. As we were leaving to go our separate ways my momma told Jenise, "friend or whatever. I like you, and I want to see you again." Then they hugged.

****

"Ethan!" I heard someone calling my name.

I took a deep breath then I turned around to see Jenise coming with a big smile. "Yes?"

"I got a ninety-eight on my final!" She smiled proudly.

"Congratulations!"

"You dang right! Thank you! Studying with you is good for my average. Now, I would like a celebratory dinner please."

"You can't demand a celebratory dinner." I said trying to cover up my amusement.

She faked surprise, "Ethan! We are friends. It's not demanding between friends. If I was some random chick I could understand."

"You're so spoiled!" I said shaking my head and walking away.

"Only cause you spoil me *Big Daddy*." She smiled.

I cracked up, "Big Daddy?"

She put her arm undermine as we walked. "Yes, I know you make those girls call you daddy when you're doing it."

I stopped walking, "how do you know?"

"Duh! Girls talk."

"They talk about the wrong stuff." I said as I continued to walk.

"Like you guys don't talk?"

"We're guys we're supposed to talk."

"And they're nasty girls. Go figure."

I looked at her out the corner of my eye. "What they say about me?"

She smiled, "I'll tell you while you make us dinner."

"I can't today, I have to go to Oakland."

"Ooh! Can I come?"

"Good grief woman!" I exhaled, "do you have to go everywhere I go?"

"You're my best friend, of course I do." She smiled.

"I thought Grace was your best friend?"

"Grace is my sister, besides she's so busy with T these days I hardly see her."

"I'll need to leave you with my momma for a few minutes. I gotta meet up with someone."

"As long as that's ok with her, I like your mom." She smiled.

"Yeah she likes you too."

"Hi Ethan!"

"Hi Blu!" Two girls said walking past and shooting me wanting looks.

Jenise frowned, "what's wrong with you?"

"They don't know who I am. That's disrespectful!"

"Next time speak up then. Don't sit over to the side complaining but you don't do nothing." I said, "You got classes tomorrow?"

"Nope, lots of homework though."

"Pack an overnight bag. We'll study tomorrow."

She smiled real big, "ok!" She got real excited.

I took her to her dorm, she packed her bag. She said Grace left her a note saying she was spending the night at my place as well. We dropped her bag off at my place then we headed to my mom's shop. My mom got so excited when she saw Jenise. I looked at the time and I told them I would be right back. Jenise sat in a chair and started chatting with my mom and her customers.

I drove over to Oakland High and I parked next to Troy's car. The lunch bell rang and he came right out. Troy said he only had half of what I needed. He said Malcolm had the other half with him. He got in my car and we drove over to the middle school. Malcolm was standing over to the side waiting. "I had no idea you were in middle school."

"I get that a lot." He said dryly as he put his bag in my trunk.

"Am I picking you up?" Troy asked him.

Malcolm shook his head no, "library." Then he walked back to the school.

Troy drummed his fingers making a beat on the car. "Who is Whispers?"

"He works for the family."

"What he want with us?"

"He's recruiting you."

"The way Frank got everything set up, it makes no sense for a cat from San Francisco to recruit us. What about Bick or somebody over here?"

"My father speaks highly of you and your cousins. All of you are hard workers and you've impressed him. Malcolm had the drop on that sucka before everyone else."

"I know! Malcolm dropped him Fuzzy finished him. That was a good day." My father was meeting with this family who have been trying to move in on my family's territory. We only sell grass to the lower markets. We're too close to Berkeley not to take advantage of that market. The heavy stuff is only sold to high-end customers. Even though EVERYONE in the Bay Area knows this. There's always some wanna be big shot who tries to challenge our throne. They were with my father at this meeting when one of the guys thought he was going to take my father down. My father already had the guy on his radar when Malcolm dropped him, Fuzzy finished him, and Leonard had the next guy down. Then Troy asked who was next. When my father told Whispers about it, Whispers has been trying to reach out to them. Their grandmother is a piece of work and has been interfering. So my father told Whispers to recruit them. That old lady loves the money her grandsons bring in besides her other hustles, but she's afraid of losing control of them.

"You two are so young to be so lethal." I said.

"Ain't that like the pot calling the kettle black?"

"I didn't kill anyone in middle school."

"True, but you were capable of it."

"True, my dad is impressed with your work. I can see you all having the whole East side if you continue like you have."

Troy shook his head. "We gotta get away from our grandma first. There are only so many moves we can make with her watching. She holds on to Malcolm for dear life."

"He's her favorite?"

"If she could have one I guess he would be." Troy said looking around.

"I'm going to try to move out this way next year. I might not bake anymore, I'll have to see."

"Alright. Keep me posted." Then he got out the car.

My momma's customer had Jenise and my momma in stitches as she told them some story very animatedly. I stood over to the side letting them finish. "Ethan you're always so serious, you know that story was funny."

"I wasn't listening. What time is your last customer today?" I wasn't interested in the laughing fit they were sharing.

She dried her hands on her apron as she walked over to her books. "I have a press and curl at three. She's got a lot of hair, I'll be off around five."

"Jenise and I will make dinner."

"I'm making dinner?" Jenise said pointing to her chest.

"You don't cook?" My momma asked.

"Eating is more of my specialty."

"You're going to learn something today." I told Jenise to come on.

She put on my momma's apron, washed her hands and waited for instruction. I smiled to myself cause she looked cute. I showed her how to slice the beef into thin slices. I chopped my herbs and spices. Salted the water for my pasta. I prepared my French bread. I seasoned the meat then I poured red wine over it. Jenise's eyes got big as she watched me. I explained that the alcohol would cook out and the flavor was going to be amazing. Then I poured a glass. "Taste it, you have to use good wine. Cheap wine will do, but good wine is better."

"Um, um Ethan! I don't want to."

"You've drank a small child like serving before with me. Did you start binge drinking behind my back?"

"No, but...."

"You can have this small amount. We're going to drink this with dinner." Her eyes pleaded, "You'll be fine Jenise."

She took my glass and took a tiny sip. "It's good." Then she put her arms around me and laid her head on my chest.

I rubbed her back, "look at that. You survived." I kissed the top of her head.

She let go as momma walked in the door. Momma excitedly said the house smelled amazing. I told her to wash up and Jenise and I would set the table. Jenise suggested putting the dishes on the table instead of making our plates in the kitchen.

Everything was delicious and momma kept smiling at me cause she really likes Jenise. After dinner Jenise cleaned the kitchen. Momma asked if Jenise and I were a couple yet. I told her that Jenise was just a friend. She kept rolling her eyes like I was putting her on or something. When Jenise sat back down momma brought her hair stuff and started brushing and combing Jenise's hair. Jenise was in heaven when momma massaged her scalp. Then she braided her hair all over her head up into a bun they told me when I called it a donut. Jenise said she loved it. We didn't leave momma's until almost eleven when she kicked us out.

Jenise said she didn't bring pajamas cause she liked sleeping in mine. I was putting my clothes away when she kept engaging me in conversation. I sat on the bed and before I knew it I had dozed off. Jenise was laying on my chest and she wouldn't let me go. I was irritated at first. Then I decided to go to sleep.

Then next day we were in the library all day. When I said I was tired early she put my pajama top on again and pulled back the covers. I frowned. She said she likes sleeping with me. "You are the ultimate pesky little sister you know that don't you?" She smiled, "I'm better than a little sister. I'm your best friend."

"I didn't choose to be your friend." I said as I laid down.

"I chose you, but who cares." She snuggled into me to fall asleep. "Goodnight *Big Daddy*!" We both laughed.

****

T looked at me angry, "why would you take Jenise to Oakland? I'm not hearing the end of it. You brought a girl home and I've brought no one!"

"It wasn't planned." I said looking at my mail.

"Think next time!" He said angrily sweeping the kitchen floor.

I went in my room and I sat on my bed. I took a deep breath, and then there was a knock at the door. "Go away Jenise!" I barked.

"Come on Ethan! I wanna know too." She whined from behind the door.

"Just open the door and go in." T said.

She opened the door just as T and Grace started kissing, then she closed it behind herself. She climbed on the bed next to me and sat Indian style as she anxiously waited for me to continue. "Open it!" She said excitedly.

"I didn't ask you to come!" I said annoyed.

"And here I am! I'm here to support you on this, you need me. Open it!" She said staring at the envelope.

"No! Get out! Let me open it in peace!" I said.

"Your bark is bigger than your bite. You know you're happy I'm here. Stop toying with me and open it."

I shook my head and I opened my envelope. My eyes scanned the letter. Jenise watched my face looking for a yes or no. I decided to torture her for interrupting my alone time and I read the entire letter. Jenise had my arm entangled in hers as she waited on the edge of her seat for my answer. I looked at her, I smiled. "I got in!" Jenise screamed and dove on me for a big hug. "I KNEW YOU WOULD GET IN! There was never a doubt in my mind!"

"Right. That's why you caught the bus and drug Grace over here." I teased.

"She was coming, I tagged along."

"Why didn't you call me? I would've came and got you?"

"You would've waited until you read the letter and then you would've tortured me in the car until I could get you alone to ask." She started to celebrate again and then she stopped. "Next year you're going to be all the way in Berkeley. Will we still be friends?"

"Of course we will. Everyone else will still be here." I exhaled, "you could transfer to Berkeley."

"Yea right! My scholarship is here. I'm gonna miss you my brotha! Dito isn't as much fun since he broke up with that girl." She scratched her chin. "I don't get it. He didn't like her, he broke up with her."

"They say his momma was a piece of work. I barely remember her. I remember she wasn't nice, I could tell she didn't like me. I told him to take this down time to think about what it is he's looking for."

"What about you?"

"What about me?"

"When are you going to get a girlfriend instead of all the bed hopping like you do?"

"You all in my business. When you gonna get up off your nun costume and get you a man?"

"As long as guys think I got to put out just to be with them, I won't have one. My temple will remain clean." She said. "Besides, Jamal and I have a plan; and I know he wants me to wait on him. I'd rather wait for him then be like most of the girls here."

"You like dangling your virginity in front of these guys. You are such a tease!"

****

"Let's rap," I said to T as I sat on the couch with a drink. T sat down with his drink and he waited. "You ever been with a virgin?"

T smiled real big at me and then he leaned forward in his seat. "You and Jenise gonna do it? FINALLY! You two drive us crazy!"

I smiled, "what are you talking about?"

"Your little best friend act is sickening. It's about time you two got together."

"T, Jenise and I are not together. We are just friends. I'm asking because I got my Master's Program acceptance letter. I'm leaving Stanford next year."

T stared at me for a minute, "I don't like it." He shook his head, "what you wanna know?"

"Everything, I know you can't treat a virgin like anyone I'm used to dealing with."

T leaned forward to stress the seriousness of his next words. "She has to want it."

He watched my eyes. Then he explained that male or female when you don't know what to expect you become very idealistic about the whole experience. He said if my virgin wasn't ready, it could do more harm than it ever could do any good going there with them. He said her body would tell me if she was ready. He told me I was still going to have to be patient. He said some can handle you going in, and then the others, which is most, you have to gradually work your way in. He explained that every movement was new so you gotta go easy on her. He told me to keep checking with her and making sure she was ok. He said to remember to assure her that everything is ok and to be gentle and patient. I frowned at him when he mentioned oral; I've never gone down on a girl. He said you don't do that for everyone only the special ones. Our quick talk turned into hours of conversation. T gave me pointers on things I hadn't thought of. Way too much ammunition for a single man. When Dito pounded on the door Grace, Jenise, and a new girl followed him. Dito introduced her as a friend, but the way they slobbed each other down made all of us too uncomfortable to stay in the room with them. T and Grace slipped into his room closing the door. Jenise said she wanted to hear a record in mine. She made me sit through another letter from Jamal. I told her I would be happy to actually meet this guy and determine whether she's been exaggerating his personality. "One day, it's not like he can drive out here for the day or weekend for that matter."

"Let's plan a weekend in Stockton. You can take us around, show us where you grew up."

"There's nothing to do in Stockton though." She said sadly.

"The party will be wherever we are. I can't promise that Franky won't bring Georgette to guarantee he's getting some that weekend. Dito could bring this girl."

"What about you? You gonna bring somebody?"

"I could, I wouldn't want Jamal to get the wrong impression."

"My parents think we're going to get married, I don't see it though. Can you imagine me on a farm?"

"Yes, hair wild and running with the animals." We laughed, "seriously though. It's clear as day that you're waiting on him."

Jenise looked away, "we had a long talk before I left. No alcohol, no drugs, no men."

"What does he think about all of us?"

"Well..." She looked around the room. "He thinks that it's always the group of us. He has no idea that you and I are ever alone. He'd die if he knew we sleep in the same bed."

"Where does he think you sleep?"

"Over girlfriend's houses of course." I shook my head at her. "Oh come on, he'd never understand that we were just friends especially if he saw you."

"Saw me?" I held my smile prisoner.

"Yes, a handsome, educated, black man."

"With all this blubber?"

"Oh come on, you're solid. Muscles everywhere, and you're toned. You're not fat, you're intimidation on two legs."

I laughed, "You're the first person to ever say that."

"It's true. You could not be my best friend if you were any other way."

"Thanks best friend." I blushed. "I can't be held prisoner in my own place. We're going back out there."

We made them come up for air, Grace and T on the other hand, well. They were behind closed doors.

In the morning, I looked at Jenise wondering if any of that was true. She was out of her mind last night.

Jenise

"Let's play cards." I announced.

Ethan brought the cards out, we played a few games. Then Dito said let's play "I never!"

When he brought out the bottle I sighed, "really? You're all going to be drunk. It's not fun being the only sober person."

"Have a little, we won't tell nobody." Dito teased.

I silently agreed and then the game got interesting. As we all sat there tipsy Dito went to the kitchen. "Blu, can me and my girl split a rice treat?"

"Sure, bring me a brownie." Ethan said.

"That's not fair! You've never let me taste your brownies EVER!"

"Cause you can't handle these brownies."

"Can I taste?" Ethan held up the brownie and I took a huge bite out of it. He told me I was going to regret it.

We started playing spoons and I remember trying to fight Ethan for the spoon. It felt like I was dreaming, cause everything was in slow motion, but then it wasn't. Since it was only a dream I kissed Ethan just like I have a thousand times in my dreams before. This is the first time he tasted like chocolate and cognac. Then I stood up and started singing, "WAIT! WAIT A MINUTE MISTER POSTER MAN! WAAAAIIIIT AND SEE!" I belted out my song and the audience loved me. I could hear the applause. I couldn't understand why Dito and that girl were making out in front of the stage. Ethan told me it was time to sleep he gave me his pajama top as usual. I braided my hair and then I waited for him to come back. "Ethan looked at me." He laid down and smiled at me. "You are so beautiful! You're the best friend a girl could ever have. One day you're going to make some lucky girl very proud."

"Right!" He rolled his eyes.

"Ethan I hate when you do that. You're beautiful and if I didn't promise Jamal I would kiss you."

"You always kiss me." He said brushing me off.

"Yes, like this." I kissed his cheek, "but I really want to kiss you like this." I laid on top of the covers on top of him. I kissed him deeply like I always do in my dreams. I opened my legs and I sucked on his neck. When his strong hands gripped my butt that's when I realized this might be real. I laid my head on his chest and his heart was pounding. The room was spinning and I wondered, if this was really real or if I was dreaming in taste. I couldn't tell if this was real or not, so I got off of him. Then I got under the covers.

"Why did you kiss me?" He asked me.

"We always kiss in my dreams." I said looking at him.

"You're high!" He smiled at me.

"You made me drink. I love it when you do that. It's so naughty."

Ethan leaned in and kissed me. His hands went all over my body and parts of this felt real.

I woke up in the dark and Ethan was sleeping on his side with his back to me. I snuggled up to him like I always do. I smiled to myself when I thought about how real that dream felt.

****

"Hello Jenise how are you?" This girl I couldn't exactly remember said.

"Hi."

"I need to ask you about Blu." She said as she leaned in.

"What about him?" I said looking her up and down.

"Is he your boyfriend?"

"Best Friend," I said still watching her.

She smiled really big, "is he dating anyone right now?"

"Dating? No." I said crossing my arms.

"Can you put in a good word for me?"

"I don't know you to put in anything for you. If you want him, you gotta make that known. I don't play the telephone game."

"Are you mad? You seem a little defensive."

"I'm just saying." I was mad, but I had no right to be. Ethan deserves a girlfriend; he's such a good guy. I just hope that she doesn't try to interfere with our friendship if they do end up together.

"Do you know if he's going to be at the party tonight?"

"He'll be there, we'll probably be on the wall as usual. You should come over and introduce yourself."

"I'm nervous, what should I say?" She said excitedly.

"Start with hi. After that I don't know what to tell you. If you can't figure it out, maybe you shouldn't speak."

"Ok, no I got it. Thanks. I'll see you tonight." She said excitedly hurrying away.

I couldn't even focus on my class anymore. All I could think about was what I was going to wear tonight. At first I wanted to wear something fabulous. Then I thought about how I didn't really have too much in my closet that fit comfortably. It's all Ethan's fault with his delicious dinners. Grace and I have gained a good ten plus pounds each. I made a mental note, we are going walking tomorrow. I will not be caught off guard like this. I exhaled and I told myself to be happy for my friend. A girl seems to genuinely like him. When I got to the dorm, I showered and got dressed. Grace and I packed our usual overnight bags and then we left with Ethan. The party was in this recreation center that had a wall outside the patio that went from low to high. A lot of Ethan's customers would approach him here. We'd hang out for a while then we'd go inside. Ethan would sit while we all danced. I was sitting on the wall making Ethan laugh like only I know how when I saw her coming. She smiled at me and I grinned back, Ethan was in an ok mood. That didn't mean she would know how to read him. I thought about when I first met him and how uninterested he acted in me until I wore him down. I wanted to see how he'd be with this girl.

"Hello Ethan my name is Nohemi." She said gently.

"Hi." he said like he was unimpressed. He didn't know she wasn't a customer.

She looked nervous, I saw Ethan recognize her nervousness. "Will you dance with me later?"

"Dance? That's a random request." He said dryly.

She smiled nervously, "I've been watching you for sometime. I was silently hoping that you would notice me on your own, but you've got tunnel vision for real. We don't have to dance if you don't want to. I was looking for an opportunity to get to know you better."

"Why?"

"Cause I think you're cute." She blushed.

Anger blazed inside of me when Ethan blushed. That was my cue to leave. I told him I was going inside. I hung out with Franky mostly. You could've peeled me off the ceiling when Ethan and that girl came in and slow danced. I couldn't believe it; he never even danced for me. I was quiet and thoughtful when we got in the bed.

"Nohemi is pretty," I said.

"I guess," he shrugged.

"You like her?"

"I guess, but I don't know her. She could be crazy." He was real nonchalant.

"You're going to make sure you find out though aren't you?"

He laid on his side and faced me, "when Lena Horne, Lola Falana, Eartha Kit, or Dorothy Dandridge walk in a room. You don't ignore them."

"Wow! She's that pretty?"

He shrugged, "I guess." Then he smiled as he thought about it. "A girl's never approached me like that before. Normally when they come, they come looking for something. She seemed like she was looking for me."

"You get her number?"

"Of course."

"You know if you start dating her I can't spend the night over here like this anymore. It wouldn't be respectful."

"Hhhmmm," is all he said then he laid down.

I tried not to show my irritation, but I thought I deserved a better answer than just a noise. Maybe he'd call the whole thing off or something. In the middle of my mental rant I realized he went to sleep.

****

"Mom, Dad this is everybody." I said proudly introducing everyone as we got out of our cars.

My parents thankfully said hello back, but I could see something in their eyes. "Can we talk to you alone for a second?" My dad asked.

"Of course," I said walking inside.

"Baby we wished you would've told us you were coming. We have news and we didn't want Jamal to tell you." My dad said.

My mom opened the door and there was a baby in a playpen. "Who's baby?" I asked as I went in to say hi. The closer I got the more I saw my dad. I turned and looked at my parents.

"Don't be angry. We didn't want you to stay home to look after us. It was an accident." My mom said.

"I have a little brother?" I said picking him up.

"Yes, but...." My dad swallowed. "He's a special needs child."

"What does that mean?" I asked looking at him, he looked perfect to me.

"He has no hearing out of one ear. The doctors say we should teach him sign language just in case." My dad said looking sad.

"If we knew you were coming we wouldn't have sprang this on you at the last minute." My mom said.

"It's ok. It's ok. I understand." I said smiling at my baby brother. I walked out the door with him and I smiled at my friends and their significant others. "I'M A BIG SISTER!" I yelled excitedly. They cheered for me and then I invited them in.

"I guess this kind of stuff happens when you don't come home for two years." Grace said as she took the baby from me. He smiled at Grace and stared at her face. Grace looked at T, "you want kids don't you?"

"Of course I do, but not any time soon." T said smiling at the baby.

I walked over to Ethan, "isn't he precious?"

Ethan smiled at my little brother. "Congratulations."

"So you had no idea that your parents were having a baby?" I shook my head no. "I would be horrified!" Nohemi said.

"That's the difference between you and her." Ethan responded.

"Blu would you take it so well if it were your parents?" She shot back.

"What's to take badly or not? He's here and they're happy."

On that note I walked away, I could tell she was getting on his nerves. My dad was showing Ethan his barbecue grill out back when Jamal walked in the front door. He was so shocked, happy, and surprised to see me. My mom called him and told him to come as soon as he could. Jamal rushed to me and picked me up with the baby in my arms. He didn't care that everyone was looking, he hugged me. I introduced Jamal to everyone; I took him out back to meet Ethan. Ethan was quiet for a minute, no one else noticed his hesitation but I did. "I'm going to go home and change. Then I'll be right back." Jamal said excitedly.

"Can you show me where the store is? I'm grilling today." Ethan said watching me. When I tried to give my brother to my mom he didn't want her. He only wanted me. So I dressed him and I brought him along with Ethan and I. Everything was the same out here, everything. "I can't believe I have a brother. I used to want a sibling so bad." I said putting little Fred in the cart.

"So that's Jamal...." Ethan smiled at me. "I knew you were a skinny chaser like everyone else."

"He's been working hard out here. What do you think?"

"He's respectful, eye contact, strong handshake. He's good."

I got excited, "I'm glad you like him."

"What do you think of Nohemi?"

"I didn't know you liked her. She's pretty." I said trying to move past my disappointment.

"Yes you did. You were there when we met. You..."

I didn't want to talk about Nohemi any more. "What kind of barbecue sauce you want?

Ethan eyed me, "are you jealous?"

"Blu! Don't be ridiculous!"

"You never call me Blu, you always call me Ethan. You're jealous?" He said jumping around excitedly.

"SHUT UP! SHUT UP!" I said looking around. "NO! What had happened was I realized that you don't care that your relationship with that girl compromises our friendship. I can't spend the night over your place any more, which means no more hanging out for me."

"Don't be ridiculous, you can still spend the night. I'll just go back to the couch."

"What about when she comes over too?"

He smiled, "you know there's a way all three of us could share the bed." He raised his eyebrows at me.

"Don't make me cut you!" Then I took a deep breath, "promise me I won't lose my best friend just because he has a girl friend."

"Promise."

When we got back to the house Jamal was just getting back as well. Jamal and Ethan seemed to hit it off. So I decided to suck it up and be nice to Nohemi.

Our weekend in Stockton turned out real nice. Everyone got a long real well. Nohemi stayed with me at my parent's house. While everyone else stayed in the local hotel. I tried to fight it, but I couldn't help it. I found myself liking Nohemi, and she genuinely likes Ethan. How could I fault her for that? I couldn't stop myself from falling in love with my little brother.

Sunday morning Jamal came over to go for a walk with me. He kept smiling at me and saying how much he misses me. I told him I miss him too. He said he likes my friends, which made me feel good so I smiled real big. "How did you lose so much weight?"

He made his muscles show on his arms. "I've been working hard." He smiled.

"I've been eating good, Ethan is always cooking and I've had more Kool-Aide than I know what to do with."

"That's ok. When you come home you'll lose it all again." He smiled.

"So then you agree that I've gotten fat?" I frowned at him.

"You're not fat, but you have picked up weight."

"Jamal you're supposed to deny it. You're supposed to tell me I'm beautiful no matter what."

41

"I didn't say you weren't beautiful."

"Fine!" I said feeling self conscious about myself.

Jamal put his arms around me. "I'm sorry, I didn't handle that right. Jenise you're beautiful no matter what size you are."

****

I was breathing hard trying to catch my breath. I went over to the water fountain on the side of the building with the bathrooms. Jamal claims it was fine that I gained weight, but I doubt he meant it. Grace and I have been hitting the track hard. Grace's parents were coming in a month. She said she'd never hear the end of it if her mother saw her in her current state. I told her how my mom didn't say anything but she was looking every time I put something up to my mouth. Now that I have more free time since Ethan and Nohemi are together, I'm determined to lose the weight.

"I got something for you to drink if you're thirsty." A guy I didn't know said. I stood up and started to walk away. "Hold on, I got something for you." He said grabbing my wrist.

His grip was hard, "let go of me!" I yelled.

He slapped me, "shut up!" He pulled me and threw my back up against the building.

"LET ME GO! LEAVE ME ALONE!" I screamed.

He punched me in my face. "I TOLD YOU TO SHUT UP!" He reared up like he was going to hit me again. I covered my face. He threw my body up against the building a couple of times and then he told me to be quiet. He started pulling on my pants when Grace ran up and hit him hard in the head with her canteen. She was screaming and making a lot of noise. Two guys on the track ran over and the guy stumbled away. They helped us and gave us a ride to Ethan's place. I wanted to go to my room so I could lay down and cry. Grace insisted that we come here instead. Ethan looked like he was about to leave, Grace called out to him as she got out the car. He was walking calmly until he saw my busted face. His face turned angry as he hurried and asked Grace what happened. He thanked the guys for bringing us and he gave them money for their trouble. He put ice in a towel and told me to put it on my face. He told T to draw the guy how Grace described him. Every time he looked at my face he got mad all over again. When T finished the picture he asked Grace and I if that was him. Grace was good with details cause when Ethan held the picture up I started crying all over again. Ethan was yelling into the phone and then Dito and Franky came. Ethan grabbed all his goodies off the plate and then they left us with Dito. You could tell he didn't like being left behind with the girls, but we all knew he wasn't much of a fighter.

The boys were gone for a long time then there was a knock at the door. Nohemi was fussing cause Ethan didn't show up for their date. When she saw me sitting with my head tilted back she asked me what happened I removed the towel and she screamed. My nose and lip were busted and my face was swollen. She screamed and ran to me. She started apologizing immediately. She got me more ice for my face and she gave me ibuprofen for the pain and swelling. I woke up when the front door opened; all three of them had fire in their eyes. Nohemi asked if they found the guy, Ethan said no then his eyes darted to me. T was in no mood to be social. Grace followed him to his room. Dito and Franky hugged me then they left. Ethan told Nohemi he was taking her home. She asked what about me. He told me to take his bed and he told Nohemi that he was going to sleep on the couch. Nohemi volunteered to stay with him, but his patience was short and he told her no. I heard the door slam and he was gone for a long time. I was sleeping when he came and got in the bed. He kissed my forehead and asked me how I was feeling. I cried and I told him I was scared that the guy will find me and hurt me again. Even in the dark I could see his face. "You're going to stay here until your face heals. You aren't going to the police. This guy will never hurt you or anyone else ever again, you understand me?" He watched my eyes.

"You said you didn't find him?" I watched his eyes cause I was trying to understand.

"I didn't, just like I'm not laying in this bed comforting you. I'm sleeping on the couch remember."

Chapter 4

Ethan

"A senseless crime has occurred. Golfers at the Stanford University Golf Course found the body of Rupert Graham early this morning. He appears to have been beaten and left here to die. The Stanford police are heavily investigating this senseless crime." My father turned off the TV. "What happened?
"He tried to rape Jenise."

My Dad sat down, he exhaled. "I understand. I wish you would've come to me. This could've been handled neater. Any loose ends?"

"The Good Samaritans. They brought Grace and Jenise here. I don't know if they really saw the guy. As long as they didn't see him we're good."

"I'll send Detective White in to interview them. He'll contact you for information." Then he exhaled, "ok so now I understand. However, you're going to have to be cleaner than this. We don't run this area and this job was sloppy. I understand why Ethan was emotional, but why weren't you all thinking?" He asked my brothers and T.

"Maybe if I would've been there I could've helped with that."

"Fernando please! You know why they left you at home." My father barked.

"To protect the girls in case anyone came to our place." I volunteered.

My father frowned at me, "you keep protecting him. What's going to happen to him when you're gone next year?"

"Blu! You leaving?" Franky said in shock.

I looked at my father; I was dragging my feet about telling Franky and Dito. "I'm going to get my Master's at Berkeley."

"But you could do that here." Franky said.

"He's manning up! Standing on his own two feet. I'm very proud of you." Dad said. Franky rolled his eyes and shook his head. When Dad left Franky and Dito went in hard on me. They were angry that I was leaving, and as usual T was the peacekeeper.

****

"It makes sense to move in here during the summer. Blu is going to move out. Ooh! Ooh! We could enjoy the summer! Go places, do stuff! Act like students. T goes home for the summer so it will be like you two have your own place." Dito told the girls.

"You might as well stay when the school year starts too." I said.

"We are not giving up our dorm room, but we could live between the two. If that's ok with you?" She said to T.

"Of course, I'll sneak back as much as I can."

"How much is the rent here? I don't think we can find summer jobs that pay enough to afford this place." Jenise said.

"You don't pay rent here." T said, "It's covered."

"We're still going to need money." Jenise said.

"Franky and I need a cleaning lady." Dito said.

"How much?"

"We can work that out, but you'll be overpaid for sure." Dito smiled.

Jenise snuggled into me on the couch. "I can't believe you're leaving me. What am I supposed to do without a best friend?"

Sometimes it's the way she says best friend that makes me ask her what she just said. "My location will not change our friendship. You'll still see me."

She smiled, "I will?"

"Nohemi is still out here."

She slumped, "you guys aren't breaking up for the summer?"

"She's going home to Tennessee for the summer so call it whatever you want." I said, and then I looked at my watch. "Speaking of her, I got to go." I said rubbing Jenise's back to move. She moved reluctantly. I grabbed my keys and then I drove to Nohemi's apartment that she shared with her roommates. When Nohemi opened the door she had on a very pretty dress, her hair and makeup were done. She tried not to smile shyly as she greeted me. I could smell food and I thought we were going out to eat. She said she ordered in. I asked where her roommates were and she said they were out for the night. She asked me if I wanted to eat now or later. I said later since she was guiding me to her room. I stopped her, kissed her, and then I picked her up and carried her into her bedroom. I want to say I was surprised, maybe that this was happening today, but that's it. I knew what I was doing when I kept pushing her buttons, turning her virgin mind into my slave. So I can now say I've been with a virgin. I laid there asking myself what the big deal was. If anything I had to be way more controlled than normal. I laid there wondering how long I had to lay there. I kept stopping myself from thinking about Jenise. I don't normally think about her when I sleep with someone else. I even felt a little guilty, but I couldn't put my finger on why.

****

Nohemi's nose is completely open now. She's worse than Jenise, she wants to go everywhere I go. She's always up under me, a benefit is that there's plenty of sex and she's a fast learner. The sex is okay, she's into it. Nohemi is a sweet girl, I care for her. She's the first girl who wanted to be with me because she wanted to be with me. Not because she was looking for something or addicted to the D. I sit here trying to figure out how my future is going to be. I see Jenise married to Jamal returning to her roots. T and Grace driving each other crazy, I keep asking him when is he going to put the shy guy act to rest with her. He said it wasn't an act and something about her brings out his shyness. Franky would probably end up being an old bachelor, kind of like our Dad. I know Dito's going to end up in Berkeley somewhere with a ginger bread family. As for me, I guess I could see myself with Nohemi. I don't really know yet.

I do know I am counting down the weeks until summer is here and Nohemi is gone. I love her, but I need a break. Random sex and freedom to just be. "Will you come out to visit me in Tennessee?"

"I can't promise a visit during the summer, it tends to be a busy time for me. I'll be working for my father."

"I want you to meet my family." She said making her face sad.

"We'll have to see. You ready? Jenise is in the car."

Nohemi frowned at me, "why does she have to come with us. I wanted to meet your parents without an audience."

"My momma has been asking for Jenise, you invited yourself."

"It's only natural that she should want to meet your girlfriend and not just your friend." She was right, unfortunately I told my momma about Nohemi after she invited herself to come. I could hear that tone in my momma's voice when she's suspicious.

My Dad's car and driver were in the driveway when I pulled up to my momma's house. When my momma opened the door she smiled at Nohemi and she said she was pretty. When I introduced my Dad, Nohemi looked surprised, it was written all over her face that I never mentioned that my father was white. I kind of thought it was obvious when she saw my brothers, and it wasn't a detail I focused on. I asked where Gwen was and my Dad said she was with Nana. Nohemi told my Dad that I must get my sexiness from him. My Dad frowned at her and then he walked away. Jenise turned her head probably trying to hold back her laughter, but my momma told her to come to the table after she washed her hands. Jenise showed Nohemi to the bathroom. Momma got on Dad's case about being rude. Dad looked at me and said I couldn't be serious about that one. I didn't know what he meant; he said she was fake and an opportunist. During dinner my Dad directed his conversation to Jenise, he had no interest in talking to anyone else at the table. I guess he was trying to make sure Nohemi didn't feel like the only person who was left out. My grandparents who live next door came in the door excited to see me. They said they saw my car outside. I told them I wanted them to meet my girlfriend, my grandmother said she was happy she was finally getting to meet her. Then she walked up to Jenise and said "how you doing baby?" Nohemi looked angry and I pointed her to Nohemi. I noticed that when we left my momma wasn't telling Nohemi she had to come back or any of the things she told Jenise.

On the car ride home no one said anything. Nohemi hurried to her door even though I walked with her, and she said goodnight and shut the door. When I got in the car Jenise asked me if I thought Nohemi was mad at her. I told her she didn't do anything so she shouldn't be.

****

"OH MY GOD ETHAN! ETHAN! ETHAN!" Nohemi called out. I rolled over and started to fall asleep. "Blu, wakeup!" She said tapping me. I pulled back my irritation, I didn't want to talk and it seemed like lately that's exactly what she wants to do when we're done. I don't want to talk; I'm all talked out. I told her I couldn't promise faithfulness while she was gone. She got mad and we had a really big fight, and then the next thing I know she's been trying her best to one up me. I see where she's going with some of her combinations. However, I've been having sex since middle school. Outside of being my first virgin, she'll never be my first at anything else. She tried to tell her parents she wanted to stay out here for the summer and they weren't having it. Ever since then she's been trying to have me pledge faithfulness to her in her absence and I refuse. "Are you going to be with anyone other than Jenise?"

I exhaled, "of course I am. Jenise is just a friend."

"It didn't seem like it with your parents. They didn't give me a chance, your mean daddy wouldn't even talk to me." She whined.

"I told you to be straight with them. That's your fault for thinking you could go in there and charm them."

"Seems like she already has them charmed to me."

"No, she has always been straight with them. She had no reason to try as hard as you did. We're just friends."

"Men and women can't be friends. Someone if not both of them feel something for the other person. They just don't act on it for one reason or another. Eventually the truth comes out. I wonder if it's her or you."

"You're being ridiculous."

"I'm telling the truth. I hate your inside jokes, and hearing from her how to handle you in certain spaces. I'm your girlfriend, and I should know you better than anyone else."

"But you don't, you don't know me like she does. Shut up whining about it, you sound dumb as all get out right now. You sitting over here whining about my friend and my family is irritating me. If this is how you want to spend our last few moments before I take you to the airport then fine. Say one more thing about them and I'm leaving. You can find your own way to the airport."

She sat up, "Ethan!" I looked at her straight-faced. "Fine! I'm going to meet someone this summer and I'm going to have mind-blowing sex all over the place. Let's see how you like it!"

I rolled over putting my back to her. "That's fine make sure he straps up first, if he knocks you up make sure you start planning your wedding before you come back. I don't care Nohemi."

She got mad and hit me with the pillow.

****

"Malcolm, Troy you stay. Thank you gentlemen." My Dad said dismissing everyone else. "Listen, I have to get going but I need you to pay someone a visit for me. Blu has all the information." He said putting on his jacket. "Why don't you all go out to the main dining room and discuss." He looked at the nosey waiter who kept coming in our banquet room.

Malcolm looked at the waiter, "maybe we should go across the street to the pizza place."

"Good thinking." My Dad said.

We said our goodbyes and then the three of us walked across the street. We sat in a booth in the corner. "Ok, what you got for us?" Troy said popping his knuckles.

"A Gabriel Harris, he lives at 112 South Cedar…" He cut me off.

"Wait a minute!" Troy smiled, "that address sounds familiar." He looked at Malcolm.

47

"South Cedar Street? By the freeway? Red and white house, he drives a brown Oldsmobile?"

I looked at the paper, that was correct so far. "You know him?"

Troy smiled, Malcolm didn't. "We just paid him a visit. He should be stinking by now." Malcolm sat back in his chair. "How do you..."

Troy tapped him, "here she comes!"

Two school-aged girls approached our table. "Hi Troy! Hi Malcolm!" The first girl said too excited. The other girl kept her eyes on Malcolm.

"How you doing ladies?" Troy smiled, "ladies this is my boy Blu."

"Hi Blu," they said in unison.

I could tell he didn't remember their names so I played along. "Ladies, and your names are?"

"I'm Janet," the excited girl said.

"I'm Yvette," the second said keeping her eyes on Malcolm.

"Are you guys waiting on your pizza?" Janet asked.

"No, we were just talking." Troy said, "but I am a little hungry. I guess we'll go see what grandma cooked if she cooked anything."

"Well we were about to order a pizza. Can we share our pizza with you all?"

"Naw, I might eat your whole pizza. We're about to...."

"We'll get two, don't leave we'll be right back." Janet pleaded pulling her friend by the arm.

When they walked away Troy smiled real big, "cute kid, but she stupid."

"I thought you said she was weak?" Malcolm asked in a non-interested manner.

"She is but she's also buying pizza. What's going on with her friend?"

"I never called her back." Malcolm said, he looked back at Yvette. "I guess it's time to call her." Then he looked at me. "So how we wanna handle this? He's gone already."

I handed Troy the envelope under the table. "As far as I'm concerned you were proactive on the job."

"Cool!" Troy said putting the envelope in his inside jacket pocket.

Malcolm looked at his watch, "I'll be right back. I gotta go to the bank before it closes." He walked out the door, got in a car and drove away."

"He got his license?"

"Nope," Troy said. Then he leaned in, "why your father want Gabriel gone?"

"I don't know but my uncle asked for the visit. As long as it's done is all we care. Are there any loose ends?"

"None, the place is clean. You staying for pizza?"

"No, there's no room for a fifth wheel here. Besides I have no interest in hanging with little girls."

Troy shook his head, "before you go. Why is Roscoe having such a hard time with Whispers recruiting us?" His relaxed demeanor was gone.

"Whispers' team handles family matters. Everyone wants to be on Whispers' team. The fact that he's recruiting you ahead of so many other qualified people is causing problems." I watched Troy's face as he processed the information.

"Whispers thinks he's my father or something?" He watched my eyes.

"You don't know your father?"

Troy relaxed, "no. It seemed like you were going to say something like that. We're good."

"Where did Malcolm go?" Yvette said looking around with her change from the pizza in her hand.

"He will be right back." Troy said turning his smile back on.

I went to my momma's house where she and Jenise were laughing and having a good time. After a couple of minutes I realized my mom was sharing stories about us when we were little. "Isn't this a conversation you're supposed to be having with Nohemi?"

"Your dad don't like that girl, I know you like her son, but be careful."

****

"You like it?" I said looking out the window.

"Yes, this is a nice place. It's just that I don't know what I'm going to do without my best friend next year." She said as she put her arms around me and pouted.

I put my arms around her and kissed her forehead. "You won't see me everyday, but I'll be around. I need some space you know?"

"I get it, I hear you got to focus when you're in grad school more than before anyways. I'm really going to miss you." She exhaled, "it's going to be weird being in your apartment without you being there."

"You never know when I'm going to pop up, just be ready for me when I do. Meanwhile I need to furnish this place." I looked around my place. "I'll take a lesser car and drive it with pride. My living space has to be decked out."

"Are you going to bake here too?"

"Probably not," I sat on the floor.

"How will you make money?" She said sitting next to me and snuggling into me.

"I've been working with my Dad more these days. He pays better, and there's no risk of getting in trouble working with him."

"How come Franky and Dito don't work with him?"

"Franky is way smarter than me, but he can't even focus on school. He needs to get it together there first. My Dad is constantly disappointed with Dito, it's not fair. Dito is smart and a hard worker, I'm sure he's going to bring him in later. It won't be the same." I felt irritated. Dito and I have sat and had a straight up conversation. I asked him if he's gay. He's not gay, but people assume that because he's different. He said the accusations and assumptions hurt his feelings. He said it made him wonder about himself for a while as well. He said there's nothing exciting about a man to him. He asked when I've ever seen him go on and on about a man. I hadn't, but if he felt that way I doubted that he would say anything. Dito said he likes women, but he seems to keep finding the ones that act like the woman who gave birth to him. He said he was looking for someone like momma.

"I don't know about Franky being smarter than you. You're extremely intelligent. When you're helping me with my work it amazes me how you understand all that." She smiled, "best friend I need you to talk to me." I looked at her. "Did you come

49

out here to get away from us? You're tired of me following you around like a lost puppy aren't you?" She smiled.

"I wouldn't move across the Bay to get away from you. You used to bother me when you followed me around everywhere. I think I've gotten used to you being around. It's going to be weird being alone, but my brothers need to figure out their lives."

"I thought you got sick of me. Cause you could commute out here, you didn't have to move. I love you best friend and I miss you already." She said

I looked at Jenise, "you love me?"

She blushed, "yes. Don't get big headed best friend."

"How's Jamal?"

"He's good, he's expecting a good harvest this season. He should be sitting pretty. Colette Stevens graduated last summer and she has her degree in etymology and she's helping Jamal and my parents with their farms. I'm told they can see a difference already."

"Colette?"

"She's from Stockton." Jenise said like she didn't want to think about it.

"Colette?"

"YES!"

"She the reason you haven't had any letters to pester me with?" I smiled.

"He's been working hard trying to turn his farm around, and..."

"Why don't you guys breakup for now? I don't understand why you put yourself through this torture."

"Jamal and I have a plan."

"Plans change. You know the distance is too much. Why do you hold on so tight? To someone you've outgrown?"

"It's better to have someone than no one."

"I'm no one?"

"You know how it is. I have Jamal, you have Nohemi. They chose us and that feels good. To have someone choose you."

"I'm no one?" I repeated my question because she was avoiding it.

"You're my best friend."

"And that's no one?"

"Oh come on Ethan, if I never would've forced myself on you would we even be friends? I know things are less than ideal with Jamal and I right now, but this will pass."

Jenise

Shopping with Ethan has been so much fun. He's let me pick out most of the furniture for his new place. Except for a few things that he thought were completely girly, he's let me pick whatever I want, he didn't care about the price tag. We keep going to all these high-end stores and then I find out that a family member owns it. Ethan was very specific about his dinette set and everything in the kitchen. Everything else he was open to, as long as it fit his bachelor theme. Ethan was hanging the artwork I picked out when there was a knock at the door. I opened the door and there was an elderly couple. The man looked at the apartment number, then back at me. "We're looking for Ethan Wallace."

"You're at the right place. Come on in!" I smiled.

"Nana!" Ethan smiled as he stepped back from the picture. Then he came and gave her a big hug.

She looked at me, she didn't smile then she looked me up and down. "And you are?"

"That's my best friend." Ethan said.

"Oh this is Jenise! She's pretty son, I thought she might've been the girlfriend." She said.

I smiled from ear to ear. She not only heard of me, she knew my name. "Thank you Mrs. Wallace. It's nice to meet you."

"Call me Nana," she said coming in for a hug.

"I'm proud of you son. This was a good move, getting away from your brothers. How's Timothy holding up? Is he going to move as well?" His grandfather said.

"T's moving along just fine. My brothers are fine too."

The old man blew air. "Franklin chases skirts like he's paid to do it. Fernando can't decide which team he wants to play for. Is Timothy majoring skirtology as well?"

"Timothy has a girlfriend." Ethan said matching his grandfather's stance.

"Annette hasn't mentioned a girlfriend." Nana said.

"Auntie Annette doesn't know about her yet. If they continue like they have she'll find out eventually."

She looked at her husband, "Franklin I think we should go see my babies. I want to drop in on Jennifer too."

"As you wish my love. Blu come talk to me." Then they went in Ethan's bedroom.

"Come sit down with Nana, tell me all about you." She said gesturing towards the couch.

I smiled at her as I took my seat. "Your grandsons did the same thing. They wanted to know all about me when they met me."

"Is that so? And you're still here so you must've said something right." She smiled.

I told her the same story I told her grandchildren and as we talked I made her laugh. When she laughed the first time she relaxed a lot. She asked me about my major in college. I told her I had an interest in etymology naturally being from Stockton. I told her my passion was in art and design. I told her I wasn't much of an artist personally, but I loved it. She smiled at me and stared for a minute. Then she rubbed my hand and said she liked me. She said she doesn't understand how I could sit back and watch the person I love date someone else. I fell silent and I moved my eyes around the room. When I started to dispute her claim, she told me to hush up and save my lie for someone who would believe her.

When Ethan and his grandfather came out of the room, she said it was her turn. She told her husband to take her seat. He sat down and stared at me like he could see through me. When I started sweating I asked him if he would like some Kool-Aide, he said sure. Then he asked me how long before I transferred out here to be under

Ethan. I didn't know what to say to that. The thought hadn't crossed my mind to switch schools. My setup at Stanford was too sweet; I didn't look to see if it was transferable. I told him I hadn't thought of transferring over to Berkeley. He watched me some more then he told me that I didn't know what I wanted to do about anything. He said he didn't like indecision. "With all due respect Mr. Wallace why would my indecision about my life bother you?"

"Cause you're around my grandson with that racket. I don't know what's wrong with you young people, but you gotta get it together!" I handed him his glass of Kool-Aide, he snatched it then he took a drink. He looked at the glass. "This is good, did you make it?"

"Yes I did." I smiled.

"Un huh, you gonna let your drink do all your sweet talking huh?" I smiled at him. "Smart girl."

****

I was in the shower singing my heart out. "SO TAKE A GOOD LOOK AT MY FACE, YOU'LL SEE MY SMILE LOOKS OUT OF PLACE...." I got in the shower after Grace and Dito left to go grocery shopping. I had the place to myself and I was enjoying it. I washed my hair and I took extra long in the shower. I wrapped a towel around my head, and one around my body. I grabbed an apple out of the fruit bowl and then I went to my room. Ethan was looking in the closet when I stepped into my room. I screamed to the top of my lungs. He cringed at my blood-curdling scream. "DON'T SCARE ME LIKE THAT!"

"I thought you would know I was here, my jacket is on the couch."

"Like I would've even seen that!"

"I tell you to pay attention to your surroundings all the time."

"You said you weren't coming out this week."

"Change of plans," he said staring at my towel.

"Can you get out so I can put something on?"

He smiled at me, and then he walked towards me. "Let me see." He said reaching for my towel.

I turned my body away from him as I held on to my towel, "no! See what?"

"What your momma gave you. What you think?"

"Um, no! What's wrong with you." I said completely embarrassed.

"Oh come on, I'll show you mine if you show me yours." He teased.

"Your what?"

"My everything, let's play doctor."

I cracked up, "you are too silly. Seriously let me get dressed."

He smiled, "or don't. We're the only ones here. I won't tell if you let me see."

I couldn't stop laughing, "no." I said backing away from him.

"Best Friend, I need a favor." He said making his face innocent, as he sat on the bed.

I cut my eyes at him, "what is it?"

"T told me about this thing, that I've never done, but I was curious about. I was wondering if you would let me try it on you? Please!"

"Stop messing with me Ethan. If T said it, it's nasty and I don't want no parts of it." I said grabbing the lotion off of the dresser.

"It was worth a try." He said smacking my butt as I walked past him.

"Why are you acting weird?" I asked, we've always been snuggly. Ever since he moved to Berkeley he has been way more touchy feely.

"I'm not acting weird, does it frighten you that I act this way even when I'm sober? You like to blame the alcohol too much."

"What way?" I said grabbing my clothes to go back to the bathroom to dress. He told me to come here with his finger. I exhaled; he was acting weird but whatever. He clasped his hands together like he was about to pray but he pointed them at my thighs, then he stuck them between them and forced my legs open and he put my knees on his shoulders. Right when I was going to say something his mouth stole my air. I dropped everything I had in my arms. "E-THAN!" I said as I tried to understand what his mouth was doing to me. I tried to grab the clarity to move, plus I felt like I was going to fall. He stood up and then he laid me gently on the bed on my back. He wouldn't let my legs go. He was kissing me unlike any kiss I've ever experienced before. My body started shaking, and then he wiped his face on the towel and smiled at me as he backed away. Then he smiled a knowing smile. "What was that?" I said trying to catch my breath.

He smiled, "did you like it?"

"What was that?"

"An experiment. I needed to test it out; you came in here all clean and freshly showered. So I figured you'd give me honest feedback."

"DON'T EVER DO THAT AGAIN!" I said trying to pretend like I didn't like it.

"How was my tongue was it too hard or not enough?" He said ignoring my pretense.

"Ethan, I don't even know what that was supposed to be." That was the truth, "can you save the sexual experiments for Nohemi?"

"How you know that was sexual? That could've been an Eskimo kiss. How you know Alaskans don't say hi like that?"

I cracked up laughing! "I HATE YOU ETHAN!"
****

Ok so now what? Every time I look at Ethan, I remember his head bobbing in between my legs. I can't focus on anything, all I know is I want to feel that again. I can tell Ethan knows exactly what he did to me too. The way he smiles at me is different now. I cringe when I think of the fact that even though it was quick he saw me naked. I dress in the bathroom now, cause I never know when he's going to pop up and I'm afraid he'll do it again. Now when he holds me he leans his body in. He brushes up against me, pats my butt. The other day he flicked my nipple and electricity traveled through my whole body. He said "Oops!" Like it was an *accident*. YEAH RIGHT!

Now when he spends the night, we go to sleep like usual, but in the morning he spoons me with it poking me in the back or rubbing up against my butt. The other day it was awake and on me. I thought he was sleep, when I turned around he was looking at me. He got up on all fours and hovered over me. It was hard and screaming at me, we both looked down at it and then he looked at me. He kissed my lips then he got up and got in the shower. I was on fire thinking of what could've happened. I put my pillow between my knees while I screamed into his. I had to take multiple showers that day; no matter what I did I couldn't wash the desire off of me.
****

"Grace you have to help me." Dito said pleadingly. "I need to break up with this girl, but I need help. She might get mad. I need you to be my Cyrano."

Grace sat her beer down. "Don't you think I have more important things to do with my time than follow you around breaking up with your girlfriends?"

Dito looked around, "no. T's not here, so that means you have nothing but time." He laughed.

"Jenise could help you," she offered me without checking with me.

"No offense, Jenise is not good with the words like you are. Let's go to my place where I can hear the words you feed me." He said taking her hand.

"I didn't say yes."

"PLEASE GRACE! I need to do this before we go on our annual camping trip with Nana and Poppa." He said.

"Why are there going to be girls there?" Grace asked eyeing him. No doubt wondering if Timothy lied when he said it was just a weekend of cousins hanging out.

"No, but I don't want this looming over my head. My Nana will pull the information out of me anyways, but I want to say I broke up with her. If I don't my Nana will worry about me. We don't want an old lady worrying about her grandson and getting sick do we?"

"Fine Dito! Fine! I get to pick the next girl out."

"What? No way!" He said shaking his head.

"Fine, then you figure it out on your own then." She folded her arms. Dito gave in and then they left.

"You're going camping with your grandparents, that's so sweet." I said feeling the drink I took from Ethan. He and Franky were sitting at the table debating back and forth smoking and feeling their drinks. I sat on Ethan's lap at the table and I took his drink again.

"Jenise have you ever had a charge?" Franky asked with a smile.

"What's that?"

Franky smiled, "show her Blu."

Ethan looked at me with extremely relaxed eyes, "I'm not going to do it."

"I'LL DO IT!" Franky volunteered.

"Stay back fool if anybody's gonna do it, it would be me. She can't handle a charge, a bite of my brownie and she was gone."

"Will it hurt?" I asked curiously.

"No," Ethan smiled.

"Ok, what do I have to do?"

Franky got excited as he hopped in his chair. "Be cool!" Ethan told him. Then he returned his attention to me. He told me to stand up. Then he told me to straddle him and to come in close. Franky sat on the side excitedly pounding the table as I did as I was told. Ethan told me to swallow the air he gave me, and to hold it as long as I could. I didn't know what he meant. He took a draw off of his joint and then he blew into my mouth. I did like he told me until I couldn't hold back my choke. When I stopped choking he said we needed to do it again. We did it three times and then he smiled and said he was turning me out. Franky smiled really big as he watched me. Then he said he was going home and calling somebody, he'd settle for Georgette if he had to. I sat there staring at Ethan while he stared back at me. I asked him how Nohemi was and his face dropped. He told me that I must've wanted to ruin his high. When I said no he leaned forward and put his head on my chest. When I stroked his head he moved his mouth to my chest. He kissed my breast, when I didn't object to that he sucked on them. When I didn't say anything he reached in and pulled my breast out of their bra and he started sucking on them. Those charges had me floating on a cloud and somewhere between reality and a dream. When I realized this was real I got up and fixed my top. I went and turned on the TV and then I sat on the couch. Everything was tingling and although I've wanted this for some time, it wasn't right. Ethan sat at the table for a few minutes hitting his joint and finishing his drink. Then he came in the living room with a fresh drink for me and the last part of his joint. He stood over me and hit it again, and then he charged me again. This time he followed it with a kiss. He took a hit for me charged me and then took one for him. When the joint was finished he put the bud in the tray and then he turned the TV off. He told me to come on. I sat there stuck scared to know what he meant. So he picked me up and carried me in the bedroom and shut the door with his foot. He asked me why I only let him kiss me for real when I'm high. I didn't say anything to that. He gently laid me on the bed and then he started kissing me. I was on system overload enjoying his touch. He took my pants off and he rolled his eyes when he touched me, he said I wanted him. I told him I always have. Then he looked at my eyes and said, Jamal? A tear fell from my eye. Then he said Nohemi and then he laid on top of me. He wasn't heavy like I thought he'd be. I kissed him and my body took on a life of its own. I opened my legs as he rubbed against me. I unbuttoned his pants and pushed them down, we were skin to skin. He was poking me on my leg and I moved until he was in position. His breathing got heavier as he found me, I kept moving and he moved until he was pressing against me. He stopped kissing me and looked at me as he pressed in on me. He was looking for me to tell him to stop, and not to do it. I was caught between what I wanted and what I needed. He kept saying how wet I was and how badly I wanted him, I denied nothing. I let my body tell him everything. The sweetest pain and discomfort ever in my life! "Jenise! I LOVE YOU!" He said in my ear as he tried to control himself. I've heard all the horror stories, my mom even told me about her first time with my dad. None of them were like this, it was uncomfortable but I was gone. Ethan cried out when he came and the sound of him feeling good on account of me sent me over and the feeling took me under. My stuff was throbbing, but he was still inside of me. I thought we were done, but he kissed me and started going again. My body picked up where it left off and I knew this was going to hurt in the morning. Ethan rolled us over and he put me on top of him. I didn't sit up; I laid there dying as I gave into the good feeling. I put my head on his chest as my heart kept pounding trying to catch up to his heartbeat.

I dozed off and then I woke up a little clearer in mind. I was still on top of Ethan and he was watching my face. Embarrassment, guilt, and happiness flashed across my face. "Did we really have sex? I wasn't dreaming that?" He shook his head no as he watched my eyes. "What's wrong?"

"No condom, not even half of one."

"What does that mean?" I asked him panicking a little inside.

"That you could end up pregnant."

My body tensed up and I got off of him. "No! No! I can't Ethan. I have to finish school. No one in my family has ever made it this far. I can't Ethan!"

"What are you saying?"

"That I can't have a baby!"

"Ok."

"You feel the same way right? What about Nohemi, grad school right?"

"Why would Nohemi matter now?" He said watching my face.

"Ethan please! No one can know about this. I don't want her to hate me." He repeated himself, "Because she's your girlfriend. I'm supposed to be your platonic friend on the side. This was not supposed to happen."

"In order to be platonic you have to genuinely be platonic. You've been sending me I love you vibes from the beginning. You had to know this would happen." The bass in his voice made my brain rattle around in my head. Then his voice cracked, "Jenise you are killing my good feeling right now. If I knew mentioning that one small minor detail was going to evoke such a dramatic response I would've waited until daylight. I mean what was this then? A going away present? Nohemi and Jamal were just as real before you put my cup to your mouth as they are now."

"I don't want anyone to know about this! I'm sorry Ethan, I...."

Ethan violently turned his body to face me. "YOU'RE SORRY? Sorry? What is that supposed to mean to me? You're too dramatic and afraid! You pushed this, I was prepared to stop. Now that you got my head all messed up you're sorry? I could choke you right now!"

"Ethan, I care about you. You're my best friend!"

"You care about me? I care about Nohemi, but I love you! I thought you loved me too! You're supposed to be the one person who didn't reject me or make me feel like there was something wrong with being me!" He angrily stood up. He kicked the bed frame with the back of his foot. The whole bed jumped across the room and slammed into the wall. He pulled on shorts, and then Grace knocked on the door. I put the covers over my head when he opened the door. "We're arguing can I help you with something?" He growled at her.

"Jenise, are you ok?" She called out.

"I'm fine, Ethan would never hurt me."

"You shouldn't be so sure about that!" Ethan said as he closed the door.

"Ethan please! I'm sorry, please calm down. I'm not saying anything right."

"Calm down? Calm down for what? What just happened here has been running through my mind ever since you kissed me the first time. If you're not adding to that dream, SHUT UP!"

"Ethan! Please!"

He looked at me breathing heavy. Even though it was dark in that room I could see Ethan like it was daylight. He looked at me snatched his pants and keys. He opened the door and Grace was pacing outside. He put on his pants and walked out the front door slamming it behind himself. Grace came in and hugged me, and cried with me. We fell asleep with her holding me. Ethan woke us asking Grace to let us talk. Ethan sat on the edge of the bed with his back to me as he bent over some. "So what's the plan if you end up pregnant?"

"I can't have a baby right now."

"Abortion then?"

I swallowed, "I could never do that."

"So then what?" He said like he was trying to exert patience.

"I hope I never have to make that choice."

"Hope is not a strategy Jenise. I apologize for being so emotional that we even have to have this conversation. I've never touched anyone without a condom, I know better." He took a deep breath, "so if you end up pregnant you're going to have the baby. Regardless of all the emotional and dramatic stuff you're saying right now, I know you can't go through with the alternative. If it comes down to that I will raise the baby. You can go on with your life and continue to make your family proud. You are going to break up with Jamal. Use the phone, call him, and break up." I gasped at him; "it's senseless to hold on to him after all of this." He shook his head as he lowered it. "I am very disappointed in you and your whole reaction to all of this. I know you're emotional and dramatic, but I never thought any of that could ever be directed towards me." He took a deep breath, "whenever you want me or need me, I'll be around. I'm not going to sit here and wait for you to realize what your heart has been telling me since we met. If you take too long you'll look up and I'll be gone."

"I can't break up with Jamal."

He looked at me with evilness in his face, "say that to me one more time." His expression scared me. "Matter of fact go call him right now and do it." When I didn't move, he got up and brought the phone in the room. His face was still evil, "CALL HIM NOW OR I WILL!" When I didn't reach for the phone, he picked it up dialed a number from memory and then put the phone on my ear.

'Hello?" Jamal said.

I looked at Ethan, how did he know Jamal's number by heart. "Its me," I said with tears in my voice.

"Jenise? What's wrong?"

"I got to break up with you."

"WHAT????"

"I've got to break up with you." I repeated.

"No, Jenise. We've got a plan. Don't deviate from the plan."

"It's not fair to you, we're so far apart and we need to let go for now. I'll be home soon, then we can see if there's anything left to salvage." Then I hung up the phone. I cried so hard.

Ethan took the phone, "when you're ready for me, come get me." Then he walked out the door and shut it.

Chapter 5

Ethan

This is like a nightmare; the best night of my life became the worst night of my life. My good feeling was quickly stolen and replaced with regret, hurt, and pain. I should've waited, this shouldn't have happened now. Why didn't I reach for a condom? They were right there! Fifteen seconds could've changed my whole life. Now, I've been stuck in this apartment waiting for Jenise to come to her senses and apologize for breaking my heart. That girl is stubborn so I should know better than to hold my breath. My camping trip was horrible; I had to fake my emotional state the entire time. Franky just knew that he set the scene for Jenise and I to move to the next level. He couldn't understand why I was angry and unwilling to talk about it. Normally I'm the one to help my Nana with the cooking, but I was very bland this trip. This time when Nana talked to me about my weight yet again, I finally told her I was tired of being overweight. I was tired of looking at myself like this. I was tired of looking at myself period, and I was over this body. Why did I say that? She made me get up early in the morning before everyone else and walk with her all over the camping grounds. She amused herself with stories about my Dad when he was little and all the trouble he used to get into. I just listened and smiled, but I didn't say much. After dinner she'd make me walk with her again. She kept making my food separate from everyone else's and before I could have anything else, I had to eat a mountain of salad or whatever vegetable we were eating. She told me I could only have water and none of the other juices and soda that they brought along. I didn't care; my appetite was pretty much gone anyways. It was late and we were laying in our sleeping bags. I was staring up at the stars without a real thought in my mind. "Psst! Blu." My cousin Malachi whispered as he moved in closer to me.

"Yes?"

"I just want to go on record as saying I know."

"You know what?"

"I know what it's like, it's a girl isn't it?" I looked at him, but I didn't respond. "I know you look at me and say who can't Malachi get? But listen to me I know the disappointment of love."

I guess his little high school mind thought he was relating to me. My situation is unlike anything he could or should know about. "Right, but my problem is which one to pick?" Malachi's head popped up. "Nobody likes the one that wants me. Everybody likes the one who got too many excuses for why we can't be together."

"Two girls?" He held up two fingers.

"Yes."

Malachi scooted his sleeping bag closer to mine. "Which one do you want?"

"The difficult one unfortunately."

"What's with you Blu? We are Wallace men! When we pick a woman there's nothing she can do to get away from us. Put your claws in and go get your woman!"

I thought about it for a minute, the kid had a point. I started laughing, "you know I can't even argue with you, you're right."

"Of course I am. Go get her!" He smiled.

"I can't do that right now. I gotta work on me a little bit."

"I can dig it! Solid!" He laid down satisfied that his words lifted my mood.

****

"Whoa! Blu! Give me five! Check you out! Where did you go?" Leonard said checking me out.

"Yeah, Yeah. I lost weight, big deal. You ready to deal with business?" I said not wanting to make a big deal out of it.

We sat at that table going over numbers reconciling the summer numbers to their distribution. Everything looked really good. As we were finishing up, Eugene walked in and he sat down at the table staring directly at Leonard. Leonard stared back, neither one of them spoke. "This one of them."

"This is Leonard Latour, if that's what you mean." I said.

"My father has recruited you and your cousins." Eugene said searching his face for something.

"I am aware of this." Leonard said staring at Eugene.

"So you will receive direction from me when the time is right. Frank is vouching for all four of you, as we all know he doesn't do that. Meanwhile, the little ones can continue on with these small distributions. You all seem to have a presence here that we don't want to lose. You and the other guy will ride with me on pick up and delivery. I'm counting on you to be good, some of these idiots start thinking they're invincible and stuff happens."

"Understood," Leonard said still watching Eugene.

Eugene looked at me, "look at you Blu I remember when you were a baby running around without a care in the world. Now look at you! I have to keep reminding myself that you aren't technically little Frank. Your old man has to be proud of you?"

"I assume so."

Eugene exhaled and looked at Leonard, "I guess at some point everything was going to get real." He exhaled again, "I'll need to meet the two little ones." He said like it tasted nasty to him to make such a request.

"I don't know about little, but they're outside if you want to meet them now."

"Fine, go get them." Eugene said sitting back in his seat. As soon as Leonard was out of earshot he leaned forward. "Blu! I don't appreciate none of this! My personal life should never affect business. Emotion has no place in business; this is how people get caught up. My father never came looking for me, and I think it's ridiculous that he's trying to stick this kid on me!" I didn't say anything; I watched the fire in his eyes from being forced to do something he didn't want to do. "I don't care about this little bastard, who cared whether I knew who my family was? I had to go out and make my way. I don't appreciate being set up like this. I…" He stopped talking when Leonard re-entered the restaurant followed by Fuzzy, Malcolm, and Troy.

"This is Eugene, he was explaining our orders." Leonard said.

Eugene's eyes bounced from person to person taking in everything about each one of them. "Have a seat." They each picked up a chair and sat next to our table their eyes locked forward on Eugene. Eugene repeated what he said earlier, and then he looked at Troy and Malcolm. "You two are a bit young to be on."

"Your point?" Malcolm said watching him.

"What I just said. This is what you want to do with your life, be runners, and hired men?"

"This is a business meeting, what do you care what we do with our lives? You supposed to come in and rehabilitate us or something? Tell us what you need done and we'll do it. Don't worry about our personal lives!" Malcolm said looking Eugene in his eyes the entire time.

"You the littlest nigga talking the biggest stuff."

Malcolm glared at Eugene, "you need to get your eyes checked. Nothing about me is little."

Eugene cut his eyes at me, "so I won't say this doesn't intrigue me. However, I meant what I said." He stood up, "You have your instructions. You two," he said pointing to Leonard and Fuzzy. "Meet me at Ace Trucking seven a.m. sharp on the docks." Then Eugene walked out. They all stood to see what he was driving. You heard whistles. His car was really nice.

"What we eating boss?" Fuzzy asked me.

"Order whatever you want." I said to all of them.

Leonard looked at Malcolm and Troy, "interesting cat."

"He don't look nothing like me. So we can put that to rest." Troy said.

"What to rest?" I asked.

"We weren't sure what kind of setup this was going to be. Last resort was the thought that he could've been my father. Looking that man in the eyes I know he's not mine." Troy said.

Leonard watched them, but he was looking at Malcolm. Malcolm didn't say anything; he looked like he was putting everything together mentally.

****

"BLU! OPEN UP!" Franky called out as he rhythmically knocked on my door.

I took a deep breath; I hadn't laid eyes on my brothers and cousin since the camping trip. When I opened the door, Franky cursed as he looked me up and down. "Come in." I said holding the door open.

Franky came in and then he stood there for a good three minutes walking around me cursing and cursing. "I'm supposed to be the sexy screw up, Dito's the sensitive one, and you're supposed to be the one who's perfect in every way but a little chubby! We can't both be sexy!" He smiled with a glimpse of pain behind it.

"Maybe those roles are played out." I shut the door, "have a seat."

Franky kept looking at me, "I can still beat you."

"You could try, I don't know how successful you'd be." Then I sat down, "why are you here?"

He put his arms up on the back of the couch. "Haven't seen you in months. What

60

happened?"

"How's Jenise?"

"Their dorm opened up a week ago. She moved back in immediately for her and Grace. Ever since T came back those two haven't come up for air. Jenise is depressed but she's not talking about it."

"She look any different?"

"Wait a minute, you two haven't talked? What's going on?"

"Nothing, we had an argument."

"About?"

"None of your business!"

"Jenise is the reason we haven't seen you? She's been moping around like a bird with a broken wing. What's going on?"

"Nothing."

"Fine, have your secrets for now. Time reveals everything. Nana and Pops came out before the trip." He shook his head, "that old man gave me such a hard time. I gotta get it together. Especially now after seeing you, I guess we could all stand to step up our game." Then he looked at me long and hard. "I can't believe you left us hanging over a girl."

"Whatever man! I've been working."

"What Dad think of your transformation?"

"He hasn't said anything."

"Which means he likes it." He leaned forward shaking his head. "Ok! Ok! This seals it; I'm getting my act together. Playtime is over." He exhaled like his mind was racing a mile a minute. "What momma say when she see you."

"She didn't say anything at first, and then as the progress started to become more and more dramatic she started crying and holding my face and kissing me. She kept telling me I'm beautiful. It was weird." Momma had tried everything she could think of before to *help* me lose weight. She hated that I fell on the sword sort of speak so that my brothers wouldn't feel bad.

"When you coming back out? I'm going to need your help to pull this off?"

"My help for what?"

"Tutoring stuff like that. I'm serious, I'm getting my act together."

"Soon...."

Jenise

I couldn't stop crying, and I couldn't explain to Grace what just happened. I didn't want anyone to know, and that included my sister. I didn't feel right being in this apartment anymore. I went out and found summer jobs, one at the grocery store, and another as an assistant to this art teacher. She was very dramatic about everything and she loved when I let my dramatics about anything fly. It was like she fed off my energy. I stayed away from that apartment as much as possible, and on the rare occasions where I wasn't working I would go for walks or whatever just to be away. I had to quickly get over my fear of being attacked again. My fear of Ethan was bigger than any attacker. When my period came I had mixed emotions, on one hand I was relieved that I didn't have to choose how my future would go. The other hand I was disappointed and I couldn't tell you why. As far as I know, Ethan hasn't come back to the apartment but since I make it a point not to be there I don't know. My dreams where he would be in the bed scared me, so at first I found excuses to sleep with Grace, and then I continued without excuses, she had to deal with my wild sleeping. Working made the summer go by faster, Dito complained that I didn't stick to the plan and I forced him and Grace to hang out whenever Franky's women interfered with the schedule. I offered no one an explanation I just couldn't deal with it all.

When the dorm opened up, I couldn't get into Grace and I's room fast enough. Part of me wondered why Ethan didn't chase me, but a bigger part was happy he didn't. I knew better than to think that when I saw him there would be any sense of self-control. All I dream about is making love to him, how good it felt, and how that night should've ended. Instead of the way I freaked out and ruined something beautiful.

I was making my bed when there was a knock at my door and then the door opened. "Its me Nohemi!" She sang with the fakest smile plastered on her face.

I tried to keep guilt off of my face. "What are you doing here? I thought you and Ethan would be tangled up in each other not coming up for air somewhere."

She looked around my room, "me too. Apparently he moved and forgot to give me the information. Do you have his new number?"

"I haven't talked to him all summer."

She eyed me, "you two were inseparable, what happened?"

"I got a couple of jobs and he was working for his father. We didn't have the time to be best friends."

"How do I find him?" She shook her legs, "I'm dying to see him."

I understood the shake now, and why females lose their minds over him, seeing her shaking irritated me. "I don't know what to tell you. Maybe he moved on over the summer. If he was still into you he would've made sure you knew how to find him or he'd find you."

"You fall in love with him?" Her eyes were evil as she looked at me.

"What? No! I'm just saying is all. Woman to woman you don't chase a man, a man will chase you if he wants you."

"Ethan wants me! How could he not? Like you said he's been busy and I was helping him out by tracking him down. Thanks for the slanted advice, I'll go find Franky and Dito." She said looking me up and down.

Then she walked out the door; I sat there trying to get myself together. I had to do some thing about Ethan. I left that whole situation dangling for long enough. Someone knocked on my door and said I had a phone call. It was the art teacher; she needed to know if I would be available this week to assist her. We went over my schedule for the week. I told her as soon as I got my class schedule next week we could go over scheduling.

****

I took a deep breath, my hands were sweating and my heart was pounding. I told myself to suck it up and just do it. The phone rang four times, just as I exhaled and was about to hang up he picked up. Sounds like he rushed to the phone. My heart dropped. I was quiet for a minute and then I went in. I told him I missed him and the silence without him was unbearable. I asked him if there was any way we could go back to being best friends and forget about that crazy night when everything spun out of control. He was quiet for a minute, I wished I was looking at him to determine if he was angry or not. He asked me how do we forget that we made love? The sound of him saying that sent electricity up my thigh. I told him we just do somehow. He didn't like that answer, I told him we could consider it an experiment like that time he kissed me like an Eskimo. "I want to do it again!" I didn't know if he meant the kiss or make love, either way my body responded against my will. I told him I didn't think that was a good idea, it would compromise our friendship. He said he didn't care. He told me to get a pen and paper, when I did he gave me a phone number. He told me to call the number he gave me for a doctor and make an appointment. He said I needed to get on birth control so that there would be no more freak out sessions like I had before. He said he's never been skin to skin with anyone before me or after me. He said we were doing it again and I needed to take care of business. I wanted to argue with him and say I wasn't going to do it, but the fact that I now needed a shower told me it was pointless to deny that I wanted to do it again too. I told him Nohemi came to my room looking for him. He said he heard about that. I asked him if they were back together and he said technically. They hadn't seen each other yet. They've talked on the phone a few times. He said when he comes back out here he's coming for me; he'll see her afterwards. I stared at the number while we talked; Ethan wasn't his old self completely. He was too busy bossing me around. That night I wondered if we could ever be friends like we were before.

The next day I went to see the doctor that he gave me the number for. The doctor was very nice and Ethan's cousin was her intern. They gave me a prescription for birth control that I got to start on Sunday the first Sunday after my period. I told myself to relax and everything was going to be ok.

****

"Why have you been avoiding us?" Dito asked sitting next to me on the couch.

"I had a lot going on. I broke up with Jamal and that was system overload for me. I had to busy myself with work and anything else to distract me."

"Un huh!" He said as he looked in my eyes. "We were friends first, don't punish me for what happens between you and Blu." I put my head down; I had no response for that.

This was the first time I was spending the night as a friend and not as a roommate since that night. Grace convinced me I needed to come out and spend time with my family cause I had been neglecting everyone. When Grace and T were ready we left with Dito and we went to the party. Grace was introducing Dito to his next girlfriend. Those two were a mess and they fussed the whole way to the party. Dito tried to act like he wasn't excited to see whom Grace picked out for him. I was curious to see as well. T and I hummed and laughed between the two of us when

63

Grace approached us. Dito was looking around and as soon as he saw her he sat up straight, it was so cute. This girl was cute, and sweet looking herself. Grace introduced her as Tess. You could tell by Dito's demeanor he was into this girl from her first hello. Grace and I high fived as we watched them like animals at the zoo. Tess had no idea that Grace chose her for Dito, she simply told her she had someone she wanted her to meet. When Franky finally showed up to the party mister bookworm asked me where I've been, I told him I had a life changing summer, and I decided to focus on my minor in Arts and make it my Major. I decided to drop Etymology altogether. I wrote my parents and told them about it, they weren't all that happy but they accepted my choice, they had to really. I was hoping to have a job or find one in Graphic Design in the city when I graduated. Now that I've broken up with Jamal, the thought of going home seemed unbearable. Franky kept looking at me like he knew something. He finally took me on the dance floor and I asked him what was wrong with him. He smiled and shook his head no. We were dancing and breaking it down on the dance floor when the room spun. Nohemi and Ethan stepped on the dance floor next to us. I looked at our table and Grace was sitting on T's lap looking at Ethan with her mouth open too. Dito was focused on Tess and T looked like he already knew. Franky laughed at my frozen reaction. I looked at Franky then I looked at Ethan. I always knew they looked a lot a like, but thin Ethan was a dead-ringer for Franky, but better in my opinion. My body was on fire immediately. Ethan gave me a hug like he normally would, he said hi and long time no see like everything was cool. Nohemi watched my eyes, as she clearly was not happy about our interaction. Ethan's eyes glided over me as he told me I lost too much weight, I looked good, and he was happy to see me. I couldn't believe how nonchalant he was acting, I told myself to get my emotions in check. It seemed like every girl was drooling over Ethan, the ones who knew him before especially. Nohemi was acting extremely possessive, but I couldn't blame her. Everyone wanted Ethan now that he's lost all this weight, but that was the only difference in his demeanor as far as I could see. I rode with Ethan and Nohemi back to T's place. Ethan was checking me out whenever Nohemi wasn't looking. That night Ethan and Nohemi left, he told me he'd pick me up from my dorm in the morning. I slept in the bed where I lost my virginity wondering what the next night was going to be like. In the morning I walked over to Dito's place and asked him for a ride back to my dorm. He went on and on about Tess. I was glad to hear that he liked her. She seemed sweet and down to earth, nothing like the girls he normally went out with. I unpacked and then I packed my bags again. Around eleven Ethan walked in my room, no hi hello or anything he kissed me deeply like it had been killing him to hold back yesterday. He asked me if I was ready for *Big Daddy* and we laughed. We got in his car and we drove to Berkeley. We went to the store to buy food for the rest of the weekend. When we put everything away he kissed me in the kitchen. He put his hand under my skirt and panties. He rolled his eyes and said I was ready for him already. He kissed me some then he said he didn't feel like it right now. I frowned at him and he smiled at me. He said I behaved badly this summer, and my punishment was that I had to wait for him. The tent in his pants said he was ready, but his mouth said he wasn't. We sat on the floor by his record player, he'd put on an album and then we'd talk. Mid-conversation he took my skirt and top off. He said he wanted me to stay like this for now. I was sitting there uncomfortable at first but I talked past it. Then he took off his shirt and his pants. Ethan was still solid, but now his body was more defined. I kind of missed his old body, but this one was fine too. As I was telling him about one of my assistant funny times he took off his draws and then he took off my bra. He looked at my breast and then he said I was as beautiful as he remembered. When I started to talk again he kissed me, I was excited and scared. Last time I was sore for a few days afterwards. He took off my underwear and then he went in. He exhaled deeply upon contact, he was completely in when my body started shaking, he smiled and then he slowly went deeper. He released three times inside of me before he needed to rest. My mouth was completely dry and I was in heaven. We fell asleep on the floor. I woke up a little cold and to the smell of food cooking. He made us dinner, and he told me to remain naked, He fed me naked and then he kept kissing me. When we got in the bed we talked for a while, and then I got up to go to the bathroom. When I came out he bent me over and my goodness I thought I was going to die, the sweetest death ever, but death. He told me to move my hips and then he resumed to pounding me. It surprised me when my body started shaking in this position, in the middle of my shaking he flipped me to my side, put my leg up and grabbed my breast as he went to town on me. My eyes crossed so many times. I now understood that I was being punished for waiting so long to call him. He was making sure I realized what I had been staying away from. We slept for a little bit and then he woke me up, this went on all night and day on Sunday. By the time he took me home, I couldn't even walk right.

****

"Let's hug it out!" Dickey said as he came in for a hug.

"Congratulations! Yay us!" I said giving him a courtesy hug. I laughed when he lingered in the hug a little longer than I expected. "Ok Dickey," I laughed.

He exhaled, "I feel like I should take you out to celebrate. Where would Ms. Davis like to celebrate?"

I shook my head, "that's not necessary Dickey."

He put his hand on my shoulder, "Jenise. Please!"

I felt like the dumbest person on the planet. It seemed like this white boy was asking me out, but why on earth would he do that? "Fine, where you wanna go?"

"Do you know how to roller skate?"

"I'm not very good at it."

"FINALLY! Finally something I can teach you." He smiled, "I'll be in your dorm lobby at four." Then he excitedly skipped away.

Dickey was having too much fun ushering me around the skating floor. I finally got the hang of gliding around the floor as Dickey skated backwards pulling me around. Then Nohemi skated up to us with the biggest smile. She was giddy with excitement as she said hi to Dickey and I. I had a sinking feeling as I searched the people on the sideline. Ethan was staring at me with the angriest expression on his face. I smiled and waved out of nervousness, what could he say to me? He was here with Nohemi. Ethan nodded at us and then he kept staring. Even though I was wobbly before, I some how found the ability to stabilize on those skates and stayed on the floor the rest of the night. I knew there was no way Ethan would come out here, or so I thought. Dickey went to the bathroom and my mouth dropped when Ethan marched out on the floor. He asked me what I was doing here with Dickey. I smiled cause Nohemi was watching us as she skated around alone. I told him we were celebrating our scores on our papers. When Ethan started telling me I better not touch him I wiggled my neck and said he couldn't tell me what to do. Nohemi skated over and asked what was the big deal about me being here with Dickey? Ethan threw his hands up and walked away.

Chapter 6

Ethan

"Oh my goodness Ethan look at you!" My Auntie Annette said standing to hug me. "Raynel, why didn't you tell me?"

Momma shrugged then she hugged me, "he didn't want me to make a fuss about it." I gave my Auntie Lauren and my Nana hugs as well, I rubbed Auntie Lauren's pregnant belly, then I took my seat amongst my cousins and uncles. Pops went over business; we went over performances of each individual business and strategies for moving each business forward. When we got to Cooper Financial, Auntie Annette asked me to take a board position. She said I would be the only Wallace on the board, when I looked at my mom and Auntie Lauren they said they were under their maiden names. Even though my Dad hadn't really said anything in a minute. The responsibilities that he passed on to me although heavy told me that he trusts me and that he was proud of me.

"Annette you know you weren't fooling anybody with that ridiculous job downtown." My Uncle Matt said.

Before my Aunt could say anything my Uncle Tim spoke. "Please explain to me why that's any of your business. Talk to me when you've successfully provided your children with any form of stability! Annette did what she felt was right for our family. How we manage that is none of your business."

"I'm just saying she would've been better off working in Emma's store or something." He said slightly chuckling.

"You mean my store that Emma manages! Matt I haven't put you in your place in a long time. Keep talking to my wife and see what happens." My Uncle said looking at his big brother like he wished he would give him the reason to get him. My Uncle Jeff sat there smiling real big.

No one said anything, not even Nana to defend Uncle Matt. Uncle Matt huffed and waited for Pops to continue. Auntie Annette blew Uncle Tim a kiss and then they continued on with their meeting.

After the meeting I followed my father's driver to a restaurant where my father and I had lunch with Whispers and Eugene. If I ever thought my brothers and I had issues with our father I told myself to think about this meeting. Eugene is a good man, but he's blinded by his issues with his father. I guess because I'm on the outside looking in I could see both sides. Whispers didn't know about Eugene until he was about twelve years old. Even then Eugene didn't feel a bond with his father, he had been scarred by his stepfather's hatred for him. He feels like any relationship they have is because Eugene went looking for him. Where Whispers has made sure Eugene was taken care of from the moment he found out about him. Eugene couldn't help but be emotional while Whispers spoke matter of factly. All of this became an issue when Whispers told Eugene to step forward and let Malcolm and Leonard know that he was their father. Eugene flat out refused. Although he was no longer seeing Leonard's mother, admitting that Malcolm was his son meant he would have to come clean about messing around with Pam, when he swore to Leonard's mother that she was the only one. Whispers told him to man up and deal with the mess he made. Eugene asked him why Pam would name him Malcolm if he was the father. Whispers said he didn't know and it was probably because she was hiding like he was. Whispers said Leonard's middle name was Eugene. He told him that those four were exceptional young men and they deserved to know where they came from. Fuzzy was the only one who knew his father and that's because he was pimping women with Barb. Barb would bring them in and then they worked together. Whispers and Eugene went back and forth for a long time. I expected Whispers to get up at any point and snatch up his son. He kept trying to reason with him, but Eugene couldn't get over how he felt he was slighted to see what the right thing to do was. Eventually Eugene got so fed up, when he stood up I could see the thought run through his mind to step to his father. Whispers gave him that cold-blooded stare that said he'd kill him, son or not. Eugene said he was tapping out and he needed to go away for a while. He told his father he loved him and he'd be in touch, then he walked out angrily.

Whispers looked up, said something to himself, and then he looked at my Dad. He sarcastically said Eugene was one of his better kids. I asked how old was Eugene when Leonard was born? Whispers said Leonard is about five years older than Malcolm. My Dad said he was so busy looking at Malcolm he didn't consider Leonard or any of the other kids. Whispers sat there quiet for a minute then he looked at me. "No matter how difficult the situation, take care of your kids. If I could do it all over again there's so much I'd do differently. There's repercussions for every action. Every time you touch a woman think about the possibility that she could carry your child. I bet you that will make you check yourself."

I looked at my father who held the same expression, like he didn't want to think of that.

****

"Where do you want to go for dinner?" Nohemi said smiling at my new body.

"I don't care, but I can't stay out too late. I got to work tomorrow and all this weekend."

"Again?" she whined.

I eyed her, "don't start! I will get up and walk out right now."

"Couldn't I come and play house? I could cook for you, serve you your dinner, and then..." She kissed my neck, "serve you dessert."

"No!" I said quickly.

She gasped, "wa! Why not? You don't trust me in your place alone?"

"No I don't."

"Wow! We've been together over a year and you don't trust me?"

"No," I said still looking at her.

"I bet you'd let Jenise be in your apartment alone."

"Jenise is my best friend, she doesn't have an ulterior motive behind her friendship with me."

"I swear if I didn't see her with Franky I'd swear you two were messing around."

"What are you talking about?"

"Oh I guess you didn't know, they're together all the time now-a-days." She smiled.

"That doesn't mean anything, we saw her with Dickey too." I said as I asked myself if Jenise or my brother would betray me like this.

"I saw them sucking face last week outside Le Maire's restaurant. I would've said hi but they had their tongues down each other's throats."

"Oh," Then I looked away. That wasn't Franky, that was me. It was one of those impulse moments where I caught her by surprise and swept her up in a kiss. Ever since I've lost weight people are constantly mistaking Franky and I for each other. I knew about Jenise studying with Franky and her hanging out with him, but she wasn't with him anymore than she was with Dito or T for that matter.

"Can we have dinner at your place when my parents come out to visit?"

"No!" She was starting to get on my nerves like she always does. "Why do you constantly try to find your way into my apartment? We can go out to eat out here, pick a place."

"I'm your girlfriend. Why can't I know where you live?"

"Because! I come out here enough where it shouldn't matter. When I go home, I go there to escape your nagging, whining, and complaining. I'd break your neck if you ever appeared on my doorstep unannounced. Since you didn't know how to call first when I was here I don't trust you not to test me. To summarize you can't know to save your life and keep me out of jail." Then I laughed, "naw I wouldn't go to jail for that."

Nohemi screamed out of frustration. That was my cue that our visit was over. She was going to be in a mood the rest of the day and evening. I didn't feel like dealing with it. I got up and I started dressing. Nohemi panicked and started apologizing as soon as she saw me dressing. It was too late I was leaving. Nohemi cried and pleaded with me not to leave. When I walked out the room her roommate and her boyfriend were relaxing on the couch. The boyfriend smiled at me like he wished he could do the same, while her roommate looked at me like I was rude. I walked out the door and I got in my car. When I parked my car Grace was walking up at the same time. She smiled and said she thought I was Franky. I smiled and told her I've been hearing that a lot lately. I hung out with Grace and T for a while, and then I looked at my watch. Jenise was going to be showing up at any minute so I walked out to my car. When her bus came and left, I started looking at my watch. Then Dito pulled up with Tess and Jenise. I immediately got excited as soon as I saw Jenise. I told myself to take a deep breath and be cool. I got out the car and met them on the sidewalk. I told Jenise I needed to show her something as I took her backpack with her things for the weekend in it. I couldn't get across the Bay Bridge fast enough. As soon as I parked in the garage I was all over her. I had to kiss her, my hands had to touch her everywhere. Doesn't matter that I've done any of this before, I needed to do it right now like my life depended on it. When we finally made it inside Jenise ordered delivery while I washed Nohemi off of me. When I got out of the shower Jenise was laying on the couch in her underwear watching a nature show. She said the take out was in the oven. I sat on my barstool and watched her for a minute. I sat there wondering how I could love her so much. I never thought about giving someone my last name until Jenise. She was definitely my future, Nohemi was something to do while Jenise got it together. Her addiction to irrelevant people is annoying at times, but it takes the edge off. "So, Nohemi thinks you're dating Franky."

"Why?" She looked over her shoulder at me.

"She says you two are always together." I smiled.

Jenise shook her head; "I'm not around Franky anymore than I'm around Dito or T."

"She saw us kissing, and she naturally assumed I was Franky."

"WHAT?" Jenise laughed, "You two don't look that much a like."

"I don't know, everybody keeps thinking I'm Franky."

"You are more handsome than Franky on his best day in my opinion." I blushed, "she's in denial." I walked over and kissed her, she smiled. "Franky can't hold a torch to you." I kissed her again, "you are the best!" She said fishing for another kiss. I was going to let her eat first, but since she's instigating I took her now. Jenise's eyes always roll back in her head like everything I'm feeling she feels. Sex with Jenise is unlike anything I've had with anyone else. I can't get enough of this woman and I let go of so much just to be here like this with her. Each time she surrenders to me holding back nothing, and I to her. This is my wife, the mother of my children, this is my forever.

****

"I'm sorry I'm late." I said hurrying to the bar, "work took a little longer than I thought it would. I misjudged my time to get here." I said hugging Nohemi. Truth was, I got to T's place and Jenise was there alone. Dito was out with Tess and Timothy and Grace took a drive up the coast in Dito's car. Nothing but space and opportunity, I served Jenise all over that apartment. I was completely spent, but I knew I wasn't spending the night with Nohemi tonight anyways so it didn't matter.

"You're over thirty minutes late son." Nohemi's father said looking at his watch.

I didn't like him already, "I know that. You must not have been listening; I just went over that with the rest of the class. Try to pay attention and keep up."

I guess because he's Nohemi's father he expects me to cower to him, but that's not how I get down at all. "Um, Ethan! This is my mother." Nohemi said trying to keep the peace.

"Nice to meet you," she said looking me up and down.

"Well where are we going to go now. They had to give our table away since you were so late. I would've left, but my sweetheart over here just knew you were coming. I guess she's used to waiting for you."

I looked at Nohemi, "this is where you want to eat. This is where we'll eat." She happened to pick a place that my Dad likes to visit all the time when he comes out. Getting a table at this extremely crowded restaurant would not be a problem for me. "Shall we?" I said pointing back to the hostess area. Nohemi looked nervous as she took my arm. Her parents walked behind us.

The host saw us before we were even close to the Host stand. "Mr. Wallace! No one called to say you were coming." The host said.

"My girlfriend had a reservation, but I was running late and we missed it."

"No! No! That will not do! What was the name on the reservation?" He said looking at his list.

"Nohemi Sindell."

"Aw I see, one moment. We will have a table for you." Nohemi got excited and she smiled real big at her parents. I didn't turn to see their stupid faces; I was dreading the night already. "Mr. Wallace we're going to sit your party at the chef's special table. Their tab from the bar has been taken care of. I apologize for the inconvenience, had we known you were coming this little snafu would've never happened. Right this way." He said leading our party to the special table.

Mrs. Sindell was impressed while Mr. Sindell was still irritated because I didn't yield to him. I told the waiter to bring me their house best straight up on the rocks, when I looked at Mr. Sindell I called out to make it a double. "This place sure is nice. You must come here a lot to get such service?" Mrs. Sindell asked as the waiter brought my drink to me.

"My father likes this place, he visited often and we normally went out to eat when he came." I said matter of factly.

"Mom Dad, Ethan as two older brothers and a cousin who attend school here as well. He has a cousin in medical school out here too." She said proudly.

"At least five of you out here at one time? Your family must be rolling in dough. You must've been born with a silver spoon in your mouth." Mr. Sindell scoffed.

"More like crystal, your point?"

"How hard did you have to work to get here? Or are you used to having everything just given to you?"

"Daddy! Ethan had a 3.8 gpa while he was here." Nohemi said in my defense.

"And that was only because I didn't apply myself like I needed to." I stared him down.

Mr. Sindell chuckled, "you probably paid the teachers off." He looked around the restaurant.

"What's your name? Elliot?"

"That's Mr. Sindell to you little boy!"

"Like I said Elliot, apparently your daughter didn't tell you who I am. I don't care what nut you think you busted that I'm supposed to praise you for, but this isn't working for me. I apologized for being late and I'm done, its over. Now, if you want to sit over there with your panties in a bunch because I'm not bowing down to you, then you need to tell your daughter to try to hook another one. You are irrelevant to my life and I don't care whether you're happy, sad, mad, or irritated. Disrespect me one more time, and I'll take you outside and show you that your boy don't exist at this table. Are we clear?"

"Daddy!" Nohemi whined, "Please be nice and get along for me."

Elliot looked away, Mrs. Sindell kept adjusting in her seat and shooting me looks like her daughter does. When the waitress came I told him Elliot wasn't eating with us tonight, and if he chose to order he needed to be billed separately at market rate. I ordered the eye of round steak with triple the vegetables instead of rice or potatoes. Nohemi ordered surf and turf and she urged her mother to do the same. Elliot ordered the chicken dish on the other side of the menu. When Mrs. Sindell attempted to share a taste of her food with Elliot I looked at her like I would hurt her. She put her head down and kept eating. Elliot was mad and getting madder as the time past. As we finished our specially created for my table desserts I made sure they remembered to give Mr. Sindell the bill for his food. After he paid I stood to leave, Mrs. Sindell asked if I was going to pay our bill. I told her it was already taken care of. Mrs. Sindell had so many dollar signs in her eyes she couldn't remember to support her husband or anything. I decided to go for broke and really piss Elliot off. I walked Nohemi to their car, and I put my tongue down her throat and I had my hands all in her butt, raising her skirt. Elliot got out of the car beyond pissed off. He was yelling at me about everything. I stood there smirking at him daring him to step in firing range. Elliot yelled and made a scene but he never came close enough to say anything to me. Nohemi ran to her father begging him to calm down like he would ever be man enough to step to me. If he had such a problem waiting for me, they should've left. Once I apologized it should've been over. He put too much importance on the fact that he thought I should be trying to impress him. He was a punk or a sissy, as my Dad would call him. I wasn't concerned.

Jenise

"You're not bringing Georgette?" I asked Franky in shock.

He shook his head like the idea tasted bad, "naw! I'm going stag tonight. It's time to tone that down anyways. She's going to be graduating this year and I don't want her hanging around here thinking that I'm looking for her."

"Franky," I batted my eyes. "Will you be my date?"

He looked at me for a minute, "I honestly don't understand what you and Blu are doing. Why is he with Nohemi and you hang out with Dickey?"

"It's complicated, oh and just a FYI. Nohemi thinks we're dating."

"WHAT? Why?"

"She saw Ethan and I together and she automatically thought it was you." I shrugged.

Franky started laughing, "did Blu tell you about the girl that approached him and tried to slap him cause she thought he was me?" I shook my head no. "Blu almost broke her hand he squeezed it so tight."

"It's something seeing him like that, but I don't think you two look that much a like. People exaggerate!"

"Right cause he wishes he was this sexy." Franky said molesting himself.

"You think you're superior to Ethan?" I put my hand on my hip.

"Huh? Don't play? Blu got the brains, I got the sexy. Don't play!"

"If you say so, that's a matter of opinion. I...."

"Jenise?" I knew that voice, and instantly my heart broke. I looked and it was Jamal. "Jenise?" He said as he took more steps in my direction. He looked like he was looking for permission to approach me.

"Jamal? What are you doing here?" I said watching his eyes bounce between

Franky and I.

"You've returned my letters, and you won't take my calls. I don't know if you broke up with me because you thought something was going on with Colette or what. I need to talk to you."

"Excuse me Franky," I said as I started walking towards Jamal.

"You still going with me to the party tonight?"

"Yes."

"Ok, I'll be back in an hour." Franky said eyeing Jamal, "Stay in this lobby." When Franky walked out the door, Jamal and I hugged real tight. Jamal kept kissing my cheek as he cried a little. "Did I do something?"

"No, baby its not you. It was all me. It wasn't fair to you to keep you hanging on. I don't know if I'll ever come back to Stockton. My life has majorly changed directions this year. I'll spare you the details, but I never meant to hurt you. I'm so sorry for hurting you."

"The person who gets left behind always gets hurt." Jamal said shaking his head, "that's what my mom kept telling me."

"I'm sorry Jamal."

"She died Jenise, I needed you."

I felt like he stabbed me, "WHAT? MY PARENTS DIDN'T SAY ANYTHING!"

"Its not like you could've come out for the funeral."

"I could've asked one of my friends for a ride."

"No, I kind of get the feeling they had something to do with our breakup."

"No, Jamal it was all me. They had nothing to do with it."

He reached out and touched my face like he's always done. "I still love you. Hopefully one day you'll remember a simpler place and you'll come back to me." He said looking me in my eyes.

I looked at the ground, "ahem." Dickey said clearing his throat. "Jenise, you left your sweater in my car." Then he looked at Jamal, "hi I'm Richard."

Jamal looked confused, "Jamal."

Dickey snapped his fingers, "oh yeah. Her ex-boyfriend from back home. Did you hitch a ride on your tractor all the way out here?"

"Get OUT Dickey!" I yelled, "he hasn't done anything to you. You will not disrespect him like this."

"Jenise, I'm sorry. I…."

"GET OUT!" I said snatching my sweater from him.

Dickey put his hands up and then he walked out trying to mask his embarrassment.

"Thank you," Jamal said looking at my eyes tenderly.

"He had no right to come at you like that. You didn't deserve that. You don't deserve any of this." I looked at his eyes. "We both know Colette came back to Stockton to be with you. She's helping make things better, give her a chance. If it doesn't work out with her, and if things don't work out for me in the big city. Maybe we'll meet up somewhere in the middle."

Jamal squeezed me tight, "I love you."

"I love you too."

Then he walked out; I went up to my room. I was dragging, as I got dressed. Why did I have to break up with Jamal and Ethan is still with Nohemi? It wasn't fair. Maybe I am just a friend to him that he gets to hump on. I waited in the lobby for Franky. He said we were riding with Ethan and Nohemi. GREAT! Just what I needed. Franky looked at my face and asked me if everything was ok. I shook my head yes unconvincingly.

When I got in the car Nohemi was complaining about Ethan's behavior when her parents came to town. I looked at him in the mirror, "You had dinner with her parents?"

"Yes! And he was a jerk the entire time! He showed up thirty minutes late with no real explanation for his tardiness. Then he humiliates my father in front of all these rich white people!"

"Where did you guys go?"

"Nohemi picked the most expensive restaurant in downtown." Ethan said as he continued to look at my eyes in the rearview mirror.

"Oh! So was he supposed to propose at this dinner? I mean fancy restaurant, your parents were there, the only thing missing WAS THE *RING*!" I flipped him off in the mirror.

"I will say the thought crossed my mind, but after the way he acted with my daddy I knew that wasn't the case. I haven't seen his apartment yet for crying out loud. Have you seen it?" She turned to look at me.

"He's your boyfriend, ask him." I said irritated.

"I have and he never gives me a straight answer."

"I'd hate to get in the middle of your lover's quarrels." I spit.

"WHAT IS WRONG WITH YOU?" Ethan roared at me.

I looked out the window, "Jamal showed up out of nowhere today." Franky said. I started crying, and Franky put his arms around me to comfort me.

Ethan started speeding to get to the party. Nohemi was screaming at him telling him to slow down. Ethan threw the car into a parking spot and then he jumped out the car and snatched me out. Nohemi screamed at him for driving crazy. "Franky, can you take her in the party, muzzle her with some punch."

"How you going to send her man away?"

"This is my best friend! Do as your told or I will deal with you later!" Ethan roared at Nohemi.

I looked at his face and it was evil, Nohemi walked inside with Franky. "Have you ever hit her?" I asked him searching his eyes for the truth, as my heart pounded.

"NO!" He said like I insulted him.

"But you're always threatening her like you will. Would you hit her?" I broke out in a sweat.

"If she provoked me I would, what did Jamal want?" I didn't like his answer.

"He wanted to know why I broke up with him. His mother died! His mother died and I wasn't there for him. I wasn't there for him so you can set the scene for a marriage proposal with Nohemi! I don't want to do this anymore Ethan."

"You must want me to hit you!" He smiled at me. His comment caught me off guard and I chuckled a little. "You can't break up with me Jenise. You're my future."

"I don't know how you think we're together when you're here with Nohemi."

"You're here with Franky." He smiled again.

"I'm serious, I broke Jamal's heart! Me! I broke someone's heart! I feel horrible! Then you're having engagement dinners with Nohemi? What is this?"

"I'll go break up with her right now. The only reason I got back with her is because I thought you didn't want me."

I exhaled, "don't break her heart on account of me. I don't want her to hate me."

"It's going to happen sooner or later." He said watching my eyes.

I stomped my feet, "I can't get over how horrible I feel. I broke his heart then his mother dies. How do I know she didn't die because she saw how hurt her son was? I probably killed his mother! I'm a murderer!" I put my hands up to my face and cried.

Ethan removed my hands from my face and he tilted my head towards him. "I'll kill anyone who interferes with us being together. I don't care that his momma died. One less person in this world to try to break us up." He said coldly.

"We aren't together!"

"Yes we are! Wait until tonight." Then he put his arm around me and we started walking towards the party. Nohemi was standing in the doorway looking at us. She opened her mouth like she was going to fuss. "Nohemi! Shut up! If you say one thing I will leave you at this party by yourself! I don't want to hear it! Matter of fact go get me some punch." He barked at her.

Nohemi was standing there with her mouth open. Franky laughed and held onto the wall to stop himself from falling. Nohemi turned on her heels and did as she was told. Franky put his arm around me. Nohemi's face looked evil as she handed Ethan his cup. Ethan looked at the cup suspiciously. "Hurry up and eat a cookie, I liked you better when you were fat!"

Ethan threw the drink in her face and Franky caught his arm, as he was about to knock the stuffing out of her. Franky pushed Ethan out the door, he had to just about carry him to stop him from getting to Nohemi. I looked at her in shock. "Does he hit you?" I did not like the look of this side of Ethan. It was making me have flashbacks.

"No, never!" She said frozen in her spot.

"I think you should leave."

"How?" She said scared as we saw Ethan still going off outside.

I took her to the bathroom to clean her up. Her makeup was running, her light pink dress and white sweater were covered in red punch, and her hair was going back from getting wet. She looked in the mirror and started crying. She said she doesn't like the new Ethan. She said his patience is gone and he's so mean to her these days. I told her what she said was out of line. She said he embarrassed her, I told her she should've let it go or said something in private once he calmed down. I braided her hair in one braid. She washed her makeup off. We tried to make her as presentable as possible. When we came out the bathroom Franky was telling Ethan a story and

Ethan looked like he was tolerating him. He looked at us and then we went on the floor. Dickey came over immediately and he apologized for how he acted earlier. I thanked him, and then I asked him to dance with Nohemi. Ethan and Franky walked up on either side of me looking at Nohemi and Dickey. Ethan was still irritated, but a lot calmer. I told him when he was ready he needed to go dance with his girlfriend. He frowned at me like the thought made him want to vomit. When Franky spotted Georgette he told me I had to dance with him. He spun me around and took me out on the dance floor. Ethan sat down and watched us dance.

****

Ethan was kissing on my neck and my mind was ready. My body was recovering but eager to be served again. It was only a little after ten o'clock, but we had been going all afternoon and evening. Ethan exhaled in irritation when the phone rang. He shrugged it off; it was kind of late for his phone to be ringing. I told him to answer it. He kept coming in for me. After the fourth ring I told him to answer. "Hello?" Ethan said trying to take the irritation out of his voice, his body tensed as he listened. "Malcolm calm down! I can't understand you!" Ethan said like he was on the verge of exploding. "Coming here? Are you sure?" He stood up, "Jenise is here, and we're going!" He shook his head then he hung up. "Get dressed, we're leaving!" He said looking for his pants.

I grabbed my backpack and I put my dress back on. Ethan asked me if I had anything I wanted to keep in the apartment. I said no then he moved one of the paintings I chose for him and flipped the switch behind it. I heard electricity and a spark then he told me to go. As we drove away I saw black smoke coming out of the downstairs apartment. I looked at Ethan and his face was calm, too calm. I didn't say anything; this fool just committed arson like it was nothing! He looked at my face and told me to calm down. We drove past a car that was on fire on the side of the street. Ethan pulled over a ways away from that car and flashed his high beams. Then the car not too far from us went up in flames and I saw three men come out of nowhere. As they approached us I heard the sound like a firecracker and they all moved, but Whispers fell. Then a gun fell from the second car that was on fire. I asked Ethan if Whispers was hurt. He opened his glove compartment pulled out a gun, he told me to get down and he got out the car. My heart was pounding as I did as I was told. I could hear them talking and then they put Whispers in the car, Whispers looked at himself, groaned then he said this was bad, he argued with Ethan saying he would be ok he just needed to get to Ethan's father's house instead of going to the hospital. No one said anything, but I could hear Ethan arguing with himself to do what Whispers instructed. Ethan stood on the gas; we drove through the Caldecott Tunnel. I had no clue where we were. Then we drove up a hill. Ethan stopped he turned off his headlights then he rounded the corner. He didn't move right away. When he let the car roll, he said they were clear then he looked at Whispers who was silently fighting to stay awake. They all started cursing and the familiar guy kept smacking Whispers' face telling him to focus. Ethan stood on the gas again and the gate opened and shut immediately behind the car. I looked at Whispers with tears in my eyes. "It's...." Then he looked at the guy, "Mal...." He

76

tried to grab his breath. "Your brother!" He pointed at the other guy. "Malcolm!" He pointed to himself. "Malcolm!" He pointed at the other guy. Ethan yelled that Whispers was hit. Whispers was bleeding heavy and he looked sleepy. Then he got angry and he started trying to breathe real hard. "Your brother! My son! Grand.... sons!" He took slow angry breaths. Ethan's Dad opened the door and pulled Whispers out. He looked at his shoulder, his face remained serious. He picked Whispers up like he was me and started walking inside. Ethan told me to get my stuff out the car. Whispers' blood was all over the back seat. The guy Whispers called Malcolm was stuck for a minute. His face looked angry then he growled from his stomach like he was in pain. He punched the backseat and the whole car rocked. The other guy was shaking his head like he was still trying to process the information.

"Malcolm, he..."

Malcolm cut him off, "NO BLU! I DON'T WANT TO HEAR IT! IF HE'S DEAD WHY TELL ME? MY BOSS JUST DIED! I DON'T NEED THIS CONFUSION IN MY LIFE!" He said from the bottom of his stomach. He looked at the other guy. "THIS CHANGES NOTHING!"

The other guy stood there with his hands in his pocket staring at him. "Malcolm! Breathe! Breathe man! There's more to this I'm sure."

"I DON'T CARE!" His deep voice cracked.

"Malcolm! Breathe! If that was our father he's gone now. Tomorrow will be like today. You can't fall apart!" He kicked the ground.

"SHE NAMED ME AFTER HIM!" He said still angry.

"How else she gonna come up with a name like that?" He said trying to make light of the situation.

"This isn't fair!" Malcolm said sounding disappointed.

Ethan told another guy to get rid of his car. He looked at me and asked if I was ok. "Why are people dying around me?"

Ethan looked very upset, "I don't know. This isn't about you." He took my hand. "I'm scared!"

"Not when you're here. You're going back to bed."

"You're not coming?"

Ethan led me inside, this house was HUGE and very fancy. Ethan moved so fast I couldn't really take anything in. He led me up the stairs and down a hallway. He took my bag and put it in a room. "We'll sleep here." Then he took me to a room a few doors over. He knocked on the door. A girl opened her door; she was completely unaware of everything going on. "This is my sister Gwen. Gwen this is Jenise."

"Jenise?" She said opening her door to get a better look at me.

"Yes," he said opening her door. "There's something going on downstairs, keep her up here."

"She a flight risk?" She looked me up and down.

Ethan exhaled, "no." He kissed my cheek. "I'll be back." Then he walked out the room.

Gwen continued looking me up and down. She walked to her bed and picked up her phone. "It was my brother.... The one who used to be fat... Yea, I'll call you back...." Then she hung up the phone. "You can have a seat."

I sat in her chair by the window then I looked around her room. She had posters all over the walls and pictures. "Jenise, who are you?"

"Ethan and I are best friends." I took a deep breath.

She looked at her clock. "Were you coming from somewhere? It's kind of late."

"You have to ask your brother."

"He ever talk about me?" She watched me.

"I know who you are if that's what you mean."

"Who am I?"

I looked at this little girl I wanted to tell her to be quiet, but I was in her room. She could rightfully say get out and then I'd have to sit in a strange room all by myself. "You're Gwen, Ethan's precious little sister."

"Precious?"

"Your brother loves you very much. I know you two don't get a long very well, but he loves you."

She looked at me like she didn't believe me. "O...k...."

"Ethan is my best friend, I'm not pulling your leg. I know that if he heard you refer to him as fat he'd be in your face. You two argue all the time. You tend to defend Franky, and you act like you don't care for Ethan and Dito. You hurt them when you do that."

She looked surprised, "Blu told you that?"

"He tells me everything."

She moved closer to the side of the bed by me. "They always make me feel like I'm just the girl. They hate me."

"They don't hate you."

"Dito does, he always wanted to go over their house. He gets so mad at me all the time." She said like it hurt.

"Dito has mother issues."

"He hates our mother so much he let that make him gay?"

"He's not gay."

She looked at me, "you're definitely Blu's friend. He's the only one who says he's not. Fernando doesn't act like anyone in my family."

"Do you act like anyone in your family?" Ethan said she didn't.

She was quiet for a minute. I guess she decided to change the subject. She asked me how long I've known her brothers, stuff like that. Then she put on records and warmed up to me. She seemed surprised that she liked me, if she only knew. You gotta be crazy not to love me. I'm lovable on purpose. I forgot why we were here until Ethan walked in the door looking so sad. As soon as I saw him my heart felt heavy. Gwen didn't ask what was wrong, but she did hug her brother. He kind of looked at her like she was weird, but he accepted her hug which made Gwen smile real big. I hugged my new friend and then I followed Ethan out the room. We went back to the room he put my bag in. This room was huge and it had it's own bathroom. He locked the door and then he hung his head. I put my arms around him and I told him I was sorry. He looked like he wanted to cry but he didn't. We got undressed and then I held him all night. At one point his breathing got heavy like he was trying to bottle up his feelings. I rubbed his back and then he went to sleep.

****

"Think about it! It only makes sense. You can come see me for a change." He said looking under the hood of the car.

"How will I explain you buying me a car?"

He looked at me, "you won't. Your sister is the only person who would ask without knowing. It's none of anyone's business."

"But Ethan! How am I..."

He picked me up and kissed me. That shut me up. When he picked me up in his brand new fancy car he brought me back to his father's place. There was a nice car sitting out front. When we got out of his car he handed me keys. He told me this was my car. The first thing I thought of after the panic subsided was my baby brother. I was dying to see him, but I didn't want to ask anyone to go out of their way just so I could see my baby.

Ethan said he realized I needed a car when he was in a mad dash to buy his. He said he could find a way back and forth to school, but he had to be able to get to me. I told him I wanted to go see my family, and he apologized for not thinking of it sooner.

Ethan was trying to shake off the mood but I could see the affects of seeing Whispers get shot and then him dying. He seems defeated, and then Nohemi came running to me yesterday just before my class. She said she tried to call Ethan and the phone was disconnected. I told her he's in the process of moving and he had a death in the family. I told her he would call her soon. She hugged me and thanked me from the bottom of her heart. Again I felt like mud. I almost got mad at her like she was purposely making me feel guilty. I told Ethan that she was looking for him and he didn't care.

Ethan said he'll make sure I have money for gas, and he would pay for anything else I needed. I told him he didn't have to do this, but he smiled and said it was done. He was about to kiss me again when the driver for his sister pulled up. She was coming from school and she was excited to see me. She handed her books to her driver then she asked me to take her for a ride. Ethan looked surprised. We rode around for awhile, that's when I realized my car was brand new too, then Gwen remembered she had her piano lessons and needed to get home. Gwen ran into her car where her driver was waiting like he knew she would come back rattled. Ethan and I walked around the back, there were dogs everywhere and the scariest part is they didn't growl, you'd look up and they were there. Ethan told them to say hi and they were loving me up. After Ethan closed the gate I sat by the pool putting my feet in. It wasn't too hot out here, but it was warm. "Where's your father?"

"Making arrangements for Whispers." He said looking out to the beautiful view of the city below.

"When does Gwen come back?"

"A few hours."

"Are you expecting anybody?"

"Why you asking so...." Then he looked at my face.

"I wanna do it in the pool." I smiled at him.

He gave me an evil smile. I started stripping while he ran and got big body towels. I got in the pool and waited for him. He jumped in the deep end and swam over to me. When he started pulling me to the deep end I told him I didn't know how to swim. He said we'd have to change that later. We had to laugh as we tried to figure the mechanics of how this was going to work. Up against the side of the pool the whole pool was moving crashing waves and I didn't think this through. My hair was wet and I was screaming. Ethan came hard, he took a ten second break and he went back in. This man was on something today. We got out of the pool and had to stop on the stairs cause we couldn't take one more step without connecting. Not the most comfortable place to have sex, but it had to happen. I passed out in that bed two rounds later. When I woke up, he was looking around the room. I asked him if he was ok. He said when I graduated he wanted to get married and start having babies right away. That wasn't my dream, but I said ok.

Chapter 7

Ethan

"Malcolm doesn't want to know, but I do." Leonard said looking my father in his eyes.

My father explained that Whispers was trying to get Eugene to come clean with them. Then he told him what he knew. He said they were pretty certain that Malcolm was Eugene's son, but there was still a possibility that he could've been Whispers' son cause Pam did after all name him after Whispers. Eugene and Whispers were supposed to go to Pam's prison to talk to her, Whispers couldn't place her based on the description of her to say whether he knew her or not; but Eugene flipped out before they could go. My father wasn't sure whether Whispers went alone or not. He said he wasn't sure about a lot of things and Eugene was being tight lipped on purpose.

Leonard explained that it was supposed to be a quiet night. Then Detective White called Whispers; he said someone was watching my building. Leonard said when the watchers spotted them, they handled them. That's when they called cause Whispers felt the car they were in was dirty as well. Leonard said he felt like Whispers was beating around the bush about something that night.

I asked if Malcolm was coming to the funeral today and Leonard said no. Leonard said he wasn't staying, but he wanted to pay his respects. At the funeral Leonard stayed to the back out the way. My father booked the biggest mortuary in San Francisco. There was standing room only. There were a ton of women crying all over the place. I couldn't think of one Wallace who wasn't here. Malcolm "Whispers" Phillips obituary was ridiculously big. Whispers never married, but his list of children was long. Then the grandchildren was even longer. The auditorium was huge and there were six sections and still his family covered at least the first three rows. Seeing how Leonard was stuck to the wall in the back I imagine all the family that wasn't in the front as they should be. My father made sure everything was top of the line for Whispers: his casket, burial suit, procession to the graveyard, and his plot and head stone. Everyone was saying how nice everything was, and how thankful they were.

Even though Jenise said I needed to have Nohemi here, I wasn't in the mood for her. I wasn't in the mood for her crap and she took me **there**. Jenise is over here crying and carrying on over Whispers. It took everything in my power to be reasonable in that moment. I don't want Jenise feeling anything for any man other than me! I was spent and then Nohemi starts in with her jealous attitude! I've seen my father handle a female a time or two. I never understood what could make him go **there** with a female especially with a mother like Nana. After Nohemi's comment all I could see was red. I was going to seriously choke her. I don't know what she thought was going to happen with her saying something like that to me. I could've killed her and I think that's why my brother stopped me. My patience is growing thin with this whole setup. Why does it matter what Nohemi feels, thinks, or cares about? It's like she wants me to be distracted by this chick for some reason I'm not seeing. There was no way Nohemi was going to be here today.

I was distracted from my thoughts when I saw the fire in my father's eyes. His eyes were fixed on Gwen and she was drooling all over herself. She was talking to my little cousins, but her eyes and everything else were focused on all the boys and men. She was subtly trying to get anyone's attention. As I walked over so did my Auntie Annette. Gwen was the only fool not to straighten up when she walked over. The look on my aunt's face as she talked to my sister told me to keep walking. Then my Nana caught my attention, she was trying to stop crying. I went over and put my arms around her. She said that Whispers was a good man and he's been around the family for years. She said he's saved their lives so many times she couldn't count it anymore. She said she knows my Poppa has everything covered, but she doesn't know if anyone will ever be as good as he was. I stayed with her until she calmed down which wasn't right away. Nana watched Jenise talking to Dito and my momma and she asked me where the girlfriend was. I sighed and said she couldn't make it. Nana asked me when was I going to stop playing games.

****

We were laying in the middle of my new bed in my new place in Berkeley. My mind was running wild as I rambled on. I was talking about our future together. I asked Jenise what kind of house she wanted and she didn't know. I asked her where she wanted to live and she said somewhere close to the city. We had a spirited debate about her working after we got married. We agreed to revisit the conversation after our first child was born. I wanted to call Nohemi and breakup with her now. Jenise begged me not to cause Nohemi would come to her for help. I heard her voice shake when she mentioned how guilty she feels about this whole thing. I told her that was another reason I needed to breakup with Nohemi right now. Jenise said it would complicate things right now for me to break up with Nohemi. I didn't get it or like it. Jenise said that it's important to her that people liked her. She didn't want to hurt Nohemi. I told her it wasn't like I wanted to hurt her either, however sometimes the right thing to do hurts other people. She heard me but didn't care; she didn't want me to do anything just yet. We went shopping for furniture and artwork. On the fly I decided to have a suit made. We went to the guy my Dad goes to in the city. He has only the finest quality materials in his shop. Jenise's eyes got big when the guy gave me a ballpark figure for the amount I was going to be paying for my suit.

She went with me a week later to try it on. Jenise couldn't take her eyes off of me in this navy blue suit. We had a lot of fun after my fitting… Custom suits she likes, custom suits she gets.

****

Jenise was telling one of her silly stories that I love to hear and laugh at. She had my undivided attention when I noticed the stupid look on Nohemi's face. "What's wrong with you?"

She looked at Franky, "does it bother you when he looks at her like that?"

Franky frowned to stop himself from smiling, "yea Blu! Cut it out!" He cheesed at me real big when she looked at me. "I mean I know you guys are best friends, but you got a real staring problem."

"The art teacher that I assist really thinks I have an excellent eye for Art." Jenise said proudly, and changing the subject.

"That's good, does that mean you'll find a job easily after graduation?" Nohemi asked her.

"She has a lot of connections, plus my professors do too and they've all said that they will help me. This summer I plan to try to find an internship somewhere."

"You're going to work again?" I said feeling irritated about our last summer lost.

"Yes!" Then she looked at Nohemi. "What are your plans for the summer?"

"I'm going home, but... I'm hoping to convince this guy to come visit me." She nodded towards me.

"I'm working! Besides I don't want to ever see your parents again." I spit at her.

"Blu! You were just as much to blame as my father was." She whined.

This girl really does bug me; outside of having sex with her I don't like her. It's amazing how I was willing to settle for her before, but now... "You heard me." Nohemi started to say something, but Jenise shook her head telling her to let it go.

Franky smiled at me, "so when y'all gonna break up?"

Nohemi and Jenise gasped, while Franky and I laughed. "We're not breaking up! I'm the future Mrs. Wallace!" Nohemi said confidently.

Jenise looked away, "really?" Franky smiled. "So you and my brother have discussed your future?"

Feeling dumb Nohemi looked at Jenise who was looking away. "He's in a mood, you need to give him 'some' so he can calm down."

"You need to mind your own business!" I didn't like the picture she was trying to paint.

"I was just saying he seems a little pent up today." She said wiggling her neck.

"Since you so worried about my brother's sex life why don't you service him for us."

"Ethan! You know I've only been with you." Her feelings were hurt.

"I don't know that, you left here threatening to sleep with everybody. My brother would just be one more to the list."

"Ethan! You know I was just talking."

"I do?"

"Yes you do, don't do her like that." Jenise chimed in.

"You need to stay out of this, you don't know her." I said to Jenise.

"Nohemi, would you give me some of your cookie? It's cool right?" Franky leaned in.

"Ethan! Stop playing!" Nohemi laughed an irritated laugh.

Franky laughed, "This was your chance. When you two breakup I don't want you knocking at my front door talking about you want revenge."

"GOD FRANKY! I'm sorry I said anything! You're not pent up!"

"You sound like the pent up one." Franky smiled at her.

She looked at me, "are you ready to go?"

"No!" I said watching her. I haven't touched her since that party. She's cried, begged, and pleaded with me and I refuse. I'm still mad at her, I'd break her in half out of anger.

She looked to Jenise for guidance, Jenise wouldn't look at her.

※※※※※※※

"You ok?" I said looking at Malcolm who looked real thoughtful.

"Of course!" He said shaking off his mood.

"I'm not! Janet's waiting for me. I'm frustrated!" Troy announced.

"Seems like these things are becoming too common these days." Malcolm said, his cousin was killed over a deal gone bad. Smoke wanted to work with them. Malcolm told him he was too all over the place and he needed to focus. Smoke was always changing directions. One minute he was straight, the next minute he was trying to hustle.

"I can't believe Smoke is gone." Troy said shaking his head sinking deeper into his depression. "You see his girl though?" Troy shook his hand to say she was beautiful.

"Yea, and she cried heart felt tears." From what I could tell they didn't have kids. She was heartbroken and completely torn up about her man. Looking at her made me want to cry.

"I want the woman I love to be that hurt over losing me." Troy said adjusting in his seat.

"Who says you'd out live her, what if she died first?" I asked, Troy frowned hard like he didn't like the idea of losing his woman.

"I got a girl who loves me like that," Malcolm said like he was thinking about it. "I doubt she can get away, but I need to see her." Then Malcolm stood up. "I gotta go." Then Malcolm walked out the door saying goodbye to the different ones he saw on the way out.

"He going to be alright?" I asked Troy.

Troy smiled, "mister invincible just came to terms with the fact that he loves his little girl. He's so hard headed. I told him that a long time ago, he didn't want to hear it though. He gives this girl money, and deals with the fact that he can't see her whenever he wants. He's never been so tolerant with anyone else, and he still tries to act like it isn't love. I don't know what else you'd call that. Delicate is not his style."

"What about you? You got somebody?"

"Not like that. I haven't met that one yet." Then he looked around at all the sad and heartbroken faces. "I'm over this, let's go get drinks." Troy said.

"You got ID?"

"If they question me I got Leonard's, let's go."

We went to a pool hall in downtown Berkeley. Since it was still early we had our choice of any table in the hall. I wanted the table in back in the corner of course.

"I'll be your server, my name is Cat if you need anything." She said putting our balls on the table as we selected our sticks.

I asked Troy if he had a preference, he shrugged and said no. So I told Cat to bring us their nicest cognac. When she walked away Troy stared for a minute and then he smiled at me. He said the waitress was checking me out. I had barely looked at her so I didn't notice anything. When Cat brought our drinks Troy asked her where she was hurrying off to? She glanced at me then she smiled, then she went back to work mode. She asked if we wanted anything from the kitchen. Since alcohol is my chosen vice, I told her no. I was going to have to eat when I got home; everything on the menu was greasy and fried. Troy ordered a burger and fries. He asked me why I wasn't saying anything to the waitress. I told him I had a girlfriend. He smiled and said "oh the *best friend*." I exhaled, I told him about Nohemi just cause I didn't like this kid thinking he knew me like that. He stood like he was proud as he listened, then he shook his head and said he understood now. I asked him what he meant and he read me like I was an open book. He didn't know the circumstances around it, but he knew I was "dating" Nohemi and I was with Jenise. I didn't confirm or deny his claim I was quiet cause I didn't like the feeling of being read like that. When Cat brought Troy's burger she asked him if there was anything else she could bring him. He said he wanted to speak to the manager and he wanted her to come back as well. Cat hesitated, and I gave him an unamused look. They came to our table looking confused. Troy said there was no one in the pool hall yet, but he had the feeling that Cat couldn't sit with us and wait on us hand and foot because of the rules. So Troy asked the manager how much he would charge us to have Cat to ourselves until we were finished playing? The manager looked confused by what he meant. Troy said he wanted her to sit out with us without her getting in trouble. The manager said it was fine for her to sit out with us until other customers came and then she'd need to divide her attention amongst the tables. Troy did all of the talking; I didn't have anything to say to this girl. Yea, she was cute and all, but I've only ever sat and talked with Jenise and that was only after I got tired of listening to her talk on and on about stuff I didn't care about. Cat kept smiling at me, and then I'd look at Troy who was smiling too. She kept trying to engage me in conversation; I would answer her questions and return to my game. This kid plays too much, and Cat looked like she enjoyed the challenge. After a while people started filling in. Soon Troy had all kinds of women at our table blowing on his stick before he shot like that was going to make him any better. Cat was eventually able to get me to talk a little, but it was nothing. We played until Troy was ready to go home with someone. I asked him about the other girl he mentioned before. He shrugged and said she'll have to wait her turn. I paid our quite large bill and I tipped Cat ridiculously for being a good sport about the day.

Something about funerals makes your mortality real. I needed to release, but T said that Grace and Jenise went out on some girl's night movie adventure and they wouldn't be back until the morning. I thought about busting up their fun, but I decided that wouldn't be right. I called Nohemi and she was so excited to hear from me. I decided I was calm enough to serve her. Knowing that I was in a mood, I grabbed two boxes of six condoms and I went over. Nohemi didn't try to pretend like we were going to watch TV or anything else. She greeted me with a kiss and desire. I didn't get a chance to acknowledge her roommate or her roommate's boyfriend. We went straight to Nohemi's bedroom and there was no talking her into anything she was beyond ready and it had been months since I touched her last, I think she was about to explode. Nohemi was bursting upon entry; it's been so long that I've only dealt with Nohemi and Jenise. I forgot what it feels like to be with someone who doesn't fit me like a glove, or curve to me. She may get on my nerves but sex with her has always been good, the only redeeming factor for her. It was still never better than Jenise, but good within its own right. I showed Nohemi no mercy and where I would be mindful with Jenise that I needed to calm down a little and not hurt her, I went for broke. I flipped her every which way. I went in hard at points; I guess it only served me right that suddenly I felt a comfortable softness. Panic hit my stomach as I pulled out to reveal a busted condom. Nohemi was still trying to catch her breath. I didn't say anything; I took the condom off like I had done with the others. I took them to the bathroom and flushed them. Then I sat on the bed wondering if I was about to be in trouble. Nohemi got up extremely happy stating that she was happy to note that I was as pent up as she was. I guess she thought today meant that I had been waiting on her. I sat there thinking about Jenise as I rubbed my face, this was bad.

Jenise

I woke up this morning feeling urgency and like I needed to go today. I told Ethan I was going to visit my family. He told me he was coming. I was happy cause I wanted him to go, but only if he wanted to. We got on the road mid-morning and two hours later we were in Stockton. When we pulled in front of my parent's house I could hear them arguing all the way outside. I looked at Ethan embarrassed and now regretting that I didn't call first. My father's voice was loud as he called my mother all out of her name and he talked to her unlike anything I've ever heard. My mother came bolting out the door as I was mustering the courage to go up to the front door. Immediately she put her eyes on the ground when she saw me. She was completely embarrassed and surprised to see me. It looked like she had been working and maybe they were done for the day, her hair was wild and her clothes were wrinkled like he grabbed her, her eyes were red and her face was puffy. He promised he wouldn't hit her again. My father came out the door behind her covered in sweat, shirt open, bottle in hand, he was drunk. I wondered how long its been since he started drinking again, he was not himself when he drank and he couldn't stop once he started. His whole demeanor was angry and then guilt flashed over his face as he tried to pull some sort of sobriety out of the air. He asked me what I was doing out here. I told them I got a new car so I wanted to surprise them and show them. I could see my father trying to pull back everything. He invited Ethan and I in. I looked at Ethan and he had a serious look like he was trying to figure out the situation. My father went and straightened up furniture that was slightly out of place. When my mother didn't follow us back inside my father's eyes blazed as he snatched the door open and yelled at her telling her to stop acting ridiculous in front of me and my friend. She reluctantly came in and stood by the door. I asked them where the baby was, and my mother looked at my father while he squirmed. He said he would be home in a little bit. "We wanted to take you out to dinner tonight. Can you go?" I asked them looking between them. Seeing them like this was breaking my heart. I didn't understand what was going on.

"Um! I don't know Taffy, we got to get up early." My father said.

"That's ok, we have to get back so it would be an early dinner."

"I don't think its…."

My father cut my mother off, "you don't think!"

Tears poured out of her eyes. "Mom, let me show you my car. Dad, can you entertain Ethan?"

"NAW! NAW! She can't go out there with you. She's gonna tell my business and…" he got angry.

"I can go outside with my daughter!" She said standing up and walking out the door.

My father hurried out of the door behind her, "so this is how you're going to act? Jenise doesn't need to know none of this!"

My mother put her hands on her hips. "She's going to find out sooner or later! Next year is her last year out there. She's going to find out and then what?"

"Mom?" I said my heart was pounding.

"Tell her Fred!" My mom yelled at him.

"No! You shut up!" My father said.

"Dad? Oh my God what is it? Am I adopted or something?" Ethan stood next to me.

"No, it's just…" Then a car pulled up.

Jamal got out of the driver's seat, and Collette was in the passenger seat. My mom started crying and walking away. "Jenise?" Jamal said completely surprised to realize it was me.

"What's going on?"

Collette got out of the car holding my little brother. She had the guiltiest look on her face as she put her head down and walked to my dad. She gave him the baby and the baby's bag. Then she hurried to the car. I ran off the porch, "HOLD ON! WHAT'S GOING ON?" I yelled at anyone who could give me a straight answer.

"I'm sorry Jenise." She said still looking at the ground and trying to get in the car.

"You're sorry?" I said catching her door as she opened the car.

Jamal walked around the car, he looked at my mom walking away. "Did they tell you?"

"Tell me what?" I looked at Jamal.

"It's not my place to say especially if they haven't."

"Go ahead and go. There's nothing to tell here." My father said.

I cursed, "If someone doesn't start talking I swear to God!"

"Oh so you move out there and completely forgot the way you were raised? You been drinking, hanging around loose women letting them poison your mind with thinking that an immoral lifestyle is the way to happiness?" My father barked at me.

"Really Mr. Wright? Right now?" Jamal snapped at my dad.

"Unlike you, I'm still a part of this girl's life. I can always take the time to point my daughter in the right direction."

Jamal looked completely angry, "you are unbelievable! Jenise is a good girl; I have no doubt that she did not go out there and completely loose who she is. She is strong willed and capable of abstaining even if you're not!"

Jamal's unwavering faith in me broke my heart. When I looked at Ethan he was standing there with his hands in his pockets watching everything especially my mom getting further and further away. "What do you mean if he's not? Dad what's going on?"

Colette put her hands over her mouth and cried. "He's mine!' She yelled.

"Who's yours? Jamal? I kind of figured that." I said not getting it.

"The baby!" She said backing up from me.

"The baby? How in God's name is that possible?"

"Your father and I had been having an affair off and on for years. I got pregnant right before you left for school. Your parents took him because I needed to finish school. I was going to be out and have him with me long before you graduated and you weren't supposed to know." She cried

I looked at Jamal with pain in my heart, "she's lying right? Please tell me she's lying!" I looked in the direction my mom went in and she was FAR away still walking. Ethan met me at the car and we flew down the street to catch up to my mom. Ethan pulled over on the side of the road in front of her. I got out of the car and I ran to my mom and I hugged her, she moaned like my hug hurt. She was crying and holding herself. I asked her why she didn't tell me. My mom said my dad threatened her and told her not to. I stood up straight, "HE THREATENED WHAT?"

"Jenise I never tested him to find out. He's been horrible since you left. He's drinking again, we don't go to service anymore, and things in that house have gotten darker and darker. Without God in our lives we have nothing, he knows this. He can see it, but he's on such an ugly path."

"Why are you still here?" I asked her completely heartbroken. I never thought I would ever ask my mom why she was still with my father.

"I don't have anywhere to go! Everything I have is his. All I know is farm life, I don't know how to pick up and start over. Besides I don't want to lose you." She said touching my face as tears ran down hers.

"Do you need medicines or anything from that house?" I asked her, I was so angry I couldn't see straight. He pinned her into a corner and then decided to show his butt.

"No, but my purse is back there."

I opened the car door. "Ethan, my mom left her purse in that house. We need to go back and get it and then I'm taking her away from here."

"You need anything else?" Ethan asked looking at my mom.

"My purse, and some family pictures. Jenise where are we going to go? I don't want you quitting school on account of me. I can stay here until I figure something else out."

"I'M NOT LEAVING YOU OUT HERE!" We got in the car, and we drove back to the house. The baby was sleep in my father's arms and my dad and Jamal were arguing.

Ethan got out the car with my mom. "Mr. Wright she's going to go inside and get a few things. I'm going to need you to stay out here and give her space."

My father looked at Ethan like he was crazy, "son maybe in the city they show this kind of disrespect, but you will not show up out the blue and tell me what's going to happen in my house!" He said giving the baby back to Colette. Then he stood up straight and walked towards Ethan. "My wife is not leaving me. If I have to put you in your place to show you some manners then so be it."

"DAD DON'T!" I tried to warn him.

Ethan let my dad walk up on him. Ethan barely moved, he grabbed my dad and put him in a crazy wrestling hold where he couldn't move. My father was breathing hard trying to get loose and he couldn't. My mom got her purse, her pictures and a suitcase full of clothes. She looked at the hold Ethan had my father in and then she ran up and kicked him in his junk HARD! Ethan let my dad go and he walked to the car. We drove away and my mom kept crying and crying. After two hours we stopped for gas and so that Ethan could make a phone call. My mom said these past three years without me have been hard. Then she said, "Bless you for never calling before you came!" Which made me cry cause I felt horrible for her.

When we got close to the Bay, Ethan told us he was going to pay for us to stay in a hotel until we found an apartment. My mom started crying; she said she could make money cleaning houses and whatever she could find. I told her about my job with the Art teacher. I told her I could pick up more hours and we could make this work.

****

Grace said she wasn't technically staying in the dorm without me. I told my mom we needed to look for a three bedroom instead of a two. So Ethan suggested that we look for a house to rent instead of an apartment. Everything close to school was too expensive so we ended up finding a nice little house in South San Francisco. I couldn't believe how reasonable the rent was for this house. We looked for something to be wrong with it, but there was nothing. The realtor said the owner owned it out right and they were looking for specific types of tenants. My mom felt it was a sign from God that he was blessing our efforts. I was nervous about how everything was going to work out.

Since Grace would be with T mostly during the school year, she would still be close to school; and the commute wouldn't be too difficult for me. My mother told Grace that our household was a Christian household and she wouldn't tolerate any shenanigans from either of us inside the house. I thought Grace would walk, but she simply said ok. We moved our few things from our dorm and then suddenly furniture started arriving. At first my mom was saying they had the wrong address and then the delivery persons confirmed that they were delivering to our individual names. Bedroom sets, living room furniture, even a dinette set all these things similar to the furniture I picked out with Ethan for his place. My mom cried when bedroom furniture arrived for her. She said she's never had her own room before; she went from her parent's house to her husband's. Ethan made sure there were no price tags on anything as they arrived, but we still knew none of the stuff that came was cheap. When Ethan showed up he wouldn't own up to anything, and then he insisted on taking us shopping for linens and things. He took us to this store in downtown San Francisco that he and I went to for his place. A woman who I'd never seen before excitedly greeted him. She hugged and kissed him on each cheek, and then she said she thought he was Franky for a minute. He told her everyone keeps saying that. Then he introduced us as his friends. Of course my mom asked Ethan how he knew her. He said the woman was his aunt; she smiled and introduced herself as Emma. She said she's seen the sales receipts from all of his purchases for his place. She told him he has expensive taste just like his father, which made him smile. Emma took us around the store and she had the most beautiful displays and items in her store. I described my room to her and she came up with a beautiful design concept based upon the picture I painted for her. I enjoyed talking with her. After awhile she started asking me for input on her displays and the layout of the store. My thing is that I always like to see clean lines, I pointed out a few things that were distorted and she loved what I saw. When Ethan told her I was focusing on Graphic Design, she asked me what that meant. I gave her an idea and she was in love. She gave me one of her cards, and she told me she was going out of town after today, but she wanted me to come back when she was back. She said I had a good eye and she needed to put my services to work. Ethan smiled proudly at me. We bought lots of stuff at Emma's store and a few others. Grace and I were covered in packages in the backseat cause the trunk was completely full. We took everything inside and then Ethan took us out to dinner. My mom said Ethan was a nice man, and of course she found a way to work God into the conversation. She wasn't as pushy with Ethan as she is with anyone else. I was happy she was actually very gentle and nonjudgmental with him. I think it's because he showed her all day that he has a good heart. He was off all day, but the opportunity to talk did not present itself as my mom stayed in the middle of all of our interactions.

When Dito, Nohemi, and Franky came to see our new place, my mom cut her eyes at Dito and me when we hugged hello. I gave them the tour of our two bedroom and technically nice sized office Grace was using as a bedroom. Even my mom looked at Nohemi slanted after awhile, she asked her if her family was religious at all. Nohemi said no proudly, then she started spouting all the stuff she learned in school about religions. That started the debate, and my mom had her bible out looking up scripture after scripture to backup her statements. Nohemi was impressed and I wanted to hide. How in the world was I going to be with and one day marry Ethan with everything my mom was saying. My mom has a devout devotion to God and I love that about her, but it hurts me when she looks down on others. She immediately found a congregation nearby and ran to it to recharge her spirit. She immediately blended into her new family and they helped her find work and anything she needed to get acclimated to her new environment. She drug me and Grace along and that night I cried to Grace because my mom would not be understanding about the past two years of my life. I'm in love with Ethan, but I couldn't share that with her now that Nohemi came and proudly shared that she was Ethan's girlfriend. Fortunately I tell her I'm with Nohemi when I go see Ethan, I don't get to see him like I used to.

My mom keeps telling me to remain focused and to never let a man have control over me like my father had over her. She was dependent on him for everything and until I rescued her she had no way of escaping. She said someone in the congregation offended him and he let that affect him in ways she never thought he would. She said he stopped going to service and then when everything with Colette blew up he wouldn't let her go anymore for fear she would tell his business. She said without God in his life my father was not the same person that I knew and grew up with. She said Jamal and Colette were courting, she said she thinks it began right after his mother passed away. That made me sad too. She said she thinks they were planning a wedding, and I couldn't help it tears started dropping from my eyes. I know I broke up with him, but knowing that he moved on didn't feel good.

****

He was leaning against his car blocking mine in its parking space. He looked upset when I approached him. He hugged me tight and he breathed heavily, he wouldn't let me go for a long time. "The condom broke." He said lowly.

I felt like fire spread all over my body. "What? How?"

"I didn't tell her."

"Why not?"

"I panicked and I didn't want her to try to trick me." Ethan looked at me with sadness in his eyes, "I'm sorry."

"You don't know that she's pregnant, stop giving up already." I said as I started fanning myself.

"What do I do? I don't want children with anyone but you."

I kissed his forehead, "no child asks to be here. We'll figure it out if she turns up pregnant. Meanwhile let's focus on business and getting our stuff together. We can't fall apart."

Ethan looked at me with pain in his eyes, "stop trying to be strong. Show me you care! I'm falling apart over here and you're acting like this is a business proposition. This is not business this is our lives. I have half a mind to have someone take her out."

"Even if you were serious Ethan that would be horrible." The break was over and the class was reconvening. "I have to go, I'll call you when I get off. Where will you be?"

He looked like he wanted to tell me I couldn't go, and then he exhaled and said he was going home. I hugged and kissed him then I walked back inside. When I saw his car drive away, I told the teacher I needed another minute. I went out on the steps and I cried my eyes out. Ethan can't have a family with someone else!

Chapter 8

Ethan

Malcolm and I were reconciling numbers and neither one of us had our heads in the game. We recognized the look in each other after we sat there staring each other down for awhile. When I took Nohemi to the airport to go home she was complaining about not being able to shake her cold. I fought back the urge to drag her to her rooftop and drop her off. I played along, for all I know she could've really been sick. When I went in that morning everything was tighter and wetter. All the signs were there whether she knew it or not. I watched her plane float away knowing that when she came back she was going to have heartbreaking news for me. Malcolm turned his head to the side and I did the same. "Smoke's funeral?" Is all he said.

"Smoke's funeral!" I shook my head in agreement.

"Does she know yet?" He asked.

"No, she has no idea. You?"

He adjusted in his chair, "she's a little girl. She's scared and I don't want this. I can't be nobody's daddy! I never had a father! I got moves to make. Roscoe is getting more and more agitated as we get stronger. I can't have him knowing how to get to me. She got a little Suzy homemaker family. She could hide there, but a baby makes me vulnerable. Word will spread so fast. If she was random I could deny her. I can't deny this girl." He said adjusting in his chair like he was fighting to hold back emotion.

"I don't love her. I have a plan with someone else."

"Can you pen it on someone else?"

"She's only been with me." I exhaled. "I told my real woman about it. She took it better than I thought she would. Now, she's distancing herself from me." Jenise is running around like she's so busy. Assisting her teacher, working, and now her mother drags her off to service. I barely see her and when I do there's not much time. When I come over her house her mother is all in our conversations and everything we do. I know her mother means well, but she's cramping my style for real.

Troy, Fuzzy, and Leonard came in and sat. Leonard said we needed to change locations cause some of Roscoe's men were circling the area in a green car. Troy suggested we go to the pool hall again. I honestly think he liked the attention he got there. The women were all over him. When we walked in Troy said he wanted our same table, and Cat was there. The people who were playing at our table finished their game and then they were moved to another table. Cat brought Troy and I drinks and then she asked the others what they would like. They said they'd have the same. Cat asked Troy if he wanted the burger he had before, he smiled and said yes. Fuzzy asked him if it was good, and he drooled as Troy described it. Everyone said they would have the same. I stuck to water and drinks. Cat paid our table the most attention and she kept finding reasons to touch me. Troy gave me a knowing smile as he told me I should try her out. I shook my head no, it felt like a setup. It was early but I didn't feel like continuing anymore. I paid the bill and then I told them they were on their own. Cat caught me at the door; she thanked me for my generous tips both times. I saw that green car pass by again. I told her it was nothing, and then I gave her another twenty to leave me alone. I went back to the table and I told them I saw that green car again. They exchanged looks and then they told Cat they were done. I told them to call me when they were finished. I walked out to my car and drove home, then I called my father. I told him this fighting within our organization was ridiculous. He agreed and he said we would discuss it soon.

That night Troy called and he said six guys were down, and that Malcolm was stabbed in the process. He said Momma Shuga was able to patch him up and everything was good and to let my father know.

****

"Blu!" My uncle's voice grabbed me.

"Yes?"

"We got a situation meet us at the dock." He commanded.

I was the first one there, I greeted the dogs. Then I made my way inside the warehouse. I sat a chair in the middle of the floor, and then I waited. My father and Uncle Jeff pulled up first with someone in the car. Then my Uncle Tim, Malachi, and T pulled up behind them. Everyone looked pissed so I knew the situation was bad. When I saw Malcolm get out of my father's car I asked him who we needed to go get. Malcolm stood up tall and walked to the chair and sat like he was ready for whatever. I did a double take; I knew he knew that the man who sat in that chair never stood again. I looked at my father. "MY DAUGHTER!" My Uncle Tim growled. I froze like a deer caught in headlights. I looked at Malcolm in disbelief. Uncle Tim hit Malcolm hard in his face, no one said anything. Malcolm didn't plead or offer excuses. I never asked Malcolm for a name of the girl, there was no reason for him to know my Uncle Tim or Uncle Jeff. THIS WORLD IS TOO SMALL! Uncle Tim hit Malcolm a few more times and then he told Malcolm he could speak.

Malcolm spit and then he spoke. "I love her sir."

My Uncle hit him again, "WHAT DO YOU KNOW ABOUT LOVE? SHE'S ONLY FOURTEEN! MY DAUGHTER IS NOT SOME WHORE YOU CONQUERED!"

Malachi stood up, "dad! I've spoken to him, he does love her!"

Uncle Tim moved across the floor lightning fast and delivered a punch that knocked his son backwards. "YOU KNEW ABOUT THIS AND YOU SAID NOTHING?" Malachi shook off the stunned feeling then he stood up while his father prepared to hit him again. "I knew they were dating. I did not know things had gone this far." My uncle hit him again as he cursed him out for not putting a stop to this whole thing as soon as he found out. Malachi explained that Malcolm and Troy helped him when Darius and his friends jumped him and Sonny at school after defending Jade. My uncle told him his sister was not a sacrifice for loyalty! When T stood up my uncle looked at him in disbelief and he fired on him before he could say whatever he had to say. From the ground T explained that he met Malcolm once, but Amber denied that they were connected. My uncle walked in my face, "he reports to you. Did you know about this as well?"

Malcolm's eyes were to the floor. "I didn't know who the girl he's in love with was until just now." I said looking my uncle in his eyes. His green eyes were glowing and surrounded by red. If this was anyone other than Malcolm, they would be dead.

"Tim!" My father said trying to be the voice of reason. "What do you want to do?"

My Uncle Tim growled then he hit Malcolm again. "Malachi, does he love her?" Uncle Jeff asked.

"Yes sir." Malachi said defying his father's anger.

"Blu?" Uncle Jeff asked me.

"Yes sir."

"That's blood!" My father said to Uncle Tim.

"YOU ARE JUST A KID! THIS IS NOT A GAME! I LIKED YOU! I WELCOMED YOU IN MY HOME! DO YOU LOVE HER?" He asked him point blank.

"More than life itself!" Malcolm said in no uncertain terms.

Uncle Tim growled and hit him again, "Tim. What do you want to do?"

My Uncle Tim looked at my father angry. "Why do you keep asking me what I want to do? You know what I want to do? Am I going to do it? NO!" He growled, "If you abandon my daughter I will find you! I will take pleasure in peeling your skin off of your body and thumping your halfway dead body in the Bay as shark bait and fish food. Do I make myself clear?"

"Crystal clear." Malcolm said.

****

"Well, well, well…. if it isn't mister mysterious." Cat said coming down the aisle. I guess she thought she was sneaking up on me. I saw her when she entered the store.

"You got a lot of hair." I said looking at her free flowing curls. She always wore it in a neat bun at work, I almost didn't recognize her.

"I'm going to take that as a compliment." She looked at my basket; I had a ton of fruits and vegetables. "Oh I see. You eat cleaner and then you drink."

"I guess," then I started to walk away.

"Do I make you nervous or something?" She smiled as I looked at her.

"Why would you make me nervous?" I cut my eyes at her.

"Cause I'm pretty." She smiled.

"You're not the first pretty girl I've laid my eyes on and you won't be the last. Nothing about you makes me nervous."

"So then you agree that I'm pretty?"

"Didn't we establish that?" I started to walk away.

"Ok, ok here let me give you my number so you can stop begging me." She said as she looked for something in her purse.

"Why would I want your number?"

"You have a girlfriend?"

"Yes."

"I'm just a friend that you call when you need me. I'm no threat to your happy relationship."

I figured it was no big deal; I put the number in my pocket. Cat kept following me around the store, so I gave in. We agreed to meet for lunch at this pizza place not too far from her job. She was never as good as Jenise, but since I haven't seen much of her this summer I figured Cat would do as a nice fill in.

****

Cat's body was definitely her trophy. She had all the lines to show off the time she spent early in the morning working out. Her mother had her in gymnastics and anything else she could think of as a child. Sex with Cat was definitely a spirited event, she was completely shocked when I not only kept up with her, but I also out did her. She said that's never happened, and I guess the fact that she was extremely flexible was supposed to blow my mind. I could tell Cat didn't expect to be hooked on me after the first time we had sex. I guess she's used to turning men out and then having them as slaves doing anything to keep her in their lives. Then in walks Blu! Every time Cat stepped out of a friend's place I could see her trying to check herself and pull it back in. Jenise and I have been reduced to talking over the phone whenever we catch each other home. That's torture cause I was used to always being with her. I told her about Cat, and she was quiet for a minute then she said I needed to focus on my last year of school instead of adding more women to my harem. I told her if she was around, I wouldn't need to add anyone to anything. I only wanted her, but she couldn't stand up to her mother so we were stagnant. She reminded me that there was a strong possibility that when Nohemi returned my life would forever change and I needed to stop trying to forget the situation I was in and deal with it.

Nohemi was barely off the plane good and she was calling me in tears. She said she couldn't bring herself to tell her parents. I picked her up from her apartment and for the first time I brought her to my place. All night I tossed and turned thinking about Jenise, did she pull away from me cause she knew like I knew that this baby changed everything?

****

I sat there watching Nohemi devour her food like she couldn't get enough. She was telling me about her parent's response to her news. I could tell she was holding back, not telling me everything that they said, but I didn't really care so I didn't force her to tell me either. "Ethan?" I heard Cat call my name.

Nohemi sat up straight as she looked at Cat. "Who is she?" Nohemi said defensively.

"Cat this is my girlfriend that you've heard a lot about. Nohemi this is a friend Cat." I said dryly.

"Send this pussy away I don't like her." Nohemi said.

Cat smiled at her, "this is why you've been busy? When are you due?"

"February," Nohemi volunteered.

"When's the baby shower? I'd love to come." Cat said.

"We're not having a shower." I said.

"Oh well I'll still bring you something for the baby." She smiled, "you go ahead and eat up for the both of you. I'll talk to you later Blu. Call me."

Nohemi nagged me the rest of the day about Cat. I waited until she fell asleep and then I left. I called Cat from a pay phone and I went over her house. I got my mid-day workout with Cat who seemed even more into it now that she's seen Nohemi, and then I went back home. Cat tried to ask me questions about Nohemi like she was sizing her up. I showered and then I ordered takeout. Nohemi woke up none the wiser.

****

Nohemi was too excited, "can you believe this?" She said pointing at her stomach. I didn't know how to feel. Her stomach went from barely there to definitely there. I was growing in her belly there was no turning back, this was happening. "No I can't!" I exhaled.

Nohemi excitedly rubbed her stomach. "I read that the baby can hear us. I think we should talk to it everyday." She said too excited. "I wonder if it's a boy or a girl. What do you think it is?"

"I don't know," I said as I got up. Nohemi's robe was on the floor. I picked it up and hung it on the door. When I went in the bathroom her towel was on the floor next to dirty clothes. I growled, "NOHEMI! YOU HAVE TO PICK UP AFTER YOURSELF! You don't have a maid!"

"I'm sorry goodness! Take it easy, it's not that big of a deal." She said watching me. "It's a big deal to me! I need order; everything has its place and should be placed in it. It makes me crazy when everything is all over the place."

"I see," she said getting up to pick up her things. "Blu can I have a few dollars? I'm meeting Jenise for lunch today."

This girl! She's pushing all my buttons this morning. "Where are you meeting?"

"On the marina at that new place."

"What time?"

"You wanna go?" She asked like her feelings were hurt. "I've been asking you to have lunch with me for weeks. All I have to do is mention Jenise and you're on board! That hurts!"

I looked at her for a minute, "you need money don't you?" I didn't care about all that other stuff she was saying.

Nohemi exhaled, "11:30."

"I'll be here to pick you up at 11:15, be outside when I pull up." Then I closed the bathroom door.

I was looking for office space today, so I decided to wear a tailor made suit. My morning floated by, the closer to eleven the happier I got. I was about to be annoyed when Nohemi descended on to the street at 11:16, but I decided to let it go. She was quiet the entire ride which I liked, cause I wasn't in the mood for her mouth. I parked next to Jenise's car, then I opened Nohemi's door for her. When we walked in Jenise was sitting. She almost looked surprised to see me. She hugged Nohemi and then she touched her stomach with a little pain in her face. When I hugged her I picked her up and spun her around.

Sitting across from her I was aching for her, it felt like forever since I've seen her.

"So, when is the baby due?" She asked.

"You two haven't talked?" Nohemi said looking between us. "I would've thought that you two have talked about all of this."

"Miss Wright is too busy for her friends these days."

"So if that isn't Jenise who have you been talking to?" Nohemi cut her eyes at me.

Jenise looked at me with sad eyes, "I've been working and going to school. I haven't had the space to be your best friend."

"That's ok, you graduate this summer. Nothing's changed on my end." I said watching her eyes.

Jenise bit her bottom lip. "So I have news." I frowned at her, I didn't like it. "I have a job offer directly after graduation."

I realized with the guilty look on her face that this whole thing was a setup. "You couldn't think that having her here would stop me from going off!" I said looking at her.

Jenise swallowed as she looked around at the other people in the restaurant. "Ethan, please calm down." She put her hands out.

"You avoided me all summer! You can't even face me!"

"Ethan, you've had a full plate this summer and you know I have as well. You need to focus on your family, we'll keep in touch." She pleaded.

"You're a coward!" I adjusted in my seat. "You can't please everybody! Sometimes people get hurt, it's life it's what happens!"

Jenise eyes turn to fire. "I KNOW THAT! THAT'S WHY I'M TELLING YOU THAT I'M LEAVING! I GUESS YOU DON'T INCLUDE YOURSELF IN THE EQUATION OF PEOPLE WHO WON'T LIKE OTHER PEOPLE'S CHOICES! IT'S THE RIGHT THING TO DO."

"No it's not!" I barked not caring that we were causing a scene.

Nohemi sat back rubbing her stomach. "Where are you going?"

"It doesn't matter, I'm not staying out here. I need to start over, rewire everything." She said not taking her eyes off of me.

I stood up, "get up! Let's go!"

"Nohemi's not finished eating." Jenise said not looking at me.

"She's going to finish eating, let's go!" I said lifting her out of her chair by her arm.

"Ethan!" She tried to move her arm but I had her and I wasn't letting her go.

"Ethan!" She said as I made her stand and walk out the restaurant. "STOP IT!" She said as I made her walk until we were out of eye shot from the restaurant and on the pier.

"How you think you're going to run away from me? You can't hide from me no matter where you move!"

"Ethan, you need to focus on your family!"

"That hoe is not my family! I'm not going to marry her! You're my wife!"

"I don't want to be your wife." She was lying she couldn't even look at me.

"Yes you do!"

"No I don't. I got off track; I had to get back on track. I can't be with you." She cried.

"You're in love with me!"

"That isn't enough Ethan. I have to leave; it's for the best. Don't make her raise your child alone. Your child doesn't deserve to grow up without you."

"What about me?"

"You're a big boy Ethan, she may get on your nerves; but she loves you. Do the right thing!" Then she walked away from me and back into the restaurant. She hugged Nohemi grabbed her purse and jacket then she ran out the restaurant to the car I bought her and left.

Jenise

I drove across the Bay Bridge as fast as I could. I bypassed the city and I went to Grace and T. I cried on Grace's shoulder, I told her that Ethan got mad at me because I told him I was leaving. She said she was glad she wasn't the only one. I told her that I told him the job was post graduation. Grace asked me why I did that. I told her he would make sure I didn't leave if he knew I was switching schools and moving this weekend. Grace said she didn't understand why I was running from him. I couldn't take it anymore. I broke down, I told her EVERYTHING! Grace gasped and then she pushed me and asked me why I didn't tell her. She said we weren't fooling anyone, everyone could see that we were in love. That made me feel worse. Suddenly butterflies hit my stomach, I looked at Grace then Ethan walked in the door. I squeezed her hand to tell her not to leave me. Ethan picked up my purse and my jacket then he grabbed my hand and pulled me up. I looked at Grace with pleading eyes. She waved bye to me, then I put my finger up to her to tell her not to tell Timothy. She shook her head yes as she put her finger up. Ethan pulled me to his car and put me in. He didn't say anything he drove. The radio was off and he focused on the road ahead of him. I sat there crying silently to myself. I love this man so much; the only way to get away from this entire toxic situation that I created was to go away. Ethan drove to San Jose to a big hotel. He tossed his keys to the valet. He led me by the hand inside; the concierge met us in the lobby. "Mr. Wallace welcome, here are your keys to your room. Please let me know if you need anything else." He said. Ethan took the keys and continued to walk. He stood impatiently in the elevator. The doors were barely open and he was pulling me out. He opened the door and shut it. I tried to say something and he rushed me and kissed me like he couldn't stand not to. His kiss was so passionate that my knees buckled. Ethan held back nothing from me, he'd let me calm down just enough to halfway catch my breath and then he'd get me worked up again. He said, "I love you Jenise! Please don't leave me!" Right as he took my body over the edge. I pushed away from him as my body shook uncontrollably. He spooned me and went right back to working me over. It was too much! I started crying and Ethan held on to me. He kept kissing me and telling me that he loved me. I laid there telling myself that this was the last time I would be a slave to his love. I looked at the time and I told him I had to get back to my mother. Ethan told me to stop avoiding him. I didn't say anything to that. He said he was going to stay in this room the rest of the week and for me to come back as soon as I could, then he put the key in my purse. As soon as I got in my car I started crying. I cried all the way home. My mom asked me what was wrong and I told her I said goodbye to some more friends. I took a bath and continued to cry, I could still feel Ethan as I laid in the tub. I tried to keep my eyes open because every time they closed I saw Ethan's face as he made love to me and that was torture.

****

"Thank you gentlemen, I'll see you in Texas." I said to the movers who were driving our furniture and my car on a flat bed out there. I watched the truck drive away and then I got in the cab with my mom.

I put on my shades and I let tears stream down my face as we drove to the airport. My mom busied herself with her weekly bible reading while I sat there trying to keep my tears silent. Ethan was going to be so mad at me when he realizes that I left. I have to stop this cycle of hurting people. All these broken hearts are my fault. Maybe Ethan and Nohemi would've been in love if it wasn't for me.

When we got on the plane my heart started pounding, I faced the window as I cried my eyes out. I cried so hard I had a headache and I passed out. I woke up as we were approaching our gate. My mom's eyes were a little red as well, but she was still in better shape than I was. Friends of my mom's from her congregation met us at the baggage claim. You would've thought they were old friends the way they greeted each other, not strangers meeting for the first time. It was a young couple; they picked up the keys to our place for us. We were renting a nice little three-bedroom house. It kind of reminded me of our farm. It didn't have as much land around it, but it was nothing like the house in South San Francisco. We put our bags down then they showed us around and took us out to dinner. I tried the best I could to be conversational, but I was dreading the moment Ethan knew I was gone. Just like I knew he was getting ready to knock on that door; I knew he'd be heartbroken. What I didn't know is what heartbroken Ethan would do. Three days later our furniture and my car arrived. My mom found a job, and I went to work and finished my courses through correspondence. I got a job in the Marketing department as a Graphic Designer of 4S's (Sweet, Salty, and Savory Snacks). It was a major competitor in the food and beverage industry. As soon as I walked in the door they had me brainstorming with the rest of their team. It was sink or swim, and I was doggy peddling my way around the pool. Sigh, Ethan taught me how to do all that. I shook my head and told myself to get it together. I didn't call Grace right away so she could honestly say she didn't know anything. I even told her I was going to Chicago just in case. My mom was a social butterfly and she immediately had friends who became her new family out here. Her new congregation seemed really nice, I just felt like a hypocrite sitting there looking wholesome and clean when I knew I wasn't.

"Jenise, we're going out for drinks. You should come." Kay said

"I'm not much of a drinker."

"Sip on some Ginger ale then, it's time to get to know you."

It was Friday and I was tired of sitting in the house. "Ok, I'll follow you."
Kay took me to a club where the disco music was pumping and everyone just knew they were the coolest. In the bathroom women were snorting powder like it was the thing to do. Kay told me to ignore them. When we sat down we shared little tid bits of our lives nothing too deep though. Kay seemed nice enough.

****

I was tired of hearing my mother nag me about it. I finally went down to the DMV and registered my car in the state of Texas. I guess this means I'm permanently a resident out here. A couple weeks later I had a dream about Ethan. It seemed so real; I could feel his hands all over me. He told me to come home cause there was nothing for me out here. It felt so real that I woke up in the morning in a sweat.

****

I was standing in the produce section going through Ethan withdrawals when Kay said, "Penny for your thoughts."
I looked up and smiled at her. The guy standing next to her looked at me like he was trying to read me. "I thought you had family coming in this weekend?"
"This is my brother Irwin."
"Hello, I'm Jenise."
"You not from around here." He said looking at me.
"I stand out like a sore thumb huh?"
He didn't respond to that he just kept looking at me. I looked at Kay for help. She laughed at her brother, "you should come over. You don't look busy."
"My mom went away for the weekend with some friends, so I guess I could. What should I bring?"
"Nothing they're cooking already. We're picking up the last few items right now."
"You like margaritas?" Irwin asked me.
"She don't drink." Kay said.
Irwin frowned, "why?"
"A lot of my family members have drinking problems, so I try to steer clear of it."
"That's different." He looked away.
"I'll take my groceries home and then I'll come by if that's ok."
"Of course." She said.
Irwin wasn't ugly; my sight is tainted forever after Ethan. Automatically I started comparing Irwin to Ethan. After two items on my list, I told myself it wasn't fair to proceed. I went over Kay's, her family was really nice. I had a good time, for the first time in a few months I felt like this could work out here.

Chapter 9

Ethan

Ok so I know it's less than ideal to plan a future with someone who has a child with someone else. However, I can't believe she's gone! She packed up like a thief in the night and stole everything. My peace of mind, my heart, my soul! I unloaded to Franky, when he told me he knew what I meant I stared at him. I thought he was making fun of me. Then he told me about the girl he fell in love with freshman year. He said she left without a goodbye, forwarding address, or anything. He said it was hard to buckle down last year cause it all took him back to when she was around. He said he wonders where she is now. I told him if he really wanted to know there was a way to find her. Then I told him how I found Jenise. I watched the DMV, she told Grace the wrong state on purpose. I told him as soon as she got her Texas ID and registered her car I had her information. He asked me if I was going out there. I smiled at him and told him I already went. Franky sat forward in his chair and asked what happened. I told him I never made myself known, I followed her to work, home, stood over her a little bit while she slept then I left. I thought about suffocating her mother so she wouldn't feel guilty anymore and she'd come back home. Franky gave me five and told me I was pure evil; I thanked him for the acknowledgment. In the end, if she was willing to run, lie, and run so far away from me what was I supposed to do? Lock her up in a basement until she saw things my way? Franky laughed and said he saw that I thought about it. I told him I priced some chains, but in the end I have to wait and see what happens. Meanwhile Nohemi's been sick with the flu, she called her momma asking her what to do cause her fever went up to 103. My momma said she needed to go to the doctor, but her momma told her she'd be fine with rest and plenty of liquids.

Franky said he couldn't believe I was going to be a father and before him at that. I said I couldn't believe it either, the other day before she was sick I was talking to the baby and it was going crazy kicking and showing out for daddy. I guess I got to accept that this is my life.

When I got home Nohemi was standing in the kitchen shaking her leg like it hurt to move. I asked her what was wrong and she said she's been cramping and sick all day. She said her momma told her to take it easy, but she was starting to feel worried, her fevers have gotten worse. I went and got her slippers and her jacket then I carried her to the car. She had nothing in her system to throw up so she was dry heaving next to the car. When we got up to the Labor and Delivery they took her temperature, and then they had her lay down. The doctor wanted to hear the baby's heartbeat to judge how the baby was doing. The doctor moved her stethoscope around Nohemi's stomach. She felt her stomach to see where the baby was and then she tried again. The doctor had her poker face on as she calmly said she was going to get a second opinion. Another doctor came in felt Nohemi's stomach and then tried to get a heartbeat on the baby. I sat in that chair rocking hoping I wasn't seeing what I thought I was seeing. They told us they needed to have an ultrasound done to determine what was happening. Nohemi was crying and she was scared, I held her hand, but I didn't know what to tell her. While they transported us to the Ultrasound room they drilled Nohemi about the past few weeks since her last appointment. The frustrated nurse asked her why she didn't come in with a fever that high. Nohemi weakly said her mother told her she would be fine and to rest at home. The nurse blew air and told her she should've called her DOCTOR and not listened to her mother. The x-ray technician measured and took pictures, and then the frustrated nurse stayed behind to get the results to take up to the doctor. Nohemi and I already knew, she turned her back to me while she cried. I sat in that chair not knowing how to feel, the one thing that I felt was ruining my life was now the one thing that I couldn't live without. When the doctors walked in with sad faces I stood up. Nohemi wouldn't turn around she kept crying and holding her stomach. The doctor said that all of the baby's amniotic fluid was gone, and her fever is a result of infection. I asked if the baby was ok, hoping that they were going to give me hope. They said they were going to start my wife on antibiotics and they would give her something to help her with the pain, I didn't correct them. They said the baby didn't make it and Nohemi needed to deliver the stillborn fetus. I don't know if Nohemi even heard what they said she laid there crying. I called her momma and she dropped the phone as she screamed in the background. I called my momma and she came right away. She hugged me and she cried my tears for me. Nohemi couldn't really exert the energy to push, her heart was broken. My momma rubbed her head and she said something quietly to Nohemi. Nohemi kept crying and then she tried a little harder. My tiny little girl slid out different shades of grey all over her tiny body with hair all over her head. Nohemi wouldn't even look at her; I shouldn't have held her or looked either. My brain was forever stained with the face of my little girl who would never be.

****

I didn't care that I messed her hair up and she would somehow have to fix herself up to run to the bathroom to try to cover up what just happened back here. What I needed right now more than anything was companionship. Nohemi is spaced out and completely depressed not that we were ever-best friends before. She shut down completely. Cat is so turned out; she'll do anything I say. I needed Jenise in the worst way, I came to see Cat to run off some frustration, and then I was going home to call Jenise. Cat looked at me while she did her best to catch her breath. "When was the last time you've eaten Ethan?" She said as she gently held my head and looked me in my eyes.

"I'm fine." I said trying to get free from her hands.

"No, you're not! It's ok Ethan. You don't have to be a rock all the time." She kissed my forehead.

"I'm fine!" I said again.

"No, you're not." She said gently, "it's ok." She rubbed my head like Jenise would do. "It's ok." I sat in the chair and blew air. She was trying to make me cry, and I refused to do it. "I'm going to be right back. Don't move!" Then she looked at me, "if you leave I'm coming to your place and I know you don't want that. Stay put."

Then she hurried out. She came back with a plate of grilled chicken and vegetables. She stood in front of me and fed me. I couldn't remember the last time I ate anything, I thanked her for the food and then I left.

Instead of going home, I went to my father's house. My father showed no empathy, I immediately asked myself why I came here. My father said that was a close call, and next time I should be more careful. As I stormed out of the house, my Uncle Tim and Uncle Jeff were approaching the door. "Whoa son! Where's the fire?" Uncle Tim said as I walked past him.

"I apologize, I've got a lot going on right now."

"Like?" My Uncle Jeff said walking back towards his car as if he knew I was following him.

"Nohemi lost the baby last week, I didn't realize I wanted the baby until not too long before it was gone."

"I'm sorry to hear that. How's the mother?" Uncle Tim said.

"She's completely shut down, she's depressed."

"Do you love her?" Uncle Tim asked.

"No, but I did love my child." I said, "She was a part of me."

"The important thing right now for that girl is to be surrounded by people who love her. You're not going to be doing her any favors playing mister nice guy in this emotional state. The kind-hearted thing for you to do would be for you to take her home. The about business thing to do would be to send her. Either way don't keep her at your house dealing with you in this space. You're a Wallace and we tend to hurt the ones we don't love especially. As soon as the doctor says it's ok, take her home." Uncle Tim said, "meanwhile. Be careful with yourself. Don't do anything to put yourself back in this situation."

****

I brought the tray with Nohemi's breakfast on it. She was staring at the wall like she has been doing since she came home. "Come on you got to eat something." Tears started pouring out of her eyes. "I know, I know, but you got to eat something."

"Ethan, listening to my mom took our baby away." She said then she started crying out loud.

I sat on the bed and I put my arms around her. "She's probably kicking herself right now. She only told you what she thought was right."

"I'm sorry Ethan, this is all my fault. You finally warmed up to the baby and then.... And then...." She buried her head into my chest.

I rubbed her head, "it's ok. You don't have to apologize to me for anything. You did your best, I'll tell you something." She looked up at me with innocent eyes. "I knew you were pregnant when you left. I didn't handle the situation right, I knew exactly when you got pregnant."

"Where did Cat come from? She's trying to get you."

"You think so?"

"You can't see it?

"I guess I can."

"Have you slept with her?" She asked me like she already knew.

"Yes."

Nohemi cried some more, "I guess we're not going to try again." I kissed her forehead there was no need to say anything. "I thought we were going to get married and be a happy family. I love you Ethan."

"I care about you Nohemi."

She laughed through her tears. "Wait until Cat realizes she can't be first. I was willing to accept that. She doesn't seem like the type to accept second place."

****

When we pulled up to the Sindell household I took a deep breath. I knew her dad was going to piss me off and it was going to take everything in my power to take the high road cause honestly right now, I wanted to beat someone. Nohemi's momma ran out the door and she cried as she held on to her baby. I told the driver to wait. I took all of Nohemi's bags inside the front door. I hugged Nohemi one last time then I walked out to the cab. Elliot and his sons pulled up as I was walking.

"Where's my daughter?" Elliot barked.

"Inside," I said as I continued to the cab.

"This is the guy?" The biggest guy asked.

I stopped in my tracks; I was definitely down for a brawl if they were stupid enough to engage me. "Leave him alone." The smart one said.

"Naw! This pretty boy disrespected our family. You dirtied up our sister, disrespected our parents. Then you come out here?"

I put my hands in my pockets; it tickled me that he called me a pretty boy. That was a new one. "You gonna keep talking or are we gonna do this? I don't have all day!" The big guy came straight at me and I felt his jaw crack when I connected with him. It sounded like a snap. He went down like a sack of potatoes. Elliot got mad seeing me drop his son like he was nothing. When he tried to kick me I grabbed his leg then I dropped down on it breaking it for sure. Elliot went down, and then I looked at the other son. He put his hands up, "I told them to leave you alone."

"You're the only smart one." I pulled money out my pocket and handed it to him. "Tell your sister I'm sorry."

When I got in the cab the driver was looking at me with big eyes. I got on the plane, and I took a cab to Jenise's job. I sat on her car and waited for her to come out. Jenise screamed when she saw me. I didn't say anything, I just stared at her. The girl she was walking with asked her who I was. Jenise looked scared as she approached me. Jenise tried to introduce me to her friend; I didn't care who this girl was. I stared at Jenise, and then I told her to give me her keys. Jenise did as she was told, then she told her friend she'd see her later. I drove to the hotel near the airport. I checked-in then I took Jenise to the restaurant. I sat in my seat and stared at her. I wanted to kiss her and at the same time I wanted to rip her head off. Jenise sat there looking scared. "How could you?"

She sunk a little in her seat, "Ethan..."

I cut her off, "you thought you were doing the right thing? You were being selfless?" She shook her head yes. "I CAN'T STAND YOU! You pursued me! You inserted yourself into my life! You kept pushing the boundaries of our friendship!

When I give in to you then you want to back pedal? Then you want to run and make it seem like I'm the one forcing all this? You run to Texas! Texas? This place is so random." I looked around. "Your whole objective was to mess with my head? You working for another family?"

"A what? I don't know what you're talking about."

"You're so concerned with breaking everyone else's heart. You don't care that you shattered mine?" Jenise exploded in tears; at least I knew she knew where I was coming from emotionally. "I CAN'T STAND YOU!"

"I didn't do any of this deliberately. I'm sorry Ethan."

"You are sorry! What woman waits until she's won to run away?"

"You have a family." She said through her tears.

"WHAT FAMILY? MY CHILD IS DEAD!" Tears came to my eyes. "SHE WAS STILL BORN AT SEVEN MONTHS! I just took Nohemi home to her family."

"Ethan!" Jenise cried harder, "I'm sorry." She started to stand as if she was going to come to me.

"SIT DOWN!" I commanded, and she did. "I'm with someone who actually wants to be with me. Someone who has time for me. I CAN'T STAND YOU!"

Jenise put her napkin over her mouth to hold back some of the sounds of her sobbing. "Ethan, I'm sorry."

"We've already established that. I'm not going to chase you anymore. I'm over this whole Jenise and Ethan game. You can keep the pieces of the heart you broke, I'll grow another one." Then I stood up and walked away from her.

Jenise

I didn't care that people were looking at me as I openly sobbed. Ethan was walking away from me and it felt so *final*. I grabbed my purse and I hurried behind him. He was standing at the elevator doors. When I got close he looked at me with red eyes and he told me to go home. I froze in place, when I didn't move he said it again and then he got on the elevator. I felt like I couldn't breathe. I knew he was on the fifth floor, but I didn't know if there was a point in following him up. I stood there crying and then I saw my hand press the elevator call button. I looked at the wall to tell me which direction room 549 was. I knocked on the door, and it took Ethan forever to answer it. He was crying and all I could see was anger and hurt on his face. I pleaded again with him to at least listen to me. He rolled his eyes and then he slammed his door in my face. I expected him to at least invite me in. He could stay mad at me, but let me try to make it up to him.

When I walked in the door my mom asked me what was wrong cause I was still crying and very hard. I told her that Ethan's baby died and she comforted me. I gave her the keys to the car so she could go to service. I couldn't stop crying, I felt horrible and it was like my body hurt all over. I didn't want to deal with myself. I pulled myself together enough to walk up the street to the liquor store. I pointed out the bottle that I always saw Ethan and his brothers drinking. I poured a small glass. Each sip reminded me of Ethan and all the good times we had. His words kept replaying in my head. He can't stand me, I not only broke his heart, he said I shattered it. When my lips started to go numb, I took one more big chug then I put the bottle in the back of my closet and I went to bed.

****

I had a headache I didn't have time for this. My tire on the front passenger side was flat. I guess I hit the curb harder than I thought last night. I went inside and called my boss. I told her I never changed a tire before, but I was going to attempt it now. I was about to change when there was a knock at the door. I opened it and there was a guy at the door, I recognized him as my neighbor. We never spoke directly, but he's talked to my mom before. He said he noticed my tire and he'd be willing to put my spare on for me in exchange for a ride downtown to his job. I happily agreed and then I watched him so I could do it myself next time. I wasn't helpless, but I've never done it.

"What's your name?" He asked as he worked on my tire.

"Jenise, and you are?"

"Greg, your mama didn't tell you about me?"

"I've seen you two talking, was she supposed to tell me."

"I thought a mama would tell her daughter when a man asks about her." He looked at me.

"You obviously don't know my mom. If you're not in or affiliated with her congregation she's not putting in a good word for you."

"I see her going to service alone, how come you don't go?"

"You watch our house?"

"Most times. It's two beautiful single women; I make sure you're ok. I saw you hit the curb last night." He smiled at me.

I covered my face embarrassed. "You didn't have to tell me you saw that."

He dusted his hands and then he stood up. "There you go."

I took him to the garage that he worked at and he filled my tire with air, and then he put it back on my car. He suggested that I come out on our porch sometimes, and maybe we could talk. I said maybe as I hurried to work.

****

"Since when do you drink?" Kay asked.

"I drank some in college, but only socially." I said ordering another drink.

"Take it easy though, you're not going to be able to drive if you don't slow down." She had a point, so I went on the dance floor to sweat out the liquor I drank already. I danced with everyone, I even danced by myself. As long as the music was loud and pumping I didn't have to deal with myself. In the bathroom I watched a couple of girls take their lines and then the peace that came over them. I wondered if what they felt, felt better than my drinks. As my curiosity mounted I then watched two other girls freak out because they didn't realize they were out of powder and neither one of them had any money. The desperation in their voices curved my curiosity. They were willing to and did whatever they needed to get more. I was still in the bathroom when they brought a guy in the stall. They didn't try to be discreet or anything. They were doing what they needed to, to get their next fix.

When I got home I had a nightcap. I thought about Ethan and how many ways he was cursing my name.

In the morning my mom kept looking at me while I poured a cup of coffee. "I thought you were leaving?"

"I'm waiting for my ride." She exhaled, "I need to get this divorce finalized."

"What's your hurry?" I eyed her.

"My freedom is important."

"Un huh, will you have scriptural grounds for divorce?"

"Adultery qualifies."

I looked at her, "you weren't with daddy since before I left for school?"

She swallowed, "not willingly."

I was sorry I asked, "oh." I stirred my coffee.

"Jenise baby, what's wrong?"

"What do you mean?"

"You seem depressed." She said looking at me tenderly.

"I've done a lot of hurtful things. I can't look at myself in the mirror."

"Jenise please come to service! There's nothing out there. It's never too late."

"Mom! I can't! It's too late! I'm sorry!" Then I went in my room and shut the door. I cried some, finished my last class assignment. Then I sat there getting more and more depressed about Ethan's last words to me. I knew I hurt him, but sitting in front of him like that was the most painful thing ever. I couldn't shake the feeling. I was trying to do the right thing for crying out loud. I called Grace she asked me if I was drunk in disbelief. "I'm trying to tell you sumtin!" My breath felt hot. "Ethan came out here a couple months ago. He MAD at me! I broke, **NO**, shattered his heart! That's what he said."

T took the phone from Grace. "Jenise? You're really drunk?"

"Yep!"

"Who were you drinking with?"

"Party for one!"

"Jenise! That's not good, don't get drunk by yourself."

"Don't fuss at my sister about the lights! She's a good girl! She made you cabbage and pancakes!"

T started laughing, "yes she did but never at the same time." Then he stopped laughing, "sis I'm worried about you. Come back."

"I'm fine, my mom likes it out here. I'm not coming back there. Ethan will run me over!"

He made his voice sad, "Blu would never hurt you."

The sadness of his voice brought my pain back. "I gotta go, tell my sister I'll call her back." I said then I hung up.

I continued drinking until I couldn't feel anything.

****

He walked over with a big smile on his face. "What made you finally come out?" Greg said sitting on the three steps to my porch.

"The weather is getting nicer." I said taking a drink.

"What you sipping on?"

"It's just a little something something. You drink?"

"Sometimes," he said looking at me. "Sometimes reality is too heavy huh."

I sighed, "yep."

"Come on," he stood up.

"Where we going?"

"If we're gonna drink we're gonna listen to good music while we do it."

"I need my purse," I said pointing to the house.

"If you say so, I'm driving. Meet me here in one minute." Then he walked towards his house.

I had a good time with Greg as we listened to music and drank. That night he kissed me when he walked me to my door.

The next time it was more drinking and a kiss and a feel, until one of the nights my mom was away at service we drank and then I slept over. There will never be a touch like Ethan's, but since I'll never know his touch again Greg's was at least enjoyable.

****

"Hello?"

"Hi this is Raynel, may I please speak to Jenise."

My heart dropped, she didn't sound upset so Ethan had to be ok. "Speaking. How are you?"

"I have a bone to pick with you miss missy! How you going to leave without saying goodbye?" I could hear the smile in her voice.

That didn't stop my voice from cracking. "I'm sorry, everything was so crazy. At the time it seemed like the right thing to do."

She told me that Franky was finally graduating this summer. I told her I was coming back for the ceremony and to get my diploma as well. Raynel got excited; she said my mother and I had to go out to dinner with them to celebrate. She told me I had to go because their sister was going to be there and the two of them steered clear of each other. When I asked her why, she said too much painful history. We talked for a long time. I told her when I came out my mom and I wanted to have my father sign the divorce papers. My mom is interested in a brother out here, who appears to be interested in her, but they try to steer clear of each other because she's not free. I told her I didn't know what state my father was going to be in when we go out there.

Chapter 10

Ethan

"Interesting choice." Franky said scratching his head.

"What's wrong with her?" I asked.

Franky looked at Dito for help, "I don't know. I can't put my finger on it. She just isn't you." Dito said. "When Grace introduced me to Tess, I knew exactly why. We've been together since the day we met, she gets me. Cat is fine for now, but it feels like you're rushing this. Give it time."

"So then I shouldn't propose?" I said pulling out a ring box.

Dito, Franky, and T jumped back like I had a gun. "LET ME SEE THAT!" Gwen said snatching the box out of my hand. "Blu, what happened to Jenise?" She said as she inspected the ring.

"She moved away," I said reaching for the box.

"I don't like how Cat just knows she got you. She's a piece of work!" Gwen said still looking at the ring.

"Blu listen to the girl!" Dito said, "Jenise could move back one day. Then you'll be stuck with this girl who's going to try to get you for as much money as she can."

I took a deep breath, "fine. I'll wait, but don't be dumb. Jenise isn't coming back, even if she did it could never be the same."

Franky looked at me like something stunk. "You digging her all like that?"

"Yes," I said defensively.

"I mean I love Grace. You've seen us. She brings out a softer and gentler side of me. However, I'm not ready to marry her right now." T said.

"You're still in school, when you're finished you're gonna marry her aren't you?"

"Yes, but..."

"But nothing! All y'all just jealous. Cat is gorgeous, good to me, and she wants me." I was frustrated.

"Jenise and I are walking across the stage together." Franky said giving me an evil knowing smile.

I felt like he punched me, I sat down while they stared at me. "She's coming? Literally coming out here?" Everyone shook their heads yes. "How you know?"

"Momma talked to her." Franky said.

"How she get her number?"

"Momma asked me, I asked Grace." Franky smiled, "you still gonna bring Cat?"

"NO!"

Everyone started laughing like I told a funny joke.

****

I stood to the side watching Uncle Tim and Malcolm talking. I don't know what they were talking about; both of them were enjoying the conversation. Their faces were serious and they were focused, Tim directed the conversation. My father called my uncle over to look at something. Malcolm sat there watching my uncle walk away. Big ole Malcolm looked young like he was watching his father. I thought about the way he took Whispers' death. I wondered if he regretted not going to the funeral. I was happy to see that Uncle Tim treated Malcolm just like he treated his other sons. Sometimes it seemed like he was harder on him than anyone else. However, Malcolm seemed to thrive under those circumstances. Malcolm and I rode together to meet up with Troy. "Congratulations on your son."

"Thank you," Malcolm's voice smiled. "All of this is outside of anything I know."

"How you handling that?"

He shook his head, "not good. Amber is over there depressed, and I can't find the words without sounding weak so I say nothing. I'm sorry to hear about your baby."

I swallowed back my emotion, "thank you."

"You ok with this?" He asked about our subject matter.

"Yea, its fine. I wasn't in love with the mother so my experience would've never been like yours."

"Its a small world ain't it?" He shook his head; "something told me to ask you why you wanted a visit for that teacher. Every time I'd think about it something else would happen. I could've put two and two together a long time ago."

"So I guess this really makes you a part of our family now."

"You got an exit strategy? Tim keeps telling me to build mine now. He says we won't be moving forever and when that change happens I need to be setup to legitimately succeed."

"Yep, I'm pretty much setup already. I keep my hands dirty dealing with you all, but I'm clean otherwise. Especially my place, always keep your place and your car clean. Make paper trails for everything you have, my father will be in your ear about business. At any moment things could blow up. We got to be prepared and think ahead. You got bank accounts?"

"About that, I don't know what to do. I have a savings account at the same bank that Amber has hers. I hadn't thought of an account until her. I don't know what to do after that."

I took him by the bank and I got every pamphlet they had on accounts. He told me his grandma opened the savings account he has. We agreed to sit down with his statements and I'd show him how I spread my accounts out. My strategic approach to doing this and then I'd help him open what he needed since he wasn't eighteen yet.

****

She has to know I'm going to be here. I wonder if she's as nervous about seeing me as I am about seeing her? I didn't want it to seem like I was trying too hard. Fortunately I've always dressed nicely so today wouldn't be any different. Hair cut and crisp just like she likes. I stood in the mirror looking at myself convincing myself to be cool. Cat put her arms around me. She said I was up early, I told her I had a long day ahead of me. I told her I didn't know how late I would be and not to wait up. She looked at my face for a few minutes. She kissed me and then she told me she couldn't wait for me to come back. When I sat in my car, I asked myself why was I feeling nervous about seeing Jenise. The way I acted last time I saw her she should be nervous about seeing me not me about her. I've been good; my head hasn't turned to another woman since Cat and I became official. I haven't walked out the door like I felt like I needed to burn off energy with someone else either. Cat is a completely better fit for me than Nohemi. Nohemi although faithful and totally in to me, was looking for someone to take care of her. She dropped out of school once she was pregnant and was completely fine with me taking care of her. She finally found her way into my apartment and she wasn't leaving. Cat on the other hand…. I laughed to myself. She moved in right away, but she still works and she does stuff with herself. The fact that I have her completely open surprises her and she can't believe it. Catalina Cuthford and I make a good team. My father doesn't hate her like he did Nohemi; he's still not fond of her like he is of Jenise. No one is, they all kind of look at her like ok… fine… but then they bring up Jenise of course when she's not there. Even if I wanted to run from the memory of Jenise my family pretty much make that impossible. When I got to Franky's he was up and clowning around with Dito and Tess. When I walked in the door they got quiet and looked at me with smiles. Then I noticed a rock sparkling on Tess' hand. I looked at Dito with a question on my face. Dito said they went to Reno on Tuesday randomly and then they decided to do it while they were there. Franky and I exchanged looks; we told him momma was going to get him. I happily congratulated my brother. He and Tess are a good match. I asked where T was and they said back at his place dealing with Grace's family. They said they came early in the morning and it's been fireworks ever since. They didn't realize that Grace was living with T, and they were speaking Tagalog until T told them if they couldn't speak English while in his place they had to get out. Franky laughed as he said Grace looked like she was about to explode watching T put her parents in their place. When I asked what he meant by explode, he said she is swimming in her undies. I frowned I didn't want to think of her like that. We beat around the bush as long as we could then I drove Franky to the ceremony since he needed to be there early. I told him I was proud of him for buckling down and getting his diploma. He thanked me, and then he took off to prepare for his climatic walk across the stage.

I sat in the stands watching people putting up decorations and getting the last minute details done. "Ethan?" I heard my name, it was Mrs. Wright.

I stood and hugged her, she looked so much better than the last time I saw her. Her broken heart was evident the entire time she was here. Now she looks rested, refreshed, and happy. "How are you?"

"I'm good. I want you to meet my friends. This is Stephen and Greg." She said proudly.

Stephen was around her age, but Greg was about my age. Greg didn't appear to be a relative of Stephen; they didn't stand by each other with familiarity in their demeanors. Immediately I knew Greg was here for Jenise, irritation ran through my blood. This girl is forever playing games. "Ethan." I said shaking their hands. Neither one of them appeared to have any clue as to who I am, but its not like I told Cat about Jenise.

"This is really nice, and the weather is just like I've always imagined California weather to be." Stephen said.

"This is your first time in California?" I asked both of them.

"It's mine." Stephen said then he looked at Greg.

"I've been out here before." Was the only comment he offered. He was looking around at everything and everyone.

"How's Jenise? Is she nervous?" I asked Mrs. Wright.

"She's been nerved up for the past month." She laughed.

"That's my best friend always nerved up." Greg's head turned and he focused on me for a minute. "My family is going to invade this section shortly, please take your seats. I'm going to be right back." Greg looked like he wanted an excuse to go with me, but we both knew I wasn't going to give him one.

As I walked away I pointed Dito and T in Mrs. Wright's direction. I walked into the auditorium where all the graduates were talking and preparing with their caps and gowns. It wasn't hard to find Jenise. I followed the sound of excitement and laughter. Jenise and Grace were holding hands and jumping around excitedly as on lookers looked at them and laughed. Jenise was in the middle of saying something to Grace when her eyes landed on me. Guilt then excitement showed on her face. She hurried to me and hugged me. It felt good to hold her even if it was just for a minute or a few seconds. I kissed her neck on purpose as I released our hug, Jenise immediately shivered even though she tried her hardest to fight it and play it off like she didn't have a reaction to me. "I'm so happy to see you."

"I saw your momma."

"You met her friend?" She gave me a knowing smile. "She wants to go get my father's signature on her divorce papers."

"You think he's going to sign?"

"No, but you can't tell her anything. She won't listen to reason, she's optimistic about this whole thing."

"When are you going out there?"

"Tomorrow, I think."

"Can I go? I want to know what's new with my best friend."

Jenise fought back a sad face. "You still want to be my best friend?"

I pulled her in and I hugged her, "we're bonded for life. We'll always be best friends." I said kissing her cheek.

Jenise cried on my chest, "I'm sorry Ethan."

I looked at Grace who was watching us and wiping tears. "I'm sorry too."

"What are you two doing?" Franky said walking up on us all loud.

"I brought a friend." Jenise said looking at me.

"So I saw, I guess I should've brought my friend too."

"Cat?" She said like she already knew.

"Yep, she moved in a little after Nohemi moved out."

"Figures." She said with a little jealousy on her face.

I squeezed Jenise a little tighter and then I let her go. "I've got a graduation gift for you, but I'll give it to you later."

We chatted a little more and then I went back out to the front. My momma and Mrs.

Wright were chatting like old friends. I could tell my momma was going to give me a hard time later about my breakup once again. We cheered for Grace Vasquez, Franklin Wallace III, and Jenise Wright when the graduates came out and crossed the stage. When the graduates came out Grace introduced our family to hers. Her cousins were very friendly and happy to meet everyone. Grace's parents were not happy at all. They kept shooting T looks like he was a thief and he stole their precious little girl. My father spoke with her parents for a little on the side. I don't know what he said, but they relaxed a lot. Jenise's friend kept watching me guess he wasn't stupid. She brought him over to me and proudly introduced him as her friend. He corrected her and said he was her boyfriend as we shook hands. Then she told him I was her best friend, I could tell he didn't like the title as much as I didn't like his. Why does he get to be her boyfriend while I was restricted to best friend? This guy is in no way better than me. I can tell that by looking at him. He's hiding something too. My brothers and T stood over to the side watching us like we were on the silver screen. Jenise pleaded with her eyes for me to be nice. "Franklin Wallace!" My father said inserting himself in our conversation.

"Greg this is Ethan's father." Jenise said as she gave my father a hug. "It's good to see you." She genuinely smiled at him.

"Who's he?" He gestured towards Greg.

"Greg is my boyfriend." She said proudly.

My father looked Greg up and down. "That's surprising," then he shot me a look.

"Your family is coming out to an early dinner with us. Follow or ride with Ethan." He commanded.

"Actually..." Jenise slowed down when she caught my father's expression, "we were going...." My father didn't turn his eyes. "Alright we'll follow Ethan. Yes sir, we are coming." Jenise saluted my father.

"It looked like you were going to try to tell me no." He said not taking his eyes off of her.

"Me? Never!"

"Good, see you in a minute." Then he walked away.

"He doesn't determine how we spend our evening." Greg said to Jenise.

"Greg, it's not a big deal. These are my friends."

"I don't know how you could ever think a white man is your friend."

"What are you saying?" I asked burning him with my eyes.

Greg sucked his teeth, "you heard me. White people aren't to be trusted."

My brothers and T stepped forward. "You realize you're talking about my father."

"Greg! Stop it! These are my friends, please don't do this right now." Jenise pleaded, "let's go. Ethan where did you park?"

"I'll bring my car around, come here." I said as I started walking. Jenise followed me. I looked at her. "Boyfriend?"

"Girlfriend?" She shot back at me.

I unlocked her door, and then I looked at her. Her brown eyes were searching mine for any confirmation. I gave in like I was hoping I wouldn't and I took her in my arms and I kissed her deeply. She kissed me back like she missed me too.

"Boyfriend?"

"Girlfriend?" She said lowering her eyes. "You love her."

I exhaled, "as much as I can without her being you."

"Same here! I thought you were going to hate me forever."

"I never said I hated you, I made sure I didn't say that. I said I can't stand you."

"It didn't sound like that. Ethan I'm sorry, I thought I was doing the right thing. Your baby deserved a fair chance, I...."

I cut her off as I started the car, "we can talk about this later. I need alone time with you. Don't make me come snatch you out of your hotel." Jenise smiled and then she showed me where the car they borrowed was. Mrs. Wright and her friend rode with Franky and me to the restaurant. Mrs. Wright was as lovable as Jenise. Her "friend" is a stupid somebody if he doesn't know there's no escaping this. Mrs. Wright has hooked him and he will forever be a slave drawn in by her no matter what he does to fight it. I know she's religious so I don't know how this is supposed to work. I thought you couldn't get a divorce if God is part of your marriage. When we pulled up to Le Maire, Mrs. Wright gasped and asked if we were at the right place. When I said yes they started pulling on their clothes as if to say they were under dressed. The host greeted us promptly with a tray of champagne. My father called out from the back of the group that he needed to add fifteen more to our reservation. The host swallowed and said, "yes sir." Then he ran to the back. Then the manager came out and greeted the Wallace group, he asked for five minutes so that they could prepare the banquet room for our additional guest. My father said the clock was already ticking. It seemed like service on the floor stopped and it was all hands on deck as they hurried to prepare our room. My father invited Grace's whole family, and we had no idea that Jenise and her mother would bring extras. Jenise kept peeking at me, but she was trying to be respectful of her man. Where I didn't care and I stared. I hadn't seen her in months, and it had been longer since I touched her. It felt like it had been years since I felt her presence. This is why I was nervous cause I knew all bets were out the window as soon as I saw her. At four minutes and fifty-five seconds the host returned to show us to our banquet room. One of our designated servers took everyone's coats, jackets, and purses if they wanted. There was a coat rack directly in the room. There was a banner that was professionally made that said "Congratulations Graduates", candles, fine china, silk linens, crystal, etc. all on the table. Our room was completely decked out. The table was in the middle of the floor and it was a long table. I waited until Jenise sat and then I sat directly across from her Gwen sat next to me and then Dito, Tess, Grace, T, Franky, so on and so forth. Greg frowned as he looked at the menu, he asked Jenise how much all this was going to cost. "I'm open to donations if you're trying to pay your portion of the bill." My father called out from across the table. He shot Greg a look, and Greg looked away.

"You've been here before?" Greg asked Jenise.

"Yes, Dito this is the first restaurant you brought Grace and I to." Jenise said trying to show Greg that I was not the center of her world out here. He'd be a fool to believe it.

Greg looked at Dito hard for a minute, "how are you affiliated with them?"

"Them who?" I could tell Dito was irritated.

Greg pointed between Franky and I. "Them."

Dito stared at his face, "get your eyes checked. The three of us look a like. We're brothers." Dito's ears started turning red.

"You're white." Greg said like he was arguing.

"And you're black. I'm glad we got that cleared up."

"What am I missing?" Greg asked Jenise.

"Wow Greg! You know how to make a wonderful first impression. Cut it out!" Jenise said.

"How old are you?" Gwen blurted out.

"29," he said matter of factly.

"Whoa! You're old!" She said trying to pull back her giggle.

Greg looked at Dito again, "and that's your wife?"

Dito smiled proudly, "YES this beautiful angel is my pride and joy."

Jenise shot Greg a look that told him to shut up, and then she pointed out some items on the menu she thought he would like as she told him off under her breath. When the servers brought in more champagne Gwen told the server she wanted some. The server told her she wasn't twenty-one and she couldn't have any. Gwen huffed and walked over to our father. She kissed his cheek then she told him she wanted some champagne. Dad signaled for the server to give her some. Momma shot Dad a look like she didn't approve of what just happened. My father waved her off and went back to looking at his menu. After everyone ordered I walked over to Mrs. Wright and I kneeled beside her seat. I told her I wanted to go with her when she took her paperwork to get signed. She didn't pretend not to be relieved when I offered to go. She shyly asked if it would be too much to ask to go tomorrow. I told her it would not be a problem at all. My father asked me what was going on. I quietly told him about what happened the last time. My father said that one of his guys was out that way; he said Tomas will be nearby in case I needed backup. Then my father looked at Jenise and told her to come down by him. When she did he asked her where she was working. She told him about the company she was working for. He told her he didn't like it, he said she needed to work for herself or work for him. He told her his brother showed him the work she did for his store. She looked confused. So I explained that my Aunt Emma Barnes co-owned the store she created the logo, remodel design, and packaging for. My father smiled and said he could see her amounting to more than just a number in someone's corporation.

Jenise

I was so embarrassed when Greg showed his butt yesterday. He said he didn't like Ethan in the first place and once he saw his father he really didn't like him. I love Greg, but I hate how he gets caught up on the color of a person's skin. He asked me how I ever survived in a predominately white college. He said Ethan, Franky, and T were fake black boys cause their fathers are white. He went on and on about how uncomfortable he was around all those white and Asian people. We were arguing really bad and then he opened his mouth and said that Raynel was a stupid house nigger. Thinking that she was better than other black people because she willingly had babies by a white man. Until that point I was trying to keep my voice down cause I didn't want my mom hearing us argue. His comment pushed me over the edge; I cursed him out so badly his ears should've started bleeding. My mom came rushing to the door just in time to see me smack Greg upside the head. Of course that made him angry and he reared up like he was going to retaliate when Brother Bolds grabbed him and told him to go walk it off. It was bad enough that we were drinking, but then he really pissed me off. I told my mom what he said, and then she stopped looking at me like I was crazy for reacting the way I did. She said she hoped he got affiliated with the congregation soon cause he'd soon learn that God doesn't see color and he loves us all. Then she reminded me that he was from the south and he knows life a different way than we do. California has prejudice people too; she said it is a lot more relaxed out here than out there. Brother Bolds said he was going to take Greg to Greg's friend's place, and Brother Bolds was going to go stay with her friends. My mom smiled and told him she would see him the next night. My mom was completely into Brother Bolds, "Stephen and I are just friends". She tried to hold on to, but I know that look in her eyes. And I know that reference to *friends* when everything else in your body is begging for more. This morning I asked my mom how we were getting to Stockton if Brother Bolds wasn't coming back until tonight. She smiled and said Ethan volunteered to take us. I couldn't hide my smile. We were staying with Sister Michaels and she had cats everywhere. Cats are interesting creatures, until now I thought cats wanted to be held and carried all over the place, but her cat Koba doesn't like people and is evil. It kept trying to trip me, and when I didn't fall I swear it hissed at me. I keep throwing stuff at this cat and it moves like a ninja. I promise me and this cat gonna tear this house down if they ever leave us alone here. Koba and I were fighting over the window when Ethan pulled up. Koba hissed at me when I finally moved out of his way. I told my mom Ethan was here and I ran out the door to hug him. He squeezed me tight and swung me around. My mom came out the door sooner than I wanted her to. Ethan asked if Greg was coming and I told him the plan was for him to spend the day with his friends while my mom and I handled business. I told Greg I would see him tonight, of course Ethan asked what was happening tonight and I told him we were going to a club in downtown San Francisco. My mom completely tickled herself by telling Ethan all about our adventures in Texas, my hilarious and dramatic responses to the insect life out there, the weather, you name it and I had a dramatic reaction to all of it. Ethan was finishing my mom's recites of my outburst without even being there. I forgot how well he knows me. Ethan made our two-hour drive in forty-five minutes. Some of the farms I remembered were gone, my mom said developers bought those farms out some time ago and they were going to build houses over there. When we pulled up to my dad's house, it had been repainted. Everything looked ninety times better. When we got out the car you could hear the tractor going out back. I told my mom to wait by the car and I stuck my head out back. My little brother was playing with a puppy, within a gated area that looked like was built for him. My little brother saw me smiled and then he started banging on a pot with a medal spoon HARD and loud. The tractor stopped and then it sound like it was getting closer. My father rushed over to see what was going on. He froze when he saw me. He looked sober and like the daddy I left behind. He looked at me with sadness in his eyes and he said he was sorry. I told him the house looks nice, he thanked me then he asked where my mother was. I asked him if he was calm and he said he was. I told him she was out front, but this was not a social visit. He sighed at the same time as he verbally told my little brother he did good and he was proud of him. He told him he was going out front and he would be back. My mom and Ethan were standing next to the car when we came around the back. My mom looked nervous, and like she didn't expect him to look better. When we got close my mom reached in her purse and pulled out divorce papers. She held them up and told my daddy he needed to sign them. He ignored her paper and walked up to her and kissed her. She tried to fight it, she melted a little, and then she started fighting again. Ethan smiled and moved out of the way. My mom's hair was wild and her clothes were all wrinkled, she was breathing hard and trying to grab her composure. She told my father he couldn't kiss her, that he no longer had that right. She picked up her papers she dropped on the ground and repeated that she needed him to sign. He told her he refused to sign them and that he wanted her back. He said he reached out to everyone he could think of for help cause he knew he had to get it together if he wanted to ever get her back. She held her papers out looking at the ground as she shook her head no and she said it was too late. She told him she was happy he was doing better, but she could not be his wife any more. My father smiled at me and said Jamal and Colette were coming in a little bit to pick up little Fred and they were expecting a child together. I felt like he punched me, I asked when they married. He said not too long after my mom left. He said they keep little Fred most of the time and he happened to be here today. My daddy looked at my momma and told her he'd do anything. She pointed the papers at him, and he said anything but that. My mom told him if he ever loved her he would sign the papers for her. He said he loved her too much to give in like that. Ethan and I sat on the hood of his car while my parents went back and forth. My mom literally ran when my father got too close to her, she was afraid he was going to kiss her again. Ethan asked me if I was ok with Jamal being married. I told him I saw it coming from the moment she moved back, but I didn't like it. Jamal stood up quickly when he saw me. He smiled and said he was going to be a daddy. I congratulated him while Colette stayed in the car looking. Jamal got little Fred from the back, he hugged and kissed my mom. While he put my little brother in the car, Colette stared at my parents. The look on her face made me wonder if that baby was really Jamal's or if it was my daddy's.

Ethan

"Why do you seem different?" Cat said modeling her dress in front of me.
"Different?" I said watching her curves.
"You were too tired last night, this morning you're gone before I wake up. You

come home, dress, and you're ready to go. You haven't chased me around in almost three days. That's not like you." She said watching my eyes.

I shrugged, "I don't know but we don't have time right now if that's what you're getting at." I said knowing it was.

Cat stomped her foot then she walked into my face. "Are you messing around?"

I could honestly say no for at least the next twelve hours. "No."

"I'm not stupid, I know how I got you. I'd be a fool to let it happen to me the same way I did it."

"That's cute," I said looking at her cheeks turning red. "Your momma's side is starting to come out. You're changing colors."

"Don't make fun of me, I'm serious!"

"Try worrying about the things you can control."

"Which is?"

"If you don't hurry up, I'm going to leave you." I smacked her butt as she walked away.

Jenise

"My friends are going to meet us there." I said, "you better be on best behavior. Don't embarrass me again." When I walked out Greg said he liked my dress. Then he told me to come on cause we were riding with his friends. He introduced Charlie and Demetria, Charlie said hi while Demetria looked me up and down. It was going to be a long night. I asked how Charlie and Greg knew each other. He said they went to high school together and they've been best friends ever since. Charlie and Demetria have been married for three years and they don't have any kids. Demetria said she's not the mothering kind. When we got to the club we barely sat down before the men were off to the bar. Greg asked where my friends were and I told him we'd know when they arrived. Charlie and Greg were in their own world catching up about the things that have happened in their lives since they've last seen each other. Demetria saw some equally rough looking friends of hers and she went over to them without looking back. Grace came over and hugged me; she told me they were in the VIP section waiting for me. I tried to get Greg's attention, but they were too into their conversation to notice me above the loud music. I finished my drink then I followed Grace. I hugged each person one by one. When I got to Ethan and his girlfriend she was pretty. She had that mixed kid hair and her complexion was a little lighter than Ethan's. She was dissecting everything about me. She put her hand out to stop when Ethan went in for his hug. He smacked her hand away and told her to quit playing. He introduced me as his best friend, "Oh no! We're not playing that game. You're with me; I'm your best friend. She's just a girl you know!"

Ethan looked at her with an unamused look, "I've shot people for less. This is Jenise, she's my best friend, deal with it!"

"Blu! I don't know who you think you're talking to! You know I don't play these games!" She said stomping her foot.

"If this is how you're going to act, take a cab back to Berkeley. You're making a bigger deal out of this whole thing than there needs to be."

"Where did she...."

"Jenise? What's going on?" Greg said walking to my side.

"Cat this is my boyfriend Greg. Greg this is Ethan's girlfriend Cat."

Cat's eyes bounced back and forth between Ethan and Greg like she was comparing them from head to toe. Greg wasn't as tall as Ethan; Greg was browner than Ethan. Ethan has curly hair; Greg has an afro and thin beard. Greg wears glasses; I could go on and on. "Did they tell you they were best friends?" She asked Greg.

Greg blew air, "she's my girlfriend I'll be her best friend before some other guy."

"Thank you! That's my point!" She said putting her hands on her hips and tapping her foot.

Ethan cocked his head to the side; she was getting on his nerves. "You waiting for me to say something? Cause I already told you. You can deal with it or you can walk. I don't care how big of a scene you make or how many outside opinions you try to drum up. This is MY BEST FRIEND and I'll end anyone who tries to interfere with that.... Do I make myself clear?"

Greg started to say something and I told him to let it go. Grace stood over to the side with wide eyes. I guess she was seeing everything differently now that she had the full picture.

Chapter 11

Ethan

Cat called herself being mad at me last night. Since she was mad I went for broke. I danced with Cat to a few songs, but then I surprised Cat and Jenise when I danced with Jenise. Jenise has only ever seen me slow dance. We were bumping all over that dance floor. Greg and his friend sat over the side drinking and talking. I had to tell myself to let it go. I know that he's hiding something, but if I found out what it was I'd have to tell Jenise. She'd break up with him, and well while I love Jenise with all my heart, the fact that she ran away from me makes me wonder about her ability to stay. I know Cat's not going anywhere, and I bought her a ring for a reason. I refuse to let either one of them go, I know it's selfish but I didn't care. So I decided to let Jenise have Greg as long as he knows to stand down. I don't like him and I'm looking for the opportunity to show him why he should always bow down to me.

When we got home, Cat huffed all over the place slamming doors, and rolling her eyes at me. It was cute. She tried to lay on the edge of the bed so I wouldn't touch her. I started rubbing her butt. "Don't touch me!" She said through tears.

"Why you mad?" I asked as if I didn't know.

She threw her body towards me. "Who is she?"

"My best friend," I said trying to make my face innocent.

"No one is supposed to come before me!" She watched my face.

"I've known Jenise since before you would've ever considered someone like me. She's my best friend."

"Are you in love with her?" She watched my face in the dark.

"She's my best friend of course I love her." I touched her face, "this is the moment of truth Cat." I put her leg on my hip so that I could play with her. Cat's eyes got sleepy. Just like any other cat, you stroke them and they are putty in your hands. "Jenise is my best friend and I will never give her up. If you can't deal with that you don't have to stay with me. I don't love her like I love you, and I could never love you like I love her. You decide what you want."

I watched her eyes get sleepy as she enjoyed my touch. "Ethan, I want to be your only."

"You're the only one here right now. That's about the best I can promise you." Then I kissed her.

Cat moaned, "you're manipulating me!" She said helplessly.

"I guess women think they have the market cornered on manipulation." I smiled.

"You love me?" She asked watching my eyes.

"Yes I do."

She lifted her leg up and brought it by her head. "Say it again."

"I love you Catalina Cuthford." I said then I kissed her.

"I want to have your baby." She said watching my face.

I got up and went to my closet. I took a deep breath cause the voice in my head screamed at me telling me not to do it. I took the ring box out. I kneeled next to the bed. "Can we get married first?"

Cat screamed, as she shot up. "Really? This is real? You want to marry me?"

"Yes, but you have to understand. I love my best friend; I'm not giving her up for anyone. If you can't be cordial with her out of your love for me then this won't work. I need you to understand your place."

She smiled real big, "I'm your wife."

"Yes, but Jenise is my best friend that I've known longer and deeper than you."

"Yes, but you're asking me." She said like the ring hypnotized her.

"Doesn't matter, I win! I'm Mrs. Wallace."

"If this is what you call winning." I put the ring on her finger.

Cat tackled me on the floor, and I appreciate her trying, but I broke her down on that floor. When I told Cat to come back on the bed cause we were falling asleep she said she couldn't move, her body was still shaking. I picked her up and put her back in the bed. Cat said she'd make an appointment to get on birth control to make sure she didn't get pregnant before the wedding. That was music to my ears.

In the morning I got up, showered thoroughly and I headed out the door. I felt especially good about the honest conversation I had with Cat this morning since it was technically earlier today. When I pulled up Jenise crept out the door with her shoes, purse, and jacket in hand. She closed the door gently then she quietly hurried down the stairs. When she got in the car, she smiled and kissed me. She said she had to sneak out obviously. I asked if anyone could vouch for her and say she came home last night? She said her momma, the lady they're staying with, and Stephen were still up in visiting in the living room when she came home. She said they sat up talking for a long time. I told her I liked her dress. She thanked me as she crossed her legs so that her dress went up more. I could not wait to get between those thighs. They were calling my name. I told her she was sitting too lady like, then I made her open her legs. I licked my fingers and then I put my hand under her dress. Jenise braced herself by grabbing the "oh shoot!" handle on the roof. She tried to tell me to stop but I had her going. Right when she was on the edge I pulled my hand back. I licked my fingers and I told her now she was on my level. Jenise was quiet for a minute, and then she excused herself to the restroom when we got to the restaurant. I smiled at her when the hostess showed her to our table. Jenise's eyes were now droopy and she started shaking her leg as she looked through the menu. I put her gift on the table, and then I smiled at her. Jenise's eyes got big as she picked up the small box with the ribbon on it. She opened it and gasped at the diamond earrings. She excitedly took them out and put them on, she excitedly turned her head from side to side to model them for me. I told her she looks good.

"So you love Gregory?"

She stopped shaking her leg, as she looked guilty. "Yes," she said sadly.

I was immediately irritated, I had to remind myself of the pep talk I had with myself. "If he asked you to marry him, would you?" Jenise started moving around like my question made her uncomfortable. "Jenise, it's me. You can tell me anything."

"As long as I thought you hated me my answer was yes. Now I feel confused."

"I may be able to help you out with that. Your little run and hide thing you did hurt me. I know why you did it, but it didn't make it hurt any less. I don't trust you not to run from me like that again at some point. I honestly thought we were over, but as soon as I found out you were coming I knew that wasn't the case." I swallowed, "by then I had already bought Cat's ring."

Jenise's body slumped like I shot her, "a ring?" She said as her eyes filled up with tears.

"Yes, I asked her this morning."

Jenise flinched, "this morning? Then why are we here? What's the point?"

I sat back, "I have to have you!"

Jenise started shaking her leg again. "But you're going to marry her."

"So…" I said looking at her.

"Ethan, I don't want to be your mistress."

"You're not a mistress. You're my best friend."

"Cat and I will never have what you and I have, but like I said I can't exactly trust you."

"Why are we even here Ethan?"

"Because I'm in love with you, you don't know what you want. You'll always be back and forth about everything. When you decide to run from me, Cat will be there for me like she was last time. She took good care of me."

"I would've taken care of you!" She cried.

"No, you are the master of running from me. This way you can have your space to be on the fence."

"What about when you have children with her?"

"What about it? She's my wife."

"You wanted to marry me and have babies with me."

"And then you ran."

"I can't believe Cat agreed to this."

"She loves me and she will do what I tell her to."

"I'm not Cat." She said rolling her neck.

"That's why I'm in love with you."

"So this is your plan? You're going to marry Cat and think you can have me whenever you want me as if you're my husband?" I didn't respond cause the moment she said it, it didn't sound right. "Ethan you have to know this isn't going to work. I don't want to live like this. I know I messed up by running, but why can't you see that I needed to run from you. You're normally so reasonable. It seems like the moment that Nohemi got pregnant your good sense flew out the window." I knew she was right, but my vision was cloudy. I wanted Cat, but I need Jenise. Right now I'm not willing to give either up.

Jenise

Ethan said our situation is what it is. He said we've both made such a terrible mess of everything. I screamed at my body for not caring about any of this and still waiting for the satisfaction that only came from Ethan. Ethan watched me as we ate breakfast; I was in my own thoughts. "Until Nohemi happened I thought I was going to be the mother of your children, your one and only wife. She was pregnant almost at the halfway point. Normally it's a wrap from there on. You're going to hold this against me for the rest of my life. You're going to marry someone else?"

"You ran away, we fell in love. I don't want to give her up." He said matter of factly.

"You're greedy!"

"No more than you are. Tell me you don't want me." I stared at him, "Jenise I love you like I have never loved another person. You're the only person who gets to hurt me like you did. I can't bring myself to trust you not to run again, but I can't leave you alone. If you could honestly say you could walk away from Greg drop him cold turkey, I'll break up with Cat and we will get married." He watched my eyes like he was internally pleading with me to say yes.

I exhaled and started crying, I looked away. How could I hurt Greg like that? I did not want to hurt him just so that I could have what I wanted. I wasn't being selfish when I ran away from Ethan, I was doing the right thing. "This isn't fair!"

His face turned angry, "what's unfair is that you can never choose me! There's always somebody in the way. This was it, your last opportunity to put me before everyone else and you've failed me again." He exhaled, "it's ok. I love you anyways, I just can't sit around waiting for you to decide."

"What would I move back out here for? I don't want to watch you and Cat play house."

"Come play with us." He smiled.

"What?"

"I'll put you up in a house, bring Greg if he'll come. I'll help you setup your business. Everyone will get what they want."

"How do you figure that's everyone getting what they want?"

"I get to have you, you get me. Cat gets to be my wife; Greg would be stupid not to propose. You don't have to break his heart. Everybody wins." He said.

"Why do you say he'd be stupid not to?"

"You are smart, educated, you've got your stuff together. To be as old as he is, I don't get the impression he's thought about tomorrow. Let alone planned for his future. He'd be stupid to think he could survive without you. I'm sure he's going to want to go wherever you go."

"And when Greg and I have children?"

Ethan slumped, "you can't!"

"I can and I will!"

Ethan was quiet for a minute, and then he started staring at me. It was like any minute I was going to see smoke lifting from his brain. "You're not on the pill now are you?"

"Why are you asking me that?" I screamed inside, how does he know that?

"You moved to Texas, you stopped taking your pill. For one you didn't have a

doctor out there and for two you didn't want to chance your momma finding them."
He sat back satisfied with himself.

"Wrong! I have a doctor in Texas. I keep my pills in my car under the seat." I was
lying but so what, he just thinks he's so smart.

He smiled at me, but he didn't say anything. I could see his thoughts swishing
around his mind. He was making his mind up about something. My insides told me
I wasn't going to like it. When we finished breakfast he drove us to the wine
country and we tasted wine until I was beyond tipsy. He drove us back to Tiburon,
which is right on the water on the other side of the Golden Gate Bridge. Our hotel
room looked out over the water and it was a beautiful day. My body was excited
and I tried to tell it to be quiet. I was still very tipsy; as I tried to find clarity he
opened a bottle of champagne. "Reunited and it feels so good!" He sang as he
poured our glasses. When I tried to say something he told me to drink up. When I
tried to say something again he rushed me and kissed me. The room spun, this was
happening. It was real, this wasn't a dream. When Ethan entered me I held on to
him, every time I tried to tell him I lied he kissed me. Ethan was in so deep I could
feel him in my throat. Sweet agony! My eyes were rolling back while Ethan kissed
me. "Change of plans, you're having my baby first!" My body started tingling and I
couldn't speak. "It's time for you to choose me first!" I wanted to say no, wait, stop,
or don't. In that moment it was so good, I would've shot my mother if he told me
to. I couldn't breathe and he kept going, he flipped me over pushed my legs back as
far as they could go, and then he went in deeper. I tried to back up, but there was
nowhere to run. This time when he came, he came so hard I thought he was going to
nut in my throat! When I tried to move he wouldn't let me. He told me, his soldiers
needed to march to do their duty. When I tried to speak he kissed me again and my
body came again just from his kiss. We fell asleep in this awkward position.

Chapter 12

Jenise

I asked Ethan what he was on. I had clearly forgotten what sex with Ethan is like. Stamina he has, and the ability to enslave my body. I was tired and sore, but my body was loving every last moment of his touch, thrust, and deposits inside of me. When it was close to midnight, I asked him to take me home. He said we weren't leaving until the morning. I asked him what about Cat and Greg. He told me they didn't matter in this moment. This was our time and we needed to celebrate the union of our souls to create someone else. I was too weak to sit up so I turned to face him. I told him a person can't get pregnant just because they want to. The timing has to be just right; I told him if I'm not ovulating, I would not end up pregnant. Ethan let me give my whole educational speech about the female body and how a woman becomes pregnant. Then he told me I talk too much and he bet me five dollars that I ended up pregnant. We laughed and then we shook on it. He told me when I got home I could do the research to figure out if this was our window or not. I decided not to worry about anything else and to enjoy my time with Ethan. We spent hours talking about everything, getting caught on the things we missed with each other, when he fell for Cat. The things he likes about her and the things he hates. Although now, his voice didn't sound too certain about anything with her. He listened very intently as I talked about Greg like he was devoting every word to memory. He told me that he feels like Greg is hiding something. I told him he was only saying that because he didn't like him. He smiled and said that too. Ethan kept kissing me and telling me how happy he was that I was back. He got really quiet when I came clean about how much I've been drinking. Then he asked why would I hurt myself just because he was upset. I told him I couldn't stand how much I hurt him. I said again how my intention wasn't to hurt him, and I thought he would understand that I was trying to do the right thing. He said he gets it, but to never be that selfless again. Then he told me he was in love with me, and hurting myself was a way of hurting him, and to stop hurting myself like that. He said alcohol is supposed to make you feel good and enhance a good feeling. He told me I needed to stop drinking anyways. He said there are recent studies that show that the possibilities of birth defects, and low birth weights are higher when the mother smokes or drinks. He said he was talking to Nohemi's doctors and paying attention to everything in the end. Then his body tensed up. He laid his head on my chest when he said he held the baby. I rubbed his head when his body temperature went up. He was radiating heat. He unloaded like he had been holding in all his emotions about the baby. He said he didn't want that baby with Nohemi. She got on his nerves so badly it wasn't funny. He said holding his baby girl's lifeless body was the worst pain he's ever felt in his life, me leaving was the next. He repeated that I needed to move back as soon as possible. He needed to know that I was ok, and I had everything I needed at all times. I asked him how he would tell Cat. He exhaled and said he didn't know yet, I grabbed his hair and lifted his head, his eyes were red. I told him I was not coming to his wedding. His face turned evil as he said I was coming and I was going to be in the wedding. That's when the argument started. We argued hard and long he was being ridiculous, there was no way I was going to happily stand by and watch him promise forever to Cat. He didn't care what I said he said I was in the wedding.

When I went home the next morning I asked my mom if Greg was looking for me. She said he didn't call once. I was relieved and then irritated. Then I looked at my mom, she wasn't drilling me about where I spent the night or anything. She looked guilty and confused. We went for a walk, my legs were still a little wobbly, the after affects of Ethan. My mom was devastated that my father would not sign the divorce papers. She said apparently she was the only person surprised by his lack of cooperation. She said she and Brother Bolds went to the beach to walk in the sand and talk. I looked at her with big eyes as I confirmed that she went without a chaperone. My mom put her head down and she said yes. She said their conversation became too emotional and the next thing she knew… she started crying. I looked at my MOM in shock and disbelief. Misses holier than thou fell victim to sin, fornication, and adultery. I hugged my mom and I told her it was going to be ok. I told her I'd ask Ethan to help her get a lawyer and get her divorce finalized. I asked her if she still wanted to be with Brother Bolds. She said a heart felt yes. She said she will always love my father he was her first love. However, she could never forgive how horrible he was to her. Then she looked me in my eyes, "I can tell he's still seeing Colette. I'm not stupid. I don't want to be involved in that hot mess anymore." I rubbed her back, but I didn't say anything. "Even though it was wrong it was perfect with Stephen. Our kiss had an undertow that pulled us out too far. Stephen tried to back pedal and I." She swallowed, "I made it happen. *Me!*" She cried a little more. "It was never like that with your father. Maybe because he was always battling his addiction. I'm so in love with Stephen, things like this don't happen for women my age. I'm not stupid enough to think this will ever happen again. Stephen is a good man, gentle, loving, and he wants me. ME!"

"So I guess you don't want spousal support? Once he gets that farm up and running again he's going to be sitting pretty."

"He already is. I called the bank to check the balance in our joint accounts. His farm is performing very well. I don't care; money can't change all that's happened. When he drinks he's mean, I gave up everything and everyone to be with him. When he kept me away from my faith I knew I had to get away." She looked away with so much pain in her eyes like she was remembering something she didn't want to speak on.

"What are you going to do now?" I asked

"Get my divorce, marry Stephen, and jump his bones daily!"

"GROSS!"

****

Greg didn't mention the fact that I was missing so I didn't either. He seemed distracted at the airport, he made a phone call then he came back in time to board the plane home. "Nice earrings, graduation present?" He asked.

"Yes, thank you." He looked completely relaxed, the kind of relaxed look that good sex gives you. I know because I recognized it on myself this morning in the mirror. Demetria didn't seem all that impressed with me. I wouldn't doubt that she hooked him up with one of her horrible friends. When we got home I decided to go with Greg since Stephen and my mom were straddling the fence about how their relationship was going to proceed. "How come you don't have any family pictures up?"

He shrugged, "I'm a man. I got pictures in a box. You want to see them or something?"

He pointed out his mom and dad. I was thankful he looked like his dad. His mom had a funny look about her. He told me that his mom always considered herself better than any brown skinned person because she was lighter skinned. Not because she was a good person. He said I was the first female in a long time that didn't remind him in one way or another of his mom. I asked him if that was based off the color of my skin. He said no, he said the way I carry myself is what caught his attention. He put a bottle of Brandy on the table and two glasses. I poured a glass without a second thought. Greg said he moved out here to get away from his mom and his family. I asked about his dad and he said his dad does whatever his mom tells him. He got angry when he thought about it. I pulled Greg to the couch and then I cuddled up in his lap. We kissed a little bit, and I was happy when it went no further than that. I was in no way prepared for more. When I went home, my mom's door was closed and Brother Bolds' car was outside.

****

"I want to move back to California." I said

Greg looked at me for a minute, "why?"

"I'm going to start my own business. I'm going to be a designer for hire."

Greg sucked his teeth, "you gonna go work for the white man!"

"Greg don't talk about my friends and family like that. They are not prejudice." Greg looked at me, and he got up and grabbed my wrists hard and put them behind me. "What would you know? I haven't forgotten that for them you lose your mind and put your hands on me. You need to think long and hard about whom your loyalty is going to be to. Them or me. DON'T YOU EVER IN YOUR LIFE PUT YOUR HANDS ON ME AGAIN IF YOU DON'T WANT ME TO RETALIATE! I DON'T LIKE BEING HIT ANYMORE THAN YOU DO, AND I WILL NOT TOLERATE SOME LITTLE GIRL HITTING ON ME! I DON'T CARE IF IT DIDN'T HURT OR NOT!" He squeezed my wrist then he let me go. I shook off the fact that he was having a moment and kind of reminded me of my father.

"JESUS!" I said massaging my wrist. "You didn't have to yell, I can hear you fine from where you are." Greg looked at me. "I can't hit you, got it. Next time what should I do? Blow bubbles at you?" I shook my head, "naw you'll get mad about the soap getting in your eyes."

"Jenise stop trying to make me laugh, I'm serious."

"I KNOW! I'll blow angry kisses at you! You better catch them too!"

Greg chuckled, "angry kisses? What does that look like?"

127

I made my face look angry then I blew kisses at him. He laughed as he dodged them. "The Wallace's are good people. They are very business savvy and I know I'm good at what I do. I need to move back. My question is whether or not you're going to come with me."

"I've had nothing but bad experiences with white people. They're horrible people who feel they're above everyone else."

"Greg that isn't fair. You can't hold bad experiences against a whole race of people. The Wallace's are different. You had to see that."

"They're different alright."

"Give them a chance." I said sitting in his lap and kissing his lips.

"I'll do it, if..." He looked at me, "if you'll marry me first."

I smiled, "you want to marry me? Are you sure about that?"

"Yes, you're the only female I've known who knows how to give me time and space to work out some things on my own without feeling threatened by my absence."

"What about my friendship with Ethan? He's my best friend and he's going to be around."

"I'm your best friend! Besides, it's not like my friends won't be around as well. I was kind of thinking about moving anyways. Texas has served its purpose. It's time to move on."

****

I stood in front of that calendar in disbelief. I counted for the tenth time to make absolute sure I was counting right. I couldn't believe it I was a week late. Greg and I were on our way to get our blood test done so we could get our marriage license. I figured they would ask me when my last period was. When I looked at the date on my calendar I broke out in a sweat. This couldn't be real, I had to be dreaming. I didn't look at my mom, I walked out the door and I got in Greg's truck. "I'm late." I announced.

"You're right on time." He said looking at his watch.

"I'm late," I repeated myself.

He sat there processing my words. "We've been careful."

"I know."

"I didn't want to have kids," He confessed.

"I didn't know that."

He exhaled, "well it's done now. Guess we gotta get married, good thing we were doing that already." He said unenthusiastically.

"You don't have to marry me. We could live together or break up, if this changes things."

"Your mama would skin me alive. We'll get married, but I'm just letting you know, I'm not in to the whole baby thing, so there's not confusion later." He said directly as if my hurt feelings didn't matter.

"We definitely need to move back to California, I'm going to need more help."

When the results came back from my blood work, the doctor confirmed that I was healthy, clean, and that I was pregnant. Greg came back healthy and clean as well.

There was some kind of mix up with our paperwork and the original judge was switched with someone else. Something felt wrong about this whole setup, but I went along with it anyways. My mom and Brother Bolds came to the courthouse with us as witnesses to our marriage. We went out to dinner afterwards, and then I guess out of habit I went home with my mom and Greg went home next door. In the morning Greg woke me up laughing saying neither one of us realized what we did. "Good morning Mrs. Carter." He said rubbing my head. "I love you so much," he said kissing my lips. He pulled the covers back and then for the first time ever I was skin to skin with someone other than Ethan. I guess it's only right after all he is my husband.

****

"Your Uncle Matthew has called my mom a few times. He said that he was going to have my father sign the papers. How is that possible, we know he won't do it." I said.

"He's a lawyer if anyone can convince someone to do something they normally wouldn't it's him." Ethan said with a smile in his voice. "So…"

"So……?" I said knowing what he wanted to know. "You think you're so smart."

"When are we due? April or March?"

I exhaled, "March."

"YOU OWE ME FIVE DOLLARS!" Ethan said excitedly. "I love you so much!"

"I love you." I swallowed, "I have news." Ethan didn't say anything. "Greg and I got married."

Ethan was quiet for a minute. "You vowed forever to Greg while you're carrying my child?" He sarcastically charged.

"You asked Cat to marry you the same day you decided to impregnate me."

"I guess it's true, people who play games get played." He said very irritated.

"What do you mean?"

"You're going to marry me! You know what it doesn't matter. When are you coming back?"

"I'll have to put in notice here at work. How hard do you think it will be to find a place out there?"

"Tell me where you want to live and I'll secure the house for you. You're going to be an employee of F. Lancaster and Associates for now. I have office space for you in my office. I've been working on acquiring a few accounts for you to start with and build your portfolio."

"Ok, I guess you've got everything figured out. You tell me when to come and I'll make arrangements."

"You should've never left!" He snapped at me.

"Hey, Ethan! Cut it out, you can keep getting mad about the past if you want to. It changes nothing. When should I come out?"

"You're going to fly out next week. I'll show you some houses. Put in your resignation at work. Is your momma coming with you?"

"Why wouldn't she?"

"Stephen."

129

I hadn't thought about him, I doubted that he would uproot and move with her when his whole life is out here. "I need to talk to her."

"What was Greg's reaction to your news?"

"He wanted to know how, because we've been careful. He said he didn't want to have kids."

"So then why did he marry you?"

"I had already accepted his proposal, and when we were on our way to get our blood test done I discovered that I was late."

I could hear Ethan breathing, "I'll call you with the arrangements. I got to go." Then he hung up.

I sat there drumming my fingers on the table in the break room for a minute. Ethan knows I can't stand for him to be mad at me. He was trying to torture me. I went in and I talked to my boss. I told her that I had an offer that allowed me to move back to California that I couldn't refuse. She told me she hated to see me go, she said I was a valuable part of her team. She asked me if there was any point to try to offer me more money. I told her there wasn't.

When I got home, I told my mom that I was moving back to California and I wanted her to come. My mom frowned and said as soon as her divorce was final she and Brother Bolds were getting married. "Mom I'm pregnant." I said watching her face.

She grabbed her stomach, "was that why you two were rushing to get married? I kind of wondered."

"We didn't rush."

She cut her eyes at me, "you still live here. You two do your business between here and there now. I was wondering when you were going to move out."

"You can't afford this place by yourself. I thought I was doing the right thing."

"I honestly thought you and Ethan were going to get married. That boy is so in love with you."

"You think so?" I looked at the floor.

"Who drives to Stockton and back in one day just for a friend? I see the way he looks at you. The way he tries to take care of you. Do you think it's the best thing for your marriage to be near him?"

"Ethan is engaged mom."

"TO WHO?" She gasped.

"A girl." She's never met her so I didn't know what else to tell her.

"You all are asking for trouble, but it's your life Taffy."

She made me feel guilty. "The point of this conversation. Can you at least move back to California with me until you're free to marry Brother Bolds?"

"Honey he wants you to call him Stephen."

"Fine Stephen."

"Let me talk to Stephen and then I'll get back to you."

****

When I got off the plane Ethan was waiting with a bouquet of red roses. He had the biggest smile when he saw me. He picked me up and kissed me. He drove to the boarder of Berkeley and Albany in the hills to this beautiful and big house. He asked me if I liked it. I looked at the house in amazement; it was a tan colored house with all the trim painted dark brown. It had a long driveway on the side of the house with a detached garage. The backyard was good size. There was a small porch that could fit a bench and the front windows were big. There was a living room, formal dining room, and large kitchen, a bathroom, and a room that could be used as an office on the first floor. There were three good-sized bedrooms upstairs and another bathroom. Ethan said there was a partially finished basement. Then he asked me if I liked the house again or if I wanted to see another one. I told him I loved it. Then he kissed me, he told me we needed to break the house in properly. Ethan kissed my stomach and said thank you over and over to me. He asked me how I was feeling. I told him I felt good surprisingly. He smiled then he focused on my stomach, he kept kissing it.

We went to dinner at a restaurant in El Cerrito. I told him my mom was going to stay in Texas. She said she talked to Matt and her divorce would be FINAL in a few weeks. Ethan told me to leave her my car and all the furniture. He said tomorrow we'd go shopping for my house furnishings. Ethan asked me if I changed my name yet, I said I was about to; but I thought I would receive paperwork to do it, he told me not to. He told me to tell Greg it was for work purposes. He said he was transferring the house to Jenise Wright, and all of my business and financial items needed to stay in my maiden name. I asked him why and he said I needed to protect my assets so that when Greg leaves he leaves with nothing. I asked him how he was so sure that Greg would leave. He said eventually Greg was going to leave he could feel it. I could tell there was more to that feeling than he was sharing.

****

I looked at his mother's house and I took a deep breath. I was scared out of my mind, I kept telling myself not to look pregnant. Raynel opened the door surprised to see Ethan and I. "I thought you had to travel for work?" She said giving us hugs. "Momma, remember that you love me." He said like he was mustering the courage to tell her. "Cat and I are engaged."

She squinted her eyes, "you mean Jenise?"

"No momma, Cat. Jenise married that clown she brought out here." He said.

"WHAT? How could you do that?" She looked at me.

"It's a long story, but Ethan told me he loved Cat so when I went home everything happened quickly."

"Jenise is going to move back out here though."

"Is your momma coming too? I really liked her." She smiled.

"No, she's going to stay in Texas. She's going to marry the man she came out here with."

"Is Cat pregnant or something? I don't understand why you would propose to her. Especially if Jenise is moving out here. I know you boy!"

"No, but she wants to get started directly after the ceremony." He said not acknowledging the rest of her comment.

"I don't understand you. It's your life Ethan. At least you're not eloping like Dito and Tess. I still grab his ear for that one, I wanted to be there for my baby."

"I need you and Jenise to be a part of the planning for the wedding."

I gasped, "I don't want to plan your wedding to someone else." Raynel raised her eye at me. "I mean," I tried to find a way to clean it up, but there wasn't. "I don't want to do it."

"But you're going to, and you're going to be happy about it. You want me to tolerate Greg don't you?"

"Yes, but…"

"But nothing." He commanded.

Raynel looked between the both of us then she got quiet. Ethan made us dinner, it was so good. When Raynel offered me wine, Ethan told her I couldn't have any, she looked at us again.

****

"I'm going to miss you." Greg said kissing me goodbye.

"You too," I said hugging him.

"At some point we should think about a honeymoon."

"You're going to want to honeymoon with me when my belly is big and round?"

He rolled his eyes, "I was thinking sooner than that. I hope it's a boy, what am I supposed to do with a little girl?"

"Goodness, I know you're not excited about the baby but you don't have to act like that."

"It's not too late to do something about it."

I released him from my hug, and burned him with my eyes. "Something like what?"

He rolled his eyes, "never mind Jenise! I forget you fear God and all that noise."

"Noise?"

"Nothing! Forget it!" He quickly hugged me again. "Call me when you land." Then he walked away.

I stood there watching him walk away. I exhaled and asked myself how this was going to end. In that moment I knew Greg wouldn't be a permanent fixture in my life.

Chapter 13

Ethan

Words cannot express how I feel knowing that Jenise is carrying my child. It feels too right in my heart, mind, body, and soul! I don't care if it's a boy or girl. All I care is that our child is healthy, smart, and strong.

I took Jenise to my grandfather's car dealership and we got her the fanciest car on the lot. I showed her her new office, and I gave her a tour around. Jenise looked overwhelmed by all of this. I told her to tell Greg the car was a company perk. This was her last trip out before her official move.

I hated to send her back out there, but she had to wrap up her job and then pack up her things. Greg's friend Charlie flew out to Texas to help him make the drive out here, since he needed to bring his truck and his things. I enjoyed the extra few days alone with Jenise when she came back. Cat has been so busy and focused on the *wedding* that she hasn't noticed how all over the place I've been.

Cat was rambling off ideas for the *wedding* that didn't sound like anything I wanted. She and her mother have been running in the wrong direction. They wanted this ridiculously small and hugely expensive *wedding*. It didn't feel right to me to have everyone breaking their necks to come to this. I was struggling with how much I even wanted to pretend anymore. I tried to ignore my conscience that told me to call this off. The whole scene is ridiculous. I want and need Jenise now more than I ever did before. Now that she's pregnant she can't run from me. Right? My uncertainty is what allows Cat to continue to exist in my presence.

****

I have been wearing expensive custom made suits since before this girl was a thought, but she feels the need to pick out my clothes. Cat came out of my closet with my navy blue and grey pinstriped suit and a white shirt. I frowned at her, "I know you're nervous but I'm not wearing that." I took the white shirt from her. I brought out my pale grey shirt, and Cat exhaled like she didn't realize the white shirt looked amateur and ridiculous with this suit.

"I'm nervous. I haven't seen my father in a few years. His last words to me were so mean and hurtful." She said fidgeting with her dress.

"What was he upset about?" I asked her while I dressed.

Cat put her head down, "he found out that I was sleeping with his friend's son. He said I was acting like my mother whoring myself around." She took a deep breath. "She cheated on him, broke his heart and then they got divorced. I went from being a daddy's-girl to no daddy all at once, he divorced my mother and my brother and I." Tears filled her eyes. "When I reached out to him when I was eighteen it felt so good to have my daddy back. Of course my mother made it difficult for us, and then the straw that broke the camel's back is when he found out that not only was I not a virgin, but that I was sleeping around. He's convinced that white women are the devil and he's so in love with his new wife and new children. He would say that they're pure Nubian blood and act like he preferred them over my brother and I. My mother isn't happy that I want to invite him to our *wedding*. I want him to give me away, but I don't know where his head is at."

"Maybe this isn't the time to have my momma and Jenise there."

"No, it will be perfect. My daddy will see that although you're mixed too, you are comfortable with being black." She smiled.

I exhaled; she always finds a way to remind me that my father is technically white. I can only imagine how confusing it has to be to look at your parents in color. My father is just my father; I forget that people associate him with a color until dumb comments like these come up. I'm not confused about who I am, I am a black man. I tell her to stop looking at people in colors and to just look at them for who they are, but how do I change the way she was raised to look at people? "If you say so."

We arrived at the restaurant at the same time as my parents and Jenise who rode with them. I could tell Jenise was uncomfortable about this whole thing. When we walked in the door a very blonde woman was standing and tapping her foot like Cat does when she's impatient about something. "Mom!" Cat said hurrying to her to hug her.

Cat looked like her momma but not exactly like her. I was curious to see what her father looked like to put everything together. "Ethan these must be your parents. Hello I'm Cathleen, this lovely young lady's mother." She said sticking her hand out.

"Raynel, nice to meet you."

"Frank." My father said uninterested in saying anything further.

"Jenise," she introduced herself. "Its nice to meet you as well."

"Well aren't those some names, what do they mean?" Cathleen asked.

"I don't understand?" Jenise said.

"They're not everyday names I figured they meant something."

My momma flashed my father a look, and he glared at Cathleen. "What does Cathleen mean?" Jenise asked.

"I forget," She said not getting it.

"Mother! Please stop!" Cat said through clinched teeth.

"No offense right? I was just making small talk." Then she looked at her watch. "We might as well sit at our table. You're father was never on time before, and it looks like some things never change." The host showed us to our table, and then Cathleen asked our waitress to bring a couple of bottles of champagne to toast the happy couple. My parents shot me another look, cause we all knew she wasn't paying nor could she afford to pay the bill. "So for the guest list, how many guest were you thinking? I was thinking a hundred max."

"Frank and I have rather large families we were thinking much bigger." My momma said.

"Oh, you have like sixteen brothers and sisters right?" She said looking at my momma.

"What do you mean by that?" I said not liking her tone.

"Most of the black families I know are large like that." Cathleen said

"MOTHER! You are embarrassing me!" Cat said turning red.

My momma looked at me, "you know! I think it's a little premature to think about dates and sizes."

"How about you leave the stereotypes at the door." I said to Cathleen.

"Actually I'm one of eight, and my family is a lot larger than my wife's. How about you stick to being that girl's momma and stop acting like you know my wife before she tells you." My father said.

Then a man walked in with his family, I could tell he was Cat's father. He was the difference in Cat's face. "Hello I'm Edgar Cuthford." He said to the table.

"Nice to meet you, I'm Ethan Wallace. These are my parents Raynel and Frank Wallace, this is my best friend Jenise."

"Nice to meet you all, this is my wife Shawntay, our son Landrell, and daughters Shandrell, and Shanice." He said proudly.

"Nice to meet you, have a seat."

Cat got up, "thank you for coming daddy." She approached him cautiously.

He looked at Cat like a father would look at his baby girl. "I wouldn't miss it." Then he hugged her tightly.

Cathleen rolled her eyes and shifted in her seat. "Our son Edgar couldn't make it. He'll have to meet your little wife and kids at the ceremony."

"I already know my stepson, he comes over every Sunday." Shawntay said full of spite.

Cathleen looked at Shawntay with evilness in her eyes, "why would my son want to associate with someone like you?"

"The same reason every man comes running to me after knowing you, to get away from you!" Shawntay said with her hand on her hip.

"Ahem!" My father said looking at Edgar. "You can try to control this situation, or I will HANDLE it!"

"Cathleen please! Shawntay please have a seat sweetheart, don't let her push your buttons." Edgar said.

"Daddy, Ethan and I are getting married." Cat said with tears in her eyes.

Edgar bucked his eyes, "ok." He said taking a deep breath. Then he turned to me and I stood again. "Nice to meet you. This is my first baby girl, thank you for loving her." He said looking me in my eyes. He was reading me and most importantly reading the love that wasn't there.

"Thank you for raising such a lovable young lady." I said giving him back what he was reading in me. He didn't raise her, he got the point. He sat down next to his wife. "Originally, we asked everyone here to talk about the wedding. For now I think we should focus on getting to know each other. For the record though Cathleen, I know you have visions of a small wedding. However, my family is rather large. So we'll have to have a much larger affair when we eventually have our ceremony."

"Eventually?" Cat snapped.

I shot her a look to tell her to calm down or I would embarrass her in front of her family. "Mr. Cuthford, Edgar, will you walk your daughter down the aisle?"

"Of course! It would be an honor." He said looking at Cat. Cat got up and ran to her father and tearfully hugged him.

My father looked at Jenise then me; he shook his head at me. Jenise was sitting between my momma and Shanice. Jenise was quiet most of the time, only really speaking when she was spoken to and talking to Shanice. When everyone's food came out the smell of Shanice's fish dish was strong. Jenise turned green as soon as the smell hit her nose, then she ran out of the dining room. My momma hurried out after her, and my father kept his eyes on me. Cathleen stared at Edgar and Shawntay with evil looks because she was jealous that they were together. When they came back to the table I asked Jenise if she was ok, and she nodded and said yes. My momma switched seats with her. Then my momma cut her eyes at me.

Jenise

Of course! I haven't had one episode with morning sickness until now. Of course the girl next to me, as sweet as she can be, orders the red snapper dish. She was so excited about her fish she kept telling me about the description. As soon as the smell of her fish hit my nose my mouth started watering and I knew I had a small window of time to get to the bathroom. Raynel came in the bathroom as my breakfast poured into the toilet. She rubbed my back as I kept going. She gave me a cool paper towel for my forehead and one for my mouth. Her eyes were locked on mine when she asked me how far along was I. I told her I was still within the first trimester; she stood in front of me searching my eyes. I told her what Greg said when I told him about the baby. She listened but her eyes said, "yea right." She hugged me and told me she was happy for me. When we got back to the table I saw her flash Ethan a look. When he looked at me I told him with my eyes that I didn't say anything.

I don't understand how Cat's mom was ever married to a black man when she doesn't seem to think very highly of us as a people. Ethan and Mr. Wallace were on her all dinner. Mr. Wallace took her comments the hardest. The straw that broke the camel's back was when Ethan asked, "Would anyone like to order dessert?" Edgar's children looked to him to say whether it was ok. "No, we're good. Thank you for everything, you've done enough."

"Edgar please, I can see in the children's eyes that they want dessert. It's the least I could do." Ethan insisted.

Edgar looked at his kids who were pleading with their eyes, "oh alright."

"I don't know what kind of dessert they're going to order. It's not like they know about crème brûlée or tiramisu, now if they had some sweet potato pies on the menu then they'd be all over it." She said laughing to herself and I guess looking to Mr. Wallace for confirmation. I don't know how she was missing the clue that he did not like her.

Mr. Wallace's eyes blazed, "what's your name again?" His voice rumbled the table. "Cathleen."

"I've had about enough of you and your derogatory stereotypical statements. Ethan, I refuse to spend the rest of my life with this woman at the family table. This whole thing is nonsense, I don't understand what game you're playing!"

Cathleen looked at my father hard for a minute. "Why do my comments about them bother you so much? Your son don't look mixed to me, you got something to share with us?"

I could see my father's eyes turning black. "What does *mixed* look like to you?" Before she could answer he went in. "You need to stop putting people in boxes. My son is MY SON, the closest reflection to me out of all of my children. He's not here for you to judge, criticize, or humiliate. You are the reason why we have so many problems in this country. You thought it made you special having a black man in your life, and he treated you like you were a queen. You thought it made your children superior didn't you. Until you learned that regardless of the color of your mate you would actually have to put in work to make the relationship work. Now you're sitting over here mad that he's moved on and is happy with his new wife and family while you hold on to this child for dear life, poisoning her with your outlook and way of thinking. I'm not here to try to educate you on how to be, but you would benefit from staying on my good side." Mr. Wallace looked at Ethan. "I don't have the patience to play this game. You were raised to be straight with people regardless of who it hurts. You can pretend over here all you want, but you're going to have to leave me and your momma out of this." Then he stood up, "sweetheart are you ready to go?" Raynel gave him her hand as she stood. They were my ride so I stood up as well.

"You're leaving too?" The little girl said with sad eyes.

"I'm sorry sweetie I have to go, I rode with them." I smiled at her.

****

My technical start time is 8am, however I normally get here a little after 6am and Ethan is always waiting with breakfast for me. He kisses my stomach, we eat, and sometimes we make love all over that office. Then by 8:30am the rest of the staff starts pouring in and we're working hard separately.

Greg finally found a job at a garage in the city. He was so testy without a job for awhile there. Charlie and Demetria come over all the time. Mostly to eat up our food and leech off of us, and by us I mean me. Greg doesn't make a whole lot of money. His contributions to our checking account do not cover his withdrawals. I've only said something when he's overdrawn our joint checking account.

Ethan told me to only put so much in our joint account. He told me to put the rest of my paychecks, bonuses, and savings in the accounts he opened for me under F. Lancaster business. He gave me company credit cards and a card in my name with no explanation. I opened a credit account in my name just so that I could have something of my own. I appreciate everything he's doing for me. Ethan does stuff and then he fills me in. I try to look at all that he's doing for me and not to focus on my lack of choice with anything.

****

"Where have you been?" Greg said standing in the living room when I walked in the door.

I looked at the clock on the wall just past his head and it was just after six no later than I normally came home. "Work."

"I went by your job to surprise you. Your boyfriend said you were out."

I frowned, "Ethan is my best friend."

"Doesn't matter, who were you out running the streets with?" He was angry.

"BACK UP! I come home every night, the only times you break your neck to be here is when your friends are here."

"How would I know I come home and you're gone."

"I go out with my friends, just like you go out with yours. You don't check in with me to say you're going out." I said

"But I'm always where I say I'm going to be."

"That's when you tell me. You don't always tell me where you're going, and when you're coming back."

He looked at me with anger in his face, "where were you?"

I took pamphlets out my purse. "I found a doctor today. I had my first appointment. You could care less or I would've told you about the appointment." I threw the pamphlets at him and I walked to the kitchen. I was thirsty and all this talking wasn't helping me. I got a glass out the cabinet and I put ice cubes in my glass then I poured boiled water from my pot into my glass. It tasted like heaven. I repeated my ritual until it felt like my thirst was finally being quenched.

Greg walked in the kitchen looking guilty. "I'm sorry." I looked at him while I continued to drink. "I was talking to some guys at work and they were telling me about Carmel and Monterey. They said they were nice honeymoon spots. I was thinking we could go."

"Oh," I said feeling bad for flashing an attitude so quickly. "You want to go for a weekend?"

"I can't really take time off from work yet, but we could drive up Friday after work, and come back on Sunday."

"Sounds good. How much is all this going to cost?" I asked.

"I don't know, I figured you could find out for us. Don't forget we need to go soon before you start blowing up."

"Gee Greg, you sure do know how to make me feel loved." I said sarcastically.

We ate leftovers for dinner, and then Greg said we've been running so much since we got out here that we haven't had sex. In that moment I was happy that Ethan and I didn't fool around this morning, otherwise I would need to clean up.

Greg may have not been into the pregnancy but he was into the sex. He could barely keep his eyes open he was so into it. I decided to soak in the bathtub while he went downstairs to watch a game. Is it wrong that I wanted to wash him off of me? He was ready for bed at the same time that I was. He looked like he was thinking, "what if we made it a couple's weekend?"

"Couple's weekend?" I looked at him like he had to be crazy.

"I think it would be fun if Charlie and Demetria were there." He smiled.

"I guess I could invite my sister and T."

"The white people? Why?" I glared at him, he put his hands up. "The not completely white people."

"Stop that! Your friends are rough, and no matter how hard you and Charlie try to

force it, Demetria and I will not be best friends. It's not anything against her."
"Just them, not the other ones." Greg said like he was doing me a favor.

When I called Grace the next day, she said it sounds good to her; she'd have to check with Timothy to make sure. Ethan came in my office as I booked our rooms over the phone. "Where are you going?" He asked as soon as I hung up the phone. "Don't get jealous." I watched his eyes.
"Well when you start like that I automatically become enraged with jealousy." He halfway smiled at me.
"We're going to Monterey for the weekend in a little over a month from now." I watched his face.
Ethan turned up his face like something stunk. "What is that? Is that supposed to be like a honeymoon or something?"
"Kind of, but then it became more like a couples weekend. His friends, and Grace & T are going too."
"I mean I'm a couple, how come I can't go?"
I frowned at him, "I don't want to be competing with your bride all weekend! NO! I haven't done anything with my sister since I came back. You're going to have to sit this one out."
"If I was there we could sneak away together." He smiled.
"Is it just the thrill of not getting caught with you? Why would that whole set up sound appealing?"
He exhaled, "I could hurt your feelings right now, but I'm going to walk away from you." He said throwing a tantrum with his hands as he stood up.
"Oh whatever! You really need to think before you speak!" I said slamming my papers around.
He shut my door and locked it, and then he pulled my chair from behind the desk. "Are you trying to make me mad?" He searched my eyes with pure anger in his. I didn't answer him. "Do you really question that I love you or why? Is that what this whole thing is about? You were always the one holding us up; all I've ever wanted was you! All of your firsts should rightfully be with me. Since you're doing this honeymoon thing with him in about a month. In two weeks we are traveling for business. I'll give you the information when it's all set up. Ask me something stupid like that again!" He put his face in mine.
"Is it just the thrill of not getting caught with you?" I smiled.
He kissed me deeply, "forever the smart aleck!'

Ethan
"I need to discuss something very important with you." I said.
Jenise sat up straight watching my face. "Ok."
I sat next to her in the chair facing my desk. "Everything with us is so crazy. I need to know once and for all where you stand." I grabbed her hand, I told my heart to slow down. I locked in on her eyes. "Jenise do you... Tell me who I am to you."

She swallowed, "what's wrong Ethan?"

"Answer the question first." Her breathing picked up, she adjusted in her chair. "I know it isn't easy for you to speak from your heart. I realize that I'm always speaking for you. I really need you to tell me. Do you love me?"

"Of course I do." She said looking at me.

"Tell me, please."

She turned her body towards me, "Ethan I am so in love with you that I turn my back on everything I know just to be near you. You have always been amazing to me. I don't understand how someone like you even thinks anything of someone like me. Words could never convey how sorry I am for ever hurting you. You are the one person I could never live with myself for hurting, and you know how much I enjoy hurting people."

I kissed her, "we are bonded for life. We're about to be a family. There's one problem, and his name is Greg."

"But you're going to marry Cat."

I picked up the folder on my desk. "I decided that we should be married." She looked at me confused. I talked it out with cousin Matty, he consulted with his father. "I had divorce papers drawn up on your behalf." Then I showed her the signature sections where Gregory Carter already signed. "Greg already signed them." I watched her eyes.

She took the papers from me and inspected the documents. "How did you do this?" I explained how when that idiot showed up here I was trying to figure out how this was going to go. I told him that the paperwork was for spousal benefits and that I was going to give them to you to have him sign, but since he was here he could sign right away. He didn't read it, he signed blindly. I told her as soon as she signed it she was divorced and free to marry me. I told her my uncle and cousins worked out all the legal aspects, then I asked her if she would sign. I didn't know how to tell her that she wasn't really married. Or that the paperwork was basically his consent to waiving any rights he might think he has to anything that she owns. He didn't even own his paychecks once he deposited them in their joint checking account. Jenise got nervous like I knew she would. I exhaled; I told her that we wouldn't break up with Greg and Cat until we were ready. She said Cat was planning our *wedding*, and I told her it was going to be a commitment ceremony and she wouldn't know the difference. If we even made it that far.

Just like the phony ceremony I had set up for Jenise and Greg. I knew if he asked she would go through with it. Tomas almost didn't make it there in time. As long as Cat thinks she has won she would be fine. Jenise stared at the papers then she looked at me and said she needed a drink. We laughed then she took the pen out of my hand. I could hear my heart pounding as she signed each line. I kissed her and thanked her for finally choosing me. Jenise looked at me and said she chose me when she let me impregnate her. Then she asked why I needed to marry Cat since she was going to technically be my wife. I exhaled and I told her I was being selfish, besides I knew she wasn't ready to leave Greg. She told me she got to decide when she broke up with Greg and I couldn't force her to do it before she was

ready. I exhaled; I guess I should be happy I didn't have to force her to sign.
****
"So! You finally come!" My father said glaring at me. "Sit down."

"What do you mean, finally?" I returned his look at him.

"What are you doing? You're not learning from your mistakes, you're making more."

"It's my life!"

"Why are you even pretending like you're going to marry Catalina?"

"Because I care about her," I cleared my throat. "I love her."

"Are you in love with her?"

"No."

"So why?"

"I just told you why. Don't do this, you're not the loving, let me offer you advice on matters of the heart kind of father. Everything outside of momma and Gwen are unemotional movements."

"You're right," he sat back in his chair. "You're here because I did to your momma, the same thing you've done to Jenise."

"What I did to Jenise?"

He blank stared at me, "don't play dumb. It doesn't suit you. You know exactly what I'm talking about. I know that's my grandchild."

"What did you do to my momma?"

"She was dragging her feet about us. That's how Franky happened, when she still didn't move her feet then you happened. Then she got smart otherwise there would be a lot more of you."

"So what do you want me to say?" I looked at him.

"Look at me son, you don't win like this. Sure I get to see your momma when she feels like dealing with me. However, I'm reduced to a privileged boyfriend. Most people don't even realize I'm married."

"Your situation was different. Jenise and I will not end up like you and momma."

"Right because your momma never ran from me. I love Jenise, but she is confused about how you handle matters of the heart. Her parents messed her up good. Her father's an abusive drunk, and her momma is too rigid. Then Jenise is little Ms. People Pleaser. She needs to figure out who she is before she can be what you need. That baby is going to complicate things." He said getting under my skin. Does he mean that my brother and I were complications to his relationship with my mother?

"I came here to discuss business."

"One more thing, since your heart isn't in this whole thing with Catalina. We need to cancel the whole idea. What's the point of pretending? This is dumb and beneath us."

"Fine."

Then my Uncle Jeff walked in the office irritated. He sat in the chair eyes blazing.

"Who is Victor Cardell?"

"He has runners all over, why?"

"Competing markets?"

"No," my father waited.

Uncle Jeff exhaled, "Sophia!" He exhaled again. "Even though she was a baby, I really wonder if it's possible that she could remember the nonsense with her mother and I." We waited for him to get to the point. "She got this sorry excuse for anything, male in our house as her husband!" He growled, "then she's cheating on him!"

My mouth dropped, "she's cheating?"

"Sasha is this other guy's kid. I can't stand this little twerp and I was tolerating him because of my grandchild. HE'S NOT EVEN THE FATHER!"

"Victor?" My father asked.

"No, one of his sons. I was about to take him out when they said he was a Cardell. I wanted to find out how big of a war I would be starting."

"The Cardell family is big like ours, never as good. We've had no problems with them; they've respected our space so we've respected theirs. He handles dirty work for Matthew from time to time. This is what you want to do?" My father said plainly.

My Uncle tried to control his breathing. "I'm **MAD**! Let me think!"

"Your grandchild links us by blood. Think it through."

Uncle Jeff looked at my father. "You're calm because you keep your daughter locked up. Wait until she gets out."

"I know exactly what I'm dealing with, and that's why she stays locked up." My father said.

"Why not talk to her?"

My father stared at me; "I hope you have a little girl so you can understand the feeling you speak so matter of factly of."

"I thought you took her home?" My uncle asked.

My father looked at me, "I took Nohemi home like you told me to. I'm dating Catalina Cuthford, and Jenise is having my baby."

"Whoa! That was a lot of names. The baby is on purpose?" I shook my head yes. "What happened to the good ole days when people waited until they were married to have babies?"

"You must be talking about thousands of years ago. Cause for the last nine hundred years babies happen when they happen. Especially in this family." My father said.

Jenise

"Aloha!" The girl in the grass skirt greeted us as we exited the plane.

"WHAT? WHAT?" I screamed grabbing Ethan's arm. "This is amazing!" I said looking around at everything. He was very secretive about where we were going. He put a blindfold on me and ear plugs on me until we were airborne. The pilot would say the temperature is very lovely where you're going, stuff like that but he wouldn't say where. I had no idea we were coming to this tropical paradise.

"I love you baby!" He said kissing me.

"I love you!" I said kissing him back.

The taxi took us to our fancy resort on the beach. "Here you go Mr. & Mrs. Wallace, the honeymoon suite awaits you." The attendant at the desk said giving us our room keys. The bellhop took our luggage up to our room and then Ethan tipped him. I ran around our suite from room to room admiring everything and screaming. I went to the fruit basket and I immediately had to have some pineapple. Oh my goodness! Talk about the best pineapple I've had in my entire life. Ethan talked to my stomach while I devoured the fruit. We put on our bathing suits and then we went down to the beach.

Everyone kept greeting us as Mr. & Mrs. Wallace, it felt great! "You want to know what I have planned for tomorrow?" I nodded at him. He exhaled, "so Dito and Tess are out here as well. In the morning I'm going with Dito while you and Tess find Dresses and do all the girly things. At two o'clock on this beach we're getting married. Dito, Franky, and Tess will be our witnesses."

I smiled at him, "you don't have to do this."

"It should be us minus the extras. They aren't forever fixtures in our lives anyways."

I frowned, "isn't Cat going to have babies?"

"Maybe," he said watching my face.

"That makes her permanent."

"It didn't make Gwen's momma permanent." He mumbled.

"Yea, where's her mother?"

Ethan shook his head, "don't want to think about that." Then he got down on one knee. "I don't think there's a more retarded and butt backwards couple than us. These are not the circumstances that I ever envisioned us doing this under, however when I think of my wife all I ever see is you. You are my wife, the mother of my children, my future. I love you more than life it's self, even when you drive me crazy. My heart needs you to say yes and we'll figure the rest out. Jenise will you marry me?"

"Yes," I said without thinking about it.

Ethan kissed me, and then he told me to come. We went back in the hotel and to a room on the side. The girl inside smiled and greeted us. Ethan said he wanted to get tattoos. I started to run out, but Ethan caught me. Ethan and the technician were laughing so hard at me. I was convinced that he has lost his mind. I told him I was not getting a tattoo. Once I calmed down he explained that they would be really small. His initials on the inside of my finger and mine on his, and a small band that would be covered with our bands. My mom wasn't going to be happy, no matter how small it was, but I agreed. Ethan got his first, and he sat there watching like she was brushing his skin with a Rose petal. From the moment that needle hit my skin I was exhaling like I couldn't take it. Ethan fell on the ground laughing at me and I was moving everything but that hand trying to cope. It wasn't the worst pain and it was over rather quickly. The technician gave us ointment for our fingers and she told us what to do so we'd scab and the soreness would subside faster. Ethan kissed me then he admired his hand. We stood up to leave then he stopped. He told the technician he wanted another one. He wrote down my name, and he told her he wanted it on the left side of his chest. I told him not to do it, and he waved me off. He took off his T-shirt and showed the technician where he wanted it. I sat there in amazement as he got branded with my name. It was on his chest, Cat was definitely going to see it. I kissed him as I looked at my name permanently inscribed on his heart. I couldn't wait to get back to the room. When we got in the room he told me he was not going to touch me today. He said we had to be strong. I smiled at him evilly. Ethan made the couch up nicely to sleep out there on it. I went out and kissed him goodnight. I put everything I had in that kiss. Ethan's eyes were big as he looked at me like I was bending his arm. I laid on top of him, kissing him, and then kissing his neck. Ethan said a very weak, "no wait, stop, don't!" As he stroked my back and enjoyed my touch. Even though I tried very hard Ethan weakly fought me off successfully. I awoke to Eskimo kisses from my man. The best way to wake up. Once I was satisfied he said good morning to our child. He said my stomach looked like I ate a burger. It was barely noticeable.

He left when Tess came excitedly; she said the whole thing was exciting but only because it wasn't her. I understood what she meant. Then she asked if she could ask a hard question. "How can you be so sure that Ethan is the father? You were with your boyfriend before and after."

"I was so nerved up before my graduation we barely touched each other. It had been a month since we did anything before I connected with Ethan and I was down for two weeks after. Greg and I were always cautious when we were together, and Ethan." I smiled, "he did this on purpose."

We found a white dress that looked perfect for the beach; they put a big white flower in my hair. Then Tess and I put on makeup. I walked on the beach barefoot. The officiant had us cracking up when he spoke in his native tongue during our ceremony. He was a real fun guy and I loved all the smiles he got out of my man. The photographer took tons of pictures of our ceremony and us. We had dinner on the beach. Our table was set on top of a wooden platform that was anchored just off the beach. When the tide rolled in we floated. When they opened the champagne I looked at my glass with sad eyes. It was only the beginning and I was missing alcohol. The five of us promised that this secret went no further than us.

Chapter 14

Ethan

Ok I know I started this but coming home was the worst part. I hated that she was going home to another man and all that he was probably going to want from her after missing her for a week. I kept changing the channel in my mind. Jenise looked like she was waiting for me to say that she didn't have to go home to him too. For the first time I thought about how hurt Cat would be and I hated myself. My selfishness was getting on my nerves.

When I entered the door Cat turned soft music on and then she turned off the lights. She tried to light a match in the dark and burned herself. I couldn't help it I laughed heartily at her. She had on her sexy Teddy and she welcomed me home. I told her I had to show her something. I unbuttoned my shirt and I showed her my tattoo. She smiled until she realized it didn't say Cat or Catalina. She walked up close, her face was angry and tight, then she asked me why I had the wrong name on my heart. I shrugged then I told her it was a dare. Cat went off and acted like she was going to call off the wedding. I said nothing; I stood there watching her. I didn't care if she threatened to call anything off, I knew she wasn't crazy. She asked me if Jenise and I had matching tattoos I told her that was a good idea. I said I was sure her husband would love that. Cat froze then she asked when Jenise got married. "You are unbelievable! If it's not related to the wedding you really haven't been listening have you?"

"Planning a wedding is a lot of work." Then a guilty look flashed across her face. "What?"

"We can talk about it later, come to bed." She said trying to regain her sexy stance. "Nope, what is it?" I said sitting on the couch.

She straddled me and kissed my neck. It didn't even feel as good as when Jenise touched me. I was unaffected. When she looked at my face she deflated. "I lost my job."

"What? Why? How?"

"Some of my appointments kept me running late. I showed up late one too many times."

I was irritated, "you need to work. I don't exactly care what you do, but you need to do something."

"Can I focus on the wedding first? It'll be easier after that."

"No! After the wedding you're going to be focused on getting pregnant and the baby. You will not sit up and get fat under my watch. You have to work even if it's only flipping burgers, do something!"

"That's too much Ethan!"

"I'll make it easy for you. My momma will plan the rest of the wedding that way you can focus on what's important. You need to find a job!" Here was my chance, "Matter of fact let's postpone until six months after you've found a job to make sure that you can take off for the wedding."

Cat gasped, "what? Why?"

"Did you think we would get married and you would lay up and spend my money? I've got news for you if that's what you thought. I'll provide the house, presents, and gifts from time to time, but you need to work. Matter of fact, I've been meaning to get those documents. You've got paperwork to sign as well."

"Paperwork? Ethan what is wrong with you?" She looked at me in disbelief.

"Losing your job was the wrong move. You just set off so many alarms in my head."

"I'm sorry, man! You think I'm after your money?" I blank stared at her. "I'm not a glorified prostitute. Could you be any crueler?" She got up angry.

Internally I smiled; I didn't want to touch her tonight anyways. She stood there staring at my tattoo for a minute then she huffed as she walked away.

****

"Where you wanna go for lunch?" Dito asked looking at my books on the shelf.

"Don't matter to me, you choose." I said looking at my paperwork.

"I'll ask Jenise where she wants to go." He said then he walked out the door.

My stomach was starting to grumble when there was a knock at the door. "Surprise! I came to take you out to lunch!" Cat smiled.

Dito and Jenise walked in the office. "Cat? What are you doing here?" Dito asked giving her a hug.

"I came to have lunch with you." She said to me.

"Cat I didn't invite you here." I didn't have to look at Jenise to know she wasn't happy about Cat being here.

"Since when does your wife need an invitation?" She looked at Dito and then Jenise.

"You two go ahead," I was irritated.

"Don't change your plans on account of me. Can't I tag along?"

"Fine!" I grabbed my suit jacket.

"Jenise, that's a nice dress." Her compliment sounded like it was coming from her mother.

"Thank you," Jenise said giving her a look.

We walked a couple blocks over from the office to a little cafe. Cat was watching everything so I slid in next to Jenise on purpose, which left Cat sitting next to Dito. "To what do we owe the honor?"

"I haven't popped by in a long time. Is it a crime to want to have lunch with you?"

"It's not a crime." Then I smiled, "at least now you're listening."

"Listening?" She tried to play innocent.

"She saw my tattoo the other night and then she realized she's been ignoring me." I smiled bigger.

"Oh the drunken dare, I'm sorry Cat that was my fault. I really shouldn't drink and dare."

"Fernando, you're responsible for that?"

"Guilty as charged. You should be happy I didn't ask for something embarrassing."

"I think a tattoo of another woman's name on my man's heart is embarrassing enough." Then she cut her eyes to Jenise. "I feel guilty, we haven't had a chance to get to know each other. I've been so busy with the wedding. Thank you for volunteering to help with the planning."

Jenise looked at me, "you didn't tell her?"

I had no clue what she was about to say, but I knew I wasn't going to like it. "No."

Dito chuckled, "I'm sorry honey. I had to bow out of the planning for your wedding. Ethan was supposed to tell you. I've got to plan my baby shower." Then Jenise kicked me under the table.

"Oh yea, but the latest development is that Cat is going to give the planning reigns to my momma cause she's got to find a job. Of course you can help my momma. Come on you're my best friend, do it for me."

"No! You're too big headed with this whole situation. I can't!" Jenise said wiggling her neck.

"Uh oh there goes that attitude." Cat said sitting back.

"Excuse me?" Jenise said like she was gauging whether she should be offended.

"That black girl attitude, no wonder you're just his best friend. Who would want to deal with that?" Cat said thinking she was right in her thinking.

Jenise's eyes turned evil, these pregnancy hormones definitely gave her balls of steel. "For your information the only reason you sit over there as the bride to be is because I turned him down MANY! MANY! MANY! MANY! Years ago! Many! You just got here, you're just another pretty face in the rotation!"

"Many years ago?" I said.

"How many was that? A lot of *many* or a little *many*?" Dito said.

"Many?" I shrugged.

"Why didn't you tell me?" Cat said looking at me.

"You heard how many many's she said." I laughed.

"You do realize you're black don't you?" Jenise spit at her still mad.

"Of course I do, but I don't have to act like you do. Men don't like women who act like that." Cat said convinced she was right.

I shook my head, "please stop talking. You have no idea how dumb you sound."

"You're supposed to be on my side!" She said turning red.

"Not when you're wrong. Cut it out Cat." I said waving her off.

"Excuse me," Jenise said moving like she wanted to get up.

"You're not excused." I said turning my attention back to Dito.

"Ethan! I will kick you in your head right now. I gotta pee!"

"I swear that's all you do is drink and pee."

"The baby's probably sitting on my bladder."

"You're really pregnant? How far along are you?" Cat asked rolling her eyes over Jenise.

Jenise rolled her eyes and then she kicked me. "Move!" She said through clinched teeth.

I smiled and stood so she could go to the bathroom. I watched her cause I knew she was leaving. When she went in the bathroom I looked at Cat. "Lean in baby so I can whisper something to you." Cat leaned in. "Need I remind you that if you push my best friend away you're going to have problems with me?" I said not whispering in her ear. "I'm not saying you have to be best friends, although that would help. When you piss her off, you piss me off." Then I kissed her cheek. "Stay on my good side." Cat looked embarrassed as she sat down but she didn't say anything. I looked just in time to see Jenise walk out the door.

Jenise

Ethan plays too much! I'm not helping with his wedding I don't care what he says. I picked up a box lunch a few doors down from the cafe then I went back to the office. The receptionist said my two o'clock was here early, I looked at my wrist and it was twelve thirty. She said they went over to Franklin's office. When I passed Franky's I saw a man and a woman with a baby. I was confused, I peeked my head, "I'm so sorry to interrupt Franklin, the receptionist said that your guest are my two o'clock clients."

"Tim Wallace," he said putting out his hand to shake mine.

My eyes bounced between the two of them. "You're Timothy's parents? Nice to meet you, I went to school with him." I smiled as I shook his hand.

"This is my wife Annette and our grandson Andy." He said proudly.

"Nice to meet you."

Mrs. Wallace looked at my lunch in my hand. "Nice to meet you, go ahead and eat your lunch, we're early. Let us know when you're ready for us."

I hurried back to my office and I scarfed down my sandwich. As I was finishing and about to go wash my hands Cat opened my door knocking on it as she came in. "Are you on the phone?"

"No, but I'm busy." I said giving her attitude.

She came in and closed the door behind her. "Look, I was out of line at lunch. I wanted to apologize. I tend to get very jealous when it comes to Ethan because I know how good I've got it." She looked at me as if she expected me to say something to that. "Look, Ethan really wants us to get along. So I would appreciate it if you accept my apology."

"Why? You're only apologizing because he told you to. You didn't see anything wrong with what you said and your assumptions. What if I defined you by every mixed kid stereotype out there? How would that make you feel? Get to know people for who they are and stop pre-judging them."

"Mixed kid stereotypes?" She crossed her arms.

So I did the same, "it's beneath me to stoop to such a level. I know Ethan wants us to get along, but you are not Nohemi so I don't see that happening."

Surprise splashed over her face. "Is that what it is? You want his stupid ex to come back? Blu moved up to a better make and model."

"Can you get out of my office I have business to tend to."

She exhaled, "ok, ok. I'm sorry ok. Blu's changing and I don't know why or what I did to cause that. Everyone is guilty until proven innocent."

I opened my door, "you should ask me if I care."

Mrs. Wallace was pacing the hallway with the baby; she looked at both of us. Cat looked at her and rolled her eyes as she walked to Ethan's office. The look on her face was like *NO SHE DIDN'T!* I apologized for her rudeness then I invited Mr. & Mrs. Wallace in. We had a very spirited conversation about the new design and logo for Ace Trucking. Mrs. Wallace showed me some of the ideas they bounced around and I helped them sharpen them up and make them look professional. Mr. Wallace got very excited as everything came together. He had us cracking up, Mrs. Wallace shook her head while she laughed saying her husband was so silly.

Ethan looked surprised when he came to my office and saw his Aunt & Uncle.

"Your dad told me to come check Ms. Wright out and we are quite impressed." Mr. Wallace said.

"Mr. Wallace chose…"

He cut me off, "I keep telling you it's Tim."

"I'm sorry, Tim chose this design but with this font. Mrs.…." I looked at her and she shot me a look as well. "Annette likes this placement best, so I was putting it all together right now to give them a feel for the placement."

"Jenise is amazing isn't she." Ethan said smiling at me.

Annette and Tim exchanged looks, "Blu?" Cat said from my doorway.

"Who is she?" Annette asked Ethan.

Ethan exhaled, "this is my fiancé Catalina, Cat for short."

Annette frowned, "you don't say." She looked Cat up and down. "What does your mother think of her?"

"Uh, uh, uh…" Ethan stammered.

Tim chuckled, "how you doing darling? I'm his Uncle Tim."

"Hello," then she looked at Ethan. "Are all your aunts and uncles on your dad's side in interracial relationships?"

"AW! CAT! YOU BLEW IT! I'm sorry." He said as he pushed her out the door.

Annette looked at me, "so who are you?"

"I'm his best friend." I said keeping my attention on the design.

"I need to call Raynel." She said rubbing the baby's head.

****

Greg said everything was picture perfect in Carmel Valley, it was so beautiful. I had to agree. We were the first couple to arrive and we sat down by the water watching the sunset beautifully. Greg had his arms around me and he kept kissing my cheek. It had been so long since we've been like this with each other I was eating it all up. The affectionate and loving guy I fell in love with was back. I think I *love* him.

Charlie and Demetria found us on the beach first and I put on a happy face to see them as we said our hellos. I got excited when I saw Grace and Timothy. Grace and I hugged each other really tight. Then I introduced everyone. "Where are you from?" Demetria asked Grace.

"Hunter's Point." Grace said.

"You used to work at that grocery store? On the corner of 3rd and…." She snapped her finger trying to remember.

Grace smiled at the recognition, "you're one of Marcy's cousins?"

"YES!" Demetria said excitedly.

"Oh wow! This is such a small world!" They hugged like old friends. "This is my MAN Timothy!" Grace said proudly.

"Nice to meet you." Demetria looked at me, "I guess you are alright after all. Grace will cut you first and ask questions later."

I looked at my sister, she shook her head. "She's exaggerating."

Demetria was still rough, but we were getting along a lot better on this trip. Dinner was nice, a couple times I saw Timothy looking at Greg like he was trying to figure something out. Then he'd look at me with no expression. I had no idea what that look meant. Grace and Demetria entertained us with stories about their neighborhood. They talked about the known hustlers in their area, people who've died. Grace smiled at Timothy and said she let the roughness of the city go, and she looked forward to a calm and peaceful life with her man.

Ethan sent a big bouquet of flowers that was delivered to our room that night. Greg swallowed his irritation by changing the subject. I smiled when he said Grace and Timothy weren't as bad as he thought they'd be. We cuddled looking out the window at the beautiful view of the water. Greg went to bed claiming he was too tired to make love. I was enjoying the affection, and I was relieved that it was stopping there. No complaints from me on this one.

Grace and Timothy had an early morning couples massage Greg and Charlie got Demetria and I up early to go walking all around the beach. Greg and Charlie told us stories about their teen years. Greg was so happy and I was having a good time. We met up with Timothy and Grace; we were trying to determine where we wanted to go for lunch when Greg asked me what he was doing here? I looked up to see Ethan and Cat approaching us. "Why?" I said.

"Hello newlyweds, I arranged for lunch on the beach for the lovely couple. The rest of us could eat in the restaurant." Ethan said taking control.

"Mr. & Mrs. Carter please follow me." One of the staff members dressed in all white said to us.

I looked at Greg; I was going to do whatever he wanted. Greg stared at Ethan for a minute, he was beyond irritated. Then he grabbed my hand. "I know you're her friend, but this is my wife. I appreciate the gesture, but we're not going out there. You can't just show up in the middle of our honeymoon and determine how we spend our time. You all go ahead, my wife and I will see you tomorrow." Then he led me away, I shot Ethan evil eyes as we walked away. We went back to our room and Greg paced the floor going off about Ethan showing up. I told him I told Ethan I didn't want him out here and this was our time. In the middle of his angry tangent Greg looked out the window and out to the beach. He cursed. "LOOK AT THIS!!" When I looked out the window there was a beautiful table set up just before the sand. The table had a beautiful table cover that flowed on the ocean breeze. The light kept sparkling off of the Crystal and silverware. The spread on the table was beautiful, staff stood by tending to their every need. I guess they decided to take our reservation cause all three couples were sitting at the table. I felt myself get jealous at the thought of Demetria and Cat possibly getting along.

We left the room, we found a little restaurant. I explained again to Greg that I had nothing to do with Ethan's pop up. Greg calmed down when he got excited about getting together with his friends in the future. I was happy he was happy.

In the morning I called Grace's room. She suggested that we go get manicures and pedicures. I asked Greg if it was ok with him. He said it was fine and that he'd see if Timothy wanted to walk the more difficult trails by the beach with him.

In the spa I whispered everything to Grace. It felt good to be able to purge like I did. Grace asked why they weren't invited to Hawaii. I told her it was a surprise to me, and I had no idea. I asked Grace if Demetria and Cat hit it off, and she started cracking up. She said they can't stand each other. That made me feel good. After our pedicures the men were standing in the lobby talking. They agreed then they walked away. Grace and I asked what was going on. The men agreed to a quick game of touch football down on the beach. Cat had on her bathing suit and a pretty sarong. She put on sunglasses and she let her big hair float on the air. She looked very pretty and her stinking stupid body looked amazing. We sat on the sidelines as the men took off their shirts and then took their places in the sand. They flipped a coin and it was Greg and Charlie's ball first. They hiked the ball and before Greg could attempt to pose like he was going to throw the ball Timothy tagged him. Demetria and I yelled our boo's and we told our men it was only the first down. When it was Ethan and Timothy's ball, they hiked the ball; then Timothy ran backwards, he threw the ball straight and hard. Ethan caught it and they celebrated their touch down. That's how the game went; Greg and Charlie were no match. When the game was over Cat greeted Ethan with a victory kiss. That's when Greg saw Ethan's tattoo. Greg shot me evil eyes, but he didn't say anything.

After lunch we were leaving so that Greg could go to work the next day. I told the hostess we needed a table for eight, Greg frowned at me. I told him we knew they were coming so we might as well include them. Sure enough Ethan and Cat walked up holding hands and looking satisfied with each other. We were sitting for a few minutes when someone's food hit my nose slightly. I lowered my head for a minute. I didn't want to run out of here. When Ethan asked me if I was ok, I said yes as I tried to suck it up. I pinched my nose, and then Ethan told me to switch seats with him. When I did I felt so much better and then he looked around. He said he couldn't smell that smell from his seat. Cat looked at me then Ethan who was now across the table. "So have you discussed names?" She asked Greg.

"She's barely showing, I don't care what she chooses." Greg said irritated.

"You don't care?" She looked at him horrified.

"Babies aren't my thing." He said waving off her conversation.

Cat looked at me with sad eyes. "Oh." Then she looked at Greg, "will your family come to the shower?"

He looked at Cat annoyed, "they don't care."

Cat grabbed my hand and she turned red. "Wow!"

"Greg's family is not close, they never have been." Charlie volunteered.

Ethan and Timothy exchanged looks. "How far back do you and Greg go?" Ethan asked.

"High school."

"Why don't you talk to him about how he treats his wife?" Timothy asked.

Charlie squinted, "that's their relationship. It has nothing to do with me."

"I just find it interesting that you have an opinion and input on everything in his life but his relationship, kind of like you've got something against Jenise. I'm trying to understand if you had a falling out or something." Timothy said sitting straight up and looking annoyed.

"Jenise is fine I guess, but I don't get into Greg's relationship; and I don't let him into mine." Demetria looked at Charlie like he was lying but she didn't say anything.

Ethan sat forward, "oh come on. We're all family, you can tell us what happened."

"Nothing, I got in the middle once and he had an ugly breakup. I stay out of his relationships."

"Since we're in each other's business. That's a very interesting tattoo on your heart." Greg spit.

Ethan smiled, "you like that? When you getting one?"

"Why do you have it?" Greg asked.

"It was a dare, I couldn't back down, you understand. Besides that woman is my best friend. I'll always carry her in my heart, seems fitting that her name rest there as well."

Greg looked at me then Ethan. "Why are you here?"

"I was devastated when Jenise told me she got married and I wasn't there for her. I came to pay for everything as my gift. I know how much money she doesn't make."

"We wouldn't be here if we couldn't afford to be here."

Ethan looked at me, "he doesn't know how you had to scrape your pennies together just to be here?"

"Ethan, please stop broadcasting my financial business across this table." I said through clinched teeth.

"He asked, so I'm telling him." Then he looked at Greg, "anymore questions?"

****

I didn't get to the office until 8am and then I cursed Ethan out so badly I expected Raynel to show up wanting to fight. He had no right showing up on my "*honeymoon*" causing problems. Ethan didn't apologize and I knew he wouldn't cause he didn't feel he was wrong. He said I shouldn't have been surprised that he showed up. I continued going off until the receptionist showed up then I went to my office and worked with my door closed the rest of the day. I left without saying goodbye. I got home a little earlier than normal and Greg was cutting the lawn like I had asked him to two weeks ago. He asked me how work was, and I told him about how badly I went off on Ethan. He smiled when he said Ethan took that from me. We were hugging in the yard when Ethan pulled up in front of the house. "HOW YOU GONNA LEAVE LIKE THAT?"

"Like what?"

He was beyond angry, and I realized that anything concerning me leaving suddenly would rub him the wrong way even if it wasn't intended that way. "YOU KNOW

WHAT I'M TALKING ABOUT!"

"Who are you yelling at?" Greg said moving me behind him.

"Hold on Greg. Ethan I'm sorry, I didn't think of it like that."

"Don't apologize to him! You had no right invading our time together like that. You may be her little boyfriend but this is MY WIFE! You need to get in your little car and go!" Greg said.

Ethan's eyes turned black as he marched towards Greg. "Ethan! No!" I said jumping in front of Greg. "You are wrong, please get in your car and leave." I pleaded. Two minutes hadn't gone by and the police were rolling up to my house. "What seems to be the problem?" The officer asked.

"Jenise come here!" Ethan commanded. I asked Greg to talk to the officer. Ethan's eyes were red when I walked to his car with him. "DON'T YOU EVER WALK AWAY FROM ME LIKE THAT AGAIN! I WILL FIND YOU AND MESS UP YOUR EVERYTHING IF YOU EVER THINK OF RUNNING FROM ME!"

"I'm sorry, I was coming home to rest. I didn't think of you taking it this way. I'm sorry!" I pleaded with him to leave with my eyes.

Ethan was beyond angry, the look in his eyes made me scared. "Don't you ever be stupid enough to think you can ever leave me again. Do I make myself clear?"

"Yes Ethan."

Chapter 15

Ethan

Victor and his brother walked in tall and determined. They gave each of us eye contact as they approached. Victor sat directly in front of my father and his brother was next to him, their men sat on either side of them filling up the opposite side of the table. "Frank, thank you for agreeing to meet with me." Victor said.

"Victor, Vern." My father said.

The waiter approached our table. "May I bring you something to drink?"

"Courvoisier XO double up." Victor said.

"Same." His brother and all of his men said.

"So Vic, what's going on?" Eugene said.

The waiter sat their drinks in front of each of them then he closed the door behind him. "Roscoe is one of your men?" Victor ran his finger around the inside of the rim of the glass before he put it to his lips, his brother did the same.

"Correct." Uncle Jeff said.

"He's approached my family, he wants a few of your kids gone."

"He approached your family, where do you sit?" Uncle Tim asked.

"I have no desire to feud with The Wallace's. Your family has respected mine, and I want to give that same respect back. I also understand that there's personal business I need to discuss with Jeff." My uncle nodded. "We have no interest in fighting with your family."

"So that we're clear, who's his target?" Eugene asked.

Victor looked at his man to say, "four of your previous foot soldiers. Leonard and da, and da..." The guy snapped his fingers as he tried to remember.

"Got it, we know who you're referring to." I said.

"You want to get in bed with us?" Franky asked.

Victor looked at Uncle Jeff. "We're already family."

We discussed go forward strategy and the immediate results of our alliance. My father told Uncle Tim to prepare his son for battle, Eugene looked annoyed.

****

"ETHAN!" Cat yelled as she exploded.

"Now go find a job!" I said collapsing on the bed next to her. Then I got up and took my condom off. Wrapped it and flushed it.

"Baby why do you still wear those now that I'm on the pill?"

"No babies until we're married. Two methods work better than one." I said laying back down, besides I knew she was lying about the pill part. I'm too busy at work and then everything else to worry about her. Today was different though; I couldn't put   my finger on why.

"I'm not having very much success finding a job." She said sounding defeated.

"Keep going until you find one. It doesn't have to be fancy, just get a job." Then I looked at the clock.

"How come you can pay for Jenise's honeymoon without a second thought?"

"She has a job and that was a one time thing." I said.

"You're paying for stuff for her shower."

I didn't realize she knew that, but I didn't care either. "Your point? Trust me, you don't want to start comparing yourself to Jenise."

"You act like she's perfect."

I got up cause this conversation was going nowhere fast, plus I needed to meet up with my momma. This was an impromptu pop up at my place to see what Cat was up to. I busted her on the couch watching her afternoon stories instead of pounding the pavement for work. Her busted face was so cute I decided to break her off for the first time in a month. Cat's still good to me and takes care of me. I just don't like the idea of this. Staying at home all day, watching stories, laying around like a literal cat. Once the baby is here I would like to move closer to Jenise. I want to take the baby to the park, and be around as much as I can. I was hoping Cat had a job by now. It's to the point that I'd rather deal with a dirty house than to have her home all day. And we know how much I love a dirty anything. My thing is, I know she will not be a permanent fixture in my life. She's going to be devastated when we separate; and I will feel better knowing she has some sort of skill set to fall back on.

I told Cat to get dressed so she could come with me. We showered and then we eventually made it to my momma's shop. Jade greeted me with a big hug and kiss. I introduced her to Cat. "Cat this is T's little sister Jade."

Cat smiled weakly and said hello. Jade looked at me like she didn't understand what was wrong with Cat.

My momma was finishing up someone's hair and Jade was shampooing the last customer of the day. My momma shot me a look. "Cat, I wasn't expecting you today."

"Blu finally let me tag along." She smiled.

"When you going to come sit in my chair?"

"Oh, um. I have a hairdresser already."

"You must go once a year, cause your hair always looks like that." My momma said.

Jade and my momma's customer smiled and then looked away. "My hair looks bad?" Cat said touching her hair.

"Just because your hair is curly doesn't mean the wild and curly look works for you. You should at least tame those curls. Look at Jade's hair." Jade's hair was down and curly, but it didn't look like a bush like Cat's. "Her momma wouldn't let her or her sister walk around looking like that, but I guess it matters how you're raised."

"Momma you're in a lovely mood today." I smiled.

"Why is it so hard to find a job? I see help wanted signs everywhere. I've lost interest in this wedding idea."

"Good thing we got the shower to distract you." I said rubbing Cat's hand.

"Who's shower?" Her customer asked.

"Ethan's best friend is having a baby. Her family is coming out from all over to show their love and support. Jenise is a good girl, confused about something's but nothing but goodness at the heart of her."

"I guess you don't like me very much." Cat said sadly.

"I can't stand your momma, and then the things you say. You sound like her. Ethan tries to explain you a different way. However, I'm tired of him building you up so that I'll give you another chance and then the first thing out of your mouth upsets me."

"What do I say?" Cat asked with her eyes wide.

"You don't think very highly of black people as if you forget that you are black. My son is not different or better than any of these other niggas running around here getting over on people." My momma rolled her eyes.

"Momma why I gotta be a nigga?" I asked laughing.

"Ethan!" She looked me in my eyes. "I know! I know you! I know what you do! You act just like your father!"

"But momma my daddy's white." I said laughing.

"That don't matter, he's the original nigga in this piece! I had hopes for you, I thought you were the one to be different, but you act like all of them!"

"All of who?" I asked still laughing which was only making her madder.

"My daddy, cousins, uncles, your father, uncles, and cousins. ALL OF YOU ARE **HORRIBLE**!"

"Momma, what did Dad do this time?"

"Same stuff he always does. I want him to leave me alone, but that's too much like right!"

That was my cue to leave. "Ok well, I'm going to get going before the curling iron starts flying. I'm leaving a blank check on your books. Let me know later how much you write it out for." My momma cut her eyes at me. "I love you momma," I said as I kissed her cheek.

"Who's Jenise?" Jade asked me.

"My best friend." I smiled kind of guilty.

"Oh," Jade said reading my eyes.

I put my arm around her shoulder, "we haven't talked in a long time. Make sure you come to the shower, I want you to meet her."

"I've seen her, she comes here to get her hair done. I didn't know she was your best friend." Jade looked at me like her momma would.

"Momma," I called out. "Can Cat come for a press and curl?" I said looking at Cat. "Put her on my books." Momma said.

When we left I told Cat she was going to have to do a better job with my momma.

****

"Malachi?" I said taking my seat. "What you doing here?"

"Shooting the breeze with my brother." Malachi said.

"Your Dad know that you're here?" I asked making sure.

"Of course, he just left." Then Malachi turned his attention back to Malcolm and Troy. "Like I was saying. I understand, I get it. That's still my sister. Both of my sisters are precious to me."

"I know that, and you know I love your sister very much." Malcolm said.

"Yea, but you've got an interesting way of showing your love. I don't like the dancer no more than you do, but I don't know about helping you."

Troy started laughing hard, "they let her go out with that fool and you've been on lock down." Troy threw his head back and laughed.

"Amber's dating someone else?" I asked.

Troy laughed harder, Malachi shook his head. "It's her dance partner, he's fruitier than a fruit cake, and confused at that. He got a crush on Amber."

Malcolm smiled, "he try to flex his little muscles at me. I popped him in the mouth last time. He knows Amber will automatically believe I'm picking on him if I get him."

Troy shook his head, "she got you letting people slide, and she ain't even said nothing. You whipped!"

Malcolm exhaled and squinted his eyes at Troy. "Mali, you're my only hope."

"I'll do this. Let me talk to my sister. I'm not going to tell her anything. If she let's on that she's open to the idea of you then we'll talk."

"Alright," Malcolm clapped his hands together. "So let's plan the night."

Malachi started laughing, "she hasn't said she wants you."

"My good girl wants me." Malcolm said confidently.

"She wants the dancer actually." Malachi said smiling.

"Should I come back?" I asked not caring about their high school games.

"Let's put a pin in this." He said to Malachi. "You got news for me?"

"You're going to be the connection to the Cardell family. Victor wants his boys with Dalenna to remain as clean as possible." I said.

"He does them no favors by babying them." Malcolm said.

"His sons his problem."

"I know Richard, he could be so much more."

"His sons his problem." I repeated. "We're going to seriously shop locations. You're going to get your Barber's license. Personally, I think you should go to school. You've got potential to grow an empire. Don't limit yourself to the things you can only see right here in front of you."

Malcolm nodded his head, "Tim says the same thing. We're just niggas from Oakland." He said gesturing between him and Troy. "Mali's gonna go to school, we got kids and responsibilities."

"Troy you got a kid?" I asked.

"It's a complicated situation." Troy shot Malcolm a look.

"Meaning you don't like the mother?"

"Right." He adjusted, "Cardell family." He redirected our attention.

"Since you're out of school, you should be the go to for them. Everything passes through you." Malcolm said to Troy.

"What about Fuzzy and Leonard?" Troy asked.

"Fuzzy does as he's told, Leonard wants to slow down."

"What about Mali?" Troy asked.

"Let's talk it out with Tim. Mali you think you can handle it?" Malcolm asked.

Malachi frowned, "Of course! He'll be fine with it. I have my minor details that I keep an eye on. Timothy's been slacking." Malachi said.

"Remember, stay clean. Keep your cars, houses, and bodies clean." I reminded them.

****

"How's my baby?" I said putting my arms out to hug Jenise. Her face was full, but this morning she looked a little pale. "You feeling ok?"

"I caught Greg's cold." She said sniffling.

I felt her forehead and she was warm. "No! No! You gotta go to the doctor!" I felt panicked.

"Ethan, I'm fine I have a cold. There's nothing the doctor can do and I can't take anything." She said dismissing me.

"Jenise!" I tried not to yell. "We're going to the hospital right now." I grabbed her hand.

Jenise didn't say anything she walked with me. Even if I was just being paranoid, I'd rather be safe than sorry. We went to the garage and got in my car.

When we walked into the triage, most of the nurses looked at me. "We need someone to make sure she's ok."

I recognized the nurse that stepped forward; it was the frustrated nurse that helped with Nohemi. She took us into a room, she gave Jenise a gown and she told her she'd be back in five minutes. Jenise sighed then she got undressed. She complained about having to take her clothes off. The nurse came back and she went down her checklist of questions. She took Jenise's temperature and blood pressure. I heard her giving the doctor all of Jenise's information. The doctor came in, she felt the baby, then she listened to the heartbeat. She let us listen as well. When the doctor confirmed what Jenise said that she only had a cold, the pressure on my shoulders relaxed a lot. In the parking lot I grabbed Jenise tightly and I hugged her for a long time. She didn't try to say anything or pull away. She let me hug her as long as I needed to.

Jenise

The closer my due date gets the more nervous Ethan gets. As soon as I hit seven months his panic became real. As irritated as I was, I can never accuse him of not caring. He was focused on the baby and me, he completely missed how all those nurses were looking at him in his tailor made suit. The nurse that helped us did her best to remain professional, but I saw the way she looked at him. It is nice when he pays me this kind of attention. Greg doesn't care, I asked him to sleep in the other room so I wouldn't get sick and he refused. He's such a baby when he's sick and he wanted to stay up under me the whole time. As soon as he was feeling better he was up and out the door going to work and hanging out after work. He didn't even come home last night. I know I have no right to question him, so I don't.

Ethan followed me home, and then he went to the store. He brought me soup, juice, fruit; he set me up nicely in my room. He told me he'd come back after work. I swear I took a nap and I woke up to him taking my cold soup away. He brought back a fresh bowl of soup and then he spoon-fed me. He read a few chapters to me from my current book since I didn't feel like going downstairs to watch television.

When eight o'clock hit he asked me where Greg was, I shrugged cause I didn't know. I told him I couldn't question him otherwise he might start questioning me. Ethan gave me a look but he didn't say anything.

****

I kind of figured something was up, but I had no idea it would be on such a grand scale. Ethan flew my cousins in from all over, my mom, and aunties. I wondered why Raynel kept asking me questions about my mother in-law. I'm so happy I didn't know, Greg said he hadn't told his family about the baby, but he doesn't talk to them. Demetria was the only female representation for Greg here besides me. I was so happy to see everyone I hadn't seen them in years. "Who's the princess?" My cousin Trinity asked me nodding towards Cat.

"My best friend's fiancé." I said with a smile.

"Your best friend ugly with money?" She said like she was telling me instead of asking me.

"You tell me." I nodded towards Ethan and my stepfather as they walked in the door carrying my crib.

Trinity fell into the chair next to me. "Oh good lord that man is fine!" She wiped her mouth. "You didn't want him?" She asked in disbelief. I was struggling with how to answer that. "Please tell me he has a brother?"

I was thankful she didn't make me answer the previous question. "He does actually."

Her eyes got big, "uglier? Finer?"

"Ethan's the ugly one of their bunch. His other brother is married though."

"Wait is that your mother's new husband?"

"Yes, Trinity please be nice."

"I can't believe she's married to someone else." She said observing him from head to toe. "Why aren't you talking to your father?"

I shrugged, "just haven't. We weren't ever really close."

"Don't you think he might need you right now? He's in Stockton without any family."

"He has my little brother."

"HE HAS A SON? From your mom?"

"No, someone else." Clearly no one, as usual, has told her about the things my father does.

I could see her resolve to judge my mom melt away. She walked over to my mom and hugged her real big. Then I saw her going around to my cousins and aunts on my father's side telling them what I told her. One by one they came up to my mom and hugged her. They even met Stephen and were friendly.

Cat came over and sat next to me. "This is a beautiful turn out."

"I can't take credit for it. I only showed up."

"How did you get Ethan to do this? If he pushes back our wedding one more time I'm going to scream." She said.

"Raynel did all this." I tried to chew back guilt.

"Yes, she planned. He paid."

"Oh, I guess you need to get in good with his mom."
Cat sighed, "she wants to do my hair, but I keep canceling."
"Why? She's done mine and I loved it."
"She can do your kind of hair mine is different."
I rolled my eyes, "ok Cat. If you say so." Then I looked at her, "just so you know... White women go to her and trust her with their hair. I'm sure she could do *little miss in between's* hair. Maybe you should start understanding that you are just like everybody in this room and stop thinking you're different."

****

Ethan's been on my case, he's told me to call him as soon as I go into labor. Where Greg doesn't always come home and he knows I could go into labor any day now. I was so happy when my mom came back. She set up my nursery with me. Greg looks embarrassed whenever my mom looks at him. He normally disregards everyone else, but he loves my mom.

I was going to my checkup when lightning hit my stomach. I fell on to the car, my mom's eyes got big. She helped me to the passenger seat and then we made our way to the hospital. I asked her to call Ethan. She told me I meant Greg and she asked for his number at work. I couldn't remember so she got his number out of my phone book in my purse. I heard her get irritated with someone as she explained that she was his mother in-law and his wife was in labor. I asked her to call Ethan cause it would take Greg forever to get to the hospital. Ethan got to the hospital so fast. He rubbed my head and kissed my cheek, he whispered words of gratitude and appreciation in my ear. My mom stood over to the side frowning at us. When Raynel came in she distracted my mom's glare on us. She asked my mom to come with her to the cafeteria for a quick moment.

I kept saying my mom is going to know. Ethan said none of that mattered right now. He kept kissing me and staying right by my side. I labored for quite a few hours, and Ethan never left me. My mom kept asking where Greg was and I told her he wasn't dependable. When it was finally time to push, five good pushes and the baby was out with STRONG lungs. The doctor said it was a girl. She had a head full of hair and she was hollering like she was angry. When the nurse gave Ethan the baby my mom and Raynel held on to each other as they stared at us. The baby looked just like him.

Ethan

When the nurse put my baby girl in my arms nothing else seemed to matter. I didn't care who was looking or what anyone had to say. I was a father, my daughter looked up at me with the most innocent look. No one else mattered in that moment. I gave the baby to Jenise's mom then I proudly put my arm around my momma. She was staring at me the whole time. Then she grabbed my ear and pulled me out the room into the hallway. "Ethan what is wrong with you?"
"Nothing's wrong with me." I tried to smile.
"Why does that baby look just like you? Like me? That's my grandchild, I can feel

160

it."

"Isn't she beautiful, I've never seen a more perfect creature in my life."

My momma slapped me, that pulled me out of my daydream. "What are you showing her? What will this situation teach her about love and family? I swear your name should've been Franklin! Especially with some bull like this! I wish my suspicion wasn't right, how could Jenise do this? How could you?"

"Momma this isn't Jenise's fault, I did this."

"Why would you do this?"

"I thought I loved Cat, she was the only one there for me taking care of me with that whole Nohemi explosion. Jenise ran from me, I was prepared to never see her again until she came back. I did this to her, she didn't have a choice."

"Unless you're telling me you raped her, she had a choice." She searched my eyes.

I ran my hand through my hair, "momma I don't want to get in to the details with you but she didn't have a choice. Kind of like you didn't have a choice with the two kids you had."

My momma lowered her head and deepened her voice, "why would he admit to you what he's never admitted to me?"

I was surprised, I thought with the way he said it to me, he told her. "Wait maybe I misunderstood."

"Did he have Dito and Gwen on purpose too?" She searched my eyes.

"No, he said they were accidents."

"What about Cat?"

"Cat's not going anywhere."

"Maybe not for now, but this will get old."

When we walked back in the room I was in shock, Jenise's momma was holding the baby and she was going completely off. She handed the baby to my momma, stuck her finger in my chest, and slapped me hard. My momma shot me a look like I better take it. My momma started crying as she looked at the baby. Jenise's momma said she did not raise Jenise to live like this, and she didn't know how her daughter would ever sink to such a repulsive level of scandal. Jenise laid there crying her eyes out. I tried to tell her that this was all my fault, but she wasn't going for it. She said Jenise was just as much to blame as I was. When her rant was still going an hour later I had enough. "Mom, I love you but if you don't stop it! I know you're upset, I know you're disappointed. It's done, its over, no matter what you say at this point nothing's going to change. We don't need this right now. You can be mad, sad, hurt, all that, but I don't want to hear another peep about it. It's done!"

Jenise's momma looked at me surprised that I said anything. She sat down quietly for a minute, and then she stood up. "Where is Greg? What are you going to tell him?"

"Ask me if I care about Greg? Who is Greg supposed to be to me?"

"Prove it! Be a man; take your wife and child home, stop playing these games. Honor them!"

I looked at Jenise who was sitting over on the side crying. "Ok, Jenise when you come home. You're coming with me."

Jenise

My mom might as well have cursed me out for how badly she went off on me. The whole time I'm thinking, she knows how quickly things can get out of hand, how you can end up losing yourself in a moment and then things spiral out of control. I didn't say anything because this was my mom and whether she understood it or not my situation wasn't right. Everybody was so hurt and upset and it was all my fault. The birth of a baby should be a happy occasion. Not the all out cursing and screaming scene that we were having. My mom had Ethan up against the ropes; of course he was going to say that we were coming home with him. He didn't care at all about hurting Greg, I did. He'd hurt Greg but he'd still have Cat. He wasn't ready to leave her alone and there was no denying that. I don't have the energy anymore to fight. They want me to devastate Greg fine, I'm in so much pain right now it doesn't matter. I probably won't be able to look at myself in the mirror ever again, but does it matter? When they put my baby girl in my arms nothing else mattered. She was beautiful, and she looked just like her daddy. Ethan couldn't deny this baby even if he wanted to.

Grace came first thing in the morning. Ethan was sleep on the couch in my room. He needed to go shower, he asked her not to leave until he came back, he wanted to make sure someone was with me at all times. He kissed the baby goodbye and me, and then he said he would be back. Grace looked at Erica Rainise and she said she looked just like Ethan. I didn't feel happy like I should've felt; each time that door opened my heart stopped thinking it could be Greg. I didn't know what he would do when he found out, and I wasn't looking forward to knowing once again I was devastating someone.

Ethan said he hired some guys to move me out of my house, and then he had all of Greg's things boxed up and set on the porch. He changed the locks to the house. This was happening and I didn't want this to happen like this. I was backed into a corner what could I do.

Chapter 16

Ethan

I sat in the car looking at Jenise's ring. My heart started pounding at the sight of it. When I saw this ring almost two years ago it called to me like it begged me to purchase it for my love. I bought it before my world turned upside down. Jenise was that one person to see me when everyone else was looking for what they could get from knowing me. She never asked me for anything other than to be my friend and to be in my space whenever she could. It's not like Jenise is the most gorgeous woman to walk into a room. However, as far as I'm concerned there could never be another woman more beautiful. When Jenise ran, I took the ring out of my safe deposit box to have something that reminded me of her near me. I'm going to give her this ring with all my heart. She's the only woman I feel like I could give all of me to. I just wish I could trust her not to be a flight risk right now. Jenise doesn't know how to deal with pain or the idea that she's let someone down. I know she's worried about how much she's going to hurt Greg. All I know is he better stand down and let it go. Jenise was never his woman; the sooner he accepts that the sooner he will let it go.

My family is just as it should be, Jenise is my wife, and now we are truly one with the birth of our daughter. I couldn't stop smiling, Erica looks just like me. No one can deny she's my child; I can't wait to hear her call me daddy. After my momma stopped cursing me, and hitting me. She got so excited about the baby; she's always wanted a little girl. I hadn't thought about what I was going to do about Cat yet. Not only was the wedding off indefinitely, but also I was done with her. I've been the first man not to fall all over himself for her. The first man to turn her out, and the first man she couldn't live without. She was going to have to do without me cause I'm done. I just haven't figure out how to do this yet.

When I walked past the gift shop, I decided that flowers would be a good gesture to enhance my ring. I bought an arrangement that I thought would look nice, and a teddy bear that wore a sash that said, "it's a girl" across it. As I approached Jenise's room I could hear someone crying loudly. The closer I got the louder and more familiar the cry became. These weren't happy tears, and I jogged to the room. When I opened Jenise's door she was hugging Demetria and they were both crying. When I asked what was wrong, Demetria turned her face towards me. She had been beaten.

Jenise

How could this tiny person belong to me? Where did she come from? How could someone so precious belong to me? I said, "Good morning Erica, how is mommy's baby?" She stared at me like she was studying my face. Ethan got up around 5am and he said he was going to go to the new house to shower, change his clothes, and see if my mom needed anything. He said she was very excited about her task of setting up the new nursery. She has my car, and he made sure she had money. Mom told me that she and Raynel were going to get a few more things to make the nursery more girly. I have no idea what the new house looks like, Ethan says it's not too far from my house cause he was planning on moving there after Erica was born anyways. Ethan donated all the furniture from my house to a nonprofit, he got new beds for our room and the guest room where my mom was staying, he said the kitchen was his, but I could decorate the rest of the house once I felt up to it. I didn't know when that would be so I smiled and said ok. I told myself not to think about him sneaking off to be with Cat before he came back. I didn't want to think about it. I thought about Greg and then I felt sad.

Breastfeeding is HARD and frustrating, the baby is hungry but she's not latching on right. A nurse came and helped me. She rubbed my back when I started crying cause I couldn't stop thinking about how frustrating this had to be for Erica, she was hungry and she couldn't figure this out. Maybe I'm doing it wrong and she's not eating because I can't get this right. My nurse told me to relax, she held Erica until she calmed down and she told me to breathe until I did as well. When I was calm and Erica was calm she told us to try it again. Erica latched on perfectly and I cried as I thanked her. Erica ate well on both sides and then I felt so accomplished as she burped and proceeded to sleep while I changed her.

As soon as 8am rolled around there was a knock at my door. I told the person to come in; my heart sank when I saw it was Demetria. She had on shades and her hood, she forced a smile. "Charlie mentioned that your momma called Greg's job looking for him." So just in case I doubted that he knew I was here she confirmed that he knew. Demetria took off her shades and jacket. She set them on the couch that Ethan has been camping on then she turned around to face me. I gasped as soon as I saw her face. Her entire face was swollen, both of her lips were busted, her left eye was blackened, and she had knots on her head. "I know it looks bad, but you should see your husband." She said trying to make light of the situation. She said Greg has been spending more and more time at their place. She said she doesn't like when he stays over cause she and Charlie always end up in a dumb fight about something and then they disappear for a night or Greg instigates arguments between Demetria and Charlie. She said Greg can be a real jerk sometimes. She said Greg was really irritated that my mom called his job and where he was just about to come home; he was back at their house. She said Greg was in such a mood that he didn't even want to go out. She heard Charlie tell Greg that he wanted to go to a club, and he got irritated when Greg didn't want to go. She said she grabbed some clothes then she left before they did and she went to a friend's house and got dressed to go to club Luxurious. She said right when she didn't think they were there she saw her husband. He was alone and watching the dance floor. She said she was going to go up to him and say something flirty when she saw a young guy approach him. She said she wasn't going to think too much of it until she saw Charlie flick the guy's chin, and then put his hand on the guy's thigh. She said the young guy went and danced with other people all the while keeping his eyes locked on Charlie while he watched and smiled. She said it looked like the young guy told his friends something then he left with her husband. She followed them to a fleabag hotel and she listened at the door until she knew for certain what was happening in there. She said she cried all the way home, Greg was up in the living room looking irritated when she came home. She said Charlie came home in the morning and from the moment he walked in the door they were arguing. Greg was mad that Charlie went out last night. She swallowed. She said they thought she was sleep. She said she walked in on them kissing. We both cried so hard there was only the sound of our tears for a long time. She said she went off on both of them, and she ended up in Greg's face. She said she hit him and she told him she was going to tell me. She said Greg fought her like she was a man, and Charlie pulled him off of her. She said he doesn't know that she knows that I was in the hospital so he probably went home to change and get his lie together before he came here. I hugged Demetria and we cried so hard together. As we were trying to get it together Ethan walked in the door with flowers and a teddy bear. I could see the alarm on his face as soon as he saw Demetria.

Ethan

"What happened to you?" I asked Demetria.

"I came to show Jenise what her husband did to me." Demetria said through tears.

"I'm her husband." I said loving the way that sounds.

Demetria didn't pay my words any attention. She said he's probably going to go home change and then come here.

I walked over to the phone, I called Malcolm's number and there was no answer. I called Troy's place and his momma said he wasn't home. I called Fuzzy's and he answered on the second ring. I told him I was at the hospital and I needed backup immediately. Fuzzy said he was on his way. When the nurse came in I told her we were going to need someone to come check Demetria out to make sure she was ok. The nurse jumped when she saw Demetria's face. She hurried out the room to get a doctor. "Why did he do this to you?"

"I hit him, and this was his retaliation." She said still crying.

"Why did you hit him?"

She opened her mouth and closed it. She looked down at the ground, "I can't say it again. It took everything in me to tell you Jenise. I can't say it again."

I looked at Jenise, "has he ever hit you?" I got angry at the thought of it.

My anger scared Demetria as she looked at me with big eyes. "No," Jenise said as she cried.

"Would you tell me the truth if he did?" I said getting madder.

"You know me, you would've known before anyone else if he did." She said.

The doctor came in the room and checked out Demetria, when the doctor asked Demetria who did this to her she said Gregory Carter with so much hatred and venom. The doctor explained that she had to call the police and she had to report the incident. Jenise was watching my face cause she knew I did not feel like this was a matter for the police. I wanted to know what was going on, but Jenise and Demetria kept crying and not talking which was irritating. When Erica woke up she was ready to eat. Jenise had to pull herself together to focus so that they could work on their feeding technique. I went out in the hallway so that Fuzzy wouldn't walk in on them. When he got there I started to explain how we would approach the situation when Greg rounded the corner. He was beyond angry and visibly upset. I told Fuzzy that was him and as he approached and I told Fuzzy Greg doesn't come in this room. Leonard came out of the waiting room and he was walking behind Greg, Fuzzy pointed at Greg and Leonard tapped him. Fuzzy walked over to them. The doctor was on the phone calling Demetria in when I told her the guy was here. I told her my family could detain him until the police got here. Greg tried to flex at Leonard and Leonard hit him so hard everyone heard it and they ran to see what the noise was as he hit the ground. Greg may have been strong and a good fighter, but he was no match for Leonard or Fuzzy. I guess he learned today no matter how good you are, there's always somebody better. One of the nurses told Leonard and Fuzzy to hold Greg in an empty room. Greg started yelling that he was here to see his wife and he didn't understand what was going on.

I went in the room as Fuzzy hit Greg, which dropped him again. Fuzzy told him to stop being hard headed and to sit down like they told him to. Greg was on the verge of passing out; he stayed down for a minute. When he looked up and saw me he started cursing and saying it was all lies. I didn't say anything I just looked at him. He said he needed to talk to Jenise. He said he told her he wasn't into the baby thing and she didn't expect him here, he didn't understand why all his things were packed up on the front porch. I told him it was because he didn't live there anymore, and that Jenise belonged to me.

"To you?" Greg said standing up straight I could see his adrenaline starting to pump.

"Jenise is my wife and she just gave birth to my daughter."

"Jenise and I got married almost nine months ago." Greg said

"And your marriage was annulled a little over a month later. Jenise and I are married, and that's my baby."

"That's impossible!" Greg spit as the wheels of his mind started turning. "Jenise would never do that to me."

"After all you've done wouldn't she." I said.

That made Greg angry and he charged me, Leonard and Fuzzy smiled. Greg ran into both of my fists and then passed out on the floor. That's what I told the officer who entered the room right as Greg was falling, he was completely knocked out. The doctor and Demetria came in the room, the doctor asked her if this was the man who assaulted her, and if she wanted to press charges. She said yes and yes. They woke Greg up to arrest him. Greg was saying he needed to talk to his wife.

Demetria looked at him evilly, "the only reason you should be talking to Jenise is to explain who Melvin is." Even though the officer had Greg cuffed he tried to charge Demetria, Leonard dropped him again and he was out... AGAIN!

I looked at Demetria and I asked her who Melvin was, "my husband's date at the club last night."

I eyed her as anger started to turn in my stomach. "What does that have to do with Greg?"

Demetria looked embarrassed as she cried, "according to what I heard in their argument." She said referring to Greg and Charlie's argument. "They were each other's first and only until my husband decided to take things further with Melvin whom they always only ever flirted with."

If the police weren't standing there I would've beat Greg until I felt better. Greg started stirring on the floor as he tried to regain consciousness. "Jenise is my wife, your dissolution of marriage paper work is in your box marked personal items. Stay away from her if you know what's good for you!"

Jenise

Ethan didn't say anything to me when he finally came back in the room. I asked him where Demetria was and he said she went to the police station and then she was going home. He took Erica and sat on the couch with her. He was angry and wouldn't look at me. I didn't know if Demetria told him anything, I laid there silently crying. How come I didn't know? I felt dirty and stupid.

Grace and Timothy came to the hospital to see the baby. Ethan and Timothy went in the hallway while I fed the baby. Grace held me while I cried some more; I thought I was out of tears but here where more and they were pouring out of me. I told Grace how our mom's came in and got on both of our cases. Grace said that Raynel tells them that they need to tell Timothy's mom about them. She said Timothy refuses and says that his mother won't like the idea that he's serious about anyone. I told her I've met his parents and I didn't know if that was true or not. I told her that Annette was very nice to me, but I saw her evil side when Cat got on her nerves. I told her from what I could tell she was very nice, but she has no patience for dumbness. I told Grace that they actually acted a lot a like. When Ethan and Timothy came back their faces were serious and sad. I could tell Ethan told him. I felt embarrassed for not knowing or having a clue.

****

"Mrs. Wallace we're going to send a lactation nurse out to check on you and the baby, to make sure everything is going smoothly. I know your *FINE* husband is going to take good care of you both." The nurse said helping me to the wheelchair. Ethan blushed and then he gave me Erica. When we got to our new house I sat there taking it in. It was bigger than my house and a lot nicer. I smiled at the house, and then my mom and Raynel came out on the porch completely excited for me to see what they've done. The living room was empty and huge, the dining room was already setup with a huge table the chairs were beautiful, china cabinet that was empty, and in the kitchen there was another table and high chair. I could see a coffee pot so I knew Ethan already had his favorite room setup. My mom covered my eyes as she led me into the room. They yelled surprise and I looked around the room and I smiled for the first time. Everything was beautiful, and I could tell they put in a lot of effort. The walls were painted like a park. There were trees and animals all over. I asked who drew the pictures. "Timothy and Grace came by after they left the hospital. Timothy drew everything and then we colored them in. Do you like it?" My mom said so proud.

"Yes mom, it's beautiful." I said looking around.

I sat in the rocking chair holding Erica. My mom and Raynel looked over my shoulders on either side of me, and Ethan snapped pictures. Ethan made us dinner; he said it was a housewarming dinner so he held back nothing. Creamy sauces, *rich* food and dessert. He kept watching me as I looked around trying to take everything in. When I reached for the bottle of wine, he said I couldn't drink any. He said while I was nursing the baby still ate what I ate. I sat back angrily cause a glass of wine was all I wanted. My mom looked at me but she didn't say anything. It was like she was trying to figure me out.

That night Ethan came to bed and he put his arms around me. As soon as he touched me I started crying, I felt like I had been holding in those tears all day. Ethan held me and let me cry as long as I needed to. I didn't have to explain anything to him. He let me cry it out and he didn't try to stop me or make me talk it out which I appreciated. My mom got up with Erica and I went in and sat in the chair. Once Erica latched on my mom asked me if I was ok, I exhaled and said yes. She said that wasn't too convincing. I looked at Erica who was watching me. I stroked her cheek, my mom patiently waited for me to get it out. When Erica finished eating she burped her and I laid her back in her crib. My mom put her arms around me and kissed my forehead. I wanted to tell her, but I couldn't talk about it.

****

My mom came and laid on my bed. I was still crying. She rubbed my back, "baby. You and Greg barely knew each other."

"Doesn't mean that I didn't love him."

"I know, are these tears of regret?"

"Kind of. I know that without Greg there wouldn't have been urgency on Ethan's part and Erica wouldn't be here. I don't regret Ethan, it's hard to put into words."

"You're scared aren't you?" She said looking me in my eyes.

"I'm not good enough for him mommy. Ethan is.... He's larger than life, and I'm just a little farm girl from Stockton who was supposed to marry Jamal and spend my days working hard on a farm. Greg was lowly like me."

My mom huffed, "that boy has issues. If Erica had been his child and he didn't show up like he did..." My mom clinched her lips. "I wouldn't be responsible for what I did to him." I knew that look. That was the look that had me wondering how I ended up on the ground one time when I decided to get smart with her. Greg didn't tolerate anyone hitting him though, I wondered if he would've been crazy enough to hit my mom. She was the only reason he didn't run when I told him I was pregnant.

"Honey how was this supposed to work? How were you going to explain Erica?"

"I don't know, I wouldn't let Ethan discuss it. I was getting tired of the game. I didn't want to force Ethan to choose."

"Why not?"

"Because if he didn't choose me, I'd have to live with it."

****

"I have to go to work, I'm sorry for waking you up. I gotta give you something that I've been holding on to for a long time." Ethan said, I continued to lay there and look at him. "I need to tell you a story so bare with me then you can go back to sleep." He kissed my forehead as he laid next to me. "I never told you about the moment I wanted forever with you. I should say the moment I accepted that you have forever infected me and I knew I couldn't live my life without you in it. I got out of class and I didn't bump into you anywhere along the way to my car. That's when I realized that I was looking for you. I got in my car and slowly drove away with the windows down in case you called out to me. I ended up at the Stanford shopping center and wandering around. I went inside the jewelry store and browsed the showcases. I thought about buying a gold chain, you know stuff like that." Then he showed me a ring box, he took a deep breath while looking at it. "Some how I was looking at rings. I was just browsing until I saw this ring." He tapped the box with his finger. "I felt like a girl, and you know how many moments I have like that. In the middle of all of these rings this one stood out to me as unique, different, and beautiful. When I saw this ring, I thought about you. I looked at the ring and as I was about to buy it, I told myself to snap out of it. We were just friends and I didn't want you getting the wrong idea. Although I didn't know what that idea was supposed to exactly be. I took your ring, remember that one you couldn't find for a minute and then suddenly you found it? I took it as a size reference. I couldn't risk that someone else would see this ring and want it for their self. I bought it and figured I'd give it to you as a graduation present. Then that summer happened." He got quiet for a minute, "one day… One day you'll understand how much I love you. However, this morning I have to give you one of the tokens I selfishly held on to for myself." He put the box in my hand, and watched my face. I opened the box slowly and the diamond sparkled at me before I got the box completely open. It was a gold band with diamonds all around the setting and a big center emerald cut diamond in the middle. The wedding band was gold and with slightly larger diamonds all around the band. "Although nothing tops that tattoo," I smiled. "This is yours to have, now that I get to come home to the real thing." I smiled and kissed him. This ring was beautiful and I kept staring at it. I kept replaying his story in my mind. My ring was bigger and more beautiful than Cat's. Ethan got up satisfied with himself and he went to the bathroom to shower. I went and got Erica and brought her to the bed. Ethan was in the shower singing off key and everything. I showed Erica my new rings, "when a man loves you he shares with you from his heart. It doesn't matter if all he can afford is a solid band; if he gives it to you from his heart you cherish it. It's not as easy as people think to fall in love with someone. It's even harder to fall in love with a good guy. When you find your love you have to know you deserve it. Baby, don't be like your mom. I don't feel worthy of any of this."

****

"You are going to get so sick of me." Raynel said hugging me.

"Impossible," I said smiling.

"Send me pictures as much as you can. I'll come back as soon as Stephen can get away," My mom said hugging me goodbye. "Ethan you take good care of my babies now." My mom said gently touching his face. "I'm sorry baby." She said apologizing for her actions in the hospital.

"It's ok, I understand." Ethan said, and then they hugged.

My mom loved Erica up one more time, and then she got in the car with Ethan to go home to her husband. When a month passed my mom and Raynel dressed Erica up in a pretty springtime dress then we went shopping. I think we were all equally excited to be outside. They helped me pick out the rest of my bedroom furniture. Ethan came home to a fully decorated bedroom and I was tired. "Let's get Erica dressed and then we'll do a little shopping." Raynel said excitedly.

I was happy my energy levels were picking up again. If I could figure out how to forget about Greg that would be great. Ethan sent a copy of the divorce papers to Charlie's since Greg wasn't understanding that we weren't married any more and he showed up at the office. He said Demetria is still there with the two of them. I felt sorry for her.

I got dressed and then we went to the mall. Raynel asked me if Ethan and I were going to her husband's party in the summer. I told her I didn't know, it depended on if we felt Erica was old enough for an evening away from us. She told me she was not going. She said he invited her when he thought of it, but she felt there was too much going on at the party. When I asked her how so, she said she was aware of how Frank spent his time when she didn't feel like dealing with him. She said someone was planning the party for him and it wasn't her, so she knew some bottom feeder was going to be there and she'd rather not deal with it. She looked really angry when she said that, and I think that anger is a cover for hurt feelings. To make her smile I suggested that we look at dresses for pictures for Erica. Raynel got so excited, and completely into the idea. She picked out the most girlie dress possible, shoes, and tights. Of course she had plans for her hair. I think Erica grew all that hair in anticipation of bonding with her grandmother.

****

I sat at the dining room table staring at the bottle of wine. Ethan walked in the door with groceries in his arms. He stopped walking and looked at me. He asked me what was going on. I told him I didn't want to breast feed anymore if it meant I couldn't have a glass of wine. He sucked his teeth; I told him the doctor said I could have half a glass of red wine. Ethan continued to the kitchen, I told him that his mom said she drank with him and Franky and they're fine. I told him it was only half a glass, and Erica would be fine. He looked at me and asked what else the doctor said. I told him that she said everything looked good with me. He asked me how I felt, and I said I felt like having a drink. I don't know how in the world I stopped drinking cold turkey, but I needed a little wine if I'm supposed to take the edge off and keep this up for another year. Erica woke up from her afternoon nap like clockwork and I made my way up the stairs while Ethan stood there watching me. She wasn't really crying, she was fussing to let me know she was awake and ready to be held. When I came back down stairs Ethan had opened the bottle and he poured me a little wine. I got so excited when I saw it. I fed Erica first while he made dinner. We talked about our days today, while I enjoyed my long awaited drink of wine. He had his bonding time with Erica, I drank lots of water after my wine, and then I fed her just before bed. As we got ready for bed we talked about the first time we had sex and how nervous he was. I had no idea he was nervous. I was too gone and into the moment to notice. We laughed at how stupid we were, and I reminded him that he kicked the bed and the whole bed hopped across the room hitting the wall. Ethan laughed he forgot all about that. I wanted to ask him about Cat, but I didn't want to ruin the mood. We were laughing and talking and then we were kissing, touching, and Ethan was rubbing me. We made love for the first time since the baby was born. At first I was scared it was going to hurt, but just like the first time it was uncomfortable at first but Ethan made it enjoyable. Apparently when it comes to my body I do whatever he says.

Chapter 17

Ethan

"Hello?" She said with tears in her voice.

"What!"

"Blu, I don't understand what happened. We're in love." She pleaded.

"No, you're in love with winning and my money."

"Blu! I'm in love with you. How could you leave me?"

"I gave you two months to get your stuff and move out."

"Where am I supposed to go? I don't have a job."

"I told you to find a job. Did you think I was playing?" She started crying. "All is fair in love and war. Cat, I don't wish you any harm. Go quietly and I may actually smile when I see you in the future."

"I can't believe this!" She cried.

"I was on my way out to lunch, take care." I hung up the phone.

Franky and Dito were waiting for me in the hallway. When they looked at me they said Cat! At the same time. We got in my car and went to my house. Franky and Dito raced to the door to get to Erica first. Jenise knew the routine, she opened the door as she saw them racing and she moved out the way. I hugged and kissed her while Franky frowned at Dito who got to Erica first. Jenise looked at my face she could tell I was irritated but I didn't say anything. Jenise had sandwiches waiting for us, which we devoured. "So Jenise, you two coming to the party?" Franky said smacking on his sandwich, "I need you to check out this girl."

"A girl? You getting serious about someone?"

"It will never be like when we dated, but she ain't half bad."

Dito dropped his sandwich with his eyes stretched wide. "WHAT?" He looked between them like something tasted nasty.

Everyone belly laughed while Dito tried to figure out what was so funny. "You never told Dito about us?" Jenise teased.

"How could you?" Dito's voice squeaked. "And then you?" He looked at me, "stop playing!"

I explained that Nohemi saw Jenise and I together and she assumed that I was Franky. So sometimes Franky would come out with us. Dito relaxed, it looked like his head was going to pop off. Jenise asked me what time I was coming home while Erica enjoyed playing with her uncles. I told her I wasn't sure then I asked her why. She said she missed me was all, and then she raised her eyebrows. Electricity shot through my legs. I kissed her neck and I told her I was coming back as soon as humanly possible. I hurried my brothers into the car.

Dito asked how Jenise is holding up. I told him that she has her good days; today was definitely a good day. Dito said Greg would always stare at him whenever he was around which wasn't too often. He said he figured it was because he was thinking of more racist comments. I looked at Dito in the rear view mirror and asked him if he thought Greg was trying to figure him out. Dito got irritated, he said it gets old. He's not gay and no amount of staring from anyone was going to change that. I told him I wished he would've told me sooner. Franky got mad and said he couldn't believe Greg was still breathing, and I was getting soft. That irritated me; I told him there were police involved. I told him as long as Greg stayed on his side of the bay he'd breathe.

When we got to the office Cat was waiting in the lobby. Looking desperate she begged me to see her. Franky and Dito stood there smiling at her when everyone knew she was hoping to get me alone. "I guess no one told you." Franky said smiling, "I love being the bearer of bad news, but my brother is already married." Cat turned white, "WHAT? You're joking?" She begged me to say he was.

I held up my ring hand with my diamond encrusted gold band. "I'm married, and you're unemployed. Get out of my office before I have someone throw you out!" Cat screamed to the top of her lungs, then she stomped her foot like she was throwing a tantrum. People on the floors looked at her, people in their offices came out. Cat was creating a scene. I told the receptionist to call security. Cat threw her hands up and walked out. Franky was too tickled. He told me it was a good thing I cut her loose when I did cause she was getting too comfortable and she gained a little weight. I shook my head at my brother for being so superficial. His women had to have their hair perfectly done all the time. Dressed in the best clothes, and always on point like little dolls.

****

"Come on Erica. Smile for daddy, come on." I said tickling her chin. Erica gave a big smile full of gums while the photographer snapped away. We were taking our family portraits today. It seemed like an all out war to get down here. Jenise swears she looks different and I promise she doesn't. She has no stretch marks and she's back to her college size. Somehow she swears there's something different and I tell her that she's mistaken. If anything, it's her guilty conscience. I know she has a drink daily as much as I can figure it's around lunchtime. Which is why I try to come home as often as possible. She is depressed still and I can't put my finger on why exactly. Maybe she doesn't love me as much as I thought she did. Sometimes there's questions that you're too afraid to know the answer to. Her mother calls everyday to talk to her and to read scriptures with her, most times that helps. Then she calls back to talk to me sometimes. She asks me how I'm holding up and how I'm adjusting to being a father. I always give her the same answer, "my life is perfect. I have the woman perfect for me as my wife and we have the perfect daughter." Her mother says that Jenise has the mommy blues, which tends to happen to women after they give birth. There's not a whole lot of information out about it, but when I mentioned it to her doctor she seemed familiar with it. Her doctor suggested therapeutic or psychological help. Therapeutic I can handle, I shower Jenise with all my love and attention. I know what it feels like to feel disconnected inside. I lived that daily until she was in my life. I want to be able to help her like she's helped me. I just don't know how. Jenise reluctantly agreed to take a year off from work, and when I come home I try to keep work, family business, and our family separate. I tell Jenise I love her as much and as often as I can without feeling weak or soft.

"Wallace's you are the most picture perfect family!" The photographer said blushing.

I decided that it was time for my father, mister too busy to come, to see the baby. So we took a trip to Walnut Creek. My father came to the door with a frown. The dogs approached us curiously. I greeted them then Jenise and the baby got out the car. My father's frown disappeared and he backed away from the door slowly. As we entered the house Gwen pulled up with a new driver. My father sat in his chair with his eyes locked on Erica. I handed her to him. "Your grand daughter Erica Rainise Wallace." All of his tough guy, extra hard exterior melted as he looked at her. "This little angel definitely comes from your momma." He said as he stared at her face.

Gwen stood in the doorway looking hurt by his comment. Jenise went over to her and put her arms around her. I expected Gwen to act like a brat like she normally does, but I guess his comment hurt too much to do anything but quietly cry in Jenise's arms. "You got a new driver?"

"Daddy got rid of the other one." She said through tears.

"Why?" I asked my father. His eyes turned black and he held up one finger. Rule number one had been broken or compromised. Knowing my father he didn't just fire the driver, if he was alive he had to know it could only be temporary. "Why would anyone be that stupid?"

"Excuse me Mr. Wallace." The housekeeper said, "your parents are approaching." "What is this pop up on Frank day?" He said then he looked back down at Erica and smiled. She grabbed his finger and my father stopped breathing.

I went out and gave Nana a hug. She was happy to see me since she hadn't seen me in awhile. I told her I had a surprise for her inside and I hoped that she wouldn't go off on me too badly. Pops looked at me like he already knew. Nana saw Jenise and gave her a hug hello. Pops started burning a hole in me with his eyes. When we walked into the living room and she saw my father holding Erica, Nana turned red. "Ethan who is that!"

Pops exhaled, "when did you two get married?"

"MARRIED? Without me? Franklin! What's wrong with your children that they think it's ok for them to marry without me? Thank goodness Jennifer came to me! I don't appreciate this one bit!" Nana said with my collar clutched in her fist.

My father looked at me, "you're married?"

I exhaled, I decided to go the path of least resistance and use my big brother's line. "It wasn't planned, it just happened." Jenise looked at me.

"What happened to the other girl that I knew I wasn't going to like?" Nana said.

"I've been in love with Jenise for years, remember we talked about it. When the opportunity presented itself I had to make her mine once and for all." I told my Nana, Jenise watched me.

"Am I the last person to know about this?"

"No, Jenise hasn't met even half of the family."

"Alright then, we'll throw you a reception." Nana said shaking her head yes as she

agreed with herself. "Why weren't you at Jennifer's wedding?" She asked Jenise.
I went to Jennifer's wedding, but I went alone. I was still with Cat and I purposely didn't bring her. The closer it got to the end of Jenise's pregnancy, the more I pulled away from Cat. "She wasn't feeling well."
Nana smacked me upside the head. "How come you didn't stay with her?"
I rubbed my head; this woman isn't going to stop until she's laid me out. "She was..."
Pop's cut me off, "now you know how I feel about being lied to. You honestly think I'm going to sit here and allow you to lie to my Queen?"
Nana's eyes turned evil then she grabbed my ear. "Look me in my face and tell your story!"
Jenise backed up against the wall. Gwen started laughing at her. "He's in trouble not you."
"I'm not too sure about that." Jenise said not moving off that wall.
I told them the whole truth and everything I could think of. Gwen went to Jenise and interlocked her fingers into hers. I didn't think our story provoked bonding but apparently it did for Gwen. Nana looked Jenise up and down for a good minute.
"You're in over your head aren't you?"
"Yes ma'am." Jenise said nervously.
Nana searched Jenise's eyes, "baby blues too?"
"Ma'am?" Jenise didn't understand.
"That's what her momma tells me." I said.
"My mom talks to you about me?"
"She mostly asks me how I'm doing and things like that."
"I want you to come meet someone, when you're ready of course." Nana said walking to Erica. Nana picked up Erica and hugged her gently. "She's mine I can feel it!"

****

I shook my head no at the six thousandth dress Jenise picked up. She's never struggled with clothes like this before. She kept picking up these matronly looking dresses. I didn't understand what the malfunction was but my wife wasn't leaving this store with some old lady looking dress. I told Jenise to switch places with me. I gave her Erica and I browsed the racks. I brought six dress options to Jenise. She stretched her eyes as she looked at the dresses. She felt the need to remind me that she was Erica's momma. I understood that but she was also my wife. I didn't pick out anything too revealing, but it was a lot better than the old lady stuff she was picking. She didn't look happy as she went to the dressing room. She came out in the first dress, and although I liked it she said it was uncomfortable. Then she came out in the second dress. "Is that a smile I see?"
"You don't think it's too much?" She asked as she twirled in the mirror.
"I love it, do you?"
"I like it, but I feel like I should try on the others." She said giving me the first real smile in months.
"Suit yourself," I said loving the moment.

Five out of six dresses ain't bad. Jenise stayed in such a good mood, I decided we needed to go out to dinner. Maybe a little dancing to celebrate the night. I called my brothers and they were all in. Malcolm and Troy were unavailable as usual. Ever since Malcolm and Amber got back together outside of business I don't see him too often. I get it, but I also make sure to give him a hard time whenever I can about it. We took Erica to my momma's house. My grandparents came over to spend time with her as well. With all the arms ready to hold her I knew she was coming home spoiled in the morning. My momma said the first thing she was doing was braiding up her hair. Jenise and I smiled, but I didn't know how she was going to manage that on a five month old. When we got home I chased Jenise around the house grabbing feels and making her anticipation of tonight grow. Her smile had my heart completely going, I couldn't wait to get her home, half of me wanted to call and cancel. I decided that part of the anticipation was the evening out. Jenise saved the best dress for the party at my father's house. It was time to go but I couldn't walk out that door without a taste. Jenise ran again, laughing and giggling, much slower with those heels on. I caught her in the hallway and laid her down on that Persian rug. I delivered long savory Eskimo kisses until I couldn't any longer. Jenise begged me to stop as she pawed my head. We had to take our clothes off and wash up. In the shower Jenise said she wanted to try kissing me. I looked at her in disbelief, and amusement. I told her she didn't have to do it right now, but she went down on her knees. As soon as her mouth touched me I realized how much I missed this, I hadn't thought about it until now. I didn't want to set my hopes on it in case she didn't like it. Jenise backed up when her jaw got tired, we were in that shower for a long time, and we were unusually late to our own gathering.

Tess was a glow with her baby bump and happy for the night out. Franky was with the girl he told us about earlier, she was pretty, but she reminded me of Cat. Leonard's girl was nice, she was a good match for him. She was just as serious and goofy as he is. Fuzzy's woman was not a polished lady, but completely his speed and still a lot of fun. We were having a good time drinking, dancing, and eating. Then Victor Cardell slides into the club with his lady on his arm. "I heard there were Wallace's in my house, I had to come down and party with you all." He said gesturing for bottle service. "No Troy tonight?"

"Not tonight," Fuzzy said watching Victor.

Tess, Franky's girl, and Leonard's girl went to the bathroom.

Victor looked around the club dancing to the music. His demeanor became serious then he looked at Leonard. "That's him." He nodded towards a little boy.

Leonard looked in the direction that Victor motioned in. "I take it you're talking about the one looking. Call him over."

"Leonard, I don't want my lady around family business." I said.

"I understand that, but he's here." Leonard said, I knew he was right, but I wasn't happy.

The guy walked over, his eyes swept over everyone like he was making a mental impression of each person. The look in his eyes made me angry. "I don't like him." I said to the table.

176

"Victor who do we have here?" The guy said in a cautiously cocky tone.

"Sammy, you were fired a long time ago. Why do you continue to come around here?" Victor said.

"Fired? What for?" Dito asked.

"None of your business cracker!" Sammy said.

Fire blazed in Dito's eyes, "surely you could do better than that. Or maybe that's why you were fired."

"Who is this guy?" Sammy asked.

"You don't EVER ask me questions. Little BOY I will break you down right here and right now!" Victor sat back with fire in his eyes. "You don't ever disrespect my guest! You've got a lot to learn about how business is handled. You've got ambition which is fine, but you know nothing about respect!" Victor waved his hand, and one of his men grabbed up one of the guys at Sammy's table. "Him or you?"

Remorse flashed over Sammy's face. "Alright Victor I'm sorry."

"Him or you?" Victor repeated, "if you don't choose it will be both!"

Sammy exhaled, "him." Then he looked as his man was snatched up and taken out. "I guess I have to tell you, since you're too stupid to get this on your own. Come to my club again and I will kill you! If I see you around anyone of my family members, I will kill you! I don't trust you! Matter of fact if I feel like you're plotting on me, it's over!"

Dito stood up, "next time before you pop off at the mouth you might wanna do your homework to know who you're looking at." He said as he walked around the table. He walked up on Sammy and punched him in the face; I looked at Franky in disbelief. "My momma is black, don't you ever call me a cracker again!"

Victor put his fist up to his face to muffle his laugh. I was impressed Dito put some real power into that punch, Sammy's knees buckled. Jenise put her hand on my thigh under the table. Victor's men took Sammy and his guys out of the club. "Your momma's black?" Victor asked Dito.

"We're all brothers."

"DITO! I didn't know you had it in you!" Fuzzy said cracking up.

"My last name is Wallace, nothing about me should be surprising."

****

Jenise collapsed on my chest trying to catch her breath. I put my arms around her giving her a minute to breathe. I started to roll us over, she protested cause my momma just did her hair for the party tonight. So I put her legs on my shoulders then I stood up holding her by her wrist. Jenise was rendered speechless as I went to town on her. When we laid down again she kept rubbing my back and shoulders. She said she was going to be walking funny tonight. I kissed her gently and I asked her if I hurt her, she said only because she asked me to. We laughed and I kissed her again. "Ethan who was that kid that night?"

I kissed her forehead, "nobody." She gave me a come on look. "That's Victor's problem."

"I've seen him before." She said, I popped up and looked at her. "I mean I've seen him around before."

"Around where?"

"I've been trying to remember, but I've seen him before."

"Around the house, around where?"

"I don't know Ethan, I've seen him around before is all."

I kissed her lips, "as soon as you remember you let me know." Then I looked at the clock. "If we start getting ready now we might make it in time to say we went to my father's party."

We cleaned up and then we dressed. I sat on the bed and watched Jenise put her makeup on. I couldn't stop smiling.

Jenise

I love when Ethan looks at me like that. When I'm lost in him everything feels right, everything feels good. The moments when I can't be lost in him hurt, and I don't know why they hurt. Other than the fact that I feel like I'm covered in guilt. Sometimes I wonder what Nohemi is doing, and I wonder if Cat knows about me. It's not like she ever liked me, but she got so close to have it all ripped away. I know that's not my problem, but it doesn't take away my guilt. I turned to Ethan I asked him what did he think about my makeup and as usual he said I was beautiful. When we got to Frank's music was playing and people were there, but everyone was kind of standing around. When Ethan and I stepped out in the backyard Gwen came hurrying over. She explained that there had just been a fight. I expected her to say the men were fighting, but when she said the women I frowned at her. She pointed to her cousins and Aunts who were fighting. She said a woman had been flirting with her Uncle all evening and she took it too far. Then I saw Timothy talking to a woman over to the side of the party. I almost didn't recognize him while he was talking to this woman. His stance and everything was totally different than any way I know him to be. I wondered why he hasn't brought Grace around yet, all this time that they've been together she should be at his family gatherings at least. Timothy's mother walked over to him while he was talking to this woman, she didn't smile or anything. She said something, but I could tell by her body language she was giving both of them a hard time. The woman got up and walked away almost stormed away, and Timothy looked irritated. Gwen took me by the hand and introduced me to so many people I couldn't possibly keep them all-straight. "These are Timothy's sisters Jade and Amber. This is Sophia and this is Tatum. Everyone this is my sister in-law Jenise." They all said hello and we chatted for a little bit, then Gwen said we'd be back. "That's Amber's boyfriend over there." She pointed to the guy from that night Whispers died, even when he's having fun he looks serious. "Isn't he delicious?" Gwen said like she's thought about it more than she should.

"That's your cousin's boyfriend." I said confused.

"For now, what does Amber know about keeping a guy like that? Everything about him seems so powerful, I bet he's amazing in bed." She said like she was salivating.

"Gwen you shouldn't think about her man that way."

She gave me a yea-right look. "I'm kind of seeing someone right now."

"How? I thought you had an escort wherever you go?"

"I've found ways to make it work. The only problem is that if Amber finds out she might feel something about it." I waited for her to explain. "Ok so there's this guy that she only sees during the summer, and he has a little crush on her but its not like they've ever done anything outside run around Nana's neighborhood together. Amber's in love with Malcolm, its not like she would ever do anything about Tag. Tag is such a hunk I can barely control myself."

"You seem to be like that about all men in general." I said as I watched her shoot eyes at the guy with Malcolm. "You need to slow down."

Gwen frowned at me, "I thought you would understand. With everything you and Blu have been through."

I was irritated, "then you should understand the point. Back stabbing and scheming doesn't end well. Your brother lost a child; he has to live with that everyday. And I was married to a sexually confused man who tried to keep me drunk so that I wouldn't catch on to him. We gotta live with that everyday. It's a horrible way to live." I said honestly.

"Yea, yea, yea…. In the end you still have each other so it couldn't be all that bad."

"If that's what you think you've missed the point completely."

****

I'm only going to have one today, to be good I made sure it was a mixed drink. I made sure I fed Erica well before we came down here. I'll give her some cereal later, like I normally do. My waiter put my drink in front of me and I felt good looking at the glass. The first sip is always the best, my waitress is so used to seeing me she greets Erica with a hug hello. When I finished the first glass I felt nothing, not even a slight buzz. So I asked for another, even though I said I was only going to have one, the first one was a tease. The second drink was still teasing me, so I had to have the third. There it is, that wonderful buzz feeling. I paid the bill in cash and then Erica and I walked home. I brushed my teeth and gargled. Erica and I started going over the flashcards that Raynel bought her; then Ethan came home early. I told myself to be cool; he does this from time to time. I guess to keep me on my toes.

Ethan made dinner like he normally does and he kept looking at me. He was about to say something when the phone rang and I dove for it. It was my mom; she was confirming her flight information with me for our reception this weekend. My mom was so excited to come back and see the baby. Stephen was coming too and he said he couldn't wait to meet his grand daughter. She asked me if I changed my mind about inviting my father and I told her I hadn't. I didn't want to deal with him at this point. I couldn't believe of all people she was asking me to be kind to him. If anything its probably because it doesn't have to be her. She's remarried and has happily moved on with her life, she's replaced him. There's only one person who causes your birth, no other man could replace him. I didn't want to deal with it. When Ethan talked to my mom his voice was low and he was upset about something. I didn't want to hear about it so I tried to go to bed early. While Ethan and Erica were having their bonding time, I took a drink of my secret stash brushed my teeth and got in the bed. I awoke to Ethan putting his arms around me and kissing my neck. I didn't feel like making love with the irritation of my father swishing around my brain. I kissed Ethan patted his arm and tried to go back to sleep. Ethan asked me how I was feeling, I told him I was tired hence why I was going to sleep. Ethan squeezed me so tight, "Jenise I love you. I know sometimes it seems like we get so busy with our day-to-day lives that it gets hard to see. I've been in love with you since that first Kool-aide challenge in my kitchen. I was so used to being overlooked and under appreciated, that everything I felt for you confused me. I always wanted to be more than just your best friend. You are my first kiss, the first person I've ever told that I loved them, you're my everything. I don't know or understand what's going on with you, but I want you to know. I'm not stupid, and I'm not blind. I see it, and I don't like it. I need a moment to regroup and figure out my line of reasoning on it. I want this madness to stop; it's insulting that you would think you could pull one over on me. Or that I wouldn't know or notice what's happening with you. I notice everything about you. I don't want to fight about it, I just need you to stop." I didn't say anything; my heart was beating hard and fast. "This is me being calm about it. I doubt I will be so calm the next time we discuss it if you continue down this path. We have to put everything in it's proper place. There's a time and place for everything. If you can't control it, I can and will control it for you." Then he kissed me.

****

"WAIT A MINUTE! WAIT A MINUTE! I THOUGHT HE WAS ENGAGED TO THAT PLASTIC FEMALE AND ONLY YOUR BEST FRIEND? I CAME HERE TONIGHT THINKING I WAS MEETING YOUR HUSBAND?" Trinity said trying to find some sobriety.

I tried to speak past my own buzz. "Ethan is my man! My husband! You must've gotten it confused." I smiled.

"No! No! NO! I may be drunk, but I'm not crazy! I know you said he was getting married to the other girl. Cause if you said he was your husband I wouldn't have dreamed about him. I came here thinking I was going to seduce him!" She laughed.

"His brother is right over there." I pointed to Franky.

"He has player written all over him, I don't want that one." She pouted.

"Oh well, Ethan is mine and I ain't sharing!"

"Fine cousin, be stingy. Chastity and I are going to move out here in a year or two. Round up some good ones for us."

My mom walked over and took my glass out my hand. She painted a smile on her face and she told us to come dance with her. Everyone was dancing and having a good time. Poppa spent most of the night watching me, and Nana came out on the dance floor with us. She told me when I sobered up she needed to take me out to the firing range with her. She said we needed quality time alone together.

Chapter 18

Ethan

My father and I looked at the numbers; I shook my head with a smile. My father told Malcolm that his operation was impressive, and it was time to open his shop. Malcolm sat back and let my father's words sink in. I explained that his organization was growing; putting the Cardell's under him has only improved his operation. He needed a cover for his deposits; he couldn't leave that money sitting around his house or somewhere. My father mapped out the structure for the business. Malcolm asked questions, good questions as usual. Malcolm showed my father locations that he had in mind for his shop. The location on East 14th was the best option. I saw a glimmer of Malcolm's version of excitement as he and my father talked out the deal. When he realized we were making this happen today setting the wheels in motion he got lost in his thoughts for a little. Uncle Tim and Uncle Jeff stopped in. They saw my father's car outside as we stood in the middle of the property. "What are you going to call your place?" Uncle Tim asked Malcolm didn't hesitate, "Drew's!"

My uncle smiled really big, "that's an excellent name son."

Malcolm inhaled deeply like Uncle Tim's approval gave him more wind underneath his wings. Once we filed his Fictitious Business Name, opened his business account, etc. my father took copies of the paperwork. Everyone congratulated Malcolm on his next step forward. I asked him if he was sure about going into business with Moses. Moses is known from around the way as an opportunist. Malcolm said Moses would serve his purpose for now, and if Moses was crazy enough to cross him that was his last strike.

****

"Erica and I are with your mom out here in the city. She finished her day early and now we're shopping." Jenise said sounding so happy.

"So there's no need to hurry home to make dinner?"

"Not unless you want to have leftovers tomorrow. Wait until you see what I got for you!" She said excitedly.

I smiled, "you got something for me? What is it?"

"Un Un! I have to show you!" The deepness in her voice made me want to come through this phone.

"You gonna show me tonight?"

I could hear the smile in her voice, she laughed. "Ethan I'm no good at this."

"No, no. Don't break character, you're doing well. Keep going." I laughed.

She inhaled deeply and giggled a little. "Yes, I'm going to show you tonight; and you're going to love it!" Then she laughed shyly.

I was already turned on. The naughty shy girl routine was enough for me. "I can't wait!" I tapped my pen on the desk. "I'm going to work a little longer since I'm not hurrying home. I'm going to stop by my Uncle Tim's to go over some business and then I'll be home waiting for you. Kiss daddy's baby for me."

"Will do."

"I'll kiss you myself when I see you."

"I'll kiss your mom too."

Yikes! "Don't tell my momma I forgot about her. Kiss her for me as well." I laughed. My momma seems like she means it this time. All my life, my dad has been in and out of the picture as the man on her arm. Sometimes you would think they were getting back together and other times she'd scream at him as soon as she saw him. I couldn't tell who was more confused him or her. My father always has women around, except for when things were going well between him and my momma. When things are going well, he's happier than normal, which means he shows more human decency. He isn't as cold blooded as normal. When they're on the outs everybody dies, I mean that literally. I think my momma is tired of playing the game. I'm her baby who's grown with a family of my own. Lately she's not taking his calls and refuses to see him when he pops up. I wish I understood what sadness looks like on that man; he seems to have one face and one face only. He rarely smiles, and the only time I've seen smiles with him involved my momma and now Erica. Everything is so matter of fact and logical. I know Franky, Dito, and I get our ability to express emotion from momma. I mean I felt them always, but my expression of them didn't really happen until Jenise.

I pulled up to my Uncle's house as he did. He looked up to the window and Auntie Annette was in it looking down at us waving. We waved back, "nothing is better than coming home to my Queen." He said proudly.

"You two have been married a long time and you still feel that way?" I asked hoping to glean anything I could from his next words.

"Marriage ain't easy son, as you will learn if you haven't already. Sometimes you lose yourself and at one point or another both of you end up doing the unthinkable. Forgiveness is the hardest thing to come by, sometimes love doesn't even help."

"How do you forgive in those spaces?" I was hanging on to his every word.

"Remember that you can't make permanent decisions when you're emotional. There have been times when we were so done with each other, never at the same time of course. I've done things and so has she. Our love for each other was our only saving grace."

"I've heard about you, what could she have done?" I hoped he understood that I needed information and I wasn't trying to pry.

"As parents you only want to give your children better than you had. That's what you try to do, the parents who care to be better anyways. My Queen and I didn't always see eye to eye on the raising of our kids. Children can and will change your relationship, if you don't stay connected they can be the end of your relationship." The look in his eyes said that was as much as he was going to elaborate and I would have to fill in the dots myself.

We went inside and discussed business when we heard tires screech outside, and then banging at the door. Auntie looked out the window then she opened the door. It was Malcolm and he had on shorts and a jacket, which was completely open, he was shirtless and barefoot. His lip was busted and he was upset. I looked at Uncle

Tim and he didn't move or say a word, if looks could kill. Malcolm asked if Amber came here? Auntie Annette said no, then the phone rang. She spoke for a brief moment then she hung up. She looked at Malcolm with evil eyes then she took the phone in her bedroom. Malcolm stood there upset and trying to think, but you could tell his thinking was clouded by emotion. My Uncle said nothing, he watched Malcolm. When Auntie Annette came out of the bedroom she charged Malcolm. "How could you?" She said punching him in the face. I looked at my Aunt in amazement; I had no idea she could hit that hard. Malcolm took a step backwards but he didn't react. "This is nonsense Malcolm! You keep hurting my child! She was not born for you to treat this way!"

"I…" Malcolm searched for words but he had none.

She hit him again, "we welcome you in to our family and this is how you act? I WILL KILL YOU MYSELF FOR HURTING MY FAMILY LIKE THIS!" She said as she hit him again.

Malcolm's eyes got big as he looked at the pain on my aunt's face; both of them had runaway tears at the same time. "Momma I'm sorry! I do love her… I…. I just…. I just…."

"You're a stupid little kid playing grown up games. Stop playing house and be a man!" She hit him again.

Malcolm came forward and put his arms around my aunt's neck. He loosely hugged her while laying his head on her shoulder, "I don't know why momma! I'm no good to anyone!"

I rubbed my fingers over my mouth. This is a side I've never seen of Malcolm or would ever imagine. My Aunt put her arms around Malcolm then she punched him in the back a couple times then she rubbed his back while she cried. "You messed up!"

"Take your hands off my woman!" Uncle Tim said tired of their love fest.

"Tim!" Auntie Annette said as she rubbed Malcolm's back.

The look in my Uncle's eyes made my Aunt put her hands up and Malcolm released her as he tried to get his emotions in check as he faced my Uncle. "One day you will learn that YOU can't be the toxic element to your environment. It's a hard lesson to learn, but for the sake of your life you need to learn faster."

"Yes sir." Malcolm said.

"My little girl is going to come home heartbroken and confused. The only reason you will live is because I think letting you exist in this state would be more powerful than killing you. You will see it in her eyes; you are the one who's hurt her unlike any other. Malcolm we love you like a son, but until Amber has forgiven you, you have to leave."

Malcolm looked at my Aunt with pleading eyes. She looked at Malcolm and then she looked at her husband. "You heard him." She said with tears streaming down her face.

"I'm sorry momma." Malcolm said looking at her tears. He took a deep breath, and then he walked out the door.

My Aunt and Uncle were extremely upset and there was no point in staying. I told my Uncle I would call him, I gave my Aunt a kiss on her cheek and then I walked out the door. All the windows in Malcolm's car were broken; he was standing by the car thinking. Malcolm looked at me with red eyes. I told him to come by the office in a couple of days. He nodded in agreement, and then he got in his car. He sat there for a minute, I guess hoping that Amber would come home before he left. When he realized I wasn't leaving until he left, he pulled away slowly. I followed him home, and then I went to my house. Jenise was in the garage she had just gotten home. She was taking her bags out of her car. She looked at my face and asked me what was wrong. I told her about the whole scene at my Uncle's house. Jenise watched my eyes for a minute, then she asked me how was Cat. I looked at her with surprise in my eyes, I told her I didn't know. I told her that I didn't know where Cat was and I didn't care. I told her for the I don't know how manyth time, that all I ever wanted was her. I didn't need Cat or anyone else as long as I had her all to myself. I could see the doubt in her eyes. I asked her why she didn't believe me. She said because I was Ethan Wallace, then I reminded her that she was Jenise Wallace and all that I needed in my life.

Erica was exhausted and trying to fight sleep so that she could spend time with her daddy. Her little fist clung to my shirt for dear life. I had to wait until she completely fell asleep and released my shirt before I could lay her down. I anxiously walked into the bedroom to see Jenise standing in the middle of the floor in a red nighty. She smiled shyly and asked me if I liked it, I told her I loved it. When I walked to her she told me I couldn't touch her. I frowned and told her I had to touch her. She shook her head no then she pushed the middle of my chest and pointed me to the shower. I did as I was told and when I got out she was waiting by the shower door. She dried me off, kissed my tattoo, and she smiled at my body. She told me that she loves that I didn't get skinny. She said she wouldn't have liked me like that. I pointed to my calves; I said that they said it was impossible for me to ever be skinny without being sick. So I guess tonight she likes pushing me instead of telling me how we're doing this. She pushed me to the bed and then she took the silk belt from her matching robe and gently but firmly tied my hands to the headboard. I smiled at her and asked her what this was supposed to be, and she replied an experiment. Then she went down on me, she stopped to tell me to tell her when. I bucked my eyes at her. Then the room spun! She had to have read a book because this was so much better than her first attempt in the shower. I still had to remind her to be careful of her teeth, but my baby was getting the hang of it and daddy likes! When I said "OK!" She hopped up and stared at my dick like it was a volcano. We had to laugh at her. When I didn't blow she climbed on top of me and worked those hips until I did. Then she leaned forward, "now that you're warmed up, are you ready *BIG DADDY*?" I laughed cause I couldn't believe this, it wasn't... CRAP IT'S OUR ANNIVERSARY! I COMPLETELY FORGOT! Jenise smiled at me as she saw the realization in my face. She kissed me and said it was ok, and I could make it up to her in the morning. She mounted me again this time with her back to me, and all I could do was watch her. Hearing how in to this Jenise was, I was rendered speechless. When Jenise thought I was completely spent and she couldn't come up with any other way to work me she released me from my bondage. I was too turned on to stop just yet. Jenise gasped in disbelief as I grabbed her in a bear hug. I stayed on her G-Spot until her eyes rolled backwards in her head. I nutted so hard she should've had a headache from the charge of my soldiers. "HAP-PY AN-NI-VER-SA-RY BA-BY!" She said trying to catch her breath. "Happy Anniversary baby!"

****

The next morning I called Dito and I told him I wasn't coming in. He laughed at me and told me I made the rookie mistake and to be on guard cause it would be used against me later. I got up and I gave Erica a bottle so that Jenise could sleep in, she earned her slumber this morning. I bathed my baby girl in the sink, her favorite thing to do is splash the water and then she looks so surprised when it splashes in her face. It is the cutest thing; I had to get tasteful pictures of her bath. As I dressed her my mind suddenly drifted off to my first daughter. I was back in that hospital room holding my tiny little baby. She looked a lot like Erica, with the differences that came with coming from Nohemi. I have no doubt that I would've loved her as much as I love Erica, but I wouldn't have been whole. I was looking at my lifeless child when Jenise touched me and asked me if I was ok. Erica was trying to make a break for the bedroom door as she tried to speed crawl away. Jenise grabbed her then she came back and looked at me, she asked me if I was ok again. I tried to lie and say yes, but Jenise knows me better than that. She asked me what happened, and I told her nothing. I told her I was admiring Erica and then everything went black.

Jenise sat on the floor in front of me and she said she understood. I asked her how she could understand? She said it wasn't the same thing, but sometimes out of nowhere she'd have thoughts about things from her past. She'd realize things that she hadn't realized before, and they would render her immobile. I still didn't see the connection. She said that her father's been a drunk her entire life and she just realized it recently. She said her momma would try to conceal it from her, but sometimes it was too much for even her momma. She said she thought her momma's tears were because of something she did so she'd try really hard to make her momma smile. I nodded my head but it wasn't the same. I appreciated her trying though. She told me to go shower and she'd play with Erica. I got in the shower and let the water beat me in the face, that fast I was emotional and my happy feeling was gone. I tried to strategize against myself on how to get my happy feeling back. Jenise stepped in the shower and I asked her where Erica was. She said she was sleep in the crib, she hugged me and kissed my cheek. She told me she was so sorry for my loss and she didn't wish that kind of pain on anyone. Her touch made me relax, I was going to explode trying to hold this in.

Jenise

Ethan always tries to be so strong. This morning he wasn't my rock of massive man, this morning he was like cement. A beautifully paved sidewalk with a sudden crack in it. I felt good being the one to help him through this. As it should be because after all I am his wife. My body wouldn't allow me to even think I could go again, it screamed at me and called me names for even thinking it. Fortunately Ethan was satisfied with my hugs, kisses, and my ears. We got dressed and we went out to breakfast. Ethan was focused on Erica and me, but mostly Erica. He was watching everything she did with so much appreciation and love. He was so focused on Erica that he completely missed how impressed our waitress was with him. He ordered his breakfast without really looking at her; he paid all of her extra efforts no mind. Where I was boiling and trying to calm myself from her blatant disrespect, Um? Hello! I'm right here! I asked for a Mimosa and she brought me lemonade. I ordered a Denver omelet and she brought me eggs, bacon, and toast. I looked at my plate completely irritated. "THIS IS NOT WHAT I ORDERED!" Embarrassed she pulled out her pad where she wrote down our order. "That's what I have written down."

"Oh so because you were so busy trying to get my husband's attention and you wrote down the WRONG thing does not mean I have to eat it!"

"What did you think you ordered?"

Her tone grabbed Ethan's attention, "I heard exactly what my wife ordered. She wanted a Denver Omelet, with a fruit cup instead of potatoes, and a Mimosa. What you can do for me right now is send out your manager!"

"But I can fix this!" She pouted.

"Your opportunity to fix this was to get it right in the first place. Manager now!" He growled at her.

Other people in the restaurant started looking when they heard Ethan's about business tone. The manager was a very tall and thin white man, he looked extremely nervous approaching our table. "Mr. Wallace you wanted to see me?"

"I'm not happy! Your waitress is sloppy and unprofessional. She copped a tone with my wife after she got her order completely wrong. It's not enough to make sure I'm catered to, if my wife is not happy, I'm not happy!" He said then he looked at him.

The manager took a deep breath to calm himself. "Mrs. Wallace I apologize for the entire mix up. I will wait on your table personally. I'm told you wanted a Mimosa, could I interest you in a Peach Bellini?"

I put my hand under my chin, "I'm listening."

He described what sounded like a Mimosa with a kick up in Peaches and Vodka. I agreed as my mouth watered at the sound of it. I told him I wanted a Denver Omelet, then he offered a spinach, broccoli, artichoke, and chicken omelet made with white wine. He had me at the wine. Whenever my glass was half full he brought a fresh one so that I wouldn't have to wait. My food came out piping hot and my fruit cup was upgraded to a fruit bowl and he brought a small bowl for Erica to enjoy some as well. Ethan watched everything looking as serious as his father would, and every bit as intimidating. I savored every bite and when the manager asked me how everything was I told him it was better than he described. He looked relieved, he apologized over and over to Ethan. He told him our breakfast was on the house and he hoped that we would feel comfortable coming back especially since our waitress had been let go. Ethan told him he'd think about it as he took Erica out of her high chair. I was completely tipsy and in heaven with Peach Bellini's now. Ethan apologized for not paying attention sooner and I told him it was ok, the manager more than made up for the inconvenience.

Ethan took me to a jewelry store in the city, when we stepped on the display floor, he told me to pick out my anniversary present. I jumped up and down clapping my hands. The white people in the store looked at us with questioning eyes, as if we didn't belong. Eventually a salesperson approached us cautiously. Ethan got annoyed immediately and again he asked for the manager. The manager came out with an inquisitive look on his face. "I'm Ethan Wallace, I believe you know my family." The manager looked like he didn't know whom he was referring to. "Franklin, Jeffery, Timothy, Matthew, Dale Wallace! Take your pick!" Surprise and shock spread across his face. "My apologies! Yes! I am familiar with your family. I didn't realize you were a part of that family tree." He said looking Ethan over.

Ethan was going to need to relax after this, this man has clearly pissed him off. "Bring me your phone!"

The guy hesitated; it looked like he was arguing with himself the whole time he walked towards the phone. He sat the phone in front of Ethan on the display case. Ethan snatched the phone and dialed a number on the rotary phone. I couldn't help but notice that his fingers were too big to actually fit inside the number circles. Ethan didn't say hello, he told the person on the phone that he brought me to this store and after waiting thirty minutes for service the manager acted like he didn't know their family. Most importantly he doesn't understand where this black man fits into their family tree. Whomever he was talking to yelled on the other end. They spoke for a minute more then they hung up. Ethan gave the phone to the manager as he glared at him. The phone rang and the manager answered it. His eyes darted to Ethan and then he turned red. He was very apologetic to the person on the phone and then he said he understood. He set down the phone and swallowed. The manager said the owner was on his way to personally assist us. Meanwhile he tried to show us jewelry and Ethan glared at him, he refused to speak to him. A white man in very expensive clothes hurried into the store, he marched right up to Ethan apologizing for his manager's ignorance. He took us into the vault where the really expensive jewelry was. He told me to pick out whatever I liked. Everything in there was too fancy for my liking; I would feel like I needed protection whenever I tried to wear any of it. The owner was trying to sell me on the big diamonds and the gaudy looking stuff. I pointed to my ring, I told Ethan I wanted something to go with that, and nothing in this store felt like a good match. Ethan smiled and said we were leaving. The owner apologized over and over again, and as we walked out of the store the owner didn't hold back from going in on the manager. We drove all the way back to Stanford to the store where Ethan got my original ring. The same salesperson he worked with before remembered him, and was more than happy to help this young black couple pick out jewelry. Erica even got a gold bangle and small diamond earrings. I was very happy with my necklace and matching earrings.

My second pair of diamond earrings from my husband.

****

No! No! **NO**! I was literally screaming at the calendar. Count it again! Obviously I counted wrong! My eyes crossed and I threw myself out on the bed kicking and screaming! NO! I'm not ready to have another baby! I'm not ready! It's all my fault I should've gotten back on the pill when the doctor suggested it. Ethan just finally stopped riding me about drinking as long as I didn't give Erica that milk. I knew we had entirely too much fun on our anniversary! Too much! I should've known better than to think anything but a baby was coming from that night. I laughed to myself as I thought about how good I got him for a change. I guess all I could do was pat myself on the back, I did this to myself.

The smells from the kitchen were intoxicating. Ethan invited his cousin Sophia and her family over for dinner. Her mom was at Raynel's shop with little Sasha. Sasha immediately became mother hen to Erica. She's not all that much bigger than her and yet she wanted to take care of her like she was. Lauren, Sasha's grandmother, suggested that we get the girls together to play. I told Ethan about it and he was quiet for a minute. The next thing I know they're coming over for dinner. I went down to the kitchen and I asked Ethan if he needed help with anything and he told me to make the salad. He looked at my face and asked me if I had been crying and I said no real fast and I turned my back to him. I finished the salad put it in the refrigerator, and then I went out to Erica who was having a ball in her big play pin. Ethan opened the door when they arrived. They were so young; I immediately wondered how they managed. Sophia immediately became excited about the smell of dinner. She put Sasha in the play pin with Erica and she followed Ethan in the kitchen as they talked in detail about our meal. Charles stood there looking awkward and unsure of what to do. I told him to have a seat in the living room with the girls and I. He looked around the room taking in our huge family portrait. He said our picture was nice as he continued looking around. I didn't know what to say to this kid so I asked him how school was going. He said it was fine for now, but he was considering dropping out to find a better paying job. I asked him what his wife thought about that and he shrugged. He said they hadn't discussed it. I frowned because I didn't like the idea of him telling me, a stranger, something he hadn't told his wife. I told him he should discuss it with his wife before he did anything. He rolled his eyes and looked at the kids. Sasha was trying to pick Erica up as if she was a lot bigger than her. Ethan and Sophia put dinner out on the table. We put Erica in her high chair and we stacked the phone book and encyclopedias in a chair for Sasha. Sophia was singing Ethan's praises as she sampled each dish. Ethan encouraged her to look into culinary courses after graduation. Charles said nothing and kind of looked around the room as he ate. He clearly wanted to be anywhere but here. Sophia and Ethan were looking at me and asked what was wrong at the same time. "I guess he's sacrificing his education so that you could get yours." I said quietly.

"Sacrificing your education?" Sophia said looking at Charles.

He exhaled, "I told her I was thinking about dropping out to get a better job."

"Why would you tell her that and you haven't discussed it with me?" Sophia said looking at him like Ethan looks at me sometimes when we're fussing.

"She asked." He said nonchalantly.

"You're an idiot! Can you at least try to act like you have social skills for one night?" He kept eating like he tuned Sophia out. Ethan was watching and getting upset. "If certain people were here you'd be mister personality though!"

"Sophia," Ethan said gently. "Pull back Nana's fire. He's an idiot that's established, but you married him. You didn't have to."

"I was pregnant and hormonal, clearly I wasn't thinking straight." She snapped.

"Give the boy a break." Charles's head snapped at Ethan. "Look at that, he does have a reaction. When you start acting like a man, I'll address you that way." Then Ethan turned his attention to the rest of us. "For dessert we're going to have crepes!" He smiled. "I got some homemade preserves at the farmer's market and I made a cream cheese custard."

"Sounds delicious! I make preserves too. We need to talk more cousin, I never had saffron before, and I love it."

Ethan smiled, "you make preserves too? Check you out!"

I smiled at Ethan for diffusing the situation. I could tell he didn't like Charles but there wasn't much to like. Charles showed no shame; he used his finger to lick his plate clean. Once he was fed and enjoying his wine he mellowed out some and at least acted like a person. The girls enjoyed their meal and desserts as much as everyone else. Each drink of my wine and port with our dessert was bittersweet. Ethan wouldn't let me drink anymore for the next year plus, and I was just getting back into the swing of happiness. Plus! This meant more time away from work and I wanted to go back in a few months. Ethan's grandparents were begging me to go back to work so that they could have time with Erica. I couldn't stop pouting. That night Ethan put Erica to bed then he stood in the middle of the floor staring at me. I tried my best to ignore him, so he stood there not moving; his mind was going fifteen thousand miles a minute. He squinted his eyes at me, "I told you I don't like games."

"I'm not playing any games." I said avoiding his eyes.

"You're hiding..." He took a step back looked me up and down on the bed. "When was your last period?"

"Ugh! Ethan! Seriously?" I said throwing the covers over my head. I started crying immediately.

Ethan laid on the bed next to me. He pulled my covers down to reveal his huge smile; he started laughing when he saw me crying. "Why are you crying?"

"I don't wanna have another baby yet. We just had Erica! I didn't even get back to work! All my clients are going to forget about me. It's not fair!" I cried.

"It's not the end of the world, it's just our love taking on the form of flesh and blood again. I'm excited!"

"You don't have to be pregnant!"

"I would have our babies if I could. As long as you're the one knocking me up."

"Yea right, until you have to go without drinking."

He stopped smiling, "that's what this is all about isn't it?"

"Kind of..." I said peeking at him.

"What happened to the girl who would barely sip her wine with dinner?" He put his arms around me.

"You happened!"

He exhaled, "I created a monster didn't I. You can't drink it's not good for the baby."

"Then walk the walk with me. You can't drink as long as I can't." I looked at him.

Ethan acted like I shot him and he closed his eyes. I pushed his shoulder asking him to agree. He opened one eye, "SSSHHHH! I'm dead!"

I laughed, "it's only fair! You need to know and understand how it feels."

Ethan faked cried, "I can't stop drinking! It's who I am!"

"You say that now wait until you start feeling dry!"

Chapter 19

Ethan

She wasn't kidding! It's not easy, a couple times we resorted to taking a couple of tablespoons of red wine to take the edge off. Jenise tearfully called her momma and told her about the baby. Her momma and stepfather got so excited for us. My momma screamed her excitement into the phone. Dito congratulated us, while Franky belly laughed. Grace asked us to slow down and wait for them. Gwen got excited and she's been coming over a lot more often. My father said that Gwen has been calmer since she's been visiting with Jenise. I asked Jenise what they talk about and she said girl stuff. Gwen doesn't get on my nerves as much. We still end up arguing about something dumb. If Dito is around her claws come out. Dito has no patience for her either so they go at it back and forth pretty badly.

I was looking at paperwork when I heard a commotion outside my office. Franky walked past my office swiftly. I walked quickly to the lobby; Greg was demanding to speak to Jenise. I exhaled then I looked at Dito with an annoyed expression. "Why are you here?"

"I need to talk to Jenise." He said glaring at me.

"She's not here."

"Tell her to get down here!"

I looked at my brothers and both of them threw their hands up like they were asking me what I was going to do about it. All the employees who have no idea who they're working for were watching. I told everyone to go back to work. As everyone was walking away I hit Greg fast and hard in the center of his chest. Everyone heard it, no one saw it. We were standing in front of the receptionist's desk and she had just turned to reach for the phone, she jumped and then she looked at us trying to figure out what happened. Both of my brothers smiled in approval of my quick movement. Greg stumbled backwards trying to catch his breath. He sat down on the couch struggling to breathe as he held his chest. Dito called the receptionist to his office and they walked away. Franky stood to the side watching. "What do you want with my wife? I'm tired of you coming here. Piss me off and I'll make sure you watch your little boyfriend die and then you join him!"

Greg looked at me like I insulted him. "You need to dismiss gossip! I don't know what you've been told."

I hit him in the face this time, "don't insult me! I've done my homework. I've seen you two with my own eyes. That poor girl is confused and trapped in the middle of your nonsense!" Demetria was still there. I stood over him wishing he would give me the reason to finish him.

Greg took a deep breath then he stood up. "I have nothing to do with Charlie and his wife. I'm here about my wife."

"You don't have a wife."

"I didn't sign anything, we're still married. She had my baby. I have rights to my child."

I had to restrain myself! "You country bumpkin! You don't have to sign for a divorce and still get one! Besides you were never married. Unless you knocked up Demetria you don't have a child. Jenise had my baby. I keep telling you this, why is that so hard for you to understand? I don't like repeating myself!"

"Maybe it's because the Jenise I know and love wouldn't be heartless and cruel. She loves me!"

I stepped in his face, "you're such a sissy! You don't know her. If you knew her you would know that when I'm involved I'm all that matters. Get out of my office and don't ever come back! Next time you walk into this building you will not walk out." Then I walked away from him.

Franky frowned at me; I guess he figured I was going too easy on him. He grabbed Greg by the collar and then he shoved him through the doors. I heard Franky telling someone to show him why he didn't want to come back. I went back to my office. I was looking at paperwork when I heard Franky talking. "Look who I found." He said with a smile.

Eugene walked in my office straight face as usual. Franky sat on the edge of my desk still smiling. "I know your father, how his boys smile so much is beyond me." He shook his head, Franky smiled bigger to annoy him. "Malcolm is distracted." His voice had my attention. He's trying to be a family with that little girl while that kid is building. Victor's waiting for the word, and Malcolm is not paying attention not even Troy. How you have these kids running things is beyond me. We...."

I cut him off, "how we have these kids running things? They're brilliant young men. Hard working and our distribution and connections have more than tripled by putting them in front. You can call then young all you want, but respect the work they've put in."

"I'm not saying they're not good. He's not focusing! He needs to leave the girl and her kid alone at least until we put that kid down."

I shook my head, "I would never advise him to turn his back on his son. You know it is possible to run business and be a father."

My comment made him mad. "Look! There's no good reason to hold back. He's building, it's only going to be weak for so long. I don't believe in holding my breath." He stood up. "Let me know when we're striking." Then he walked out of my office leaving the door open.

Dito looked at him walking away then he came in and shut the door. Franky wasn't smiling anymore. "What's going on?"

Franky laid out the brief conversation we had with Eugene, then I called Malcolm. "This is Malcolm." He answered his phone.

All three of us stared at the phone, in that moment the unintentional raspiness of his voice made all of us think of Whispers. "It's Ethan, Dito, and Franky. We need to talk."

"Alright. One moment..." His voice was muffled for a minute. "Let me guess. Eugene came by your office? They told me he came by here."

"He did, what are we going to do about the kid?" Franky said.

Malcolm was quiet for a minute. "He doesn't have the manpower to do anything."

"You and Amber looked comfortable at Jade's graduation. It only takes one person." Dito said.

"I do all of this for her. Fernando that is a good point. Amber and I plan to make some moves so I'll need security for her since she'll be under my wing and no longer under Tim's."

We exchanged looks, "you sound like you're about to plunge." Franky said in disbelief.

"Why you say it like that?"

"Malcolm you're still young, I know you want Annette and Tim to be happy. But you can't rush into marriage to make someone else happy. You've got to be ready or else it's not going to work and you'll still have Tim on your back." Franky said.

"I hear you," his voice was thoughtful. "Troy is here let's switch gears."

We talked for a while, the numbers looked good. We talked about squashing a few fires that were smoldering on the sidelines. As we were wrapping up Malcolm excused himself when he got a phone call.

We spoke a little longer then I made my way home. When I walked in the door Jenise had her feet up on the sofa and Erica was brushing her hair. My girls smiled at me and Erica screamed with excitement. I never tire of her excitement to see me. I kissed Jenise and then Erica latched on to me and wouldn't let go. Her laugh was contagious just like her momma's. "How's my favorite girls?"

"Good! I like pudding!" My babygirl said.

Jenise forced a smile, and then she turned her body to face me. "So the guy from the diaper service came by today." I listen for whatever she was going to say next. "We chatted for awhile, he's excited about the increase in order. He gave me the paperwork so I can increase our order." She looked at my eyes sadly. "I saw that kid walking in front of our house. He tried to look casual, but I spotted him. He saw me see him, he got in a car and drove away."

I released my air slowly so I wouldn't yell and scare Erica. "Jenise! Why didn't you call me?"

Her eyes filled up with tears, as she rubbed her stomach. "I have no good excuse, Erica had to potty and I got distracted."

Erica was watching my face. "Did you pee-pee in the potty for daddy?"

She shook her head yes with a proud smile. "She almost made it but at least she's asking." I kissed Erica and I stood up. Jenise's eyes stretched wide. "What are you going to do?"

"I'm going to make some calls." I went in my office.

I called Malcolm and he didn't answer at the shop or his place. No answer at Troy's, Fuzzy's, or Leonard's. Franky wasn't home, Tess said Dito barely made it in the door when he answered the phone and hurried right back out. She didn't know what was going on. As soon as I hung up the phone Dito walked in my office. "We've got to go! Amber's in the hospital. All I know is she was driving Malcolm's car." Dito said completely pissed.

I took a deep breath, "Jenise saw Sammy in front of the house earlier today. They can't stay here."

"Let's take them to momma's house. Dad still has it on detail." Franky said walking away. He picked Erica up hugged her deeply and then kissed her cheek. He told her he was so happy to see her, but Dito and I heard the worry in his voice. Jenise wouldn't stop rubbing her stomach as she silently watched me. I went around the house double-checking that it was secure. When I got to the basement one of the windows looked like someone was trying to get in. I reinforced the window, secured the breadbox, and then I rechecked everything around the house. Turned on the lights and television as if we were home. I told them about the window, we walked around the house and then we left in Franky's car. I nodded to the man on his post as we approached my momma's house.

"Why does it take all three of you to bring Jenise and my grandchildren? Where's Tess and my grand baby?"

"Tess and William are secure." Dito said directly.

"What's going on?" My momma asked while Jenise listened closely.

Franky explained that Amber was in a car accident and we needed to secure everyone and find out exactly what happened. I kissed the three most important women in my life then we left. We speculated all the way to the hospital. The night was crazy as we all came together to discuss next moves I kept thinking my house was compromised, and of all of us, why was my house compromised. I knew I was missing something and I couldn't figure it out.

Jenise

"Can I ask you something?" I said taking another swig of my drink while Gwen led Erica around the pool.

"Sure," she said keeping her attention on Erica.

"Why don't you come over Raynel's?"

Gwen turned red matching her hair. "I'm not welcomed over there."

"Why not?"

"Fernando can pretend all he wants, I know she's not my mother! I don't even know her, and you're the only person to mention her to me. I barely know her name. Fernando says I act like our mother, and I don't know why that's a bad thing. We both came from her, one of us if not both of us should act like her."

"Where's your mother now?" I asked.

Gwen looked away, "she went away." She said as a tear fell.

"I'm sorry. I didn't mean to put you in a bad place." I said getting out of my lounge chair.

Gwen looked at my very pregnant belly under my swimsuit. "Tag and I did it." She forced a smile.

I gasped, "you're barely in college!"

"How long did you and my brother wait?"

"That's not the point."

"Then what?"

"You should at least love the person. You're just trying to win."

"Jenise, Amber is not concerned with Tag she's got Malcolm."

"Ok, but now you're going to be wondering if he's concerned with Amber. What kind of a man does that?" Gwen gave me a yea-right look. "Your brother never hooked up with any of my friends. And ESPECIALLY not my family!"

"Well that's probably because he hasn't had the opportunity to. All my brothers and my father are heartless when it comes to women. You shouldn't assign Ethan so much honor."

"Gwen! Look at me!" She did reluctantly. "I'm here because your brother wanted me here. You need to start looking at the heart of the men you're surrounded with before you end up bitter and alone. Your father loves you so much; your brothers love you too. YOU make it difficult for them to love you. You make it difficult for them to be around you. As unpleasant as Sophia's husband is they used to come over all the time for dinner. That could've been you too, but you push everyone away. I don't know why you do that."

"You've only been here a minute. You don't know my family or the things they do."

"Well you see that's where you're wrong. I may have been slow before, but I'm paying attention. I'm noticing the things going on."

"Yea right!" She rolled her eyes.

"Why you think I asked you to show me how to give head?" Gwen frowned, "I know he was with all those freaks and although he never asked or even tried to push me in that direction I've got to stay on my toes. I'm paying attention to everything, and you need to wise up. Your brothers and father love you, and I hope your cousin doesn't feel some kind of way about this selfish guy using you to make her mad."

Gwen was quiet for a minute, "well I'm using him too."

"Really? How?"

"I wanted to get all that virgin stuff out of the way." She smiled devilishly at me, "and now that that's out of the way I can hone in on my craft. I don't want to be good, I want to be THE BEST!"

"Well if that's the case. Pass me your notes when you're done." I smiled at her.

****

Oh my God! I woke up this morning and my stomach grew. Ethan had to help me roll on my side just to sit up. This baby likes to eat. I scream every time I go to the doctor and I step on the scale. Out of sympathy for me Ethan has put on a little weight as well. It's so weird, seeing him a little bit thicker reminds me of college and how much I wanted to be all over him but I couldn't. Now I can be, but this stupid stomach is in the way. Sometimes we end up fussing and it's only because I'm miserable.

We can't go back to our house, Ethan hasn't said why but I don't question it. My man said we had to go, so we went especially after hearing about his cousin. She's going to be ok, but everyone is on high alert. So we've been at Raynel's since that night. We're in Ethan's old room; I love sneaking to quietly be with my man. I just hate that this gigantic stomach is in the way. All the things I fantasize about doing to him never turn out right. We always end up laughing. Erica sleeps with her

Grammy. She gets excited when it's bedtime cause Grammy reads to her until she falls asleep. Then her greats spoil her rotten. Whether it's her Nana or Poppa or her Gram or Grampy or Frank; Erica is showered with love.

This baby has me so blown up I move slowly. Ethan decided to take off work today. We're looking at new houses, and then we're going to get a few things for the baby. Ethan liked the first house but I didn't. There were trees all around the house and I know he was thinking privacy, but I was thinking of all the bugs.

Now this second house!!!! Ethan and I looked at it with big eyes. It reminded me of Frank's house just not as big. From the street you see the driveway and Ethan said he wants a gate. The drive way is kind of long it has a two-car garage. The house is big and old looking. The previous owners raised their children here. The wife died and the husband is in a home. The kids were selling the house cause it was just sitting and none of them wanted it. I smiled at Ethan to let him know I wanted it and we hadn't even walked inside. The yard was open and spacious. Around the back of the house was a breath taking view all the way out to the Bay. You could see the Bay and Golden Gate Bridges. I grabbed Ethan's arm to make sure he was seeing what I was looking at. Ethan was looking around at the grounds thinking about things I could careless about. I wanted this view; I wanted to come out here with a drink in my hand and reflect on the beautiful things that God has blessed me with. I want this house. Everything inside the house is old and outdated. I could see Ethan calculating stuff in his mind. Erica studied her father's face and then she mimicked his expression. As the realtor opened the door he explained that the house has been closed up for sometime. The house didn't stink it was just closed up and stale. Everything needed to be upgraded, it was not move in ready. I didn't care, I knew Ethan's house has to be his castle and anything we did to this house would make it grander than it already felt to me. Ethan told the realtor if we considered this house they would have to discuss the asking price. He said the only thing this property has going for it's self was the location. That was also Ethan's cue to stop smiling so much. So I did like Erica and mimicked Ethan. The next two houses were nice and more up to date but I wanted the old broke down house. I could see the potential for so much with that house. The realtor asked if we wanted to place an offer on any of the houses we saw today. I pinched Ethan even though I kept my face straight. He didn't jump or react, he exhaled and said yes. When he told the realtor how much he wanted to offer, the realtor and I frowned at him. He said the house needs a lot of work, he said he has an untrained eye, but he could see that even the plumbing was going to need work. The realtor and Ethan went back and forth. He had a good point; even though the house needed work the property itself was worth more than Ethan was offering. Ethan probably wanted to walk and do some research. I knew in order for him to agree to see the house he did some digging on it already. Ethan conceded and came up a little more on his offer. The older gentleman shook Ethan's hand, he told him he had no idea Ethan was so prepared. Ethan looked at him and told him he was going to take that as a compliment. I had a huge smile as we drove to the mall. "So I take it your mind is made up?" He said watching the road.

"I want that view, and we have space to build out during the remodel if we want. To answer your question yes."

"If we go with that one we'll have to stay with my momma longer. Don't you want to bring the baby to our home?"

"Home is where you're loved, as long as your mom is ok with it, I am." I said excitedly cause Raynel and I already discussed it. She loved having us with her, and coming home to her grand baby. She was in heaven when Tess brought little William over.

Ethan and Erica walked slowly with me as we picked up basics for the baby. The layout of this department store was very clever. They put the toy department next to the baby and kids clothes. Erica was luring her father in that direction. Ethan told me to stay close.

Ethan says it doesn't matter to him if this baby is a boy or a girl. I have a feeling he wants a son though. I was admiring this little bow tie when I heard my name.

"Jenise?" It was Cat. She was smiling at me and it seemed genuine, I was confused. She had bags in her hands and it looked like she wasn't finished shopping. "I almost didn't recognize you. I guess you're just spitting them out." She said scanning me over.

I couldn't stop staring at her; I didn't know what game she's playing. "I guess you could say that."

"I mean I know Greg wasn't happy about the first one. I guess he decided to go for it again?"

"Greg?" I frowned at her; Ethan was standing to the side watching. She hadn't seen him yet.

"Your husband duh!" She nervously laughed.

"You're shopping?"

She laughed nervously again, "yes. My boyfriend." She held up her bags. "How's Ethan?" Her eyes filled with tears.

"He's great! He..."

"Tell me the truth did Nohemi come back? I figured I'd give him time to get tired of her, I know he's coming back to me. It's just a matter of when."

I rubbed my stomach as I shot Ethan a look. "He's coming back to you? Why?"

Cat spun around in her short dress that left nothing to the imagination. Her figure was very cute and tight. I felt very fat in that moment. "There's only one me."

Ethan picked up Erica and he walked over to us. Cat was so busy talking she didn't notice him until he stood next to me. Cat looked at Ethan in disbelief, she was so busy taking in his size that she didn't notice Erica. "This is Erica." I said, my baby looked Cat up and down and then sat back like she wasn't impressed.

Cat looked at Erica with her mouth slightly open. "Erica?" She shook her head at Ethan. "HER?" Her face turned completely red.

I couldn't tell for sure who she was raising her hand to but her temper got the best of her. Ethan grabbed her wrist and her hand turned completely white. Ethan gave Erica to me. "Cat I will break your arm off if you ever think you can raise anything more than an eyebrow to my wife and child!" He said twisting her arm behind her.

"WIFE?" Cat yelled, then she cursed. I was about to tell Ethan to let her go when a guy hurried towards us. It was the kid, as soon as he saw Ethan he cursed and ran for his life. Ethan chased after him out of the store and into the mall. I dropped my items and started heading towards the car I didn't know what else to do. "Jenise!" Cat was crying and shaking out her arm before she picked up her bag. "You?" She spit at me like I was beneath her. "I knew better than to trust you! All that bestfriend crap! You fattened him up so that you could feel like no one else would want him." I stopped walking, she pissed me off. "The only reason he lost weight in the first place was for me! You don't even know him!" Store employees came close.

"I know you're a backstabbing two faced female dog! I can't believe you stole my man!"

"HE WAS NEVER YOUR MAN!" I yelled from my feet.

"Yes he was! We lived together and everything."

"You moved yourself in, he never invited you. You got so used to being taken care of you've resorted to sexing that little boy for everything he can give you! One day your age and lifestyle is going to show on your face and body, you better have a plan B."

Cat got mad and started charging at me with my baby in my arms. A older white man intercepted Cat before she got to me. "Aw heck naw! What is wrong with you? This woman is pregnant and has a baby in her arms! You better get out of my store before I call the police!"

Cat kept coming, "I don't care! Call the police!" She yelled.

Erica put her arms around my neck as she looked away. The man grabbed a fist full of Cat's hair to stop her. Then he told someone to call the police. Mall security came just before Ethan came back he was beyond angry. "That's your little boyfriend? Where does he live?" Ethan wouldn't calm down; he didn't care who was watching us.

"He comes to my place, I don't know where he lives."

"I guess you finally found a job that pays well enough for now."

"What?" She looked confused.

"Laying on your back!" He spit. The onlookers oohed and snickered. "Your place is in your name?"

"Sir, I'll handle all the questions here." The officer said dismissingly.

Ethan glared at him, "who do you report to?" The officer ignored him and went back to his pad. "Is your place in your name?"

"Sir! Don't make me have to speak to you again!"

Ethan looked at the officer then he looked at Cat like she better not make him have to repeat himself. "Yes." She said trying to hide her question in her tone.

"Someone's coming and you better cooperate!" Ethan said.

"Sir! I warned you!" The officer said turning his attention to Ethan, he took one step.

"You might want to get on your little walkie talkie and run the name Franklin Wallace by your dispatch before you take one more step in my direction. I'll use your dead body to beat her with!" Ethan said standing tall. The officer turned red, "oh so I see you're smarter than you look. Good now! Why don't you do this?

This prostitute…" Cat gasped like she couldn't believe he said that. "… is hiding a criminal who tried to kill my family member. Do your job; find out where her underage boyfriend ran off to. You better hope you find him before I do."

I guess that was the final confirmation that I needed, I smiled at Ethan and he kissed me.

Tears started pouring out of Cat's eyes, "he's not my boyfriend." She said to the officer but loud enough for Ethan to hear.

"Are you having sexual intercourse with a minor?" The officer asked her, Cat looked at the officer like he was crazy…. but she didn't respond.

Ethan told me to come on, he took Erica from me and he kept looking around as we walked out. When Ethan got in the car he gripped the stirring wheel. "He threw this old lady in my way. I would've had him if I was heartless."

I reached over and I hugged Ethan, I kissed his cheek then his lips. "I love that no matter what you always do the right thing. That kid will be dealt with, but you helped the old lady and she will never forget it. Was she hurt badly?"

"She said she was ok, I told her to go to the doctor and I gave her my card to send me the bill. She wasn't dressed like Nana, probably on retirement and looking forward to her moments of fresh air. Even though she refused I gave her everything in my pockets. The fact that she wasn't looking for me to give her anything I gave her more. What happened with Cat?" He looked at me.

"She tried to charge me and the store manager happened to be right there when she started coming. He grabbed her by her hair."

"WHAT?" Ethan looked like he was about to blow a gasket. I grabbed his arm and held on for dear life.

"Baby, she's going to be dealt with let's go home."

As soon as we walked in the door, Ethan went straight to the phone. I don't know who he called, but he took off his nice clothes and put on jeans, a T-shirt, and a jacket. He kissed us and said he would be back later, he was still angry.

I told Raynel what happened and her eyes were big then she picked up her phone, when the person didn't answer she hung up. She was angry just like Ethan and I've never seen her like that. She was vowing all the things she was going to do to Cat the next time she saw her. I had never seen her like this. When the phone rang she was going off to the person on the phone. She told them she didn't know where Ethan went. When she got off the phone Erica was watching her taking in all of her Grammy's emotions. Raynel picked her up and hugged her up. Dito and Tess walked in the door. Erica got down from her Grammy and ran to her Uncle Dito. Dito sat next to Raynel and put his arms around her. Tess sat next to me with William in her arms. Dito assured his mom that everyone was safe and this was temporary. They had some kinks that needed to be ironed out. Dito's calm but strong manner calmed Raynel and she laid her head on her son's chest. Tess looked at them like she had no idea what they were talking about. I guess she felt it at the same time and we turned our eyes to give them some privacy. Tess and I went into the other room. She asked me how I was feeling and I told her I felt fat. I told her we saw Cat. Tess asked me how she looked and I gave her a look. She smiled and said that good huh? I wouldn't care what she looked like if she didn't make it seem like it was such a big deal that she looked like that. Tess said it didn't matter what she looked like Ethan was done with her.

That night Ethan came home with the things I had picked out earlier. He said he went back and personally thanked that store manager for protecting his family. I told him he missed Dito and his family. He said he knew, he said whenever his mother gets upset they send in Dito to calm her. He said that Dito is the best at it. I asked him when was the last time he saw Cat, and he said when she popped up at his office, He said she knew he was married, she didn't know who to. When I asked him why, he said it was none of her business what he did with his life. I asked him when was the last time he slept with her and he exhaled and then he said before Erica was born. Ethan was trying to answer all my questions, but I could tell he didn't want to talk about Cat. To keep the peace I let it go.

****

Our bedroom pushed open like Erica does when she's ready to deal with us in the morning. I could hear her little feet as she approached our bed. I prayed that she chose her daddy and not me. I needed to sleep longer. When I felt the tugged on the covers on the other side of the bed, I told myself to hug her up later. She whispered, "daddy, daddy". Ethan rolled over and said good morning to his princess. She asked him to read her a story. Ethan whispered and told her they had to be quiet so that they didn't wake me. He got out of the bed and I watched them walk out of the room hand and hand. I smiled to myself and just after I fell back to sleep they came back. They sat on the floor with their backs to me. Ethan whispered as he pretended to read the extremely large book to Erica. He told her a silly story about three baby birds and their mother. In a very kind way he told the story about his mother and his brothers. He said there was a beautiful songbird who was very lovely and everybody always said how lovely she was. One day she met a buzzard, who immediately fell in love with the beautiful songbird. Nobody liked the buzzard because he was different, but the songbird loved the buzzard very much. One day they had an egg to protect, and the buzzard wanted to fight off all predators, but the songbird didn't want war so she hid the egg. Erica clapped at the story and Ethan reminded her that they had to be quiet. He told her that buzzard brought her another egg, and the songbird fell in love with the egg as if it was her own. Then they had another egg and that egg was him. Erica giggled, as she listened to him tell her how the little chickies practiced karate, scratched the ground for worms, and jumped on the Buzzard's head and ran to the songbird to protect them. In a very light hearted and funny way he explained to Erica how sad he was growing up cause the buzzard and the song bird could never figure out how to get along. He said this made all the little chickies sad. He said one chickie would do karate on big trees. One chickie was very kind and gentle cause he understood the songbird's pain. The last chickie was very sad, but he could fry up some mean worms and twigs. He made the songbird happy with his fancy worms. The last chickie was sad because of all the fighting. Then one day he met a chickie who kept jumping on his head. Every time the last chickie looked around the new chickie kept messing with him and she wouldn't leave him alone. At first the last chickie was mad, but then he realized he wasn't mad at all. The last chickie realized that the new chickie made him very happy and he loved having her around. The new chickie was very scared to be honest with her new friend and she tried to fly away. Do you know what the last chickie did? He asked Erica, she shook her head no with the biggest smile. He grabbed Erica and tickled her, he grabbed the new chickie like this and he loved her up and begged her to stay. The last chickie grew into a buzzard and the new chickie is the most beautiful songbird ever. Now they have a chickie named Erica and they're waiting for the next egg to hatch. Erica continued giggling she had no idea what her daddy just said to her. I closed my eyes when they got up. Ethan kissed me then he made Erica give me a juicy kiss. "I know you ain't sleep. You stopped snoring." He said kissing me again.

Chapter 20

Ethan

"How did you find her?" I asked Troy.

"It may take a minute but I find people." He said irritated. "My baby momma makes sure of it!" He mumbled.

Malcolm closed the door behind him, "we ready?"

"He knows that Cat is compromised he won't go there."

"We're going to make sure of that." Malcolm said deadly serious.

We got in Troy's car in silence. "Malcolm, please remember she's just a female mixed up with this fool. She doesn't know about Amber." Troy said looking at his cousin.

"He killed my child, tried to kill my Queen, I'd kill his dog if it sniffed in my direction." Malcolm said directly.

"Be cool Malcolm. Franklin wants to go in on his whole family, don't move too fast." Troy said.

"As long as Sammy is mine!" Malcolm said.

We parked on the corner across the street from Cat's place. Troy pulled out his papers and looked at the license plate on the car in the driveway. "Malcolm you stay here."

Malcolm blew air, "I'm going! I'm gonna choke the life out of her too!"

Troy looked at Malcolm, "if you ever want to get Sammy you're going to have to calm down. Stop being so emotional and think about this. Blu and I are going to go. You keep an eye out for him."

Troy and I got out of the car. It was quiet and we could hear music as we approached the door. I knocked on the door listening for how secure the door was. I could kick this door open if I needed to. "Who is it?" Cat called out.

"It's me."

She opened the door quickly, she was sweating and in her exercise clothes. "Blu?" She said with big eyes. I walked in the door with Troy right behind me. "Come in?"

"Where's your boyfriend?" I said while Troy looked around the room.

"I don't know, what's the big idea trying to out me in front of the police? Were you jealous?"

I tilted my head at her, "Jenise told me what you tried to do. I could kill you right now, this is not a social visit."

"What's wrong with you? Blu, it's me! The woman you asked to be your wife! Now you're acting like I slept with your friends and people. What did I do that was so horrible that you suddenly dropped me like I was a bad habit? We were in love."

Troy folded his arms and smiled real big like he was going to enjoy this. "Do you even hear half the things that come out of your mouth? I was rebounding from Jenise when you and I started messing around. Out of appreciation for your kindness I tolerated you gradually moving yourself in to my place. Jenise showed up with a boyfriend and what can I say, I choked. You didn't try to get to know my family, I told you, you needed to do better. You quit your job you didn't get fired. Then you speak to my wife like you did. You attempted to harm my children!" I didn't realize I was moving closer to her until I realized my hands were around her neck choking her. Troy's call back to reality is what brought me back. I released her. "Now you're living off some wannabe punk who's had the gall to come up against my family! You sent him to my house!"

Cat was crying, "no I didn't!"

"You're the reason he tried to break into my house, knew what car Malcolm drove, and someone shot at Troy!"

"What?" Troy said angrily, "my momma was in the car. CHOKE HER!"

"No! No, I didn't. I don't know where you live." She pleaded.

"But you told him about Malcolm's car, and me?" Troy said trying to pull back his anger.

"I was just talking, I didn't know it meant anything."

Troy clapped his hands real loud and the sound echoed off the walls. "You better be happy I don't hit girls!" He squeezed his fist. "You better be happy my momma wasn't hurt otherwise I could careless about my rule."

Cat looked at Troy with big eyes. "Troy I'm sorry, I didn't know. I wouldn't intentionally hurt you." She was looking at him the same way she looks at me. I've always seen it, but for whatever reason I ignored it before.

I frowned at her, "and your crush on Troy!"

"Eeewwllll! You nasty! Blu I didn't know about that." He said backing up.

"I know," then I looked at her. "You got with this kid and you ran your mouth. You knew who my realtor was. You're so busy thinking you have the upper hand with this kid that you didn't notice he was working you for information. You stupid trick!" Cat kept crying and apologizing. True she had no idea, but she never ran her mouth so much about her past with me. Only if I asked and I guess that was the difference.

Troy took a picture off her bookshelf. "Who's this?"

"Sammy's family."

"Slowly tell me each person's name." Troy held the picture in her face.

Cat gave him information like he asked. Troy put the picture in his pocket he gave her the frame and told her to put another picture in there before anyone noticed it was missing. Cat kept staring at me with pleading eyes. I could smell her desire mixed with her sweat from across the room. It used to be a welcoming aroma, now it smelled like putrid fish! He walked to the door Cat grabbed my hand kissed it and fell on the floor, as she knew I might hit her. She tearfully told me that she still loved me and that she was going to be waiting for me. Troy pulled me out the door; I guess my intolerance was all over my face.

****

The bed was shaking, at first I thought it was a small earthquake but when the shaking kept going I realized it was Jenise. I thought she was shaking her leg, but she didn't respond to me. I popped up and even though it was dark I could see her eyes focused on me. She was trying to quietly breathe. I asked her if it was time and she shook her head no. That's when I realized this was early, four weeks too early. Jenise watched my face like she was looking to me to tell her this was going to be ok. I kissed her gently and I told her she's perfect, and everything was going to be ok. I told my momma that I was taking Jenise to the hospital to get checked out cause she was having some pretty strong contractions. My momma got up lightning fast and went in my room to Jenise. She touched her face and hugged her just like I did. Then she said she was going to take Erica next door to my grandparents and she would meet us at the hospital. Jenise was quiet the whole way to the hospital, which made me nervous. As she was getting on the bed her water broke and Jenise started crying really hard and loud, she was scared. Seeing her break down made me feel so helpless. Her doctor came in the room ready to go. She checked her and she said the baby was going to come today and not to worry because she was 36 weeks almost 37 and the baby could survive perfectly fine at this point. That helped Jenise calm down. I called her momma from the hospital and she had just gotten off the phone with my momma. She was worried and said she was coming as soon as she could. I told her I would have a ticket ready for her and Stephen whenever they got to the airport. Then I called my receptionist, even though it was the middle of the night, I asked her to get the tickets and call all my appointments for the rest of the week and to let them know I would be unavailable. I rubbed Jenise's back and everything she asked me to do until she asked me to stop. She labored all day, and that evening she started pushing. I expected to see a little baby resembling a premature image. The doctor said, "whoa! Folks your body said this one is going to be too big so let's kick him out early." She held up a big and screaming undeniable baby boy. Jenise looked at me for a reaction, we honestly thought we were having another girl. My momma started crying and reaching for the baby because we were both in shock that they said it was a boy. I have a son! A little man! Immediately I wanted to cut all of the hair off his head. He looked exactly like Erica and I wanted him to look more masculine. He stopped crying when the doctor put him in my momma's arms. I reached for my camera and took pictures. The look on Jenise's face when she held our son for the first time was priceless. I could see her love for him already, and she wasn't as spaced out this time around. The doctor had warned us of low birth weight since he was early, but clearly this boy was an eater and was on his way to hugeness. He was early and weighing in at almost seven pounds. He looked at me with a serious face as I stared back at him. It was a little me, and my momma confirmed that he was. Janise's parents made it in the morning. She was surprised as well that he was so big. She said he was going to be a big boy if he would've stayed in to full term. He had no problem latching on like we were warned that he might, when they tested him they said he was definitely premature, but he was perfectly ok. When the nurse asked us about circumcision, Jenise looked to me. I agreed to it and the nurse put in the paperwork. I felt like little E looked at me with a frown. The nurse wheeled him away, and when he came back he was mad and sucking on his pacifier hard. When Jenise and I were alone she exhaled and said she was afraid something was wrong with him and that's why he was coming early. She said now she sees he was just impatient.

Jenise

A little man. Even his cry is different than Erica's. Even though he's so little he's so big. He wants to eat all day. He eats and then he wants more, most babies lose weight after they're born he continued to gain weight rapidly. It was like he told me to feed him and not to stop no matter what. Erica is full of kisses for him and she shows him all of her toys. As soon as she saw me feeding little Ethan she didn't want me anymore. She kept saying baby's milk in her baby language. Plus Raynel and Ethan's grandparents keep her pretty full. Nana and Raynel say he's just like Ethan was. My mom and Stephen were excited to have one of each. My mom kept watching me and asking me how I was doing. I told her I felt a lot better this time; she kept hugging me and kissing me.

Some how she was always around when I would be staring at Raynel's liquor cabinet. I missed drinking terribly and nothing would've celebrated the birth of a MAN from my womb more than a glass of wine. It doesn't matter; Ethan says the baby needs to nurse for now so I still can't drink. This boy acts like he's trying to suck me dry though. It's like he knows that if he tries to nurse and I'm on the dry side to cry and then my milk comes RUSHING in. He's gained so much weight in such a little span of time. Ethan's still cooking all his heavy cream sauces and rich foods. Even my mom and Stephan gained weight from eating Ethan's food. Where I think EJ nurses so much he's gaining my weight for me and I keep shrinking. I'm not complaining about that part at all. Running around behind two babies is definitely a lot of work, so I guess it's justified. I feel like I'm running even with all this help. Ethan's grandparents take Erica during the day. They go to the zoo and anywhere else they can think of regularly. My mom and Stephan help with EJ. Today my mom and Stephan are going to South San Francisco to spend the day with friends from my mom's old congregation. Raynel went to work; I kissed Erica and sent her on her way with her Gram and Grampy. My mom kissed me and told me she would be back later. When everyone was gone I looked at EJ and he watched me. I bathed him while I waited for him to get hungry which didn't take long. I nursed my beautiful baby, watched him watch me. He seemed to know I was putting him to sleep so he fought to hold on as long as his little body would allow him to. As soon as he passed out I tried to calm my breathing. I went in the kitchen and I made a little breakfast. I kept breathing, I needed someone to show up or call me. Tears came to my eyes as I felt myself giving in. I told myself to stick to a small taste of just wine. I started to reach for a bottle then I ran out of the room. I laid on the bed and cried, disappointed in myself I returned to the wine cabinet. As I reached for the bottle again the phone rang. I tried to clear the sound of my quandary from my voice. It was Ethan and he was calling me to check in like he normally does. I tried to sound happy and upbeat, but he wasn't buying it. "What's wrong?"

"I'm wrestling with myself." I said in defeat.

"Can we give the baby three months?" He pleaded, "I know it's hard. Remember I'm right here with you. I had no idea how hard this is until walking it with you. We can do this Jenise." The walkie-talkie in his office made noise. "Hold on." He was listening for a minute. "Gwen is there."

"Where?"

"There, she's walking up the stairs right now. Let her in, then let me talk to her."

I went to the door surprised cause Gwen doesn't come here. When I opened the door Gwen was barely knocking. She looked relieved that I answered. "What time does she come home? I don't want to be here when she does." She said to me.

"Hi," I hugged her then I handed the phone to her. She spoke to Ethan, rolled her eyes, and then gave me back the phone. Ethan told me he loved me and he would be home as soon as he could.

Gwen brought an outfit for EJ and an outfit for Erica. Then she smiled, "how much longer are you down?"

"I go to the doctor in two weeks. Everything should be good to go." I said.

"Birth control?" She asked

"I'm going back on the pill."

"Ok so class is in session." She smiled real big. She took a book out of her bag. "You're coming back with a vengeance if I have anything to do with it."

My brain was swirling around with everything we went over. She buys books, etc. anything that talks about sex. She tries what she reads and then she shares her notes with me. Talking to her did redirect my craving to my husband instead of the bottle. Gwen and I laughed and chatted about everything. She held EJ with a ton of pride. She kept kissing him and smelling him. I asked her if she thought she and Tag were going to get married. She frowned and said a definite NO! She said Tag is just her tester, she said she didn't see forever with him. I asked her why she said that. She said he's used to females falling all over theirselves for him, bending over backwards to be with him. She said he thinks too much of himself to be the kind of husband she needs. She said she wants to marry a good guy, but she wasn't ready to meet her good guy yet. Since she has a taste for the bad boy right now she should at least make it work for her.

Ethan

You know that feeling when you feel like you're forgetting something? I started feeling that way last night. I spoke with my father as usual. He thanked me for bringing the kids to see him. Tess decided that we all needed to rally around my father so he could interact with all of his grandkids last weekend. My father actually smiled and more than once. I cooked and it was a good time. Erica loves her Poppa, and she has his undivided attention. Jenise was able to keep Gwen on good, for the most part, behavior.

This morning I sat and stared at Jenise for a long time while she slept. Our house was coming along and everything was happening the way it should. The house was being remodeled from the pipes up. Jenise is really excited, and Timothy and my Uncle Dale collaborated on the remodel consulting mostly Jenise. When I told her she couldn't have these fancy and ridiculous fixtures cause they took us over budget, somehow my father volunteered to cover any over budget cost. Jenise loves being spoiled and it wasn't hurting anything so it was fine. I just wish I could shake this feeling. I called Malcolm once I got to the office. He was in his office about to go out to meet with Victor and Troy. I asked him how my little cousin was doing and he said she was mad at him as usual. When I asked him what he did he said same thing as usual. He said he was going to sit Amber down tonight and completely "punk out" as he called it. He said she had her dance class tonight so she should be calmer. I wished him well on that attempt.

I don't know if I gave my weird vibes to my brothers but we ended up sending everyone home early and quitting. The housing market has tanked in this 80's economy, so I rented Jenise's house out. I drive by it randomly from time to time to make sure the house still looked nice at least outwardly. Then I drove a few blocks over to our old house. The real estate office did their job and made sure we had quality renters in all of my properties.

I was talking to my grandfather who was too tickled about his conversation with Erica about the baby, when Leonard pulled up. We were talking business until he looked at his watch and said it was time for him to head over to the apartment before Amber got home from school. I told him Malcolm said she had class tonight. He said that was right. He smiled and said he needed to go see his girl and then he'd go over to the apartment. Jenise was sitting at the table when I walked in the door. She was talking to my grandmother making her laugh as usual. She had a glass with what looked like it was grape juice, but I picked up her glass and took a drink to be sure. Then I kissed her hello also checking for alcohol. I made dinner, I put every heavy cream sauce in this decadent meal, no alcohol and one more week without my woman was wearing on my soul. I get it! I get it! This is hard! Something has got to give! I did my best to stay away from Jenise who was all personality tonight and I wanted to eat her alive. I heard my walkie-talkie in the other room. When I walked in the room I heard people yelling and going off. "Leonard's down! Leonard's down!" Fuzzy roared through the device. "I'm on his man's tail!" Malcolm roared through the mouthpiece. "I'm right behind you!" Troy roared. "I see you, we're right behind you!" Victor's man roared. "Fuzzy! Please make sure she's not inside!" Malcolm sounded like he was on the verge of tears. I couldn't pull my shoes on fast enough. I grabbed my walkie talkie, "where am I going?" I said.
"Blu?" Malcolm asked.

"Yea, I'm here."

"I don't know if Amber is in this car or in the apartment!" He said, "for their sake they better hope she's not in that apartment. IF ONE HAIR IS OUT IF PLACE!"
"The baby with her?" I asked hurrying out the door as everyone looked at me with questioning eyes.

"Yes," he said weakly. Then Malcolm growled.

Dito pulled up as I came down the stairs. He said Franky was following them and this was all out war. When we got to the apartment Fuzzy was still outside holding Leonard crying his eyes out. There were a couple guys down but not dead by Leonard's feet. Best I could tell these idiots thought they could over power Leonard and he broke them down when someone else opened fire on him. Two pops later,

Dito grabbed Fuzzy and they took the elevator while I skipped stairs up to the top. The door was wide open. Everything thrown about all over the apartment. My heart slowed down and I scanned the room. If I saw the slightest drop of my family's blood! Every room was torn up, if Amber tried to hide anywhere in here there's no way she was successful. Fuzzy found Amber's *Dear John* letter on the floor. He read it over the walkie-talkie. Malcolm said they could still have them. He said they pulled into a garage and he was going in. Fuzzy told him to wait for us, and Malcolm said it was *too late*. He didn't respond anymore. I asked Franky where they were. He said they were in West Oakland. I knew where he was describing. Fuzzy didn't want to leave Leonard. We told him he had to come the police were coming. My Uncle Tim's voice was clear and angry. He wanted to know where his child and grandchild were. "MALCOLM! WAIT! WAIT! MALCOLM!" I couldn't tell who was yelling but it was all out chaos. When I pulled up I could see the gunshots lighting up the rooms in that house. I heard screams then silence. A guy tried to run out the house holding his chest. Fuzzy grabbed him like a rag doll and threw him back in the door as he shot him. Dito and I secured the outside of the house. When I crept into the house I called out to Franky and he called out that they were upstairs. People were all over that house. Malcolm was breaking Sammy with every hit. He swore he didn't have Amber. The police were coming we told Malcolm to finish him and to come. Malcolm looked like he had lost everything and he wasn't letting him go easily. Franky told Malcolm we were going to check her friend's houses. Malcolm said she wasn't there. He didn't believe Sammy and he had no real reason to. As much as I wanted to personally snatch Sammy from the opposite end, I told everyone to fall back this wasn't discreet. Troy and Fuzzy were losing it. Dito was completely red, I told him we had to find Amber. Franky asked where Cat was, I told him to follow us. Uncle Tim chirped again asking where his child and grandchild were. "We're still trying to find her sir." I didn't know what else to say.

"MALCOLM IS DEAD! HE HAD ONE JOB! ONE JOB TO PROTECT WHAT'S MINE! AND HE'S FAILED ME FOR THE LAST TIME!" Uncle barked into the walkie-talkie.

"I understand, but she may be hiding. She left a note at the apartment." I said hoping that offering calmed him some.

"He better hope for his sake that she is. Report to me IMMEDIATELY!"

"Yes sir!" I said. When we got to Cat's, Dito didn't wait for us, he kicked the door open and charged in. Cat was sitting on the couch like she was waiting for someone. It was after two in the morning at this point. He had her by her hair and demanded to know where Amber was. Cat tearfully said she didn't know. Cat kept her eyes on me as I took in the room. There was a play pin in the corner and a few items that weren't there before. "You were going to keep my cousin."

"I didn't know who the girl was but they were supposed to be bringing me a little boy and possibly the mother hours ago. He's dead?" She watched my face.

I picked up my walkie-talkie, "Sammy doesn't have Amber. She's hiding." I looked at Cat, "you didn't tell Sammy we knew where you are?"

She shook her head no, "why would I?" Her eyes pleaded with me. "Blu..."
"Either fix this door or run. This is going to get ugly." I said then I walked away.
Dito came out the house hotter than fish grease. "They were going to kill her!"
"Her hot temper worked to our advantage." I said.
"Amber is ok, where is Malcolm?" Pops asked.
"He's in custody, I couldn't get him to stop." Troy said in defeat.
"How many did we lose?" Pops asked.
There was silence for awhile, "just Leonard." Troy tried to say above his emotions.
You could hear everyone breathing. "Did anyone contact Eugene?" Pops asked in a
heavy voice. No one answered. "Blu where are you?"
"West Oakland." My brothers looked at me. They knew if I told him we were
walking away from Cat's and she was still alive they'd make us go back.
"Go to Eugene." He commanded.
"Yes sir."
Dito asked why we were going to Eugene's. He got quiet when I told him that
Leonard was his son. Dito said he didn't want this for his son and neither did I for
mine. Franky parked behind us. Eugene buzzed us in and I got a lump in my throat.
How do you tell a man his son is no more? I just talked to Leonard hours ago. When
we got to the door Eugene's stare gave me chills. He asked which one and when we
said Leonard he slumped and dropped his eyes to the floor. He turned around and
shut the door in our faces.
Franky gave me a ride and Dito went home since he was close to home out here in
the city. We rode in silence. When I came home Jenise was up nursing the baby.
She was crying my tears for me. She quickly put the baby to bed and then she came
for me. At first I was trying to ignore what my insides were screaming for until
Jenise took us there. She ignored my hesitation and put my hands on her. She didn't
even know what happened but the devastation in my face was clear.
****
When Malcolm sat down he looked defeated. He shook his head, "I can't believe
I'm in here."
"Do you have a plan?" I asked him trying to refocus him.
"Blu! They're moving me to the county jail, they got me. What's there to plan?" He
shook his head.
I looked at him irritated. "If you don't stop all this sissy whoa is me stuff! We got
our team on top of it. Look at where you're sitting? We're in the chief of police's
office. You're family is here! Suck it up man! I've got a plan if you don't."
Malcolm stood up. "How's Amber?"
"Sophia says she's ok. This is a lot on everyone." I snapped my fingers, "focus. I've
got a reading list for you. Even if you don't technically have the degrees behind
them doesn't mean you can't have the knowledge. College is in session."
"Should I propose?" Malcolm said still lost in his thoughts. I waited for him to get it
together. When he looked at me he exhaled. "School?"
"Yes, make sure your business keeps growing. We can't continue like this. I don't
want this for my children, do you? All this over some rocks and powder, it don't

209

seem worth it. You gotta know how to do more than push rocks."

Malcolm looked at my eyes, "you think I'm going to be in here that long?"

"Not as long as you could but longer than I want you to be." I said honestly.

Malcolm took a deep breath. "Ok..."

He said it needs to be business as usual for Troy. He said he needed to lean on Amber for the shop. I told him I could run that for him and he said he needed her hands in there, I was too busy. I knew he was also testing to see if Amber would double cross him.

Jenise

I couldn't even cry. I took it like a champ. I drove straight to Ethan's office. It seems like a lifetime ago that I worked here. My office still has my name on the door, "Jenise Wright." I opened Ethan's door and let myself in. He looked surprised and happy to see me. He hugged me and then I started laughing. You know that laugh when it hurts too much to cry. "So the doctor says I'm pregnant, that's why it's been six months and no period." Ethan's mouth fell open. "Yep, so I figure that one night did it. And I've been taking the pill all this time for no reason. It's not my fault if this kid comes out drunk! I didn't know!" I put my arms around myself. "I still can't believe it!" Then I cried. Ethan put his arms around me and kissed my forehead. We were both in shock. "Oh and I deliver right after we move in. Unless this one comes early too."

"Thank you for loving me. I'm sorry Jenise this is all my fault." He said holding me.

"I guess I'm going to know what it's like to have twins." I tried to joke. "If you were ugly none of this would've ever happened!"

Ethan started laughing, "it's my momma's fault."

"No! It's Frank's! What's wrong with you? It's always the man's fault." I said burying my head in his chest.

"That's right, I forgot."

"We might as well have one more after this."

"Ok.... Why?"

"I might as well change my name to Irma."

"I think Jenise suits you just fine."

I put my arms around his shrinking waist. "One more and then we're done. Deal?"

"Let's talk about this when you're more rational."

"I am. I want to do the SURPRISE! We're, happy tears, pregnant once. I want to consciously choose it instead of having it chosen for me by you or my body."

Ethan nodded his head, "I understand."

"You also understand you're off liquor again too!"

He sucked his teeth, "Jenise!"

"If I gotta do it so do you!"

****

"Are you nervous?" I asked Grace watching her face.

"Yes and no," she shook her hand. "Yes, because of the whole big reveal after all of the secrets. No, because I have nothing to hide." She said confidently.

"Timothy's siblings and dad are really nice, and I hope once you and his mom get past the awkwardness of your first hello you two will hit it off. She's really nice, and Timothy's her baby. Her first born, when you have a son you'll understand what it's like." I said trying to explain it.

"I hope your right. I wish you were coming. I told her I was resting up and getting ready for Jade's wedding the following weekend. I told her also, that I couldn't expect Ethan's grandparents to watch my babies two weekends in a row."

Grace looked at Eric, and she kissed his cheek. "I'm getting pregnant as soon as we get married. You promised to have one with me."

"Eric and your baby will still be close in age. Heck Erica, and EJ are not too much older." Grace blank stared at me. "Of course, that's the dream any ways. To be pregnant with your sister." I smiled.

"Our dream anyways." She smiled.

Timothy and Ethan walked in with the kids. "We got to get going." He said looking at Grace.

"So are we going to work them in or rip the Band-Aid off?" She asked Timothy.

"I already told Amber and Malachi. It will only make it worse if we beat around the bush."

"You guys are coming back after the party right?"

"Yep," Grace said nervously grabbing Timothy's hand.

Ethan walked them out and then he took Erica with him as they went out to the grill. Eric was born perfectly fine even though I was drinking for the first part of my pregnancy. Good healthy weight and all his mental faculties so far. Eric and EJ stare at each other all the time. I already know they're going to be wrestling all over my house and I'm going to be yelling at them for being disobedient. I always imagined a big family since I came from such a small one. I never imagined having three babies back to back though. That part is a little hard. Erica is barely out of diapers, and then I have the two little ones. EJ has been trying to walk already though. It seems like he's trying to grow up too fast. EJ is a little man, always has been. I can see Eric following in his footsteps. We had dinner outside as a family and it was beautiful. We could see the fog from the city creeping up on us in the Berkeley hills. Ethan called the puppies as he put a plate down with the bones from our meat. We went inside and Ethan sat with the kids and read them stories while I nursed Eric. This is my family and this is my life.

Grace and Timothy came back looking whooped. Grace said Timothy's mom wasn't mean, but she kept watching her all night long. Grace got excited and she said now that Timothy's family was aware she wanted to start planning the wedding. Timothy shrugged and said ok. Grace and I squealed as we started making a list of the next steps. We were too excited.

****

Jade's wedding was beautiful. Grace and I took a lot of notes from their ceremony and reception. The look on Ethan's face when Amber introduced him to her boyfriend was scary. You would think Malcolm was his family member or something. Fortunately Malachi and Dito were able to calm him down while Amber was oblivious to her big cousin's reaction to her news. I went to the bar and I got a drink for Ethan and I. I handed him the drink and then I waited for him to drink before I took mine. I could tell he was done with the evening. He rolled his eyes at me and then he drank. I was sitting with Gwen when Nana came over. Gwen instantly got quiet and looked at her grandmother trying to determine whether she was in trouble or not. Nana scanned Gwen for a long time, then she told her to go get her a drink. Then Nana sat next to me, she patted my hand. She asked me how the children were. I told her they were good. She inhaled then she exhaled as she looked at me. I started shaking my foot cause it's like I was an open book and she was the only one who stopped to read me. She tried to smile at me, and then she told me I needed to see someone. She said babies and alcohol won't fix what needs a little tweaking. She told me the sooner I saw someone the better. I told her I've been doing a lot better. She pointed to my hand, she asked me did I have to have my drink or did I only want it. When I said I wanted it, she told me to pour it out. I started sweating, Nana patted my hand; and then she walked away. I was irritated.

Chapter 21

Ethan

I bumped Franky as the men of Grace's family approached us. "So you tell me, man to man. What type of man is your son?" Grace's father said to Uncle Tim.

Uncle Tim stopped talking and looked Grace's much shorter father up and down, then he tried to pull back a frown. "You've met my son, and you approach me to ask who he is? You're looking at me you should see my son. The apple doesn't fall far from the tree."

"That doesn't tell me anything." Grace's father snapped.

Uncle Jeff folded his arms and smiled. Uncle Tim chuckled to himself to remain calm. "I understand how you feel. One of my babygirls just got married. It makes you mad even though you're happy for her. You know exactly what type of husband you've been and you wonder about the man she's chosen. There's no one better than my son. But! If you would prefer to fight about it we can step outside, but I'm sure you want to look decent for your pictures. Take a deep breath, it's ok." He warned.

"It's one thing that she's marrying this guy she barely brought home, but they're moving to Chicago. She has no family out there. No one to protect her when he's acting like a jerk." He was so angry his chest was pumping up and down.

Uncle Tim smiled at him and put his arm around Grace's father's neck. "I know what you mean. My daughter and son in-law said I do, and then they ran off on their honeymoon. Then they went back to school. She's my sweet little angel, how can she hold up ok with this young guy cause we know how they act. My son appears to love your daughter very much. You should take some deep breaths before you approach him though. He doesn't have a daughter so he may not be as understanding about your approach."

"My brother is basically trying to warn you that if his daughter calls him he's not responsible for what happens." Grace's uncle said.

All of us started laughing. "You clearly have no idea who you're talking to. For your sake I hope she never calls you either." My Uncle Jeff said.

We were locked in a good old fashion stare down until Uncle Tim started laughing. I think he laughed to keep himself calm cause no one else laughed. Then Grace's aunts came and told everyone to take their places cause it was time to start. When we took our places Sophia stood with little Sasha and Andrew waiting to tell them when to go down the aisle. Timothy proudly took his momma's arm and stood next to his father. Grace's father said something and the three of them looked at him with the same look. Malachi chuckled and lightened the moment while Grace's mother told her husband to zip it. Uncle Tim gave Grace's mother a hug and welcomed her into the family all while watching Grace's father daring him to say anything. Sophia held on to the kids and asked if they needed to handle business first. Everyone looked at Grace's father. His wife snapped her fingers at him and told him to get it together. She told Sophia to start; Sophia released the kids who did their best to follow instructions as they walked down the aisle. Then Timothy and his parents went. Then Malachi walked Grace's momma down the aisle and took his place as the best man next to Timothy. Then the women and Grace joined us. I walked with Amber while her boyfriend watched from the audience. What I can't decide is whether I don't like him because I feel a sense of loyalty to Malcolm or if I just don't like him. Troy is way more relaxed about this fool than I am. Troy says that this chump is just a space filler for Malcolm and Amber needs to see that there is no one better than Malcolm for her. I say I want him gone before things get too deep. I don't know why they let Amber run around all wild while the rest of them are held tightly. My father would've never let this fool step foot on his property if she was Gwen. Erica better never bring some transitional guy home to me thinking I'm going to be ok with it. I was making myself upset thinking of all the ways I would kill the first boy who points his erection in my daughter's direction when Jenise stared at me until I looked at her. She asked me if I was ok, and I nodded. She was beautiful, momma did her hair, and although I wouldn't think to put a black woman in pink and such a light version of it at that, Jenise is stunning. She proudly stood next to her best friend adding a splash of color to the bridal party. The rest of them were the same complexion as Amber, outside of Jade who was just a little bit browner than Amber. Grace was a beautiful bride and I was happy for my cousin. During the mother son dance my Auntie Annette put her arms around her baby's neck and rested her head on his shoulder. She was not happy about him moving so far away. She kept asking Timothy to consider moving home sooner than later. She even kind of made it seem urgent. Timothy kissed his momma and told her they would be back. We showed out on that dance floor, all the Wallace's were front and center. Jenise and Grace had such a good time, as Grace never experienced all of us together before. All the cousins set the party off nicely. Grace's family was cool too and once they relaxed we all got along quite nicely. Grace was on the dance floor and Timothy was on the side comforting his momma who was sad because she was losing her son. No more summers where she would be the woman in his life, he had a wife and would soon have a family of his own. Jenise said Grace told her that seeing how Timothy's been with his momma she now sees why she wasn't brought around as much. Auntie Annette wasn't mean to Grace, but it was hard for her to let go of her son. Someone asked Malachi when he was getting married and if looks could kill. Auntie Annette told him he had plenty of time to worry about marriage later. Malachi nodded that he understood, his momma couldn't handle another woman coming and taking her baby away.

****

I stood in the mirror flexing. Not bad! Not bad at all! I smiled as I took myself in. Who knew that chubby little kid could ever have a life so sweet? A beautiful wife who loves me, three of the best kids, a good career where I get to be a jack-of-all-trades. I dabble in a little bit of everything. It seems like every time I turn around my father wants to open another business. Who knew owning something as simple as a gas station could be so tedious but so lucrative? That's just one avenue of all of the ventures that we have going on at once.

214

****

Jenise turned over; I knew she was going to look at the clock soon. This was going to be her first physical day back in the office. I came home one day and she was fed up with all of the babies. Diapers, pooping, feeding, she was over it. We found a preschool for Erica that would accept her just below their regular age requirements. My father demanded that someone be at the school day in and day out with his first born grandchild, so my cousin Edwina *volunteers* at the school even though my father pays her very well to be there daily. Once Erica was adjusted to school then Jenise felt confident about leaving the boys with my grandparents who lived next door to my momma and she worked not too far away. Jenise said she wanted to come back to a flexible schedule at first and then she'd go from there. At first I didn't want it and I was against it. Jenise was unhappy and I could see it. The straw that broke the camel's back is when I came home one day and she was depressed. As soon as she saw me she clocked out. She went up to our bedroom with a bottle and drank until I took the bottle away from her. "Oh right! I forgot to ask your permission to have a drink. Is it ok with you Mr. Wallace if I have a drink or eight?"

"What's wrong with you?"

"I need to get out of this house. I can't do all day every day babies, babies, babies! They cry, they whine, they poop, and they sleep! I didn't go to Stanford to be a housewife. Why would you think this is a fulfilling life for me?"

"What's wrong with taking care of our family?"

"Nothing, but there's more to me than being a maid!"

I was floored, "a maid?"

"Yes! You came home the other day. No hello, no hi, all you wanted to know is why Erica's toys were still out in the yard. You've got the money hire a maid."

"I guess I should pay for the things I want done right." Now why did I say that? Jenise's head whipped at me, "you must want to fight!"

I frowned at her, "don't be stupid."

"I want to go back to work. I'm not good here!"

"You're perfect and exactly what our family needs."

"What our family needs is a happy mom. If all you wanted was a stay at home wife you should've married Cat!" I threw the bottle at the wall and it shattered. "Another mess you think I'm going to clean up. I'm not going to do it!"

"How dare you sit there and talk to me like that! Is that what you want? You want me to go get back with Cat?"

"If all you want is a pretty little wife who wants nothing more than to sit at home and wait on you and you're children, YES!"

"Why do you have to be drunk to talk to me? I can't even deal with you right now!"

"Doesn't matter whether I'm drunk or I'm sober you don't listen. As long as you think your way is the right way you don't care. You don't listen to me no how." She started crying.

I exhaled, "your dramatics are worse when you drink."

"I'M NOT THE ONE WHO SHATTERED A BOTTLE ON THE WALL!" She

yelled.

I walked out the room and slammed the door. I walked outside and walked laps around the house. I stopped walking when I realized all the kids were outside mimicking me. These innocent little faces had no idea what was going on. I don't want them knowing about their mom's drunken states from time to time. I started running and they gave chase. The dogs laid back and watched us running around in the dark. I scooped up my kids and hugged them up. Erica put the boy's pj's out while I bathed them. She knew not to come in the bathroom while they were naked. She stood outside the doorway talking with us. When it was Erica's turn in the tub the boys played just outside the door and I made sure this girl who loves the water didn't drown herself. She was almost four and growing too fast right before my eyes. When all the kids were bathed, I read them a bedtime story and then I kissed Erica, while giving my boys high-fives goodnight. I cleaned my kitchen while I tried to think of argument after argument for why she needed to stay home. I was trying to fight a losing battle. She wasn't happy, and I was mad. I cleaned up the mess I made, and then I went to bed. Jenise cried on her side of the bed and I did my best to act unaffected by her tears. In the morning, I told her to call my father and ask him where he got his maid. She was hung over and not in the best mood. I slammed all my doors on purpose and went to work for a little bit. I didn't want Jenise to come back to this office on the off chance that Gregg was somehow watching this office and waiting for an opportunity to confront her. Franky had him roughed up real good after that last time he came. However, I knew better than to think that just because I didn't see him meant he had forgotten about her. I called Franky and Dito in and I told them we needed to build another office. They waited for me to finish before they spoke. I told them this office was fine for certain aspects of our business, but we needed to expand to a larger office. Franky read between the lines and told me he had office space for us in an office closer to the freeway basically on the opposite side of Berkeley from where we are now. He said that Jenise would have a bigger office there than she does here. Dito was all for it as well. Franky said he needed two weeks to get everything up to speed and then we could move right in. I called my momma and asked her if she would mind hanging out with her grandkids while I took my wife out to dinner. Of course she was happy to be with them, she said she would be to my house in an hour. On the way home I kept asking myself if I was doing the right thing by giving in. When I walked in the door, Jenise was waiting with another bottle in her hand like she couldn't wait to get upstairs. I took a deep breath and I told her to put the bottle back. When she started to argue I raised my voice and told her to GO PUT THE BOTTLE BACK! All of the kids froze and looked at me with big eyes. Jenise rolled her eyes and did as she was told. Then she stood in the dining room with her hands on her hips and tears in her eyes. I told the kids Grammy was coming to visit with them. Jenise looked surprised then angry. I told her to go upstairs and to get herself ready so that we could leave when my momma came. I decided to keep it simple and make a couple of homemade pizzas for my momma and the kids. My momma buzzed at the gate as I was taking the pizzas out of the oven. I kissed the kids then Jenise and I left. We rode in the car in silence. When the waiter asked if we would like to start with a cocktail, I told him wine would be fine, as Jenise had her mouth open to order a drink. I chose a nice Chardonnay to sip on while we chose our entrees. Jenise sat there glaring at me. "So this is what you're going to do now? When you're not happy about something you're going to drown your sorrows in a bottle of liquid courage? You want to be treated like an adult then act like one. As adults we use our words, speak." I sat back and watched her face turn all kinds of colors. "I have tried talking to you, but you don't listen. If it's not your way then it's no way. You want me to play some Suzy Homemaker character from the fifties then I figure I might as well play the roll completely. Take care of the kids during the day and drink my sorrows away at night. I was just playing the role sweetheart." She sarcastically grinned.

"I'd believe that if drinking wasn't your answer for everything. Eric sat up on his own, let's drink to that. Erica didn't wet the bed; let's drink to that. I changed my nail color, let's drink to that."

"This is coming from the man who made me drink when I didn't want to! Don't start none, won't be none!"

"Ok, are you ready to order?" Our waiter asked not noticing the tension between us. "NO!" We said in unison.

"At least we agree on something." Jenise said rolling her eyes, folding her arms, and sitting back in her chair.

"You're that unhappy with me that you'd rather wake up every morning with a hangover than be happy with the family that I provide us with?"

Jenise deflated a little as she picked up on what I said. "Ethan," she said gently. "You are a wonderful husband and father. It's nothing against you. Me going back to work has nothing to do with you."

"What about when you decide to have another baby? You going to start work to stop it again?"

She put her head down as she tried to pull it together. "My sister...." She started crying. "Grace is having a hard time, once she makes it past the first trimester I will get pregnant again, but I will not stop working. Plenty of women work and have careers. I'll be my own boss so I can dictate when my schedule will be."

I touched her hand; I know the fact that Grace and Timothy are having a hard time getting their family off the ground was affecting Jenise as if it was us. I couldn't fault her for feeling that way. When Dito and Tess miscarried with their last child you would've thought it was my child that was lost. It brought up all those feelings I try to keep buried. "Ok, let's start over." Jenise looked at me. "Let's have this conversation over."

"Ethan I would like to go back to work." She said watching my eyes.

"What about our family?" I watched her.

"Erica is in preschool, and the boys will be with your grandparents, with your mom helping out as much as she can."

"Are you rejecting me? The house? I need to understand."

"I'm only rejecting the stay at home part. I want to be more than just a mother and a wife."

I took a drink of my wine. "You want Wright or Wallace on your door?"

Jenise smiled really big, "would it offend you if I kept my business name as Wright?"

"It doesn't matter."

She leaned forward and kissed me. Now... Now, she was happy. She happily ordered her food and the rest of the evening went well.

This morning I told myself that this wasn't personal. When Jenise's alarm went off she got up excitedly. She got ready for her day with the biggest smile. We took the kids in their separate directions and then Jenise's eyes got big as we pulled up to our new building. We parked in the gated garage and then we went up to the almost top floor where our new office was. Most rooms had glass walls; I figured that was so that the light from the Bay shined through the office. Jenise's office was next to mine, the wall between our offices was glass; with a regular wall on the opposing sides. She made silly faces on the window at me, and then she got Windex to clean the smudges she left on the glass. Jenise looked out the window with a smile watching the water for a minute. I saw her pray for the first time in a long time, and then pull books off of her bookshelf. She spent most of her day reading and then I watched as she picked up her phone calling someone from the back of her book. She wrote down information and then she came to my office. "I need to take a class." She announced. "The books I have are kind of dated. I called information and got the number to the company who published the books. They're releasing a new books, but its part of a class. The class sounds interesting, it talks about incorporating computer design. It...."

"What are you building to?"

"I just missed the class in California. They're going to call me with information about the next classes." She smiled nervously.

"Are you done?" I asked irritated.

"For now." She said smiling and walking backwards out the door. Not even a full day in and she comes to me with this nonsense. When her phone rang Jenise excitedly answered it. It looked like she was writing for a long time. When she hung up she smiled at her list. When she turned towards me I was already staring at her. She called me and went over the dates and locations, Chicago, Phoenix, New York, Charlotte, and Tulsa. I hung up the phone, I had no words.

Jenise

"This is Jenise." I said answering the phone.

"Hello Jenise this is Emma Barnes how are you sweetheart?" Her voice smiled.

"Hello! I'm good, how are you?"

"I'm so happy you're back. You're timing couldn't be more perfect. I want to open a New York store. I need your expertise."

"Meaning you need me to come out to New York?"

"Of course! I'll pay you for your time, I'll pay for your flight and hotel."
"I took some time off to have my kids. I feel a little rusty. I was going to take a class as a refresher. If you wouldn't mind there's a class in a couple of months in New York. If Ethan's ok with it, maybe I can kill two birds with one stone."
"Of course sweetheart, whatever's easiest for you and your family."
We chatted for a little longer. I told her about my kids, Emma was quiet and then she told me she was happy for me. I asked her about her travels over the past few years. As usual she travels the world like I go to the grocery store. We talked for awhile then we got off the phone. I picked up the phone and I called Grace. I needed help thinking of how to present this to Ethan. When Grace answered the phone she sounded really happy. My heart fluttered, she has been trying unrelentingly to make it to her second trimester and this time we were holding our breaths again. "I was hoping this was you. We just got home from the doctor. I'm officially seventeen weeks almost eighteen." We screamed into the phone.
Ethan looked at me, and when he saw my smile he went back to his meeting. "I'm so happy for you. When will you announce to your families?"
"This momma's boy called her from the doctor's office. I'm going to call my mother when we hang up. It's happening! Jenise! I'm going to be a mother! Timothy and I will live on forever!" She said with tears in her voice.
"I'm so happy for you. I'm giving you a hug through the phone. I wish you weren't so far away. I'd come over with goodies like you've always done for me. Are you sure you won't move back?"
"Not right now, my parents and Timothy's would be too much to deal with. Timothy's mom is his first love I guess, as it should be, but I'm his wife. When Annette and I get along my mother has a fit. It's always something, and being out here just he and I is different. We need the space to bump heads right now."
"Ethan and I still bump heads." I volunteered. "When should I start trying?"
"Give me a month or two."
"I'll stop taking my pill after my next period."
"You don't have to. I know you're just getting used to being back at work. You could wait."
"Grace I want to do this with you. I haven't had any control over my own life in years. I want to do this; it's going to be so exciting. For me it will be my first pregnancy. All first for me. Plus I don't want this baby spaced out too far from the others."

****

This man is trying to kill me! Ethan was acting like this is the last time we'd have sex. We put the kids to bed, made love, fell asleep, he woke me up, he knocked me out, he woke me up. I don't think I can cum any harder than right now. I wrapped my arms around Ethan as I tried to catch my breath. I kept kissing him and telling him I would be back in three days. Ethan's heart was pounding and I could tell he was holding something back. He had every number I could think to give him. I held on to him and when he was ready again I kissed him, I needed him to CALM DOWN! He could go, but I was tired. He let me sleep, but when I got in the shower he followed me. I wanted to complain, but honestly I love it. I knew when I came back he would be backed up and ready.

Franky laid on the floor in the nursery with the kids. He came over to help Ethan with the kids while I'm gone. I talked Ethan's ear off with excited energy the whole way to the Oakland airport. The girl at the check-in counter caught herself when I asked her whom she kept smiling at. Ethan never notices all these females who bat their eyes at him hoping he would look in their direction. I guess that's a good thing, but some of them are bold. I started frowning and then Ethan touched my cheek. We waited at my gate, Ethan said this was the first time we'd be apart since we got married, and then he looked at me and reminded me that he was trusting me. I kind of couldn't believe he thought I'd run from him now after all this time and three and a half kids. Oh yea, I think I'm pregnant but I haven't gone to the doctor yet. It's on my to do list of things to do when I get back. I kissed my husband one more time, and then I boarded my plane. As soon as we were in the air I went to sleep. Ethan basically kept me up all night. I woke long enough for my meal, then I went back to sleep. As soon as I stepped off the plane Emma was right there waiting with a smile. She said I looked exactly the same. I told her Ethan and I have that argument all the time, I swear I look different and Ethan swears I look the same. She said she agrees with Ethan. Emma took me to this dinner theater place. They had a whole R&B Soul Revue theme. We enjoyed our meal with good music. Emma took me to my hotel room. She said she would escort me to my class in the morning and she'd pick me up at the end. I called Ethan and I talked to the kids and then he and Emma discussed their agreement about my appearance. That night I realized this was the first time I've ever been alone. I was scared for half a minute and then I enjoyed the quiet. I sat in that bed thinking about my life. EVERYTHING changed when I kissed him. I love being Ethan's wife and the fact that he comes home to me. It just feels like I'm going to have to fight for more independence. I know he's taking it personal and this is about me. I called Ethan and he answered on the first ring. He and Franky were relaxing with a drink. The kids were in the bed. I told him I didn't want to interrupt, and he assured me I wasn't. We talked a little and then I could finally fall asleep.

In the morning Emma took a cab with me to my class. I confirmed the end time with her then I got on with my day. It was like grade school all over, everybody loved me. I learned a lot in the class and people were practically taking my business cards out of my hands. Quite a few of my classmates kept asking what I was doing after class. I told them I had plans, and they really didn't have to put on that they liked me. Everyone laughed as we walked towards the front of the building. Emma smiled at my group, and they took that as an invite to ask about our plans. Emma told them where we were going and they asked if they could join us. She didn't care. So six of my classmates joined us for dinner. When one of the guys asked where I was staying I quickly said I was staying with Emma and her husband. I didn't know this guy and I didn't feel comfortable telling him I was alone in my hotel. Then I took out pictures of Ethan and the kids. I proudly showed pictures of my husband who barely smiled in our family portrait. One girl said he looked very serious, I told her he was very serious most of the time. When the night was over, mister where are you staying put us in a cab. Emma told the driver to take us to some place, but it wasn't my hotel. When we got there we walked a few blocks over and then we took a car service to my hotel. Emma said that guy gave her the creeps. She said he was watching everything and he asked too many questions. I was relieved that I wasn't the only person who thought so.

The next day armed with new and more modern concepts I looked at Emma's plan for the new store. She said Tim and Annette were on board with her vision for the new brand for both stores. She mentioned that her brother Elmer Jr. was going to manage the store. We took a late lunch cause our creative juices were flowing. I was mid-sentence when I saw her. She was smiling painfully as she looked at me. I put my hands down and took a deep breath. I told myself to keep my demeanor the same and not to change as she approached us. The closer she got the clearer it became that she was going to hug me. I stood up and hugged Nohemi who immediately started crying. I rubbed her back, and then I introduced her to Emma. "You live out here now?"

"No, I'm actually moving to the west coast in a few months. I got a new position at the bank I work for. Meanwhile I'm training my replacement out here. How about you?"

"I came out for a training class and to meet with my client."

I could tell by the way she inhaled she was about to ask me about Ethan. "How's Ethan?"

"He's good."

She looked at my hand, "you're Mrs. Wallace?"

I got a lump in my throat. "I am."

She nodded, like she needed a minute. "You have kids?" Tears came to her eyes.

I found myself wanting to say no, "yes." I said quietly as tears came to my eyes as well.

"Do you have pictures?" She asked painfully.

I took out my wallet; Nohemi covered her mouth and cried a little as she looked at our family picture. "You have a beautiful family."

"Thank you, what about you?" I prayed she was happily married.

"No, I just broke up with my boyfriend. Moving back to California is me starting over." She took a deep breath to pull herself together. She tried to smile, "I'm happy it's you and not that Cat girl!"

I smiled, "thank you."

"It was nice meeting you Emma. Jenise take care." Nohemi said as she hurried towards the bathroom.

I excused myself and I followed her. I needed to make sure she wasn't exactly mad at me. I know it shouldn't matter at this point, but I couldn't help how I felt. I hugged Nohemi and we cried together really hard. I invited her back to our table. She said after Ethan took her home her depression got worse and worse. She explained to Emma that she lost her baby at seven months pregnant. Emma grabbed her other hand and tears poured out of her eyes immediately. The three of us sat there holding hands crying and listening to Nohemi tell us how hard the past almost six years have been for her. I secretly rubbed my stomach thanking my womb for never betraying me and losing one of my babies. Emma and I rode in silence. We couldn't discuss anything anymore. Emma kept crying and she said she'd call me when she was ready. She didn't come up to my room like normal. I hugged her really tight, cause it was clear that she was upset. When I got to the room I called Ethan in all out tears. He was so quiet you could've heard cotton hit the floor. I kept talking and talking until he spoke. He spoke slowly and he told me he couldn't wait for me to come home. He said that he and the kids missed me. I guess he had nothing to say about Nohemi.

Ethan

"Ethan, a Juan Rosales is here to meet with you."

"Send him in." I said searching for my difference in the sheets. The receptionist showed Juan in to my office. His eyes swept my office then his eyes locked on mine. "You came straight here?"

"That was Malcolm's instructions." He watched me.

I chirped Troy and I told him Juan was here. "Malcolm said you're going to be his intelligence. He seems to feel that you're trustworthy." Juan nodded. "Where are you going next?"

"To my lady."

I nodded, "of course. Let me get you on your way." I took out the folder. "Let's get your employment forms squared away."

Juan read each form thoroughly before he signed anything. While he took his time with the forms I went back to my other paperwork. "Signing bonus?" He raised an eyebrow.

"Malcolm said he's going to be trusting you with a lot. With that you can't be worried about small things. As part of your employment package there's a signing bonus that should initially set you up nicely. You can marry your girl and move forward with your plan."

Juan pushed his chair back from the desk. He got on his knees an started praying. He was thanking God in Spanish for blessing him. He stayed like that for a long time. I don't speak Spanish but I understand it. He got up with red eyes; he shook his legs as he signed his paperwork. Troy came in the door, "did I see you praying to Ethan?" He said with a smile in his voice.

Juan smiled at Troy as he stood up. "I'm a little overwhelmed." They shook hands hard.

"I have an apartment unit for you in my building if you don't have a place."

Juan roared deep and loud, he blessed Malcolm in Spanish. "Yes, it will only be temporary though."

Troy put keys in his hands. "Malcolm says you're our missing brother. That means I'd give you the shirt off my back, and you would do the same for me."

"What about him?" Juan pointed to me.

"Big brother."

"Yes, yes we're family. You girls done yet?" I barked. I had paperwork to do then I had to get to the airport to my woman.

Troy laughed, "let's get the paperwork together so you can show your parole officer that you got a job, etc."

I gave Juan his letter of employment, the check for his signing bonus. Juan stared at the check for a minute. Troy told him they were going to the bank to open a checking account for him. Then I gave him the envelope with cash in it. I told him Malcolm said it was pocket change. Then I went back to my work.

I watched Jenise's plane pull up to the gate. Just like I thought her eyes were swollen when she got off the plane, she's been crying all night and day about Nohemi. Her eyes softened when she saw my flowers. I don't allow myself to feel anything about Nohemi. She's a part of my past, and I don't want to get caught up in feelings about her. I can't run from my child no matter how hard I try, but I refuse anything more. I kissed Jenise then I made her look me in the eyes. "You have no reason to feel guilty! You sacrificed everything so that her child could have a chance. You paid the price already, don't take this on yourself. She has to get past it just like we have. You hear me?"

Jenise's eyes started clearing up, "yes *Big Daddy*." She smiled. I chuckled and hugged her tightly. "I brought the kids toys. Do you think that will help them forgive me for going away?"

I put my arms around her and squeezed her tight, "the kids are going to be happy to see you. All they need is you."

When we got to Erica's school, she threw her doll in the air and she ran top speed screaming "MOMMA! MOMMA! MOMMA!" Jenise smiled really big as she picked up Erica and kissed her. The boys had similar reactions.

We had a picnic dinner in the yard. We put the kids to bed together. Then we walked hand in hand to our bedroom. Jenise jumped on me pulling at my clothes. She locked on my eyes, "what do you think?" She said as she slowly took me in. "Survey says?"

Her warmth, extreme tightness, and slipperiness made me gasp. "You think?"

She kissed me then she smiled excitedly, "I think so! I'm excited." Then she locked in on me, that night she was all over me. She took everything I had until I had nothing else, which had never happened before. Then she rolled over satisfied with herself.

Jenise

"Gurl! I mean I understand! With a man that pretty I don't doubt that I would be spitting out all these pretty babies too. I just never thought of you as a baby-making machine. Last time I saw you, you had one. Now you're on number four. How many babies are you going to have?" Trinity said.

"This is it." I said rubbing my stomach.

Ethan walked out of the house with a tray. "Ladies, your beverages."

"Ethan do you have a brother as fine as you?" Chastity asked bluntly.

Ethan blushed, "I have two brothers, one is married and the other is single." Then he walked away before she could ask another question.

"You remember his brother, he looks just like him; but he got playboy written all over him." Trinity said.

"Oh yea!" Chastity said, then she took a drink of her drink. "This is so good!" She smacked her lips. "So..." She shot Trinity a look.

Trinity exhaled, "we talked to your father. He had no idea that you were married or have a family. He wants to see you." She said bluntly.

Fire blazed over me. "I don't want to see him right now."

"Why are you avoiding him?" Trinity asked.

"Hello! You know what happened." I said like it was self-explanatory.

"That was between him and your mom. She can divorce him, you can't divorce your parents."

"Yes I can, and I did. You two have no idea what it was like growing up with him as a father."

"My uncle was a good father to you. Shoot at least you had a daddy! Growing up with his sister as a mother was no picnic either." She said getting mad herself, "but we would never turn our backs on her like you've done him."

"Cause there's more to the story then you understand."

"Like?" Chastity asked.

I rolled my eyes, "it's none of you guy's business. He's your uncle and he should be able to be that."

"You're so wrong!" Trinity said, "when was the last time you went to service? You need to remember how to forgive and let go!"

I hopped out that chair like I wasn't pregnant. "OH SO I SEE! YOU TWO CAME OVER HERE TO JUDGE ME AND GANG UP ON ME!" I rubbed my stomach. "IT'S NONE OF ANYBODY'S BUSINESS HOW MANY KIDS ME AND MY HUSBAND DECIDE TO HAVE! ESPECIALLY IF I'M NOT ASKING EITHER ONE OF YOU TO SUPPORT THEM! WE CAN AFFORD TO HAVE THIS BABY AND TEN MORE IF I DECIDE TO CARRY THEM! THAT'S NONE OF YOUR BUSINESS! YOU'RE JUST JEALOUS! WHETHER I DECIDE TO SPIT IN MY FATHER'S DIRECTION AGAIN IS NONE OF YOUR BUSINESS EITHER! THE STUFF THAT HAPPENED IN STOCKTON IS NONE OF YOUR BUSINESS, AND YOU CAN'T POSSIBLY THINK HE TOLD YOU THE WHOLE STORY WHEN IT'S NONE OF YOUR BUSINESS! MY RELATIONSHIP WITH GOD IS NONE OF YOUR BUSINESS EITHER! YOU WILL NOT USE MY ATTENDANCE TO SERVICE AS AN EXCUSE TO JUDGE ME! IF YOU CAN'T GET IT TOGETHER I WILL THROW YOU OUT OF MY HOUSE AND NOT EVER LOOK BACK!" I said not even believing I went off like that without a drop of liquor in my system. I believe the baby made me do it.

Trinity put her glass down and stood up. "I am jealous! It's been a long time and trying to walk on the straight narrow has me dried up bitter and mean. Still doesn't take away from the fact that there's nothing holding you back from coming back to service. Comeback." She pleaded with her eyes.

"And I feel your father should at least get to see his grandchildren. Our father doesn't care about us; my kids won't have a grandfather. Your kids know your husband's family. What about us? And yes I'm jealous that you get to have SEX until you're tired of it with that fine husband! I want a husband! I want to have sex!"

"There's more to being married than just having sex." I rubbed my stomach.

"Do you get to have it?" Trinity asked, I nodded yes. "Do you love it?" I nodded yes, "the rest is just details."

"You better be careful before you slip up. Or worse, married to someone just to have sex."

"YOU GOT DOGS?" Trinity said with tears in her eyes.

All of the dogs slowly walked towards us then they faced the front of the house. A car came around the driveway. It was Frank; his driver hurried out and then opened his door. "Excuse me," I told my cousins.

I walked to the car; Frank looked me up and down. "Again?"

I smiled and rubbed my stomach. "Of course."

He shook his head, "you're not rabbits. Where's my boy?"

"Your son is right here, my boys are inside." Ethan said coming out to his father. Frank and Ethan walked inside, Erica ran outside to be with us girls. "Did you say hi to Frank?" I asked her.

"Yes," she said climbing into Chastity's lap.

"They call their grandfather by his first name?" Chastity asked.

"That's what he wants."

"Erica you are so pretty! How you get to be so pretty?"

"My momma," Erica smiled.

That night I was sitting in the bed reading my baby book tracking my baby's development. Each pregnancy has been different and Eric's was over not too long after I figured out he was there. I barely had a stomach with him, but he was still seven pounds at birth. This baby feels brand new even though I've done it before. I'm excited, and Ethan's excited that I didn't ask him to abstain from drinking this time. He just got back to his comfortable weight; even though I love his cuddly size I know he doesn't like it. I could tell he was dreading the words; he was completely shocked when I told him he could keep drinking. This time I don't want to drink, I feel really good. I know a lot of that has to do with the fact that I'm pregnant with my sister, and this is the first time I've chosen to be pregnant. Even the sex is different. I'm not as big as I was with EJ or even Erica. Ethan knows this is our last pregnancy so he better get all the pregnant loving he can while it's here. Somehow I seem to keep knocking him out though, I feel so powerful.

Ethan got in the bed and he asked me why my cousins have to flirt with him. I told him they were just playing. He said it makes him uncomfortable cause it doesn't feel like playing to him. I told him that was because he was so sexy they couldn't help theirselves. He told me he was serious, as if I was kidding. "Ethan you are so fine! Tell me you know it!"

"Goodnight Jenise!" He tried to sound like he was over the conversation.

I pulled him on his back. "Ethan! You don't know it?" I asked in shock.

"Goodnight!" He closed his eyes.

"Oh no! This won't do!" I got on top of him. "I need to go on record, excuse me sir if you could stop pretending you're sleep for this. I need your attention." I tapped his shoulder until he opened his eyes. "There's my beautiful baby." I smiled at him, while he blushed. "Ethan you are so fine that the first time I saw you I wanted to take my panties off and throw them at you." He chuckled, "Baby you are so fine! And then I got to know you and I couldn't help myself. You're beautiful inside and out! You are the only person who could make me do all of the unthinkable stuff I've done." I kissed him, "and then...." I shook my head, and licked my lips. "Then you put it on me!" He chuckled, while I laughed. "I love you so much, and I understand why someone else would want you, but you're **MINE**!"

****

"Jenise! He's here! Grace and the baby are doing well." Timothy said.

I screamed with excitement. "Timothy kiss her for me! CONGRATULATIONS! Tell her to call me as soon as she feels up to it."

"Hold on she's reaching for the phone."

"Niecy Pooh he's here! He's beautiful! He's mine!" Grace said crying, which made me cry. "He looks like both of us! I'm so happy! I'm a mom! I'm a mom!"

I was crying and Ethan came to my office to see what was wrong. "Yes you are! I can't wait to meet him."

"We're coming as soon as we can travel."

Chapter 22

Ethan

I kissed Jenise who was all smiles as she looked at the baby. "Hello Elaine! Welcome precious!" She said as she kissed the baby who was looking around taking everything in.

"Both of them boys were born with girl hair. Where's her hair?" I asked looking at her.

"That's just her way, Elaine is different." Jenise said still smiling at her.

The doctor knocked at the door. "Good afternoon Wallace's how's everything going?"

"Good!" Jenise sang.

"Your surgery was very routine. Your healing should go according to plan as well. I'm going to miss delivering all these pretty babies." She smiled at Jenise and the baby. Jenise was so focused on the baby I know she wasn't completely listening.

"You would think this is your first baby. It's so nice to see you so in love with your fourth child."

It was nice to see Jenise so in love with the baby. She hadn't responded to any of our children like this. I was trying to appreciate it and not question it.

****

"Hey son how was work?" Jenise's momma said bending down to greet the kids. They hugged her and then ran to the family room.

"Hey, how was work." Jenise said with the baby in her arms and she was all smiles. "It was good."

"I was going to make myself useful and make dinner but Jenise warned me not to step in your arena."

"He cooks too?" Trinity called out from the family room.

I looked at Jenise, "all you're missing is Gwen."

"I'm here big brother!" Gwen responded.

"Where's your car?" I called out, "where's all of your cars."

"Juan called and told us to put all the cars in the garage." Jenise watched my face.

I looked at Jenise's momma, "the kitchen is mine. Especially dinner, I will consider requests."

"I have a taste for roast. Can we consider that for tomorrow."

"Ooh mom Ethan's roast is melt in your mouth delicious too."

"Is that what my ladies want?"

"YES!" Trinity yelled from the family room.

Gwen looked at her, "so you're coming back tomorrow?"

"As soon as I get off work."

"Don't you have service tomorrow?" Jenise's momma said cutting her eyes at her.

"Um!" Trinity smiled.

"Right, take your behind to service!"

As I made dinner Trinity found an excuse to come watch me. Jenise and her

227

momma were in the family room with the kids. Gwen came in the kitchen watching Trinity the whole time. This is probably Gwen's first visit where we didn't get into an argument at all the entire visit. I know a lot of that has to do with the fact that she was watching Trinity. Trinity was going on and on about the fact that she loved watching a man in the kitchen. She kept leaning against the counters, and trying to show off. All the stuff Jenise didn't do to get my attention she was doing. Jenise was so preoccupied with the baby that she wasn't seeing any of this. I chewed back my irritation, whenever she asked me questions I looked at Gwen to answer. "I guess you don't talk much?" Trinity asked.

I looked at Gwen, "can you hand me the lemons and the oranges in the refrigerator?"

"I could do that for you daddy I'm right here." Trinity said opening the refrigerator and bending over. I looked at Gwen and she turned red matching her hair. "Here you go baby."

"I'm not interested." I watched her eyes.

"WHAT?" She gasped.

"You're doing too much! I suggest you go back in there with your family. Don't make me have to send you." Then I washed my lemons and oranges in the sink. Trinity left but Gwen stayed. A few minutes later Jenise came in the kitchen asking what happened, so I told her. She said Trinity didn't mean any harm. Gwen didn't say anything she stood there watching us.

****

Juan knocked on my door. "You got a minute?"

"Sure," I said.

"So Pamela Latour, who is she?"

"You're asking because?"

"Barb! She's been going to visit her a lot lately. Looks like she's getting out soon. Her sheet is pretty extensive."

"Ok," I said waiting for him to get to the part that brought him in here.

"Eugene has gone recently as well. I know he's been zeroed out lately. I was just wondering if he could be turning."

"Eugene is Leonard's father. He had unfinished business with Pam."

Juan sat there quiet for a minute as he processed. "Switching gears. This Charles character, Victor wants him gone. Does he have anything?"

"Nothing substantial, why does he want him gone?" I exhaled, "I'll talk to Victor, we got to let him hang himself."

"I'm leaving Friday, I'll be back Saturday night." Juan said watching my eyes. Malachi called earlier this week, he needed backup while he handled someone by his school. Juan and a couple others were flying out under fake names, handling business, and coming right back. Everything paid in cash no paper trail. "Right, do you think you'll need anything else?"

"No we got everything, we'll be there on time." Juan said walking out.

****

Malcolm walked out tall and although there was no smile on his face, it seemed as if he was. He and Troy hugged, patted each other really hard on their backs, and then he and Fuzzy did the same thing. He kept inhaling and exhaling. We gave each other a half handshake half hug greeting, then we walked to the car. Malcolm watched out the window as we drove away. "I'm never going back in there!" He said strongly.

No one responded or said anything at first. "You are a well read and educated black man now, there's no reason for you to ever go back."

"I need a hair cut," He said looking in the passenger side mirror on the visor. "Does Amber still have that fool at her place?" He asked wasting no time thinking about my little cousin.

"Yes, Malcolm maybe you should wait before you see her. You haven't been out an hour yet. You might be a little too raw for her right now." Troy said.

I looked at him in the mirror; Troy had concern on his face. "You're right! Your old grandma still kicking up dust?" Malcolm asked.

"Everyone pretty much avoids the house as much as they can. Renee says she's ready when you are. They've been fighting and she pulled a gun on Renee talking about Renee was stealing from her. She did that mess in front of the kids and everything. She pulled the trigger and then started laughing when she said she must've forgot to reload her bullets. Then she told Renee next time she wouldn't forget. That was the last time she came to the house." Fuzzy said.

"She can't stand me, she told my momma she was going to shoot me if I ever came back. She said I betrayed her with the whole Amber thing, and then she said she knows the girls been hiding at my place." Troy leaned forward. "Here's what I don't understand, the dock walkers are at least twenty strong. She got a couple of fools in there as stand-in pimps. What she need with her grand daughters?" Troy asked.

"If she would put on her own daughters, our momma's… Why would her grand daughters be safe? That kind of business you always need fresh and new. Obviously she lost her touch, she can't distribute properly." Malcolm said.

"Her product ain't even clean. All it took was for a couple of people to OD on her stuff and the word spread like wild fire. Nobody's messing with her." Troy said.

Malcolm was quiet for a minute, "if her product ain't moving. That should mean she's holding somewhere. Sounds like we need to take that off her hands." Malcolm said.

"What we supposed to do with it? Its cheap crap!" Fuzzy said.

"Dump it in the Bay. If we rob her, she gotta some how make up for that money. Maybe her supplier will take care of her for us." Malcolm said like he was talking about some person he didn't know.

Fuzzy leaned back shaking his head, "that's our grandmother."

"She's my enemy! She set me up! It's time to do what comes next, don't go getting soft on me now." Malcolm roared. It was quiet for a minute, "everything good on the Cardell side?"

"SMASHINGLY WELL!" Troy joked trying to get Fuzzy to smile.

Malcolm looked at me. "I need an audience with your father and grandfather, I've got ideas that I want to put into action. Thank you for getting Mitigated up and running for me."

"Anytime, Juan is a good worker. He comes in does his job. He asks questions from time to time. He's good at what he does."

"He still in the building?" Malcolm asked Troy.

"Just until he buys his wife the house she wants."

"Good! I'll be happy to see him when I can." Malcolm said watching the road. "I'm never going back in there! Never!"

****

I went home for lunch, Jenise was singing. I could hear her downstairs. I stood in the doorway watching her perform for Lanie. I couldn't help but want to ask what made this experience so much different from the others. She's in no hurry to drink, she enjoys breast-feeding the baby. At night she used to ask me to take turns with her, the baby always slept in the crib. Lanie is always in our bed. That's not such a big deal right now, but when our rotation picks up again Lanie's gonna be a problem. I stood there watching quietly. All the kids have Jenise's crazy laugh, just different versions of it. Lanie's is contagious just like Jenise and you have to join her. The two of them were so in love, I backed away from their moment and I went to the kitchen. Jenise heard me in the kitchen and called out to me. She came down with a very happy Lanie in her arms. Jenise kissed me and said I was home for lunch earlier than usual. I told her she never knows when I'll pop up.

Jenise smiled excitedly as she said Grace made it to her second trimester, but the doctor put her on bed rest. I told her that was a mixture of good and interesting news. I asked how she was supposed to be on bed rest with an infant? She shook her head, she said Timothy is like me and does as much as he can and it makes all the difference in the world. I looked at Lanie and I asked if I could hold her. Jenise frowned at my request as she gave me the baby. She asked me why everyone keeps asking her that. I told her because she isn't as sharing with Lanie as she was with all the others. She said it's probably because Lanie was so lovable she wanted to eat her up. I played with her for a little bit; I wanted to see if there was something different in this baby's eyes. I wasn't getting it, and I didn't want to seem like I was knocking Jenise for loving our child. It was just different. "Don't you go to the doctor soon?" I asked looking at the baby.

Jenise's hesitation made me look at her, "I went last week. You don't remember?" I looked at her waiting for her to say more. "The doctor says everything looks good. I just don't feel ready." She said looking guilty.

"You don't feel ready?" I didn't understand.

"Yeah, you've been patient like you always have and I appreciate it. I just don't feel ready to pick up where we left off yet." She put her eyes on the floor.

"I don't understand," I really didn't.

"I need a little more time, I promise it will be worth the wait." She half smiled at me.

I stood there staring at her, I didn't know how rejected I should've felt in that moment a little bit or a lot. How in the world could a baby's love replace me? I gave Lanie back to her and I walked out the door. I had the receptionist screen all my calls after that. I told her to tell Jenise I was busy. I picked up Erica and the boys after work and the four of us went out to eat. The kids had a ball. Erica told us about her teacher and how funny she was. The kids ate pizza until they were stuffed, and then I took them to get ice cream. All three of them passed out in the back of the car on the way home. I picked up Erica and I made those boys walk. They held on to each other as they walked inside. Jenise didn't say anything she stared at my face as I walked in the door. I put the kids to bed and then I got in the bed in the guest room, I locked the door. Jenise jiggled the handle trying to open the door. She was calling me but I didn't respond. I was angry, but I was hurt. She could've talked to me about how she was feeling. Why she wait for me to ask her and then she comes to me with some bull. We didn't even wait six weeks after EJ, which is also how Eric happened. However, I'm not unreasonable she could've talked to me.

Jenise

I walked back to our bedroom feeling horrible. I know I hurt Ethan's feelings and I wasn't trying to, honest. I'm scared! Even though the doctor said everything was healing nicely and there was very slim chances that my tubal could have healed on its own. My mom and cousins were talking about this lady who got pregnant after she got her tubes tied. They didn't even realize how much they scared me. Grace said I'm overreacting and that if the doctor said I was good I was good. What am I supposed to do? Try it and then when I end up pregnant go Oops! I don't want to have any more babies, I am so done. I don't want Ethan thinking I'm rejecting him, and unfortunately I think that's exactly how he's feeling right now. I love my husband more than any person in this world. He's the last person I would ever want to hurt. Outside of walking in the room naked I don't know how to fix this, and I don't know if that would save me either. I kissed my baby girl and then I laid down, I hoped Ethan would calm down and come to our bed. In the morning I heard him in the closet getting a suit for work. I ran to the closet, Ethan looked right through me and continued on with his morning routine. He normally kisses me goodbye and he didn't even acknowledge me. I spent the morning upset, I tried to call my mom, but Stephen said she was at work. Grace was more than likely sleeping and I always waited for her to call me. I heard the housekeeper come in and get to work on the house. The buzzer for the gate rang and the housekeeper said it was Gwen. Gwen came in the room and took the baby from me, and then she looked at me. She asked me why I wasn't up and dressed by now. Normally Lanie and I would be dressed even if we weren't going anywhere. I was trying to hold it back, but I was about to burst. So I told her and Gwen's eyes got big. She asked me how close Trinity, Chastity, and I were. I said they were my cousins and they were the closest things to sisters I had for a long time. She said even though they were my family I should be careful. She said Trinity especially was doing everything she could to get Ethan's attention whenever she came over. She said if my family is acting like that I needed to imagine how other females acted towards him. She told me to get back on the pill if I was so scared, but I couldn't keep him waiting in limbo like that. All this indecision made me thirsty.

Gwen told me to take Ethan out to dinner without the kids. I didn't like the idea of leaving Lanie, but under the circumstances my hands were tied. I found a dress that fit, and then I nervously fixed my hair. Gwen asked Franky to get the boys for us. Then we went to the school and picked up Erica. Then Gwen dropped me off at the office. There were some big and mean looking guys in Ethan's office. Whatever they were talking about it was serious. Ethan looked up and saw me waiting. He didn't smile, he stared for a minute then he went back to his conversation. I thought about going to my office. I decided to wait instead. When the men left his office Ethan stood in his doorway watching me with his hands in his pockets. My husband is unbelievably handsome and I'd be a fool to let him walk around feeling like I didn't want him. He watched me as I approached him, "*Big Daddy* will you go on a date with me?" Ethan looked at me, but he didn't respond. I exhaled cause he wasn't going to make this easy on me. I kissed him, and he accepted my kiss, but there was no passion on his side. I backed up, "UM! Ethan! Do you see the dress I'm wearing? Did you notice my hair? I know I smell good! Stop trying to play cool and kiss me!" I smiled at him. Ethan didn't smile back, but when I kissed him again he was more eager. So he's playing hard to get now? I felt even more thirsty now, cause this was all for him even though I was terrified. Ethan remained quiet as I told him which restaurant I made reservations at. I preordered the roasted crab especially for him because I know how much he loves it. I had them bring the Chardonnay to go with our meal.

Ethan saw that I had them bring out all of his favorites, he looked around the table and I knew he couldn't hold back his appreciation any longer. "Why Jenise?" His eyes burned a hole in me.

I couldn't beat around the bush I had to come clean. "We are two of the most fertile people I know. I look at you and I get pregnant. We've had a lot of babies in this short period of time. I'm afraid of getting pregnant."

"You just got your tubes tied." He said finally taking a sip of his wine.

"Yes, but did you know some women have been known to get pregnant even after they've gotten theirs tied? That could be us!" I said putting my hands up to my neck.

"Having my children scares you that badly?"

"This isn't exactly about you."

"Yes it is! You rejected me while I watch you give everyone else what they need. What about me?"

I slumped in my seat, "it wasn't my intention to reject you. You're a better husband than I could've ever dreamed of having. I'm so sorry for making you feel anything less than amazing."

"You should've come to me, instead of making me have to ask you." He said irritated.

"I know, you're right. I'm sorry." Then I smiled, "how's the wine?"

"You're not drinking?"

"Lanie's not three months, besides I want to give her a year before I cut her off."
"What is that about?" He watched my eyes.
"That?"
"You're completely different this time."
"Lanie is our last child, our last everything. I feel like she completes us."
"You know you aren't supposed to have favorites." He watched my eyes.
"I don't have a favorite, Lanie's just the last one. She's the baby."

****

"Are you busy?" Chastity asked.
"I just put Lanie down for her nap, what's up?"
"I just got off the phone with your father." She paused; I guess she thought I was going to say something. "He asked me to give you his number. He's begging you to call him." She pleaded.
"Why do you guys do this?"
"Cause you have a father who wants a relationship with you, I would give anything to know how that feels." Her voice cracked a little, as she got emotional.
"What's his number?" I said in defeat. Chastity got really excited when I took his number, I told her I wasn't calling today maybe not even this week. I would think about it.

I called my mom and as soon as I heard her voice I started crying. I told her that Trinity keeps asking me to call him and I didn't want to talk to him. My mom was silent for a minute, probably praying for the tact to say the right thing. "Jenise, he is your father, and regardless of what happened between he and I he loves you very much. He has grandkids he's never seen. That has to be eating him up. Even if it's not for you, at least allow your kids to know they have two grandfather's who love and care about them too."

"Ok Sister Righteous, now please tell me how you really feel. That was the Christian thing to say and I appreciate it. Now please give me your honest answer." I heard tapping in the background like she was debating with herself. "Call him before you go out there. Make sure he's sober when you go. Ethan needs to know more about him before then too."

"Then I'm never going. I don't know how to explain my father to anyone. No matter what I say, they always look at me like is that all? They don't get it."
"Even still, talk to your husband before you go."

When I got off the phone with my mom, I couldn't even think of taking a nap. I sat there staring off into yesterday. My parents fussing, all the tears, all the fighting. Flashes of things I've tried a lifetime to forget. If Ethan didn't hate cigarettes I think now would be the time to start. I needed something to help me calm down. When Ethan got home with the rest of the kids, Erica came in my room and shut the door. She said no boys were allowed with us. She showed Lanie, and I her papers from school. She pointed at her gold stars and she told Lanie those meant she did everything right. I told her I was so proud of her and I kissed her forehead. Erica smiled with pride. At dinner Ethan kept looking at me. Timothy called while we were eating, he told us Grace had the baby and they now had a little girl that they

233

named Tina. He said she was a light skinned black version of Grace. I told him she sounds beautiful, and he assured me that she is. I told him I couldn't wait until we could figure out our travel plans so that I could meet my babies. Ethan asked Timothy if they were going to try to catch up to us. He said maybe in a little bit; right now Grace's body needed rest. He said back-to-back pregnancies were a bit much. I told him to kiss them for me and to send pictures as soon as they could. When we put the kids to bed, Ethan took Lanie and put her in her crib. I wanted to cry as much as she was in protest of her crib. Lanie had a clean diaper, and a full stomach. Even though she wanted to protest longer, after five minutes she was quiet and sleeping hard. Ethan sat on the bed and he patted his lap for me to come sit. I curled up in his lap and put my arms around his neck. I started talking and I told him about my conversation with Chastity and then my mom. I told him I don't know how to tell him everything that happened in that house, or the things I saw. I kept saying there are no words. Ethan asked me if I wanted to see my father, he said I didn't have to if I didn't want to. I felt like I wanted to cry, but I couldn't. I said the thought of seeing my dad made me uneasy. He rubbed my back and told me that he supported whatever decision I made. I told him I could start with a conversation especially since I had the enforcer on my side.

****

I waited a week before I called my father; I waited until I had no excuse. I put Lanie down for her mid-morning nap and then I took a deep breath. I dialed the ten digits to my father's line. The phone rang four times; I was about to hang up when he answered. My heart started pounding and I waited for his second hello before I said hello back. My father's voice quivered as he asked, "Taffy? Is that you?"

"It's me." I said not knowing what else to say.

"Little girl how could you go so long without talking to me? I hear you're married, I hear I've got grandchildren. I have news too."

"Oh really, like?"

"You first, how many grandkids do I exactly have?"

"Four."

He gasped, "from my one daughter I have four more descendants. That's amazing! Tell me their names."

"Erica Rainise, Ethan junior, Eric Leonard, and Elaine Jenise."

"Leonard?"

"A close friend passed away, we named our son in his honor."

"I see, so you could name your son after a dead guy; but I never came up as an option? I guess that's fine, regardless of what you name them my blood runs through their veins."

"What's your news?"

"I remarried, the farm took off so I hired someone to oversee it while I bought a new house close by."

"Who married you?"

"I guess that's my ticket to getting you out here. You need to meet her, and I need to see my grandchildren. So when are you coming?"

****

I looked back at my babies who had all fallen asleep in the back of the car. EJ and Eric both leaned in on either side of their big sister resting on her shoulders. Her head was leaning back. Lanie was slumped to the side in her seat. I took out my camera and I snapped a few pictures. The sound of the clicking camera woke Erica. "We're here?" She said realizing that the car finally stopped moving. She nudged both of her brothers telling them to wake up cause we were here. I reminded all of them, but I was mostly speaking to the boys to be on best behavior. My boys are very energetic and curious, most times it's like they feed off of each other. Whenever they're around you know it by the chaos they leave behind. They are too strong for their own good, and running after them is always a workout. Ethan reminded them that they would be well behaved and their eyes told him they did not want to be on his bad side. As they climbed out the car on the passenger side, Erica went over their clothes making sure she straightened them out. She was definitely the mother hen to the boys and they seem to love and accept it. They mostly did as she told them to do, occasionally they would bump heads with her, but I was so pleased that they all got along and protected her like the little Princess Ethan always tells her she is.

It was warm out there already and it was barely 8am, there was no doubt that today was going to be hot. I looked up at my father's new beautiful house. It didn't appear that he was hurting for money anymore. Immediately I wished my mom had asked for something in the divorce, at least a lump sum of some sort. All those years where we went without so many wants and barely having what we needed. For him to now seem to have it all and then some seemed so unfair. Ethan stood on the other side of the kids holding Lanie; he said the new house looked nice. I didn't respond, I told them to come on as we approached the front door. His house was in a new planned development. Some of his neighbor's houses were still being built. I had no idea of what to expect when I rang the doorbell. I could hear hurried footsteps towards the door and my father's voice as he called out that we were here and he had the door. When he opened the door he seemed taller and fancier, even though he had on house shoes, a grey sleeveless shirt, and black shorts. He smiled as he scanned the children and then his eyes landed on Ethan. "I should've known it would be you." He looked at my kids again. "These are definitely all your children." He said to Ethan, "Come in, and come in."

I let everyone walk in before me, and when I stepped in the door he threw his arms around me and squeezed me so tight. "Hi dad," was all I could say as I barely hugged him back.

"Thank you for coming! I have been waiting for this for a long time." He said sounding emotional. Then he turned to the kids and smiled. "I'm your grand daddy, tell me your names." The kids said their names individually and then Lanie stared at my father like she was figuring him out.

"That's Lanie, she's a baby." Eric said like my father couldn't figure out why she didn't speak.

"Yes she is," He said as he reached for her. Lanie didn't lean in for him to hold her but he took her anyways. She watched his face like she was analyzing him and at any minute she was going to demand to be put down so she could crawl away. "I'm your Grand daddy little angel." He smiled real big. Lanie looked at him with the same expression that Ethan had on his face, like they were trying to figure him out. A woman came down the stairs with a smile plastered on her face. I don't know why I thought he was going to unveil that he was now married to Colette? I suddenly felt like the drama deepens with this vaguely familiar woman. "It's nice to meet you, I'm your stepmom." She smiled at me.

"Is that what you want me to call you? Stepmom?"

"You can call me mom." She smiled.

"Um, no! I have a mom. What is your name?" My father looked surprised by my attitude, Ethan didn't.

"Taffy, be nice." My father said almost like he was ordering me.

"Who's Taffy?" Erica asked.

"That's what we call your mom, she never told you guys the story?" The kids shook their heads no. "Let's go in the backyard and I'll tell you the story."

"Where's my little brother?" I asked as he started to walk.

My father looked at his wife. "He'll be here in a little bit. Why don't you two get to know each other."

Ethan watched my face, "you going to be ok?"

"Of course she is." My father responded.

Ethan ignored him and waited for my answer. He was going to stay if I asked him to. I wasn't afraid of this woman, but I didn't like her already. "Yes," I wanted him to go with the kids. It was like my father was this brand new person; I didn't exactly feel like it was ok to just let him be around the kids. Not so much because he would do something, but I didn't know what he would say. Plus I doubt he's forgotten the hold that Ethan put him in before. That should be a reminder to watch what he says. When they closed the sliding door behind them I looked at my stepmom, "what is your name?"

"Reba," she said quickly then she invited me into the kitchen. She took a pitcher of Orange juice out of the refrigerator, along with a fruit platter and other things for breakfast.

"Why do you seem familiar?" I asked directly.

She kept her hands busy and her eyes focused anywhere but on me. She looked guilty, "oh I don't know. Orange juice?" She asked.

"Sure." She poured a glass for me and then she took the pitcher and cups out back. I grabbed the fruit trays and walked out behind her. We set them on the table and then Reba went back inside and came back with a couple of pastry boxes. She said donuts were in one box and croissants were in the other. She told the kids to dig in. Erica asked the boys which donuts they wanted and then she grabbed napkins and handed them out. She asked her daddy which one he wanted. He told her it didn't matter. She stood there thinking as she looked at the options. She picked up a napkin and then she put a croissant on a plate for him and then she loaded the plate with fruit. She very carefully, but happily carried the plate to Ethan. She had the biggest smile on her face as Ethan appreciatively thanked her for his plate. I went back in the kitchen to my glass of juice and plate of fruit. When Reba came in I looked at her, "so."

"So…" She busied herself with making coffee. "Your father says you went to Stanford, that's quite an accomplishment."

"Thank you, do you have any kids?"

She held back a frown, "time wasn't on my side. Before I knew it I was too old. I'll leave the babies to the young people." She said dryly.

"Does my brother come by here often?"

She swallowed, "oh he's here all the time. I've learned so much having him around."

"Like?"

"Sign language," she said quickly. "What do you do now? Do you work with all those babies?"

"I'm a Graphic Designer, do you work?"

"With your father." Then she happily headed to the door when the doorbell rang. I heard a female voice ask if we were here. Reba said yes, and then they started whispering.

My dad opened the door and came inside. "Bring yourself!" He commanded them. "Come meet your nieces and nephews." He said looking down towards my brother, as the footsteps got closer to the kitchen. "This is your big sister Jenise." He pointed to the kitchen as my little brother and little **SISTERS**! Walked in view of me. I looked at him with my mouth open. "You remember my Junior? This is Yolanda and Yewandae." Then Colette followed them around the corner. She looked embarrassed as she waved hello with a ringless hand.

"What happened to Jamal?" I asked feeling bad for him, I had a flashback of how happy he was when he thought he was going to be a father.

"Come outside and meet your family." My father said to my siblings who did as they were told.

Reba and Colette came in the kitchen, Reba pulled out a stool for Colette and then she sat on the other. It looked like they do this quite often. "Obviously Jamal and I are not together anymore. He sold his farm and moved away."

"What? Where did he go?"

Colette shrugged, "as soon as his father died there was nothing holding him here. He sold his land to a developer and he made millions. He's gone and I'm sure never looking back at Stockton."

"My mom told me you were carrying my father's baby, I was hoping she was wrong, Jamal was so excited."

Colette shifted in her chair, "I told him the truth before the baby was born. What could I say when he wanted a divorce? He was right to want one."

I looked at Colette and Reba, "so both of you are still with my father?"

Both of them looked embarrassed as they shook their heads yes. "I'm his wife though."

"For now," Colette said as if she was laughing to curve what she meant.

Reba frowned at Colette, "this is supposed to be a pleasant visit."

"Alright, alright." Colette said putting her hands in the air. "I've loved your dad since I was a little girl. What can I say?"

"You're not that much older than me, that's disgusting!" I said.

"Coffee?" Reba offered.

"Not right now, it's still making me nauseous." Colette said waiting for me to grab what she said out of the air.

Now I felt nauseous, "you're pregnant?"

"Yes, we just got confirmation the other day." She said looking embarrassed again.

"What do your parents say about all of this? Why are you ok with your husband sleeping with someone else? Having babies and everything."

"My parents will not talk to me, but this is my life. I can have as many babies with the man I love, as I want. I'm not asking them for their opinion or to raise them for me. All they have to do is be grandparents, and since my life isn't going according to the way they want it to, they cut me off! Fine!" She said angry.

Ethan came to the door with a frown on his face and Lanie in his arm. "Jenise, what is all of this?" He said as he walked in the door looking at Colette.

"My father's wife, and his concubine." I pointed.

"Where's Jamal?"

"She don't know." I said as I watched my father come back in the door. "YOU ARE DISGUSTING! I CAN'T BELIEVE YOU THOUGHT MY MOTHER WOULD BE A PART OF ALL OF THIS!"

"Let's get it out so we can get past all of this. Regardless of how you feel about how I'm living my life, I'm still your father. Nothing's going to change that." He commanded.

"I don't want my children seeing this thinking this is normal! Why would you ever think I would get over something like this?"

"Because I'm still your father. In order to understand yourself you need to understand me. I have a right to know my grandchildren! I have a right to be included in your life!"

"NO YOU DON'T! You lose your quote unquote rights when you put what you want ahead of what's best for me. You haven't changed! Do you hit them too?" I looked at Reba and Colette. Colette looked surprised by the question, but Reba didn't.

"He's never hit me!" Colette said like the thought of it was absurd.

"That would make you the only one!"

"Stop making it seem like I walk around here beating on women cause it gets me off. It was never like that!"

"It doesn't matter! Either you do or you don't, and we all know you do."

"You came out here to judge me? You're not living the way I raised you to live. Your cousins told me you don't go to service, for no apparent reason at that. You still living a double life? I know you went to college and lost your mind. How many scandalous things have you done?" He shot back at me.

"You're not living the way you raised me to live either. From the looks of it, you never have. You...." a younger version of Reba's face flashed across my mind. I remembered waking up to noise when I was little and going into the living room. Reba and my father were drunk and having sex on the couch. I don't remember where my mom was, but I got in trouble for walking in on them. My father spanked me viciously and then he told me he'd spank me again and worse if I told my mom. He was drunk; at the time I didn't understand that. I started cursing and charging at Reba. Her eyes got big but she didn't move, where Colette hopped off her stool and ran behind my father. I knocked Reba on the floor and I started kicking her. When my father tried to stop me I turned on him and started hitting him. Ethan took Lanie out to the back and he came back fast. He closed the door then he closed the blinds in front of it. "That's that woman from the couch!" I yelled at my father.

My father held my wrist, "calm down!"

"Let her go!" Ethan's voice boomed.

My father reluctantly let me go, "Jenise you are an adult, you can't go around hitting on people!"

"I'll never take advice from you on how to treat people! YOU THOUGHT MY MOTHER WOULD SPEND THE REST OF HER LIFE LIKE THIS? I'M GLAD SHE HAD ENOUGH SENSE TO GET AWAY FROM YOU! YOU GOT BOTH OF THESE IDIOTS OVER HERE PLAYING STUCK ON STUPID FOR YOU! YOU DON'T NEED ME, OR MY CHILDREN FOR WHATEVER THIS IS SUPPOSED TO BE! YOU ARE A MISERABLE EXCUSE FOR A MAN!" I yelled. My father got angry and acted like he was going to react. He took two steps toward me and Ethan stepped in his path. He bounced off of Ethan's chest and fell backwards. Colette and Reba rushed to him to help him. I turned back to Reba, "you know good and well you know who I am! How many times did you sneak in my parent's house to sleep with my father? You were there when he spanked me, and you said NOTHING! You even came back! I guess you didn't realize he'd be spanking you too!"

"WAIT A MINUTE!" Colette put her hands on her stomach. "You guys told me this whole story about how you met a few years ago."

"That was how we met," my father said sitting on the stool touching his lip.

"But it wasn't recent!" Colette yelled like she couldn't believe he lied to her.

"Why are you surprised?" I asked her.

"You're an evil, miserable, drunk! And I hate you! I will NEVER come out here again! You will NEVER see my children again! You've got four replacements; you can forget I was ever born! Ethan, let's go!"

"Taffy! Don't leave! I know you're upset, but we needed to clear the air. We can get past this." My father said from his stool.

"That line may work on them, but you know who my mother is. When we're done, we're done! GOODBYE!"

Chapter 23

Ethan

I don't exactly understand all that happened in Stockton. It seems like it took every ounce of power in Jenise's body to keep it together in front of the kids. We came across a carnival on the way home. A wonderful distraction for the kids while I comforted Jenise. Every time she'd try to say anything her voice would leave her and she'd cry very hard. She kept throwing on a smile whenever the kids came around but she wasn't very vocal. The boys didn't notice, but Erica did. I bought them more than enough tickets to make theirselves sick on every kiddie roller coaster they could ride.

When we got home that night, Erica hugged Jenise. Then she asked me if I could help her make her momma some tea. I asked her which one she thought was best. I explained the different flavors we had, and she said Sleepy Time tea would help her sleep. I carried the teacup and saucer for her and she carried the spoon. Erica pushed open the door and Jenise was sitting in the same spot we left her in a long time ago. "Momma I know you don't feel good. We made you tea that's going to give you good dreams and help you go night-night."

"Thank you baby." Jenise said putting her arms out for a hug. Erica hurried over, and Jenise gently put her in her arms and cried very hard. "I love you baby!"

"I love you too momma. You're going to feel better in the morning, drink your tea." Erica assured her.

"Ok, lets get the boys and Lanie ready for bed." I said enlisting the help of my little helper.

Erica kissed Jenise then ran to come help me. We put Lanie down first and she screamed her momma's tears. She would not calm down or stay down when we put her down in that crib. She wanted her momma and she was not backing down this time.

"Can she sleep in my bed with me?" Erica asked me looking at her little sister stuck in her crib jail. Lanie has the flair for dramatics as she stuck her little arm through the bars reaching for her big sister to free her.

"If you get up in the middle of the night, you have to close your door so she won't escape. We don't want her crawling on those stairs she could hurt herself."

"Yes daddy."

"In the morning if you wake up before us, be careful taking her down the stairs. She can eat cereal with you."

"Yes daddy."

When I took Lanie out of her crib she immediately stopped crying when I gave her to her big sister. Erica put Lanie on her little hip and carried her to her room and shut the door. I put my knuckleheads to bed, and then I peeked my head in Erica's room. Little momma was reading Lanie a bedtime story, well more like reciting it from memory. Lanie was quietly laying down playing with her feet as she listened. Jenise still hadn't moved she sat there crying as quietly as she could. I kissed her and put my arms around her, which made her cry harder. She kept saying she's not like him, like she was trying to convince herself because she may have believed what he said was true. I told her she was not like him 'and she grabbed me and tried to squeeze me as hard as she could. I kept kissing her forehead and assuring her that she was not like him. Around almost midnight the phone rang and we were still sitting in the same spot. I answered the phone and it was Jenise's momma. She apologized for calling so late, she said Jenise told her she would call no matter how late it got. I put the phone on Jenise's ear, and she continued crying. She told her momma we weren't even there two hours. She told her we met Reba, I heard her momma yell the name through the phone. Jenise cried harder. Jenise was stammering as she spoke through her tears about Reba, Colette, Jamal, and her father's kids. Jenise shook her head no as she said an absolute no to whatever her momma was telling her. Jenise said no threw the phone on the bed and then she walked away and slammed the door to the bathroom. I picked up the phone and I could hear her momma crying on the other end. I asked her where Stephen was and she said he was sitting next to her. I told her I don't understand what's going on. She asked me to fly her back out here; she needed to see her baby. I told her I'd call with the information as soon as I got to the office tomorrow. I told her I'd find an excuse to sneak away tomorrow which was Sunday. She thanked me through her tears.

Jenise barely slept and when she did fall asleep she woke up screaming, "DADDY NO!" It was a long night. Jenise stayed in the bed all day, and Erica kept Lanie preoccupied with her dolls making them dance and sing for Lanie who was eating up all the attention.

"Hello?"

"Hi Ethan, this is Trinity can I speak to Jenise?"

"Naw, she not taking calls right now." I said knowing that Jenise's father more than likely called her and now she's calling on his behalf.

Trinity gasped and then she was quiet for a minute. "Ethan?"

"Yes." I said calmly knowing she was about to get on my nerves.

"What's going on? I can't talk to my own cousin?"

"You can talk to your cousin, just not today. I'll tell her you called." Then I hung up the phone before she got on my nerves. The phone rang again, "hello?"

"Why you hang up in my face?"

"Ok, you hang up first this time. There wasn't anything left to say."

"What's going on? My uncle is upset, got my mom upset and her blood pressure is bouncing off the walls. Now Jenise don't want to talk to me? What's going on? What happened?"

"Jenise is resting, when she feels up to calling you back she will. Now hang up."

"Should I come by?" I didn't like the infliction in her voice when she asked that question.

I took the phone off my ear and looked at it. "IF YOU DON'T HANG UP THIS PHONE! JENISE WILL CALL YOU WHEN SHE WANTS TO TALK TO YOU!" Then I hung up, I stared at the phone. If she called back again I wasn't responsible.

I turned the ringers off on all of the phones.

I took the kids with me to my office and I made arrangements for Jenise's momma to fly out. Her momma thanked me and said she was already packed. We went grocery shopping and Erica suggested that we buy Jenise flowers to help her feel better. Jenise hadn't move all day except for when she went to the bathroom. The food I brought her for lunch was on her nightstand cold and untouched. She said she wasn't hungry. That night while I undressed she asked me if my father spanked me when I was growing up. I assured her that he did, she asked me what they were like. I told her when we were little he had a belt, when we got older he punched us. I told her Nana had belts too, I told her we got it according to what we did. Tears poured out of Jenise's eyes as she said if her father was unhappy everybody was in trouble. She said she always tried to make him happy and to keep her momma happy. She said one time she asked if she could have a Popsicle. It was before dinner so she shouldn't have been asking anyways, but she did. As her father was about to respond her momma said no. Her father asked who Jenise was asking, and she said her father because she was hoping for a different answer. He told her she could have the Popsicle, which caused a fight. She said they were arguing and then it got quiet. Then her mom went to the bathroom. She said her momma had a bloody nose and she thought it was because her momma got mad at her. She said spankings in her house were vicious and over the top. She said the older she gets the more she remembers and realizes how horrible things were in her house. She cried and said she didn't understand if her father thought she was just going to accept everything in his life as his life and be ok with it. She didn't see the point of driving two hours for that kind of trauma. She said he had to know she was going to remember that woman at some point. Then she cried harder and said poor Jamal. I wanted to be irritated about her tears for him, but I let her get it out. Now I was irritated and using all my self-control not to say anything. Jenise was crying so hard at points I didn't understand what she was saying. I felt helpless; I wanted to fix this for her. I could take her father out, but I didn't know that him being gone was going to fix anything. I was thinking hard about the situation with Jenise, when she looked at me with red swollen eyes. "Ethan I feel horrible." I kissed her forehead, "please make me feel good."

So I did!

In the morning I asked Jenise if she wanted me to take Lanie to my grandparents. Her head popped up like she forgot about Lanie. Then EJ knocked on the door. "Momma! I need a hug!"

I frowned at him cause I told them to leave her alone. "Come here baby." Jenise said sitting up. EJ ran to her and wrapped his arms around her neck. I went to Erica's room to get Lanie. Erica had Lanie cracking up with some silly dance she was doing. I hugged my girls and then I told them to come on so I could make breakfast. I could hear laughter and when we got to the room Jenise had been tackled by both boys. They were smothering her with kisses, and Jenise was eating it all up. Erica and Lanie joined the love Fest, and I stood over to the side watching. They were carrying on for awhile when I looked at the clock, time flew. I didn't have time to make breakfast anymore. That meant we were going to have to go through a drive-thru. The kids would be happy, but I HATE drive-thru's. I kissed Jenise and asked her if she was going to be ok. She exhaled and said yes as she smiled at Lanie who was acting like the day they spent apart was more than she could handle.

I worked a few hours and then I went to the airport. Jenise's momma looked worried and concerned. If she could've grown wings and flown to my house she would've. She almost forgot about my dogs when we got to the house otherwise she would've ran out the car. I reintroduced her to the dogs. Then she hurried inside while I got her bags. I could hear Jenise's voice when I walked in the door. She was slurring as she cried. I walked in the kitchen and Lanie was in her high chair with food all over her face and the little bit of hair she has. The bottle was on the counter and Jenise was sitting at the table. I blew up; I told her if she was going to drown her sorrows in a bottle Lanie shouldn't be here. Jenise's momma kept apologizing to me. I thought I was going back to the office, but my car went in the opposite direction. I stood on the gas and I made it to Stockton in less than an hour instead of two. I banged on the door, and when no one answered I walked around the back. No one was home; the pastry boxes and platters from this weekend were still on the table with flies and bugs all over them.

I got back in my car and I drove to the farm. Reba was talking to someone in front of the house. She had on shades and her nose was swollen. I asked her where he was and she pointed towards the back. Jenise's father was yelling at some people, he was so busy ranting he didn't see me walking up on him. I hit him as hard as I could in the face. Jenise's father spun around spraying blood as he turned and then he hit the ground. "Jenise is falling apart! What is wrong with you!"

I caught a smile on someone's face, and it didn't go unnoticed by me that no one tried to help him or protect him. Jenise's father was hurt and he rouse slowly, spitting blood on the ground the whole time. "I wanted to see my daughter!" He said holding his mouth.

"No you wanted to mess with her head!"

"How could she cut me off! What's between her momma and me ain't got anything to do with her. I will not be ignored!" He said trying to get it together to stand up.

"Yes, stand up so I can knock you down again!" I was wishing he would. "I don't respect any so-called man who bullies women just because he can! Tell your nieces that if they even mention your name to my wife again I'm coming for you!"

"So you think you can bully me?"

"I know I can, I will, and I have!"

"I'm going to the police!"

"Your word against mine! I'm sitting in my office right now."

"I have witnesses!"

I looked around at his workers. I reached in my pocket and held up a wad of money towards them. "What witnesses?" He looked around at his workers in disbelief. "All you have to do is leave Jenise alone. Her momma is happily remarried, she...."

He cut me off, "SHE'S WHAT?" His eyes were big.

I smiled down at him, "leave Jenise alone! You will never see her again!"
****

"You're going to be faithful to a team that's leaving us? Come on over to the Niners." Uncle Jeff teased.

"We're not from the city! Born and raised in Oaktown! I'm following my team; even if they leave they'll be back. Shoot, I'm thinking about laying my head down and resting for a little bit too. That's all my team is doing, moving to get a rest, then they'll be back." Fuzzy said

"Jeff, you not gonna come hang with us in the Skybox?" Troy asked.

"No!" Uncle Jeff said.

"I can't believe my daughter is letting you take my grandson in that stadium!" Uncle Tim said.

"Believe it!" Malcolm replied, "Blu's coming."

The room fell silent as my father, brothers, cousins, and uncles looked at me like I was a traitor. "It's a Bay Area team, I will be dressed in red and gold of course." Everyone exploded in laughter and side comments. "You sure you want to do that?" Fuzzy asked me.

I looked at him, "like someone would ever be stupid enough to say something to me! My boys will be in red and gold as well."

"Twin terrors!" Troy laughed, "uh oh everybody better look out."

My boys had to be the most curious critters I'll ever know. My Grandmomma says they're bad, Nana says they're curious. This past summer was their first time going camping with the big kids. I thought it would be too much for them, but they were fine. They remind me of my brothers and I. We were always into something. "Are we done? I need to go get them." I asked the group.

We had to meet off hours to discuss business. Malcolm wasn't kidding when he said he was ready. We've got so many items jumping off the page. Malcolm has a laundry list of businesses that he's starting, a few flop, but for the most part they stick. Most of his items he runs by my father and Pops. Seeing them brainstorm is always entertaining.

I went home and the kids were outside playing. Nana's car was in the driveway. Gwen, Jenise's momma, and my cousins Tatum and Jill were in the living room with my girls talking. Jenise and Nana were in my room. "Blu, where's my King?" Nana said hugging me.

"With my father, they're brainstorming."

Nana rolled her eyes, "I probably won't see him until tomorrow then."

"I'm not staying I need to change for the game." I said grabbing my clothes.

"Candlestick doesn't have any games today."

I smiled, "I'm going to the Raider game."

"Dressed like a Niner fan?" She smiled real big. "That's my boy!"

"It's unity on a whole new level." I said walking towards the bathroom.

"Yeah right! You're looking for a fight!" Nana laughed. When I came out the bathroom Nana patted Jenise's hand. "Jenise is going to meet my friend."

"Friend?"

244

"My friend Joanne. They're gonna talk about something's. Then we're going to the range."

"As long as you're not teaching her to shoot at me."

I got my boys dressed, I asked Erica one more time if she wanted to go. She looked at her auntie Gwen with a big smile and said next time.

Malcolm pulled up next to us. Little Andrew got out the car quietly. He put his hands in his pockets and stood next to the car waiting for Malcolm. His face lit up when he saw my boys and me. He waited for Malcolm to come closer then he said an enthusiastic hello to my boys and me. Malcolm looked at Andrew then he looked at me. He locked his jaw like he was biting his tongue. The boys walked close behind talking about kid stuff. "I can't believe you gonna walk in my house dressed like that!" Malcolm said looking at my clothes.

"I don't know how you would expect anything less from me."

As we approached the Oakland coliseum people were looking at me like I was waving a red flag in front of a bull.

"Why are you wearing that?" Andrew asked my boys.

"Go Niners!" Eric yelled.

"That's right son!" Then I looked at Andrew, "Drew we tried to save you."

"Drew don't listen to him. You're born and raised in Oakland. Support your team." Malcolm said, "I've told you since you were a baby that this is where I'd take you, and here we are."

Andrew didn't say anything to that, but you could tell his little brain was ticking. Malcolm bought out two boxes and they were catered with tons of food and alcohol. As Malcolm's family arrived they came over and thanked him for the tickets and then they made a big deal over Andrew. Eventually little man was smiling from the outpouring of love from his family. All of them stared at our Niners starter jackets, etc. like we were lost. Malcolm kept looking at me and shaking his head. Troy and Fuzzy fell into the counter when they saw me. "WHAT ARE YOU WEARING?" Troy said laughing.

"My team's stuff, you got a problem with it?"

"He want us to have to fight on our way out of here!" Troy said shaking my hand. Malcolm put his hands out, "where's yours?"

Troy mimicked a girl's voice. "He's too little for all that!" Then he acted like he was choking an invisible person.

The game was fun; Andrew kept looking at his father who was watching him the entire time. Malcolm offered to buy my boys souvenirs, and I refused. I told Andrew he needed to come over to play with the Niners stuff, real authentic Bay Area team spirit. Andrew stood like his father and said no thanks. Tickled me to no end.

When I got home my house was still full of people. Music was playing and everyone was talking, laughing, and having a good time. Lanie was passed out in Jenise's lap in the middle of all of the noise. Erica was delirious dancing her little heart out with Tatum and Gwen. The boys happily joined in the fun. Jenise was faking it, she had a smile on. I knew it wasn't a genuine smile.

****

I watched Fuzzy hurry into his truck. I hate feeling like I'm in the middle. It's been hard on everyone after losing Leonard. Fuzzy is taking his life into his own hands by choosing to go this route, but I understand it. My little brothers are all trying to move on. "Fuzzy showed up early." I said into the walkie-talkie, as I started the car.

It was silent for a long time, "he's leaving?" I couldn't pinpoint the tone in Malcolm's voice. Did he understand what I was saying to him? Or maybe he didn't want to know.
"Yes. He's not sticking around for questioning."
"Blu, she came up against my Queen. Both of them."
"Remorse?"
Malcolm growled into the walkie-talkie. I drove out of the back of the park and Malcolm was sitting in his car in the park parking lot. I parked next to him and I got out of the car. I leaned over the roof of my car towards him. Malcolm got out of his car and leaned towards me. "I don't understand his connection to her."
"Momma Shuga put all of you through a lot. Maybe his way of navigating through it explains the connection he had with Pam."
Malcolm chewed back emotion. "I'm not going to do it Blu! I told you how evil that woman was. She let Momma Shuga put her up to anything, then the other things she's done."
I shook my head in agreement. "That's why everything happened like it did today. Would she have come after Amber if Momma Shuga didn't put her up to it?"
Malcolm was quiet like he was thinking. "I'm just saying. She didn't go out of her way to bring you problems, she just didn't know how to be a good mother."
"A decent human being period. The way Fuzzy describes her is nothing like the Pam I know."
"He's not her child, at least she was smart enough to only have one."
"Who knows, that fat lady could've had a whole litter for all I know."
I tried not to flinch, "why do you talk about her in size?"
"Blu you haven't been a big guy in years. When I see fat I think of Pam. I know it's not fair. Knowing that I came out of her isn't fair." He shrugged, "it's done now." He looked around and drummed his fingers on the roof. "I need my woman."
"So when we met you thought of Pam?"
"When we met you were a stranger to me just like everyone else." He drummed his fingers some more. "I got to know you." Then he looked at me. "What you want from me Blu? You know you're like a big brother to me, especially now." Malcolm's voice quivered. "Thank you for everything. Educating me, taking care of my family, handling my business. They say in this business we're all crooks and thieves. Thank you for letting me rest, letting me breathe freely. I…" he drummed his fingers again. "I need my woman." He looked like he was aching.

246

If there was ever a moment where I doubted Malcolm's love for Amber. This moment forever changed it. I could see his ache for Amber like I ache for Jenise.
"You going to call her?"
Malcolm stood up, "I'm beyond words. She's ready, I'm going over maybe tomorrow."
"You sure about that?"
"I know my queen. She knows I need her especially after this. I'm sure." He took a deep breath. "You need the site cleaned up?" He said like he was talking about business and not the burial site for his mother.
"No, Fuzzy took care of it."

****

I called Tomas who isn't too far from Stockton. Tomas does little quick jobs for my father and Pops from time to time, he's the one who went to run interference on that pretend wedding Jenise had. I gave him information for Fred, Jenise's father. I asked him to send me occasional invoices for random quarterly visits to his house and farm. I needed him to remember to stay away, and I wanted quarterly bonuses given to his employees for their cooperation.
Malcolm and Juan knocked on my door as I hung up with Tomas. I told them to come in. "Catalina Cuthford!" Malcolm said as soon as he sat down.
"What about her?"
"I'm gathering our information on each person. She's still in contact with Sammy's family, how much of a threat is she?" Juan asked.
Malcolm watched my face, "you still doing her?"
"No," I said. "How is she still in contact?"
Malcolm kept his eyes on me. "You feel something for her."
"You're going to read me now?" I said irritated.
Malcolm leaned forward, "I need to understand what we're dealing with. I don't understand why you're getting caught up in a question. Don't make me chase you, give it to me straight."
"Emotions I don't want to deal with. She's a rebound chick who thought she was the one for me. She gave Troy all the information you have on Sammy's remaining family members. If Sammy would've had Andrew she would've given him to us."
"She can't straddle the fence you know that. Either she's with us or she's with them."
"I haven't talked to her in years." I said dreading what he was going to say next.
"It's your call, you tell me where she belongs."
"Jason has Moses setup, it's a matter of flipping the switch with him." Juan told Malcolm.
Malcolm watched me, "how Amber get mixed up with a Mason?"
"A what?"
"There's a Mason family and a Baker family closely related and they run Richmond like the Latour's, Cardell's, and Wallace's run Oakland. He got her thinking his family so wholesome and religious. Got my son looking at him like he's supposed to be looking at me." Malcolm sat back, "I've made contact."
"Why?" I started reading him.

247

"He wants my woman, my Queen! How you let her have his baby?"

"Let her? Fool I didn't let her do nothing. You made that happen. Stop pushing her, let her come to you."

Malcolm exhaled, "momma Shuga is in custody."

"What about Pam?" Juan asked.

"She's done." He said coldly.

I looked at him and there wasn't an ounce of remorse or uncertainty in his face. "You ok?"

"Why wouldn't I be? She was never a mother to me. She hated me; my life meant nothing to her. The straw that broke the camel's back was when she went against my queen. At her age she should've known better than to listen to her momma. Momma Shuga means everybody harm, her loyalty is to the highest bidder." He said so matter of factly.

"I hear you've been spending a lot of time with Auntie Annette." I watched his eyes as they softened.

"I see my real Momma almost every day! It's been helping me." He shifted in his seat.

"Your real momma?" I smirked at him. "All her kids is cinnamon to white, where you come from?"

"I'm the other son," he smirked back.

"So you want me to talk to her?" I said referring to Cat.

"Only if you think you need to. I say she goes with them."

"How long do I have?"

"Once Moses is gone things will move fast. He's their eyes. You need to speak quickly."

****

"This is my boyfriend Richard." Sophia said proudly.

"Richard Cardell." I said shaking his hand, "you look like your father."

"Nice to meet you." He said looking me in my eyes.

"You know his father? How come everyone seems to know him except me?" Sophia asked Richard.

"Calm down, I barely know him either." Richard said calming himself.

"You don't know him, but Blu does?" Sophia said looking at him out the corner of her eye.

"You heard me," he said sounding irritated.

"We won't keep you from your meal, I just wanted to come over and say hi." Sophia said changing the subject.

"Where's Sasha?" I asked cause she was nowhere to be found.

"With her Dan-Dan," when I looked at her like what is that, "her grandmother."

"You've seen my father recently?" Richard asked.

"Yes."

"Can you tell him I want to speak with him? He doesn't seem to respond when I tell my momma to tell him, but I know he knows how to find me."

"Ok."

"Cousin, I think I want to open a restaurant."

"You think?"

"I mentioned working in a prestigious restaurant to your father and he about died. He told me he wants me to open my own restaurant."

"Is that what you want to do?"

"I'm warming up to the idea. You know how I love to call the shots. I think I want to specialize in comfort foods, but I don't know just yet. It's still all just ideas."

"Start collecting recipes and ideas, put them in a box. Make sure you take at least one bookkeeping class. I'll start writing down some of my dishes for you. I think a restaurant is a good idea for you." I looked at Richard, "I take it I'll see you around more often?"

"I've always been around, but you'll see more of me."

They walked out of the restaurant as Cat walked in. Immediately I felt like this was a mistake. I felt like someone was watching me, but it could've been my guilty conscience. I felt like I was slipping, I didn't see Sophia here, I did a quick sweep around the restaurant could I have missed someone else? Her face completely lit up when she saw me. She almost ran to the table, she slowed down when I didn't stand to greet her. I told her to sit. Cat smiled really big as her eyes danced over me. She told me I looked good, her smiled dropped when I didn't respond or tell her the same. Cat was starting to age; it was showing up all around her eyes. I asked her why she never got a job. She shrugged with an attitude. I told her I wanted to forget she existed and go on with my life. I told her that I can't do that cause she's constantly chasing money and endangering her life. Cat didn't say anything she sat there listening. I said what I had to say and then we sat there staring at each other. Then Cat said she started dying the day she came home to an empty closet. She said I was heartless and cruel for leaving her like I did. I pretended like I was playing a violin. She gasped at my lack of sympathy and remorse for the way our relationship ended. "I'M IN LOVE WITH YOU!" She yelled a few people looked in our direction.

"You're chasing money! I paid the bill, I tipped you. You came for the money and then you got turned out. There's a difference between love and lust. If you thought Troy's pockets were deeper than mine you would've went for him."

I could hear Cat's foot tapping under the table demonstrating her impatience. "Blu, I'm in love with you! I came for the money, and then I fell in love with you. Regardless of everything else you know I love you." She watched my eyes, "why else would you have proposed?"

I shook off the bad feeling as I remembered the bad place I was in. My chest started feeling heavy, I could feel the sadness that flashed across my face. I shook my head as I looked down at the table. Cat sat up with big eyes as she watched my eyes. "I was..." I shook my head no; Cat leaned forward with understanding eyes as she waited for me to get it out. "Ok let's talk. Once and for all, this is it!"

"Ok, let's talk." Cat adjusted in her seat.

"You first," I said.

"In all honesty, I was attracted to both of you. He was mister personality, and you were quiet and unassuming. You were paying and you weren't a playboy."

"An easier target." I volunteered.

"Right," she drummed her fingers. "You don't talk all that much, but I could tell you weren't happy. I was hooked after the first time we laid together. No one has ever touched me like that before or after you." She closed her eyes.

"What did you love about me other than the sex?"

I could tell she felt stupid. "You're smart, a good provider, you didn't make me feel dumb for loving you. I thought you put me first, and no man made me feel like that before."

I adjusted in my seat, "I was miserable. I was stuck in a relationship with a woman I didn't love. The woman I loved was distancing herself from me to do right for my child even though I was too selfish to do it myself. I was hurting so badly for Jenise that I told myself you would do." Cat's face cracked and turned red as she tried to pull back her emotions. "I did have a very strong like for you that was confused for love temporarily. I appreciate all that you did for me. Your kindness is what saved your life. You don't know me; you didn't really try to know me. You didn't care about my child, an extension of me. You attempted to harm my pregnant wife while she held our child in her arms. How could you claim to care about me, but then you would even think to frown at parts of me. You are like every female I've ever met. You come for something, get turned out and confuse that for love." Cat started crying. "I can't trust you."

"Trust me for what?" She looked hopeful.

"Trust you to do right by me even when I'm not looking."

"Blu, I would...."

"Listen to me! You need to get away from Sammy's people. You need to get as far away from them as you can. They don't trust you or care about you."

Cat stood up, she blew air. "What makes them any different from you?" She put her shades on, and then she walked out.

****

Jenise was crying in her sleep again. I put my arms around her and kissed her cheek waking her up softly. "Baby you're dreaming." Her sobs became real as she woke up. "I'm here, talk to me. What happened?"

"I'm tired of this Ethan! Why is this happening? I'm tired! I keep disappointing you. You have enough going on in your life; you don't need someone like me making your life harder. All I do is cause you problems." She cried.

"You're joking right?" I said rubbing her head.

She cried harder, "I wish I was. I've been sneaking out."

I exhaled, "you're not sneaking. I know where you go, when you leave, and when you come home. I know it all."

Jenise started crying harder, "I'm sorry! I don't know what's wrong with me. I can't do anything right!"

"You need more help then I can give you. We thought your baby blues were gone; they've just taken on a new form. Nana keeps stressing her doctor." I kissed her head, "you are perfect." That made her cry harder. "Do you feel like it's time to go back to work? Maybe the distraction of work could help."

"Gwen wants me to work with her. She says graphic design is a major factor in marketing."

"Is that what you want?"

"If it's ok with you. I don't know what I want anymore. My mom is so worried about me. She keeps saying my father invited us out there to mess with her."

"He didn't know your mom is remarried?"

"I thought he did. He was horrible to my mom. If it wasn't for me she could've gotten away from him a long time ago." She cried.

"Why do you say that?"

"I was the stupid kid who cried for her daddy." She tried to catch her breath in between her tears. "Being in your arms was gentle, that's what made me realize I've never felt gentleness."

"Jamal never held you?"

"Are you kidding? We had to sneak to hold hands. He knew how my father was and he never wanted to be the reason I was in trouble. I could count how many times we kissed. I love you Ethan, but I feel like I'm making everything harder for you."

"Turn around," she did. "I'm so in love with you. My life doesn't work without you in it. I was lonely and miserable without you. All these people who only came around cause they wanted something from me. None of them wanted me, except you."

"Nohemi wanted you."

"Nohemi was annoying and she wanted someone to take care of her. She didn't even appreciate my self-improvement, it made her more insecure. It was my fault that she got pregnant, but it was her plan all along. She wanted the money." She opened her mouth, I cut her off. "Cat wanted to win. Again she did love me, but again it was because of what I could do for her. Financial security, all that. She'd never love *Big Daddy*, which would be failure on her part. You gave up everything even your sense of control for me. You look at me and see me, you don't ask for much from me unless it's decorating our house, and I'm right there with you. Our home is our castle, but that's only as long as you are my Queen. You don't disappoint me. You're human, you have to have some kind of flaw."

"I disappointed you when I was drunk with Lanie."

I kissed her, "you're human. I should've taken her to my grandparents. I knew you were hurting."

"You think she's going to hate me? All of the kids."

"No!"

"My father is an evil drunk, I hate him. I can't believe anything about me is like him. I want to be like my mom. She still goes to service even when it's hard. I doubt God will forgive me!" She cried.

"What have you done that was so horrible?"

"I lusted after you from the beginning. I happily committed fornication, and then adultery. Well in my mind it felt like adultery."

"I'm not religious so you have to tell me how this works. You step out of line and you're shunned forever?"

"No," she exhaled. "God's main attribute is love. He wants you to turn away from sin and repent. He wants you to be happy. People make walking in God's love harder than he ever does. We judge, and we hold on to stuff that we should let go."

"So with all of that, why do you stay away from service? I want you to do what makes you happy."

Jenise

I bought Erica the prettiest little dress, hat, gloves, purse, and Mary Jane shoes. I put her hair in three long ponytails. I wanted to take my big girl on my visit back to service. Erica was so happy to do something just she and I. I don't know why I was nervous but I was. As soon as we walked in the door people smiled at us and introduced theirselves. I was talking to an older woman who was really sweet when someone tapped me. I turned around to see Jamal. He had the biggest smile on his face. I screamed and we hugged really big. I introduced him to Erica and I told him I had three more at home. His eyes got big when I said that. I reminded him of who Ethan was and then he looked at Erica again. "You look just like your mommy pretty little lady."

Erica smiled politely and said thank you. "What about you?"

"Too much emotional baggage. No one gets it."

"Jamal don't sell yourself short just because of Colette and even I was an idiot. You deserve a happy ever after."

He smiled, "I do don't I."

It was time for service to start so Erica and I took our seats across the aisle from him. An older gentleman brought me a bible and everything Erica and I would need. During service Erica kept peeking at Jamal. After service Jamal hugged us goodbye and then he left. "Momma who was that man?"

"I grew up with him in Stockton. Did he look mean?"

"No, but I didn't want him to talk to you."

"Why?"

"I don't know. Are you going to tell daddy about him?"

"Of course, why wouldn't I?"

"Sometimes Grampy talks to ladies and he tells us not to tell Gram about it. Then he buys us candy."

"How does that make you feel?" I was trying not to show my irritation that Ethan's grandfather would put my children in the middle of his nonsense.

She shrugged, "I don't know."

"What about daddy? Does he do that?"

"No! Ladies look at daddy all the time. They make their eyes go like this." She batted her eyes, "but he don't see them. I frown at them like this." She made her face frown, I laughed.

"Good! Your daddy is a very handsome man and those ladies should be ashamed of themselves."

"Shame on them?"

"Yes shame on them." I exhaled, "you think the boys should come next time?"
"One more time just me and you." She put her little gloved finger up.
"Ok."
When we got home, I held Erica's hand as we told her daddy about service and seeing Jamal there. Ethan didn't say anything; he looked at Erica who was watching every reaction her daddy had. He asked if Jamal was nice to her, she smiled and said yes. Ethan asked if that's where I planned to attend service. I told him that was the plan as long as he didn't have a problem with it.

****

Nana laughed hard as she looked at my target. I shot four times and only one hit the paper. "Believe it or not I've seen worse." She said as she cracked up. She showed me how to hold the gun. She explained to me how to gage how to hit my target. Next round all four shots hit my target in the center. I felt powerful and capable. When we finished we went out to lunch. "Do you really think religion replaces therapy?" She said then she took a sip of her iced tea.
"No, I'm not doing it instead of, in addition to."
"Have you called Joanne?"
"No," I sunk in my chair.
Nana laughed hard, "Erica acts just like you. Honey, I love you. You are living the dream right now and it's passing you by."
"The dream?"
"You're married to my handsome and wonderful grandson. He's not like some of them; he's so in love with you. I can't say that all of my children and grandchildren are in love with their spouses. That's why I'm drawn to the ones who are. My King is the love of my life. Franklin found me when I was broken and elevated me to royalty. I get to be a Queen loved and adored by my King. There are things about our relationship that's not for everyone, we are not perfect by a long shot." She looked off for a minute. "You are a lovable and likable young lady. I see a lot of me in you. If you don't realize what you have everything is going to overwhelm you."
"I'm already overwhelmed. Sometimes I want to stick my head in the sand and just stay there. I feel like Ethan deserves better than me. I'm not pretty enough, I come from a totally different background." I said honestly shaking my leg hoping she understands what I mean.
She touched my hand. "I come from money. My parents were rich snobs, arrogant, cold, and ridiculous. People think families with money don't have issues and most times they have the most issues. My husband's family had a little money but nothing like mine. I was afraid for Franklin to find out about my family, cause I didn't carry myself like someone of my family's status. My momma was Lady B; I wished she was my real momma so badly. People saw me with her and heard me calling her momma they assumed I was high yellow." She smiled real big. "They still do, and I love that." Then she shook her head, "anyways. My King felt inadequate because of my family's status. I had to remind him that it was he and I. I didn't need the money, I needed him. Sometimes we lose sight of what's important."

******

My heart was pounding as I held on to Ethan for dear life. Joanne walked out into her lobby and greeted Ethan and I together. I don't know why I was so scared to be here, but I was. I guess I was afraid of the things I might say and the things I might remember. Ever since we went over my father's house that day memories of things I've done my best to forget have flooded my brain. Going to service has helped me a lot, but Nana was right I needed more help. I started shutting down again. I haven't felt like myself in some time.

We talked and did the whole getting to know you portion of our conversation. She asked me if I wanted my husband to come in, and I told her he drove me here cause I didn't know what to expect. We talked for quite a few hours, when it was time to go, Ethan was going over paperwork from his briefcase. He looked surprised to see a smile on my face as I walked out of Joanne's office. I made an appointment to come back. When we got home I asked Ethan to take all the heavy liquor out of the house and only leave the wine. He didn't ask any questions, he did it immediately. This was the start of something new, a clean slate for me.

Chapter 24

Ethan

I woke up this morning with a smile on my face. Jenise was watching me while I slept. We laid there staring at each other with slight smiles not talking. Things have gone from good to great. Jenise has been going to service with the kids. I went once and my mind kept drifting off to all the work I needed to get done at home. The next thing I know she was nudging me cause I dozed off and I didn't even know it was happening. After Jamal came over and he officially congratulated me on my marriage to Jenise. I could see the dulled love he has for her still in the corner of his eyes, but we both know he knows better. He's of no threat to me. We made small talk for a little, then he went his way and I went mine. Erica and the boys watched our interaction as if they were taking cues from me as to how they should take him. Jenise is happy again, and I'm happy. Therapy has been going well for her. The only thing is she still babies Lanie. I decided to pick my battles cause she still shows love to the others and she tries to steal moments alone with each of them. So I don't complain, I love our little family. I try not to show favoritism towards Erica, she's my little Jenise. She follows me around everywhere, and she makes sure her daddy is taken care of. It depends on the day and the moment which one of my boys reminds me of me. Eric has more of Jenise's personality most times than EJ. It's those moments when I think EJ is my little clone that he breaks out with Jenise'isms and I find myself laughing at their jokes but mostly watching. Sometimes my momma refers to the three of them as the triplets cause they're so close in age. With everything that has been going on in our family I decided that the kids were going to private school. Jenise wanted them to go to regular public school like Sasha and the rest of my cousins. However, I saw that there were too many risks involved with sending them to school unmonitored and unsecured. My father's driver takes them to and from school daily.

I stroked Jenise's hair, "we can do this."

"Our baby!" Jenise said with semi sad eyes.

"It's only preschool. The sooner she learns the world does not revolve around her the better."

Jenise exhaled, "good thing I have a job to do. This would drive me crazy." Then she looked at me. "You look good today."

I exhaled, "thanks." The sudden loss of my Auntie Annette has been hard to cope with. My momma and Auntie Lauren, just about fell apart. No, everyone fell apart. Jenise has been on the phone constantly with Grace and she says that Timothy's been dealing with the guilt of moving so far away, and not paying attention when his momma begged him to come back. Jenise says that even though Grace won't say, they're going through a hard time right now. But could you really blame him? He and his momma were so close all while we were growing up. I understood his reasons for keeping Grace away while they were dating. I guess he didn't know how to manage as husband and still being a momma's boy. I don't know, but my brothers and I have been rallying around our momma so much since we lost our Auntie. It's not easy; she used to bring Timothy over all the time when we were little. Sometimes she'd keep us when our parents went out. She's always been a part of my life. We've been on Auntie Lauren and Aunt Blanche to make sure they're ok. Our Uncle Matt has been married so many times it's hard to keep up with all of them, and it's not like we had a specific bond with any of his wives.

"I'm going to get the guest room ready for my mom and Stephen after we take Lanie to school. I'll be in the office shortly after that." Jenise's mom and stepfather were flying in tonight. Jenise's parents have decided to move to California now that Stephen has retired and his youngest recently married. Jenise told me she wants to buy them a house or condo whatever they wanted. I guess Jenise thought I would object or something when she told me about her surprise for her momma. She acted like she was nervous and everything. It was her money, and why would I try to stop her from doing something for her momma?

"Do you have appointments today? By the time you finish it will be time to pick Lanie up, why come in the office at all?"

"You've got a point." Jenise said laying there thinking, then she looked at the time. "You know Mister Wallace, we have a little time before the kids are up." She rubbed my leg with her foot. "Can you think of a productive way to spend our time?" She said then she kissed me. As soon as we connected Lanie was pounding on the door. Sometimes I swear she has a daddy's alone time with momma sensor. Jenise looked like she wanted to acknowledge that little mood killer. I kept kissing her and moving slowly to keep her engaged as I waited for Erica to come get her little sister. Lanie pleaded and cried at the door. Erica came and got her, I exhaled then I looked at my wife who was trying her best to focus on me. It was time to reward her efforts. Jenise needed a brief nap before she could face the world.

I showered and then I came out of our room. Erica had Lanie dressed in the outfit Jenise laid out for her, and she was in the bathroom fixing her own hair. I watched her for a minute. Erica smiled at me in the mirror. "What do you think daddy? My ponytail up here?" She pulled her hair on the top of her head. "Or on the side?" She pulled her hair to the side of her head.

"Top."

"Ok," she smiled at me.

"Thank you for getting your sister, she must've escaped from your room again."

"I know it seems like she knew I was sleeping right at that moment. I knew you guys weren't up yet, so I got her to lay back down."

"Did everyone eat breakfast?"

"EJ didn't, he's acting weird in his room."

I kissed my baby girl's forehead then I went to EJ's room. He was sitting on his floor looking at his hands. When I walked in he said, "good morning dad." But he didn't look at me or move really.

"What's wrong with you?"

"Close the door please." I did, and then I sat on his bed behind him. He exhaled, glanced at me and then returned his eyes to the floor.

"What I tell you about looking down? You always look a man in his eyes."
EJ shook his head, "dad I can't."

"There is no room for can't! You can and you will, I taught you…."

He cut me off, " I heard momma this morning." I shut my mouth. EJ fidgeted, "I guess I've always heard you two and I never realized what I was hearing."

"What do you mean you heard us, we're on the other side of the house." I made sure it was designed that way. Our master suite was on the left side of the upstairs; our bathroom and then our closets shared a wall with their bathroom.

"I came to your door right after Erica got Lanie. I was going to ask you something about breakfast. It wasn't loud, but I heard you and momma making noises in there. Why do you have to do that to my momma? She doesn't want to have any more babies."

"Why were you worried about breakfast so early?" EJ shrugged. I ran my hand over my face. "Son I love your momma very much. What you heard this morning was an expression of that love. How do you think you got here?"

He put his little hand up, "Dad! Please!"

"Just because we're not going to have anymore babies doesn't mean that we stop loving each other." I exhaled, "tonight when you and your brother come home we're going to have a man's talk."

He looked at me with pleading eyes, "not about momma! Please anything but that!" I was tickled inwardly but I refused to smile. "No! About girls in general. By the time my dad thought to have the talk with us, we were all doing it already."

EJ's eyes got big; "you were doing it before momma?"

I looked at the ceiling; private school sheltered these kids from a lot. "We will talk about everything tonight. Now go eat breakfast."

When I told Jenise that I wanted to have *the talk* with the boys, she said she should do the same for Erica. I just about lost it! I told her she better tell her to tell all little boys to get lost! Jenise blank stared at me as I went off for five minutes about how Erica better never even think about holding hands with a little boy.

We took Lanie to her first day of preschool, Lanie clung to Edwina for a little bit, and then she eventually made friends with the other kids. I dropped Jenise back at the house, and then I went to the office. Detective White was in my office on the phone when I arrived. Franky, Dito, and Juan followed me into the office.

"What is your affiliation with Catalina Cuthford?" He asked me directly.

"We dated years ago, why?"

"She's in the hospital fighting for her life right now. She's the girlfriend of Elijah Cobb. Someone opened fire on the car they were riding in last night. The Calhoun family is trying to name your family, the only link I could find from your family to theirs is Catalina."

"Cat's still chasing money." Dito said.

"Elijah works for the Calhoun family. Are they trying to provoke a war?" Juan asked the room.

"Looks that way doesn't it?" Franky said.

"Are you still seeing Catalina?" Detective White asked me.

"No, last time I saw her was years ago before all that drama jumped off with Sammy's family."

"That was the last time?" Franky raised an eyebrow, "were you in a relationship at that time?"

I looked at Franky not amused by his question. "No."

"Then what?" Dito said rolling his hands.

"In so many words I gave her a heads up to get away from Sammy's family before something like this happened." Everyone was looking at me. "WHAT?"

"Why would you do that?" Franky asked.

I frowned at all of them, "because she didn't tell Sammy that we came by her place the first time." They kept looking, "if she would've told him things could've gone worse than they did."

"You're still feeling her!" Franky barked at me.

"Seriously?"

"You went alone?" Franky asked.

"I'm done with this. I told you no, and I meant it."

"Problem is, since she isn't gone her link to us keeps coming up. She's got to go!" Franky said.

"Because we dated years ago?" I knew why, I knew they were right. I just didn't want to know about it. I didn't even check to see if she got out safely when the dust cleared with all the drama we were having with Moses and Sammy's families. I wrote her off as stupid and went on with my life. I guess I did feel something for her, but it wasn't like anything I felt for Nohemi, and it could NEVER be anything like I feel for Jenise.

Dito frowned at me, "you're not stupid. Don't play dumb." Then he looked at Juan, "you got this?"

Juan looked at me, "big brother you alright?" I opened my hands and shut them. He looked at Detective White; "we'll go over details when we're done here."

Detective White gave us as much information on the Calhoun family as he had. He told us he would provide more as soon as he had it.

The rest of the day I filled my brain with whatever thought I could think of not to think about Cat. She is definitely a stupid somebody, I guess she finally gave up on black men and decided to go for someone white. Somehow she stayed in that fast money element though. Warning her about Sammy was the last bone I could throw her, it was done, she was gone. Before Juan left the office he got a call that Cat succumb to her injuries and died earlier that day. At least that's what I heard him telling Franky. I'd be stupid to think he didn't tell Franky that for my benefit.

When I got home Erica met me at the door with the biggest smile. She told me to close my eyes as she led me to the guest room downstairs. Jenise bought all new furniture and everything looked fantastic. I touched the bed and the quality on those sheets were up to par. I nodded my head and smiled. I asked her if her momma was going to want her own place after staying in this room. Erica is always excited about my approval no matter how small; she led Lanie in a squeal of excitement. Jenise looked at my face and she asked me if she could talk to me for a minute. I followed her up the stairs grabbing at her the whole way until I saw EJ looking at me with horror in his face. Great! Now this kid is aware and paying attention to everything I do. We shut the door. "*Big Daddy* I know how you feel about my cousins, my family really." She twisted her hands in front of her. "But! My Uncle Nelson is coming out for a visit and I really love him. I haven't seen him in forever; he's not like my father or any of his other siblings. I want to go see him." She stared at me.

"Jenise I would never keep you from your family."

"I know, but the thing is I want you to meet him." I started to say something, she put her hands out. "He's not like them. I promise you're going to love him!"

"And when I don't?"

"Five dollars says you will!" She said sassing me and putting her hand on her hip. I liked it, "I don't want your funky five dollars. You gotta come with something better than that." I said leaning back on the bed on my elbows with a slight grin.

"How come when its something you want I gotta settle for the five dollar bet?"

"You don't have to, but you go for it." I grinned.

"I'll make you dinner." She smiled.

I cut my eyes at her, "you can't cook!"

"I never said I couldn't, and since you like to do it, and do it better than I ever could, I let you have the kitchen. If I'm wrong I will cook dinner for the family the following Sunday. If you like him, you invite him over for dinner the following Sunday and you make a decadent dinner with all the fixings." She smiled real big.

"Your momma like him?"

"She loves him, and she's happy to see him. What do you say?"

Jenise was so happy and excited how could I say no. "Wait a minute, how am I supposed to meet him?"

Jenise smiled sheepishly at me, "um you gotta come to service with me and then we're going out to eat afterwards."

I fell back on the bed, "THAT PLACE MAKES ME SLEEPY! YOU MUST WANT ME TO GO TO SLEEP!" I barked staring at the ceiling.

Jenise got on top of me, "oh come on *Big Daddy*. Do it for me." Then she kissed me.

"Fine! I don't appreciate you using my weakness on me." I smiled.

"*Big Daddy*?"

"Yes darling?" I held my smile.

"Can Jamal come?"

I dropped my smile, "Jamal? Why he gotta come?"

"Cause he's met my uncle before, and he's going to see him at service. My Uncle's going to invite him if I don't tell him he can't. Since you're going to be there I'm asking for your permission first." She explained real fast.

"You know Jamal is waiting for us to breakup so he can claim you." I watched her eyes.

"Jamal doesn't look at me like that anymore. We barely even kissed and even with that I could count on my hand how many times that happened." She reminded me.

"Doesn't matter, he may be respectable, but he still wants you. How could he not?"
"I swear you love to pump my head up!" She kissed my lips.
"Whatever, I don't care. My minions will be there anyways, whatever I don't see, they will."
"EJ is truly your child. He watches Jamal all the time, no smiles just stares and glares. And if he's not looking Eric is." She laughed.
"So," I smacked her butt. "Your parents sell all of their stuff?"
"Everything! They're bringing their clothes and having boxes of their pictures, stuff like that shipped. Stephen is so excited to move to California and be so close to us."
I exhaled, "that's good. Let me go talk to this boy. It seems like no matter what I say he's going to be traumatized."
Jenise laughed, "yea and tell him to stop looking at me like that."
"Like what?"
"His eyes get big and he looks at me like he can't believe it. He acts like he walked in on us."
When I walked into EJ's room he looked up at me with big eyes and he swallowed big. "Boy what is wrong with you?"
"You and my momma have sex. I know it, I heard it! I can't believe it!" He said looking at me disappointed.
I rolled my eyes. I opened the door, "ERIC! COME HERE SON!" I called out.
"Yea dad?" Eric said as he hurried to the room.
I shut the door and told him to sit next to his brother. I opened my hands, "you two are getting older. I guess it's time we have *the talk.*"
"*The Talk*?" Eric said sitting up straight in shock. "What did I do to deserve this?" Eric said looking at his brother. "Dad! We are not twins! And even if we were, I'm still my own man! I don't think I did anything to deserve to hear you talk about *stuff*! I'm innocent!" Eric said with Jenise's humor.
I looked at him hiding my amusement. "I know you're not twins, I was there for both of your births. However you aren't even a year younger than your brother. You're old enough to have this conversation."
He put his hands up, "I don't want to. I already know what I need to know."
"What's that?"
"If I put my thingy in a girl, a baby will slide out. Momma said I can't do it until I get married. I'm going to wait."
"If you put your thingy in?" I frowned.
EJ plugged his ears, "I don't want to hear this. He did that to our momma!"
Eric gasped and looked at me, "that's right! Cause I'm here. EEEWWLLLL! We're all here! Four times dad really? You couldn't control yourself?" He looked at me in shock.
"They were doing it this morning!" EJ said looking like he was going to be sick.
"DAD? NO! Lanie can't handle being a big sister!"
I chuckled a little, "I cannot resist your momma."
Both of the boys paused as they looked at me and their mouths fell open.
"Disgusting! That's just nasty! You're talking about our momma!" They both

yelled in disgust.

"So what happens if one of them little girls at school say they wanna have sex with you?"

"I'm running! I'm not ready to be a father and a husband! I'm not even ten yet." Eric said.

I looked at EJ, "dad no!" He said like the conversation was too much.

"So you're going to wait until you get married to have sex?"

"Of course!" EJ said.

"Naturally!" Eric said.

I eyed them, "un huh!" YEA RIGHT! I won't try to derail the religious upbringing Jenise was instilling in them. "Ok, but promise me this. If there should come a time where you feel like you're ready and it happens to be before you're married come see me first. Every time you put your thingy in a girl, as Eric so eloquently said, doesn't have to result in a baby. There's things you need to know, and ways you need to protect yourselves."

"Promise!" They said together.

I pointed at EJ, "stop making your momma feel guilty for loving me. If I stop getting loving because you couldn't handle it, I'm kicking your butt!"

"Wait! Wait!" Eric threw his hands up. "Is momma gonna have another baby?"

"No," I said watching his face.

"So why did you do it?" He asked me.

"Because I love her."

"Momma lets you put your thingy in her just because you love her?" Eric frowned. EJ turned red and he punched his brother hard in the chest. "SHUT UP! I DON'T WANT TO HEAR ABOUT ALL OF THAT?"

Eric hit him back, and I watched them tussle on the floor until they both gave in. Bruises and knots upsides both of their heads. "Go ahead dad." Eric said not giving into his older brother.

"Your momma and I are in love and we express that love to each other regularly."

"Can I be excused?" EJ said angry.

"No, you need to hear this so we can talk about it later." Eric told him.

"I don't want to hear this. You know what he was just doing?" EJ spit.

"What?"

"He was smacking momma's butt as they came up the stairs!" EJ said pointing his finger at me.

Eric gasped, "why would you do that to our momma? She's like our momma and stuff."

"She's my woman first!"

Eric threw his hands in the air. "I give up, I'm with you brother. This is upsetting, how can we make you stop? Don't do that to our momma, she's a nice lady. She don't deserve to be treated like that."

I was going to gross them both out but I decided against it. "When you two are ready, come see me. In the meantime, if our bedroom door is closed and we're both in there. Stay away from the door." EJ grabbed his stomach like he was getting

261

sick."

****

I was on the phone with my Uncle going over the meeting minutes from his stockholder's meeting, when Jenise walked into her office. I glanced in her direction and something was off. I knew she was going to my momma to get her hair done, but I was not prepared for what I was looking at. Jenise stood in the window looking at me as she touched the back of her head where hair used to be. She chopped almost all her hair off in a modern haircut. She asked me the other day of what I thought of Shari Belafonte's hair. I said it looked fine, I should've known when she kept pointing to short hairstyles looking for input that it meant she was going to take the plunge. I didn't hate it; I didn't know how I felt. She watched my eyes through the glass for approval. When she couldn't read me she modeled through the glass for me, doing silly dances. When I hung up the phone even her walk was different. She twirled and asked me what I thought. I told her it looked fine, and that I would have to get used to it. I stared at her hair asking myself why it looked different. She volunteered that she put a relaxer in it to keep it straight and maintain her style. I said ok, I mean what else could I say? She chopped all her hair off and she liked it. It didn't look bad, I just was not expecting to see her with all her hair missing. When I brought Erica and the boys home they all gasped, then Erica screamed asking her momma what she did to her hair. She said she cut it off and she asked her if she liked it. Erica immediately asked if she could cut her hair too. I said "NO!" Before Jenise could answer. "Momma! Why did you do it?" Eric asked with big eyes.

"You don't like it?" She asked him.

"NO!" He said bluntly.

Jenise's smile dropped, "I like it momma." EJ said watching his momma's disappointed face.

"I LOVE IT!" Erica said with stars in her eyes.

"What about you?" She said to Lanie, "do you like it?" Lanie shook her head yes, but she agrees with anything that Jenise says.

That night I put the kids to bed and Jenise grabbed me before I could get in the room good. She threw my clothes off of me and she was immediately ready and frisky. After round three, I told her I loved her hair, Jenise smiled a satisfied smile as she drifted off to sleep.

****

"Uncle Nelson this is my husband Ethan!" Jenise said completely proud.

Nelson looked up at me, he was a little shorter than average. Light skinned with lighter brown hair, thick mustache, and freckles. His suit was a nice off the rack suit, which he coordinated down to his wing tip shoes. "It's nice to meet you." He said giving me eye contact the entire time.

"You as well." I said reading him. He was cautious about me, just like I was cautious about him.

Jenise introduced him to the kids; all of the kids immediately liked him. Jenise's momma came over quickly with her arms extended the entire way. "Evelyn! It's so good to see you!" He said genuinely.

"Nelson! It's good to see you too." She said squeezing him tightly. "This is my husband Stephen."

They said their hellos and Stephen and Nelson were doing the firm handshake of manhood test. "Good morning Ethan." Trinity said to me in a tone that made my skin crawl.

Nelson caught the tone as well and shot his niece a disapproving look. I heard Chastity explaining that she had been meaning to call Jenise and make payment arrangements. Jenise shushed her and then she told us all to move to our cars so that we could go out to brunch. Jamal and Nelson greeted each other on our way out of the auditorium. Jamal said hello to me, and tried his best to be normal. The girls rode with Jenise's parents, Jenise stared at me with a smile. She wanted to hear me say that I liked him, but I only just met him. I told her it was too soon. Eric leaned forward, "momma can I ask you a question?"

"Of course sweetheart, you can ask me anything." Jenise smiled at him.

The tone in his voice told me I wasn't going to like the question. "Do you like having sex with Dad?"

Jenise gasped and I swerved, and then I did my best to grab my composure. EJ turned towards the door and put his book bag over his head like that would shield him from this conversation. "Eric, you got to learn to pick the proper time to ask your questions."

"I figured it was ok cause there aren't any girls around." He said honestly.

"So I'm not a girl?" Jenise asked him.

"No, you're my momma!" He frowned at her.

"I am a momma now, but I'm also a woman who used to be a little girl. To answer your question, yes I do."

EJ whimpered in the corner, "why?"

"Because I love your father very much! I could never love anyone like I love him. When you get married you will know what I'm talking about." She said in a gentle manner.

"What if I don't wait until I get married? What if I fall in love and we can't wait for the wedding?"

"Part of love is controlling yourself so the other person doesn't get hurt." She said. "Everybody can't be as strong as you and dad were."

Jenise gave me a guilty look, "son. Here's the truth, you are a smart and handsome young man. When you feel like you're ready to have sex come see me. There's a lot of things you need to know before you fall in. Sometimes things happen and you can't wait for marriage to have sex. Sex without love is just sex, it can feel good and you can like it. However, without love it leaves you feeling empty and not whole. When I fell in love with your momma, she was my missing piece to the puzzle of my life. I couldn't live without her, and I couldn't be happy without her. At all cost we had to get married, honestly I've always loved your momma with everything in me. I did not exercise control like she's teaching you all to. Listen to your momma because my way broke a lot of hearts and caused a lot of unnecessary hurt and pain." Jenise smiled a guilty smile as she glanced at me and then out the window.

When we got to the restaurant Stephen asked me why I swerved and everyone was looking at me with the same question in their eyes. I said it was a slip up, Jenise walked away quickly too embarrassed at the thought that I might say why. Nelson asked Stephen and I to stay behind while everyone else went to the table. Nelson stood as tall as he could looking both of us in our eyes. He basically told us that he loved Jenise and her momma very much, and he was happy to see that they appeared to be very happy. He looked between both of our eyes as he said he knows that our women went through a lot being in a family with his brother. He said he can only imagine what it's like to try to manage the after affects of Fred. Stephen and I looked at him then we looked at each other. I cut my eyes away as Stephen and Nelson fell in love with each other giving each other manly props on the things they've heard and observed about each other. I wanted to get away from these girls! "I'm going to be out here for awhile, maybe we can take the boys fishing in the next couple of weeks." Nelson suggested.

"They can't, the kids are going to my grandparents house for a month starting next weekend. It's a tradition that started when I was young. They bring all the grand and now great grandchildren together for a month, and one weekend they go camping. It gives the kids an opportunity to bond and connect, reinforcing our family bond and connection. And it gives the parents much needed down time. If you're still here when they get back we can definitely plan something."

"So that means that you and my niece will be available for some adult play." He smiled real big.

"Depends on when, Jenise's schedule is a lot more flexible than mine."

When we got to the table, it looked like Jamal was looking for an excuse to switch seats. Chastity and Trinity were on either side of him, and he happily stood up and offered Nelson his seat. Then Jamal came and sat between Stephen and I. He was shaking his head like there was no way.

We were talking and enjoying our meal when Trinity walked down to our end of the table and bent over to say something to Jenise. As soon as I saw skin I turned my head, then you heard Nelson explode in anger as he did everything but snatch Trinity up. He yelled at her and told her to follow him. You could hear him fussing as they exited the restaurant. Jenise's momma asked what happened. I said Trinity was revealing too much of herself. Chastity sat there looking scared for her sister. Nelson came back still angry, and then he lectured the children, and indirectly Chastity on how to get the attention of, and be a, good man. He told the girls that if a man will turn his head cause they're prancing around in front of him, they will do that when any other woman does that as well. I nodded my head to some of the things that he was saying, and then I noticed Jenise smiling at me. I rolled my eyes, FINE! I invited Nelson to our house for dinner the following weekend. Jenise was over joyed.

Jenise

Trinity was so embarrassed; I could only imagine how embarrassed she was going to be when Chastity tells her about Uncle Nelson's speech.

"Evelyn, I really like this husband of yours. But you know in bible times you were supposed to be my wife when my brother dies." Uncle Nelson says with a smile.

"Good thing it's not bible times, besides I haven't killed your brother yet." Stephen said almost smiling himself.

"Death would be too good for him. He's miserable and determined to keep misery around him." Uncle Nelson looked at Ethan, "he's been having a hard time. Although Stockton is this quiet little place. He's caught the attention of this little gang it seems. He's their only target, they rough him up and then they disappear. Nobody knows where these people come from or where they go. Sounds like he's finally getting a taste of his own medicine."

I glanced at Ethan who stood like this was new information to him. "What do you mean a taste of his own medicine?" Chastity asked.

"Your uncle is a bully and worse when he's been drinking. Now he's being bullied." Uncle Nelson said.

"Uncle Fred has always been nice to me." Trinity said.

"That's because you never lived with him. You don't know that other side of him. He's a great guy until you live with him. Evelyn, I don't know how you lasted so long."

I felt guilty looking at my mom; she stayed with him because of me. "Nelson, I loved Fred very much. I wanted a happy family life with him. I kept giving him chance after chance to redeem himself. In the end everything worked out for the best. I'm married to a good man, and my daughter is healthy and happy. Everything is exactly how it should be."

I looked at my Uncle Nelson, he looked disappointed; he's always been nice to me. I love him very much. I remember him and my father always arguing, could those arguments been a result of underlying feelings towards my mom? Uncle Nelson was married for awhile, he never had any children of his own. Ethan was looking at me like he was reading my thoughts.

When we got home Erica brought the barrette box into the family room and sat on the floor in front of my mom. Lanie sat on the floor next to them watching with big eyes. My mom greased Erica's scalp then she started braiding her hair. Lanie kept asking Erica if it hurt. My mom kept peeking at me and smiling, she knew where my head was. "What was that?"

"You know that moment when you have the option to choose which one you want? I chose wrong." Then she thought about it, "not exactly wrong because I have you. You can't go back and change things anyways." She smiled bigger.

"Why didn't you tell me?"

"Same reason you felt the need to think I didn't know about you and him," she nodded towards our family picture. "It wasn't a big deal or anything."

"When did you tell Stephen about all of this?"

"I've told him everything and from the beginning. Nelson's like Jamal, it's in the past."

Lanie and I watched my mom braid Erica's long hair into long braids. When it was Lanie's turn, Erica held her hands and did her best to distract her. Lanie went from no hair to a head full of it, and she screams bloody murder when you touch it. Nana doesn't care and she combs it anyways, Lanie acts so traumatized it would be best to send them to Nana and Poppa with braided hair. Ethan followed me up the stairs.

"What was Chastity talking about?" He watched me.

I knew he heard her, I forced a smile. "I leant her money and she hasn't paid me back yet."

Ethan blank stared at me, "I thought we discussed this."

"She needed to have emergency dental work done. She was in a lot of pain." She could barely talk when she came to me I knew she was genuinely hurting.

"How much?"

"Two thousand," then I threw my arms around him. "Forgive me *Big Daddy* I have sinned!" I smiled hoping he wouldn't get too mad.

"I know it's hard especially for you. You think my cousins don't come to me with sob stories about their financial woes. She's never going to pay you back. You can't loan her money again."

"Yes *Big Daddy*, I won't." I smiled relieved that he gave in so easily. "So you like my uncle?"

"He's alright so far. A little in love with your momma, guess I can't fault him for that."

My eyes perked up, "you think my momma is attractive?"

He froze in his spot, "so that we're clear. You get a lot of your ways from your momma. I am acknowledging that. I am not acknowledging whatever sick and twisted thoughts you might be having."

"So if my momma wasn't married and something happened to me, would you hook up with my momma? You got a secret crush on my momma too?" I said tickling his side.

"You play too much and that's not even funny. Shower?" He put his hand out.

****

Tess and I arrived at Nana's the same time as Ethan's cousin Sharon. We hugged hello, Ryder was beyond excited to see his cousins. The kids excitedly greeted each other. Lanie held onto Erica for dear life, acting shy with her cousins as they greeted her. When we walked inside Nana was hugging Sophia and Amber both of them were red from their tears. Tess and I started to back away as Sharon hurried to her cousins and hugged them. Nana told us to come in and then her eyes turned tender towards her grandchildren. "I don't wish the term widow on anyone but you have to know you are better off without him, both of you are." She sighed, "battle of the losers and the biggest loser lost." Neither of the girls said anything initially. Nana lifted Sophia's chin and she told her not to feel guilty. She told her he was an idiot and he should've made better choices. She said it was one thing to have secrets; it was another thing to go against our family. Sophia nodded her head in agreement. Nana told us to sit down and that she would make drinks for us. My insides panicked a little because I had done so well these last few years I was afraid of a relapse. Still I said nothing and I couldn't bring myself to watch as she mixed our drinks. She sat fancy glasses in front of each of us. I took a sip and I was delighted to find that it was a fruity punch. Amber asked me if I was pregnant, I guess she noticed that my drink was made differently. I explained that I have a tendency to over do it on alcohol, so I try to stick to wine and then mixed drinks only on special occasions when I'm with Ethan. As we walked away from the house Sophia said we should get together at least once to celebrate that the kids are gone. "MOMMA!" Darryl screamed running out the door top speed, and jumping down all the stairs like it was nothing. Tess and I gasped cause there were a lot of stairs and he could've hurt himself.

"Yes baby?" Amber said not alarmed at all by her little man's actions.

"HOW MANY TIMES I GOT TO TELL YOU, THAT YOU CAN'T LEAVE WITHOUT GIVING ME MY KISS?" His little self said like he was her boss.

"I know baby, I'm sorry." She said giving him a hug.

"My kiss!" He said turning his cheek and sticking it out for her. She kissed his cheek and he acted like she knocked him down. "Oh momma! You knock me out!" He said with a big smile.

Just like that Darryl lifted Amber's mood and she was smiling at her baby. Darryl waved bye to us and ran back in the house with all the big kids. We agreed to talk to the men in hopes of them being onboard. I got home at the same time as Ethan. He smiled at me, and I told him what the girls and I discussed. He said we should have everyone over so that everyone could relax. I called Sophia and Tess and I told them to tell everyone. Sophia called back to discuss food with Ethan. Tess asked what I was going to wear; I took the phone in my closet. I told her I didn't want to look like a mom tonight. Tess laughed and said she didn't either. I stayed on the phone with her until I came across this little asymmetrical number. I totally forgot about this dress. I started singing Vanity's song Seventh Heaven when I looked in the mirror. Tess was cracking up; I got butterflies in my stomach as I thought of Ethan's reaction when he saw me dressed like this. We've been acting like parents lately, which is fine. I want to get back to the chasing each other around the house stuff, even though my parents are downstairs. We found the most exquisite condo in Oakland for them. It has a doorman, valet parking, completely plush all around. All you have to say is condo to Stephen and his eyes get big and he gets quiet. I'm paying for it and all they pay is the homeowner association dues, taxes, and utilities. By the time they pay all of that it's about a little less than what they would've paid if they bought something on their own. Ethan handled the negotiations but I listened closely to hopefully pick up pointers on how to do it. We're in escrow right now, and then we get to go SHOPPING!!!! I want my momma to have everything she's ever dreamed of. Especially since she took the high road in her divorce. Makes me mad every time I think of it. I took a deep breath and refocused my attention on my dress. Tess said she and Dito would come over in a few minutes so we could get ready together. When Ethan came in the room I could smell chocolate baking. My face dropped, I asked him if he was making brownies. He smiled but he didn't answer me. I asked him if he could make a batch without any *special seasoning*. He said of course. My momma invited my Uncle Nelson and my cousins. When Tess came we giggled up to my room. Eventually my room was female central. All the women came up to my room to primp and prep. Gwen asked her cousin Caddy who the guy she was with was. Caddy gave Gwen a stern smile and said a friend. She warned her she better not try any of her crap. My mom's mouth fell open when she saw my dress. Raynel clapped her hands and then she told me to sit. She freshen up my hair. I was loving my hair cut. Sophia asked how Amber got here cause she didn't see her car outside. Amber said she came with Malachi and her Dad. Chastity asked who was single downstairs; she said it was crawling with handsome men. Everyone stared at Chastity and Trinity not saying anything for a minute. Then Sophia told them they should assume that every man down there was spoken for so they didn't end up in trouble. When everyone said they were good we emerged from my room at the same time. As soon as I saw the lowness in Franky's eyes as he swept up his girlfriend I tensed to think of how my mother would react when she realized what the men were up to down here while we were upstairs prepping. Uncle Nelson and Stephen were in the kitchen with Ethan, his cousins, and his uncles. Uncle Nelson had a drink in his hand and he animatedly told a story. The closer I got the more I recognized the story. He was telling them why they called me Taffy. It was the dumbest story, but it was one of those stories that made my parents and apparently Uncle Nelson smile. To summarize my uncle brought me salt-water taffy, and even though my parents told me I could only have one piece after dinner. I thought I was sneaking and I went and ate the whole bag. My stomach ached and I couldn't believe my parents knew it hurt because I ate all that candy not realizing that my face and clothes showed the evidence of my disobedience. First Uncle Nelson started calling me that and then it stuck. It was the dumbest name to me so I never encouraged it. Ethan was grinning at me with low red eyes. When my Uncle and Stephen turned around their eyes were low and red as well. I looked at my mom, who was none the wiser. I frowned at Ethan until I realized he was drooling over me, quickly I forgot what I was supposed to be annoyed about. Raynel took my mom by the arm and they walked outside with Auntie Lauren, and Auntie Peggy. Ethan had the stereo pumping through the house, and people were dancing, playing cards at the dining room table, and dominos at the family table. Then others were dancing in the living room. Chastity and Trinity were dancing in the living room with cousins of Ethan. There were so many people all over the house I walked around taking it all in. When I walked outside Frank was talking with Uncle Tim and Uncle Jeff. The three of them were standing in a circle talking seriously. Uncle Jeff smiled at me and called me over holding his arm out. He put his arm around me and then he kissed my cheek. "When did you cut all your hair off?" Frank asked with big eyes.

"Oh it's been a little while now. I wanted something different." I smiled.

"I wouldn't have recognized you." He said looking at me.

"Does that mean you like it?" I asked with a smile.

"I like long hair." He said bluntly.

"Your hair cut looks good on you sweetheart, don't mind his opinion." Uncle Tim said.

"Yeah, I like it. It makes you look more mature." Uncle Jeff said.

"She's still just a kid." Frank said.

"Thanks dad, I love you too." I smiled.

Frank rolled his eyes and looked back in Raynel's direction. She was chatting with my mom and the Aunties. I could tell she knew Frank was staring at her but she refused to look. I swallowed air when I saw one of the cousins hand my mom a brownie and she quickly took a bite. I wanted to scream "NO! STOP! DON'T!" But everything happened too fast. I buried my head into Uncle Jeff's shoulder, I couldn't watch. When they figured out what just happened they laughed and asked if she knew what she just ate. I told them no and she didn't indulge in things like that. I told them I asked Ethan to make a regular batch of brownies, but I doubted that's what my mom got. I kept my head in Uncle Jeff's shoulder peeking out at them to see if there was any change. The next thing I know someone said something funny and they were all laughing hysterically. When the music started to change Uncle Tim said this was his song, and he took my hand. He led me back in the house just as the music changed. "Ain't no mountain high enough! Ain't no valley low enough!" I don't know what I expected, but I couldn't stop smiling as Timothy's dad glided around me in our living room feeling the song. Amber and Sophia came and danced on either side of me. As if this was a family personal best almost everyone joined us and two stepped all over the living room, with the exception of just a couple of people everyone was on the beat. Ok so I take it everyone in this family likes to dance. Amber stopped dancing when Malcolm, Troy, and a girl I didn't recognize walked in the door. Gwen was watching them as well; she had a little evilness in her eyes. She went upstairs, while Malcolm and Troy and the girl went in the kitchen. Gwen came back down with her purse and jacket. I asked her why she was leaving; she forced a smile and said she had a date. When I asked with who she gave me a look that said I knew who. I asked why she was leaving and she said this party was last minute and she had no plans of staying longer than up to her date. She hugged me and then she hurried out the door. I didn't mean to, but I wondered in that moment if Gwen had finally gotten to Malcolm. Then he shows up here alone and she knew that meant he was going to be around Amber and she couldn't take it. I went outside and I watched Gwen drive away. As I walked around the back, I caught glimpses of my doggies patrolling the perimeters of our property. They were on the clock and taking their positions seriously. When I walked around the corner, I smiled at Raynel and Frank acting civilized towards each other. I knew she had to be high to be cordial in his presence. He was talking and all the ladies were smiling. I chuckled as I heard a tiny bit of his charm as he spoke. Then Ethan put his arms around me and he gently squeezed me as he kissed my neck from behind. "WHERE DID YOU GET THIS DRESS?" He rumbled in my ear.

My body immediately tingled, "it was in my closet."

He pressed his body in on mine, "you make me want to send everyone home! I love this dress!" Then he nibbled on my ear.

I closed my eyes, "*Big Daddy* don't start none won't be none."

"You think I'm joking, I'm about to send them home."

"Why would you do that, people are just now getting here."

He squeezed me a little tighter, "I don't care what other people are doing. I need to get between these thighs."

I turned around and faced him, "let's sneak off for a minute." I said as butterflies hit my stomach.

He kissed me deeply, "Jenise you are a bad girl."

I took three steps back holding his hand, "yes *Big Daddy*! Now come do me!"

Chapter 25

Ethan

"Here's what's not making sense to me," my father said. "Why are we responsible for this guy's fury?"

"Good old fashion jealousy. The Calhoun Family has wanted in on our territory for a long time. We have reason to believe that someone in the Calhoun family was aiming for Elijah when Cat unfortunately stepped in the way. They need more funding to come after us, so I'm assuming that's the purpose that staging this whole event served. Elijah Cobb comes from money, clean money." Franky paused, "well I should say washed money, more than I can say clean. The Calhoun's want our North West territory, Sausalito, Marin, Novato, Petaluma, Santa Rosa, to name a few."

"Stop holding my hand and give it to me straight, I don't have all day for this nonsense!" Pops said.

"Blu they're trying to name you as the shooter." Dito said apologetically.

Everyone in the room looked at me for a response. "Ok, why?"

"They're hoping for either response, war in which Elijah's family will definitely step up. Or cooperation from us." Malcolm said.

"Since neither one of those will be happening, what's our response?" Franky said.

"We need a meeting with the Calhoun Family. I want Victor, Vern, Eugene, our South Bay, East Bay, and Valley heads all there. I need to give them a gentle reminder of why they don't want to mess with our family. They have bitten off more than they can chew by letting their minds wander this far. Blu get rid of the girl, she brings too much drama." Pops said.

I looked at Juan, "she is gone."

"Yes, and now her family is up in arms. They're under the impression that Cat was still connected to Blu and they're making a fuss." Malcolm looked at Juan then he wrote something down, he showed it to Juan.

"Tell them to shut up or silence them! I don't have time for these petty arguments with people who don't matter." Pops said, then he changed the subject to distributions and business. Before he ended the meeting he advised that even though the family as a whole was going straight there were some crooked lines that my father would manage. Pops said no one would muscle us out of anything.

I was beyond irritated that this kept seeming to come up. I didn't want to feel anything about Cat, I wasn't responsible for her demise. Her need to be taken care of is what got her in this position. Her daddy issues, heck her issues with her mother as well is what led to this end. I was still sitting there uneasy. When our meeting was over, my uncle Matt assured us that everything would be fine and it was business as usual. We drove out to the Belmont area and we had lunch at Pop's restaurant. I was eating in my normal silence listening to the conversations at the table when two women walked past our side corner table following the host to their table. It looked like they were on lunch and a business lunch at that. The second woman's walk was familiar but I turned my eyes. The woman dropped her napkin and as she bent down to pick it up her eyes caught mine. Immediately my appetite was gone, I sat back and she looked like she didn't know how to respond either. We were staring at each other for a minute. I excused myself and I walked over to their table. "Blu!" She said as her voice shook.

"Nohemi." I said, "business lunch?"

Nohemi shook her head out of her trance from yester-year. "Yes, this is my boss Kaley Kelson."

I nodded at her, "nice to meet you. I didn't want to interrupt, but I figured I should speak."

"How's your family?" She blurted out. "I saw Jenise in New York years ago."

"My family is wonderful, do you have a family?"

"Not yet," she twiddled her fingers. "Ethan can I talk to you for a minute?" Nohemi said standing.

"Sure," I said not wanting the emotional scene that I knew was about to follow. As I followed Nohemi out, I saw Malcolm watching us walk. We walked back to the hallway before the restrooms.

Nohemi looked at me, "I can't believe you're here. It's really you." She said looking at my face with tears in her eyes.

"What did you want to say?"

"You were always in love with Jenise weren't you?" She searched my eyes for the truth.

"Yes."

"Why were we dating if you wanted her?"

"She wasn't ready for me. When things escalated she didn't want to hurt you."

"Did you ever care about me at all?"

"Yes."

"But not like Jenise?"

"Never like Jenise." I said watching her eyes water.

She took a deep breath, "I thought I loved you. I thought we were in love. Wasn't until my last boyfriend that I understood that what we had wasn't exactly love. You were in love with a girl who was supposed to be just a friend. And I...." She blew air softly to catch her breath. "I was so concerned with making you love me, that I wasn't being true to myself."

"Ok," what else was I supposed to say to that?

"I did love our child and I didn't do it on purpose."

"I know," I guess she needed to say that, cause I never questioned her love for the baby.

"You saw her, can I ask you what she looked like?" She pleaded with her eyes.

"One of my biggest regrets is that I didn't look at her."

"You did the right thing, her image is stained on my brain." I looked at Nohemi, "she looked like me, with your nose and lips. She looked like both of my girls."

"Both?" She whispered like she was trying to remember. "Amina looked like you."

Hearing the name she chose shouldn't have affected me, but it felt like she shot me.

Putting a name to my baby girl's face stung like I couldn't have imagined. I slumped into the wall and I could feel emotion welling up inside of me. "She stays on my mind. I think about how old she'd be. I look at my girls and I wonder what her little personality would've been like. I know it's for the better. Things would've gotten messy." I said lowly.

"Jenise left because of the baby?" she answered her own question.

"I made her come back to me. I can't live without her in my life." I don't know why I felt like I was pleading with Jenise to come back in that moment.

A tear fell from Nohemi's eye, "you're right. That would've been messy. Blu, why don't I hate you?"

"I can't answer that for you." I looked at my hands.

As if this conversation wasn't emotional enough, she says. "How did Cat take it?" I shook my head, "I can't! I can't talk about her right now." I was falling apart. Nohemi reached out for me and we hugged. Her smell hadn't changed, her perfume was different. The essence of her was still the same. She was crying in my arms and my tears were being held captive by my manhood. I had that, "someone's watching" feeling again. I looked around and then I saw Malcolm coming around the corner. He saw me hugging Nohemi, he didn't say anything. He went into the restroom. I whispered, "Amina" to myself. A beautiful name for a beautiful little girl.

"Thank you for being honest with me." She said as she reluctantly let me go. I shook my head in agreement. She touched my cheek, "I really believed that we were in love."

"Why did you love me?" I wanted to see if her answer was as superficial as Cat's. She locked her eyes on mine, "you're so smart. I loved talking to you; even your version of silly was intellectually stimulating. You possessed seen and unseen power, everything about you represented your power. You were always a gentleman with me, as strong as you were you were gentle. Unless I made you mad. Even then you didn't hurt me, but you definitely moved me out of the way." She half smiled, "you were so good to your mother and even though I tried to believe you. I loved the way you were with Jenise. The way you would look at her sometimes, I wished you would've looked at me like that even once. She'd argue with you when I wouldn't, and to see you give in to her... I wanted that for us. You are the prototype that I compare all other men to. Sometimes I think the mold was broken after you were created."

"So why did you break up with the last guy?"

More silent tears came out, "he said I was holding back. I know I was, I didn't tell him about Amina. A few times I said her name in my sleep. My holding back led to his holding back and eventually we had nothing in common anymore. I have so much emotional baggage I don't know that I'll meet anyone who I can trust enough to unload."

"I can't tell you that you will. I can only apologize for being a selfish kid. I would have the head of any young man who thought he could treat my girls the way I treated you. I was out of line, I apologize."

"Blu you were as good to me as you could've been under those circumstances. I get it."

Malcolm walked out of the bathroom not looking at me at all. Then Franky came around the corner, "Nohemi?"

She looked surprised, "Franky? Oh my God!"

Franky hugged her, "what are you doing here?"

"I'm on a business lunch and I noticed your brother. I didn't look at the rest of your table." She smiled through her sadness, "are you married with a family too?"

"No, I'm still single, but I am seeing someone seriously right now. Did Blu tell you about his family?" He smiled.

"Actually I saw Jenise in New York a few years ago. She showed me a picture of their happy family." She tried to say like she was happy about it.

"That's good. So you're married with a family as well?"

"No, not yet."

Franky cut his eyes at me. "I see," then he clapped his hands together. "So what else is there to talk about?" He tried to say nicely.

Nohemi's tears were back, "nothing. Nothing at all." She shook her head. "Thank you for talking to me Blu, Franky it was good to see you again." Then she walked into the women's bathroom.

Franky looked at me with fire in his eyes, "outside!" I followed him out the door. We walked by the cars and then he turned to face me. "Are you trying to get caught up in some kind of affair?"

My face held no expression, "no."

"You can't be having emotional conversations with your ex's! I'm not married and I know that! That's a recipe for disaster."

"Nothing was going to happen."

"Getting caught up is not a matter of being strong or weak. Matters of the heart will betray you every time."

"I wasn't in love with Nohemi!"

"Yes but you loved your child together. Stay away from her Blu, you'll end up in trouble if you don't, mark my words."

Jenise

Gwen was so excited, she happily moved into her new office down the hall from me. Since we were business partners it only made sense for her to setup shop here. Dito didn't like the idea and he said he and Gwen would be arguing all the time. When I suggested that Gwen and I looked for our own office space, suddenly Dito was quiet. He worked between this office and the other Berkeley office. When Dito is here he keeps it moving, sometimes Gwen would say stuff to try to get under his skin, but he'd ignore her. Franky and Gwen get a long a lot better now, and they barely argue. I think most of that is because she yields to him the most. She stays out of Ethan's hair, and now she relies on me to communicate with Ethan for her. We went over our business plan with Ethan. Gwen wants to eventually have a Marketing firm, for now she's doing independent consultations. When we gave

Ethan our plan, he asked how big or small did we want to run. Gwen said the bigger the better. Ethan picked up the phone and called his cousin Sophia. She came to the office the next day and he had the three of us meet. At the time Sophia was finishing up her schooling shortly and she was ready to dive right in to owning her own restaurant. Apparently she and Ethan had been talking about her idea in detail for some time. Initially Sophia wanted to start off small, and then work her way up to bigger. After all it's the 80's and businesses have been flopping all over the place in this economy. Ethan wouldn't hear of it. He told her to believe in herself and her ability to pull this off. I sat there listening to my man not only empowering his little female cousin, but empowering the three of us to dive in and take the risk. He showed us numbers, demographics, he advised on real estate locations and everything. Sophia, Gwen, sometimes Amber and I looked at location after location. We picked out locations for both of their ventures. I tell Gwen it's amazing to watch her mind go when she's in work mode, she's tenacious about everything until it's perfect in her mind. I helped Sophia maximize the space without making it appear as though her customers would be sitting on top of each other. Amber's school was a lot of fun to design as well. The family called Gwen and I the dynamic duo, cause our package together seemed to work wonders. Sophia's was always busy, and Amber's school had a waiting list for hopeful future students. I went from working gigs here and there to always busy. Sometimes Gwen would come over and have dinner so we could work together.

Gwen told me that this next client we were meeting with was potentially a long-term client. We spent all last week perfecting our portfolio so that when we showed our resume if you will, there would be no room for doubt about whether we could handle their account. Raynel touched up my hair and my dress complimented my whole business professional look. Gwen came in with shiny red curls and a grey power pants suit looking amazing. We were getting ready for our client in my office when the receptionist buzzed me and said our 10am was here. The plan was that Gwen would sit next to Mr. Perry while I sat at the desk. We told each other to take deep breaths then I told the receptionist to show him in. Gwen and I took our places then we waited. The receptionist came in my office with the goofiest smile on her face. I didn't understand it until he walked in. Gwen's weight shifted from one leg to the other abruptly, and I swallowed. This man was gorgeous and neither one of us was expecting that. I wasn't expecting him to be black either. I've spoken with him over the phone a couple of times to set up this appointment, but his voice gave no indication of an ethnic twang. "Mr. Perry nice to meet you." I said extending my hand to shake his.

"Thank you, thank you very much." He said shaking my hand.

"I'm Jenise Wright," I motioned for him to sit.

"And I'm Gwendolyn Wallace," she said sitting and then crossing her legs towards him.

"Nice to meet you both, Ernest Perry." He said looking between us with his almond shaped eyes on his brown skin. He was shorter than Ethan, and on the somewhat thin side, but not really. His hair was nicely and professionally cut, tapered on the sides low on the top. His suit was off the rack, but who am I kidding. Only my man could afford tailor made to fit suits.

"Would you like coffee, tea, Pellegrino?" I asked.

"Ah, yes. A Pellegrino would be nice thank you." He replied as he sat his briefcase down to open it.

"I'll be right back." Gwen said going to get his beverage.

I turned to my computer to bring up my information for him. Ethan walked into his office looking at the papers in his hands. When he noticed someone sitting in my office he looked over. He sat down and looked at us for a few minutes. I refused to look at him. I knew he wanted to know who was in my office. Gwen came back with Mr. Perry's drink and then she shut my door. Ethan stopped looking as hard once Gwen sat down, but he kept looking through out the course of our meeting. Gwen was in Ernest's space and I couldn't stop laughing inwardly. He looked at Gwen a couple of times, but he didn't seem interested. Little miss gets what she wants didn't let that bother her or slow her down. When noon hit the caterer arrived as planned with our lunch, I love Sophia. Not only is her food delicious, she's always on time. We had plenty of options for him to choose from and then we fed the rest of the office. Amber raves over Sophia's meatball sub so I picked it up and the aroma slapped me in the face. Mr. Perry had a pastrami sandwich, potato salad, and garden salad with another Pellegrino. Ethan's lunch was sitting on his desk untouched as he watched us like a hawk. Mr. Perry said he liked our presentation, and he liked the ideas that he saw. His only hesitation was that we were a small team and he wondered if we could handle an account as large as his. "Mr. Perry…" He interjected, "Please call me Ernest."

Gwen smiled, "Ernest. Even if you went with a large corporation your demands would be met by a team our size. I am more than confident that we can handle all of your company's needs and desires. You've seen our work and our portfolio is only growing. What you need to ask yourself is whether you want to work with us today or if you want to work with us tomorrow. I have no doubt that if you pass today you will come back begging us tomorrow. The difference between today and tomorrow would simply be the cost. It will cost you less today than it will tomorrow." Then she grinned.

He looked at his paperwork, "your pricing is very competitive."

"That's because today we're reasonable, tomorrow we will be demanding."

He closed his folder, "sounds good. The fact that you handled the Ace Trucking account does show that you can handle the workload. I'll present your information and I will get back to you by the end of the week." Then he stood.

Ethan stood up, I knew he was coming over. He walked into the office, "Ethan Wallace," he said extending his hand.

Ernest looked at Gwen, "Ernest Perry is this your wife?" He gestured towards Gwen.

Gwen frowned, "no. He's my brother."

"He's my husband," I said proudly.

We all noticed the disappointment in his reaction. He did his best to recover. "Oh well, that's good. Nice to meet you." He looked at Gwen, "you'll be hearing from me by the end of the week. Good day everyone."

"I'll walk you out." Gwen said.

As soon as she closed the door behind her Ethan rushed me and kissed me deeply. I was caught off guard by his kiss, and he took my breath away. I held on to his shoulders. "Um… Um…" I said trying to find my words.

"You know good and well you were in here teasing." He grinned at me.

I tried to look innocent, "I don't know what you're talking about."

****

Gwen ran in my office champagne in hand, "WE GOT IT! WE GOT IT!" She ran to me and hugged me. We did the happy dance in my office and then we opened the bottle. When the bottle popped you would've thought that was the call of the wild. Everyone came over to congratulate us and open more bottles. Ethan and I shared a glass and celebrated with everyone else. That night Ethan and I had our own celebration.

Ethan

Pops looked at his watch, he said if they were five minutes late we were leaving. We were at a random and neutral location. The host of this restaurant quickly sat us back here in this room off to the side. They poured water glasses for us and put out breadsticks. Pops told them it wasn't necessary as we were not there for a social visit. Vern kept looking around and saying he had a bad feeling about this whole thing. Victor told his men outside to be on standby through his walkie-talkie. Pops pointed around the barren room, he said it looked like this is normally a storage room as he pointed to the cement floor that was unlike the nice floors outside this room. Vern said they could've at least painted the walls, as he nodded towards the scuff marks on them. Victor's walkie-talkie chirped and someone said they were here.

The Calhoun family members filled the tables in front of us. The waiters brought water pitchers and quickly filled their glasses, and placed breadbaskets in front of them. The workers did not eat or drink. The family reached, I exhaled cause they were idiots and obviously low budget. Pops spoke immediately getting to the point. "All of this nonsense stops today! Your attempt to set us up was amateur and botched."

Levi Calhoun sat forward and cleared his throat real hard. "That's where you are mistaken. We didn't try to set anyone up. Everything happened this way." He cleared his throat again, "since we have an audience with you, we'd like." He cleared his throat again. "We'd like to be brought on just like the Cardell's." He coughed, then he took a drink of water.

"Good water?" Pops watched him drink. "You seem to misunderstand the type of organization I'm running here. If we don't invite you, you can't muscle your way over. This is a family business," a lot of them started coughing. Pops looked at Victor who stood up and walked towards the middle of the room where the men were now choking. He ran his finger around the inside of the glass. He looked at

Pops and said it was tainted. Their men drew their guns. Pops ignored the guns and tilted his glass towards himself then he ran his finger across the glass, he said his was too. Levi started foaming at the mouth along with the others who drank. Victor told the workers to lower their guns. Pops asked their group of workers who didn't drink who did this? Victor chirped his walkie-talkie but didn't say anything. When no one spoke up more of our guys came in the room, and Pops said this was the last time he was repeating his question. One guy tried to say "E..." And he was shot before he could finish. The workers and the stupid Calhoun's in the room died and we left. I called Malcolm and Juan, I told them it was a setup.

Jenise

"This is Jenise," I said as I answered the phone concentrating on my computer screen.

"Mrs. Wallace this is Griselda Huldenberg the Principal at your children's school. We need an audience with you and your husband if he can come. We need you to come immediately!"

My heart dropped, "are my children hurt?"

"Your children are fine, but the matter is URGENT and we need to speak with you immediately!" She said sounding stressed.

When I popped up out of my seat Ethan looked at me. I grabbed my purse, I saw him lock his computer and then come to meet me. I told him the school called and what they said. He told Franky we were gone and we hurried out. My mind was racing with all the possibilities on the way to the school. My children were always well behaved and their highest performing students. Whenever we visit the school all of their teachers rave about our model students. Ethan reached over as he drove like a normal person and told me everything was ok and to calm down. He said they weren't hurt and everything after that was just information. My heart dropped when we pulled into the parking lot and there were two ambulances there. The lights were off and they weren't running, at least there was that. When we walked into the office Erica was sitting in the waiting area crying and looking at the paramedics. When she saw me she ran to me and buried her head in my chest. I could feel heat from Ethan, it wasn't going to do any of us any good if we were both emotional. I could hear a parent yelling and cursing. The secretary smiled a nervous smile and said she was happy we were here. And as she went to say something to the principal I heard EJ's voice booming out of the office cursing someone out. I looked at Ethan in shock because EJ was our calm child. Ethan hopped the little gate that was stupidly locked like someone couldn't step over it if they wanted to get to the back. Then he opened it for Erica and I. Erica wouldn't let me go, and now I was holding on to her. As we passed the nurses office, all of the paramedics were in there with a bunch of little boys in their uniforms. All of them were banged up pretty badly and two were laying on the nurse's beds. Erica squeezed me harder and would not turn her face towards that office. When we walked into the Principal's office EJ was standing in a man's face cursing him from the bottom of his soul. Eric was standing next to him like he was waiting for someone in the office to test them. Their jackets and shirts were ripped, but I didn't see anything else physically wrong with them. Ethan asked what was going on, and immediately EJ stopped cursing. He looked like a miniature Ethan with his soul on FIRE! There were two men and four women in the office, all of the women looked scared and the men were angry. The man that was yelling before stood up angry and started yelling again, it was the same voice I heard moments ago. Ethan put his hands in his pockets, "let me give you a second to get it together. Clearly I don't have a clue as to what's going on here. However if you step in my personal space one more time, there will be problems." Ethan said trying to control his temper. I looked at EJ and Eric, Eric was holding EJ back. The Principal asked everyone to please calm down so she could explain once and for all. One of the mom's asked why my boys got to be in the room while their boys were confined to the nurse's office. The Principal looked at her and said the boys were in her office as a safety precaution for their children. She said she could send them out, but she didn't think that was wise. I needed to know what was going on and now.

The Principal explained that one of the boys had a crush on Erica. She explained that they were mutually infatuated with each other. However, as young romances go it was quickly over. She said the boy had choice words for Erica because another boy expressed interest in her. She said my boys responded in defense of their sister. She said they were trying to be peaceable but the situation escalated until it was a group of boys against my sons. She said the only way they could stop our boys from breaking the other boys was to remove Erica and the main aggressors. She said my boys viciously beat the other students without any remorse for their actions. Ethan asked her why it sounds like our boys were in trouble for defending their sister, especially if they didn't start or provoke the fight. The Principal gestured towards the parents. "How could you think your sons could beat on my child viciously and walk away with a smack on the hand?" One mother said, "I will withdraw my funding from this facility!"

"Me too!"

Me too!" The other parents chimed in.

"So because your child got beat up you want my children who didn't start the fight to be disciplined?"

"Have you seen how severely my child was beaten?"

"Next time they won't be so stupid, please explain the problem to me." Ethan said ignoring the other parents.

"My son is a brown belt, and this is unacceptable!" One father said.

Ethan looked at him, "so let me guess. You're child was the main idiot wasn't he? He thought daddy's money spent would protect his idiotic ways? Regardless of how well you train there's always someone better."

"Oh yeah, well I'm a black belt!" The father said standing in his stance.

"Mr. Stout PLEASE!" The Principal said trying to get control of the room.

Ethan chuckled to try to remain calm, "Please! You don't want to see me. Who you think taught them?" He said disregarding the man.

"I'm not playing!" He said then he smacked Ethan's head.

Erica and I moved back towards the wall, and my babies moved forward. Ethan was out of his seat so fast. The father expected Ethan to take some pose, but Ethan reached up grabbing the man by his chin, and he kind of tossed him up where he hit is head hard on the ceiling and it dented. Then he grabbed his neck as he came down and slammed his head into the wall. "I'm not playing either! All of your training could never save you from me!" The man was bright red as he couldn't breathe and he gasped and struggled to get free. "This is your first and only warning! Next time I will hurt you!" Then Ethan released him. "Now I want all of you to shut up so that we can sort this thing out." Then he calmly sat.

The stupid man laid on the floor in disbelief holding his neck, while the other parents cowered in the corner with big eyes. The Principal's hands were shaking as she tried to get her composure. My boys went and proudly stood on either side of their father. It was clear as day that her hands were tied, although our boys weren't in the wrong this whole thing wouldn't go away. So Ethan told her he was removing his children and his financial support from this school. He said he didn't feel confident in this school's ability to protect his children from this kind of bigotry and evil mob mentality. We got Lanie out of class and then we took our herd out to dinner. Ethan was still upset and I was shaken as well. The boys looked at Ethan with big eyes thinking that he was upset with them. "Ethan and Eric, I am very proud of you. You stood up for your sister and you handled the situation as you've been trained to do. My question is why you went so hard?"

"There were too many of them Dad. We needed to put each one down without the risk of them getting up again, and we had to move quickly." Eric said.

"It's true Daddy, it seemed like they kept coming and coming." Erica said

Ethan cut his eyes at her, "I thought I told you no boys!"

Erica gasped and the disapproval on her father's face brought her to tears. Erica cried very hard into her napkin, "Daddy! That wasn't very nice!" Lanie said running to hug her big sister.

Ethan stared at Lanie, but she didn't back down. She rubbed her sister's back and stared back at him. "You heard what I said! No boys!"

"I'm sorry daddy, it will not happen again. Please don't be mad at me!" Erica pleaded.

Ethan turned in his chair like her tears were melting his anger prematurely. "It's done, eat your dinner and your mother and I will discuss next steps." He said pushing back in his chair.

When we got home Erica was completely depressed because she thought her father was upset with her. Lanie followed her around trying to cheer her up. Ethan wasn't upset about the school anymore; he was upset completely about the boys. I told him to stop letting Erica stew in her guilt, I told him to go talk to her. Make sure that she understood that he still loved her although he was disappointed in her. Ethan didn't want to but he went in Erica's room, Lanie was her little protector and she asked him if he had spoken with me first. Ethan glared at her and told her to get out, Lanie looked at me and I shook my head yes. She kissed her big sister's cheek and then she slowly walked out looking her dad in the eyes the entire time. Ethan kneeled next to the bed and softly spoke to Erica who was still all tears and apologies. We couldn't hear what they were saying but when they hugged Lanie clapped and said Ah! Then she ran back to her sister and joined their hug. I left them alone and I went to Eric's room where he and EJ were going over the high lights of their fight today. I guess they really are Twin Terrors like everyone calls them. They looked like my babies to me. I hugged and kissed each one of them and I thanked them for protecting their sister. I asked them if they knew about her having a boyfriend, and EJ said no. Eric crossed his arms and stroked his chin, "I had a suspicion momma, but I wasn't sure."

"A suspicion?"

"Yes," he walked in a circle. "She was acting different and I saw her talking to him. More times than I was comfortable with, this whole thing caught me off guard this time. Next time I will not be caught slipping again."

"Next time?" EJ asked him.

"Let's face the facts, our sister is pretty. Some stupid fool is going to try to run up again." He stopped in his tracks, "UNLESS!" He shouted pointing his finger to the sky, and then he looked at me. "Unless! You stop allowing her to shower, comb her hair, and only let her wear raggedy clothes." EJ frowned at Eric while he stood there like his plan was actually a good idea.

I chuckled, "boy you are hilarious!"

He put his hands out, "I'm serious!"

I crossed my arms and nodded my head, "that just might work!" Eric smiled at his brother. "Of course she couldn't go on this unkempt journey alone. You would have to hold yourself to the same standards as your sister. No weekly visits to Drew's, old hand me down clothes, and no showers!" I smiled.

Eric gasped, then he chuckled, "oh momma. I was just kidding. I'll think of something else."

"I thought you might see it my way." I gave them kisses and hugs. As I walked out the room, I heard Eric telling Junior that Lanie was going to be the problem because she showed their father no fear. He had a point.

I went to the room and prepared myself for anything when Ethan came back in the room. Gwen called while I was waiting, I told her what happened at the school. She confirmed that I probably wouldn't be at work tomorrow so that we could sort the whole schooling situation out. I heard the boys outside tending to the dogs still talking like they were preparing theirselves for further retaliation. I told Gwen I'd never seen Ethan even slightly in action. I told her how he tossed this not so small man up in the air like he was nothing. He caught the guy off guard and he was unable to recover. Gwen didn't sound impressed, but I can only imagine what she's grown up seeing. Even though the guy deserved it, I didn't like seeing Ethan like that. I won't mention it, cause I understand the situation. Lanie came barging in my room and sitting herself in my lap. She didn't care that I was on the phone she just wanted to be held. After awhile Ethan told her to come on cause it was time for bed. Lanie pouted trying to get me to say otherwise. I told Gwen to hold on, I told Lanie to get before her father got after her. Lanie whined all the way out the room, when

Ethan couldn't stand the whining anymore he told her to zip it. Immediately she stopped whining, but I knew she was going to cry into her pillow and that made me feel bad. I hung up with Gwen then my phone rang again five minutes later. It was Grace and she sounded upset. She never tells me what's going on with them, but I can always hear it in her voice. I let her talk about whatever she wanted to talk about. She didn't have anything major to say, she just wanted to talk to her sister. I understood and I flowed with her. When she asked me how my day was I didn't hold back I told her everything. I could hear her breathing heavy on the other end. She was going off about the whole situation. I told her that Ethan and I hadn't discussed next steps yet. I told her Ethan was more concerned about Erica's interest in boys than anything else in this situation. I didn't go into details about the boys fighting or Ethan snatching up that man like he was nothing. From our conversations I don't get the impression that Timothy tells her anything about how his family is. I don't know why he doesn't share, but he doesn't. It's not like Ethan tells me either. However, I see all the different things that happen. Whenever Malcolm comes to our office I know it's serious. Ethan finally came to our room after all the kids were down for the night, he still looked upset. I told Grace I had to go and then I watched him. Ethan paced back and forth like he was trying to find the words. "My baby girl is precious to me!" Then he stopped, "I am the first man in her life right?" I nodded yes. "She learns love from me, I show her what she should expect from other men. If she ever tries to bring a little punk-sissy-pathetic excuse for a boyfriend home, I will end him and lock her up!" I frowned at him. He exhaled, he crawled on the bed and put his head in my lap. "Tell me if this is too ridiculous." He swallowed, "I want to take Erica on her first date. I want to give her a barometer of what's acceptable and what isn't. If I show her how she should be, how she should feel maybe she will choose better in the future. Does that sound crazy?" He searched my eyes for understanding.

"Ethan! That is a WONDERFUL idea! It will be exciting and special bonding time between you two. I'm pretty sure she still thinks you're mad at her, I would."

"You would?" His eyes were sad, then he sat up. "Should I go back and talk to her some more?" He said inching off the bed.

"No, she was sneaking. So she needs to sit in it for a little bit. But you should...." I looked at the ceiling in excitement. "You should bring her flowers and genuinely ask her to go out on a date with you." I swallowed as I thought of more. "Then I'll take her to get her hair done, and we'll buy a new outfit. I'll have a mother-daughter talk with her the whole time. Then you arrive and you demonstrate how the little punk should interact with her parents." Ethan chuckled and repeated little punk.

"Then you should open the car doors for her. Take her somewhere nice to eat. Go see a movie, tell her how much you love her. And then when you bring her home walk her to the door hug her and tell her how much you enjoyed your evening." I was salivating I was so in to the idea. Ethan asked me who was more excited, and I said I was. I told him I wished that my father would've been a real person with me. When we couldn't agree to an alternative, Ethan put his foot down and said the boys would go to public school with their cousins, and the girls would go to the all girl private school not too far from our house. I wanted them all go to public school and not be sheltered from the ways of the world, but Ethan wouldn't hear of his girls being vulnerable.

Ethan

Erica is going to think she has the corniest dad ever, but I couldn't see another way around it. It had to happen this way. I dropped Jenise at the house and then I went to the store and bought roses. When I rang the doorbell I could hear commotion, when Erica opened the door Lanie was being very nosey trying to see who it was. She said, "it's only daddy."

"Hello Erica, I'm your father and I'd like to take you out on a date tomorrow night. Are you available?"

Erica's eyes got big and she looked back at her momma, then she looked at me. "Yes?"

"Great! I will be back at seven to pick you up. Is there anywhere specific that you would prefer to eat before I make reservations?"

"No?" She said with big eyes.

"Ok, see you then."

I didn't wear a suit, but I was nicely dressed. When I rang the doorbell Eric answered the door. He looked me up and down. "I hear you're here to take my sister out on a date?"

"Yes, I am." I said as I saw Jenise and Erica waiting at the top of the stairs.

"Dad! He's here." Eric said dramatically as he stepped to the side to let me in.

EJ came around the corner with my robe on. "Who are you?'

I chuckled, and then I got my composure. This little guy was playing me? "I'm Ethan sir."

"Yes, but who are you? You've come to take my little girl out for an evening and I don't know you."

I shook my head in agreement. "Well sir, I am very responsible, hard working, and I like your daughter very much."

"I don't care about what you like." EJ said doing a very good version of me.

"I understand sir, I value your daughter's happiness very much. I understand that her happiness is closely connected to yours, so I would not intentionally do anything to get on your bad side cause that would not make you happy and in the end it would not make her happy."

"Dad that's good, I'm going to have to remember that." Eric said breaking character. Everyone frowned at him and he pulled it together.

EJ looked me up and down then he called Erica down. I want her back here by curfew, and she better come back with the same innocent smile that she's leaving with."

"Yes sir." I said as I watched my angel walk down the stairs followed by her momma and little sister. I handed her a single long stem rose. Erica smiled at the flower and then she thanked me.

"I want to go!" Lanie whined.

"It's not your turn sweetheart." Jenise said.

"But it's just daddy why can't I go?"

"Cause it's not your turn." Jenise said returning her attention to us with a big smile. I put my arm out to Erica. "You better be on best behavior. You never know when and where me and my brother are going to pop up. Guaranteed, we're going to pop up!" Eric said.

I opened Erica's door for her, while everyone watched from the doorway. Then I got in the car and I turned the music down low, "how was your first day at your new school?"

"Irritating! I don't know anyone so I ate lunch alone."

"You'll have new friends in no time soon."

"I hope so, I never thought I'd be so relieved to see my baby sister at my school." She said looking around as we drove. I took her to a nice restaurant for dinner. I told her she doesn't want to assume that her friend has tons of money. I told her even if she's been here before she should ask the guy what he recommends, to see where he's at. I told her it does not make him less of a man if he can't afford the fanciest meal, however if he recommends something extremely expensive not to order it. I told her some guys were stupid and figured that if they were paying then they were owed something later. I said if she gets that vibe from a guy then she needs to remind him about the big black man who will be waiting for her return. I opened every door held her chair for her before she sat. I focused all my attention on her, I told her any guy who gave any less then this was not worth a second date. Erica listened like she was studying for an exam. At the end of our date, I walked her to the door and I told her I had a good night. She smiled and said she did too. I gave her a hug and a kiss on her forehead. I told her I loved her very much and I only want her to accept the guy who's worthy of her. Some little punk who would lead a mob in attacking her family isn't worth spitting on as she passed him on the sidewalk. I asked her if she understood. She said she did, then she said goodnight and stepped inside.

****

Nohemi is on the table pushing and she's screaming in pain. Then my baby girl slid out grey like before, but suddenly she started breathing and crying. The doctors hurry and take her from me and they start working on her. Her heart starts flat lining, and they're trying to revive her. I call out to Amina telling her to breathe for her daddy. I apologize for being so careless and so dumb. I'm screaming her name and then Cat walks in the room with a syringe and she delivers a fatal shot to my baby girl and laughs as my baby stops breathing. I'm trying to get Cat to knock her head off and someone is holding me back. I wake up cause my struggle is real, and Jenise is sitting on the stool of her vanity staring at me with big eyes. I try not to, but I start crying. Jenise hurries to the bed, and she hugs me. The warmth from her body lets me know that I am covered in a cold sweat. She rubs my head and she rocks me in her arms. I asked her why she moved so far away. She said I was fighting and I pushed her off the bed. She said she was moving to get out of the way. Then she asked me who Amina was. I said, "Nohemi" and then she hugged me tighter. She said she didn't realize we had a name for the baby. Jenise held on to me, and then she sang a song I've heard her sing to Lanie thousands of times before. It was simple and repetitive. I hugged her tighter then I laid still until she thought I was sleep and she went back to sleep.

Jenise

The driver for the girls arrived, and then they were off. The day seemed uneventful as usual, until I saw her in the grocery store. I focused my eyes like they were out of tune. "Nohemi?" I said as I got closer.

She looked surprised and then she smiled, "Jenise, hello!" A guilty look flashed across her face.

"What are you doing all the way out here?" I said watching her face.

She exhaled, "my boyfriend lives out this way. I'm here getting things for his dinner." Then she nervously laughed. "It's a small world isn't it?"

My eyes narrowed, "how small?"

She put her fingers up, "tiny." I waited for her to say more, what was she saying? "I ran into Jamal a few months ago. We've been talking and we decided to make it official about a month ago." I gripped the cart; "I didn't recognize him at first. We only met that one time and it wasn't until he reminded me of when we all went out to Stockton that I remembered who he was. By then I already had feelings for him." She said apologetically. "I was actually going to come to service with him this weekend. I understand you two attend the same congregation. How did that happen?" She was trying to shift the conversation to comfortable conversation.

"It's a small world, like you said." I said standing there staring at her. "Where have you been? When I saw you in New York you were on your way out here. Have you been out here all this time?"

"Pretty much, but I've been on the Stanford side of the Bay where I live currently. I only come out this way for Jamal." She looked between my eyes, "why do you look mad?"

"I don't trust you around my man. Are you trying to get to Ethan?" I asked bluntly.

"What? No! Ethan and I are over you know that."

I searched her eyes, "and I also know how it is when you're not honest about your feelings for him. To be fair let me warn you. I am not you, I will end you if you even think about batting one pretty little eyelash at my man!"

Nohemi frowned, "geesh Jenise. I never treated you like this."

"And you see who has him and who doesn't. Maybe you should've." I said not taking my eyes off of her.

"I'm not a fighter Jenise." She said honestly.

"There's more than one way to fight! I'm not playing with you Nohemi, I have no tolerance when it comes to my man!" My breath has never seemed so heavy in my life.

"Ooh! Jenise they have artichoke…." Gwen was talking until she realized I was frowning at Nohemi. "What's going on?"

"She's dating Jamal." I spit.

"Jamal?" Gwen rolled her hands.

"My ex! I'm not playing with you Nohemi, so help me God! I swear on everything I love!" I somewhat yelled.

"Jenise, I thought we were friends?" She pleaded.

"No not un! Not when it comes to my man. I'm very aware of your past, and I'm not playing this game with you." Ethan's been dreaming about their daughter for the past six months or more. I may be overreacting but at this moment I don't care. I'd rather be safe than sorry!

"I'm sorry you feel this way. I never did anything to make you feel I wasn't trust worthy. It's not like I slept with your boyfriend behind your back or something. Your point has been taken and I will keep your warning in mind. Good day." Then she slithered away.

Gwen didn't say anything she watched me for a little bit. When we got in the car on our way back to the office she turned off my radio. "SO that was Blu's ex?" I nodded, "and you feel some type of way about her even thinking about him?" I nodded. "Jenise, I'm confused. Why is it ok for you to threaten her within inches of her life for even thinking about Blu. But you bring your cousins in the house all the time when all they do is throw themselves at him. ESPECIALLY that one who was all in the kitchen drooling over him during your six week down time when most men stray. If you want to get a man that's the best time to strike, she did it. In your house while you and your momma were in the other room. You down played it, and always do, but this chick shows up and you look like you wanted to slash her pretty little face. She hasn't even seen Blu."

"My cousin wouldn't..."

"Ah! Don't you even fix your face to tell that lie! You know she would if Blu went for it. Stop playing dumb. I know those are your cousins, but take it from me. They'd do Blu if they thought he'd go for it."

My whole body was on fire. "I guess you would know." I snapped.

Gwen smiled, "we both know what I'm capable of. So if I'm telling you, you should pay attention." She clapped her hands together. "Now! Why is she worthy of all this anger?"

"She was pregnant, she lost the baby at the end of her pregnancy." I tried to pull it back but my tears broke free. "He's been dreaming about them! Her and the baby, and then she appears." Gwen's face twisted and she sat back in her chair. "What?" Gwen shook her head to say nothing. "WHAT! DON'T GET QUIET NOW!"

Gwen made her voice soft, "is he seeing her again? I mean he's been dreaming about her then she suddenly appears? It could be a coincidence, but you should check."

When we got back to the office Juan and Malcolm were waiting. "Good afternoon ladies, we're your one o'clock today." Juan said.

"I didn't know we had a one o'clock." I said looking at the receptionist.

"I just inserted us, we can wait if you need more time." Juan said while Malcolm watched my eyes.

"Now is good isn't it." Gwen said to me telling me to get it together. "Gentlemen let's go to Jenise's office." Gwen said directing them.

We went to my office and Ethan wasn't there. "We want to open a few offices. A main office in San Francisco at first. Eventually we will expand to additional offices and kiosks. We'd like to query you for a proposal." Juan said.

"We need you to work with Dale because our locations will need to meet certain requirements." Malcolm handed Gwen papers.

She looked at the papers, "you want to purchase a building in downtown San Francisco?" She bucked her eyes. "That's going to take millions!"

Malcolm didn't flinch, "your point?"

Gwen smiled like she was impressed. "Malcolm this is beyond hustling for nickels. I'm impressed and I don't get to say that too often."

"Ok," Malcolm said as he watched my eyes as I kept looking for Ethan to return to his office. "Do you think you can provide the type of service we're looking for?"

I tried to smile, "of course. We need a couple of days to look at your requirements, can we get our proposal to you by end of week?" I asked.

Juan looked at his list of possibilities, "yes. We'll need it first thing in the morning. Your proposal will be our final proposal for review."

Understood, we aren't the only company bidding so we needed to be on top of our job. "He's with his father and Pops." Malcolm volunteered. I didn't say anything to that. "We're headed there now. Do you need him?"

"Where are they?"

"Everyone's meeting at my office at the shop."

"You don't need to be there with them?"

"I'm going now, did you want to come?"

This is probably the longest conversation I've had with Malcolm in my life. Maybe it's showing on my face that I need to see Ethan. "Yes." I said picking up my purse.

"So I guess we'll discuss next steps once you come back." Gwen said, but I ignored her.

We got into Juan's car and I asked him about his family. This man loves his family very much. "¿alguna vez te digo que puedo hablar un poco de español? (Did I ever tell you I speak a little Spanish?)"

Juan smiled, "that's very nice where did you learn?"

"los niños que juegan con. Entiendo más de lo que puedo hablar. (The children I played with. I can understand more than I can speak.)"

"Did you teach your children?"

"Un poco (a little bit)." I felt extremely rude for not including Malcolm in the conversation. "Malcolm how are your boys?"

"They're good." He said looking around.

When we got to the shop all the men were there. Even Amber's little ones were there. When Ethan looked at me I felt guilty for coming. I don't know where I thought he'd be. I walked back out the door and to Ethan's car. He walked out searching my face for the answer to the unspoken question of why I was here. I tried to think of a reason to cover my butt. At a lost I kissed him as hard as I could. "I miss you!" That was the truth. He's been working hard lately. Everyone's been hunkering down around the office. His cousin Malachi and Franky used to run hard together with their girlfriends. Now everyone's so busy and serious. "Come home with me."

Ethan shook his head, "I'm working. I can't just leave."

"Please Ethan! I miss you!"

He looked beyond irritated. "What's wrong with you? You never interfere with me working!" He said irritated. "I need to focus! You're over here thinking about yourself! I'll take you back to the office, but I don't have time for this!" He opened my door.

When he got in the car, I said. "I miss you, I don't understand what's going on. Why would you come to Malcolm's shop instead of coming to the office?"

He took a deep breath, "we're tying up loose ends. Pops wants to go straight, and he wants to go yesterday. He wants everyone set up to succeed, even my cousins who don't know nothing about working or being a credit to this family. It's frustrating putting them in the equation when they took theirselves out!" He exhaled, gripped the steering wheel. "Hard work used to be what we had in common at least I thought that's how we bonded. You don't understand that I've been working?"

"I didn't know missing you was a crime. You've always worked hard; you've been just here. You started having nightmares and shutting down. Did I do or say something?"

He cut his eyes at me, "my child has nothing to do with this."

"You're mad, and it feels like you're mad at me. What are you not saying?"

"I just told you everything I could tell you." He pulled in the garage. "I'll be home late." Then he unlocked my door.

I couldn't help it; I cursed him out so badly. He was looking at me but he wasn't listening. I slammed his door and stomped inside the building. Gwen paid no attention to my pout; she barged into my office excited about business. She had more than enough enthusiasm for the both of us. When I dove into work it did feel like a good distraction. I called my mom and asked if the kids and I could come over for dinner. She excitedly said yes. She said she'd pick them all up and then I could come over when I got off. I was hoping she said that. Gwen had appointments for tomorrow set up already to meet with potential realtors, etc. Malcolm's project was a little out of our scope, but Gwen loves challenges. "See if you can get your hair freshly done."

"Ok."

"Did Ethan tell you we're all going camping this year?"

"All of us? Why?"

"My daddy said it's mandatory that everyone is there. He wouldn't explain why."

"This is the first I'm hearing of it."

"Is your mother-in-law going?"

She asked with so much venom it made me jump. "Like I said I don't know anything about any of this. What is the issue? Why don't you like her?" Gwen was quiet, when my desk started shaking I looked at her and she was lost in her own thoughts. Her breathing was heavy, and she was red all over. "Gwen?"

"She's not my momma!" She stood up, "I've got to go!"

"Wait! Whoa, what was that?" I called out to her.

"I've got a date! See you tomorrow!" She stormed out.

When I walked in the door Lanie was standing in the corner facing the wall. As soon as she heard me she ran to me. Right before she got to me my mom grabbed her, popped her and told her to get back in the corner. I asked my mom what was going on, and she said Lanie was being a brat as usual. Lanie cried out to me to save her. "Why don't you spank her?" She asked me frustrated.

"I don't hit any of my kids." I said not wanting to have this conversation.

"You're not doing her any favors by not disciplining her. That's your problem child and then you baby her!"

"Hi mom how are you? My day was hellacious, this isn't helping me." I said as I started feeling thirsty. I walked in the kitchen and poured a glass of water. I closed my eyes and exhaled because I was wishing this was vodka.

"Hi momma, I got one hundred percent on my test today." Erica said watching my face for a reaction.

I hugged her; "you are my good news child today. Thank you!" I kissed her forehead. Erica gave me the hug I needed.

"Momma I thought public school was supposed to be easier then private? I'm about tired of all this homework! Every time I turn around this teacher wants ANOTHER report!" Eric complained sounding like his father earlier. While EJ sat there watching me like his father would.

"Sit down momma, I'll heat up your plate." Erica said patting the chair at the table.

"Moommmmyyyyy!!!!" Lanie cried out, "save me!" She pleaded.

The look on my mom's face made all of us jump. Erica ran to Lanie and told her to calm down. Lanie dramatically leaned on her big sister shaking her head like she couldn't take it anymore. Erica rubbed her back and told her if she straightened up maybe grand mommy would let her out of the corner. Erica hurried back to the kitchen, she heated up my food, and then she sat a small plate in front of me. I thanked my mom for dinner, when she released Lanie from her corner. Lanie came and dramatically sat in my lap putting her arms around my neck. "Jenise send her in the living room." My mom said with her eyes on Lanie. I didn't want to send her away but I did as I was told. "Why do you baby her?"

"She's my baby." I said looking at my hands.

My mom lectured me about my blatant favoritism towards Lanie although I argued that I'm good to all of my babies. I was over this day! I kept swallowing my thirst. I mentally tried to check in with myself like Joanne has showed me to. There were so many moving pieces in this day that made me want to tap out.

When we got home I put the kids to bed and Lanie bolted for my bed. At first I thought to send her to her room cause I knew Ethan would be upset when he saw her. At least she wanted me around. I snuggled with my giggly girl. We hugged and kissed each other and then we fell asleep. I awoke to Ethan taking her out of the bed. He was irritated, but he handled Lanie gently. When he got in the bed, I tried to pretend like I was sleep. Ethan started talking anyways, he apologized for his behavior earlier. He said he's stressed out, frustrated, and he's tired. He said after the camping trip we needed to go away, he was going to need to unload.

Chapter 26

Ethan

Detective White said there were a lot of moving parts. He said they're anonymous tips arriving at the D.A.'s office trying to place the gun that shot Cat in my hand. However, there was not enough evidence to prove that I did anything. The fact that I dated her once upon a time was not enough to prove anything. Then the fact that Cat's body was cremated right after they called the time of death, but there's no cause of death. They have record of what brought her into the hospital but not how she died. The police had pictures from the crime scene, a whole bunch of nothing. They keep saying her family is angry but when I ask if it's her father or her mother, it's not them. So who then? This brother that I never met, possibly? Detective White, Pops, and my father sat there going over information. While I tried to put everything that didn't make any sense to me together. I got a page from code 415; I exhaled staring at the code. I could call and ask why she was paging, but I knew why. I could ignore it like I often do, but I was tired and beaten down. I didn't want to think about any of this. I'm tired of fighting, now that she's entered my brain, if I ignore the page, I'll have a nightmare tonight. I didn't want to put Jenise through that, I excused myself. I picked up the phone in Dito's empty office, when she picked up the phone I said, "two o'clock." Then I hung up and went back to the weeding out of my future. Pops told Detective White he wanted Elijah Cobb down. My father said that might bring on retaliation. Pops said we weren't going to pull the trigger, he said simply that we were going to expose his renegade ways. I walked out of the office with them. Pops asked where I was going, I said out. Then I got in my car and left.

****

"Talk to me," I said looking in Timothy's eyes.
"There's nothing to say. Sometimes we're good and sometimes we're not." He said taking a drink of his beer.
I leaned against the rock I was standing next to. "When it rains it pours, right."
Timothy looked at me with his father's eyes. "Say it ain't so Blu?" I looked away, "Blu! No!"
"It's too much! This whole going straight business is one thing! Pops always told us to plan for the day when our covers would be our only way of life." I ran my hand over my head. "I've been prepared for this." My chest got heavy, my voice cracked. "Have you talked to Pops?"
Timothy stood up straight, "what?"
"He's got to tell you."
"Blu don't play! Tell me!" I shook my head no. "It's been a minute since we've tussled, but I'm about to thump your body over this rock if you don't spill it!"
"Timothy you are a smart man. Look around, pay attention. When do we ever come together like this outside of weddings and funerals?"
Timothy slumped into the rock. "I knew something wasn't right about all this! He

catch something from one of those tricks?"

I shook my head no, "his prostate. He ignored it too long. By the time he went...." I had a lump in my throat.

Timothy stared off angrily for a long time. Levels of pain, hurt, and anger registered on his face. "What's happening to the people I love? I know Pops is getting up there, but I'm not ready for my rock to be gone. So what? Am I supposed to go home with this weighing on my heart? Grace has been through enough." He looked away. "Dito and Tess look strong."

"They are, who would've thought old soft hearted would be the strongest?"

"I bet you it was all that time he spent with your momma that we teased him about that made him a better man."

"You were right behind him on the momma's boy roster."

He exhaled from the deepest part of him. "I haven't been behaving like Annette's son! Sometimes I look in the mirror trying to figure out who that man is staring back at me. I thought this softer version of me was necessary to have a happy family life. Grace has been through so much. She didn't need the raw Wallace experience. My kids," he fake laughed. "They're so square!"

I chuckled, "at least you don't have the twin terrors. Something is wrong with them. They terrorize people."

Timothy laughed for real, "that's just you and Franky."

"I don't remember being that bad though." I exhaled, "I do know that if something were to happen to me my girls would be safe. They're crazy!"

Timothy smiled, "crazy?"

"Yea! I thought Jenise was instilling Holy thoughts in them. They had one fight at that private school, that is shut down by the way, and it's like they developed a taste for blood. They don't always start it, but boy do they finish it." I shook my head chuckling proudly. "My Dad gets such a kick out of the stories."

Timothy looked at me, "is it Cat?"

My smile immediately went away. "Cat's dead!"

"SERIOUSLY?"

"I can't talk about it!" I warned.

"The only females you showed feelings were her, Jenise, and.... Nohemi? NO! I thought she was under a rock?"

Everything felt like it was on fire. "Amina," saying her name hurt.

"WHO'S THAT?" His eyes were stretched wide.

"My babygirl who never was." I said feeling like I was back in the hospital. "I look at Erica. My angel! My most cherished and precious possession. Lately I can't stop wondering who she would've been. Would she act like Erica? Erica looks like her." I exhaled, "or that other one."

Timothy frowned at me, "how you gonna call your child the other one?"

"That's Jenise's baby. She may look like Erica, but she don't act like her. Since all this nonsense has started it's like Jenise indulges her more and that pushes me away more. It's a lot going on over here! My ex is killed because of me, your momma suddenly leaves us, and momma refuses to deal with my dad. You would've thought he caused Auntie Annette's death by the way momma scowled at his tears. I don't even understand why he couldn't hurt like the rest of us. Dito and Franky have stepped up with this whole going straight thing. Didn't stop Pops from putting me in charge after Dad. The main businesses he divided between my dad, yours, Uncle Jeff, Uncle Dale, and Auntie Martha. The rest are getting the fluff stuff that we all know they're gonna piss off."

"Uncle Matt?"

"He's too greedy and distracted. Outside of the law he's an idiot. Jennifer will be good though; she can practice at a moderate physician's pace. You know how proud they are of her despite her parents." Timothy was waiting for me to get to it. "Jenise has been drunk all weekend."

"She's not the only one though, thank the Amber Special." He said with a smile.

"Jenise is a alcoholic, she's been doing so GOOD these last few years. I know she's weak because of me. I can't bring myself to tell her. I want it to just go away."

"Since when do you punk out? That's not your style." He looked at me.

"Probably about the same time you did." I spit back at him.

"Fine! Insult me if you must, but you need to be real with that woman and stop cowering in the corner."

"Honestly, do I have to tell her?"

"You're taking a lot. You're burying your head in work, running from emotions. I know first hand it doesn't work. She'll find out if you don't tell her."

"If I tell her, she'll think it's more than it is. Jenise is so dramatic! I don't even know how to explain this." I shrugged, "it doesn't matter. No matter how I try to spin it, I'm wrong I know that."

"I don't think Grace loves me any deeper or harder than Jenise loves you. Grace has stood by me through all this. She don't like me most times but she's working with me. I've had to swallow my pride as well. Just talk to her."

Jenise

I really like her, she's smart, funny, and down for her man! How could you not love someone like that? Rosalind is Amber's good friend and she's dating Troy. They are so cute together. I'm having the best time on this camping trip. Open bar! I wake up sipping, sip all day, and go to sleep sipping. Nana's been too distracted to notice, and Ethan is all over the place. I keep hugging Grace and squeezing her. It's been too long. I see my kids from time to time, but they're out with their cousins having a ball. My boys don't stand out as the crazy ones here. All these kids are crazy, I'm so relieved. I don't know why I stopped drinking, this feels good. Everything is funnier, I'm hilarious! And every time that hangover feeling starts I grab another drink. It is a little upsetting that Ethan hasn't noticed or said anything. Not that I want him to be mad at me, but he's been so focused on work that he barely notices me at all. I was laughing when my mouth suddenly started watering. I hurried to my cabin and made it just in time to the toilet. I sat on the floor for a minute trying to get myself together. When I went to the sink my face was covered in icky sweat. I had to focus for a minute cause with my short hair slicked back and my makeup melted away I saw my dad's face. The way he looked when he was drunk. No wonder Erica kept staring at me earlier. This is not a good look; I'm growing my hair out IMMEDIATELY! I took a shower and changed my clothes because of course I suddenly had to pee as I ran to the toilet. I grabbed ibuprofen and water; I'm done with drinks. I put on my shades, and tried to shake off the depression that had jumped on my back. When I walked out of the cabin Poppa was walking up. He asked if Ethan was inside, I told him no. He stood there staring at me for a minute then he told me to follow him. His simple demand sobered me up real fast. I felt like I was in trouble. He told me to sit in the chair he pointed out and then he brought a chair in front of that one. He told me to take my shades off. He stared at my eyes hard, I wanted to run away. So I did what Jenise always does, I smiled at him. He flinched when I smiled then he sat back in his chair. He asked me how I was getting along with Joanne. I told him she has made all the difference in my life. He nodded then he asked me if she was helping me why was I drunk at his send off trip? "Sir?" I didn't understand.

"I'm telling you something I've only told my wife and boys." Then he ran his hand over his hair. "I have cancer, I might have a year. Might! My sons and grandsons have been working hard to assure me that my family, my legacy will continue to be strong without me. I almost believed it then I look at you."

"Poppa? You're dying?" Tears violently flew out of my eyes. "No! We need you! Ethan!" Suddenly it all made sense. Ethan's frustration, short temper, and depression. "Ethan's been devastated and not saying. I thought it was me!"

Poppa stared at me unmoved by my tears. "Here's my dying wish for you!" There was no friendliness in his voice. No warmth or compassion, he just told me he's dying and he doesn't seem to care that it's hurting me. I tried to be quiet so that I could listen closely. "I need you to get some self esteem about yourself! My grandson's happiness depends upon you! And you're so busy trying to make him and everybody else happy! I know the good book teaches you to be selfless, but you take that to the extreme. I like you Jenise, you spend so much time worried about whether I do or don't that you have nothing left to give yourself." He snapped his fingers, "cut it out! Everybody's not going to like you. Sometimes you're going to step on other people's toes." He shrugged, "oh well! It happens! Both parties will live. Blu needs you right now and you're over here falling apart."

I kept crying, "you're right. I thought he was having an affair or something."

His brown eyes electrocuted me. "What if that was the case, is this how you fight back. You whimper away in the corner? You don't even try to fight for your man?"

"I tried, he sent me back to work."

"What happened the next time?" I sank in my seat. "What would he have done if the shoe were on the other foot?"

My eyes got big. "Do you think Ethan would ever hit me?"

He frowned at me; "you can't play nice because you're afraid of getting hit! If he EVER hits you, you better make sure he knows better than to ever go there with you in the future. I don't care how much I liked my son in-law, if my daughter held back because she was afraid of what he would do!" He shook his head while he locked his jaw. "My boys know it would never be a fair fight, I raised them better than that." He exhaled, "that's why you don't spank Lanie? Your father hit your momma and you're afraid?"

"One time Ethan got mad at a girl and Franky grabbed him. I don't know what he was about to do, but it scared me."

"What does Blu's reaction to some female who probably deserved it have to do with you? I'm not saying it couldn't happen, but you determine how that ends. If you accept it, it will keep happening. You can't back down to him. What kind of women will your girls be if you don't show them? And if you don't discipline that little one! She knows how to conduct herself when she's with us, but I know it's not the same anywhere else."

"Is Lanie really that bad?"

He actually laughed as he said yes. "She tries to play on your goodness. Those last two girls of mine tried to be like that. We were on them and they still caused problems. You've gotta get a hold of her."

I looked at Poppa with tears pouring out of my eyes. "I'm going to miss you!"

He turned his eyes, "I know." He said lowly.

I jumped out of my chair, threw my arms around his neck and kissed his cheek. "Who's going to intimidate me now?" I said as I sat down.

Poppa was red cause he was trying not to be emotional. "You've grown from a little girl to a lovely young lady. Don't worry I've instructed Frank on his intimidation in my place. You're covered."

I gasped as I cried harder. "You're joking with me! Poppa!"

I hugged him again. He kissed my cheek, and then he pushed me away. "Go away Jenise you're getting on my nerves!" He said with wet red eyes.

"Yes sir," I said stealing one more kiss then making my way back to my cabin to cry my eyes out.

Ethan

When I went to the cabin to get ready for dinner Jenise was in tears. I could smell the alcohol on her breath, but her eyes were clear. When she said she talked to Poppa my shoulders got a little lighter. Jenise and I sat in the middle of the bed holding each other while she cried my tears for me. We got to the banquet hall just in time to be considered early. Erica watched us come in. She ran over and hugged Jenise when she noticed the clarity in her eyes. Then she went back to helping her little sister select her dinner. The evening was moving along fine until the pictures. Dito put his head down when a picture came up of his birth mother and my father. Tess rubbed his back and started talking to him. Franky walked straight out the banquet hall, I think the whole scene hit him too hard. Or he went after Tatum who left when pictures of her ex showed on the screen. Or both! All the wedding pictures made me feel bad that Jenise and I don't really have any. I didn't gather that the thought crossed her mind, but if we make it out of this situation whole I'm going to have to make it all up.

Jenise

Gwen slithered into my office and shut the door. I was worried about her after the camping trip. I don't exactly know what happened, but she said she was done with Tag and every other guy.

Then that night she came over and cried for a long time not speaking. I stroked her curls and waited for her to release. She just kept saying she had no right to hurt that little girl like that. Then she kept saying she was hurting. At one point she cried loudly. Ethan came in the room; he looked at Gwen laying across my lap. He didn't say anything, he walked back out. A couple hours later Nana and Raynel walked in my bedroom. Gwen was pale and her nose and eyes were red. Lanie screamed, "momma! I need you!"

"Go to your dad!" Nana said, the look on her face made Lanie swallow and walk away as Raynel closed the door.

"Sit up!" Nana commanded, Gwen did as she was told. "What did you do?" Gwen cried harder, "I saw all those angry looks in your direction. You could've peeled Amber off the ceiling! Did she beat you up?" Gwen shook her head no, "what did you do?"

"I don't understand why you had to show all those pictures? Amber and Tag, Amber and Malcolm, Amber and David, me and Dito." She cried harder, "my father and my mother! My father and her!" Her body started shaking like it did before. "You could see it all! Dito and I are the other kids! At least Dito still gets to have a mother! My whole life has been punishment for something I had no control over! Everybody got a momma except me!"

Raynel's stern face started to melt. Nana looked at Raynel, "Gwen cut the crap! You've always gone out of your way to be difficult. Don't sit here and act like the helpless victim. What did you do?"

"Is it because I'm not black?" Gwen spit, "it's reverse racism!"

Nana slapped Gwen so hard my whole bed shook and Gwen went flying head first off the bed her feet were straight up. Nana cursed her out so hard for saying something so dumb. She said the color of her skin was not the issue. "Who did you go after Malcolm or his friend?"

Gwen cried harder and when Nana reared up like she was going to hit her again Gwen screamed, "Troy!"

I gasped thinking of his girlfriend and her daughter. They were the cutest family; I didn't get a vibe that he would look in Gwen's direction. "What makes this time different? You're always after someone else's man. You came to your Poppa's send off with Tag! You know how I feel about that!"

"That little girl screamed at me with a broken heart. I could've cared less about his girlfriend, but I wasn't...." She cried into her hands. "All my daddy says is I act just like her, it's not like he says that nicely. Now I'm hurting little kids? I can't shake it off."

Nana said this information couldn't go beyond this room. She said it could bring harm to Troy if Frank found out. I looked at Raynel with big eyes. I guess Gwen was looking to make Raynel feel some sense of motherly inclination towards her.

Raynel said she couldn't promise anything, and then she shrugged. Nana and I looked at her, Raynel swallowed then she climbed on the bed. She told Gwen one day they'd sit down like women and discuss everything. Then Raynel clinched her teeth, she told Gwen she was going to have to give up a lot of her ways. She told her Frank's love and affection was not a competition sport between them. Raynel said she stayed away in an attempt for Gwen to have her father in her life. She said things could've been a lot worse if she didn't.

"NOTHING EXCUSES YOUR NOT COMING TO OUR TRIP!" Nana exploded suddenly and we all jumped.

"Irma, Frank and I are not together!" Raynel said in her defense.

Nana's eyes might as well have been red. "That weekend was not about rekindling anything between you two. My husband is dying and we wanted all of our family there! I will never forgive you for not being there!" A tear ran down Nana's face.

I was speechless, I looked at Raynel. "HE'S WHAT?" Raynel and Gwen said at the same time.

"You were so busy being absorbed in your world that you didn't see that he was…" Nana broke down. "MY KING!!!!" She screamed, and then she sat on the bed sobbing hard. We ran to her, "I can't do this on my own! I can't imagine life without him. I'm tired of being strong! I can't do this! A world without my King doesn't make sense to me. You all want to cry and fuss about all these things that don't matter. I'm about to lose the love of my life! HE CAN'T LEAVE ME!"

"Irma, I'm sorry! I didn't know." Raynel cried.

"Raynel, I need my family! All of it, put your differences with Frank aside. I need you!"

"Yes momma!" They hugged crying.

****

"We're so happy you finally moved out here!" Erica said to Uncle Nelson.

He put his arm around Erica and kissed her head. "Thank you sweetheart." Then he exhaled as he looked at me. "How have you been?"

"Ok, you know how things go good then they're interesting, then they're good again."

"Have you met Chastity's boyfriend? Trinity doesn't like him. I can't tell if she's just jealous or if I should be concerned."

"Last time I talked to either of them they were trying to borrow more money and they already owe me a small fortune."

My Uncle nodded, "like you owe them something because you're the first to go to college."

"Yes, I worked my butt off to get there. Then I worked even harder to stay there." I shifted in my chair. Family I know of but was never close to even have their hands out.

"See why I refused your help?"

I slumped, "Uncle Nelson none of that applies to you. You've always been good to me. My kids regard you just like I always have. " I smiled at Erica, "she's making her first dinner in your honor."

Carey Anderson

Uncle Nelson smiled real big as his chest swelled with pride. He kissed Erica's forehead again, "you all are so good to me! I love you too babygirl."

"I'm going to help her!" Lanie said joining their hug Fest.

"What are we having for dinner?"

"Beef Wellington with roasted fingerling potatoes with herbs and garlic and salad." Erica said proudly.

"Ooh!" Eric said perking up and rubbing his stomach.

Uncle Nelson's eyes got big, "how do you know how to make that?"

"My daddy makes it all the time. I told him I wanted something special for your dinner."

Jamal walked out to the parking lot. I haven't spoken a word to him since I found out about him and Nohemi. He doesn't say anything either, he just looks at me. Whenever Nohemi comes to service with him she stares at my girls like she's in a trance. One time she grabbed Erica and hugged her while she cried. Once Erica saw me looking she relaxed and let this stranger hug her in our place of worship. Lanie refuses to play along, she doesn't like Nohemi and she's rude to her. I explained to them that her baby died a little before it was born and she thinks they remind her of her baby. Erica felt bad for her, Lanie did not care. Looking like her daddy she said she did not want Nohemi touching her. Erica would avoid Nohemi as well but she wasn't mean about it.

He watched me as he approached us. EJ almost growled, as Jamal got close. I looked at him; Jamal's expression was somewhat like he wanted to talk to me, but there's nothing to be said. He and Nohemi are together; if she makes him happy then they'll probably get married. They've been together at least a year since I found out about them. Jamal said hello to Uncle Nelson, shook his hand, nodded at me and started to walk away. "Hold on son! What am I missing?" He looked between the two of us.

"Nothing, he's dating and keeping a respectable distance. Isn't that right?" I raised an eyebrow at him.

"What was disrespectful about the way things were?" He looked confused.

"It's complicated." I didn't want to go into any of this in front of the kids. "Girls get in the car, we're going to pick up daddy in a minute." Erica opened the car door to do as she was told while Lanie stood there with her hands on her little hips. I cut my eyes at her, "you heard me!" Lanie kept her eyes on Jamal as she slowly did as she was told. "Boys, can you get in Uncle Nelson's car please?" They got in the car and both of them looked like they had their hands on the door in case they needed to jump out.

"When did my name get put on the terrorist list?" Jamal frowned.

"Kids pick up on vibes. What's changed?" Uncle Nelson asked.

"He's dating Ethan's ex and I don't want her around Ethan. She can't see Erica without getting emotional."

"She lost her child, I guess you can't empathize with that." His eyes were serious.

"My point is she can't handle seeing Erica. I don't want her around Ethan."

"You mean anymore." His face was drop dead serious.

298

I grabbed my purse like it would change what he just said. "You gonna marry her?" If he said yes then it wasn't as bad as he was alluding to. If he said no they all die! "I don't know!" He watched my eyes. "It depends on what you do."
"Why?"
Jamal looked at Uncle Nelson like he was wishing he wasn't standing there. Uncle Nelson gave him a big toothy smile. "Call me tomorrow, my number's on the congregation list." Then he looked at Uncle Nelson, "it was good seeing you again." Then he walked away.
Uncle Nelson put his hands on my shoulders. "Don't jump to conclusions without talking to your husband. Even then you only do what your heart can handle. You've got a beautiful family." He gestured towards the kids who were all watching me. Why did I have to have so many?
When I got in the car, Erica quietly watched me while Lanie sang along with the radio from the front seat. Lanie went inside to get Ethan; Erica didn't move she just stared.
Ethan was quiet when he got in the car, which wasn't unusual these days. He didn't notice that I was quiet; he was lost in his thoughts. I followed as he picked produce and herbs and explained to the girls how to pick them and why. When we were in line he put his arm around me and told me I looked nice then he kissed me mechanically. I looked at him hoping he'd notice my expression, but he didn't. When the groceries were loaded he exhaled. "On top of everything right now," then he looked at me. "Why didn't you tell me?" His eyes held irritation and pain. "Gwen?"
"Gwen?" I swallowed immediately thinking of Troy.
"Who's the guy? I can't be in all places at all times. Who's the guy she's dating?" I internally sighed a sigh of relief. I explained how they met. We were having lunch with Mr. Bell and his associate when Gwen's friend kept looking in our direction. He was very handsome and polished, I imagined Ethan being like that if he was white and smiled half as much as this guy did. Gwen was ignoring him at first until she realized that he was sitting with a female. Once our clients left Gwen smiled giving him the green light to approach. At first I thought he wouldn't because he wasn't alone. When it was time to go the woman headed for the door and he came to our table. He said a polite hello to me, and then he introduced himself as Martin Zaragoza. I liked his name, and the way he kept his eyes on Gwen like she was a flame that he was drawn to. I didn't know if he sent the woman away or what, but he wasn't in a hurry. He charmed her seven digits from her. Gwen on the other hand was trying to play unimpressed, but I could tell she liked him. When he left I clapped in excitement, but she tried to play it off like it was nothing.
The next morning she came in my office all flushed. Her complexion was completely pale, I was afraid something had happened with one of our clients. She said she was up most of the night talking to Martin. She wrung her hands together and she screamed at me. Ethan looked at us, shook his head and went back to his work. We were always screaming and acting silly. She said she didn't know what to do; he's a nice guy in charming guy's clothing. She said she doesn't know what to

do with a nice guy, she's used to dogs. She said he kept telling her how much he loves her red curly hair. How beautiful she is, and he appreciates how smart she is. When I asked her when she was going to see him again she said that night.

THE NEXT morning she came in flushed again. She said their date went GREAT! She said it was different on this side of the fence. This was the first time that a man was pursuing her, talking to her, asking her questions about herself, and listening. When she said she didn't sleep with him that night, I think I lost color.

They dated almost every night for four weeks before they slept together. I know that seems like no time, but in Gwen time that was like three years of no sex. The morning after Gwen called me from the lobby all shook up about it. She cried as she said it was beautiful. Normally Gwen gets pretty graphic with her details about the sex. This time all I got was that it was beautiful.

"Oh that's just Martin he's a very sweet guy."

"JUST MARTIN!" Ethan was in big brother protective mode. "Why didn't you tell me?"

"Just because she's your sister doesn't mean that I report back to you about all the things going on in her life. How would that encourage sisterly bonding?"

Ethan was more irritated than he should've been about the whole thing. "You're my wife, you don't keep secrets with anyone from me!"

"But you keep secrets from me." I watched his face, which didn't really tell me anything cause it rarely changes.

"You're trying to pick a fight."

"No, I think you're trying to pick a fight with me."

Ethan looked at me, "so now you're going to play echo with me. Everything I say you're going to say it back?"

"Come here," I said patting the bed next to me. Ethan frowned at me, so I patted the bed again. He reluctantly came closer to me and as soon as he sat on the bed. I attacked him; part of me was now looking for the signs that said my husband had exerted all of his energy with someone else. His kisses were the same full of love and passion for me. I kissed my name on his heart wondering if his tattoo still carried the same weight. He was at a full salute, nothing like he was tired or this was a second or third erection. Ethan is still in love with me, I could feel it in every thrust. I was thoroughly confused.

In the morning Gwen came in my office flushed again. "I'm late she whispered." with horror in her face.

"How? Are you sure you counted right? Could it be stress?"

"I'm... I... I have a doctor's appointment late this morning. The only way this could be possible is if that acne medicine interfered with my birth control."

I looked at her with big eyes, "I've heard of that happening. Crap Gwen! What are you going to do?"

She laughed hysterically, "keep it. Marry Martin? I don't know. Is it wrong that it feels kind of perfect? I feel like if I go to the doctor and they say I'm not pregnant, I'll feel cheated."

"You want to have children? You've never said either way."

"Jenise I want this, I just didn't know it until now. Am I crazy?" She looked at me for approval.

I gave her a hug, and then Ethan looked at us as he walked into his office. "Oh and a heads up, they know something. Ethan came in the room last night with his panties in a bunch about Martin."

Gwen's cheeks turned red, "life in a bubble is getting old for me. There's always someone watching. They give you the bigger office and fascinating view so then we'll always have to meet in here. They're watching who we bring in, who we meet with, who we see. We need our own office!"

"Should I start pulling listings?"

"No need, I have a list. Can you take me to my doctor's appointment then we can go look from there?"

My brain started ticking, "I can drop you and pick you up. I need to run an errand in the in-between time. Page me when you're done."

"Sounds like a plan." Then she went back to her office.

I took out my coin purse and the congregation list. I went downstairs and across the street to the pay phone in the lobby of the building over there. I told Jamal where to meet me and what time. Ethan was on the phone when Gwen and I left, I dropped her off at her doctor's office, she excitedly told me to wish her well. I went inside the "A Cup of Tea" bistro off of college in Berkeley. Jamal was waiting upstairs in the far back table like I told him to. He stood when he saw me, he looked nervous. I hugged him hello then I sat down. Jamal didn't beat around the bush he dove right in. He started by telling me that he still loves me, I wasn't expecting that, and I couldn't understand why he'd still feel that way. After all these years? My fifteenth wedding anniversary was coming, how could he still possibly? The look in his eyes told me it was true and not to question it, so I sat there waiting for him to move past it. He said quite simply that my choice determines what he does. If I choose to stand by my husband then he and Nohemi would try to work things out. However, if I wanted out he wanted me. I frowned as I tried to let the foreign thought sink in. I asked him what he knew. He said he knows that they meet up from time to time; it's not consistent enough to put a pattern to it. He said whenever they meet up Nohemi is emotional and somewhat depressed afterwards. He said sometimes she calls him in the middle of the night cause she's had a nightmare about the baby. I asked him if he had proof that my husband was sleeping with Nohemi. He reminded me that he said they saw each other, he didn't say they were sleeping with each other cause he didn't know. "Jamal I love my husband! I don't want you holding on for false hope. Even if for one reason or another Ethan and I separated, I couldn't come to you. If you're going to marry Nohemi then marry her. Don't wait on me to make that decision."

"We both have baggage. Mine is losing you and then being stuck in the Friend Zone for the past what…. eight years, or so? Watching you play happy wife and mother to someone else when you were mine. You can't be happy sitting during service alone. Then all that mess with Colette! Nohemi is beautiful, smart, and she has her own money that she's worked hard for. Just like you she has a weakness for Ethan. I understand it though; I don't fault her for it. I get it; he's a better man than I am."

"Why would you speak of yourself that way?"

"He's tall dark, doesn't smile, and a commanding presence. I'm just your average guy on the side trying to get some genuine loving from someone good."

"Nohemi is good. She was good to Ethan when she had him. She needs to understand what it feels like to lose you to appreciate you."

"So how do you want to move forward?" He said not overlooking that I didn't say Ethan wasn't better than him. There's NOTHING wrong with Jamal, he's a good guy. I'm already married to the love of my life, whether we come out of this intact or not.

Chapter 27

Ethan

"You sure you want to do this?" I said looking at the ring box.

"It's time and I'm ready!" Franky said with a full smile.

I moved the box in my hand, "marriage is dumb. Why did I marry Jenise again?"

"Because regardless if you had that tattoo on your heart or not, she is the only woman in there." He reached for the box. "You haven't confronted her yet?"

"How can I without it backfiring on me? I have to ask myself if a couple of meet ups with Jamal is worth the backlash."

"I'm surprised you're so calm about it. I'm surprised he's still alive."

I shook my head, "I can't deal with one more thing! Pops, Momma and Dad, some little boy's calling for Erica, Gwen's getting married. My wife... I know what I've done, I can't confront her."

There was a knock at the door, I gave the box to Franky and then I told the person to come in. Malachi peeked his head in. "Please tell this fool he's making a mistake! What's the hurry Franky, we're young we've got plenty of time to settle down and have babies."

"Speak for yourself young-buck. I'm in my forties and not getting any younger. My oats are sewn, I'm ready to settle down and become boring like my little brothers." Franky said.

"Boring? I'm not!" I had to think about it, he had a point. "Well so what, I like..." I shifted in my chair.

"Denise and I are not ready for marriage." Malachi said shaking his head.

"You mean you aren't. She's ready, believe me." Franky said.

"Fine, fine. Tomato, Tamato! I'm not ready, Denise should understand?"

"Do women ever understand?" I huffed.

Malachi looked at Franky to ask him what was wrong with me. "Blu, I don't know why we can't go twist this guy's cap backwards on General Purpose!"

I looked at my brother, "when will you calm down?"

"When you learn to react! You see that fool didn't show his face at our office anymore after my proper send off. You like to coddle these fools too much!"

"This isn't about him, it's about Jenise."

Malachi bucked his eyes, "Jenise is stepping out on you?"

"It's not like that..."

Malachi cut me off, "I'm with Franky! Denise tried that crap! Her little friend will never walk again. She knows better!"

My eyes bounced between them. "You two need to calm down! If I react this backfires on me."

"SO WHAT! You ain't got your woman in check? What's good for the goose is not good for the gander."

I looked at my little cousin and his young reasoning. "You let me know how that works out for you when you're married with children. I need to think this through unemotionally and you all are not helping."

"I guess, but you're always a shrinking violet when it comes to Jenise." Franky said, "in the middle of all of this you're letting her move their office."

I shook my head not wanting to discuss it anymore. Jenise knocked on the door smiling as she pushed it open. "Gentlemen," she nodded.

"See! Another reason you shouldn't leave us. How are you going to see my dashingly good looking face daily if you and Gwen move?" Franky joked.

"You'll still see me." She said putting an envelope in front of me on my desk. She winked at me and then she floated out.

"Ok, that's confusing!" Malachi erupted.

I eyed the envelope suspiciously. "Very!"

"If you don't open it, I will open it for you." Franky said diving for my envelope. I looked at Jenise and she was watching us covering her huge smile. Franky and I played snatch the envelope. I got it and I told Franky to calm down. I neatly opened my now crinkled envelope. There was a handwritten letter inside.

Dear Ethan,
I think you're SO cute! Will you go out on a date with me?

☐　　*Yes*

☐　　*No*

　　Jenise

"What does it say?" Franky asked as he watched me blush.

I cut my eyes at Jenise who was trying to act like she wasn't watching. With Franky and Malachi over my shoulders I checked the yes box. I gave my letter to Malachi who fought with Franky over who was going to deliver my response. I couldn't stop grinning as Jenise waited. Franky gave it to her, and then she told him to hold on as she wrote something else. She shook her finger at him and then he ran back to me. I opened the letter.

Dear Ethan,
I am excited. Please wear something sexy! I will pick you up tonight; tell your family not to wait up.

Jenise

I couldn't stop blushing as Franky and Malachi excitedly jumped around. I really did feel like Jenise teleported me back to grade school. We acted like kids for a little longer, and then I got back to work. Pops called me checking on financials for Cooper Financial. He was still fighting and I cherished every extra moment with him.

When I went home Erica was doing homework at the counter and watching Lanie make dinner. I put the keys to my car in Erica's hand. I told her that her mother and I were going out tonight. She wasn't sixteen just yet but she was driving and I'd send her to the store from time to time. EJ and Eric drive as well, but those knuckleheads would go on a joy ride just for the fun of it. I kissed Lanie's forehead and I asked what she was making. Her eyes danced around the room as she said "Lanie surprise." Lanie likes to play mad scientist in the kitchen. The stuff she comes up with although delicious sometimes lacks the polished presentation that I hold my dishes to. We let the boys taste first and when they don't fall out on the floor from poisoning then we take courage and taste. I told her I was sorry I was going to miss tonight's experiment.

EJ met me at the stairs; his eyes were serious as he told me he needed to talk to me. He followed me to my room, he shut the door. A little bit of worry spread across his face. He said he needed to talk to me about sex. I couldn't help it a smile spread across my face. I asked him if it was love or urges. He said both; I shook my head in understanding. I asked him to give me until tomorrow. I told him we would talk and I'd make sure he had what he needed. EJ agreed and then he walked out. I showered and then dressed. Jenise pulled up as I walked down the stairs. I told the kids I was gone, and they had no idea when we were coming so I didn't want any stunts. They all tried to hold innocent expressions. I knew that meant they were going to sneak and do something. When I got in the car I kissed Jenise's cheek hello.

Jenise

Ethan looked very good when he walked out the door. I told myself to smile. Even though I wasn't dreading the outcome of tonight, I hated that this had to happen at all. Ethan kissed my cheek when he got in the car, he smelled delicious.

We rode in silence and I took us to a lounge on the boarder of Berkeley and Albany. Ethan didn't say anything, he started staring at me. He knew where we were; this is where he normally meets Nohemi for lunch or whatever. I took his hand and I firmly linked my fingers in amongst his. His hold was firm, but he came with me willingly. I didn't look at him. We walked to the back hand in hand to Jamal and Nohemi. Jamal's face changed immediately as soon as he saw us. Nohemi dropped her head. Ethan let me scoot into the booth first as he looked at Jamal. Ethan's face was serious while Nohemi sat there crying. I was torn between feeling bad for her and wanting to hit her. "Jamal this is my husband whom I love deeply. Ethan you know Jamal and Nohemi."

Ethan looked at me, "the point of this?"

"I don't want to play telephone or run in assumptions. I want to know what's going on. I want the complete truth!" I said looking him in his eyes.

"Jenise this is emotional." He said cause I knew he refused to show emotion in front of them.

"Nohemi is over there crying enough for everyone. Speak on it matter of factly. This ends tonight!"

"This isn't what we discussed." Jamal said to me.

"I want them both here, no more he said she said. You've been stringing this along long enough." I looked at Ethan, "I know you know I've been meeting with him."

"Yes," Ethan adjusted in his chair.

Ethan

"Timing is everything, and at the perfect time for nonsense, confusion, and gut wrenching despair she shows up releasing my babygirl that never was' name..." Jenise interrupted me, "did you sleep with her?"

I put my hands out, "no. But it's not that simple."

"So your dick belongs to me, what about your tongue?" Jenise said bluntly.

"Yours."

"Ok your explanation?" She said looking like she was in a business meeting.

"*Stuff* did happen."

"Do you want to be with Nohemi?" She asked watching Nohemi.

"No."

"This wasn't about getting back together." Nohemi said over her tears.

"Then what?" Jamal looked at her irritated.

"My.... Our daughter died! Time doesn't heal that. Neither one of us have dealt with the loss of Amina." She cried, "you wouldn't understand. All of your children are living and healthy!"

Jenise looked at me, "there's nothing you can do to change what's already happened. She is not worth losing me!"

Jenise

Nohemi looked at me, "ignoring the past won't fix the present either."

Did this trick just get smart with me? My rage started in my stomach, traveled up my neck and came out of every opening on my head. "I do recall making you a promise!" I reached in my purse and pulled out my gun. "I told you to stay away from my husband didn't I?"

Nohemi and Jamal's eyes got big as they looked at my gun sitting in my hand on the table. "JENISE!" Jamal exclaimed as he pushed back in his seat.

"This is what I needed you to understand the first time I told you... I WILL END YOU! ETHAN IS MY MAN! MY HUSBAND! I GAVE HIM LIFE FOUR TIMES! WHY WOULD YOU THINK THE OLD JENISE IS STILL HERE SITTING BACK AND PATIENTLY WAITING FOR YOU TO DECIDE WHEN YOU'RE DONE WITH HIM! I STEPPED DOWN ONCE! I WOULD NEVER BE THAT STUPID AGAIN!" I let my thumb rest on the metal, "NOW I MADE YOU A PROMISE! DO YOU THINK I'M A LIAR?"

"NO! NO YOU'RE NOT A LIAR!" Nohemi was trembling.

I gestured towards Jamal, "What about you?"

"You crazy!"

"But not a liar right?"

"Jenise!" Jamal pleaded.

I looked at Ethan who sat there looking unamused by my actions. "ETHAN! DO SOMETHING!" Nohemi pleaded.

"I swear to God Ethan if you say anything in her defense I will shoot you too!" I spit at him.

Ethan

I'm sitting here looking at my wife hanging on to the last thread of her sanity. They got the nerve to say those crazy twins act like me. All I see is Eric in her right now, extremely emotional and about to snap. I should've never let Nana show her how to use those things. I knew she was upset, and it was my fault. I slowly reached out and gently put my hand on hers. Jenise was trembling so lightly, she was on the verge of snapping in the middle of this crowded place. Her grip was tight but she released the gun when I took it from her. I dropped the clip, and Nohemi started crying hysterically when she saw the gun was loaded. I put the safety on and then I put the gun in my pocket. Jenise was angry but she was not crying.

I turned my attention to Jamal, "so let me guess. You were trying to convince her to choose you with all of this?"

Jamal wiped his forehead with his napkin, "of course."

I looked at Jenise, "do you want him?"

Jenise flared her nostrils at me, "WOULD I BE HERE TRYING TO KILL HER IF I WANTED HIM?"

"Let's have this out once and for all like adults."

"Meaning what?" Jenise wiggled her neck, "you're sneaking around with your ex. You're supposed to be the adult here?"

I took a deep breath, "answer the damn question Jenise!"

She rolled her eyes so hard I just knew she was about to fall asleep. "Jamal you are going to make someone a wonderful husband some day, but I already have one." Then she looked me up and down, "at least I thought I did!"

"We will deal with us later." Then I looked at Nohemi who was completely traumatized. "Do I even need to say goodbye?"

"You might not, but I do!" Jamal turned his body towards her. "I told you everything that I've been through and here you go taking me through something else. So you didn't have quote unquote sex, what did you do?" Nohemi shook her head looking down at her hands. "ANSWER ME!" He hit the table.

I nodded at Jamal; he was trying to be tough. He was going to make her pay, but I could see love for her in his eyes. It was masked by hurt and anger. If he didn't care, he would've gotten up and walked away. "He wouldn't respond to me." She said lowly. I looked at Jenise who was focusing hard to hear her.

"What does that mean?"

"He...." She took a deep breath so that she could talk. "I'm sorry Jamal, I tried to sleep with him. It wasn't about sex, it was.... It doesn't matter because he didn't respond to me no matter what I did."

Jenise looked me up and down, "since when you don't respond?"

"To you!" I made my point, Jenise relaxed some and some of the crazy left her eyes.

"So you were acting out, how is sleeping with my husband supposed to bring Amina back?" Hearing Jenise say my baby girl's name hit me like a whip.

Nohemi shook her head; "he's the only other person on this planet who lost what I lost. I hurt every day; some moments of pain are louder than others. Most days I can fake it. There are no words to explain this, I wasn't trying to steal your husband, and Jamal I wasn't trying to hurt you."

"BULL! You were trying to get back at me for everything that happened while we were in college." Jenise said.

"YOU LIED TO ME! YOU SAID YOU WEREN'T DATING HIM!" Nohemi's cheeks were bright red and her eyes were now swollen.

"No I didn't! I wasn't dating Ethan then. I was still technically with Jamal."

"You were sleeping with my boyfriend behind my back!"

Jenise pursed her lips, "not at first. It did end that way though, and you know what. I'm sorry about that. I didn't mean for it to happen in the first place. Ethan wanted to break up with you immediately and I begged him not to. I was devastated when Ethan told me about the baby. My fear of hurting you caused all of this." She internalized it for a minute. "The difference between you and I though. I would've never let my selfishness affect children. I ran away so that your daughter wouldn't have to live in a separate house from her father. You could've cared less about mine because they're not yours! I almost felt bad for you until I realized you had the opportunity to move on. Start over, and you're so busy looking backwards that you jeopardized your future."

"I DON'T CARE ABOUT ALL OF THIS! WHY IS YOUR PAIN MORE IMPORTANT THAN THE PAIN YOU'RE CAUSING ME? HE DON'T WANT YOU! HE'S NOT GOING TO! I WANTED YOU! I WAS GOING TO MARRY YOU!" Jamal got up and walked out.

"You better go chase him! Cause I'm getting my gun back and the bullet in the chamber has your name on it!" Jenise said in a scary calm voice.

Nohemi didn't hesitate; she slid out of the booth and ran out behind Jamal.

Jenise

I was too angry and hurt to be scared. I stared at Ethan who stared back at me. "We need to leave before we tear down this restaurant!"

"Get up then!" He didn't move.

I angrily slid around the table and got up. A few people looked at us cause they heard us fussing in the booth, but for the most part the music was loud. When we stepped outside Ethan snatched my keys from me. I hit him upside his head, he looked at me out the corner of his eyes but he walked on. "YOU MAKE ME SO SICK!" I ran in his path, and he stopped walking. "YOU THINK I'M GOING TO PUT UP WITH THIS?"

"No," he said like my question was dumb.

"How could you do this to me?" I said as tears finally fell from my eyes.

Ethan

Seeing Jenise cry knowing it was my fault hurt worse than anything I could think of in this moment. Worse than losing Amina. I threw my arms around her hugging her, she accepted my hug at first then she started fighting to get free. "I don't want to have this conversation on a random sidewalk."

"I'm not getting in that car with you! I gave you space in there, I can't give you anymore!" She was still fighting me.

"You want me to talk to you here? Get in the car and I'll take us somewhere." I released her to open her car door.

Jenise looked at me and then she started walking. I grabbed her arm, "ETHAN YOU ARE ABOUT TO LOSE ME! I COULD CARELESS ABOUT WHO WALKS PASS US RIGHT NOW! WHO SEES YOU CRY! IF YOU WANT ME TO GET IN THAT CAR YOU BETTER GIVE ME A REASON TO."

"Our family is a reason to!"

"Our family was not a reason for you not to, why should I care about our family?" She put her hands on her hips. "You don't care neither do I!"

"I care Jenise!"

"You've got a funny way of showing it! Why would you let her touch you? Because she pulled on your emotional strings? Who's next? The girl from your first wet dream?" Then she swung at the air. "You made a liar out of me! I planned on shooting her!"

"That would've been dumb!"

"I don't care! I warned her! And she proceeded like I wouldn't. Being closer to God does not mean I will ignore her mistakes or forgive her! Being closer to God does not mean I won't snap! I HATE when people assume that my life means I'm a push over!"

Eric said the same thing once when he was trying to explain why he beat this kid within inches of his life. "I couldn't live with the guilt of you being locked up." She tilted her head to the side. "NIGGA PLEASE! YOU NEVER LEAVE HOME WITHOUT SOMEONE TO CLEAN UP YOUR MESS! YOU JUST DIDN'T WANT ME TO SHOOT HER! YOU BETTER MAKE SURE SHE'S GONE, I WILL SHOOT HER REGARDLESS IF I STAY OR NOT!"

I grabbed her arm, "you can be as mad as you need to be, but you can't leave me!" Jenise snatched her arm and swung at me. "YOU DON'T CONTROL ME! I CAN LEAVE IF I WANT TO!"

"You can try and argue with me about your right to leave me all you want to. I'm telling you right now, it'll never happen. Moving to Texas didn't stop me from walking around in your house. You could try leaving the country and when you wake up each morning I will be right there!" Jenise was confused because she looked like she wanted to smile. I did NOT want to have this conversation outside in front of strangers walking by. I also didn't want witnesses to me throwing her butt in the car and the police being called. The headache! I leaned against the car, took a deep breath. "You want me to explain stuff that is all stacked on top of other things. I don't know where this begins Jenise. That's the honest truth."

To kill me more her tears were back. "Start where you forgot about me!"

"I could never forget about you! I couldn't get it up, not that I wanted to." I looked around, "when do I ever have a problem with performing?"

"I don't know you are getting older." She held back a smile.

"This is not funny Jenise." I chuckled, "I've never been that lost in my life! My little girl died! She's dead! Gone! Your touch has been my only comfort for so long and in that moment I lost you for nothing. I should've never listened to you! I did that to her, and then the trauma. Death is all around us these days. Cat tried to save my family and I reward her by having her killed." Jenise gasped and moved closer to me. "It doesn't bother me of course when random people die. Leonard, Whispers, my... Auntie...." I shook my head, "it's too much!"

"YOU COME TO ME! YOU DON'T DO THIS! THIS IS UNACCEPTABLE! I'm so mad at you Ethan!"

"I know, if it helps. You are taking this a lot better than I thought you would." She smiled through her tears, "why would you flirt with me if you knew we were coming here?"

She scratched her head messing up her slick ponytail. I now understand the style; she came prepared for a fight. "I don't know," she exhaled in defeat. "I'm not going anywhere," she cut her eyes at me. "This time! I kind of figured it was something like this. Once Poppa told me about his prognosis I lightened up on you. I know you weren't seeing her very often anyways. This is your one pass Ethan!"

"Understood."

I reached out for her, "DON'T TOUCH ME! I'm still mad at you!" She snatched her keys back from me and drove back to the house.

So I know I told these fools we were going out. True to teenager style people were in my house. I told Jenise to block the gate with her car. We walked in the front door and Eric was letting a little girl kiss all over him on the couch out of the sight of the others. Lanie, Erica, and a boy and girl I did not recognize were at the table playing cards. When the girl at the table saw us she hopped up and ran right into the sliding glass door window. The stupid idiot didn't realize the door was closed. I told the boy to sit while Jenise had Eric by the ear. I asked where EJ was, Erica swallowed and said upstairs. Jenise had Eric's ear in the death grip of fury. I told them to stay put. I quietly opened the door as some little girl was going to town, working her head sucking the life out of my son. She was shirtless and on her knees. EJ was so focused on her doing her job that he failed to notice me standing there. It's something about getting served in your room. I stood there waiting for him to finish. As he finished, I cleared my throat. The girl tried to scream as she swallowed and started choking. I put my hand out and told the little girl not to move. I did not want her to turn around. I told EJ to fix his clothes and to bring his friend downstairs.

Jenise had Eric's ear as she yelled at him asking him if this was what he had in mind for her expensive couch. "Do you have any idea how much this couch cost!" She yelled at the little girl, the little girl shook her head no with big eyes. "Touch it!"

When the little girl didn't move, she jerked Eric's ear. "TOUCH IT!" The little girl gently stroked the couch. "I spent $7000 on just that part of that couch. You think I want some disrespectful and nasty teenagers getting your juices on it?"

"Jenise."

"WHAT?" She looked crazy!

"The boy's ear!"

She forgot she was holding it. "Sit your nasty behind down!" When EJ and the girl came down the stairs Jenise's eyes turned red! She told EJ to come here so she could rapid fire slap him upside the head. Both of the boys sat side by side on the couch. Honestly my mom has caught me and my brothers doing way worse. I was reminiscing when Jenise called me back to the room. "Oh something's funny to you?" She said wiggling her neck and crossing her arms. "Tell the others to get in here!" All the kids quickly came in the room. "I don't know you!" She pointed at the strange kids. Then she turned to the boys; "I don't want hoes in my house!"

"Jenise!" She didn't have to say or do any of this in front of these strange kids.

"Jenise what? Would you be so calm if Erica had a boy here doing what either of our sons were doing?"

Ok I was now on her level of going off.

"But all I was doing was beating them at cards." Lanie whined.

The look that came across Jenise's face scared me, and Lanie immediately straightened up. Jenise went off on all the kids. You would've thought she's spent her entire life cursing with her colorful combinations. I held the dogs back and I moved her car when Jenise sent the intruders out. Jenise's tangent intensified while she went in harder on the kids. Finally Lanie erupted in a plea for mercy singing everyone's thoughts. Everyone was on punishment! Then she stormed upstairs. The kids all looked at me with big eyes as if I could save them. I reminded them that even Lanie was in trouble there was no hope for anyone.

Jenise was still fussing to herself when I walked in the room. She was in her robe and just out the shower. She was beyond angry with everyone. I had two choices, curl up and rollover and accept her right to anger. OR! Demand the affection I desperately need from her right now. She can be as mad as she needs to be for as long as she needs to, but I can't handle her denying me. As if she heard my brain ticking she looked at me and said NO! I didn't turn my eyes I kept looking at her. NO! She kept saying NO! I told her to come here, I could see her mad at me and arguing with herself. So I kept wagging my finger waiting for her to come to me. I knew better than to go to her, she was ready to punch and I was not in the mood for that. I felt beat down and depressed. At least if I made her feel good I could try to sleep tonight. Jenise turned her back to me as she sat at her vanity and put her facial stuff on. I didn't care I like the way it smelled. I was sitting directly in her mirror so every time she looked up she saw me. She yelled a few more curse words at me and then continued on with her nightly routine. When Jenise got up her robe hung on to the chair showing off her naked thigh. Jenise angrily tugged at her robe for betraying her. When she walked past me I put my hands out and she huffed as she tried to remain strong. I could see her weakening even though she was fighting as hard as she could. She told me to leave her alone cause she was still mad at me, I told her I understood that. I told her this wasn't about me. She rolled her eyes and said NO! When she walked past me again I tugged on her robe, she stopped and frowned at me. I looked up at her innocently and I said, "but it's Wednesday!" Jenise's eyes rolled back in her head as her mouth defiantly said, "Hump Day!"

"All I want to do is give you an Eskimo kiss then you can continue being mad at me." I watched her eyes.

Her eyes said, "YES!" but her mouth said, "no." I sat on the bed watching her inner struggle as it became apparent.

****

"What were you thinking bringing that girl to our house?" I asked EJ.

"You two never come back that fast, it was a bad call." He watched me, "she was very angry."

"Yes she IS!" I said looking out the window. "Park over there." I pointed to the parking spot furthest in the lot. We got out the car and we walked to a bench over looking the Marina. I handed him a brown paper bag. "This is not a license to go out and screw all women over. I just don't know if it's realistic to think my son would wait until marriage. Was yesterday the first time you got head?"

"Yes," he said opening the bag.

"Now-a-days you can't let females lick you without a condom, she could've had herpes or worse."

"Isn't it the same difference if I kiss her?"

"That depends on you. Your mother was the first female I ever kissed or let kiss me. Kissing is intimate and personal; it's up to you whether you kiss them. I'm just telling you what I did. Understand?"

"Yes," he took the three boxes of condoms out the bag and the zucchini. He looked at me quizzically.

"The cheap ones are for practice. You need to learn how to put them on and you wear them like your life depends on them, cause it does. Always bring your own, never use hers. Pay attention to your environment if something feels even kind of *different* pull out and inspect your condom. YOU DO NOT TOUCH ANY FEMALE WITHOUT A CONDOM! I don't care if you love her or not! I don't care if she's on the pill, or has some spongy thing pushed up her stuff. DON'T BE STUPID!"

"Yes sir," he continued looking at everything.

"You have a better head on your shoulders than I did at your age, but you're about to enter a world where women are vicious, heartless, and cruel. Some women think because they know some new tricks that's going to keep you coming back. Nothing a trick can do will make you stay, all they do is get you in trouble."

"What made you love momma?"

I inhaled, "she didn't want anything from me but to be up under me. She followed me around all the time, making me laugh, and well you know how she is. She paid attention to me as a person. She did this so well I almost felt like she was part of a trap. I asked her if she was a cop even. I didn't talk much then."

He cut me off, "then?"

"I talk more now than I ever did before."

"Wow!"

"She was the first person to show me genuine unbiased affection. She infected me with her ways; I didn't even realize it was happening until it happened already. It was too late, she had me, and she didn't even realize it." I looked at my son who was processing all of this information. "Who are these for?"

EJ shook his head, "they're not for her. I," he scratched his head. "I want to be ready for her. I want to know what to do when its time for her. The not knowing is worse than the waiting."

"Practice doesn't make perfect in this case. You may know what to do, but it's not going to matter when you're with her." Then I thought about it, "well at first anyways. If she's new to sex she won't know what she likes. She won't know her body; she'll have to learn how to ask for what she wants. It is not one size fits all when it comes to this. Sex can be hardcore and over just as fast as it starts, making love takes time. I'm going to give you instruction for sex, cause it's important to know how to handle yourself, and after all you must carry on the Wallace man legacy. However, when it comes to making love, you're on your own. That's a learned behavior nothing can prepare you for that." I showed my son how to put a condom on and how to take it off. Then I explained the basics. Things I wish I knew my first few go arounds, when my dad finally blessed us with the information my whole game plan changed. EJ asked questions and I broke everything down to him. I told him this was a lot to absorb all at once so he could come back whenever he needed to ask me questions. He told me about the girl he likes; he said she's innocent and sweet. She reminds him of his momma. He disappointedly said he wasn't ready for her. "It seems like every time she looks at me I can hear her calling me lord on her heart."

"What?" I didn't know what he was talking about.

My son quickly explained a bible passage to me about Abraham and Sarah. How much she loved her husband that she called him that on her heart. I told my son I didn't understand why if he honestly felt he had that why he needed to mess around. I told him girls like that girl yesterday would not make him feel any better about himself. I told him to never pass up on love for cheap thrills. Then he reminded me that her family goes to his congregation, and that he couldn't touch her until he married her. I blew air, cause this fool isn't even in high school; he's still got college to get through. I patted his back and I repeated myself, "hoes will not make you feel any better about yourself. If you're going to wait for her, then you should wait. It's not impossible."

Jenise

I was sitting at my desk staring at my computer while my body was still rocking. I HATE ETHAN SO MUCH! My body was on fire, but I wasn't ready for anything more. All I could do is sit here mad, hurt, and angry. His reason why was WEAK! I guess that's what made it feel sincere for me. If he had some smooth explanation then it would've felt rehearsed like he knew it was coming and he was prepared for it. I called Nana and Sophia answered the phone. I thought she was visiting, but she explained that she moved to be with Nana. Kind of stole my thunder cause I was going to offer for her to stay with us. I guess it's for the best that she doesn't have to move or leave her home and way of life. I asked how Poppa was doing, and Sophia said he's in his office working. She said he seems so strong you'd never know… then her voice trailed off and became painful. I was right there with her. Sophia invited us over Saturday for dinner and to meet her boyfriend. I knew Erica would be excited to see Sasha, I asked if Amber was coming as well. She said it depends on how she's feeling; I didn't want to pry so I didn't ask and Sophia didn't offer. When Nana got on the phone I told her Ethan took my gun and I needed another one. So of course I had to tell her what happened. Nana belly laughed so hard, I could see her turning red laughing at my recollection of last night. She was laughing hard and then suddenly her laughter stopped and then she said I should've shot the girl. I assured her I was going to, and then she smiled through her voice. Nana asked me what I was going to do next. I told her Ethan needed a break from everything here, I decided as I was talking to her that he and I needed to go away just the two of us. Nana said she agreed with my decision, she gave me the name of the travel agent she normally uses and then to make sure I called her to tell her what amazing place I was taking her grandson to. I asked her if it was a good idea to go away right now with Poppa's situation. She said he's doing really well and he's still fighting to stay with her. She told me to let her know our dates and nothing would happen back home until we got back. I called Nana's travel agent and then I made an appointment. I went down to her simple nice office and I explained that my husband and I needed a luxury vacation from everything and everyone. She took out brochures for Hawaii, the Caribbean, and then I saw it. It was unlike anything I've ever seen before. The French Polynesia, Bora Bora! The water looked warm and clear, and it looked like a peaceful and tranquil island. That's where I needed to go with my husband, we both needed to get away and just purge. We've been going since college, working, babies, families, we needed time to ourselves. When she gave me dates I called Uncle Nelson and I asked him if he could stay with my kids for two weeks while my husband and I went away. He barely let me finish before he said yes. He loved spending time with my kids, and they him. Uncle Nelson although lovable wouldn't take any of their crap. I could see one of those boys paying Lanie to distract my mom or Raynel while they snuck out. That wouldn't be the case with Uncle Nelson. Then I called Dito and I asked him if he could clear Ethan's calendar while we were gone. Dito told me to consider it done. I handed over my credit card and not even flinching when the travel agent gave me the total for our FIRST CLASS all the way trip. I knew Ethan was going to love it! I worry about cost way more than he does, but it's the way I grew up. When I got home, Erica and Lanie were walking around sad and pitiful cause they were on punishment, no videos, no television period, no music. The only thing they could do was read, and Lanie always asked Erica to read to her. Eric on the other hand was in the kitchen making the house smell delicious. He was just trying to butter me up as

well. I asked where their father and EJ went and they said they had to run an errand. When Ethan and his twin came home, they wore the
same expressionless expressions on their faces. They followed me with their eyes trying to judge what kind of mood I was in. Lanie set the table beautifully; she brought out my expensive China. Water glasses along with wine glasses that they drank grape juice out of were placed on the table to go with dinner. Lanie did everything except tuck my napkin under my shirt when I sat down. She lit a lavender candle hoping it would calm me, and then they set the dinner on the table. They think they're slick, braised lamb shanks, over spicy polenta, and a green salad. Lanie said she and Erica made a banana pudding for dessert. Eric volunteered to say a dramatic prayer over our meal and then they passed each dish to me first. They watched me as I took my first bite, I couldn't help it my eyes rolled in my head.

"You like it?" Eric asked excited.

"It's delicious baby." I said quickly, as I dug into my plate.

"I couldn't stop thinking about you all day. You are the best momma a guy could have. I wanted you to enjoy this meal from the bottom of my heart."

"That and you realized that spring break is coming and you don't want to be on punishment while you're out of school." I snapped.

"That too, but you got to admit this is a delicious please forgive me meal!" He smiled big.

"You know how to grovel." I cut my eyes at Ethan. When we finished eating Lanie set the pudding dish in the middle of the table. "I have news. Uncle Nelson's going to come stay here next week for two weeks. Your father and I are going away and he will be here with you." I looked at my boys, "don't get any special ideas just because you're taller than him. He will bring you down to his level, and if I find out that anyone." I looked at Lanie, "so much as poked their lip out at him you're going to have to deal with me. Understood?"

"Yes momma!" They said in unison.

Lanie made her face real pitiful, "momma. So, you're going to leave us here on punishment while you're away?" She clasped her hands together and pleaded with me to say no.

"I don't know, it depends on how you conduct yourself while I'm here. If I feel like you're sneaking or breaking your restrictions then yes! And one person will mess it up for all of you."

Everyone looked at Eric; he blushed and put his head down.

"Where are we going?" Ethan asked when he came up to the room.

"Bora Bora!" I showed him the brochure.

"Do you think now is the time to leave? Poppa…" He exhaled.

I told him I talked to Nana earlier and she told me to book it.

When we went over his grandparent's on Saturday Poppa was in good spirits, he looked very good. Ethan relaxed a lot. Ethan, Troy, and Malcolm tried not to like Travis, Sophia's boyfriend, but you could see they were fighting a losing battle. Once Troy caved it was a wrap, Malcolm didn't appreciate him caving but Troy shrugged. Travis is a good guy and very sweet. He was as square as they called him, he lacked the spice that Richard brought, but I figured she wanted something different. Sasha was very fond of him, which was all pluses in my book.

I told the kids they were off punishment as we walked out the door. We closed the door to them celebrating and retreating to their corners. When we got to the airport Ethan informed me that he changed our flight plans and we were no longer flying commercial. He said he leased a jet for our trip to save us time. It was going to take 27 hours to get to Bora Bora, now it was going to be much less. Everything was still FIRST CLASS but now even the setting was more intimate. We talked, we slept, and we ate. Everything was as beautiful if not more than the brochure made it seem. We had our own private pool in the middle of our bungalow. This was a clothing optional trip, and most times we opted to go without. It's kind of hard to be mad at naked Ethan. Ethan period, but naked Ethan stood at attention whenever I looked at him. I was strong the first night, but I gave in and it was over. I was tired from holding on to my anger anyways. He promised me never again! I promised him if there was ever a next time, somebody was dying.

Chapter 28

Ethan

This trip is everything I need right now. Jenise and I talked deeper and harder than we have ever before. She wasn't letting me slide on anything. I had to sit through her explaining how badly I hurt her as if I didn't already know by her demeanor in the lounge that night. If I tried to one word answer her she'd go off, seeing her in pain reminded me of my momma. My momma still isn't feeling my dad, and that's not the ending that I want for us. So I dug deeper and spilled everything I could from the depth of me. When she saw how hard I was truly trying, she cut me a tiny bit of slack and I do mean tiny. She wasn't holding back too much and I had to feel the effects of all of my wrongs. She was right; I should've come to her immediately. We've been together too long and been through too much to suddenly choke up like I did. I didn't relax until she did, I felt like at any moment she could throw her hands up. The things she explained about her family situation while she was growing up made me wonder how she ended up so lighthearted and silly. When I told her stuff about my family I didn't realize she hadn't connected certain dots, but I guess if you didn't live my life you wouldn't. Only Jenise could make me laugh at the idea of my little sister turning out her now husband. I hated to go back, but we needed to return to real life and our family. We promised each other a family vacation and a couples vacation each year. Jenise called home before we left the hotel. I could see the stress lines on her face as she tried to calm the person over the phone. Jenise turned pale as tears fell from her eyes and she watched me approach her. My heart was pounding, as I knew before she said, that it was Poppa. I told myself to be strong and deal with it. Jenise looked at me with tears pouring out of her eyes, "Troy!"

Jenise

Ethan blinked for a long time like he didn't understand. I told Erica who was crying her eyes out that we were getting on the plane and we'd be there shortly. Ethan stood there frowning like he didn't understand. I gently led him by the hand into our cab. Once we were in the air Ethan asked me to explain what I meant. I told him as much as Erica told me. I couldn't describe the look of pain on Ethan's face. I wondered about Rosalind and her daughter, Malcolm, Fuzzy, and their whole family. I don't know if they're his sisters or cousins, but Tiffany and Penny were always around him when they were younger. I held on to Ethan as he looked out the window most of the time. A few tears fell from his eyes, but I figure he was waiting to hear that I had it wrong. Honestly I was hoping the same.

When we got to the house Uncle Nelson gave me all the funeral information as he gave us his condolences. Ethan changed his clothes then he got in his car. I asked him where he was going and he told me he'd be back. The look on his face said to leave him alone. He burned rubber as he exited the gate. Uncle Nelson said Ethan was more than likely going to be with his family. Uncle Nelson has taken the kids over Troy's cousin Renee's house everyday to be with their family.

Erica was very sad about the whole thing. She said that Tanisha was telling her on the camping trip how much she loved her stepfather. She said she was sad because she couldn't imagine living life without her daddy. I asked her how Tanisha was holding up, and she started crying she was devastated. I hugged my baby girl who was crying her cousin's tears.

There were so many people at the funeral; I helped Sophia with the food. All the men were in their own pain, little words and lots of liquor. The kids all congregated around Tanisha and another little girl. There was another man, who spoke with Frank and the Uncles. He watched Malcolm, it was like he wanted to approach him but he didn't. When he came through the food line he put his eyes on me and then he kept looking at me. Whenever I looked up to get a location on Ethan and the kids he was looking. I was talking to Uncle Tim through his shades; I could hear that he was upset in his voice. He was saying he was so tired of funerals when Ethan walked over and said he needed to go. He had enough and needed to go home and lay down. Uncle Tim said he'd bring the children home later for us, cause the kids all seemed to need each other right now. When we got home Ethan undressed in the middle of the floor down to his shorts, letting his clothes lay where they fell, and climbed in the bed. I knew he was beyond words when he didn't pick up after himself. I climbed on the bed on top of the covers and I rubbed Ethan's head and kissed his lips. A tear fell when he said he can't live like this anymore. He said he couldn't continue like this. He's tired of losing people he cares about behind nonsense. I rubbed his head as he yelled, screamed, and cried out loud about the loss of his little brother. The buzzer from the gate sounded and I jumped, Ethan exhaled. I went to the monitor and it was Raynel, I could see Dito, and Franky's car behind hers. I told him it was his mom, Ethan didn't respond. I buzzed them in and then I picked up his clothes off the floor. I opened the door and Raynel hugged me, the men and their women followed her. They all went up to my room; I was about to go up when Frank opened the gate. I stood at the door waiting for him. He approached the house slowly. He asked how Ethan was doing; I said he was very upset. Frank stood in the doorway looking like Ethan when he's a little unsure of how to react to our boys when they're emotional. They care, but they don't know what to do. "Frank everybody's in the room, just go in." Frank exhaled and then he slowly walked up the stairs.

****

Car doors slammed the kids were home. They were all excited about something and making a bunch of noise. I put my book down and waited for them to walk in the door. "MMMMMOOOOMMMMMMMMAAAAA!" Lanie yelled as she walked in the door first.

"I'm in here!" I called out. The boys and Lanie ran in all talking at the same time. No one would let the other person talk first. They were too excited, and then Erica walked in, her hair was a mess, her clothes were wrinkled. She's normally neat and always put together; she was angry and unamused by her sibling's excitement.

"What happened?"

"Drew's STUPID girlfriend!" Erica huffed as she threw herself in the chair. "Momma you should've seen it! That girl was getting on everybody's nerves. She was just a little dumb chick as far as I was concerned. She started picking at EJ when Drew wasn't paying attention. I don't know what she said, but all I know is I heard the slap. WE ALL DID!" Eric was too happy.

Lanie put her arm around my shoulders rubbing them, while shaking her head. "Erica beat her up pretty bad momma."

EJ sat next to Erica and put his arm around her. "Thank you for defending me." Erica kissed her baby brother's cheek, "nobody messes with my babies!" Erica looked at me, "I'm sorry momma. I didn't mean to disappoint you."

"Come here," I put my hands out to hug her. I made her sit in my lap. "I would've been disappointed if you let your brother fight a girl because you were too afraid to get your hands dirty. Of course I want you to use your words first and try a peaceable way out, but it's not possible every time. Was Drew upset with you for fighting his girlfriend?"

"I hope not, he didn't seem mad." Erica looked horrified at the thought of her cousin being mad at her.

"He better not be!" EJ's voice boomed. "She wasn't supposed to be there in the first place."

"Darryl kicked her in the leg when Drew was picking her up." Lanie laughed.

"What's funny about a boy kicking a girl?" I frowned at Lanie.

Lanie explained the way he did it. He was acting like he was helping her up and he kept pushing her down. The way Lanie described it made us all laugh, but I still didn't agree with a boy hurting a girl. Lanie doesn't like anybody, but since they all agreed they didn't like her and Erica tries to like and get along with everyone I have to assume she's as horrible as they were saying. The kids went out back, the boys wanted to show the girls some counter moves. I was happy to get back to my book. Then the buzzer for the gate rang. I recognized Sophia's car and the old school car that Andrew drives. Both cars were loaded up with teenagers. I exhaled and buzzed them in. All I wanted to do was sit back, relax, and enjoy my book. It was getting juicy and these kids keep coming. JoJo was running to the door as I opened it with a smile on his face. We hugged and then the kids poured out the cars. JoJo apologized for the intrusion; he said Erica left so fast you would've thought the police were coming. He asked if I minded if they hung out at my house. I could tell they sent him in here to smooth things out. I told him it was fine and I'd order pizzas for them. He smiled real big, thanked me, and then he announced loudly that I said it was cool for them to stay. I didn't recognize all the kids out there. So I ordered the pizzas and then I went outside. Darryl introduced his cousins; I relaxed knowing that everyone out there was related. I gave Tanisha a big hug and I kissed her forehead. She squeezed me tight and then she excused herself to the bathroom. Sasha hurried after her with concern on her face, Drew was right on her heels. Erica and Donzae were sitting to the side bonding over their dislike for Drew's girlfriend. Donzae was telling her about the time the only thing that saved the girl was that

Drew was paying attention and checked her immediately. Donzae said she couldn't stand that girl and her happy thought is of one day beating that girl. I told them not to focus on violence; Erica listened while Donzae pleaded her case for how much this girl deserved everything she got. I looked up just as Darryl flipped my baby, just as I was about to scream I saw him grab her so that she fell softly on the grass. Lanie's eyes were big and she asked him to show her again. Darryl asked Ryder to show her and then she could try it on him. Lanie laughed an evil laugh as she took it all in. It was too much and too many kids, it seemed like they were all so angry and my peaceful talk was only for my benefit. I went back inside, Andrew had his arm around Tanisha rubbing her shoulder with Sasha on the other side of her as she calmed herself. I didn't want to upset her again so I grabbed a couple slices of pizza, grabbed my book and I went up to my bedroom. I got comfortable in the middle of my bed and got back into my book. The kids turned on the outside speakers with the stereo and they sat around eating and listening to music. When Ethan came home he closed the door and stood there staring at me. He was upset, but I knew he would be. They went over Poppa's today, he's getting worse and worse. When Gwen had the baby she made Martin take her directly to Poppa and Nana. It was so heart touching watching her apologize for all of her nonsense. She assured Poppa that Nana would be loved and pampered for the next forty years without him. Nana rolled her eyes at the idea of forty years without her King. Since I had to work this morning Ethan told me to come home and relax when I was done. The look on his face was heart breaking. I put my book down and Ethan told me to stay put as he paced for a minute. He said today was system overload. He said Poppa could go at any minute now and although everyone was expecting it, it was still eating everyone alive. He said he's worried about Nana and his Uncle Tim. He said for the first time since she was a teenager Nana was going to be alone. He said his Uncle Tim has leaned on his parents to help him with the loss of Auntie Annette. Then he asked me when my last physical was. I sat there trying to remember, when a half of a second passed without an answer Ethan told me to schedule it immediately. I told him I would and then he climbed on the bed and buried his head in my stomach. "Sometimes I wish we could still have more babies."

"More?" I couldn't believe it.

"Life is the only way to offset death." He exhaled, "I know I'm just upset; but a little Franklin would be nice right about now."

I rubbed his head, "how about you give it your best shot." I smiled.

He smiled the best he could, "challenge accepted."

When we woke up the kids were still outside. Ethan dressed and then he went down to the kitchen. I followed him and watched as he stood in the middle of the kitchen like he needed to make something. He kept clapping his hands together looking around.

He started putting items on the counter, I sat on the stool watching him as he pulled items and I could see him making up his mind about what he was making. I sat up straight when he pulled cognac out of his spice cabinet. He looked at me and said it was for cooking only. My eyes stayed glued to the bottle. I saw myself running to the bottle and guzzling it before he realized I was out of my seat. I haven't had a drink since the camping trip. I've been growing my hair out since then and I have nice length on my hair. I told Joanne my hair was a reflection of a better me and I planned to let it grow as long as it wanted to. I still have Raynel perm it for me, so now I see the length as it grows verses a huge Afro like before that I styled however I wanted or mostly pressed.

I drummed my fingers on the counter as I watched Ethan intently. He mixed sugar, heavy cream, and spices in a bowl then he poured a large amount of the cognac into the mixture. He smiled at me while he stirred then he took out the ice cream maker. I smiled as he poured the mixture in and turned it on. Next he made caramel sauce using some of the cognac again. THEN! He took the apples off the counter basket, peeled them then he sautéed then in brown sugar, butter, and cognac. As they cooled he added blueberries and spices to the mixture. He put pie tins on the counter and put his pre-made crust in them, baked them a little then he filled them with his mixture. Darryl slid the door open with a big smile. "Something's calling me!" His eyes danced around the kitchen. "COUSIN! What CHA making?"

Ethan didn't smile, but he doesn't smile very often. "Pie!"

Darryl smiled bigger. "EJ and D-Rick act just like you. Look at them," he pointed to his brother and my baby sitting side by side, serious expressions as they talked about something. "They are having the best night of their lives!" Darryl started laughing. Then he looked at me, "how did you end up with such a serious guy?"

I smiled, "his seriousness pulled me in."

He sat in the stool next to me and put his hand on his chin. "How? It's not like he makes you laugh. What did he do to make you smile?"

"You think the only way to a woman's heart is through her smile?" Ethan asked.

"It's not the only way," Darryl winked. "However, I have to beat girls off with a stick just because I make them laugh. Most times I'm not even trying. I'll do like this," he stopped smiling and looked me in my eyes. Knowing something funny was about to come from his lips I started laughing. He didn't smile he put his hands towards me looking at Ethan. "See! I don't have to do nothing and women laugh."

"It's because I know something crazy is coming next. I'm ready." I patted his hand. "Being funny is a gift, embrace it."

"You have the gift as well, so I know you understand."

I blushed, "you think I'm funny?"

Ethan shook his head and went back to his pies. "Cousin, you've made me hurt right here!" He pointed to his stomach on the side. "You made me bust my gut so many times it's pointless to allow it to heal. Ryder and Eric are natural laugh machines." He leaned in, "Lanie is CRAZY!" He whispered, "and if I'm saying it then you know it's true."

"Why do you say that?" Ethan was listening closely.

"Take the fight today, even though Erica was handling that girl. It took two people to hold her back as if E was losing."

Ethan's eyes turned red, "Erica had a fight?"

"Whoa cousin! Did you miss the part that she won? She beat that girl down so fast!

It was beautiful!"

"Why was she fighting? Who did she fight? Where was her security?" Ethan said moving closer to us.

"We call *IT* Toya! *It* tried to jump bad with EJ, and E wasn't having it. Security was right there, but since E had the upper hand the entire time they made sure our scene was contained to just us."

"I don't want my daughter fighting!"

"That girl is a beast! I wouldn't worry about her fighting. She dang near killed the *IT* we call Toya! It was beautiful!" He gestured with his hands like he was describing a movie. "It started with a slap. Then she punched her. Then she hit her again and kicked her. THEN!" He wiped drool from his mouth. "THEN! Then she slammed her and literally kicked her butt until Eric grabbed her."

Ethan was not amused, "I don't want Erica fighting. Don't fail me again!"

"Got you cousin! It won't happen again. Now this no smile policy, how firm are you on that?" Ethan didn't smile, Darryl looked at me with no expression. "How do you live like this?"

I shrugged, "I love him! I smile enough for the both of us."

"EVEN MALCOLM SMILES AT MY MOMMA!"

I gasped, "he does? What's that like?"

He patted my shoulder, "it's scary cousin. It's like watching a dog walk on its hind legs."

"Ethan smiles," I looked at him.

"I do not!" He said washing his dishes.

"Watch this," I said walking to the sliding glass door. I called Erica inside. I put my hands on her shoulders and I brought her in the kitchen. Erica looked at me and I told her to watch her daddy. Ethan frowned at me and then I put Erica in front of me. Darryl was leaning on the counter. "Say hi to your daddy."

"Hi daddy?" Erica said not understanding what was going on.

"No like you normally do." I patted her back and winked at Darryl.

"*HI DADDY*!" Erica said putting her father in a bear hug.

Ethan immediately gave in to the affects of Erica and smiled as he hugged her back with wet hands.

"THAT'S AMAZING! I WANT A DAUGHTER!" Darryl said cracking up.

When Ethan's pies were cooled and ready everyone came for pie and ice cream. I savored every bite, as the cognac flavor was there just enough to taste it. The kids stayed pretty late.

In the morning Nana called and told us to hurry. Everyone ran out the house. The street was full of cars and more family was arriving as we parked. Ethan and all the kids ran top speed into the house. I wanted to run, but my legs wouldn't carry me anywhere fast. All of Ethan's aunts and uncles were in the room and then as many grand and great-grand kids who could fit. Nana was laying in the bed holding Poppa's hand. Everyone was crying and Poppa was trying to apologize to Nana for leaving her. I couldn't take it; I took myself out of the room. I picked up Beth's granddaughter who was crying on the couch. We held each other tightly and cried our eyes out. Suddenly everyone was exiting the house to the backyard, through the front door, and the side door. People poured out the house howling at the dawn. Lanie found me in the living room and she buried her head into my chest as she cried angrily. Sasha cried heavily as she turned the coffee pot on. The hospice nurse asked Nana how long she wanted to wait before someone came to pick Poppa up. Nana calmly told the nurse that they could come now. Nana was crying but she wasn't falling apart like a lot of her children, grandchildren, and great-grandchildren were. Amber was sitting at the table like she was trying to maintain her sanity. Every time the door opened she looked at it like she was looking for someone. Nana sat down at the table next to her and she grabbed her hand. When they looked at each other they started crying.

****

When Nana went in the bathroom I asked Sophia how Nana's been. Sophia looked worried, she said Nana puts on a brave face but she's not doing well at all. You could see her broken heart all over her. I hugged her and I told her everything was going to be ok. I had to say something. Although I remembered how she broke down at my house when she was talking to Raynel. Sophia said everyone is going through it right now. She said Amber was depressed before Troy, then their friend died right after that. I asked how he died, and she said he had been sick for sometime. She said he didn't have proper medical coverage and he was too proud to accept Amber's help when she had three kids to care for. She said his stubbornness cost him his life. I asked her how Malcolm was holding up, and she said they hadn't seen him. She said he didn't even come to Poppa's funeral. Then I told her he was there. He was in the back with Uncle Tim at one point. Sophia turned red and started going off. She was so hurt for her cousin. She said even Richard paid his respects to her and Sasha for their loss. The fact that her boyfriend was there didn't stop him from doing the right thing. Sophia was still going when Nana came back. Sophia asked Nana if she knew Malcolm was at Poppa's funeral? Nana said of course he was there; he came and hugged her and everything. Sophia went off more. Lanie came and sat quietly next to me absorbing all of Sophia's fire. When Sophia stopped for air Nana told her to calm down. She pointed out that Sophia was only seeing Amber's side. She reminded Sophia that Malcolm keeps losing people closest to his heart. When she mentioned Leonard both of us slumped. Then Nana told us that Malcolm and Leonard were not only cousins but also they were brothers cause they had the same father. I asked her if Malcolm was part Jackson and Sophia started laughing. Nana said Malcolm's poor heart is so broken losing Leonard, Whispers, Auntie Annette, and now Troy. Sophia retracted her claws, and then Nana reminded Sophia that she and Poppa were the closest things to grandparents that Malcolm knows. She said it wasn't right that he shut down, but Amber needed to cut him some slack. Sophia said he needed to say something. Nana said he's flying blind; it's not like he knows how to deal with everything he's feeling. Then she told us he's come by quite a few times and he always acts like he's mad. Nana said he's in a lot of pain right now. Sophia asked about Amber's pain, Nana said she has us. Ethan and the rest of the kids came in the door with groceries. Sophia joined them while Lanie and I stayed with Nana. Lots of people came over, some I barely recognized cause there were so many. You could see irritation on Nana's face when a lot of them came in the door with new clothes, new jewelry, and new fancy cars. She rolled her eyes until she couldn't take it any more and then she went off. She went on a loud tangent about how ignorant, wasteful, and disrespectful they were. She said her husband worked hard so that they could have comfortable lives and they run out and waste his money on clothes, cars, and flashy jewelry. All things that could be lost, stolen, and have no real value. Nana told them to go get educations, make better investments. "Make all his hard work stand for something! Otherwise get out of my face! You act like you've never had money before!" Then she stormed away into her bedroom and slammed her door.

Lanie looked at me with big eyes. She asked why Nana was mad about their clothes. I explained that there was nothing wrong with looking nice, but the way her cousins were running after labels was a waste of money. Then I reminded her of how her daddy explained her savings account to her. She got excited reciting how he explained how interest worked and why she wanted her money to work for her. I smiled big at my undercover daddy's girl. I told her that Poppa gave her money when he passed away, then I asked her what she did with it. She smiled and said she and her daddy went to the bank and put it in a special account that would help her money grow. I explained that a lot of her cousins didn't do that and that's why Nana's upset. Lanie's eyes stretched with understanding.

When the food was ready Sophia brought a plate in to Nana who was too upset to eat. Sophia tried to keep it together as she begged Nana to taste something on her plate. Uncle Jeff asked Sophia if Nana's been eating, and when she said no, Nana called her a tattle-tale. Lanie started crying like only she could, and then begged Nana to eat. Nana ate some just to shut Lanie up. Uncle Jeff picked big ole Lanie up like she was still a baby and kissed her cheeks over and over thanking her for being a brat.

A month later Nana caught a cold, then it turned into pneumonia, and just like that she was gone. Everyone took it pretty hard. Almost six months to the day after losing Poppa she gave up. Lanie told me she was going to make her Nana proud of her. She promised to be responsible with her money. That way all of Poppa's hard work wouldn't be wasted on her.

****

The doctor gave me the results of all of my blood work, etc. She told me that I was in good shape for someone who rarely worked out. She told me it would be a good idea to get in the habit just for general health overall. She told me that I needed to get mammograms regularly since I was now in my forties. My cholesterol levels weren't bad but they weren't exactly good, so I needed to be mindful of that with my daily diet. Overall I was pretty healthy, but it was now important to come in at least annually for checkups to keep an eye on everything. I watched her eyes for a minute then I told her to tell me. She assured me that the concern on her face had nothing to do with me, and that I had nothing to worry about.

I still had that sinking feeling though. When I got back to the office, Gwen asked how everything went. I told her it was fine. Gwen asked me to come in her office and then she shut the door. She walked up to me and whispered. "Jenise this is ridiculous! Every week its something new, Ethan has done everything except burn the building down. We can't stay here! We have to move!"

I put my hands up, "what are we supposed to do? I asked Ethan about it and he said it wasn't him."

Gwen blank stared at me, "and you believe him? Even if it's not him, I don't put it past those other two either. They're all guilty of being control freaks. THIS IS TOO MUCH! Martin is all over me at home, and then my brothers are all over me at work. I need to be able to breathe. You don't feel stifled?"

"I kind of like looking up and seeing my husband everyday. It's a wonderful view for me."

Gwen bucked her eyes, "is it you? Are you the one throwing the monkey wrench in our machine?"

"No! No! No! Calm down, I'm with you. I'm just saying it's nice seeing my husband daily. I'm also ok with rushing home to see my man when I need to. What do you mean Martin's on you when you get home?"

She turned red, "I'm not used to being the object of someone's affection. He loves me and Peyton so much, sometimes it feels wrong. I know my father loves me, but there's a certain way he was with the boys verses me. Heck there was a certain way he was with Jade and Amber verses me."

I backed up, "don't start Gwen!"

She shushed me, "keep your voice down. They probably, no I know this office is bugged."

"Why would they bug your office?"

She frowned at me, "did you even pay attention to how detailed Malcolm is with each of his offices? He and Juan got everything locked up."

"Who cares, we have nothing to hide."

"I just don't want my brothers controlling me. You may like how Ethan controls you, but I don't."

"As a matter of fact I do." I put my hand on my hip. "It's like vindication for me, cause I'm an honest person with nothing to hide. Ethan watches, and he doesn't control everything. However, I'm not stupid enough to fight over something so dumb. You just want control to say you have it, who cares? We are very well taken care of and watched over. I happen to like knowing whenever I step out the door I don't have to worry about what some stranger may do to my children or me just because I was in the wrong place at the wrong time. I like knowing that if someone spits in my direction they will be dealt with and I have no one to fear. You just want to fight, I don't."

"Uh…."

"Come here," I grabbed her arm and I pulled her out of her office and we marched right into Ethan's office. He was typing on his computer when he stopped and looked at us. "Ethan, Gwen and I would like to move into our own office next week. Everything that's been happening in the spaces that Gwen has secured for us is unacceptable. I need you to make sure that our next location is safe and worthy of our business."

Ethan sat back, "ok."

"Isn't there a vacant office just above this one?"

"Yes."

"We want it, we'll go up today. Layout how we want it constructed. We move in on Monday."

"Monday? We got to…"

I cut him off, "Ethan you can make this happen. Don't tell me you can't. Pay whomever overtime, it's what we need." He huffed, "either that or we can go out find our own place and rush in. We could be in the way of the next pipe bursting or whatever other disaster that hits our soon to be office."

"Fine."

"Thank you," then I pulled Gwen back out of the room. "Now was that hard?"

"No, but…."

"Stop giving Martin a hard time for loving you. You love that he loves you like he does. Stop giving him a hard time about it before he stops. Then you'll be devastated!"

Gwen was quiet for a minute, and then she smiled wickedly. "You are not the boss of me." Then she walked to her office smiling.

When I sat at my desk, I had work to do. Something wouldn't let me work, so I called my mom. She was resting, but happy to hear from me. I told her what the doctor said about my visit. I could hear her holding her breath cause she knew I was about to ask her about her checkup. She said she had a follow-up appointment next week. I asked why she needed a follow-up appointment. My mom exhaled and then she said that the doctor thinks she may have seen something in her mammogram, she came in for a biopsy and she was going for the follow-up. I asked her why was I just now hearing about this? She said with everything that Ethan and I have been dealing with she didn't want to burden me with nothing. She said as soon as they told her it was nothing she was going to tell me everything.

Chapter 29

Ethan

I'm staring at this phone lost in my thoughts. Lately my mind shifts stations constantly and I have to try hard to focus. Grandparents get older and eventually you have to let them go. The fact that I had mine well into my forties is outstanding. Jenise lost her grandfather when she was a teenager, and the others long before. It seems like everyone has thrust their selves into work. Meanwhile I went and got a physical and so did Jenise. Jenise convinced her momma and Stephen to get them. The doctor asked Jenise's mom to come in immediately to discuss her results. Jenise and Stephen went with her, and now I'm staring at the phone waiting for word. I should've went with them, I can't work right now anyways.

My Uncle Tim knocked on my door as he opened it. He asked me if I had time for him. Of course! He sat in my guest chair quiet for a minute. He adjusted a few times then he ran his hand through his hair. I went back to work while he found the words. When he was ready probably twenty minutes later he leaned forward. As he was about to say something my phone rang. I asked him to hold one moment. I barely said hello when I heard Jenise's tears over the phone. She said they found a lump during her mother's mammogram. Jenise tried to say something else and she couldn't talk she was crying so hard. I stood up, I told Jenise I was coming. Uncle Tim asked where he was taking me. I ran my hand over my face to pull it together, and then I asked him to take me to the hospital. We rode in silence for a minute then I told him they found a lump on Jenise's momma. Uncle Tim said he was sorry to hear it. I needed to think about something else, so I asked him what was up with him. He said he's been thinking about the future. He said his boys could run his company when he's gone. Then he asked me if it was crazy to want his girls and Malcolm over Cooper Financials? He said that was Annette's baby and it would only be right to have her kids over it. I told him that was a wonderful idea. He said he wanted to loop Jade and Malcolm in now and put Amber's name down. He said she's working so hard right now, and he doesn't want to burden her with being in one more place. Then he smiled, he said he doesn't know what he'd do without his girls, and both of them remind him of Auntie Annette. I could see why he said that about Jade she was so loving and nurturing. I had to ask how Amber reminded him of Auntie Annette. He smiled with so much love in his eyes. He said when his babygirl was born she was different than all the others. He said he saw himself right away, he said a father should see himself in his children at least initially. I thought about Lanie as he spoke. She was always different, look like me yes, but definitely different. He said Auntie Annette said Amber was her the moment she laid eyes on her. He said he realized it the first time her little temper flared. He said Amber is so much like her momma she couldn't change it if she wanted to. He said both of them fell for Malcolm immediately. I listened to my uncle describe my little cousin in a way I never saw her. Listening to him explained so many questions. I never understood why they let her bump her head so much.

When we got to the hospital he parked and came inside with me. The three of them were huddled and crying angry tears. I hugged Evelyn tightly as she held on tight to me. Uncle Tim asked who their oncologist was, and then he suggested Auntie Annette's. He said even though the cancers were different he was very confident in this doctor's abilities. Uncle Tim stayed with us the rest of the afternoon. Jenise's momma had to demand that Jenise come home cause Jenise would not leave her, not that I was making her. However, in that moment I saw how Lanie acts like her. Her attachment to her momma was undeniable. When we walked in the door Lanie immediately called for her momma. Jenise had nothing to give her, she ignored her. I asked Lanie what she needed, and she boldly told me she needed her momma she did not say daddy. All the kids froze and gave Lanie "sucks to be you!" looks. Before I could react Jenise came out of nowhere snatching Lanie's not so little body up. Everybody looked with horror in their faces as Jenise scared the daylights out of that little girl. "YOU WILL NOT SPEAK TO YOUR DADDY LIKE THAT EVER! YOU HAVE A GOOD FATHER WHO LOVES YOU, TAKES CARE OF YOUR BRATTY BEHIND, AND HE DOESN'T BEAT YOU UP! HOW DARE YOU DISRESPECT HIM AND ME BY EVER THINKING IT'S OK TO SPEAK TO HIM LIKE THAT! WHAT IF ONE DAY HE'S ALL YOU HAVE?"

The teenagers looked at me for an explanation. I gently approached my wife and I asked her to put my baby down. When Jenise put Lanie down, Lanie tried to run to Erica. Erica told her no, she said Lanie went too far! Lanie looked at EJ who had no sympathy for her in his face. Lanie fell on Eric's shoulder sobbing. Erica shook her head no at Eric and he swallowed. Eric gently told her no as he pushed her away. Lanie looked at me as her last resort. "I'm sorry daddy!"

"Stop with the waterworks!" Lanie tried to pull back the sounds of her heartfelt sobs. "I think your momma has made her point. However, mark my words. You don't want to have to deal with me if you EVER twist your mouth like that at me again. You're getting to be too old for this. You're not a baby, and I will not treat you like one. Do you understand me?"

"Yes daddy," she said as her big crocodile tears fell from her eyes.

"Daddy what's going on." Erica was reading me.

I looked at Jenise who was falling apart; she turned on her heels and walked up the stairs. "Your grandmother has breast cancer. The good news is that they think they can get it all with surgery. The not knowing until then is the hard part." Fear and shock ran across all of their faces.

"Momma thinks she's gonna get it too, doesn't she?" Erica had empathetic eyes. I hadn't thought of her taking it that way, however it explains her little speech to Lanie moments ago. "She hasn't said that."

"She just did." Eric said running up the stairs to my bedroom.

The rest of the kids followed her running into my room. I went up behind them while my brains screamed all kinds of obscenities at me. My brain couldn't handle the idea of Jenise ever coming down with anything more than a cold. Teenager and preteen bodies were tangled up on my bed. It looked like a five car collision as they held on to each other. Jenise was crying, and I could definitely hear the girls, I couldn't tell if my boys were crying. EJ put his head up and told me to join their grief fest. I opted to sit at Jenise's vanity. Jenise came and sat in my lap, which then brought all of the kids. They were not going to make me cry. "Lanie let's go get dinner for everyone."

Lanie's head popped up, "you want me to go with you?" She wiped her red eyes. "That's what I said isn't it?"

"Okay..." She said slowly scooting off the bed. She stood and took two steps. "Daddy are you tricking me? Are you going to take me outside and beat me?"

Eric started laughing, "cause you know you're disrespectful behind deserves it."

"Just go," Erica shooed her.

Lanie nervously followed me out of the room and out the car. When I opened her car door for her she smiled widely. She got in the front seat and buckled her belt. When I sat in the driver's seat Lanie was happily bouncing her legs. She stared at me for a while then she exhaled. "Are you mad at me?"

"Mad?"

"I always think you're mad at me cause you don't talk to me." She watched my face.

"Who do I talk to a lot?"

"Nobody really, you watch us a lot. Then you tell Erica to drive you or the twins."

"I haven't given you much Lanie time have I?" I hadn't thought about it like that.

"NOPE!" She smiled.

"Probably because you're always hogging your momma from everyone."

"I'm the baby, aren't I supposed to hog my momma?"

"No, I was the baby until your Auntie Gwen was born. I didn't act like you."

"Why does everyone say I'm bad? Do you think I'm bad?"

"Yes!" Then I smiled as she gasped. "You constantly test limits, and if someone says something you don't like then you run to your momma."

"I'm sorry, I didn't think you liked me."

"What does *like* have to do with anything? You're my daughter."

"That's what Erica says, but I don't know." She looked out the window.

"I like you Elaine, how about we start over?"

"DEAL!" She smiled really big, "but can you do me a favor?" I looked at her. "Call me Lanie? Momma says I'll like my name when I'm grown. I don't think so but we'll see."

Lanie talked my ear off the rest of the car ride. When we got to Shylight Lounge, Lanie looked around with big eyes. She'd never been here. The manager greeted us and then he asked who my pretty young lady was. Lanie smiled bigger as I told him she was my babygirl. Lanie did an excellent job ordering for everyone. She told me, now Erica wasn't the only one who knows what I like.

****

"Nelson Wright, is he important?"

"He's Jenise's favorite Uncle, the only member of her family that I actually like besides her momma. I'd say he's important. Why?"

"He's been calling a lot, I was just wondering if he was her father." Eugene watched my eyes.

"As far as I know Fred is her father." I exhaled, "Evelyn is sick. I'm sure he's concerned about her. Do you know something I don't?"

Eugene looked around, "your wife has a way about her. I'm sure that's how she hooked you."

"Your point?" I watched him squirm.

"Gregory Carter!" I looked at him, "he's still looking for her. What she do? Make him some red sauce? How many years has it been?"

"Are you trying to irritate me? I know exactly who my wife is, and why he's still sniffing. I'm telling you to cut his nose off or put him out of his misery. I have more important things to fill my day. Give me updates on Elijah, I'm not worried about that nonsense."

Jenise

My mom is all that I have. Everything about me is just like her. Everything that happened to her happens to me. I started developing at the same age she did. I'm shaped just like her. I have all of her allergies. My beauty mark is even in the same place as hers. I have no doubt that breast cancer is in my future. It's a matter of when. Ethan keeps trying to convince me otherwise, but he doesn't get it. The doctor said my mom might not lose her hair. However she's been shedding like crazy. Stephen shaved his head first, and then I held her hand as he shaved hers. My mom says we got to be positive and that positivity is the only way to beat this. On the way home, I went by the beauty supply. I bought clippers then I waited for Ethan. He walked in the door asking how my mom was doing. He looked at the clippers in my lap then he waited. I gave him this whole speech about it being just hair and I wanted to show my mom that I support her. I told him I wanted to discuss it with him first cause after all he was going to have to look at me like this. Ethan didn't say anything. He took the clippers from me and laid them on the bed. He hugged me tightly and kissed my neck. He took his suit off and hung it in the closet. He put a towel on the bathroom floor and he turned on my clippers and shaved his head. He told me I didn't have to do it and he would keep his head clean until my mom's hair started growing back. When I told him I wanted to do it, he said it was fine. However, I needed to consider why I grew my hair back in the first place. He said it might be more of a head trip seeing my father's face in the mirror than it would do me any good. I hadn't considered that. I kissed Ethan as I rubbed his head. He asked me if I liked his haircut. I told him I loved it.

My mom received a clean bill of health, her cancer was in remission and life was good.

****

When I got out of the car there he was again. Ethan said he's Whispers' son Eugene. All I know is he always stares at me without speaking. I don't know what his problem is. I nodded at him and then I walked inside the restaurant. Uncle Nelson was waiting at our table. Worry and concern were all over his face. He stood up and hugged me tightly. "How's your mother?"

"She's well, her cancer is in remission so we're good."

"Why didn't anyone tell me?"

"Because she didn't want to worry you. You've got your hands full dealing with Trinity and Chastity."

Uncle Nelson exhaled. "She's not happy with this guy. I wouldn't be surprised if he's hit her. I know you all haven't spoken in a while but I'm asking you for me. Please come with me to talk to this girl. You'll be my example of a healthy relationship."

"Ethan and I go through our stuff. We drive each other crazy sometimes."

"You don't have to down play your relationship for her."

"Ethan is a good man, I love him to death. However, he's a control freak. He's so controlling that his surroundings have to be neat at all times. If an item is out of place then you know he's losing it. I thought I was pretty neat before Ethan, but he takes it to a whole other level."

Uncle Nelson smiled, "what were you fussing about this morning?"

"MY FREAKING VANITY! It's mine! He doesn't use it. He was all pushed out of shape because I was rushing and I didn't put my makeup away. We fussed over the phone my whole car ride here."

Although I was serious Uncle Nelson belly laughed and told me that love was wonderful. I asked him if he ever planned to remarry. He snatched his eyes away from me, and then he said the woman he was waiting for married someone else. I frowned at him, I told him that was nasty. He looked me in my eyes and said he didn't care. He didn't touch his plate as I choked down mine. "I'm not going to lie to you. I'm still in love with your mother. The only other person like her on the face of this earth is you. I am so proud to be your Uncle. You're as close as I get to being related to Evelyn." It kind of made my stomach turn hearing my mom's name drip off his lips with so much love in it. "It's not fair to anyone else to pretend with them. I tried that, remember?" He looked at me. "She was a good woman who deserved a husband who was in love with her. I did what I had to do to make sure she was free to remarry."

"But Uncle Nelson you're a good guy. Why would you wait? Stephen and my mom aren't separating."

"My heart wants what it wants. I'm getting older, hopefully I'll die soon."

"You better not! We need you alive and well."

Uncle Nelson was stuck in his thoughts for a while. "Why do you think she chose Fred over me?"

"Does it matter? Knowing won't change anything." I said lowly.

"I know she told you. I deserve to know. I've played the role of the supportive uncle for years. I need to know."

"I'm not saying she didn't tell me. What she said is she chose wrong and then she had to fix that because if there was no him there'd be no me." My Uncle shifted in his chair. I put my hand on his. "I can only imagine how hard it has been for you. Thank you for never letting any of that stop you from being good to me. If it weren't for you I don't know what I would do, or who I'd be."

"What do you mean?"

"In a lot of ways Ethan reminds me of you. In a quieter more smoldering way of course." I smiled, I could tell he wanted to push the issue, but he dropped it.

We finished eating then we took Uncle Nelson's car to his place and then we rode together to Chastity's apartment building. When I got out of my car a man I didn't recognize looked at us like we were crazy for being here. I hesitated; Uncle Nelson asked what was wrong as he looked at the guy. That other guy Eugene pulled up, he left his car in the middle of the street as he walked over. Uncle Nelson hurried over to me and put me behind him as he asked what was up. The Eugene guy put his hand up disregarding my uncle as he asked the unknown guy in front of us for his credentials. The guy rattled off something and then he spoke fast. Uncle Nelson asked what was going on. I reached around him and I told him we needed to go. Then a different man started walking towards the building. He was almost inside the courtyard when he glanced at us then he did a double take. "Jenise?" He said calmly, as he frowned.

"Who are you?" The first guy said to Greg.

Greg looked at him like he was crazy, and then he looked back at me. "Hi?"

I looked at the Eugene guy, who had no patience on his face. "Leave," he told me. I told Uncle Nelson to get in the car. "Hold on! Where are you going? You know you need to talk to me." Greg said calmly.

"How you think you're going to tell her anything!"

"You don't know me! You don't know what's going on here. That's my wife!"

Greg and the first guy started arguing loudly. Uncle Nelson frowned at me when I didn't dispute Greg's claim. Chastity ran down with her cordless phone in her hand. She started yelling at the first guy about him stalking them. Uncle Nelson moved closer to them as he looked at Chastity who was in complete tears. It didn't make sense that she was so upset about a stranger outside her apartment then she turned to Greg and slapped him so hard everyone stopped breathing. Greg wasn't expecting it and he stumbled backwards. When he straightened up, I knew that look in his eyes and I remembered Demetria's face the day that Erica was born. Uncle Nelson grabbed Greg's arm as he started to raise his hand and Chastity braced herself to be hit. I looked at the Eugene guy next to me, he apologized to me. "I don't remember your name." I wanted to be sure, and not assume.

"Eugene," he watched me.

"What do you mean? Why are you apologizing?"

He looked at Chastity, and then he told me I was about to see. When Chastity saw that my Uncle had Greg she started screaming again. "I went to the doctor!" That made Greg madder. "You bastard! I'm positive! How could you do this to me?" She threw her phone at him.

"What do you mean by positive?" The guy standing in between Chastity and Greg asked.

"HIV!" She screamed.

The guy backed up from her putting his hands in the air. "Whoa!" Even though his back was to me I could tell Uncle Nelson was upset. His hand on Greg turned into a grip and then he hit Greg so hard he fell no he flew backwards. Greg fell and when he tried to get up his legs didn't agree with him. He had no choice but to stay down. Uncle Nelson grabbed Chastity and hugged her as they both cried. Eugene looked at me with sad eyes. Then he took out his big cellular phone, no doubt calling Ethan. He told him what happened and then the police pulled up. Greg was still on the ground struggling to get up. Chastity screamed to the police that she wanted to press charges because Greg knew he was HIV Positive and he didn't warn her or try to protect her. She kept saying he's trying to kill her. All the stereotypes did not apply here. Greg didn't look sick, he didn't look gay, my brain hurt. Eugene moved his car out of the middle of the street to behind my car blocking it in. I asked him if Ethan was coming and he asked me if I even needed to ask him that.

Greg insisted that Chastity was lying. She said her doctor gave her a ton of pamphlets and medications to begin immediately. The officer asked how she knew to go to the doctor if he didn't tell her. Chastity looked at Greg and said Demetria came to her job. She said Charlie was Positive as well. Then Chastity screamed at Greg asking if he protected his side chick, then she tried to hit him again. Chastity said they were at the hospital when Charlie died, and the funeral and Greg said nothing. She was crying about how she was supportive and giving him everything she had and none of it was ever good enough. She even tolerated him cheating on her with a *woman*. Then she screamed ***WOMAN***! She had no idea that there was anything between Charlie and Greg. Greg kept saying she was lying. When he stood it was like he tuned Chastity out. He kept trying to talk to me, ask me questions. I looked at him and asked him why would he hurt my cousin? He said she wasn't me, and then he said he needed to talk to me away from everyone. It took the unnamed guy, and the officers to hold Uncle Nelson back when he said that. Greg didn't flinch or seem like he even cared. His eyes were locked on me. "All these years! All these years Jenise! You disappeared into thin air and then surrounded yourself with an electric fence! Why would you leave me? You abandoned me!"

"Charlie," was all I could let come out my mouth.

"You're my wife, I laid with you. You had our child, don't let them brainwash you. You know how much I love you! Did anything about me seem feminine when we were together?"

"You're in love with Charlie."

"He was my bestfriend, you got it all confused."

"Greg you're talking to me. I know about being in love with your bestfriend! Ethan is my bestfriend!"

"Is? He was just a friend!"

"Just like Charlie was just a friend. If you love me if you ever loved me how could you hurt who I love?"

"I didn't infect her, if anything she infected me!"

"Ok, so then how do we explain Charlie?"

Greg caught himself as he almost gave way to tears. "Don't let them brainwash you. Ethan probably set this whole thing up."

Ethan pulled up behind Eugene's car, time seemed like it was creeping past.

Although I know Ethan didn't obey the speed limit to get here, it seemed like he got here really fast. When he got out of the car I noticed he had black leather gloves on but I didn't pay that any attention. His face was angry as he walked up on Greg. I braced myself and sure enough Ethan dropped Greg again! Ethan was livid I didn't understand everything he was saying. He said all Greg had to do was leave me alone and he couldn't do that. He said he gave him too many warnings and hints and he was too stupid to get it. I had no idea Greg was an issue after the hospital. I looked at the officers who were watching like they were stuck. Ethan didn't even acknowledge that they were there. "I WANT HIM GONE!"

"Uh...." One officer regretfully stepped forward. "We already called in that we were bringing him in. This young lady," he pointed to Chastity. "She wants to press charges against him. He knowingly infected her."

Greg couldn't get up, but he laughed like a crazy person. "You gonna try to kill me like you tried to kill Cat!"

"Tried?" I looked at Ethan.

"He's been cheating on you this whole time with Cat and that other girl No-No or whatever her name is."

Ethan kicked Greg hard. "Stand up so I can knock you down again!"

Greg laughed again, "I have proof! I've got pictures of him with both of them! Jenise I tried to warn you about those white people. You gave me up for a lie! He's been using you all this time! Using your name for fake businesses and stuff like that. He just proposed to Cat again! He's going to leave you!"

"Wait a minute! You just said he tried to kill her now he's marrying her?"

"Jenise baby please listen...."

"BABY???" Ethan kicked him again.

"I have pictures!"

"Where?"

Ethan shot me an irritated look cause I know he didn't want me to humor Greg at all. "They're in my car, in the glove compartment." He threw his car keys on the ground.

I asked Chastity to show me which car. The envelope had female writing on the front. I opened it and pulled out pictures. Most of them were old, even the one of Ethan and Nohemi hugging looking like they were both crying or upset. I knew this was not a recent picture. Ethan looked pained in each picture. They were normally sitting somewhere talking and sometimes leaving together. Then the pictures of him and Cat. They were in a restaurant I'd been to with Ethan before. He had his wedding ring on in the picture. He never mentioned Cat. Then there was the picture of him with his head shaved. He was holding a door open for a woman. I asked out loud if this was supposed to be Cat. I walked back to Ethan as he watched me. "Is this supposed to be Cat?" I held up the picture.

"Cat's dead!" He barked.

Greg started laughing, "no she's not."

"What is your point? Do you honestly think Jenise would have you after living as my wife all these years? You got in the door behind a misunderstanding. Doesn't matter what you say you're going to die!"

"Jenise, Cat is alive and he's been hiding her. He's still with her! They've been toying with us all these years. Think about it, they were engaged and then you have my baby and he claims it."

"So you infected me to get back at my cousin? How could you? Greg I loved you, I trusted you."

Greg's face turned evil, "YOU ACT LIKE MY MOMMA! ALWAYS COMPETING WITH THE NEXT FEMALE INSTEAD OF STAYING IN YOUR LANE! You assumed I was cheating with Cat. Worried about dumb superficial stuff, the world won't be missing anything when you're gone. I did the world a favor!"

Uncle Nelson came flying through the air and he kept beating Greg. Greg towered over Uncle Nelson when they were standing. I screamed for Uncle Nelson to stop when Greg started bleeding. Ethan was looking at the pictures I handed him. "This is not Cat!" He held up the picture, "I don't know who she is. I was holding the door open for her that's all. The rest of these pictures are old." Ethan kicked Greg again then he took his phone out of his jacket pocket. He moved the screen down until he landed on Cat's number in Greg's contacts.

Ethan

I felt stuck seeing her name. Jenise took the phone from me and called the number. I could hear Cat's voice when she answered. "Did you do it?"

"Cat, it's Jenise."

You could hear the phone hit the ground. "Hello?"

"Cat?"

"No," her voice shook. "You've got the wrong number." Then she hung up.

I called Malcolm, "this is Malcolm."

"CAT'S ALIVE?!?!"

Malcolm was quiet for a minute. "Is that right?" I gave him her number and I told him to find her. "Are you sure you want me to do that? If I find her you know what happens next."

I looked at Jenise who was staring in my mouth. "She's been watching me and my family. If she wanted to live she would've left me alone." I looked at the picture of Cat and I. She was wearing her engagement ring. "I need proof she's gone this time."

"Jenise is with you?"

"Yes."

"Call me later, meanwhile I'll get to the bottom of this."

"Ok, I'm going to hand Greg over to Eugene."

Malcolm was quiet for a minute, "he surfaced again?"

I knew he was talking about Eugene, but I was focused on Greg. "Cat has been feeding him information. Watching me and Nohemi, taking pictures. Not sure how but she set up this whole relationship between Greg and Jenise's cousin. I wouldn't say he resurfaced, he's been lurking."

"Death is too good for him!" Chastity blurted out. Then she started crying, "I want him to feel all the affects of this disease! I want him to slowly rot away!"

"Did you hear that?" I asked Malcolm.

"I did, let me call Matthew and Ryan."

I told the officers to take Greg into custody. They put on rain coats and gloves then they cuffed him and put him in the police car. Jenise looked at me with tears in her eyes as she held on to Chastity who was sobbing uncontrollably. Nelson put his arms around her and then we went into her apartment. Chastity showed us all of the medications that her doctor put her on. She said that her doctor assured her that as long as she took her medications like she was supposed to, she would enjoy a long and healthy life. I asked Nelson to hold on to Jenise's car and to excuse us cause we needed to leave. When we got in the car Jenise asked me how much of what Greg said was true. I told her the only part that was true is that apparently Cat's alive. Jenise asked me to take her to Demetria's place. When we pulled up she asked me when was the last time I verified her address and I told her it had been a couple months. I walked with Jenise up the stairs to the door. No one answered, Jenise asked me to take her to Demetria's job. She didn't ask me if I knew, she sat in the seat exhaling lightly like she was trying to calm herself. Eugene told me that Demetria was running around like a woman scorned, but I didn't put the pieces together. I needed this situation contained and kept small. When we pulled into the parking lot Jenise took my hand and interlocked her fingers in mine like she always has. When we walked in the office Jenise turned on her personality. She explained that she was one half of the Meridian Marketing company. The people at the front desk were smiling and willing to give her whatever she wanted. Jenise asked for a tour of their printery she told them she was touring local printing houses in an effort to determine which ones would meet their needs for their clients. A salesman came out hungry for business. He proudly showed us around the facility. Demetria was working hard and focusing on her machine. Jenise gently steered the salesman to Demetria's machine. Demetria broke out in a sweat when she looked at us. She kept looking at us as we finished our tour. Then we went outside to wait. Jenise put her arm around me, and laid her head on my chest. I knew she was upset but she was trying to keep it together. Demetria came out the door with her purse on her shoulder and tears and pain in her eyes. Jenise went to her and they hugged and cried. They got in the backseat together. Demetria asked Jenise if she saw Greg? When she said yes Demetria cried and asked if she was ok. Jenise asked her if it was all true. Demetria explained that Greg got sick first and then Charlie, then their friend Melvin. She said Melvin couldn't afford his medication, but she honestly thinks he didn't want to take it. She cried as she told us about Charlie getting sick and passing. She said Greg has been so angry since Charlie passed away and he's been harassing her. Like he's mad that she's not sick or something. She said she and Charlie stopped having sex about two years after everything came out. She said he stopped wanting her like that. She said once he started showing signs of being sick the most they'd do is kiss. Jenise cried as she shared her day. Demetria's eyes got big as Jenise spoke. She said Cat popped up at her place one night in the middle of the night. She came crying to Greg cause her boyfriend was cheating on her. That morning it was all over the news that she was dead. She said Cat turned all kinds of colors as she wondered why the news was reporting that she was dead. She said they scrapped their pennies together to send Cat away because her boyfriend was looking for her and she was scared. She said Charlie would ask Greg how Cat was and Greg was always short with his answers in her presence. She honestly didn't know where Cat was. She said a few times men came to their place looking for Cat, and they moved when their place got shot up. Jenise asked Demetria what she was going to do now. She said she was working to move to Virginia where her sister moved. Jenise asked if she needed anything from home cause she could take her to the airport right now. Demetria cried loudly as she said no she didn't need anything. It was all game, I knew Demetria had money. Elijah was giving her money, I never understood why before, now it was clear. He was paying her to be his eyes, I kept my mouth shut. Jenise withdrew cash from the bank and she handed Demetria an envelope. Demetria called her family to tell them she was coming. We took her to the Oakland airport. As we walked I made eye contact with the Mitigated staff all over the place. One supervisor came out and watched us. I put my hand on Demetria's shoulder and I told her to have a safe trip. The supervisor nodded and then she fell back. Now I didn't have anything against Demetria and she was the one to inform Jenise of everything she needed to know about Greg. The fact of the matter that she's still a woman scorned and now a loose link to us she couldn't float freely on the wind. We stayed with her at the airport for three hours until she boarded her plane. Jenise told her about our kids. She was reassuring herself how much better her life was with me verses if she would've chosen Greg. We turned to walk away as the supervisor went down the ramp to get Demetria. I put my arm around Jenise as we walked out of the airport.

Jenise

She put a badge in my face, "Detective Dartnell, I need to ask you some questions." I sat up and looked at Gwen. "Me?"

"Yes, you're Jenise Wallace aren't you?"

"She needs a lawyer!" Gwen said as she started turning red.

"Good thing you're meeting him here today isn't it." She smiled.

"How do you know who we're meeting with?" The detective smiled as she helped herself to a seat at our table. "We didn't invite you here. You can't sit down and harass us."

The detective looked at me. "You are so sweet. You do a lot for the community with your congregation. Don't let this family ruin you."

"What is that supposed to mean?" Gwen snapped.

She looked at Gwen, "you know what I mean." Then she looked at me. "I'm here because we have a man in custody a Gregory Carter. He's being charged with the first degree murder of Demetria Lake." I gasped and tears immediately poured out of my eyes. My tears startled the detective, "I'm sorry honey. I thought you knew she passed away." I shook my head no as I cried into my napkin. She stopped talking and rubbed my shoulder. "I'm sorry," she was quiet for a minute while I cried. "I'm sorry I thought you knew. Mr. Carter continues to insist that he's innocent."

"He beat her up before." I said through tears.

"He insists that you and he are married and that you have a child. However, we cannot find record of your marriage. I show that you shared an address at one point, but no marriage records."

"That's because they were never married." Ryan said setting his briefcase down. "Why are you here questioning her about something you know isn't true. You have the police reports of his previous violent acts against Mrs. Lake and Ms. Wright. He continues to deny that he infected Ms. Wright and that he was in a homosexual relationship with Mr. Lake. Although Mr. Lake died from complications of the same disease he's carrying. Your job is pretty open and shut. Why are you here?"

"Something was telling me to follow up."

"If any of his claims were true you'd be able to back them up with paperwork somewhere. Please leave."

The detective looked at me, she mouthed that she was sorry then she walked away. Ryan hugged and kissed Gwen and I then as he showed me a paper he told me to talk to Ethan if I had any questions. We waited for Matt Jr. and then we went over business. That didn't stop tears from streaming down my face. How did Greg get out of jail and then get on a plane?

When we got in the car Gwen kept squeezing my hand. Ethan met us in the garage. He hugged and kissed me. We got in his car and he took me to Oakland to the top of the hill. The view of the Bay was breath taking. He put me in his arms. He kissed my cheek. "This is what you need to know. Your marriage to Greg was never legal; Demetria didn't get on the plane. She didn't tell you the whole truth about her situation. She was trying to get over on you. I'm sorry I didn't tell you she died."

I stared at my unemotional husband; his face was cold and matter of factly. "Ethan, where's your heart? This was a living person."

"My heart is with you. Demetria was not your friend or concerned for your wellbeing. She came to the hospital because she was angry not to protect you. She never reached out to you to make sure you were ok or safe. My priority is to make sure you're safe."

I exhaled, "so we were roommates at best?"

"Everything you bought and had was in your name. Outside of your joint checking account in your maiden name what link is there from him to you?"

"Our addresses on our credit history."

"He ain't got no stinking credit!" Ethan and I laughed. "Seriously though, you understand? Everything he's saying is ludicrous."

"Got it!"

****

"What's in it for me?" Gwen smiled.

"Name your price!" He said watching her.

"We're huge NINERS fans! And I have an even bigger family. How many prime

338

seat tickets can you get me for the season?"

"I can guarantee four, but I will see what I can do about getting more."

"DWAYNE don't play with me, four guaranteed and as many more as you can secure?"

"Yes, I might have to shake down some of the others. I'll let you know by next week."

Gwen smiled at me; "you want to come to the preseason game Saturday?"

"Can't, we've got plans." We were going to go to the State Fair in Sacramento as a family.

Gwen started to say something when my office door opened. Martin had fire in his eyes, and Gwen sat up straight. "Martin?"

"Woman! Don't you ever in your life hang up in my face again!"

Dwayne and I exchanged looks. "I was over the drama. Man! Get over it!"

"Gwen!" I'd never heard his voice that deep. Normally Martin has his nice guy voice on. This was a different side. "I need to speak to you in private! **NOW!**"

Gwen turned red, but she didn't argue back. She walked out leaving my door open and shutting her office door. We could hear them fussing. "To be married," he smiled.

"You ever been?"

"Once, when it was good, it was good."

"So," I folded my hands. "What do you want with my little cousin?"

"I've been fascinated with her for sometime. I would like to meet her. She's very talented and I think I might be her biggest fan."

"Un huh! You're about to get in over your head." I warned.

"Why is she crazy or something?"

"Amber's great, no one better. However, she's very protected. You'll see. You better come correct!"

Dwayne was about to say something when Lanie walked in my office. "Who are you?" She asked with big eyes.

"I'm Dwayne, and you are?"

Ethan and Erica walked in behind Lanie. "Where's Gwen?" ETHAN asked with his eyes locked on Dwayne.

"In her office with Martin." I blushed and I don't know why.

"Ethan," he extended his hand, "you look familiar."

"Dwayne Reed, nice to meet you. I'm an assistant coach for the Niners."

"Right! You're the reason all these girls been at the game." Ethan was sizing him up. "How's our season looking?"

Erica and Lanie shyly stood on either side of me while looking at Dwayne. "We've got some new legs, and it's looking pretty good."

"As long as we beat Oakland I'm good. The Superbowl would be nice, but Oakland at least."

"Consider it done." Dwayne and Ethan looked at us at the same time. I felt embarrassed for my girls. "You never told me your name little lady."

Lanie blushed hard then she turned to me. "My cheeks won't stop this weird thing they're doing! Help!"

I chuckled, "that's called blushing baby."

"Oh man! I don't like this!" She tried to push her face even. "I'm Lanie."

"And you are?" He stood to extend his hand to shake Erica's hand.

She shyly shook his hand, "Erica." Then she squealed, as she couldn't pull back her blush.

"Don't do that to my daughters." Ethan said unamused by the whole scene.

Dwayne smiled and both of the girls melted, which made him blush. "It was nice meeting you all. Jenise, I will be in contact with Gwen next week. I'll see you all soon. He stood shook Ethan's hand again.

Ethan looked at his girls, "I'll never understand women. He's just a man."

"He was cute!" Lanie said before she could catch herself.

Ethan stared at her until she backed down. "Um! Dad says it's going to be hot in Sacramento, so we were hoping you and Auntie Gwen were free to go to the mall?" Erica was trying to save her little sister.

I glanced at my calendar, "hang for about an hour and then I can go. I'll ask your Auntie when she comes out."

Ethan frowned as he looked across the hall at Gwen's door. "Call down when you're ready. Girls come downstairs." He commanded.

After awhile Martin came out the office and he did not look in my direction. He walked out the office quickly. I knocked on Gwen's door and she quickly opened the door and closed it behind her. I still smelled the smell of sex as she exited her office. Gwen still had little sweat beads on her hairline and neck. Her hair looked like she tried to smooth it. I smiled, "you are a BAD girl Gwen!"

Gwen smiled, "you better believe it!" She went to the bathroom, got the air freshener sprayed her office and then she was ready to go.

Ethan

I advised the boys that today should be pretty laid back, but I still needed them to be alert. We needed to get away from the Bay where everything was getting to be too stressful.

Apparently Elijah has been looking for Cat over the years. Sometimes he'd find her and somehow she'd escape. Run to Greg to help her hide again. Now that Greg was locked up for the first-degree murder of Demetria that handicapped Cat. Once Malcolm found Cat I initially told him to get rid of her. Something told me not to, I told him to put her somewhere. I didn't want to know where, but somewhere that she couldn't bother me. I didn't feel right putting her down even though the family who never liked her anyways wanted her gone. With Cat in "custody" this Elijah person is losing his mind cause he can't find her. No one serious is stupid enough to go up against us. This Elijah cat is beyond ridiculous!

Nelson came with the reformed Trinity and Chastity. The reality of Chastity's life woke both of them up. Both of them have reconnected with their congregations and turned their lives around. Chastity even met a man at one of her support group meetings. She ministered to him, and he's joined her congregation. He's probably going to propose to her at the fair. I don't want all that girlie gushing on our day of fun, but if I reject it I'll be the jerk. It's only ok when it's me an Jenise and I never need an audience for us. Thank goodness for my boys cause Nelson is too attached to these girls to not get caught up in their girlie feelings.

Lanie sat forward and kissed her mother and I. "Do you have your seat belt on?"

"Yes daddy!" She sang happily, "I love you guys so much."

Jenise smiled and turned sideways, "we love you baby."

"This girl at my school is falling apart because her parents are getting divorced. She has to choose which parent she wants to live with and everything. She cries and cries, I feel bad for her. I asked D what it's like having your parents in separate houses."

Jenise looked guilty, "what did he say?"

"He doesn't like it, but he doesn't know any different. He said he would love it if his parents lived together, but he doesn't think it will happen. Thank you for never making me have to choose." She kissed us again.

"It's not easy to stay together, it takes a lot of work." Jenise said like a good mother would.

"Daddy you agree?" She asked like she could hear my thoughts.

"In the case of your mother, it's easy." Jenise shook her head disagreeing with me. "It's in the book of the Wallace Family. Our women may think they have a choice but they really don't. I've told your mother there's nowhere she could go that I wouldn't find her. She tried one time to run from me. I think she learned her lesson."

Eric perked up, "momma you ran from dad?"

Jenise squinted her eyes at me, "yes. But...."

Erica sat forward behind me, "where did you go? Why did you leave?"

I grinned at Jenise while she gave me irritated eyes. "YOUR DADDY! Was seeing another woman and I couldn't take it so I left."

"DADDY!" Lanie said in shock.

"Where did you go?" All of the kids were on the edge of their seats, suddenly our lives were interesting.

"Texas, and then I come out to my car after work one day and there he is." Lanie gasped, "sitting on my car looking mad."

"That's right! She was stuck with me." I looked at her.

"So then what happened? Did he drag you home by your hair?" Lanie asked.

"Drag me by my...." Jenise looked at Lanie then me then back to Lanie. "Something is wrong with you! Do I look like the type of woman who would enjoy being dragged by her hair?"

Lanie and Erica laughed, "momma. Well.... how do I say this?" Eric was trying to choose his words. "You're weird. You went from our sweet and loving momma, to this crazy lady it seems like over night. You see me kissing one girl and you lose it!"

Jenise gasped and turned around in her seat, "do you have any idea how much that couch cost?"

"But then you gave it away the next year."

"To buy an unsoiled couch thank you very much!" She wiggled her neck like I like, I patted her butt so she'd sit down.

"Ok, but my point is since that night, Dad is getting checked like every day. It took some time, now even Lanie gotta watch her step with you. You're crazy momma!"

"What's your point Eric?" She tried to hold back her grin.

Eric gasped dramatically, "uh… that you're crazy!"

"Is it ok with you that he calls you crazy? I'll pull this car over and handle him if it's not."

Jenise smiled proudly at me, "good job baby!" She put her arms out and kissed the side of my face. "You guys your daddy made a funny." Then she kissed me some more.

"Un huh!" The kids said sounding like we grossed them out.

"So is that when you got pregnant?" Erica asked.

Jenise froze, and I regretted the backfire. "Oh come on, we can all count! We've known for a very long time that you were pregnant when you two got married."

"NO! AND SHUT UP!" Jenise fussed then she sat in her seat facing forward.

Of course that made Lanie laugh, and before long all the kids were laughing. Jenise shook her head at me as we wondered what was so funny? Maybe it was the joy of knowing that they busted their parents out or something.

When we parked our security parked around us, to the common eye we didn't look like we belonged together with our team. EJ rode with my momma, Evelyn, Stephen, and Uncle Tim.

We told the kids to stick with us at least while we entered the park. Chastity, her friend, and Trinity waved bye and went their way. We walked around getting a general layout. There was a gazebo with microphones and speakers. Lanie asked Eric to do a song with her. Eric told her he would do it if she convinced everyone else to do it as well. Lanie got her momma, and sister to agree. Eric folded his arms and smiled and told her she had to convince EJ and I. EJ and I looked at each other and walked away. Lanie asked us and we said no. They huddled for a minute, and then they broke. Each person took their spot placing us in the center of their box. Jenise moved in closer to EJ asking and then begging him to sing with them. I shook my head at EJ when he crumpled. They cheered in victory while my son my own name sake would not make eye contact with me cause he knew he let me down. Then Lanie stepped forward begging, her brown eyes pleading with me to just say yes. As the irritation of her cuteness worked on me, then Erica started in. I DON'T SING! Jenise is the one who sings and got them singing. In the end I agreed to stand on the stage with them as they sang. My momma and Evelyn were all smiles as I stood to the side with my arms folded as my family pretended to be the Partridge Family and sing their family song. It seemed like girls flocked to the area when they heard my boys singing. When Eric winked at EJ it was clear that this was all part of his plan. Jenise called Nelson up and they had their little mini concert. At the perfect break in the music I went down to the audience with our mommas, Uncle Tim, and Stephen and admired my family on the stage. I was happy when the singing was over, a steady stream of little girls seemed to follow us around. When our mom's and Jenise wanted to stare at a pregnant cow who has been laboring for the past twelve hours, I told the boys to watch after their sisters and to go have fun. I told them to meet us in the front at nine. I didn't want to get on the road too late since it was an hour drive back to the Bay from here. Uncle Tim, Stephen, Nelson, and I sat at a table enjoying beers while the ladies stared at all the pregnant and newborn animals. I sat back and took my wife in. Her hair was now ridiculously long, to the middle of her back. I hadn't thought about it before, but I liked it long. I didn't mind it short, she was definitely feistier when it was short. However she seems to be calmer with her hair long. Jenise's mom looks good; you'd never know she had a bout with cancer. She wears her hair pressed now; she said she didn't want chemicals on her hair after going through chemo. I don't understand how Nelson endures this kind of torture. His love for Evelyn was obvious, and yet he always remained respectful of her marriage to Stephen. Jenise came over excitedly telling us that a cow was delivering. All of the men looked at her in disgust! Nelson told her it wasn't pretty when humans do it, why would he volunteer to watch an animal do it? Jenise shook her head disappointed as she went back to the women to watch the miracle of life within the animal kingdom. Chastity and group found us hysterical and excited. Chastity held up her hand like she cut her finger off as she screamed and cried that she was getting married. Nelson caved just like I knew he would. I turned my head as the women excitedly gushed over her proposal. Uncle Tim shook his head and said Malachi needs to hurry up and get it together before Denise gets tired. He said she's been patient, but time is ticking. I reminded him that Denise is young and they have time. Nelson asked Stephen how he and Evelyn met. Stephen told the story of the congregation gathering where they were casually introduced. Stephen explained that he had just gone through a bitter divorce. His ex-wife turned his boys against him, and his daughter didn't want to make waves, but she was the only one who saw through their mother and her manipulations. He explained that he wasn't trying to look at Evelyn as anything other than a friend especially when he learned that she wasn't free to marry. He said the harder he tried to fight it the more everything about Evelyn pulled him in. I understood exactly what he meant. I looked at my wife who was laughing and talking with my momma and hers. My desire for her in this moment is the furthest thing from her mind. I needed to get her on my level, so I watched her until she looked at me. I asked her if they were ready to go. I put my arm around her neck as we walked. Jenise smiled at me, and then she continued her conversation. As we went from exhibit to exhibit, I kept grabbing and touching her. At first she only smiled, but once I lingered in her personal space one too many times now she was understanding the message I was sending her. It was now my job to tease her, until we got home. I love this game.

Jenise

He plays too much! My mom is telling Raynel about all the blankets and things we knitted back in the day. While I'm stuck watching Ethan who's trying to act like he's not intentionally messing with me. First one to cave gives up the power, and then he's sniffing for me, I'll let him keep sniffing. I smiled to myself at the thought of my husband, after all these years he's still attracted to me. I think it's amazing. My mom and Stephen have only been married a little longer than us, but they're old. Their story is different. The last twenty plus years of my life have been all about Ethan. He thinks he's going to make me pant after him, not tonight! It's my turn! When we turned the corner away from our parents, I turned to him and kissed him. I kissed him just deeply enough to make my point, then I stepped back smiling. Ethan said he was ready to go, and I told him we couldn't leave yet. I told him we couldn't leave until I got my caramel apple. Then I drug him a long the rest the day, brushing my chest up against him. Ethan pulled me into his arms. We were having a good time in our little game. It was time to meet the kids and I bought caramel apples. Ethan looked excited; well his version of excited, to go home. Then his phone rang, his entire demeanor changed and I immediately knew it was something with the kids. They hadn't come to the front yet. When Ethan took off, I took off right behind him. Security was running along side us in the same direction as the Ferris wheel and other rides. Kids and our security were fighting everywhere. A few women were doing their best to hold Erica and Lanie back. They were both trying to get to their brothers. Eric had just knocked someone out with one punch, I looked at the guy I guess he was going after when the guy reached around his waist and I saw something shiny. The guy's hand was shaking as someone tackled him and the spark went out of his gun. Eric ducked and then I saw Erica fall. A sound I've never heard come from my husband before bellowed from within him. He was on his way to the girls, and then he changed paths and now he was heading for this guy. I ran to my baby who was laying on the ground screaming, the woman with her ripped her shirt open to make sure Erica hadn't been hit. Erica was screaming for her daddy saying she was ok. Her left arm of her jacket looked like it had been burned, the bullet passed through her clothes just missing her skin and pierced the wall behind them. Raynel and I ran to Ethan who was about to literally break the neck of the shooter. Raynel called out to him and told him that Erica was ok. This still didn't stop my husband from picking the guy up and driving him head first into the cement. He wasn't going to stop there but Raynel grabbed him. Police were everywhere with their guns drawn. EJ and Eric backed up with their hands up, Ethan looked like someone I've never seen. Murder was in his eyes and it took a minute for him to come back to us. Onlookers were giving police statements about what happened. A gang member set his eyes on Lanie, and when Lanie popped off at the mouth telling him she wasn't interested he was embarrassed and angry. He tried to slap Lanie and she knocked him down which then made the situation worse. Eric tried to warn the guy to go away, but he came back with reinforcements as the kids tried to come to the front of the fair grounds to meet us. Ethan went off on EJ and Eric in the parking lot; he said that had they been looking after their sisters like he told them to, the whole situation would've never gone as far as it did. Ethan was beyond angry. Uncle Tim was the only person who could get Ethan to calm down. He reminded Ethan that they had some tactical training, but they weren't professionals. Once Ethan and Uncle Tim walked over to the side of the parking lot away from us, I put my arms around Eric. He said he never would've moved if he knew Erica was in the line of fire. While I was consoling Eric, EJ was silently pacing. Looking like his father as he took everything in. It seemed like everything went silent as Frank and his driver pulled up. There was nothing but seriousness on Frank's face. He asked where Erica was and I told him she was in the car with my mom and Raynel. Then he asked where Ethan was. I pointed in the direction he went in with his uncle. Frank told me to stop babying Eric and then he told my boys to go with him.

Chapter 30

Ethan

When I finally calmed down a few days later, Uncle Tim talked to my children. Apparently this gang member thought Lanie was a lot older than she actually is. Her little preteen body doesn't reflect her age. I'm living a father's worst nightmare. Although our relationship has improved tremendously I still don't put it past Lanie to turn out just like Gwen.

****

He waved his hand telling me to drop it. Elijah Cobb was no longer an issue. If life has taught me anything, nothing is that simple. There are always repercussions for every action. I didn't appreciate how cavalier my father was being about the whole thing. He said things should return to normal now. The thought of "normal" put a lump in my throat.

Erica's going to be going away to school soon and I'm in knots. I'd rather she didn't go to school at all. I have enough money that she could live comfortably for the rest of her life and never work. Jenise says my attachment to Erica is ridiculous and I needed to let go. I told her to talk to me when it's Lanie's turn.

My phone rang, there's a "Frederick Wright Jr. here for Jenise." The security guard in the lobby said.

"Send him to my office."

"Who is he?" My father asked.

"Jenise's little brother." I tried to think of how old he should be now.

The receptionist showed an almost tall and thin young man into my office. He had a hearing aide on his left ear. When he saw my father and I he looked at the receptionist, "I think there's a mistake. I was looking for Jenise Wright."

"You're in the right place." I pointed towards the chair for him to sit. "To what do we owe the honor?"

He sat then he leaned forward. "I'm not here to start any trouble. I just want to see my sister."

"Why? It's not like you know her."

"I want to though."

"Why?"

He exhaled, "you're the husband?"

"Who else would I be?"

"I don't know." He exhaled, "can I please speak to my sister?"

"What do you want with her?"

"To know her, all my life I've heard about her. I only met her once that I can remember. I have nieces and nephews too?"

I looked at my father who nodded, his nonverbal consent to me allowing Jenise to come. I called Jenise and asked her to come to my office. The kid sat there quietly looking around. When Jenise walked in she wore her usual smile. She hugged my father who's gotten used to her hugs. Then she looked at her brother with no recognition as to who he is. "Hello, I'm Jenise."

He put both of his hands on hers, "Frederick junior," then he searched her eyes for recognition.

Jenise's eyes got big then she looked at me. "My father's son?" He shook his head yes. Then Jenise touched his chin like she does to our boys. "Of course it's you!"

Then she pulled him into a hug where she rocked him from side to side. "Hi baby, how are you?"

"I'm good now that I see you!"

"How did you find me?"

"My mom and I met Jamal and his wife. My mom asked him if he's heard anything about you. He told her you were doing well. So we searched until we found you."

"How's your father?"

"Your father is fine I guess."

"What do you mean you guess?"

He glanced at my father and I then he refocused on Jenise. He's drinking again. He cut my mom off because I beat him up for hitting her."

"What name do you go by?"

"Red."

"Red? That's cute. Are you in school?"

"No, my mom couldn't afford it, and he doesn't care. He wants me to grovel."

"So you came here instead." My father said.

"I wouldn't say that."

"I wasn't asking, just telling you what I see."

"Who are you?"

"Her father."

Jenise smiled wide, "I love you too!" Then she looked at me. "What's the deal here?"

"Your dad thinks he's found a loophole. I told him to stay away so he indirectly sent your brother. Look at the way he's dressed, he's not hurting for money." The kid was covered in labels. His outfit cost about four hundred at least, and his doggone pants were hanging off him. "Do you want to see your father?"

Jenise quickly said, "NO!"

The kid looked back and forth between us. "So, what does that mean?"

"I'm so sorry babe, I refuse to let Fred back into my life."

"What does he have to do with me?"

"He sent you."

"No he didn't! I'm my own man." He said defensively.

"Then your mother sent you." Jenise watched his eyes as he turned his head. "Fred is still controlling you. He's just going through your mom. Fred is a horrible person and I want nothing to do with him."

Red stood up, "he's getting old and he's sick. Please come and say goodbye."

"That's what this is about, isn't it." Jenise put her hands on his shoulders. "Give him my regards, but I..." Jenise started crying.

"Time to go!" I said grabbing his shirt collar and pushing him towards the door.

"You can tell your father he made his point. He better die, before I make mine!" When I released Red's collar, my father grabbed it. "I'll see him out. Take care of her."

"He's diabetic and he refuses to take care of himself. He's on dialysis, and there's something with his heart. He won't be around too much longer!" Red pleaded.

"He can die knowing how much he ruined me! I'm done!" Jenise said through her tears.

I closed the door and Jenise cried into my chest. After awhile she called Joanne and asked for an appointment. I drove Jenise to the office, and she held my hand taking me into the room of her private conversations.

****

"Mr. Wallace there's a Cathleen Cuthford here to see you." The receptionist said. I looked at the monitor, and Cathleen was pacing in the receptionist area in her normal impatient manner. I stared at the screen for a minute. I was trying to weigh how much I didn't want to talk to her. There was a young girl with her who looked immune to her behavior. The girl sat in the chair flipping through a magazine. My Uncle Tim asked me who it was. When I said it was Cat's mother he asked me if I was going to let her in. I took a deep breath; my mind ran a thousand miles a minute trying to figure out why she was here. "Send her in."

Cathleen came in my office the girl stayed put. I could tell she was anxious when she walked in the door. She looked a little confused when she looked at my uncle. "I'm sorry, Mr. Wallace you look great!"

"Thank you?" Uncle Tim frowned.

"She thinks you're my father."

"This isn't your father? I'm so sorry." Her hands shook a little as she reached out for my uncle's hands. "I'm Cathleen, Cat's mother."

"Nice to meet you." Uncle Tim said pointing to her seat, "have a seat."

"What do you want?" I said looking back at the monitor.

She took a deep breath; "I'm not going to beat around the bush with you." She started gesturing. "I don't know why you and my daughter broke up so suddenly all those years ago." She exhaled trying to fight back emotion. "Cat immediately got with the bad news kid, and well we know how that ended. I'm here because all these years I was under the impression that Cat's daughter was the bad news kid's baby." My head whipped back to the monitor. I looked for a sign of Erica or Lanie in this girl. All I could see was Cat. "I've had Zoey since she was a baby. Cat's life has been too crazy to slow down and care for anyone, not even herself. However, she's always managed to have money sent for Zoey. I don't know where Cat is, and the guy who was bringing the money suddenly stopped coming. I reached out to the bad news kid's family, they demanded a blood test." She wrung her hands, "he's not the father. I know it doesn't speak greatly about my daughter. I doubt you're the father either, but I need to be able to cross you off the list."

"Who else is on the list?" I asked staring at the monitor. I know I shouldn't have but I thought of Troy.

She laughed nervously, "I hit a brick wall if it's not you. I know that would be hoping for a miracle."

"Why would you hope that I was the father? You never liked me."

"Whether I liked you or not you've made a good name for yourself. The low-life's that my daughter chooses to associate with are just ridiculous...."

I put my hand up, "bring her in here." When Cathleen walked out, I looked at my Uncle with pleading eyes.

"Call your wife down here."

"Jenise, I need you to come down here." I said as soon as she answered her phone. Sensing the urgency in my voice she hung up without another word.

Cathleen nervously walked back into my office followed by an uninterested teenager. All I saw was Cat, a head full of short hair but wild just like her momma. She glanced at me then my uncle and then she looked at me again. "You're Ethan Wallace?"

"Yes, and you are?"

"Zoey Cuthford as far as I know." She tried to look uninterested, but she couldn't take her eyes off of me.

Jenise walked in the room and she slowed as she saw Cathleen. Then her eyes darted to Zoey and then Uncle Tim. "Cathleen, this is my wife Jenise. Jenise this is Cathleen and her granddaughter Zoey."

Jenise's nostrils flared, then she stood by me. "So I take it we're just finding out about this?"

"Nothing's for sure of course, I was hoping that Ethan would be willing to take a blood test."

She put her hand on my shoulder, "of course. We need to know for our own peace of mind. How old are you sweetheart?"

"Sixteen," Zoey hadn't taken her eyes off of me.

"Call Franky in here." Uncle Tim said.

Jenise walked over and asked him to come. He was smiling until we introduced him to Cat's mother and her grand daughter. "We need your doctor." Uncle Tim told him.

"How soon?"

"Today if she can manage." Franky went away, then he came back, he told us to go now. "Whelp, folks lets move this party over."

"Who are you?" Zoey asked Franky.

"I'm his brother, I guess that makes me your uncle."

Her eyes got big, "you think so?"

Franky looked at me, "she looks like the rest of the kids just a little lighter."

I looked at her again; all I could see was Cat looking back at me. Franky gave the address and then we got in my car. Zoey looked at my car with big eyes, Cathleen just looked nervous. I looked at Jenise and she had no expression on her face. As I reached for her hand she was reaching for mine. The warmth of her hand soothed me. We went to a doctor's office in downtown Oakland. The receptionist greeted us with a smile then he showed our group to a room.

Jenise looked at Cathleen's nervousness and asked her why she was so nervous.

Cathleen said she really believed that Sammy was Zoey's father. She said it hurt to have to un-tell Zoey everything she said. She said she doesn't know where Catalina is to ask her otherwise. She said she started relying on the support of Cat's boyfriend. Jenise cut her eyes at Cathleen when she asked if this was only about money? Cathleen said Zoey is at that age when a girl needs her father. If he's dead that's one thing, but Zoey was getting to be too much to handle on her own. Zoey cut her eyes at her grandmother, "you say racist stuff! I'm wrong for calling you on it? When you talk about black people you're talking about me!"

Uncle Tim looked at Cathleen, "you don't have any sort of filter do you?"

"Sometimes they're too sensitive. Slavery was a long time ago, they need to let that go." The words came out of her mouth so matter of factly. Everyone stared at her for a long time. She put her hands out towards Uncle Tim like she needed him to agree with her. "Why do they think we have to walk on eggshells for something that happened so long ago and we have nothing to do with. I'm not racist! I married a black man for crying out loud!"

"We? I'm not sure about what *we* you're talking about. But **We**," he gestured to the rest of us in the room. "Have had to deal with ignorant comments like yours for too long. Marrying a black man and having children doesn't exempt you from being a racist. You were probably curious like the rest of them. The closest you'll ever come to enlightenment is by picking up a book. I suggest you do that right away."

Her mouth fell open even Zoey stared at him. "**We?**"

Dr. Bissell hurried into the office. She apologized for the wait. We explained that we needed a DNA test, etc. The doctor swabbed Zoey and then me. She told us she'd get the results to us as soon as possible. We went out to lunch, and Jenise got Zoey talking like only she could. Her personality started to show that's when I saw it. That look that both of my girls get from my momma. I looked at my Uncle who shook his head at me as if he could read my mind. Zoey started staring back at me, "you don't talk much?"

"This is me talking."

She smiled, "that's cool."

Jenise stayed with me when everyone left. As soon as we were alone she started crying a heartbroken sob. She said she already knows. I felt like garbage, I apologized as I held her. Jenise squeezed me and then she said it wasn't my fault. She said that was a highly crazy and immature time in all of our lives. She asked me how we were going to explain Zoey to the kids. "Let's face it. They already know I was pregnant when we got married."

"Right, but I don't want them getting ideas. That was a crazy chaotic time in all of our lives."

"You think our kids are angels? Especially your sons! EJ is truly living up to your name. He likes that little girl but he's running around. Eric is a regular little playboy singing girls out of their panties."

"None of that matters we are the parents. We're held to a higher standard." I exhaled, "we're going to tell them straight forward this is what it is. You have a sister born between Erica and EJ. Deal with it! Erica's still the oldest, Lanie's still the baby, and the twins are still the twins. I don't want to focus on how it happened. Let's direct them to embrace her and welcome her."

When I was alone, I called Malcolm and I asked him if he still had Cat stashed. He simply replied yes. I told him there's been a new development and I needed to think about what to do with her when I calmed down. Malcolm told me to take my time. That night I remembered the last time I slept with Cat. I dismissed her tightness and wetness for desire for me. I didn't give it a second thought. If she wanted my baby so badly why would she chance everything by cheating on me? She couldn't have thought Zoey was my child or else she would've been in my face. If she thought there was a possibility that Zoey was mine wouldn't she have spoken up? Maybe I some how wanted this little girl to be mine and she wasn't. What if Cat somehow got to Troy? Zoey could be his daughter. How much of Cat is in this child? She didn't seem arrogant like Cat. She seems depressed and unsure of who she is. I guess that's right, she doesn't know her mother and she doesn't know who her father is. How is she supposed to be happy and up beat in that space? I kept tossing and turning until Jenise put her arm around me. I apologized for waking her. She said she wasn't sleep; her mind was turning over trying to understand everything. I apologized again for everything; I was disappointed about the whole situation. I couldn't believe how calm she was about this whole thing. Jenise exhaled and said she was only calm outwardly. As I got lost in my anger Jenise shot up. She said what if all the white girls I turned out in college got pregnant? She said we needed to figure out how many kids I actually had. She asked me how many girls did I have at Stanford. I told her I didn't keep a tally. Jenise asked me if we should run an ad "looking for Wallace Spawn! If this is you call this number..." Then she hit me with her pillow cause it took me a minute to truly grasp that she was joking. I was mentally spent. Jenise stroked my head and she told me she loved me and everything would be fine. "Is she dead?" I shook my head no. Jenise exhaled, "good." Then she kissed me again, "that explains why you didn't fall out in tears."

****

Two days later Dr. Bissell called and confirmed what we already knew. It still felt like someone shot me. Cat couldn't have known otherwise she would've used Zoey as her way back in, right? That night we sat the kids down. Jenise ever so gently delivered the news to our group. "So you're not pregnant?" Lanie blurted out. Jenise put her hand on her hip, "why would you think something like that?" Lanie raised her eyebrows, "well... You guys have been a lot more cuddly and spending so much time behind closed doors."

"Whatever! She's coming tomorrow evening and staying the entire weekend. Make sure she feels included, and each of you should make an effort to know her." Jenise directed.

"Daddy are you ok?" Erica asked watching my face.

"I'm fine, you all appear to be taking this a lot better than we thought."

"That's because we always knew you were a pimp." Eric smiled, "you sweet talked our momma to get with you even though she was a good girl. This isn't surprising. Are there any more?"

351

I looked at Jenise, she exhaled. "Your father lost a daughter a year before Erica. The baby died before she was born."

"It was that lady HUH?" Lanie sat back on the couch. "I didn't like her! How could you be nice to her?"

"Your father and I weren't together when that happened. She lost her daughter she's suffered enough."

"What about Z's momma? You gonna have to beat her down so she know her place!" Lanie laughed wickedly.

"Something is wrong with you!" Jenise said unamused.

"My momma's not fighting anybody!" EJ said staring at me.

"Nobody's fighting anyone. Zoey has been through a lot, please show her love you guys." Jenise pleaded.

Jenise and I went to Zoey's school to pick her up the next day. I stood outside the car waiting. Zoey smiled a nervous smile as she approached my car. "So I guess the results said you are my father?" Her eyes showed relief.

"Is that ok with you?"

Zoey threw her arms around me and buried her head in my chest. She cried hard, I looked at Jenise and she was wiping tears from her eyes as she watched. "Can I come live with you?" She said as she looked at me.

I opened the car door for her, "you want to leave your grandmother?"

"What did I miss?"

"Zoey wants to live with us."

"You've met my grandmother. I think she means well, but she makes me feel bad about being me. She borderline hates me, she doesn't even know me. Plus I don't know you or the others. How many are there?"

"You have two brothers and two sisters. Let's see how this weekend goes, you may change your mind." Jenise said as she watched my face.

"Anything has to be better than Cathleen. She deals with me out of obligation. If we didn't find you she was probably going to kick me out anyways. Watch how she sounds."

When we got to Cathleen she had the DNA results in her hands along with the rest of her mail. She was relieved just like Zoey.

Zoey asked what she should bring for the weekend, and sure enough there was a "funny" look on Cathleen's face. Cathleen asked if we wanted to keep Zoey longer in a joking manner, but we all knew she was serious. "Of course I want my daughter! I was trying to be considerate of you."

"I've raised my kids! I need to be free! It wasn't fair for Cat to leave her here. I don't care how much you can pay for child support my freedom is more important to me." I put my arms around Zoey as she had a "told you so," look on her face. "That's ok grandma! That man you're chasing doesn't want you, but you will learn that the hard way. Then when you're old and you need someone you better hope my mom comes back because I'll let you become a ward of the state."

Cathleen didn't care how she was affecting my child. Out of anger I was about to say something when Jenise went off. She walked in Cathleen's face and everything. Zoey ran to Jenise and thanked her. Only thing Cathleen wanted to hear is that Zoey was leaving. Zoey barely halfway filled a suitcase with the things she owned while Cathleen's place was furnished with expensive things, no need to wonder where her child support was going. Jenise rode in the backseat holding Zoey as she cried.

When we pulled up to the house Erica was waiting in the doorway. "This is your house? Wow!" Zoey said looking around.

I introduced Zoey to the dogs as she got out of the car. "This is your oldest sister Erica, Erica this is your sister Zoey." Erica smiled really big and hurried and hugged her. They squeezed each other and rocked from side to side.

I had no doubt that Erica would warmly greet Zoey this way. It's that other one that I'm looking for. EJ and Eric hugged Zoey and introduced theirselves. Lanie was nowhere to be found. They showed Zoey to what used to be one of our guest rooms. I went to Lanie's room. She was laying on her bed doing her homework with her headphones on. I tapped her foot as I shut her door. "Talk to me about it." I sat on her bed.

She took a deep breath, "I don't want to share with another person. You're my daddy, now she's going to need time to get to know you. She's going to hog you and try to take you away from me."

"We're all going to have to adjust. I guess I should tell you now that she's moving in."

Lanie shot off the bed, "DADDY! Now she's going to live here? What if she's crazy?"

"Is there really anyone crazier than you?"

"Good point, but how is that going to affect the bathroom rotation in the morning? Don't I get a say?"

"Her momma is gone. Her grandmother was raising her and she just washed her hands. You are the only family she has. Be nice Lanie."

"All that says to me is that she's gonna be even more attached to you."

I smiled at my babygirl and I had her sit on my lap. "It's nice to know you love your old man this much. We'll still have our time alone. And they'll all be away in school and it will be just the three of us probably."

"I love you very much daddy. I will give this chick a chance for you. But if she gets on my nerves I will treat her like anyone else."

"If that's the best you can do, why would I complain right now? Let's go."

When we went down the hall all the kids were in Zoey's room listening to her tell them a story about how she embarrassed herself at school one day. Jenise introduced Lanie as she walked in the room like someone was forcing her in. All of the kids dove on her and smothered her with kisses. Lanie tried to fight it, but she was fighting a losing battle. Zoey was too happy to fit in somewhere for the first time ever.

****

"You all came back at the perfect time! Jenise could use having her sister around."

"It is good to be back!" Timothy said looking around. "You only want to upgrade the kitchen?"

"No!" Jenise yelled from the living room. "The whole house! Everything!"

I exhaled, "how long is all of this going to take?"

"Depends on how extensive the remodel is."

"Even if we're all out of your way? Our family vacation is coming up." Jenise said walking into the living room with Grace in tow.

"How's Zoey adjusting?" Grace asked.

"You mean Lanie, Zoey is fine and just like the rest. Lanie has melt downs frequently."

"Sounds like we need to have a chat one psycho to another."

"Un un! You just got here and you're calling my baby names."

"Just moved back, but I've always known you gave birth to me. Your heart was missing my craziness so much that you poured all my energy into that one." We all laughed, "if you or I don't talk some sense into her she could end up with a thug, and I know you don't want that."

Jenise and I smiled at Timothy, "as in you didn't?"

Grace put her arms around Timothy, "my baby may be a lot of things. But he is no thug."

On that note I walked away laughing.

Jenise

"At night you tie this scarf around your hair. Does she have a satin pillowcase?" Raynel asked me.

"We all do." I was enjoying watching Raynel and Zoey bond. Zoey was so nervous about meeting Raynel as if she wasn't going to love her just like the rest of us do. I kept waiting for signs of Cat in her personality. Fortunately this child is mostly Ethan. She loves her siblings and like Erica she's very patient with Lanie who has her good days and she has her bad. Zoey calls me mom even though I told her she didn't have to. After the talk she and I had to have about everything she erupted into tears and thanked me. Her grandmother taught her nothing about hygiene and her room.... I thought Ethan was going to have a heart attack. He walked in and just about ran out. We were packing up the house for the remodel. We left her room for last, thinking it would be the easiest since she'd only been in there a couple months. Like I said Ethan walked in and then he walked out. Clothes were everywhere. I sat down on the bed and had a gentle conversation with her about how much of a neat freak her father is. Her eyes were big as she asked me if Ethan was mad at her. I told her he was more surprised than anything. She said her grandmother did everything around the house cause she was afraid Zoey would break something. I helped Zoey pack her room up as we talked about anything she wanted to. She asked me if I hated her. I told her she was a part of Ethan and I loved everything about him. Whether or not she and I got along depended on her. This poor child has spent her whole life waiting for her mother to come for her. She held her breath when I told her I've met her mother. She asked me if we fought. I wanted to say, "please I didn't need to, cause she had nothing on me." Instead I just said no, and that we obviously had our differences but we never came to blows.

"I didn't realize the silky pillow was for my hair. I like how it feels on my face."

"Believe it or not your hair is a lot like Erica's. Over the years I've instructed her on how to care for hers. How do you want to wear your hair? Long? Short? Medium?"

Zoey's eyes got big. "My hair could grow long like Erica's? I want long hair just because I've never had it."

Raynel told her how to take care of it. Then she told her to call her anytime or ask Erica whenever she was in doubt.

Lanie and Tina sat over to the side whispering about who knows what.

****

BAM! My eyes popped open as Ethan got up quickly to check on the noise. BAM! I grabbed my hotel robe and I scurried out the bedroom behind Ethan. EJ had Lanie pinned to the wall while she was kicking and fighting to get around him. Eric was holding Zoey on the opposite side of the table. Erica was at the table covering her mouth as she cried. Ethan told the girls to sit then he sat at the head of the table. "I already know this is nonsense. Why would you disrespect me like this?" Both of the girls looked at Ethan with shocked faces. He was tired of them fighting already.

"You're sisters and both of you are parts of me, you disrespect me when you fight."

"She was talking about my mother. I don't know if the things she was saying we're true or not. But she has no right to say them!"

Ethan's eyes burned a hole in Lanie. "Why?"

"She's trying to steal my sister!"

"That's not possible, why would you think that?" Erica said over her tears.

"You guys are always whispering about stuff."

"We can have conversations that don't include you. You don't have to be in the middle of everything we do or say." Zoey spit.

Lanie chuckled then she jumped on the table and swung at Zoey. Ethan caught her hand, flipped her on her back and pinned her to the table. He was telling her to calm down. Zoey's eyes were big as she looked at her father in fear. "Elaine I don't know what else to do with you."

She cried hard as she screamed, "LANIE!"

"ENOUGH!" I yelled, "since you two are always fighting regardless of who starts it, you two are going to be conjoined twins. Let her up." I told Ethan.

"Conjoined?" Zoey looked at me with her mother's face as if what I said was ridiculous.

Eric crossed his arms as he put his hands over his mouth. "Momma? I don't...."

"Shut up! Get up Lanie!" She got off the table. "Now hug and kiss your sister."

Lanie gasped, "no! No! I can't do that. You're gonna have to beat me. I'm not doing that."

I popped her upside her head. "Do it!"

"Momma I will take the licks! I'm not doing it!" Lanie called herself putting her foot down.

I kept popping her as she backed away until she was up against the wall. Then I remembered this child has to be reached another way. I exhaled then I looked at

Zoey who was watching in horror. "Come here." She walked over nervous about what I was going to do. "Give her a hug and kiss." Zoey swallowed and then she put her arms out to hug Lanie. Lanie acted like she was doing karate as she blocked Zoey's advances. "Zoey, because you did as I said we're postponing this reconciliation." Then I turned to Lanie, "go get in the shower."
Lanie grinned and then she hurried to their bedroom. She took her clothes in the bathroom. When the water started I took her suitcase out of their bedroom. I took out her brightest colored shirt, with and equally bright but completely miss-matched short pants. I went in the bathroom and switched her clothes. I took everything cute out of her suitcase. Lanie liked to pair funky clothing pieces with her nice things to create her own style. Today she was going to the amusement park as Punky Brewster meets Rainbow Bright. I only left the crazy looking clothes in her suitcase. Fortunately she couldn't fit any of the other girl's clothes, but I still told Erica not to lend Lanie anything. Eric followed me back to my room he said this was cruel and unusual punishment. I asked him if he wanted to spend the rest of our trip breaking up their fights? Lanie snatched the bathroom door open as she hurried out in her towel to her bedroom. She screamed a blood-curdling scream. "Momma no! I'm sorry! I'm sorry!" She ran to Zoey and kissed her hand. When I didn't react she screamed as she hugged and kissed her sister. EJ and Eric hurried to their room and they stood in the doorway watching with smiles on their faces. "I love her momma! I love her! Look!" She kept violently hugging and kissing Zoey full of enthusiasm. Erica ran to Ethan and buried her face in his chest as she laughed. "Zoey! I love you! Love your stinking guts! Ooh I love you so much!" Then she looked at me, "please no momma."
Through clinched lips I said, "you told me no! As if you thought I was going to take that from you. The clothes in the bathroom are what you're wearing today. And if I don't see love for your sister all day, you'll be wearing the same clothes everyday." "Momma no! I'm sorry! I don't know what's wrong with me. I'll never do it again!" She cried as she held onto her big sister's neck for dear life. Zoey stared at Lanie as if she was stunned.
"The next time you think to open your mouth to defy me you'll remember this. If you purposely get your clothes dirty or anything else you will wear these clothes in their jacked up state. I suggest you make the most of it."
Lanie screamed to the top of her lungs. Then she ran to her father, she pushed Erica out of the way then she wrapped her arms around Ethan. "Daddy!" She kept kissing him. "My beautiful and all powerful father. The man responsible for my life. Daddy! Help me! Please! Please daddy! I won't disrespect you anymore. I just don't want Zoey to come in and take over. I...."
"I'm not trying to take over Lanie. You're the only one who treats me like an outsider. I'm just trying to belong somewhere."
If looks could kill, Lanie stared at Zoey for a minute. "Fine!"
Zoey got up and ran and hugged Lanie, kissing her all over. Everybody laughed while Lanie looked like she was going to explode. Even Ethan started cracking up. "Uh Lanie? That doesn't look like love to me." Tears poured out of Lanie's eyes as

she forced herself to hug and kiss her sister back. "Now I appreciate the love fest after, but..."

Ethan cut me off, "baby; step into my office."

"Yes! Please go! Listen to your man!" Lanie pleaded as I walked back in the room with Ethan.

Ethan smiled at me, "I know you want to make her wear the clothes anyways. I think she's gotten the point. I really don't want to look back at these pictures and see her dramatics all over them."

"You just want her to see you saving her. What message will that send to Zoey if I go along with that. I want, no we want the fighting to stop."

We talked some more then we told the girls to come in. Lanie was still in her towel awaiting her fashion fate. I told Lanie I didn't want to give her another chance to obey, but her father talked me down. Lanie ran to Ethan and hugged and kissed him. I told them the choice was theirs. They could quickly become best-friends today and show us that they're inseparable all day or.... Both of the girls ran to each other and said they didn't need to know the or else. Ethan smiled at his girls then he told them to carry on with their morning, Lanie kissed her clothes as she walked out. I locked the door, took off my robe and laid back down on the bed. I told Ethan that was not the way I envisioned waking up this morning. He stood there looking at me not saying anything. I could feel the heat from his eyes as I tried to ignore him and get back to sleep. When Ethan got on the bed I told him I was sleep. He laid next to me and started rubbing my back. I warned him that I was sleep and to leave me alone. He said he could help me with that. I whined and said he was going to make me more tired. He started kissing my neck, and then the kids started knocking asking what time we were leaving. They were excited to show Zoey around the park. I exhaled cause they weren't going to leave us alone now. I told them to give me an hour. Ethan watched me get up probably thinking I was leaving him hanging. I turned the shower on and then the radio. I looked at Ethan and I told him he better come and get it.

****

It was barely dawn as we approached. Grace excitedly stood next to Timothy as we got out of the car. I was already looking at my house in Aw! I could see the expansion as we pulled up to the gate. I grabbed Grace's hand as everyone gathered in front of the door. Timothy told us he appreciated our patience as he got the job done right. Then he opened the door for us. Immediately I noticed that the upstairs was longer due to the renovation. We were still on the left; all the kid's rooms were on the right. There was another full sized bathroom upstairs. Every room in the house except the guest room and bathroom downstairs were now bigger. Ethan said he wanted the boys on opposite sides of the house, and the girls in the middle. All of their rooms were exactly the same. Lanie and Zoey wanted to be next to Erica so she chose the room in the middle to keep the peace. Ethan claimed the last upstairs room as his office. Grace showed me all the nuances in the house as we picked the colors for each room. We had to come early so all the painting could be done today so we could move back by end of the week. The kitchen was completely redone with new appliances and more space. Ethan was on the phone telling the movers to bring our things in two days. I looked at Ethan and I told him I needed to redecorate everything. He didn't say anything but I knew he always loved what I did. Ethan and Timothy talked to the landscaper about the new yard design. Meanwhile the house painters got to work on the house. Tina and Grace came with us as we browsed furniture stores with my paint samples. When I explained the concept of drapes verses blinds to Zoey I also explained how she was expected to care for them before I let her choose. Erica gave her ideas for her orange and brass themed room. I have to admit I didn't like the colors when she picked them. As I saw the stuff they picked for her room Grace and I applauded them for pulling it off. Lanie's colors were yellow, green, and stark white. Her room was going to be bright and airy. Eric asked Lanie and Zoey to collaborate on his room. He gave them specific instructions on how he wanted his room to look. But he didn't want to risk the ridicule from his father and brother for coming with us. EJ told Erica that she knew what to do with his room. Erica's room was lavender and she picked pastels to compliment her soft manner. She opted for blinds and a pastel blue chiffon fabric that she got yards of at the fabric store to drape accordingly along the framing of her window. I could've done those boys rooms, but I'm sure they asked their sisters to make them feel special. While we shopped Grace told me about the problems she's been having with her family. They seemed to feel that since Grace was back that she needed to spend every free moment with them. Grace said that she and Timothy are doing so much better and now that they're back it's supposed to be the icing on the cake. She said her father challenged Timothy and to her surprise Timothy put him in his place effortlessly. Grace smiled as surprise was still all over her face. When she said she was rooting for Timothy as if she forgot it was her father. I looked at her in disbelief as I confirmed that Lanie was just like her.

****

"Mmmmoooommmmmmaaaaaa!" Lanie yelled from her bathroom.

"What I tell you about screaming like that?"

She put her big brown eyes on me, "sorry momma. I'm just frustrated!" Her hair was all over her head. It looked like she tried to do something and ended up in a war with her hair. "I need help!" She pointed to her head.

I tried to hold back my laughter, "what are you trying to do?"

"I don't know, something cute."

"Lately you care so much about how you look when we go to service. This wouldn't happen to have anything to do with that new family? Would it?"

The Jamison family moved to Berkeley from Palo Alto. They have a son about Lanie's age and one a little younger. Now that I think about it Lanie has been my number one partner to service. Erica, Zoey, and EJ come as well, but they don't come as religiously as Lanie has been coming these days. Now that I think about it, her little shopping sprees have been somewhat centered around what she's going to wear to service. Lanie put her eyes to the floor, "maybe."

I smiled, "he is a little cutie pie isn't he?"

"I think I might be too much woman for him."

I couldn't help it, I cracked up! "Too much woman?"

"Yes, sometimes he doesn't say anything to me."

"He does seem shy."

"Yea, he's not like daddy. Daddy just doesn't talk much. Not because he's shy, he's just sitting there thinking of mean things to say half the time. Dorian is just shy. That makes me want to grab him. I don't know why."

"Grab him?"

"At the congregation picnic, he was following us around. We were walking up this hill and he started falling so I grabbed him and pulled him up. His eyes got big and after that I kept grabbing him when he was about to step wrong. I couldn't have my man falling off the hill."

I cracked up, "your man?"

She blushed, "yes momma. Why is this funny?" Her eyes were serious as she looked at me. "It seems like all the boys like Erica and girls like her. I'm not that sweet and I'm not that innocent."

I crossed my arms, "explain that."

Lanie's eyes danced around the room, "I mean. I don't know how to be gentle like that. Erica's got that never been kissed look down real good, I don't. She's been kissed and I haven't."

I closed the door, "you can't be saying that. What if your father hears, he'll have a heart attack."

"Come on! Erica's almost in college, he can't think she's never been kissed. Just like you can't think EJ and Eric are still virgins."

Irritation ran through my veins, "funny how you're telling me everyone's business except your own! I don't want to know that my sons are taking advantage of little girls. I don't want to know that you want some boy putting the most diseased part of his body in yours!" Lanie turned green, "stop trying to grow up so fast. You are not a woman little girl. Erica and the twins are a lot older than you. There's certain things they will experience that you need A LOT of time before you experience. Right now you should focus on enjoying being a little girl. You will be an adult soon enough and once you're an adult you can't go backwards." Then I started taming her hair.

She watched my eyes in the mirror, "are you mad at me?"

"No, but I don't want to know that my sons are squishing about in little girl's guts, or that my daughter is letting a little boy get close enough to her to put any part of his body in hers. It all leads to trouble, and its not the way I'm trying to raise any of you. Are you sexually active?"

She gasped, "what? Momma no! I haven't even been kissed."

Ethan opened the door, "GOOD! And you better never!"

Lanie and I jumped, "where did you come from?"

Ethan focused on Lanie, "who did Erica kiss?"

Lanie stiffened, "nobody! I was just saying that to have something to say."

Ethan gave her that fatherly death stare, "when is it ever ok to lie to me?"

Lanie flinched, "I'm sorry."

"Who?"

Lanie put her eyes on the floor. "Daddy I love you so much! You're an amazing father."

"Who?"

"You are the best father, there's no one better than you. I tell the girls at school all the time about how good of a daddy I've got."

"ELAINE!"

Lanie gasped, "DADDY! We've discussed this!"

"Answer me!" Lanie kept her eyes to the floor. Ethan took the comb from me. He put it in her hair and started pulling it through.

"DADDY!" She screamed in agony. "Ok! Daddy! Ok! I'll talk. I'll talk!" She said grabbing for the comb.

"What's going on?" Erica said walking into the bathroom. Zoey was peeking in from the hallway.

"RUN! Save yourself! Daddy's gonna torture you too!" Lanie said with tears pouring out of her eyes.

Erica started to run and Ethan called her back. Still holding Lanie's hair in one hand and the comb in the other, Ethan asked Erica who's the boy she's been kissing on. When Erica stood there looking stuck, Ethan put the comb back in Lanie's hair. As he pulled the comb through again Lanie screamed again. Erica started crying and she begged her father to stop. Zoey looked terrified by the whole scene. Now this would seem horrible if Lanie's hair was tangled. This girl just takes tender headed to a whole other level. The comb passed through her hair nicely each time, but Lanie don't like getting her hair done period. Lanie started screaming that this was child abuse. To save her sister Erica sang like a canary. Ethan told Erica to invite the boy over. When she hesitated he warned her that if she didn't, he'd make her go to school right here in the Bay and she wouldn't be allowed to date until she was fifty years old. Lanie stood there crying her eyes out as if she was reliving the whole experience. Zoey looked beyond scared as she watched Ethan walk out of the bathroom. Her fearful expression made Ethan stop walking. He stared at Zoey as she stood there trembling. I swallowed then I told Erica to fix Lanie's hair. Ethan told Zoey to follow him. I walked behind them into our bedroom. I put my arm around Zoey's shoulders as I had her sit next to me on the bed. Ethan started breathing hard every time he attempted to say something. "JENISE YOU KNOW MY QUESTION YOU JUST GONNA SIT THERE AND LET ME STRUGGLE?" I cut my eyes at him, "I'm here for moral support not to be your mouth piece."

"You know I'm going to say the wrong thing and mess this whole thing up. Can you spare us that trauma?"

Zoey grabbed my hand with her sweaty hand as she kept her eyes to the floor. "Dad?"

He exhaled, "yes."

"I..."

Ethan exhaled and then he put his hand up. "We're not going to go into details about this. Do they know?"

"Erica does..." She kept her head down. "My grandma made me get rid of it."
Ethan looked at me with fire in his eyes. "JENISE!"
I rubbed Zoey's hands, "how do you feel about that?"
"It's all a blur to me. I know I'm not ready to be anybody's mom."
"Where's the boy?"
"He's in San Francisco we broke up."
"Why?"
"He moved on and I tried to kill him." She slightly squeezed my hand.
"You did what?"
"He was trying to act like I didn't matter. I thought we were in love and finally I had someone to love me for me. He changed up and then he came over my house unannounced. I stabbed his arm, he had to get stitches. Then I found out I was pregnant."
"Why aren't you and Lanie bestfriends?" I exhaled, "I'm sorry you went through that. I don't know if your grandma ever talked to you about waiting. What we're trying to do here is raise all of you with a sense of value that you assign to yourself. You are very valuable to your father and I. Ethan took Erica and Lanie on their first dates. He's going to do the same for you. This is your roadmap to follow when you choose to allow someone close to you. Do you understand?" She shook her head yes. "Also we're going to get a physical for you and we're going to have more conversations."
"Ok," then she looked at Ethan with tears falling down her face. "Are you mad at me?"
I raised an eyebrow at him. "No, but you will conduct yourself like you're my daughter. You are loved and you don't need some little boy between your legs to give you what I give with no strings attached. If it's not love you will not stoop to a degrading level of self-loathing. When you need love, you have a family now. If he doesn't love you like I love Jenise you will not do it. You understand me?"
"Yes dad."
"Come here," she walked over slowly. "I'm sorry I didn't know about you sooner. You are just as special to me as everyone else. When Jenise and Lanie leave, you and I are going to spend some time together."
"Can Erica come?"
"You afraid to be alone with me?"
"She explains you to me so I understand how to react. I would be lost without her."
"That's fine as long as she wants to go."
"I'm sorry daddy."
When she started crying I told Ethan to hold her. He held her like a baby. Then I went back to getting ready to go.
When Lanie and I got in the car I told her she looked nice. She thanked me then she turned to me. "Did you guys beat her?" She had a big smile.
"Should I beat you?"
"No! I was just asking."
"I don't understand why you two aren't the closest, both of you are the same kind of

crazy."

Lanie snapped her fingers, "is that what it is? That's why we fight over Erica. Got it!"

"Got what?"

"I got her number now. Don't worry momma everything is fine." Then she laughed a wicked laugh.

When we got to service Lanie's eyes scanned the room until she found Dorian who was working alongside his father. As soon as he saw Lanie he blushed and Lanie stared at him.

****

My mom has been awfully quiet over here in her corner. Something's wrong I can feel it. Zoey and I picked up her graduation dress and then I told her I had to go check on my mother as urgency washed over me. Zoey's eyes got big as she looked at my mother's building. I told the doorman to tell them Zoey and I were coming up. Stephen opened the door as we approached. He hugged me but he didn't look me in my eyes. He said hi to Zoey as he hugged her. He had a drink in his hand. My mom said she was in her room. Stephen told Zoey to come with him. My mom was laying down, then I saw the chemotherapy machine sitting on the nightstand. She sat up slowly as she tried to smile at me. She said her cancer was back and so Stephen convinced her to get the double mastectomy before it spread. I asked her why she didn't tell me. She said my plate was full with blending my kids and my house renovation. She didn't want to burden me. When I started freaking out she said she didn't want this either. She said her doctor was pretty confident that they got it all.

Zoey knocked on the door, "mom are you ok?"

I put arms out to tell her to come to me. I held her in my arms like a big baby. I held on tight as I rocked her and I told my mother how much I loved her. My mom cried and said she knows.

Zoey drove us home and I went straight to bed. Ethan came in the bedroom on his phone. I could tell he was talking to Stephen. "I understand your reasoning but Jenise is very attached to her mother. You guys have to do a better job of communicating over there. She has me; we will deal with whatever comes up. Please no more bombs like this."

Zoey bumped the door open with her hip as she brought a tray to me with tea on it. "Mom, I brought you some tea. Erica and Lanie are on their way." Zoey said setting the tray on my bed.

Ethan came over and kissed me then he gently rubbed my head. "I'm sorry."

"Thank you," I said hugging him back.

Chapter 31

Ethan

Our silence was the most comfortable silence I've known in my life. We didn't feel obligated to chit chat or fill the car with needless noise. Good music and open road. When a Torrie Rowe song came on the radio, Malcolm quickly changed to his CD player. "Isn't that your girl?"

"My rotation, nothing more."

"How my daughter feel about that?" Malcolm shook his head as he blew air. My Uncle Tim chuckled, "I really like Dwayne." Malcolm's grip got tighter on the steering wheel. "He's a good kid. Family oriented, almost exactly the kind of kid I had in mind for my Babygirl."

"Almost!" Malcolm said at the bottom of his voice.

"Yeah, almost. Nephew, you tell me how you would feel if one of your girls were in Amber's shoes."

"Malcolm would be dead a long time ago." I said without blinking.

"Good thing you're my son HUH? Who else would be so understanding? My son is gifted, talented, and brilliant. But a total idiot with his heart! It's like you feel love and it paralyzes you." Uncle Tim exhaled, "good thing I understand where you're coming from. I don't know any other father as patient as I am."

"Amber knows I love her."

"You love her so much you can tolerate her falling in love with someone else. The thought of your momma loving someone else woke me up. You sit here and accept it like it's ok. When they get married I will not tolerate you hovering."

"Amber's not marrying that pretty boy!" Malcolm said firmly.

"If I say she can are you crazy enough to go against me?" My Uncle Tim said firmly.

My Uncle Jeff chuckled cause he knows his brother. "If it came down to it yes I would. Amber will not marry him!" Malcolm said firmly.

Uncle Jeff laughed out loud looking at his brother's expression. "Give that little twerp a chance you told me. Don't push him away you said. Sophia is happy with her little square and that Cardell kid is five hundred plus miles away." Uncle Jeff inhaled happily.

"Richard is a good cat, I hated to see him go." Malcolm said.

"You're the only one. Sophia made her choice."

"He'll be back. You can live in a fantasy world if you want, but we all know the truth. Just like Amber is in love with the knucklehead up there, Sophia's in love with Richard. Eventually she's going back, her story ends with Richard." Uncle Tim said, Uncle Jeff wasn't smiling anymore.

He irritatedly stared out the window. "How our girls end up with these, these.... Thugs!"

"They fell in love with men just like their fathers." Malcolm interjected.

When we got off the freeway in Redding we drove through the city. Down a two lane street. We parked in front of a duplex. Malcolm got out of the car and he pointed to the unit on the left. My uncles got out of the car and stood with Malcolm. I took a deep breath and then I knocked on the door. I could hear music playing on the inside. "Who is it?"

"Blu."

She hurried to open the door, and then she slowly opened it. "Oh my God!" She said barely opening the door. "What do you want?"

"Open up!" Cat cut all her hair off into a short curly style. Her face was hard and aged; she looked older than she is. She opened the door looking out to see my entourage. She shut the door behind me. She was nervous and unsure of why I was here. "So you cheated on me."

She froze in place and immediately started sweating. "I...." She looked around the room. "Yes! You were done with me anyways."

"I would've been done a lot sooner had I known." She still had her engagement ring on. "Why do you still wear that?"

"The only time a man chose me. I cherish it."

"A lot of good that did me." I stood in the living room. "Did you know Elijah has disappeared?"

She sat on the couch, "no." She was thoughtful.

"Do you get why I'm here?"

"No."

"Your mother came to my office with Zoey."

Cat's eyes got big, "Zoey's not your daughter."

"Who's daughter is she?"

"Sammy's."

I was in her face in point five seconds squeezing her wrist. "Sammy's not that little girl's father! I am!"

She gasped, "what?"

"I have the DNA test to prove it. Even if you didn't know she was mine how could you leave her with your mother?"

Tears poured out of her eyes, "I was trying to get something better for her. For us."

"Meanwhile she grows up wondering why her mother never loved her and thinking her father is dead. Your mother unloaded her as soon as she got the results. It was a long shot that she came to me in the first place. I could kill you!"

"She looks like me, I didn't see you in her at all."

"You didn't even consider the possibility!"

"No, you were always protected. I don't even know how you could be."

"If you would've gotten to know my momma like I told you to, you would've seen me all in that girl's doggone face!" Cat's hands started turning blue they were so white. I released her and I took three steps backwards. I took a deep breath, "it's done." I reminded myself. "She's graduating from high school this summer. You're coming to her graduation, fix yourself up. She's going to be angry with you. She won't accept you. But you owe her this! When she goes to college if she wants to reach out to you she will. If you run Cat, I promise I will kill you. This is the last person in the world you need to hurt. She didn't ask to be here. Your sole purpose is to be there for her. Nothing more nothing less. If you even think about mincing words with my wife it will suck to be you. Understood!"

"Understood."

****

"Erica Rainise Wallace!" Everyone cheered loud and long, I clapped. Erica, daddy's angel walked across the stage full of pride. They remained standing they barely got the Z out of their mouth when our section erupted in loud thunderous applause again, "Zoey Annalisa Wallace". Zoey looked at our section with big eyes. We could tell she was crying, Erica waited for her at the bottom of the stage. They squeezed each other tightly letting other graduates pass by them. Lanie was next to momma watching, and then I see her joining their hug. No one saw her slip away. The three of them hugged then they went to their seats. Lanie wedged herself between the two of them on the graduate floor. The faculty didn't know what to do about Lanie. Fortunately for them they let it go. Lanie held out her disposable camera taking pictures of the three of them. In closing the graduating class had Erica sing a solo. We had no idea she was going to do that. My babygirl blew everyone away. Then she told her family she loved us. It was over and our section would not calm down. The twin terrors rushed the stage followed by Lanie. Everyone in our section started down towards the stage. Jenise tapped me then she pointed out Cat. Cat was on the other side of the auditorium standing and staring at the stage. I could see that same nervousness she had about seeing her father for the first time in years all over her. The Mitigated staff member was standing next to her. Jenise interlocked her fingers into mine and then she told me to come on. She led me over to Cat. Cat stared at us like she couldn't turn her eyes away. She looked so hurt I'm assuming by how good we looked together. Jenise smiled and said hello like there was never any bad blood between them, she even hugged her. "Zoey is such a wonderful young lady. It's good to see you."

"Thank you," Cat said with tears in her eyes as she focused on Jenise. "You look good."

Jenise's eyes saddened for Cat, "thank you."

"I'll go get Zoey, you two stay here." When I got to the crowd of young and old family members I told Zoey to come. Her smile was big and full. "Come on." I held her hand and had her walk with me. She was smiling as we approached Cat and Jenise. When Cat saw us she stiffened and put both of her arms straight at her sides. Zoey stopped walking and she looked at me with fear in her eyes. "She's here to congratulate you."

"Dad there are no words! I don't know how to feel about this."

"That's understandable, stay by me."

Zoey squeezed my hand and let me lead her while she fell behind me peeking at Cat. When we got to Cat, Zoey stood behind me and close to Jenise.

"Congratulations," Cat said awkwardly.

"Thanks!"

"Is this your momma?" Lanie said approaching us. I could feel Zoey shake her head yes. Lanie smiled and crossed her arms. "Go ahead momma beat her up! I know you can take her!"

Jenise rolled her eyes at Lanie, "you are a disturbed child."

"Why isn't she hugging you? My momma would hug me."

"She's not that kind of mother." Zoey said lowly.

"You want me to get her for you? I'll do it! I don't know her!"

Lanie and Zoey started laughing. Then Zoey stood next to me, "it's not like I know her either. Thank you sissy!" Zoey looked her up and down, "you look old."

"Hard life," Cat said watching Zoey. "I used to look like you."

"Not! My sissy's beautiful!" Lanie blurted out.

"Thank you sissy as are you!" Zoey smiled giving Lanie daps. "Are you dying or something?"

"No, I wanted to congratulate you."

"Where do you live?"

"Redding."

"Where's that?"

"Up north close to Oregon."

Zoey's cheeks turned red, "why are you all the way out there? How come you stopped coming to see me? Why did you leave me behind? Why didn't you know who my father was? Everybody at least has his or her mother! You left me!"

Cat shifted her weight from one side to the other. "I don't have a good excuse for my actions. My selfishness has been out of control. I don't blame you for hating me. That's exactly how you should feel. Had I known Blu was your father things would've been so much different. It's my fault for not knowing. I hid my pregnancy from him and I hit the ground running as soon as you were born."

"Why didn't you have an abortion?"

"It was too late by the time I realized I was pregnant."

"We're happy you're here! You were meant to be here!" Lanie said looking at Zoey with very serious eyes. Zoey walked away crying, Lanie pointed her finger at Cat. "I don't like you! I'm gonna get you!" Then she went after her sister.

Tears fell out of Cat's eyes. "There are no words!"

"Zoey says that all the time." Jenise said not knowing what else to say.

"Now what?"

"You wait, it may take some time but she'll reach out to you. Be there for her when she does." Then I told the staff to take her home.

Jenise

Once Cat left Ethan and I walked in the direction that Zoey hurried away in. I looked at the stress lines in Ethan's face. We stopped walking and I asked him how he was holding up. Ethan shook his head as he looked down. He said it's not all Cat's fault. He said he shouldn't have been so selfish. His selfishness has caused so much unnecessary pain. I put my arms around him; I told him he wasn't in this alone. My fear of ruffling feathers was a MAJOR factor in all of this. Ethan put his arms around me and hugged me tightly, "I love you so much!"

I kissed his cheek and I told him I loved him. As we walked a little further we stopped in our tracks as we saw Lanie comforting Zoey. Lanie made Zoey laugh as she told her how they could go beat Cat up for her until Zoey felt better. Zoey said hurting Cat wouldn't make her feel better. Lanie told her she was crazy! Lanie explained how a busted lip could shift the hurt feelings easily. Ethan shook his head and then he told me Lanie acts like me. I smiled as I disagreed. They hugged and Zoey thanked her for trying to cheer her up. When we walked up, Zoey threw her arms around me. She cried hard as she said Cat never wanted her. I hugged her, I told her that doesn't matter cause she's here, and I've wanted her from the moment I laid eyes on her. Zoey squeezed me tighter as she screamed through her tears. Ethan exhaled and ran his hand through his hair. Lanie ran to Ethan and smashed her face into his chest. We thought she was playing at first, but she was really crying.
"Thank you for loving me. That is so sad! I know I'm different and you didn't have to try with me, thank you for trying daddy. Thank you for thinking that ugly lady was ever cute and giving me a sister who I tried to kill at first. I mean I love her now, and I'm so sad for her."
Zoey started laughing, which stopped her from crying. "I thought you were trying to kill me. Thanks for confirming."
"Anything for you sissy. Thank you for not dying. I'm sorry for all those times I tried to suffocate you."
I gasped, "Lanie you didn't?"
"Hey, I didn't know if she was going to try to get me so I was getting her first. We're cool now."
Ethan smiled down at Lanie, "you are so twisted."
"OH THANK YOU DADDY! That means so much coming from you!" She smiled wiping her face.
The rest of the family came out of the main auditorium. Frank had his arm around Erica with his version of a smile on his face. He waived Zoey over and he told them they were riding with him. He told the rest of us to meet him at his restaurant. Raynel rode with Dito and Tess. All the teenagers gathered in the other cars and followed us. In the car Ethan exhaled, then he asked me why our kids were so crazy. I told him it was the combination of two dynamite people that took our offspring to such extremes. I told him that EJ acts so much like him it's ridiculous. He said Erica and Eric act like me. Then we argued over who Lanie and Zoey act like. Those two seem to have morphed into the same person. When they started getting along, they became very close. Sometimes Erica comes in our room to escape her crazy sisters. I told him that clearly the crazy gene came from him. He argued that my love makes them crazy, and it makes him crazy too. We had a good laugh. As we were walking into Rainise's, Frank's restaurant on the border of Berkeley and Oakland, we heard a girl call out to Eric. It was his little girlfriend with her parents. Eric called us over to meet them. Lynn's parents were nice and they had nothing but nice things to say about Eric. Young love! Lynn is a sweet little thing and Eric is completely gone over this girl. Sometimes they double date with EJ and Shelby. Ethan successfully scared away Erica's friend. Lynn's parents

invited us out to get to know each other. When we went inside Grace asked what the introductions were about, and when I told her she looked at Lil Tim and asked him how come she hadn't met one of his girlfriends yet. Embarrassed Lil Tim put his head down and said nothing. I told her not to embarrass him. When she didn't listen to me, Uncle Tim said Auntie Annette was the same way with Timothy and she saw when they finally met. He told her to cut him some slack. Grace immediately calmed and then she bumped me under the table. I smiled cause Grace swears Uncle Tim is a retired ladies man. She says he's always so smooth and strong. She sighs and says she wishes Timothy would've inherited more of his rougher side though. I bite my tongue so hard most of the time. It's not my place to tell her that her husband is a reformed thug.

Frank stood in the middle of the room with both of the girls under each arm. "I am so proud of my grand daughters! Both of them have graduated and they're continuing their education. I am so proud to see all my hard work pay off to provide for my generations. My father wanted educated and well rounded off spring for generations to come. I'm honored to be able to watch that dream live on for him. I have no doubt that you're going to take the world by storm." Then he kissed each of them on their cheeks.

Then Frank stepped to the side and my Uncle Nelson came up and put his arms around the girls just as Frank had. He looked from Zoey to Erica with a huge grin. "You two make your Uncle Nelson so proud. You are dignified and respectable young ladies. Now don't go away to school and lose your minds like you've had no home training. Your grandparents and I have created a schedule of random pop ups. We expect you two to be on best behavior at all times." Then he kissed them and stepped to the side.

Then Gwen stood up with her very pregnant belly. She hugged both of them. "My girls are going to the party school. Yahoo! Chico state!" Ethan nor his brothers or father laughed at her comment. "Make sure you maintain your grades and stay at the top of your class, AND have some fun. I'm proud of you! Keep in mind that too much fun leads to one of these." She rubbed her belly. "You want one of those," she pointed to Martin. "Before you start having these." She pointed to her stomach again. "A man who loves you no matter how crazy you are." Then she kissed them, "oh and these hurt when they come out. AND your body will never be the same. AND we won't get into the head trip that happens when you have a baby." Zoey looked at Gwen with big eyes, no doubt thinking of her mother.

Then Frank told the girls their graduation gifts were outside. We followed them outside and two brand new luxury cars were now parked outside with red bows on them. Ethan cut his eyes at his father. The girls screamed jumping up and down then they hugged and kissed Frank. He gave them keys and they ran to their cars. As if they knew the cola colored car was for Zoey and the periwinkle colored car was Erica. They chirped the cars and got in. Both of the girls were crying as they looked around their cars. Franky asked if the cars had all the bells and whistles, Frank frowned at him and said of course as if the question was ridiculous. EJ volunteered the girl's cars for a weekend road trip to start the summer off.

Tina asked her mother with pleading eyes if she could go. Grace hesitated and asked me if Lanie was going. I pointed to Lanie who was getting in the front seat of Zoey's car. Grace told her she could go if Lil Tim went. Tina screamed and ran into the car with Zoey and Lanie not even checking for her brother who was getting in the car with my boys. "Wait a minute! Where are we going?" Drew asked trying to be the voice of reason.

"Drew man! We got cars and credit cards, does it matter? Are you coming or not?" Eric said.

Drew kissed his mother's cheek and then he got in the car with Derrick. The caravan of teenagers left the parking lot and then we started back inside. Grace and I were at the back of the group. I was smiling because Ethan and I now had the house to ourselves. If I know my man, we'll barely make it in the door. "Jenise!"

I spun around at the sound of my name. My chest tightened when I saw my father coming right at me. "Dad?"

"My invitation must've gotten lost in the mail!" He yelled at me.

"You know good and well that I didn't send you one." I said holding Grace's hand as my heart pounded like it was going to fall out of my chest. "Go away! I don't want anything to do with you!"

"Fred? What are you doing here?" My mom said coming back out of the restaurant and standing next to me.

"Evelyn! How could you leave me? How could you let Taffy put me out of her life?"

"She has a right to choose you or not."

"You got my brother here, my nieces. I can't be here? How could you two turn your backs on me when I need you the most?"

"You should've thought of that when you were traumatizing them." Uncle Nelson said coming out of the restaurant.

My father looked down on my Uncle. "You still trying to take over my life. That's my wife and my child! No matter what, or how much you hang around wishing and hoping they will always be mine! Never yours!"

My Uncle looked at my mother and she looked at the ground. "Fred your jealousy about me and Evelyn is exactly why you're standing on the outside and not in here with us."

"Oh so I'm crazy? I'm paranoid? Is Jenise my daughter?"

I looked at my mother who looked like my father's question slapped the taste out of her mouth. "FRED!" She started crying, "how could you?"

"You know Jenise is the only reason she put up with your abuse." Uncle Nelson barked.

My father stared at my mother, "he doesn't know about the guy?"

"Fred you know Jenise is your daughter. You're evil! She's the only reason I stayed."

"Everybody thinks you're so perfect and innocent like I'm this monster and my frustration is unwarranted. I bet you never told them about your boyfriend, or Nelson."

"Still doesn't change all that you did to cause yourself to be the outsider today."
"You're still going to defend her until the wheels come off. You're my brother! When do you have my back?"
"When you're wrong, you're wrong! I know everything and no one here cares. Leave Fred! Don't ever come back! They've moved beyond you and they're happy without you!"
Ethan stood next to me, "I warned you."
Stephen put his arms around my mom. My father visibly became unglued as he looked at Stephen and my mother. He screamed at the night. Ethan waved at invisible people and told them to remove my father. As two guys approached my father, he yelled that he was taking someone with him. He reached in his jacket and the light caught something shiny as he pulled it out. My father pulled the trigger and I saw one spark, then he pulled again. Ethan shot at my father as I was thrown to the ground with the force of fire as my entire body was covered in pain.

Ethan

Sound ceased to exist! Grace's blood curdling scream told me this was real! Jenise fell to the ground and blood had sprayed my clothes and me. Evelyn's eyes were stretched wide as she ran to Jenise in disbelief. Dito had Fred on the ground and when the realization that Jenise was hit washed over him, his everything turned red and he open fire on Fred. Hitting him in every fatal spot but allowing him to suffer. My momma slapped me and told me she needed my attention. Everyone was moving around me, but this couldn't be real! This couldn't be!

Chapter 32

Ethan

When the paramedics arrived they got her bleeding under control. In the ambulance they said Jenise's heartbeat was weakening. I held her hand and begged her not to leave me. When we got to the hospital they put me in this room and told me they were taking her into surgery. There wasn't a dry eye in here. If I would've moved that much faster it would've been me instead of her. They took Jenise into surgery immediately, and we've been waiting for any kind of news for the past four hours. Fred shot Jenise in the chest, as far as I could see, and she was unresponsive immediately. My momma held on to me and she kept telling me I was in shock cause I wasn't here. This was a horrible nightmare that I couldn't wake up from. Jenise is my life, my *everything*. I can't even... Our story doesn't end here. I keep pacing! All I can think about is this foot goes in front of this one and now the next. I can't sit still cause it breaks my heart. Nothing about this room is tranquil. That stupid fish tank makes me want to punch through it. The fish swim to one side then they swim to the other. It's like they're mimicking me and I'm not in the mood. The stupid walls are painted this blue color, which Jenise says, is supposed to help calm you cause blue is considered a "happy" color. Nothing about this room is happy and I want to tear it down. "Mr. Wallace?" The doctor said walking into the waiting room. Everyone stood around the doctor anxious to know what he had to say. I felt like I couldn't breathe, my mind kept running from me. I planted my feet. "Mr. Wallace?" The doctor said again as he waited for me to get it together. "Mr. Wallace your wife is going to be ok. The bullet just missed her lung. Thank you all for your efforts to keep her bleeding down. You did the right thing. She's in recovery right now, you can see her as soon as we move her to her room."
"How bad is her recovery going to be?" My momma asked.
"She's going to be in a lot of pain, she has a few fractured ribs. We will do everything in our power to keep her comfortable. Once she's conscious we'll go over what to expect next. Your wife is going to be ok." He assured me. Evelyn and I hugged as she cried angry tears into my chest. Grace refused to leave; Timothy explained that there were too many people and that they would come back. Once Grace gave in, Tess conceded as well. Martin had to just about carry Gwen out, cause she didn't want to leave but her very pregnant body screamed to differ with her. I was too upset to pay attention to the fact that my momma was crying in my Dad's arms. I released Evelyn to Stephen, and I tried to remain focused. Franky told me he needed to take his family home and to call him, but he'd be back tomorrow. As the others dosed off in the waiting room I was up pacing the hallway. I couldn't relax until I saw her. I needed to apologize from the bottom of my soul about everything. Then an orderly told me he was moving Jenise to her room and I could come in the back with him. Jenise was still sleep; they had a cap on her head to cover her hair. I touched her hand and her eyes fluttered. I held her hand all the way to her room. The nurse introduced herself, checked Jenise's vitals and then she left.

Once we were alone all the fear and pain washed over me at once. I held on to Jenise's hand and cried. I thanked her for not leaving me. I apologized for failing to protect her. I kept kissing her lips and telling her how much I loved her. All the things I wanted to do and say were on my tongue but now I needed her ears to hear me. I fell asleep holding her hand. When she moved her hand I woke up, her eyes were fluttering and then she woke up panicking as if we were still outside the restaurant. She looked around completely terrified and she was trying to figure out where she was, her heart monitor sped up. Once she focused on me she immediately started calming down. Her nurse came in completely calm and she spoke in a soothing voice to Jenise. Jenise looked at me with tears in her eyes as she slowly said her father shot her. It was more like she was answering her own question. Jenise asked if her momma was ok, I told her that Evelyn was safe and in the waiting room waiting for her to wake up. Her eyes turned red, I could tell she wanted to ask if her father was gone, but it was pointless to ask, she knew the answer. I leaned over her bed and I put my forehead on hers. "I have never been so scared in my life. You cannot leave me, I can't live without you!" I kissed her lips. "Those kids were going to have to figure it out cause I can't breathe without you. You were created for me; you are my reason for living. Without you I am nothing!" Jenise cried, "marry me!"

She looked confused, "we're... married."

"That was a rushed and controlled ceremony. I want you to have the wedding you want. You get to pick the date; you get to go dress shopping. It can be as big or small as you want. We need a do over."

"After all... this time... you want... to marry... me again? Are you... sure?" She asked through her tears.

"How could you ask me if I'm sure? You are the one guarantee in my life! I will always do anything for you!"

Jenise smiled at me, "can I... think about... it? Ethan... this is all... so sudden... I need... to see... if I... can get... a better... offer." I stopped smiling and I frowned at her. "Blu might... bring me... a ring."

I looked at the wall and then back at her. "You're forever joking! Leave it to you."

"That's why... you love... me."

I kissed her lips again, "you are my air, my words, my everything!"

Her nurse came back with pain medicines that made her sleepy. I came out of the room so that her momma, Stephen, and my momma could go in.

I was in the waiting room with my father, Nelson, and Uncle Tim when Eugene walked in the door. Nelson watched Eugene without saying a word. Eugene said he came as soon as he heard. "You're the guy aren't you?" Nelson accused him.

"The guy?" Eugene said standing up straight.

"Evelyn!"

"The guy what?"

"She was going to leave Fred for you?" Eugene didn't respond right away he looked at Nelson. "Who are you?"

"Are you Jenise's father? Who are you?"

"Fred is her father."

"I know who Fred is. I'm asking you, are you her father?"

I looked at my father who was leaning his face on his left fist as he watched them go back and forth like this scene was mildly entertaining.

"I'm telling you Fred is her father. She married him didn't she."

"Doesn't rule you out as a possibility."

"How did she meet you? Where did you come from?" Nelson's jealousy was all over him.

"Jenise needs to know if you are more than just her uncle."

Uncle Tim cleared his throat, "I hate to barge in on your conversation. But who are you to tell him anything when you haven't come clean with Malcolm?"

"That's different!" Eugene said matter of factly.

"Oh right, cause you're waiting to divulge that information on your death bed. Eugene we go way back, but Malcolm deserves to know just as much as Jenise does. Shoot from the sound of things they were almost stepbrother and sister." Uncle Tim said staring Eugene down.

"You've got Malcolm under your wing. You might as well leave it there."

"My son deserves to know where he comes from just as much as Jenise does. How do we know you aren't her father too?"

"I didn't come here for this! I came to make sure Jenise was ok." Eugene looked at me.

"She's going to pull through."

"Good! I'll make contact later." Then he walked out.

Uncle Tim sprang out of his seat and my father jumped in front of him. "Tim relax! Breathe!"

Uncle Tim was trying to get around my father. "Move out of my way fat boy!"

"Tim you're so angry that that's the best you can come up with? Let him go. He has to live with his choices."

Through clinched teeth he said, "I just wanna tell him something." He tried to move around my father.

My father picked his little brother up. "I know you! If you go out there right now he's going to die, and then how will he come to his senses? You think Malcolm doesn't know by now? Whispers told him, he knows."

"He won't own up to his indiscretions but he points out someone else's? I don't like hypocrites Franky!"

"Hey! Hey! Franky is my son, I'm just Frank. Franklin if you really need to call me something else. I'm not putting you down until you calm down."

"I'm calm! Put me down!" When my father put him down Uncle Tim took off running, and my father ran right behind him. You could hear them scuffling in the hallway. Nelson tried to hold it back, and then he started laughing.

Then my father and Uncle Tim hurried back in the room as a nurse followed them in the room with her arms crossed. "Cut it out!"

"Yes ma'am!" They said together like big ole kids.

Now that we're done playing I looked at Nelson. "Are you Jenise's father?"

Pain flashed across his face, "you don't know how much I wish I could say yes. Evelyn says no, so I don't push it. She only stayed with him because he was Jenise's father."

"If there's a possibility you should get tested. You see my life and the conviction that Zoey's mother held believing I wasn't the father when in fact I was."

"At this point if I push the issue how will that affect Jenise? I am her father figure I always have been. If I was her father then everything she went through with Fred would be for what? It causes more problems than it solves pushing the issue. Fred is her father, I'm just her uncle."

I didn't know how he could stand existing like that. It's important to me that my children know that I am their father, no one else but me. Especially after losing Amina how could I ever knowingly live with myself if the question existed?

****

"DADDY HOW COULD YOU?" Lanie said loudly no doubt mindful that we were in a hospital as our tribe of children filled the room. "Why didn't you send for us?" Eric grabbed a chair and then he sat next to his momma. He grabbed her hand and then he broke down. EJ looked up at the ceiling and when that didn't work he gave in to his tears as well. "I was concerned with your momma."

"He's gone?" EJ asked me with fire in his eyes.

"What do you think?"

"Grandmomma braided your hair I see." Erica said looking her momma over as her tears poured over her face.

"Of course. She braided my hair, and got me a few satin pillowcases."

"Momma! Auntie Grace body slammed me! And she put Zoey in a headlock." Lanie said like she was tattling.

"What did you do?" Jenise said with a weak smile. She was waking up from her morning nap when the kids came.

Lanie wiped her eyes, "you can't tell someone their momma is in the hospital and expect them not to react! She was trying to talk too calmly and we needed to get here. She took sissy's keys from her and when I reacted to that she slammed me and got sissy." Then Lanie started laughing as tears fell out of her eyes still. "Our relationship just turned another corner. I didn't expect her to go there."

Erica gently stroked her momma's foot. "We were dropping Lil Tim and Tina off when she was trying to give us all the information. All these hot heads were reacting and she had to get their attention so they could calm down and listen."

Jenise cleared her throat, "we need to tell you all something though." All of the kids froze with big eyes staring at Jenise. "Your fa...." She tried to clear her throat.

"Erica baby can you give me some water?" Erica grabbed the pitcher and hurried to Jenise. Jenise swallowed then she cleared her throat again. "Where was I?" She looked at each of the kids.

"Mom! You're killing us!" Zoey declared.

Jenise held up her hand and her new engagement ring blinded them. "Your father and I are getting married."

"I knew I was a love child! I could feel it in my bones!" Lanie exclaimed.

"As long as you know you can't have any!" I said.

"A vowel renewal?" Eric asked raising his eyebrow. "Why?"

"Why not?"

Eric threw his hands up, and then he looked at EJ. "He's still sensitive." Then he looked at me. "I was just asking."

"When?" Erica asked

"All of this has to be healed up of course. I have no idea yet. Lanie will help me plan while you two are away."

"Great! It's gonna be a rainbow bright wedding!" Zoey said.

Lanie kicked her butt, which made her fall off the bed. "Shut up!"

"Lanie don't kick your sister."

"Dad, you didn't see what she did to me earlier."

"I swear you two are just as bad as the twin terrors. Cut it out!"

Chapter 33

Ethan

Jenise looks so cute struggling with her sling. It's been a couple months and her doctor is very happy with her healing. The twin terrors are riding with Erica while Lanie and Zoey rode together. We're caravanning out here to Chico to get the girls squared away in their place. My father bought the property and he has some staff in a few of the units closest to theirs. Jenise and I were going to buy the girls cars, but my father beat us to the punch. So we bought their computers, phones, furniture, etc. I gave Erica's previous car to Chastity's husband as a belated wedding present. Jenise and I sat Zoey down and we explained the distance between Chico and Redding. She was going to be an hour and a half away from her mother. We told her it was *ok* for her to reach out to her and go see her. She was **not** allowed to give her money or let her stay with them in Chico. We explained that her lifestyle was *questionable* before she went into hiding but it was ridiculous to think that she would never want anything to do with her.

Jenise turned to face me, "tell me the truth. How are you holding up?"

"I don't want them to go." I said honestly.

"You've always known this day was coming."

"I know," I tried to will away the ache in my heart. "Each of them has a different place in my heart. Erica's the one I had to grow up for. My dream realized! That night with you I poured all of myself into you and nine months later she looked at me with no uncertain terms that she was my babygirl. Looking like me and acting like you. My babygirl has always made me proud I can't imagine life without her." I shook my head, "for all the wrong Cat has done. Crushing on my brother, cheating on me. The only thing she did right was Zoey. I don't feel like we've had enough time together. She's a part of me I don't want to let go of yet. I don't want her forgetting the love we've shown her, get out here and lose her mind. I know how I ran over girls in college, I want better for her."

Jenise leaned over and kissed my cheek. "Our girls will be good. Did I ever tell you how sexy your soul is to me? Who knew you could love so deeply?"

"I never tire of you telling me anything."

"Our girls are going to be wonderful additions to the world. Zoey followed Erica out here because she needs the comfort of family." She softened her voice as she prepared to give me something straight. "Baby, you remember you and I in college." I cut my eyes at her; I could feel my body temperature go up. "Please be approachable and patient. They may meet their versions of the little boy Blu who they give it all up for." I was getting mad anyways. "I've talked to them and I've made sure they're prepared for everything."

"Explain everything!"

She stroked my head, which made me calm a lot. "Let's just say everything ok. As their father we'll keep it high level. You gave them the road map to know what to expect. I gave them the tools to be prepared."

"Something's up with EJ." I changed the subject cause I was going to lose it.
"I noticed that too. At first I thought he and Shelby broke up, but they went out last night."

Jenise

"I bet you that little girl is pregnant."
I grabbed my chest. "Ethan don't play! My baby's got one more year of high school left. The twins can make it through high school without pregnancy scares."
Ethan watched the road, "if you say so. How much you wanna bet? The usual?"
I gritted my teeth, "you better not be right. Our usual five... No! I want something else when I win. I want a date night to that Jazz club in Oakland when I win. Grace and Timothy, Dito and Tess, Gwen and Martin everybody."
"Fine, and when you calm down and realize I'm right and I've saved my son and name sake from the clutches of your death grip. I want you in bikinis the entire honeymoon."
I gasped, "bikinis? You can't be serious. We're not in our twenty something bodies. I've had four babies."
Ethan glanced at me. "Your point? You scared you're wrong?"
I joined Club One in downtown Oakland; it's a nice fitness club. Unlike the meat markets that have completely turned me off. This one is low key and worth the money. Gwen goes there and she's been asking me to join her for years. Since I wanted to tone up for the wedding I joined, but now I think it'll be a good idea period. Even though he's wrong I'll wear bikinis for my baby.
Erica and Zoey pulled into their garage, while we parked in visitor parking. Ethan pointed out his father's driver. Then we saw Frank walking the grounds probably doing an inspection of the security setup. Erica walked straight up to Ethan threw her arms around him and buried her head in his chest. She started crying really hard as she squeezed her daddy. "Aw! Isn't that sweet!" Lanie said snapping a picture with her disposable camera. Ethan squeezed her back as he kissed her forehead. After two minutes and they were still going we decided to leave them to their special moment and go inside. We grabbed the boxes out of their cars and brought them inside their place. Their two master bedroom townhouse had both bedrooms with their separate bathrooms upstairs. There was a half bathroom, kitchen, dining room, living room, and attached two-car garage downstairs. Everything inside this unit was brand new and top of the line. When we were in college the boys lived in nice apartments. Frank of course provided better for his girls.
Ethan and Erica eventually came inside. Erica's eyes were puffy and completely red. She followed Ethan around their place like at any given moment she was going to change her mind and come home.
We hung artwork, put up shelves, setup their rooms. EJ and Eric hooked up their computers and got them setup for use. Once everything was done, Erica ran back to her father and buried her face in his chest again. Ethan told Zoey to come over as well and the three of them sat on the couch hugging, kissing, and having low conversations. Eric came and put his arms around me as he smiled at his sisters. EJ

wouldn't look at me, he looked so guilty. Lanie started looking at him the same way I was. My baby is always quiet like his daddy, but his spark was off. At dinner Ethan broke everyone down except Frank mister emotions of steel. Frank wasn't leaving until the morning. We kissed the girls goodnight and then we told them we'd be back in two weeks. In the car Lanie snuggled into Eric while she stared at EJ. "You know Ethan you should try to act normal if you don't want people to notice that there's something wrong with you."

Ethan glanced at me then he looked in the rearview mirror. "Spill it!"

I turned around and looked at my baby. "You know we love you right? There's nothing you can't tell us." I said gently as I stroked his chin.

"I know." EJ said as he debated with himself. He took a deep breath. "We need to sit down with Brother and Sister Clark." He looked out the window.

Fire exploded in my stomach and with my good arm I tried to strangle that boy. He's not even eighteen! I'm not ready to be a grandmother! "Jenise!" Ethan grabbed my leg after the car swerved. "Sit down!"

Lanie and Eric were squished in the opposite corner of the backseat with big stretched eyes. "How could you do this?"

"I didn't do it on purpose momma. It's all my fault." EJ pleaded with his eyes.

****

"ETHAN!" I screamed as I looked at the monitor for the front gate. It was Red, and his sisters, and their mom.

"I see it!" Ethan called out from his office then he hurried down the stairs.

"Who's that?" Lanie asked from the top of the stairs.

Eric and EJ went out with their father to the gate. I watched from the monitor. "Can I help you?" Ethan asked them looking through the gate to our walkway.

"We need to talk to my sister. We've sent letters, left messages, and she hasn't responded." Red said.

"She's been recovering!" I stroked the monitor asking Ethan to calm down.

"Recovering? She was ill?"

Ethan looked at the boys. Each of them grabbed their waist and then they walked out the gate. "She was injured." Ethan said walking up on the car. Eric left the gate open and then he told the dogs to wait.

"We didn't know that, is she going to be ok?" Red looked concerned.

"Yes. What do you want? Why are you here?"

"We need to tell Jenise that our father died, and there's some issues with his estate."

"She knows he's gone. What issue with his estate?"

"He left everything to her and her mother."

I immediately burst into tears. Why would he leave everything to us and then try to kill me? Lanie raced down the stairs to grab me as I melted towards the floor.

"Momma!" Lanie said with tears in her eyes. I held onto my baby as I cried angry tears. The buzzer from the gate was loud. Lanie answered and then Ethan asked if I felt up to talking to them. I told him to let them in. I went upstairs to splash water on my face and get it together. Lanie followed me around watching me. I could hear them downstairs talking with Eric. No doubt Ethan and his mini me were watching them not saying much. When Lanie and I came down the stairs Red and his sisters were watching us. When I got down the stairs Red gently hugged me. My sisters Yolanda, the little one Julea, and Yewandae introduced themselves. I assumed that Julea was the one Collette was pregnant with when we came. Collette said hello but she kept her distance. Eric showed them into the living room while I studied their faces looking for anything that looked like me in them. Not that you can always determine genetics by sight. Red pulled out paperwork showing my father's last will and testament. He updated his will the week before the girl's graduation ceremony. He left nothing for Red, his sisters, or their mother. I looked through the folder as my tears burned my eyes with confusion. I found a letter at almost the bottom of the pile.

*I, Frederick Dupree Wright Sr., being of sound mind and body leave all of my liquid assets to my first wife formerly known as Evelyn Wright. Evelyn tried to love me and put up with all my selfishness. She stayed with me even though I barely had anything to share with her. I don't blame her for anything she did to me. I deserved way worse. To my daughter formerly known as Jenise Wright I leave all of my real estate, farm, life insurance, and bonds. My daughter grew up without any luxuries in life. She still managed to smile constantly and try very hard to make her troubled father smile. She dedicated herself to her studies in school and she worked very hard in college. Because of me she was born and became the beautiful woman that she is today. To my son Frederick Dupree Wright II and my daughters Yolanda Wright, Yewandae Wright, and Julea Wright. I leave them with their college trust funds and the clothes in their closets. All of you have been spoiled with all the luxuries that I could provide and Red is the only one to graduate from high school. I doubt that Julea will amount to much more than her siblings as she has already begun down the same path as her big sisters. I only leave her college trust fund as well. I am completely disappointed in all of you especially coming from an educated mother. Your mother can continue to support your dead weight. **I'm done!***

Sincerely,

Frederick Dupree Wright Sr.

I gave the letter to Ethan as I continued to cry. I asked what happened to his wife. They said no one's been able to find her since the day before he died. No one's heard from her or seen her. "So you're upset because he left you nothing?" I continued looking at the papers.
"He spoiled us and then he's mad because we turned out the way he raised us!" Yolanda spit.
"So he was happy about you not finishing high school?"
"You don't have to finish high school to be a farmer."
I looked at this chubby ain't worked a day in the field little spoiled brat. "So that's your plan? You're going to be a field hand for the rest of your life?"

Yolanda rolled her eyes at me and sucked her teeth. "Get real!"

A blast of air went past me in yellow, blue, and orange. Lanie knocked Yolanda and the chair she was sitting in over. Lanie had her hands around Yolanda's neck. "I WILL KILL YOU IF YOU EVER DISRESPECT MY MOMMA AGAIN!"

Eric calmly removed Lanie's hands. "Alright sissy, she's been warned. Let's let them finish their plea then we'll kick them out. Momma gonna get you for messing up her furniture." Eric smiled at me, "we still hear about that couch." He helped Yolanda up. "You all need to mind your manners and get to the point before you piss us off."

"Red lets go. They got all this money they don't care about what happens with us." Yewandae said.

"You didn't care about yourself! Who doesn't graduate from high school? That's the easiest part!" Lanie barked.

"I messed up!" Yewandae cried.

"So," Lanie looked at their mom. "You they momma, she cries and says she messed up and that's it? My momma will do something horrible to me if I get less than a B in any of my classes and you let them fail?"

"Technically I'm your auntie and so you...."

Lanie cut her off. "YEP! My aunt and a prime example of how not to be. You surely are dressed nice, but you stupid! You don't come in nobody's house acting dumb and expecting them to help you!"

"Why are you letting her talk to us like this?" Yolanda asked.

"She's not lying." EJ said.

"Here's what's going to happen. Once you've graduated from college Jenise will consider selling you back some of your father's things. Nothing is given to anyone. If your niece graduates from college without word from you all we will assume the you forfeit our deal and we will disseminate everything amongst our children."

"HUH?"

"Distribute!" Ethan huffed.

"You can't do that!" Yolanda yelled.

"It's time for you all to leave." Ethan watched my face as he pointed to the door.

"You heard my father! If you can't get up I'll help you up!" Lanie said clapping her hands.

"Jenise, please." Red clasped his hands together.

"You heard my husband. This is for your own good. No one owes any of you anything. In life you don't get something for nothing."

"Sounds like you have a lot of planning ahead of you. I'll walk you out." Eric said walking with them out the door.

I asked Ethan to have Ryan or Sonny look at these documents to validate that they were legit. I needed to ask them if my questionable paternity would have any bearing on them.

****

"Thank you for coming over." I said putting cheese and crackers in the center of the table.

"Jenise your house is so beautiful! I've never been here before." Sister Clark said.

"Thank you Sheila, Kenneth would you like something to drink?"

"No, I'm ok. Please excuse my frankness but this feels like a setup. What's going on?"

"Jenise and I wanted to discuss the kids with you."

The Clark's looked at their daughter who looked terrified. "Shelby what's going on?"

I exhaled, "baby. You didn't tell them."

Shelby silently cried as she shook her head no. "I don't know how."

"Tell us what?" Brother Clark said as he tried to hold back his anger.

"I'm going to have a baby." Shelby cried.

"We're going to have a baby." EJ said sitting tall and holding Shelby's hand.

Her parents sat there in shock as they looked at their daughter. "So let's hear it. What's your plan." Ethan said to EJ.

"As soon as I graduate we want to get married." EJ said directly to his father.

"What about college?"

"I'm still going. I know this situation is not ideal, and I apologize for getting Shelby in trouble. I did not mean to disrespect you, or interfere with the way you raised your daughter. This whole thing is my fault and all my idea."

"Shelby," her mother said gently as she held her daughter's hands. "Are you sure you want to marry him? You don't have to marry him just because you're pregnant."

"We were talking about getting married when he graduated before the baby. Mom, I love him." Shelby said from her heart.

"I don't expect a eighteen year old boy to stick to an ice cream flavor for the rest of his life. How could I give you my daughter?" Brother Clark asked.

"You would give me your daughter because I'm not a boy. I may only be seventeen but I love your daughter deeper than any boy could understand. Whether you accept it or not your daughter and I are in love and we will get married as soon as I'm legal. Meanwhile my fiancé and child will be provided for. You only need to be her parents in this. I will take care of everything else." EJ said reminding me of his father.

"You work?" Brother Clark asked as if he was going to prove with that one point that EJ was wrong.

"As a matter of fact I do. I've been filing taxes for my income since I was fifteen. I make more than enough money to provide Shelby with anything she wants. Your daughter will be taken care of."

Shelby looked at EJ somewhat surprised herself. "I can work too."

"Only if you want to. You don't have to." EJ rubbed her shoulders.

"All of our children are hard workers. I apologize that this is happening with your daughter involved. Our son will respect your wishes." Ethan said watching the devastation on the Clark's faces as they were trying to grab some clarity.

"Shelby how long has this been going on?" Her mother asked her.

Shelby swallowed, "we haven't been doing it all that long. I'm sorry mommy."

"This is your fault meaning you pressured her into this?" Brother Clark asked.

EJ looked at Shelby, "with all due respect. I can't make Shelby do anything she doesn't want to do."

"Ethan's protecting me daddy. I wanted this, obviously I didn't think all the details through."

"No, we're in this together." My son said taking her hand into his.

Ethan looked at Brother Clark, "Kenneth?" Brother Clark looked heartbroken. "This is your daughter. I know how I would feel about my daughter in this situation."

"The only thing we really need to know from them is whether she has to move out or not. If Shelby has to move out, she'll have a place to stay by tomorrow. We don't need your permission to live our lives."

"Ethan!" I took a breath, "I know you're flexing your manly muscles right now; but put yourself in their shoes. What if Shelby was your daughter, or Shelby was one of your sisters. You're only looking at this situation from your point of view. Shelby has reasonable parents and the fact that they're so calm having just got this news right now shows that they're good parents. Give them some time to take in what you just dropped on them."

"We love our daughter very much. We'd never put her out because she made a mistake." Sister Clark said.

"Shelby's staying with us until you get married. Give me a moment to take this all in."

"So regardless, it sounds like we're planning your wedding in a year?" I asked.

"Definitely!" EJ said looking Shelby in her eyes.

"Sheila, we're family now." I touched her hand.

Ethan

"What difference does it make? You're grown. You've got this all figured out." I watched my son.

"Dad you know I have to work." EJ said like I was being ridiculous.

"Now I understand to an extent the point that you were making. However, show some humility son. Remember that although your last name is Wallace without my approval you will have to live off your inheritance. Without further education how will you make that work for you? There's a time and a place to flex, I would've broken Erica's little boyfriend or fiancé or whatever you're supposed to be down. Especially if it's at that moment that I found out everything. Calm down!"

"You're telling me to punk out?"

"Come on, when would I ever say that? I'm telling you to calm down. It's important that you get along with your in-laws, you're going to put their daughter through enough just by being a Wallace. Always be good to your woman and the rest you'll bump your head through, but that's what you have me for."

EJ looked around, "thank you. I apologize for assuming that you would employ me."

"You sure you want to marry this girl? You don't have to. You're extremely young, how can you say you even know who you are yet?"

"I've been in love with Shelby since I noticed girls. She's a good person and she's down for me just like momma has always been for you."

"She knows who you are?"

"Yes, she knows everything about me."

Malcolm knocked on the door and I told him to come in. "You know my son's getting married?"

Malcolm stared at EJ for a minute. "What does a kid know about making a marriage work?"

"Probably just as much as you do, but I'm committed to making it work."

Malcolm shook his head, "and you're going to marry Jenise twice? What is wrong with you?"

"I love her, and I'd marry her every year for the rest of our lives if it wouldn't be overkill."

"Speaking of your wife, I'm hearing things. Rumors and buzzes."

"Like?"

"Like she could be Eugene's kid or Nelson's. What does her mother say?"

"They haven't spoken about it. Everyone's focused on Jenise healing." Malcolm was quiet, "does it matter?"

"It's important to know where you come from. Pam never cared whether I knew, but she was so twisted. My boys know where they come from, and they know that I'm here for them. It's not the way I grew up, but I can see the difference in them verses me. I found my Momma and Dad on my own. However, it would be nice to know where she belongs."

"Do you know any of your siblings?"

"I know of a lot of them. Doesn't matter."

"So my son is going to be a husband, father, and student."

"All at once? How is that supposed to work?"

"You can't tell young folks anything."

"Where are you going to school?"

"So far I've gotten into all the schools I applied to. I haven't decided. Princeton, Harvard, M.I.T., are on the list to name a few."

Malcolm looked at me then back to my son. "You're going to go away to school? Do you think that's wise?"

"What's wrong with that?" EJ looked at him.

"Your class load is going to be heavy, you're going to spend a lot of time studying. Then you're going to be working when you're not studying. If all your wife has is you and the baby, you won't make it a year. I suggest you stay close to home so that she has access to both of your families. She's going to need the help."

"Why wouldn't I be enough?"

"Let me break it down for you. You've got papers due in multiple classes, you need to focus. On top of that your boss demands excellence so when you're not doing school work you have a demanding job. When will you have time for quality time with your wife and child? Little spurts here and there at best. She's going to need some help so she doesn't lose her mind. And if you're her only help she's going to get you."

"Stanford's right there." EJ was thinking. "I want us to have our own, but I guess the other side of the Bay is close enough, but far enough away."

Jenise

EJ and Shelby are getting married in August. Ethan and I are getting married in the following Spring. We have been beyond busy with all the planning for both. Lanie has been my little trooper and she's been by my side with all of my planning. This weekend needed to be relaxing, instead of full of appointments. Sophia asked Ethan to come to her restaurant this weekend to go over her menu changes and ideas. EJ was going to spend time with the Clark's, while Eric went with Ethan. So Lanie, my mom, Grace, Tina, and I went to a spa. My mom and I were sitting side by side.
"Psst mom," I said lowly.
"Yes sweetheart." She smiled.
"I know the timing is horrible but I can't take it any more. Why did my father ask you if I was his daughter?"
Pain settled over her face. "Fred is evil! He was aiming for me when he hit you. Me or Stephen." She exhaled slowly, "my relationship with your father has been tumultuous you know that, but I never went into detail about everything. When I met your father I was so young. Fred was so sweet and loving in the beginning. I fell in love so hard so fast with him. We didn't date long before we were married. We were together for a while when I realized I was pregnant. That same day Pandora's box opened. All your father's lies and secrets came pouring out. I know it's not right, at the time I wanted him to hurt like he was hurting me. I slept with Nelson, that's when I knew I messed up. I was young and everything was out of control." She shook her head looking down at the floor. "Poor Nelson, I should've never allowed that to happen. After Nelson your father was never good enough. Your father promised to behave and Nelson and I called everything off. Heartbroken Nelson moved away to give us space. Well you know your father. Our reconciliation was short lived, and that's when I met Eugene. He was this man's man unlike anyone I knew. He wanted to take us away from your father. Rescue us from everything, but you loved your father. You weren't leaving him for nobody. So I stayed. Learned about the bible and developed a conscience about my past. I came clean with your father and instead of making us closer it tore us apart. He tried to make my actions the excuse for his behavior, but he was always that way."
"You stayed with my father because of a guilty conscience."
"Yes, and I did love him."
I exhaled, "does Uncle Nelson think I'm his daughter?"
"I told him that he wasn't your father. I don't know what he thinks."
"Why didn't you go back to him when you left dad?"
"Too much pain! Your father would've lost it and he never would've left us alone. I was tired of all the drama. I'm happy with Stephen, he's good to me. I'll always love Nelson for everything he has done for me."
"If my father would've died before you left would you...."
"I would've been with Nelson in a heartbeat." Then she smiled like she was remembering something.

I turned a little green. "That's nasty!"

****

RING! RING!

"No!" Ethan said holding me as I reached for the phone.

"Jenise? It's Sheila."

"Is it time?"

"Yes, she just started laboring."

"Ok, the kids are coming." I said still half asleep.

"Why don't babies know to come during normal business hours?" Ethan fussed as he rolled over.

I went to EJ's room. He was sleep so hard he was drooling and everything. I barely touched him and he jumped hard. I told him he may have a long stretch but he needed to go be with Shelby. EJ popped up trying to focus. I woke Eric and Lanie, I told them to go with their brother. Lanie caught herself before she cursed in front of me. Lanie and Eric complained all the way out the door. I told EJ to call me when they left for the hospital. When I got back in the bed Ethan threw his arm and leg back over me. He kissed my cheek, and then I realized he was awake because of his breathing. I asked him if he was ok. He said he wasn't ready to be a grandfather. I told him it was out of our hands. He said he thought we would be a lot older when we started having grandchildren. I did too. Ethan kissed my neck, and I asked him why we couldn't go back to sleep. He told me we were young and we needed to have a proper send off back into our dreams. He got no objections from me.

When we got to the hospital Shelby was still laboring. Her father was pacing in the waiting room. Eric had the rest of Shelby's family in stitches as he told us about EJ and Shelby acting up before they got to the hospital. EJ was trying to do the things they discussed in birthing class and Shelby wanted none of it. EJ was massaging her back and then he asked Sheila to switch with him because he was getting tired. Shelby went off and threw her water at him telling him she was tired too. Lanie, Sheila, EJ, and Shelby's sister were in the delivery room. One by one, sometimes in twos the cousins on our side started arriving to the waiting room. William, Dito's oldest, and his sisters brought a big bouquet of flowers and balloons.

They were in there for hours. Brother Clark was fussing about how long it was taking, he was so worried. Raynel agreed with him that it was taking a long time. Sheila came out and said they were going to have to give Shelby a cesarean. Her contractions were coming hard and she wasn't dilating. She said EJ was getting dressed right now. Lanie climbed in my lap like a big ole baby. She was crying as she told us how horrible it was. She said Shelby was in so much pain and there wasn't anything she could do to make it better. My mom winked at me as she mouthed there wouldn't be any babies for Lanie any time soon. That was my point in sending her.

A little while later EJ was jumping in front of the window in his hospital clothes. He was extremely excited. "He's here! He's here!" Then he ran back down the hallway. We crowded around the nursery window and my baby held up his baby. His son! I started crying and I buried my head in Ethan's chest. The baby looked like my son and Shelby combined. When I finally held him this was my baby. Lanie snapped picture after picture of everything and everyone. Everyone said they wanted copies of the picture of Frank holding the baby and Ethan and EJ standing on either side of him as they all smiled at the baby.

Ethan

"I'm so happy the school year is over! Chico's fine, but we miss you dad!" Erica smiled.

"You just saw me two weeks ago."

"That was two whole weeks!" Zoey squeaked. "Thank you for coming to get us. We've got four hours to talk your ears off!"

"I know I've told you already but I am so proud of both of your grades all year long. Zoey I know you've had to work harder to get on this level of achievement, I'm so proud of you."

"Erica's had to tutor me in almost everything. Thanks sissy." Erica leaned forward and kissed Zoey who was riding in the front seat. Zoey took a deep breath, "so I saw Catalina the other day."

"Ok, so how are you doing?"

"She was telling us about the baby you loss."

"Amina," the thought stung.

"She said you took the loss pretty hard. That was also when you opened up to her." She looked out the window. "I don't understand her. If she loved you so much how could she cheat on you? All the years I felt lost. From the moment I walked in the door of your house that feeling went away. I belonged somewhere, I have family."

"When I saw you that ache from losing Amina subsided. Once we were altogether I started sleeping better. I've wanted your momma to go away, but something would always stop me from squashing her. Seeing you filled in the blanks of my subconscious. I was hurt about the child I lost, but there was someone missing. It was your crazy behind." The girls laughed I smiled. "I blamed Lanie on Jenise, I swore she was crazy because of her. Now I blame her for both of you. Two peas out of one pod."

"And I love Lanie, it's also nice to have a sister closer in age. I don't have to be far away from home by myself lonely for family like a lot of our peers." Then Erica cleared her throat. "I'm sorry for getting in your momma's face like that."

"You mean Catalina, Jenise Wallace is my mom!"

"What happened?"

"Catalina was saying little stuff about momma, I was about to check her, but Erica took care of that for me."

"I think she got jealous because Z kept saying mom this and mom that. She even bought some earrings she thought momma would like right in front of Catalina."

"She had no right, that's why I told her. From your lips to God's ears. She was out of line. Then she looked at me and said I act just like you." Zoey smiled at me real big. "The first real compliment she's ever paid me. I hope I never act like her! Using people to gain something. She has a new boyfriend and he's old. I've only heard his voice in the background. I can tell she don't love him either."

"That's her life, it won't be yours."

"Got that right!" Zoey shouted.

****

"You're a father, a high school graduate, and now you're about to be a husband. I'm proud of you for standing up to your responsibilities. Lil Ethan didn't ask to be here, and your soon to be wife will expect you to love her, protect her, and provide for her. I've laid out the roadmap for you. But don't hesitate to reach out to me. I'm here for you son."

"Thanks Dad!" We hugged.

"If you ever want a roadmap on what not to do ask your father to share with you everything I've done." My father said.

I straightened my son's bow tie on his tuxedo. He smiled proudly at me. "Thank you for everything dad." We patted each other's shoulders.

I proudly held Jenise's hand as we watched our first born son vow forever to Shelby. Watching our kids stand proud with their brother makes me anxious for my turn.

****

"I just need you to admit you wanna be like me!" Eric teased EJ; EJ did not look amused at all. "You can't stand to be four years without me can you?"

EJ looked at me unamused. "I'm starting to rethink being this fool's neighbor."

"As long as none of you even think about coming home. FINALLY I have my Grand Palace!" Lanie laughed evilly. "I have momma and daddy all to myself! This is going to be so sweet!"

The twin terrors stared at Lanie. She went on and on about her bliss. Jenise had two books in her arms. She gave the boys one each. It was copies of their baby pictures to current. Amongst everything else she worked really hard on putting the books together for them. She snuck Erica's to her before she left to school. She didn't want Zoey to feel slighted or anything. Shelby looked over EJ's shoulder as he opened his book. EJ cracked a full smile as he looked at the first page. Eric closed his and looked at EJ's book. They laughed at pictures and smiled. Then they went through Eric's book, more laughter and smiles. The twins hugged their momma and thanked her for their gifts. EJ's graduation present was his wedding. Eric got a brand new car just like his sisters did. He gave his previous car to Shelby. The boys are neighbors in the complex we all stayed in out here when we were in school.

We took all the kids out to Le Maire for dinner. Jenise spotted them and pointed them out. Nohemi and Jamal were tending to their family and enjoying their meal. Our table was towards the middle of the floor. When we sat down Jamal was looking. Once we made eye contact he came over to say hello. He knew Shelby and her family from Jenise's congregation when they all attended together. He congratulated my son on his recent nuptials. Then Jamal pointed to the table pointing out and naming their kids. Nohemi stayed at their table and she didn't look in our direction after she realized who we were. She looked happy before she saw us. I suspect that as soon as she saw me she thought of Amina. It's that pained feeling that always strikes my soul when my eyes land on her. My little girl who never was. Nohemi looks the same as she did the last time I saw her. Apparently Jamal has been good to her and good for her. Her stress lines around her eyes are gone and she looks like she's at peace with herself. Jamal looks happy as well. The longing for my wife isn't there anymore in his eyes. He looks very content with his life as it stands. His kids are well behaved and respectful looking. I guess you could say that Jenise's threat on Nohemi's life made them better. Or made them realize that they needed to be together.

Jenise

Jamal was talking to our table as I watched Nohemi stay with their family. I was happy that she didn't look rough and beaten down like Cat. Jamal looks happy and content with his beautiful family. Ethan was looking around surveying everything as usual, but he didn't look at Nohemi any longer than realizing she was there. Knowing my man I know he thought of Amina. Fortunately the thought of his child didn't seem to affect him like it used to. I internally sighed a sigh of relief. Jamal and his family left before we did, and Ethan held my hand as we stood to leave. We said our goodbyes to our children and then the three of us headed home.

"SO!" Lanie said as she exhaled a sound of relief. "Now that I've got you all to myself I think we should go over some ground rules."

"Ground rules?"

"Yes, please don't become overly strict all of a sudden just because you don't have any other distractions. I like money, clothes, and chocolate in that order. Feel free to shower me with all of the above frequently."

"You are required to spend more time with me. Call it whatever you want, but I will not have you thinking that spending time with your momma cancels out my time." Ethan said.

Lanie leaned forward and put her arms around her daddy while he drove. "I could get used to you wanting to spend time with me."

That night Ethan and I seemed brand new. Outside of Lanie being all the way on the other side of the house it was like we were empty nesters. Even our lovemaking was new and exciting. I felt like my man from college was back minus the extra loving he carried that I seemed to adore.

****

"This is really good Jeff. You have such a good eye."

He stood there tall and proud, "thank you. I'm going to knock off a little early do you need anything else from me?"

The receptionist knocked on the door, "Jeff. Your friend is here."

"Thank you," then he looked at me waiting for me to say something. Jeff has been a wonderful addition to our team. I want to think of him as a little baby, but he's definitely a man now.

Gwen was in the hallway and she told Jeff's friend to come in my office. The young man walked in my office with long and neat dreads. He was always very respectful, and quiet. "Can I touch your hair?" Gwen asked with her usual smile. He said yes, and then Gwen as usual touched his hair in a manner that made me uncomfortable. She's such a flirt, and I've warned her about flirting with men outside of her husband. She says it's harmless and just fun. My thing is, if her husband wouldn't like it if she did it in his face, why would she do it behind his back? Yussef tolerated Gwen petting him until I couldn't take it anymore. I asked them what they were getting into tonight. They said they were meeting up with Drew later. Lanie's eyes got their usual disgust when she saw Yussef, as she walked in my office. "YOU READY TO ADMIT YOU'RE IN LOVE WITH ME YET?" Yussef smiled and then he shrugged. "It's a doggone shame! My momma won't tell my daddy, we could plan our big reveal. I was going to tell you that I may look like a little girl right now, but I'm drinking milk and in the next few years…" Everybody fell out laughing. "You could at least let me get it out before you start laughing so hard." She smiled.

"Good afternoon Lanie." Yussef said.

"Good afternoon." Lanie smiled, "Jeff, my daddy wants you to swing by before you leave."

Then Lanie went out to assist our receptionist as the boys left. I closed my office door and sat at my desk. I took the ring box out of my purse. I looked at Ethan's wedding band and smiled. When I looked at the solid gold, white gold, and silver bands they were plain and my baby's not plain. To this day I love his tailor made suits, even his "casual" clothes are nice and good quality. Knowing that everything he has is top quality why would a plain band be sufficient? Even the band he wears now has a beautiful design and a couple of very small diamonds. This ring is custom made white gold, diamonds, and onyx. There's a total of two carats in diamonds on this ring. I think he's going to like it. It kind of matches my engagement ring. I sat the ring on my desk and I pushed my work aside. In this moment, almost the last minute I decided to write my own vows.

****

"Are you nervous?" Rosalind asked as she applied my makeup.

"Nervous about marrying my husband? Why?" To me it was a no brainer; if after four babies and five kids and all these years of me moving things on purpose just to drive him insane when he thinks he's had the last word. Or when he's sleeping and I'm still mad and I suddenly break out into a heart-felt song at the top of my lungs jarring him awake. I laughed thinking about how angry he would be, but he refused to even fuss to give me the satisfaction of knowing I was bothering him. "No, he should be nervous about marrying me."

"This is all so romantic, often I try to imagine what my wedding will be like."

"You didn't have a wedding with your ex?"

"Ben and I went to the courthouse with our parents. It was real quick, nothing special at all. We might as well had gone to McDonald's afterwards. It only seemed to matter to me and my mother."

"Do you think you and your boyfriend will advance to marriage?"

She exhaled slowly, "who knows. No one will ever replace Troy, however it's not like he broke up with me and I'm waiting to reconcile with him. I don't know." The room became still and cold for a moment. "I wish we could've been you and Ethan. In love since college, Tanisha…" she paused. "Our kids all under one roof growing up together. Troy and I going out dancing all the time. I wonder sometimes if we would've ever tired of going out? If we would've ever gotten tired of each other? How many babies we would've had together? I wonder if we would've been just as in love as you and Ethan? You've got such a good man, and he's so good to you. Kind, trusting, and patient. Treasure that, cause not everyone is so fortunate. I'm so happy for you Jenise." Tears started pouring out of her eyes. "You've got a good man, treasure him."

We hugged, "Rosalind you can't have me crying already. My makeup!" We laughed.

"It's ok, you're waterproof. Just lightly dab like this." She demonstrated on herself. Grace knocked on the door as she opened it. "JENISE! You are beautiful!" She said as her eyes watered.

"Don't start it off again, we just calmed down." Rosalind said.

Grace kissed me, "let's get you dressed. Ethan put me in charge of keeping you on time."

We went into my room and I put on my dress, when I stood in the mirror we all smiled. My mom and Raynel hugged me and kissed me. My girls clapped with excitement as they looked at me in my dress.

Ethan

My brothers and I stood in the mirror admiring ourselves in our tuxedos. Eric was telling us that we needed to pop our collars. "Look at my kid brother. Successful in business, successful in love, successful in life. Both of you! All these years here I was thinking that you two didn't get it, that you two didn't understand. And look at you, both of you married to the same women you fell in love with in college. Me…." He looked around the room, "which wife is that one number three or four? I can't remember." He tried to make light of his situation. "Jenise has been family since day one. I am so happy that you fell in love with her the first time. You came to life when she came into our lives. With Jenise is when you started to allow yourself to have better."

"RIGHT!" Dito interjected. "Hand me downs were ok until you got with Jenise. Then it's tailor made suits, silk shirts, fancy apartments, and then eventually a house."

"You guys know your dad used to be a pudgy boy."

"We saw the pictures." EJ said.

"Right, it was like that was the only way he stood out as different. Once he fell in love with Jenise he came out of his cocoon. People kept mistaken him for me."

"I wouldn't go that far," I said.

"I kid you not! Then all of you kept coming. For a minute it was like Jenise was always pregnant. Now look at you, grandfather about to marry his sweetheart again! Your queen has made us into a better royal family. Royals who actually get along and work so much better together." Franky and I hugged.

"Malcolm has a speech!" Darryl volunteered his father.

Malcolm stared at Darryl for a minute. "There's a time and a place for everything. Congratulations, I'm going to my seat."

As Malcolm walked towards the door, Eugene walked in. They stood there staring at each other for a long time as if they were going to punch each other if the other person blinked. "Daddy? Who dis?" Darryl said looking Eugene up and down. Eugene looked Darryl up and down, "daddy?"

"My son."

"Get a DNA test."

Derrick flew out of his seat and grabbed Darryl who instantly became enraged and lunged for Eugene. Drew helped Derrick take Darryl out the door who became unglued that fast. Malcolm's jaw tensed and un-tensed. "You should speak on what you know. In the future this will not end this way, if you ever comment on my life again." Malcolm was beyond pissed off. You could still hear Darryl going off in the hallway. "Frank, Tim, Ethan, gentlemen. I'm going to take my sons away before someone dies and spoils this day. I apologize for leaving." When Malcolm went out to the hallway Darryl immediately stopped making noise.

Everyone was looking at Eugene, "why would you say that?" Uncle Tim said.

"Oh shoot! Tim!" Uncle Jeff said moving closer to his brother.

"Eugene you've clearly upset the entire room. Why are you here?" My father asked.

"To offer my congratulations."

"Eugene, come talk to me." I motioned for him to join me out on the balcony. I shut the door, "you do know you're not Jenise's father?"

"I never thought I was her father."

"Then what's your deal? Why would you come here and upset my family?"

"Malcolm knows that's not his son right?"

"You can tell the paternity by looking at Darryl?"

"Yes." He looked me in my eyes.

"So then why haven't you come clean with Malcolm?"

Eugene was visibly irritated. "Look I came to congratulate you. I didn't come here for all of this."

"Malcolm already knows anything you try or don't try to tell him. I don't know how long anyone's going to be able to hold my Uncle Tim back. Stop doing this."

"Ain't nobody worried about Tim. Besides I knew him longer, his loyalty should be to me. Just because Malcolm laid with his daughter and got my son killed…" his voice trailed off and pain was all over his face. His breathing got heavy and he was trying to get his air back.

My Uncle Tim slid out the door, and my Uncle Jeff came out behind him. He got in Eugene's face with that look in his eyes like he was going to throw Eugene over the balcony. I looked down at the ground trying to figure out how long it would take to clean up the mess. "If you can't stand up then stand down. My son deserves better than you! I don't know why you play this game with him like you're hurting anyone but yourself!" Uncle Tim's finger came up and pointed at Eugene like it was a knife to stab him with. "Malcolm knows who you are! Instead of blaming Malcolm for the death of your son that you did not openly claim until his demise you should be blaming yourself. You knew that kid was on the move, and instead of stepping up you let it play out. Leonard's death is your fault!"

Eugene's chest kind of sunk in, but he tried his best to suck it up. He looked at me with red eyes. "I failed to protect that precious little girl when she was just a baby. I almost had her and her mother out of that house. Jenise wanted her father, and Evelyn couldn't handle me. It's a small world. The only time I've been able to relax about her safety is when she was with you." Then he looked at my Uncle Tim, "Malcolm is your son!" Then he walked out.

****

It seemed like a halo of light followed my parents, children, and wife down the aisle. Everything about Jenise was priceless. I couldn't wait until the "you may kiss the bride" part. When Jenise reached for my hand I pulled her in for the biggest and most delicious kiss I could muster.

Jenise

"… I promise that I will always love you for all eternity. No one could ever love me like you do! Forever and ever is always on my heart!"

"I love you with every breath in my soul!"

"I love you with every piece of me!"

"You may kiss the bride…"

MORE FROM THE AUTHOR

Thank you for allowing me to entertain you. I hope you have enjoyed reading my current release. If you have not read Volumes I – VIII of the Wallace Family Affairs series, please do so. Click here for a list of all the background stories. Once you have read the background stories, please checkout the current date series Together We Are Strong. Stay tune for more to come shortly.

Wallace Family Affairs
At Last (Click here)
Tracy's Complications (Click here)
Distorted Mirrors (Click here)
Sometimes Love Isn't Enough (Click here)
Love Is Just Enough (Click here)
Just A Friend
Invisible (Click here)
Look Beyond Your Eyes (Click here)
No Regrets (Click here)
First You Laugh Then You Cry (Click here)
A Heart That's Taken (Click here)
Abandoned (Click here)
Last Words (Click here)

Together We Are Strong
Season 1 Present (Click here)
Beyond The Wallace's ~ I Knew You When (**TBD**)
Season 2 What Comes Next (Release **TBD**)

Standalones
Secrets & Lies ~ (**TBD late 2016 release**)
Anthology **Short** Story (Where Love May Find You Collection) ~ (Click here)
Waiting (**TBD**)

Hopefully you've enjoyed all of the background stories for our lovely Wallace's and Latour's. Please tune in for more from the "Together We Are Strong" Wallace & Latour Family Episodes on Amazon